CITY OF LIGHT, CITY OF DARK

A RICHARD JACKSON BOOK

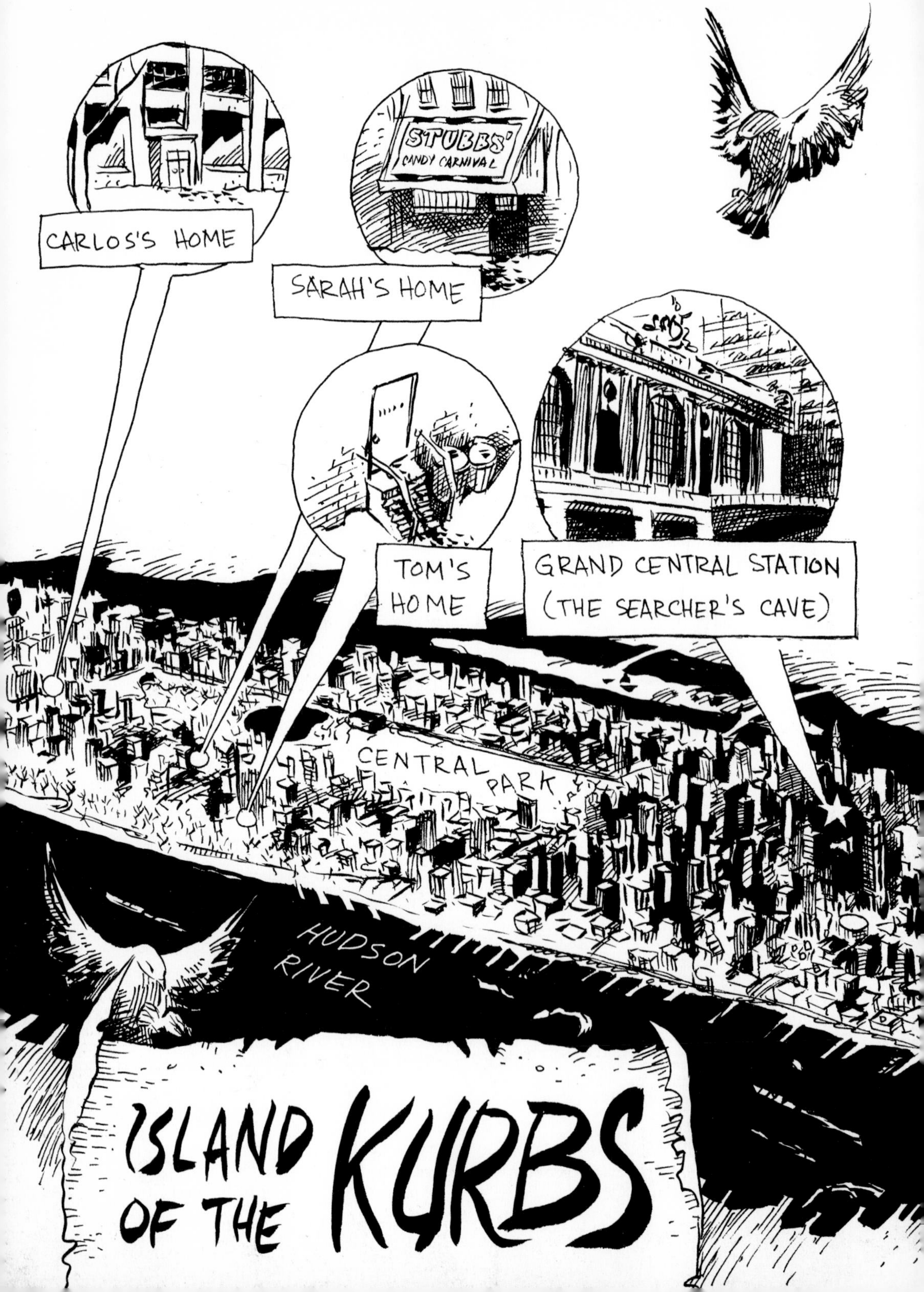

CARLOS'S HOME
STUBBS' CANDY CARNIVAL
SARAH'S HOME
TOM'S HOME
GRAND CENTRAL STATION (THE SEARCHER'S CAVE)
CENTRAL PARK
HUDSON RIVER
ISLAND OF THE KURBS

CITY OF LIGHT, CITY OF DARK

A COMIC-BOOK NOVEL

story by **AVI**

art by **BRIAN FLOCA**

Orchard Books New York

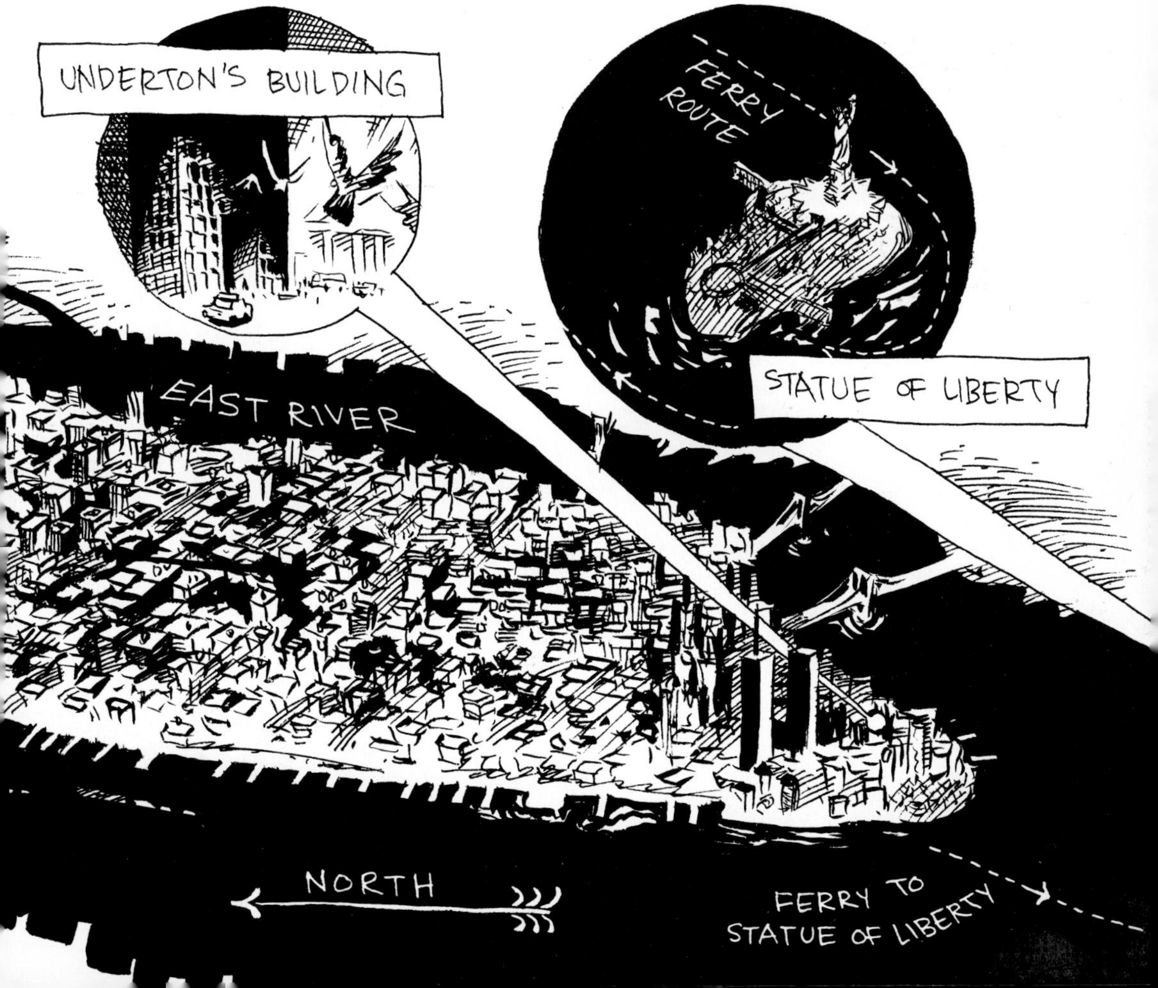
UNDERTON'S BUILDING
FERRY ROUTE
STATUE OF LIBERTY
EAST RIVER
NORTH
FERRY TO STATUE OF LIBERTY

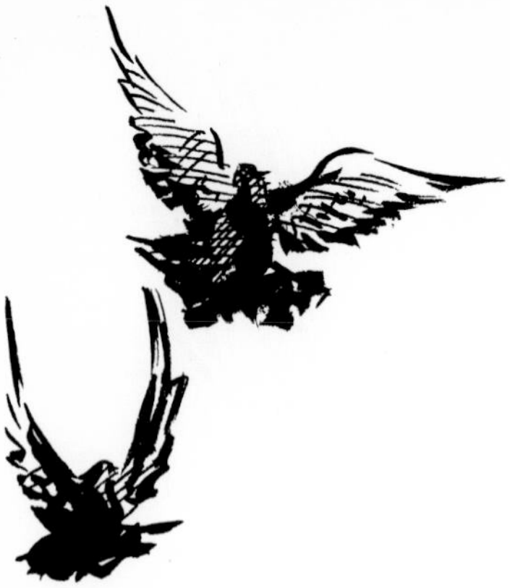

Spanish translation by José Aranda and Anthony Trujillo

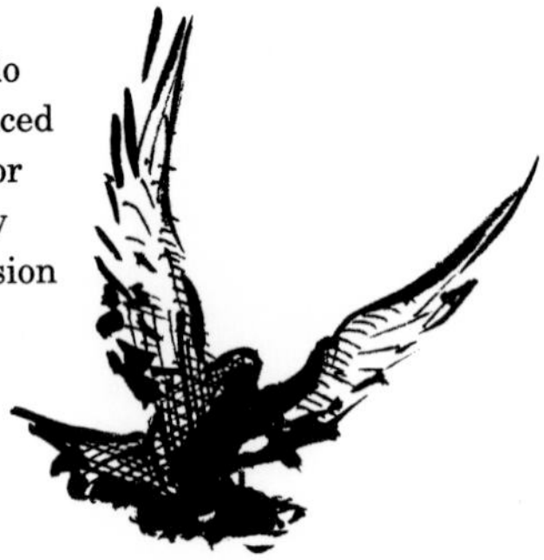

Orchard Books, 95 Madison Avenue,
New York, NY 10016

Manufactured in the United States of America
Book design by Mina Greenstein
The text of this book is hand lettered. The illustrations are rendered in pen and india ink applied with a brush.

10 9 8 7 6 5 4 3 2

Library of Congress Cataloging-in-Publication Data
Avi, date. City of light, city of dark : a comic-book novel / story by Avi; art by Brian Floca. p. cm. "A Richard Jackson book."
Summary: Asterel races against time to locate a token which will prevent the Kurbs from freezing the city.
ISBN 0-531-06800-5. ISBN 0-531-08650-X (lib. bdg.)
[1. Fantasy. 2. Cartoons and comics.] I. Floca, Brian, ill.
II. Title. PN6727.A95C57 1993 741.5′973—dc20 93-2887

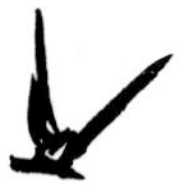

For Shaun and Kevin

—AVI

For my parents

—B.F.

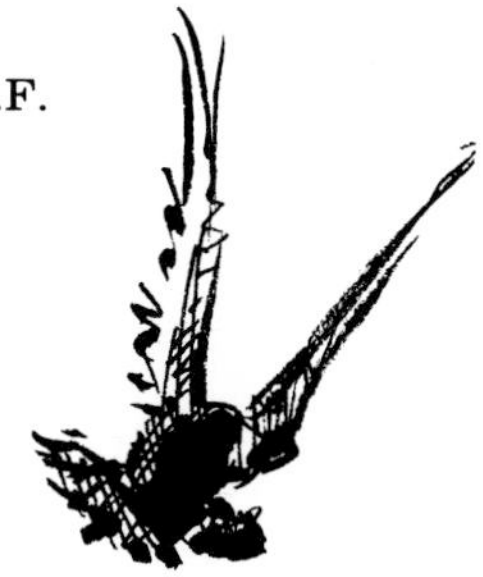

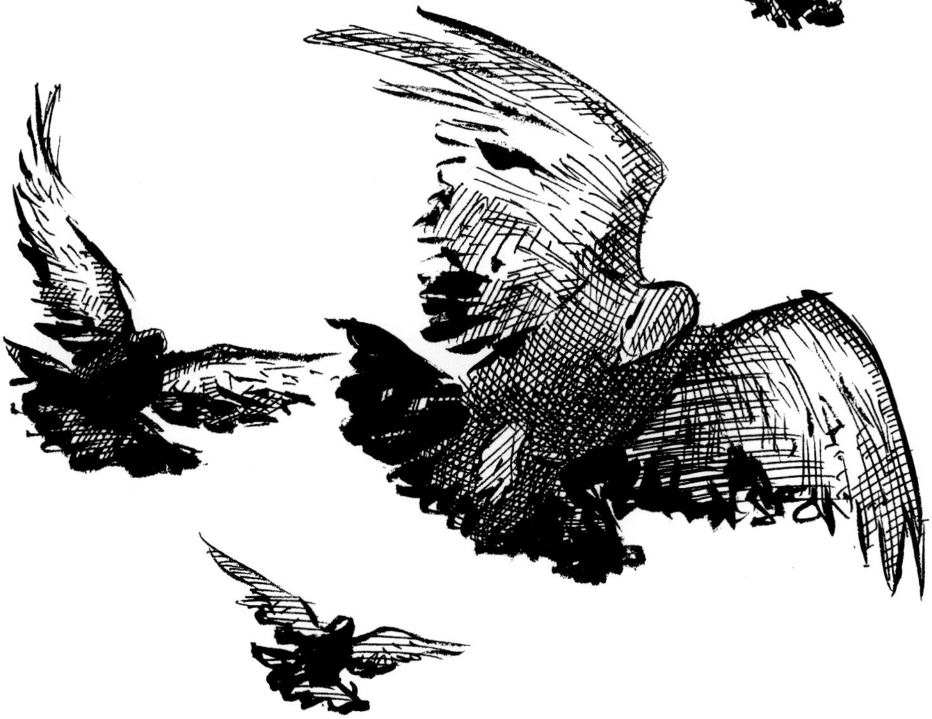

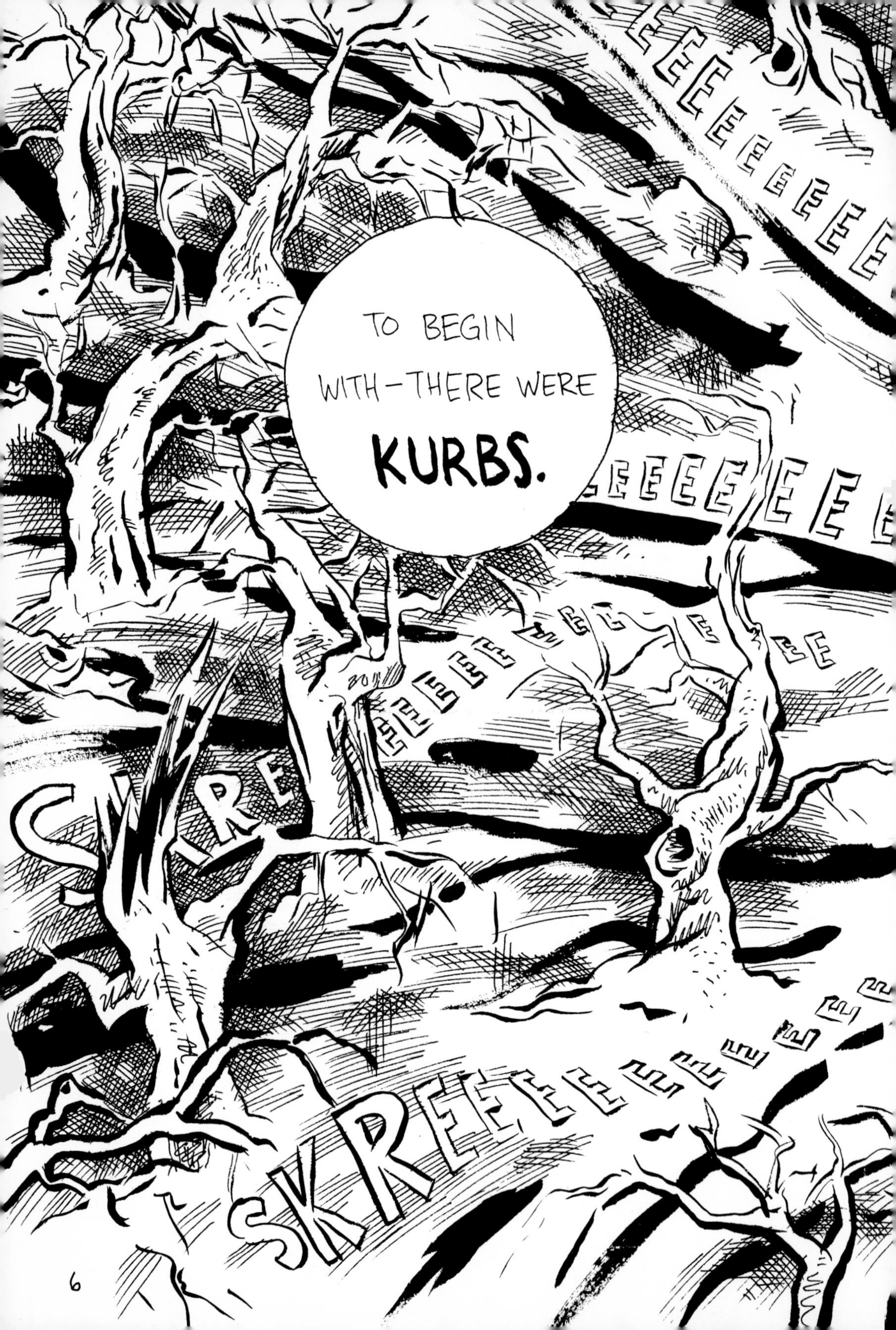
TO BEGIN
WITH—THERE WERE
KURBS.

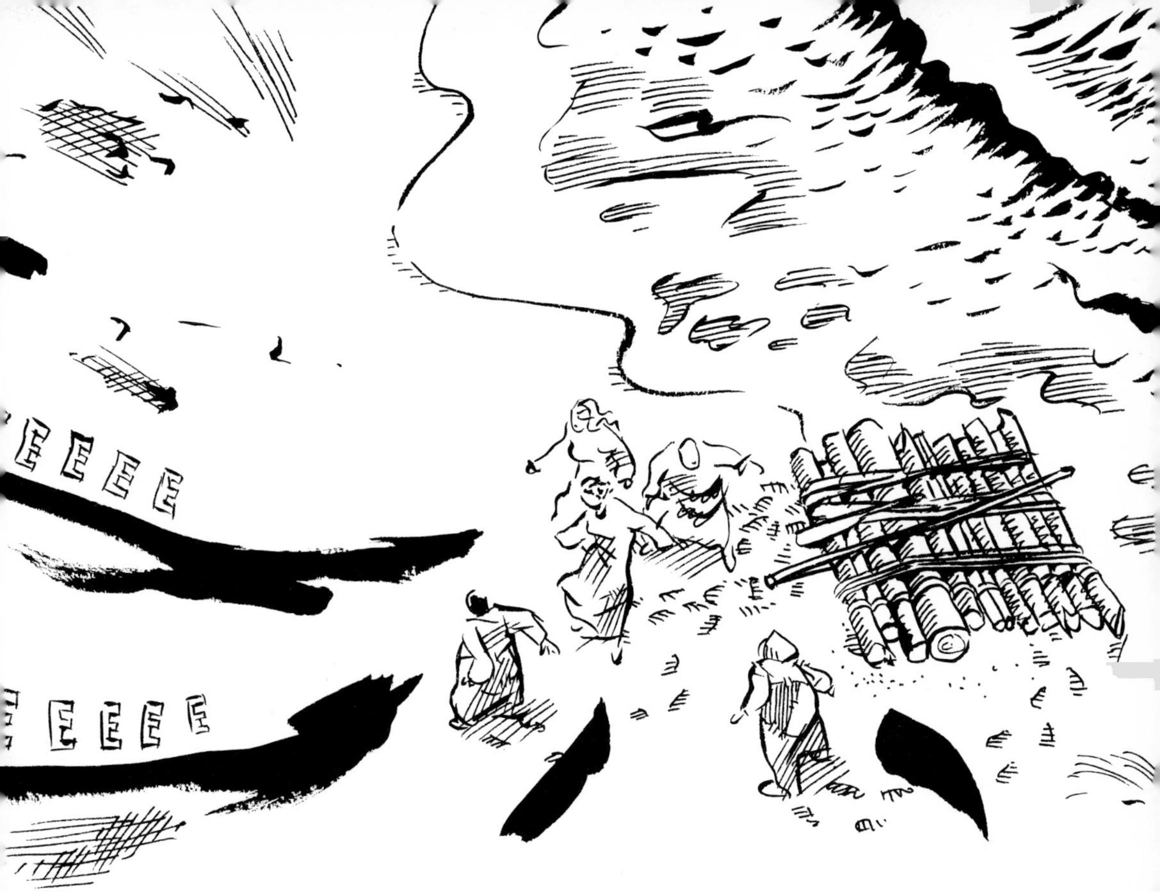

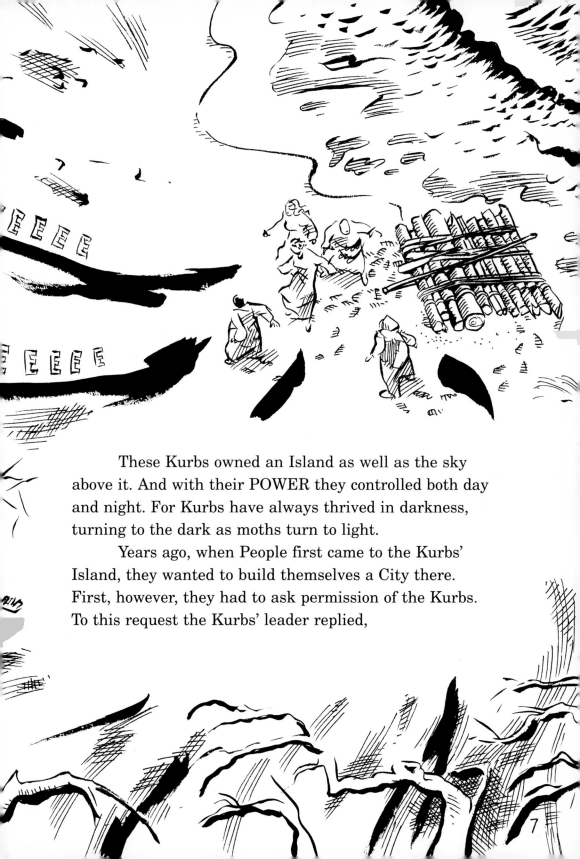

These Kurbs owned an Island as well as the sky above it. And with their POWER they controlled both day and night. For Kurbs have always thrived in darkness, turning to the dark as moths turn to light.

Years ago, when People first came to the Kurbs' Island, they wanted to build themselves a City there. First, however, they had to ask permission of the Kurbs. To this request the Kurbs' leader replied,

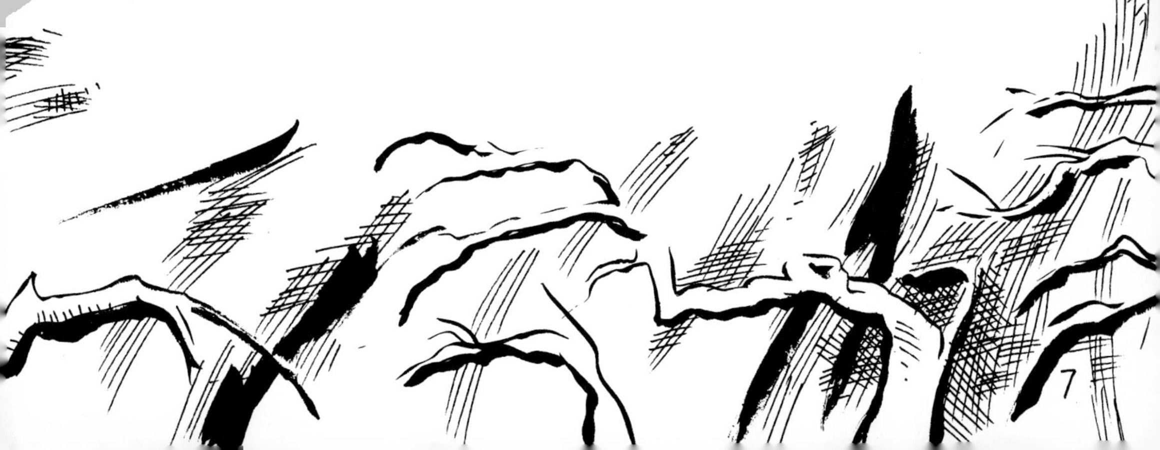

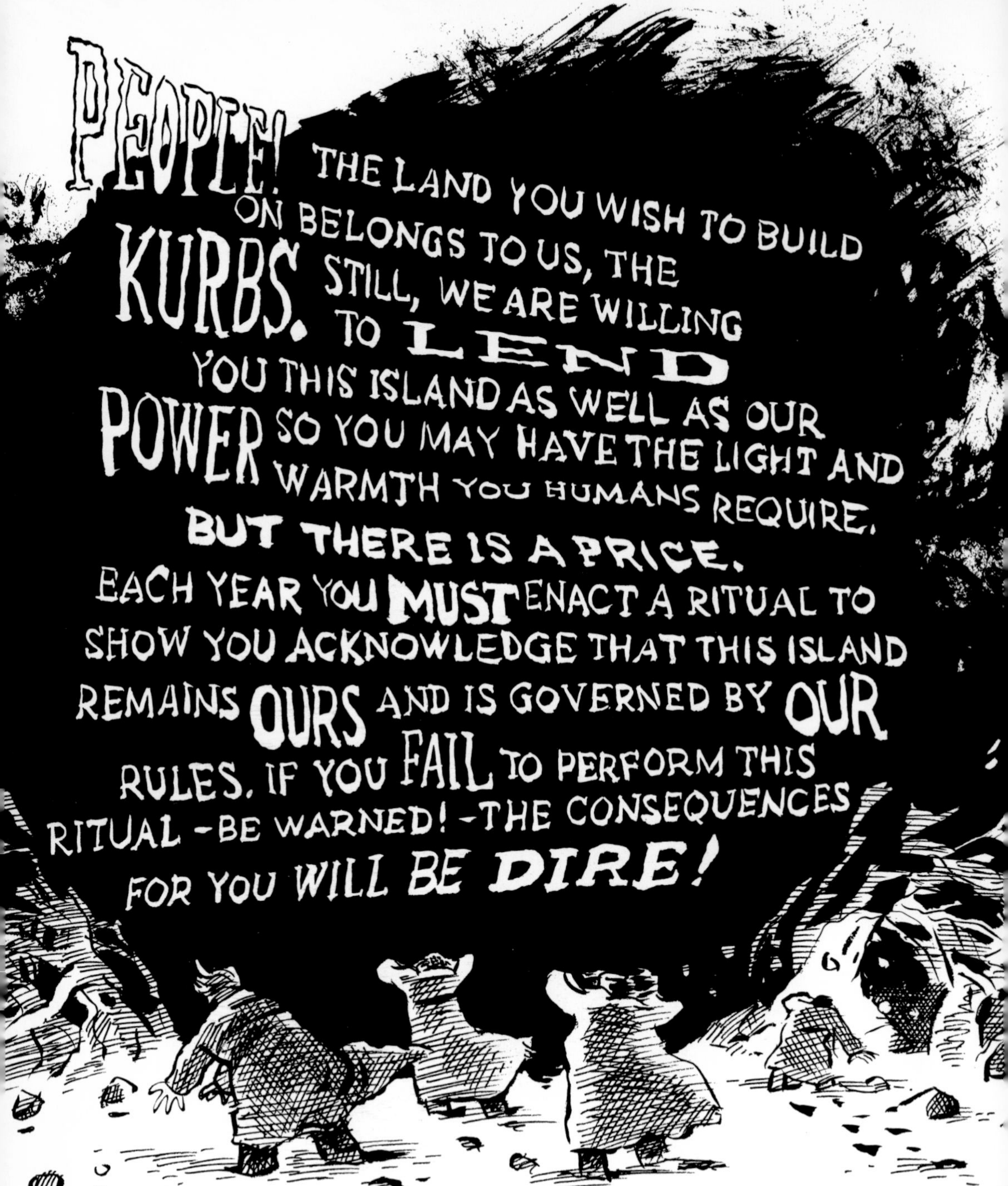
PEOPLE! THE LAND YOU WISH TO BUILD ON BELONGS TO US, THE KURBS. STILL, WE ARE WILLING TO LEND YOU THIS ISLAND AS WELL AS OUR POWER SO YOU MAY HAVE THE LIGHT AND WARMTH YOU HUMANS REQUIRE.
BUT THERE IS A PRICE.
EACH YEAR YOU MUST ENACT A RITUAL TO SHOW YOU ACKNOWLEDGE THAT THIS ISLAND REMAINS OURS AND IS GOVERNED BY OUR RULES. IF YOU FAIL TO PERFORM THIS RITUAL -BE WARNED! -THE CONSEQUENCES FOR YOU WILL BE DIRE!

To this pronouncement the People listened and finally agreed. So the Kurbs established—

The Treaty of
THE RITUAL CYCLE OF ACKNOWLEDGMENT
THAT THIS ISLAND BELONGS
TO THE KURBS

Whereas:

1) Each year, on the 21st day of June, the Kurbs shall hide their POWER somewhere in some form in the People's City.

2) The People will have six months to search for it.

3) When the People find the POWER, they shall return it to a place of safekeeping, designated by the Kurbs, no later than noon on the 21st day of December.

4) If the POWER is *not* returned, the City will grow so dark and so cold that it will *freeze.*

5) And the Kurbs will take their Island back.

Furthermore:

6) From the moment the Kurbs hide their POWER on the 21st of June, the hours of City daylight shall begin to decrease.

7) When the POWER is ritually returned to its place of safe-keeping on the 21st of December, City days shall start to grow warm. The hours of daylight will lengthen.

Finally:

8) THE RITUAL CYCLE OF ACKNOWLEDGMENT marks two halves of the human year, December to June, June to December. For the first six months the POWER shall be kept safe in a place designated by the Kurbs. For the second six months the POWER will be hidden somewhere in the city, and the People must search for it. Should the People fail to find the POWER and return it, the Cycle will be broken and the People's lease on this island shall be ended *forever.*

AGREEED _____
For the People

AGREED _____
For the Kurbs

Signed on the 45th day of the 13th moon, Kurb year 55122337.

In the early years of this agreement the Kurbs' POWER was hidden in an ear of corn, then a musket ball. Later it was put in an oil lamp. Most recently the POWER has been put within a transit token, the small golden disk used by the People as fare for bus or subway travel.

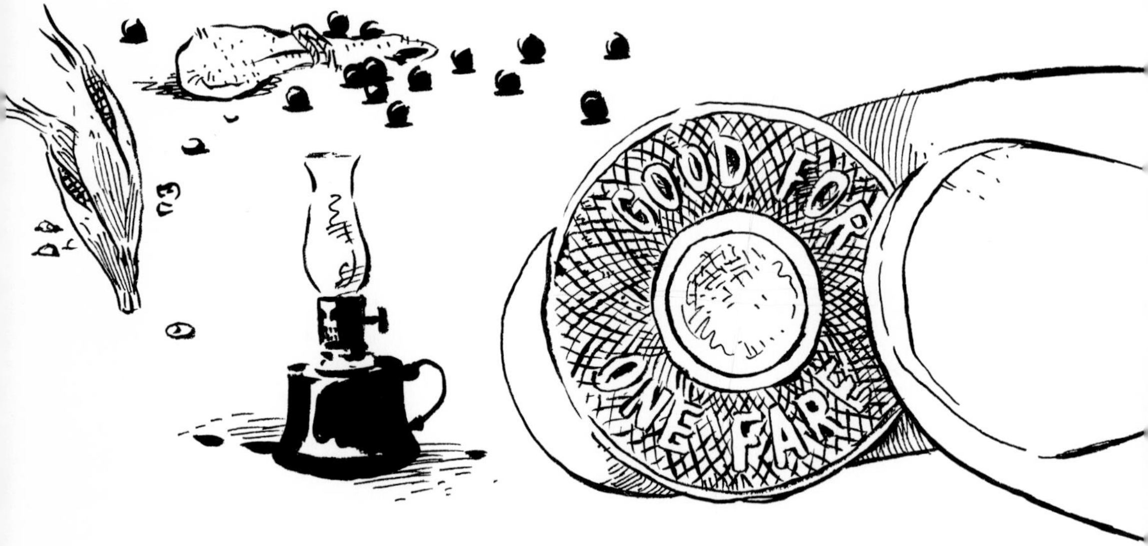
GOOD FOR ONE FARE

W*ho searches for this* POWER*?*

The People chose a woman. She alone had the responsibility of conducting the search. To help her in her searching, the People gave her powers that included special sight.

Now, when this woman had a daughter, the first thing she did was give that girl those powers. Only when the girl was older did her mother provide her with knowledge of the search as well as her future responsibilities. This meant that when the woman died, there was someone new to take up the yearly search. Thus, THE RITUAL CYCLE OF ACKNOWLEDGMENT continued,

mother to daughter, mother to daughter, generation after
generation.

Now, the means by which the woman passed on
her special powers was simple: the POWER—in whatever
its form—was held to the baby's forehead. From that
moment the daughter was fated to take on the searcher's
responsibilities.

For hundreds of years the cycle of seeking the
POWER and of returning it to the safekeeping of the
Kurbs continued unbroken. Then, eleven years ago,
something very different happened.

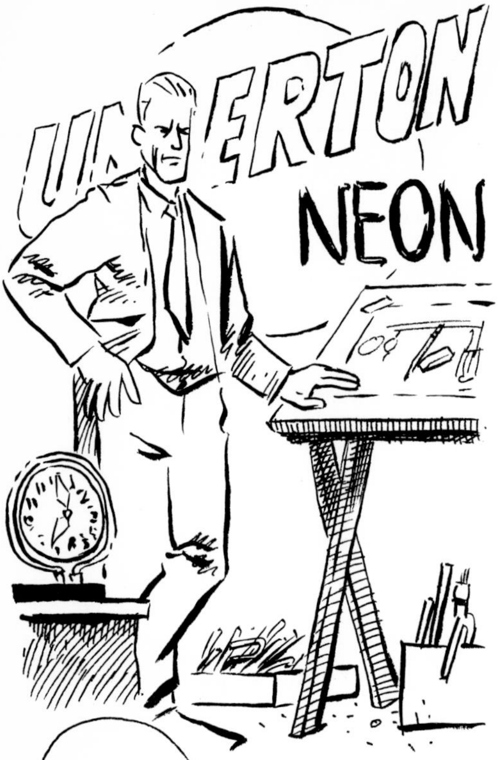
NEON

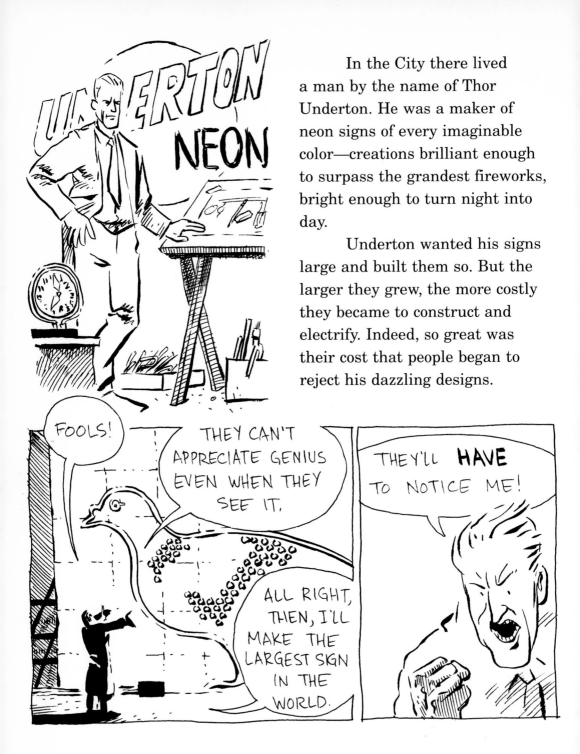

In the City there lived a man by the name of Thor Underton. He was a maker of neon signs of every imaginable color—creations brilliant enough to surpass the grandest fireworks, bright enough to turn night into day.

Underton wanted his signs large and built them so. But the larger they grew, the more costly they became to construct and electrify. Indeed, so great was their cost that people began to reject his dazzling designs.

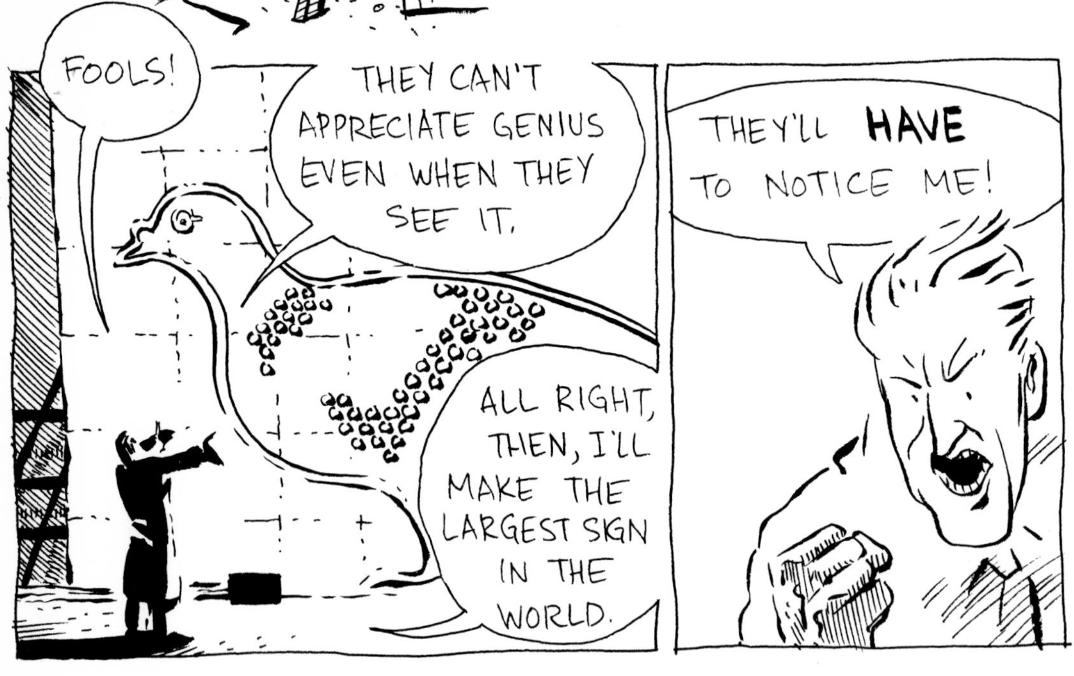
FOOLS!
THEY CAN'T APPRECIATE GENIUS EVEN WHEN THEY SEE IT.
ALL RIGHT, THEN, I'LL MAKE THE LARGEST SIGN IN THE WORLD.
THEY'LL **HAVE** TO NOTICE ME!

Underton set to work with the assistance of his young apprentice, one Theodore Bitner.

Underton had found Theo abandoned on a dark city street. He took him in, fed and clothed him, and taught him much about sign making and electricity. Naturally, Theo wished to please Underton.

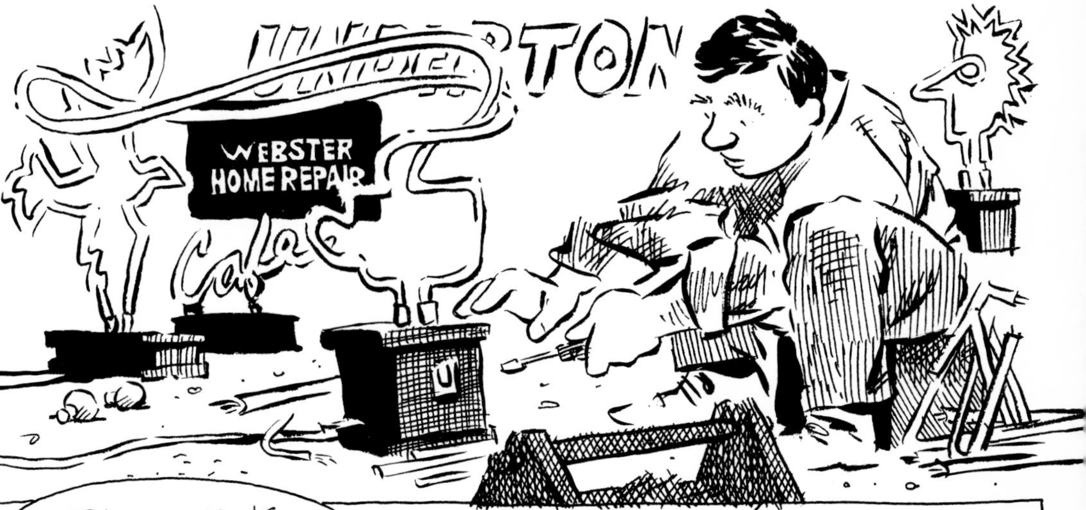
WEBSTER
HOME REPAIR
Cafe

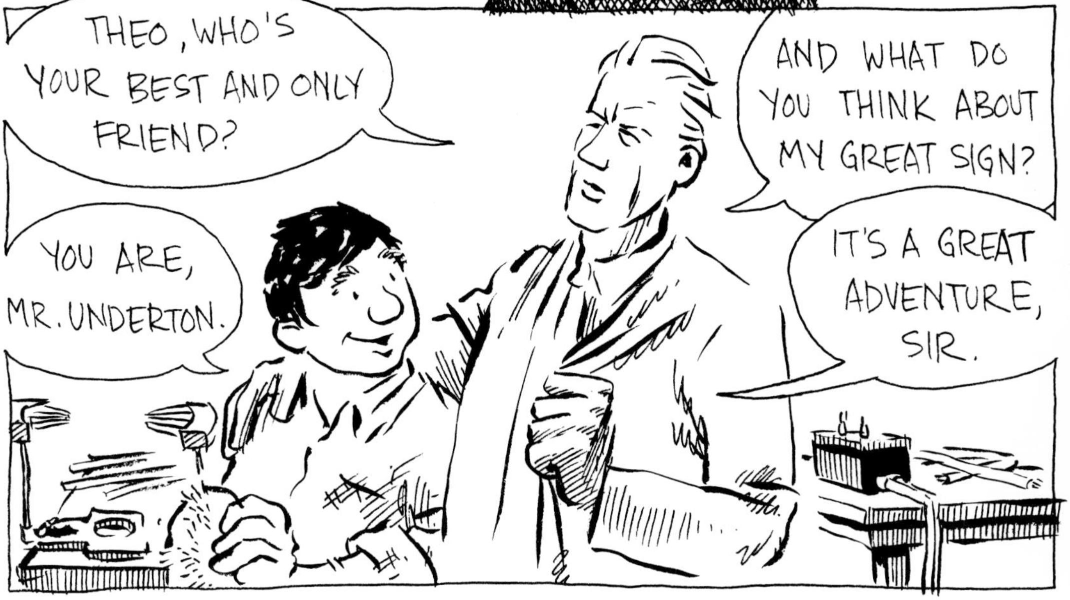
THEO, WHO'S YOUR BEST AND ONLY FRIEND?
YOU ARE, MR. UNDERTON.
AND WHAT DO YOU THINK ABOUT MY GREAT SIGN?
IT'S A GREAT ADVENTURE, SIR.

After much time and many difficulties, Underton—with Theo's help—completed his masterwork—the largest neon sign ever attempted—a gigantic spectacle of sparkling, blazing, blinking, flashing color. Its letters read,

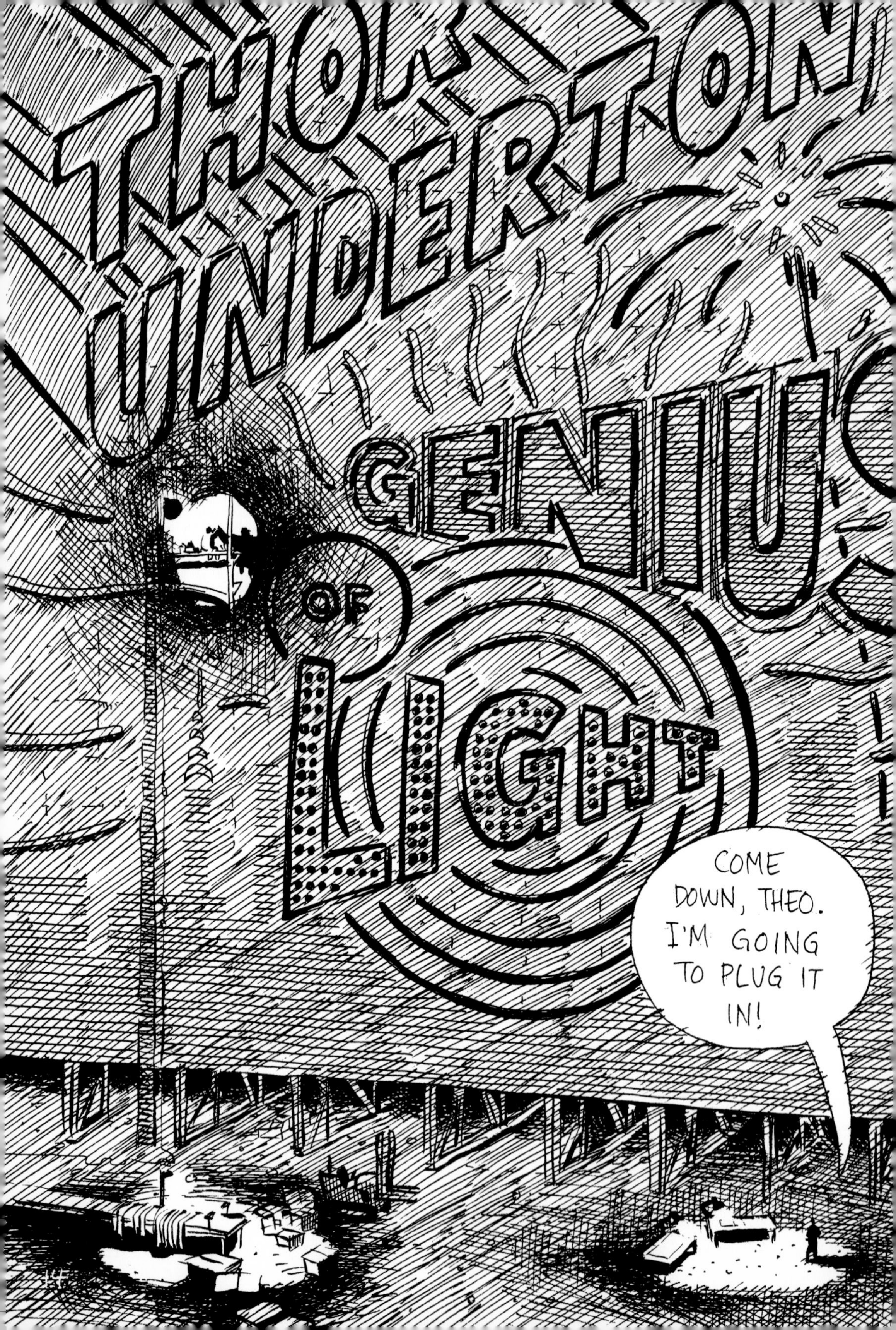
THO
UNDERTON
GENIU
OF
LIGHT
COME DOWN, THEO. I'M GOING TO PLUG IT IN!

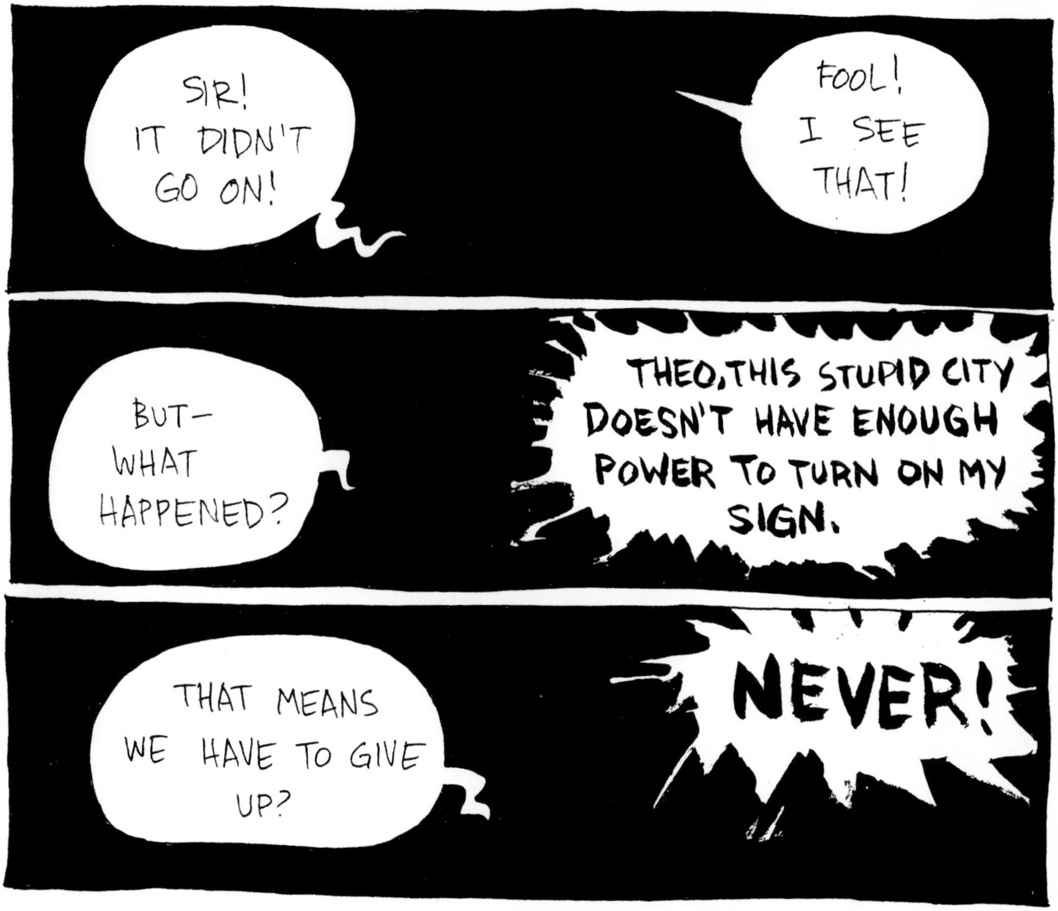
SIR! IT DIDN'T GO ON!
FOOL! I SEE THAT!
BUT— WHAT HAPPENED?
THEO, THIS STUPID CITY DOESN'T HAVE ENOUGH POWER TO TURN ON MY SIGN.
THAT MEANS WE HAVE TO GIVE UP?
NEVER!

Underton considered atomic power, solar power, sea power, wind power—nothing was enough.

Frantic, he spent hours in libraries. He consulted the Moderns. He studied the Ancients. In so doing he stumbled upon the history of the Kurbs and *their* POWER.

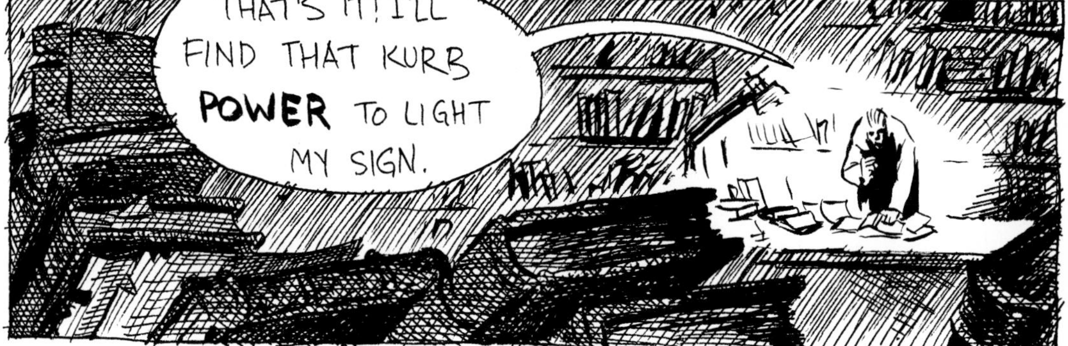
THAT'S IT! I'LL FIND THAT KURB **POWER** TO LIGHT MY SIGN.

Further research revealed that in recent times this POWER resided in a City transit token.

But would Underton be able to find the one token from among the millions of tokens that existed? He looked for a year but did not find it.

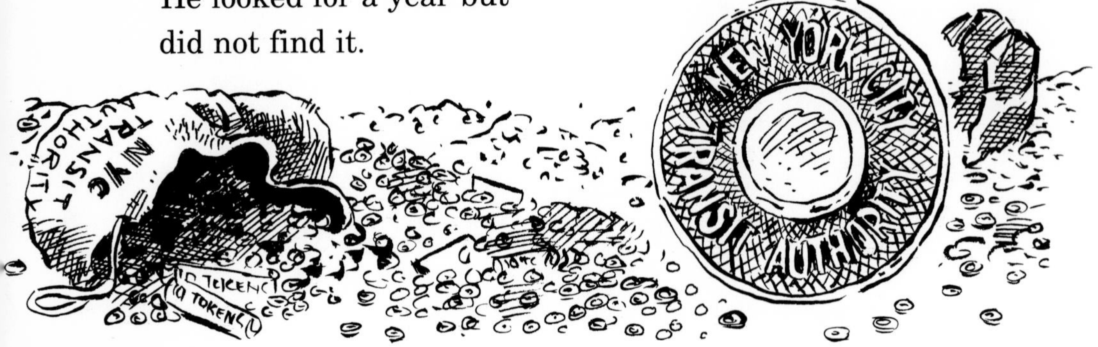
NYC TRANSIT AUTHORITY
10 TOKENS
10 TOKENS
NEW YORK CITY TRANSIT AUTHORITY

Then he learned that, at that time, the person whose mission it was to search for the token was a young woman named Asterel. He would wait until *she* found the small golden disk. Then, *before* she could restore the token to its place of safekeeping, he would take it and thus gain control of the Kurbs' POWER!

Slyly, Underton confided in Theo about the Kurbs, the POWER, and THE RITUAL CYCLE OF ACKNOWLEDGMENT.

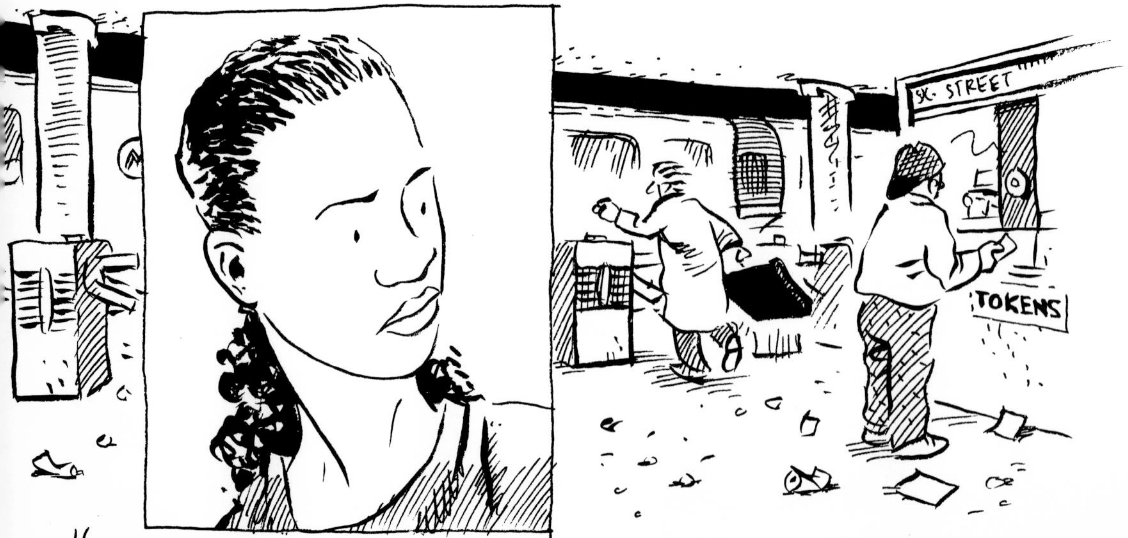
TOKENS

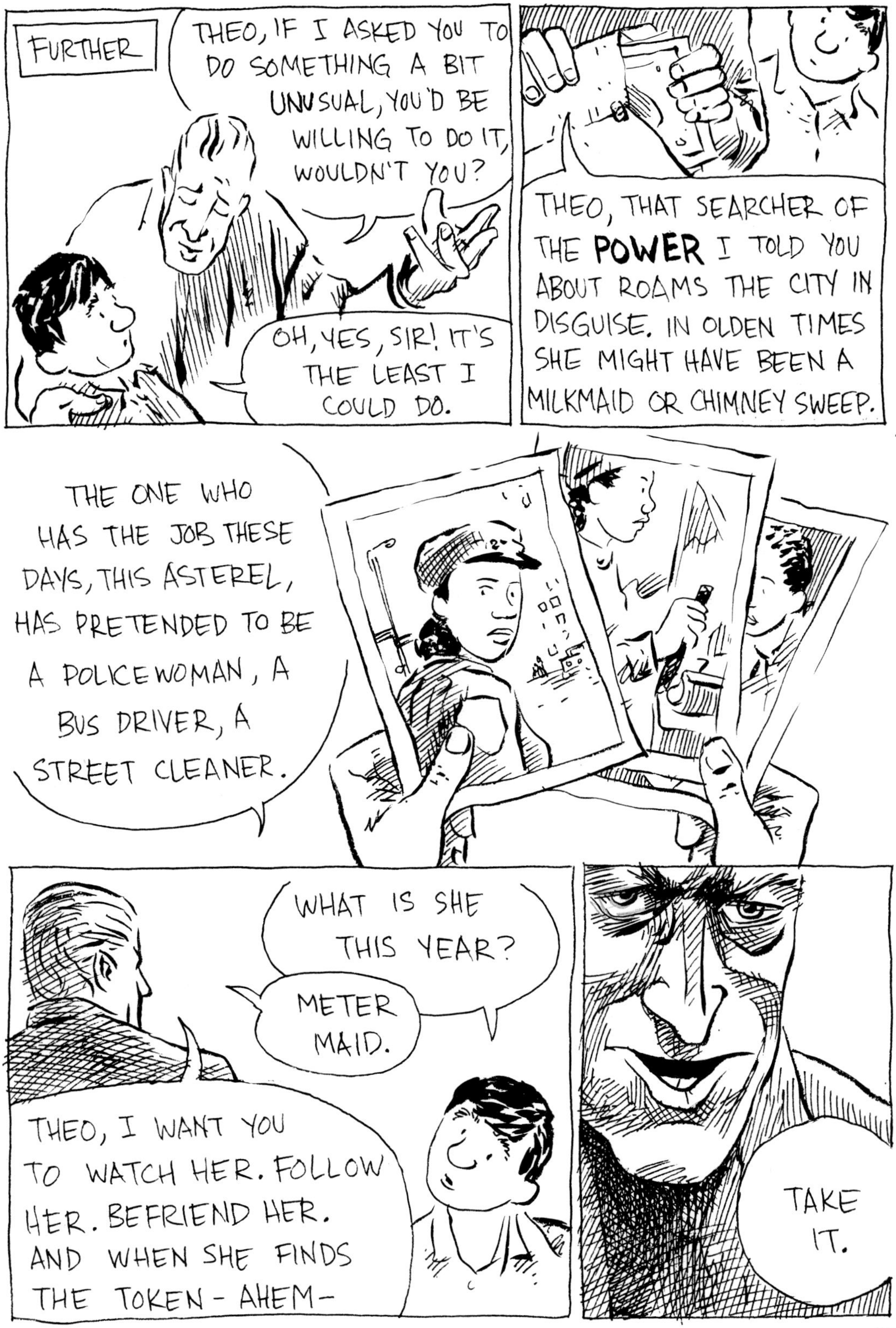
FURTHER
THEO, IF I ASKED YOU TO DO SOMETHING A BIT UNUSUAL, YOU'D BE WILLING TO DO IT, WOULDN'T YOU?
OH, YES, SIR! IT'S THE LEAST I COULD DO.
THEO, THAT SEARCHER OF THE POWER I TOLD YOU ABOUT ROAMS THE CITY IN DISGUISE. IN OLDEN TIMES SHE MIGHT HAVE BEEN A MILKMAID OR CHIMNEY SWEEP.
THE ONE WHO HAS THE JOB THESE DAYS, THIS ASTEREL, HAS PRETENDED TO BE A POLICEWOMAN, A BUS DRIVER, A STREET CLEANER.
WHAT IS SHE THIS YEAR?
METER MAID.
THEO, I WANT YOU TO WATCH HER. FOLLOW HER. BEFRIEND HER. AND WHEN SHE FINDS THE TOKEN - AHEM -
TAKE IT.

Theo had no trouble meeting Asterel: he merely parked a car by a fire hydrant. She—a meter maid—gave him a parking ticket. But once the young man and young woman met, they came to like each other. What's more, in the course of time, from January to February, they fell in love.

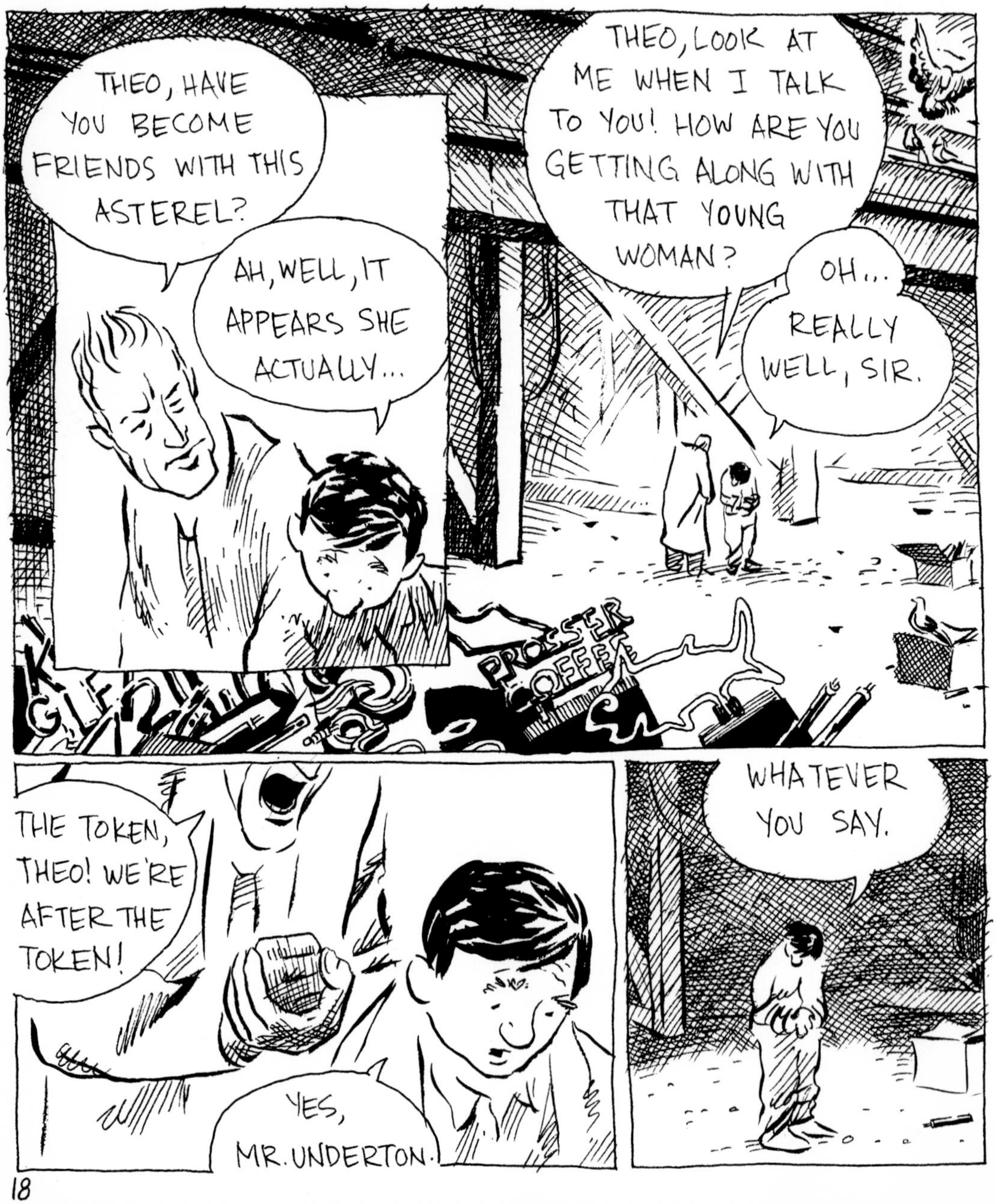

THEO, HAVE YOU BECOME FRIENDS WITH THIS ASTEREL?
AH, WELL, IT APPEARS SHE ACTUALLY...
THEO, LOOK AT ME WHEN I TALK TO YOU! HOW ARE YOU GETTING ALONG WITH THAT YOUNG WOMAN?
OH... REALLY WELL, SIR.
PROSSER COFFEE
THE TOKEN, THEO! WE'RE AFTER THE TOKEN!
YES, MR. UNDERTON.
WHATEVER YOU SAY.

But the more deeply Theo and Asterel loved, the greater grew their fear that the truth of their identities, if discovered, would split them apart. So they held fast to their secrets—he to the nature of his assignment from Underton, she to her fated mission as the searcher of the POWER.

In the month of March, they married.

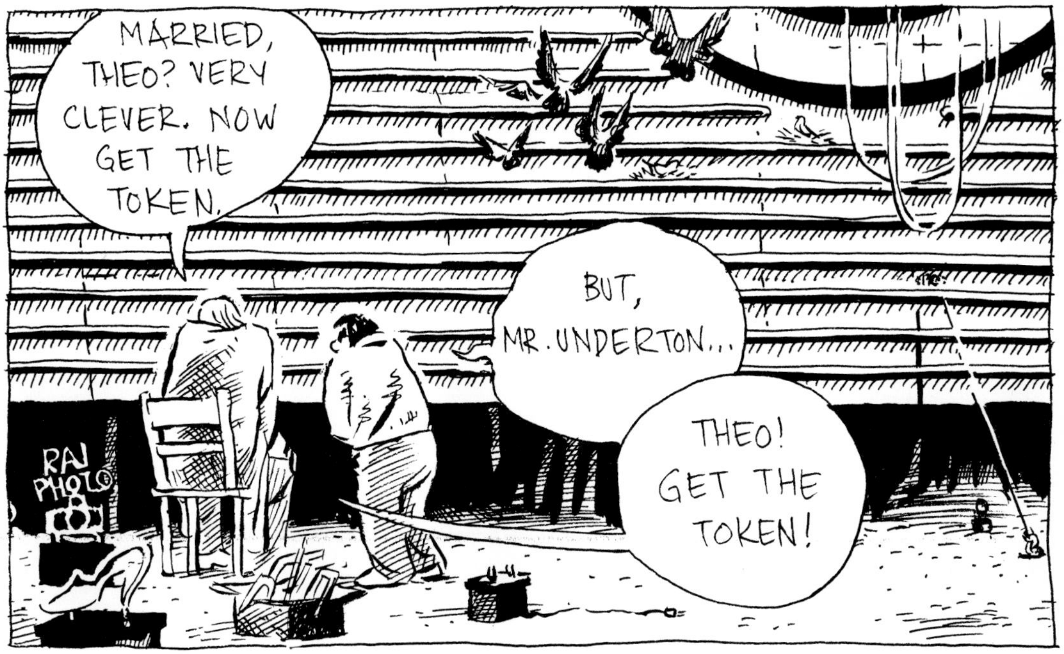
MARRIED, THEO? VERY CLEVER. NOW GET THE TOKEN.
BUT, MR. UNDERTON...
THEO! GET THE TOKEN!
RAJ PHOTO

Three months after the marriage—at the moment of noon on the 21st of June—Asterel secretly resumed that year's mission of searching for the token hidden by the Kurbs. Theo—just as secretly—spied on her, so he knew when she found the token. But he did not know why his wife slipped off to an underground hideaway beneath the City's Grand Central Station. Though he followed her there, he was unable to see her conceal the token in a hiding place of her own. The truth is, Asterel was to have a baby in December and she needed to keep the token so as to anoint the unborn child. Of that, Theo knew nothing.

In the third week of December, Asterel gave birth to a girl. "Let's name her Estella," she told Theo happily. "The word means 'star.'"

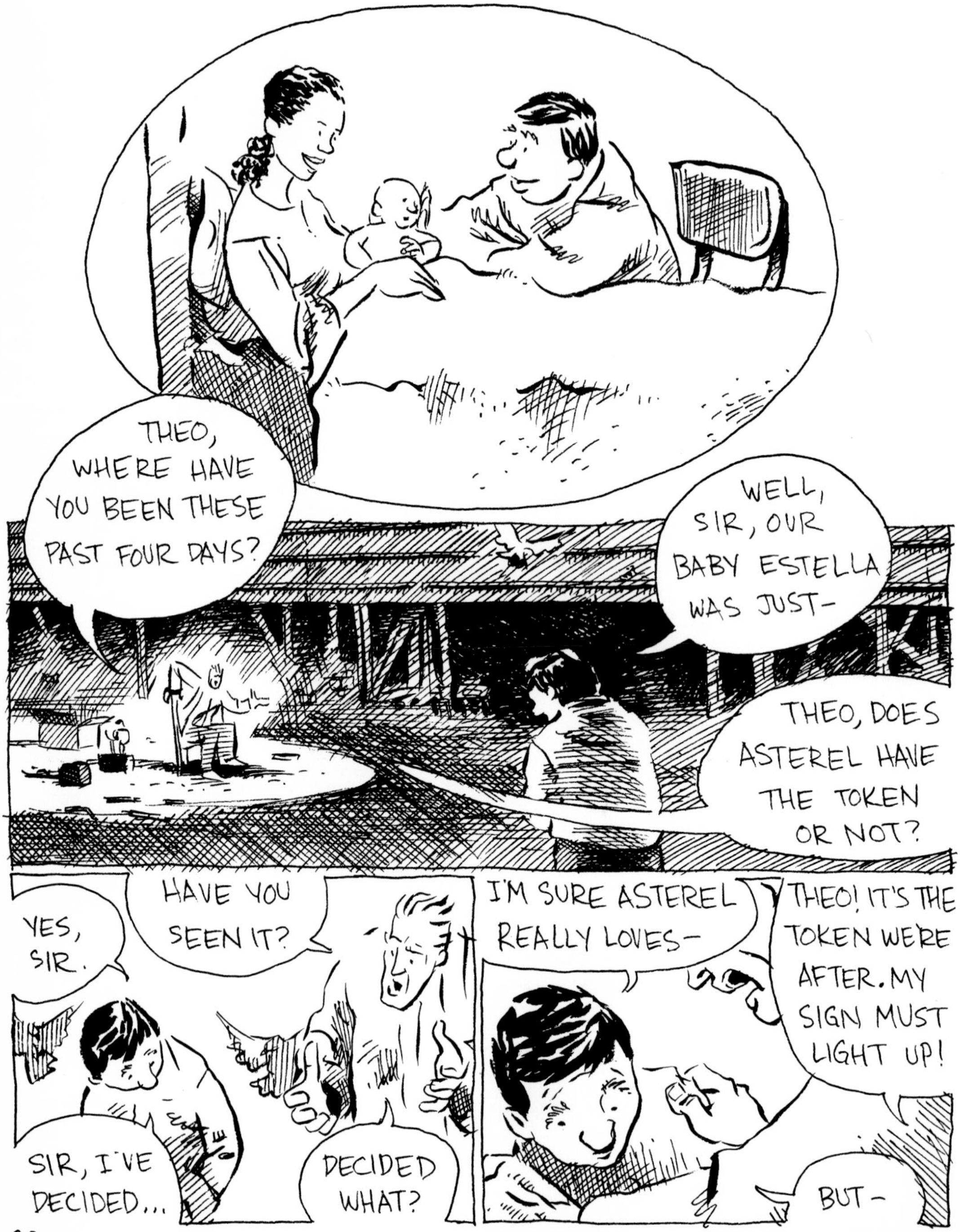
THEO, WHERE HAVE YOU BEEN THESE PAST FOUR DAYS?
WELL, SIR, OUR BABY ESTELLA WAS JUST-
THEO, DOES ASTEREL HAVE THE TOKEN OR NOT?
YES, SIR.
HAVE YOU SEEN IT?
SIR, I'VE DECIDED...
DECIDED WHAT?
I'M SURE ASTEREL REALLY LOVES-
THEO! IT'S THE TOKEN WE'RE AFTER. MY SIGN MUST LIGHT UP!
BUT-

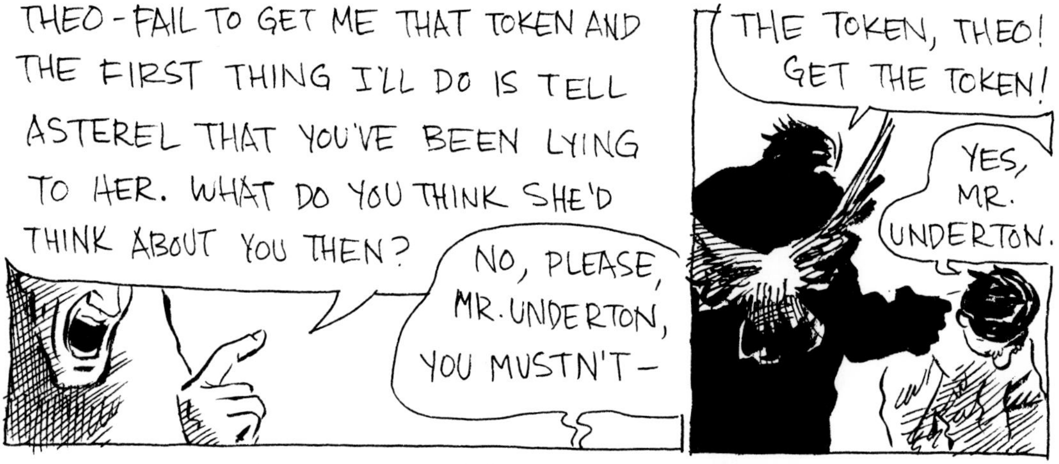
THEO - FAIL TO GET ME THAT TOKEN AND THE FIRST THING I'LL DO IS TELL ASTEREL THAT YOU'VE BEEN LYING TO HER. WHAT DO YOU THINK SHE'D THINK ABOUT YOU THEN?
NO, PLEASE, MR. UNDERTON, YOU MUSTN'T-
THE TOKEN, THEO! GET THE TOKEN!
YES, MR. UNDERTON.

By the morning of the 21st of December, Asterel had regained enough strength to make some excuse to her husband, then slip away to her underground hideaway and fetch the token. With it she intended to anoint her daughter, passing on to Estella the searcher's gift of special sight.

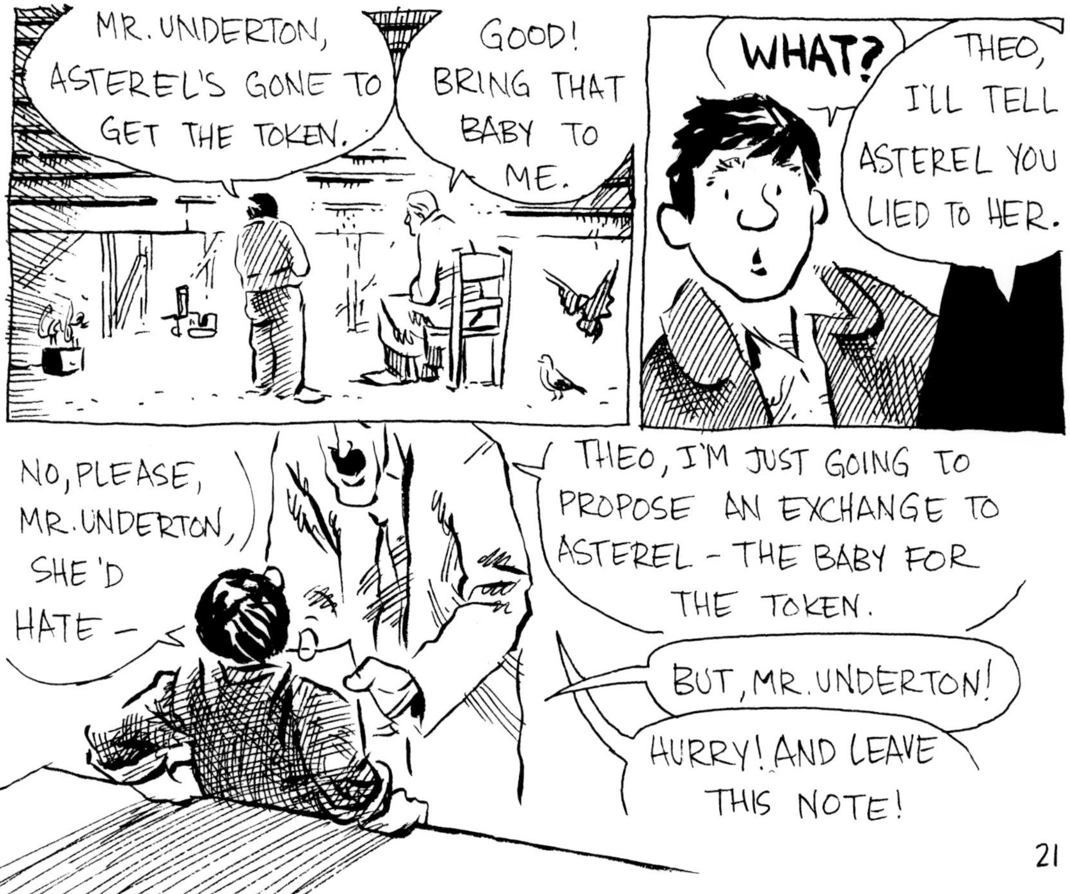
MR. UNDERTON, ASTEREL'S GONE TO GET THE TOKEN.
GOOD! BRING THAT BABY TO ME.
WHAT?
THEO, I'LL TELL ASTEREL YOU LIED TO HER.
NO, PLEASE, MR. UNDERTON, SHE'D HATE -
THEO, I'M JUST GOING TO PROPOSE AN EXCHANGE TO ASTEREL - THE BABY FOR THE TOKEN.
BUT, MR. UNDERTON!
HURRY! AND LEAVE THIS NOTE!

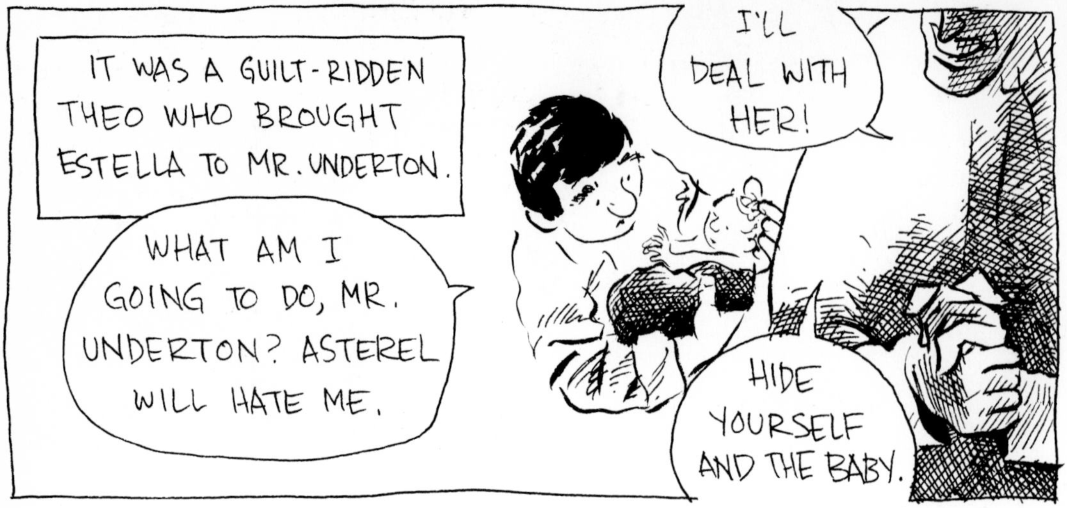
IT WAS A GUILT-RIDDEN THEO WHO BROUGHT ESTELLA TO MR. UNDERTON.
WHAT AM I GOING TO DO, MR. UNDERTON? ASTEREL WILL HATE ME.
I'LL DEAL WITH HER!
HIDE YOURSELF AND THE BABY.

Token in hand to anoint Estella, Asterel returned to the home she shared with Theo. There she found a note:

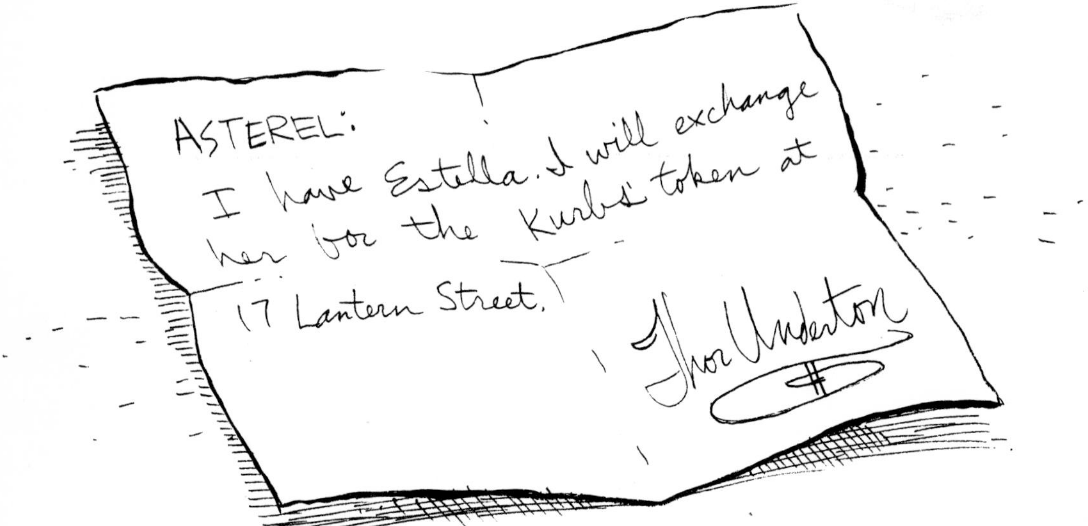
ASTEREL:
I have Estella. I will exchange her for the Kurbs' token at 17 Lantern Street.
Thor Underton

In rage and panic, Asterel raced to Underton's workshop. Instead of bargaining with the genius of light, she commenced to destroy his great sign, shattering the neon tubes into a million slivers of glass. When Underton tried to stop her and save his masterwork, he was accidentally blinded.

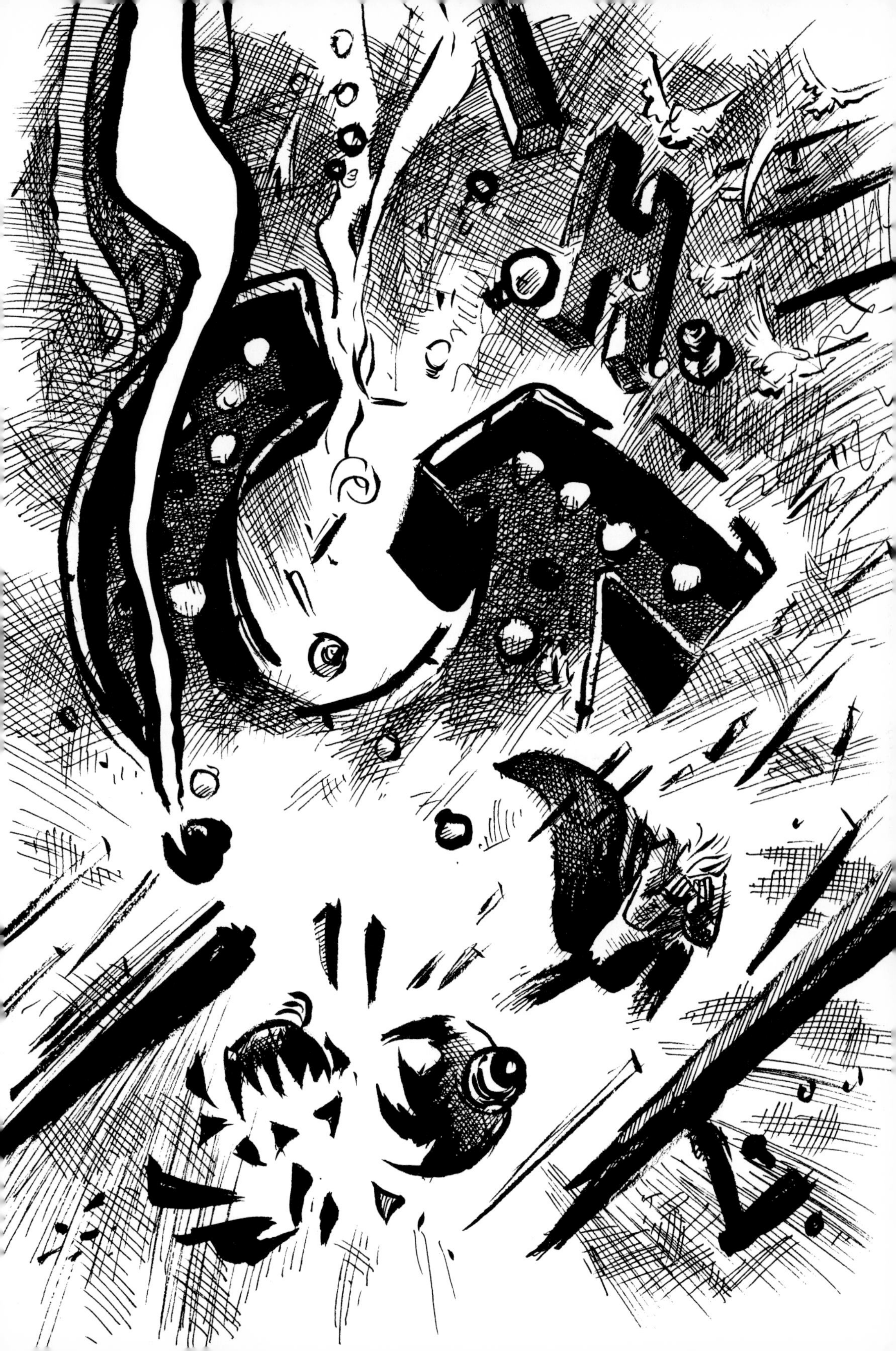

Now Asterel faced a terrible decision: should she complete the ritual of the token or set off to search for her baby? She felt she had no choice. She must save the city. In agony she fled the workshop, struggled through the City, and restored the token to its place of safekeeping. Then she fairly flew back to Lantern Street. But Underton, Theo, and her Estella were nowhere to be seen.

That was eleven years ago. In the time since—

Asterel has continued to do as she was meant to do—search for the token and complete the annual ritual. *But she has never stopped looking for her daughter.*

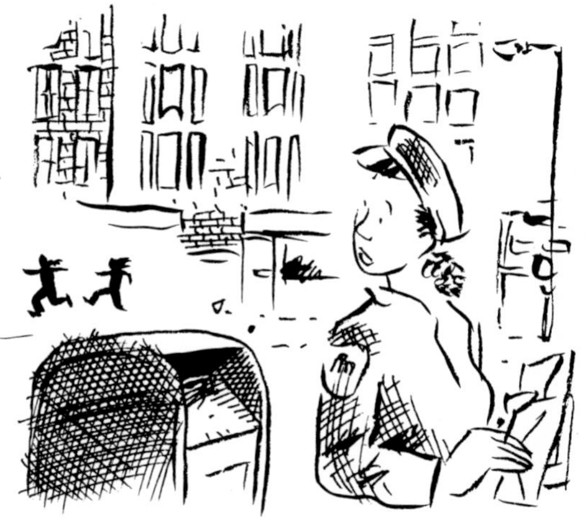

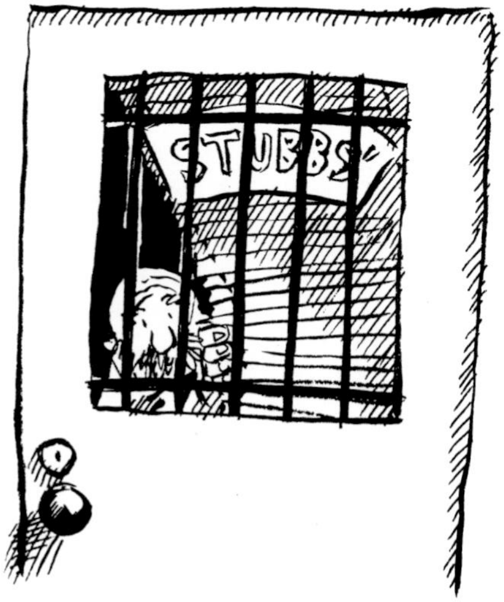
STUBBS

Theo has cared for Estella as lovingly as any father could. But, fearful that Asterel might find him and take their child, he has changed his name, disguised his face, and meekly given over control of his life to Underton. *Above all, he has tried to stay hidden from Asterel.*

As for Underton, he, embittered by blindness, has grown more and more obsessed about the token. Absolutely convinced that its POWER can restore his sight, he devotes all his time, energy, and genius to one goal: *that the token shall be his!*

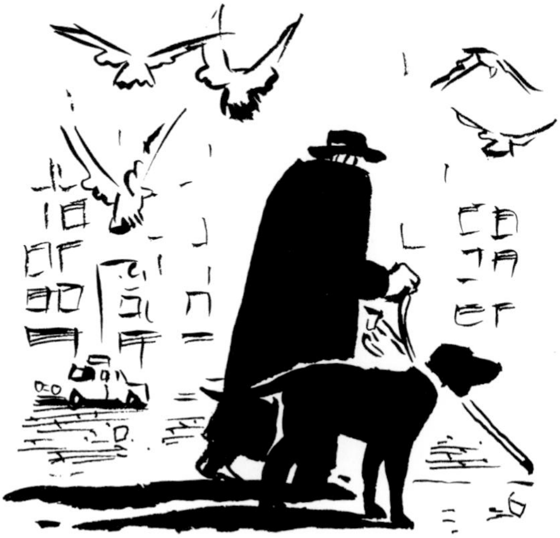

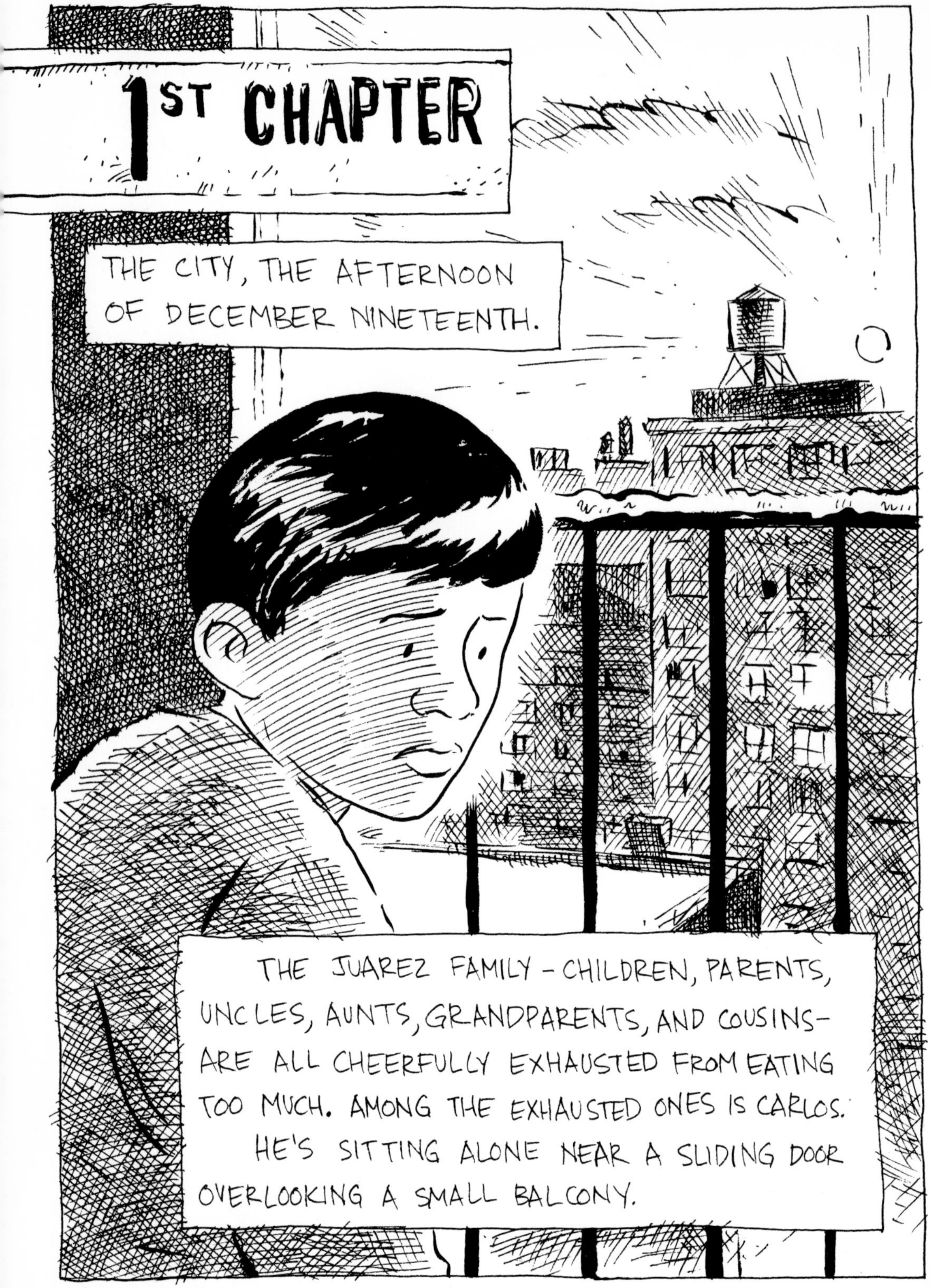
1ST CHAPTER
THE CITY, THE AFTERNOON OF DECEMBER NINETEENTH.
THE JUAREZ FAMILY - CHILDREN, PARENTS, UNCLES, AUNTS, GRANDPARENTS, AND COUSINS - ARE ALL CHEERFULLY EXHAUSTED FROM EATING TOO MUCH. AMONG THE EXHAUSTED ONES IS CARLOS.
HE'S SITTING ALONE NEAR A SLIDING DOOR OVERLOOKING A SMALL BALCONY.

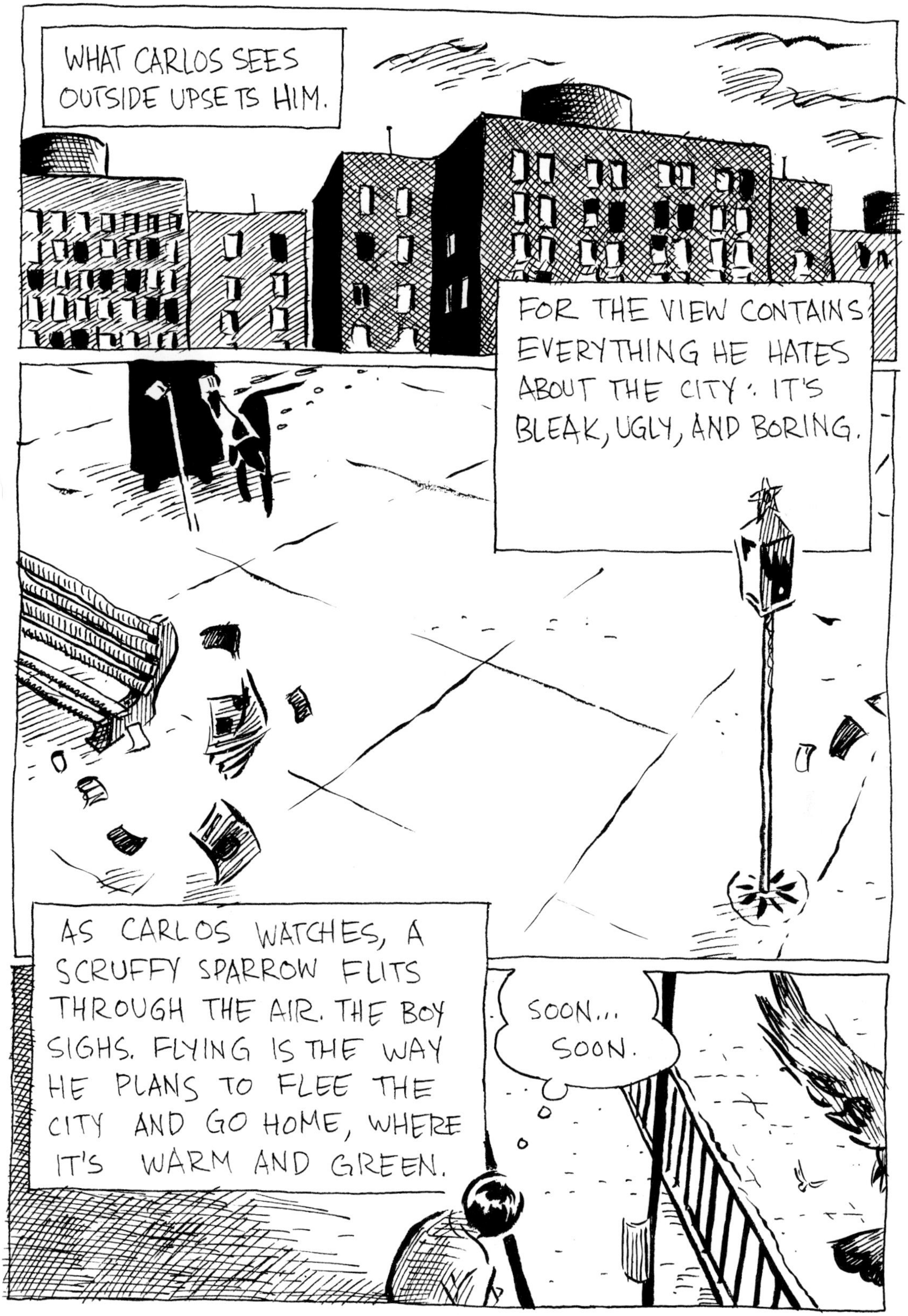
WHAT CARLOS SEES OUTSIDE UPSETS HIM.
FOR THE VIEW CONTAINS EVERYTHING HE HATES ABOUT THE CITY: IT'S BLEAK, UGLY, AND BORING.
AS CARLOS WATCHES, A SCRUFFY SPARROW FLITS THROUGH THE AIR. THE BOY SIGHS. FLYING IS THE WAY HE PLANS TO FLEE THE CITY AND GO HOME, WHERE IT'S WARM AND GREEN.
SOON... SOON.

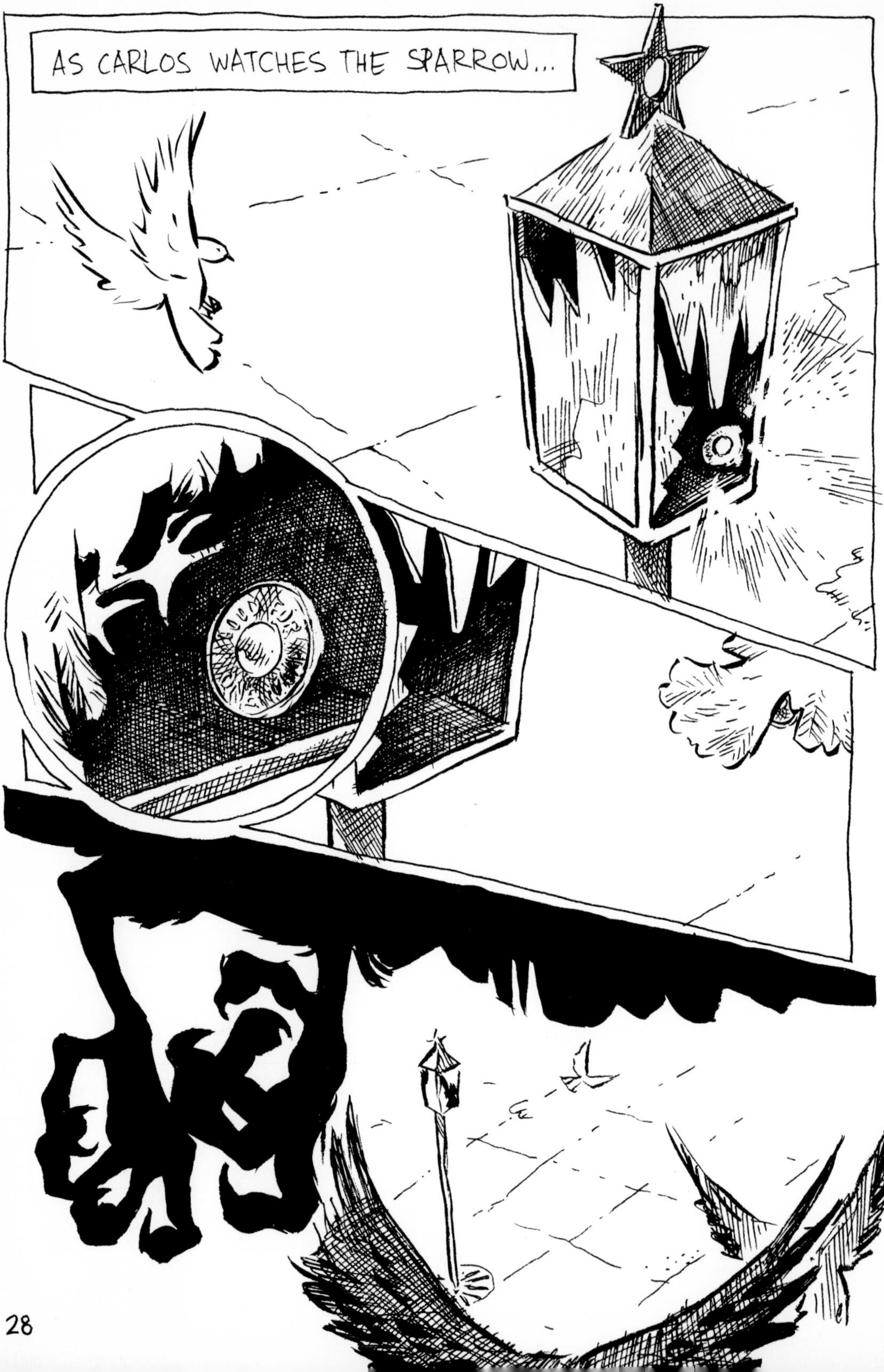
AS CARLOS WATCHES THE SPARROW...

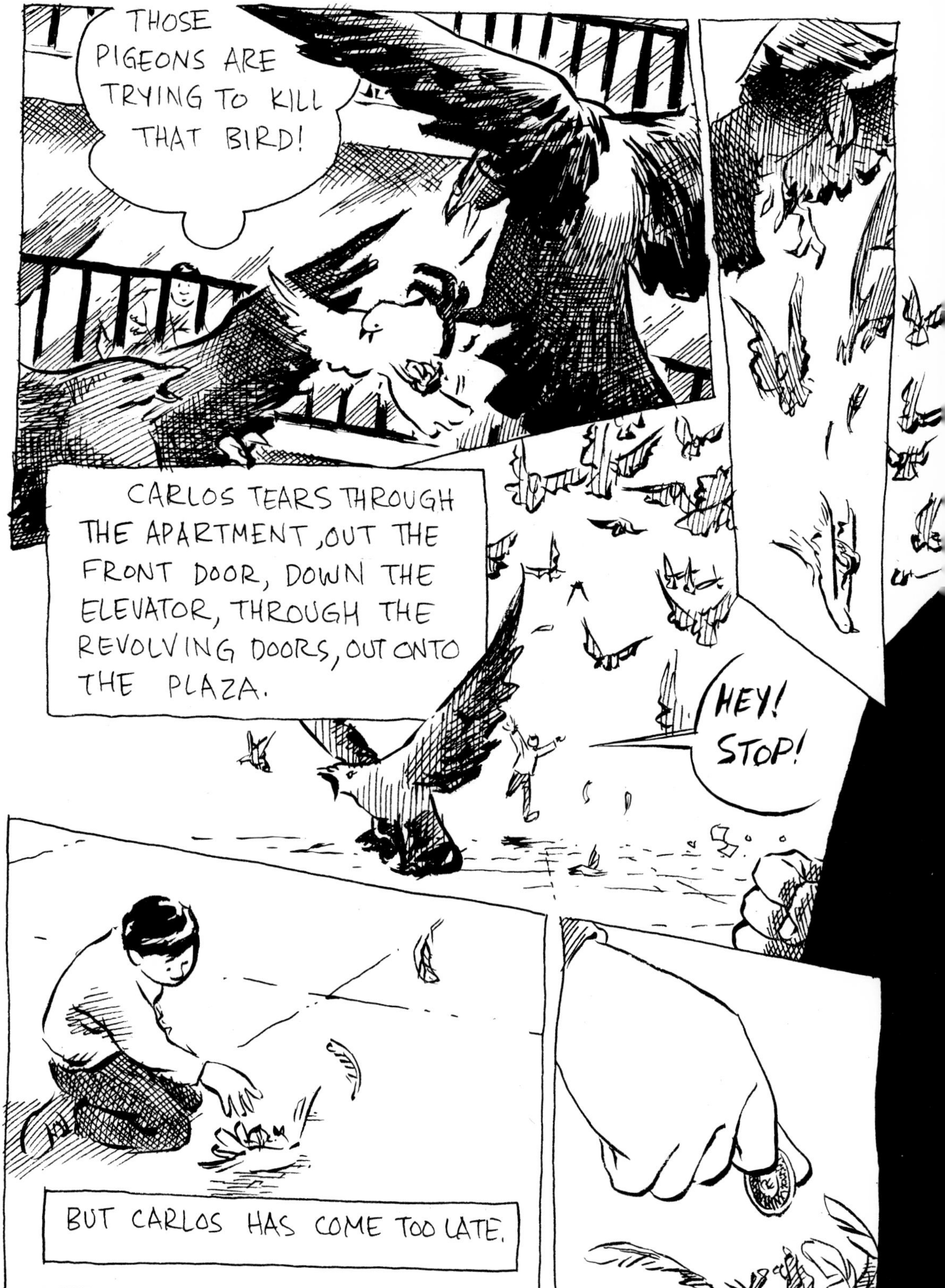
THOSE PIGEONS ARE TRYING TO KILL THAT BIRD!
CARLOS TEARS THROUGH THE APARTMENT, OUT THE FRONT DOOR, DOWN THE ELEVATOR, THROUGH THE REVOLVING DOORS, OUT ONTO THE PLAZA.
HEY! STOP!
BUT CARLOS HAS COME TOO LATE.

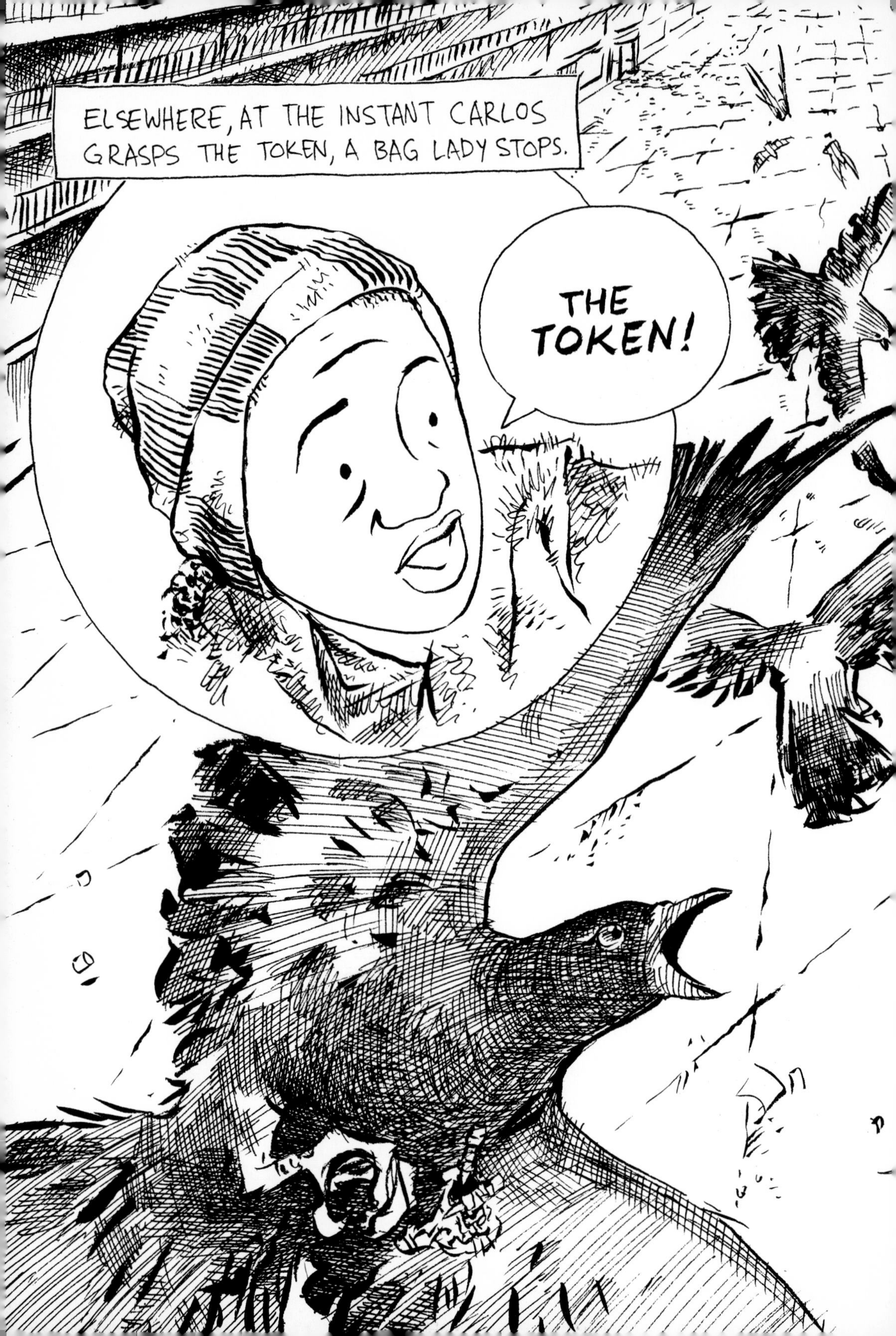
ELSEWHERE, AT THE INSTANT CARLOS GRASPS THE TOKEN, A BAG LADY STOPS.
THE TOKEN!

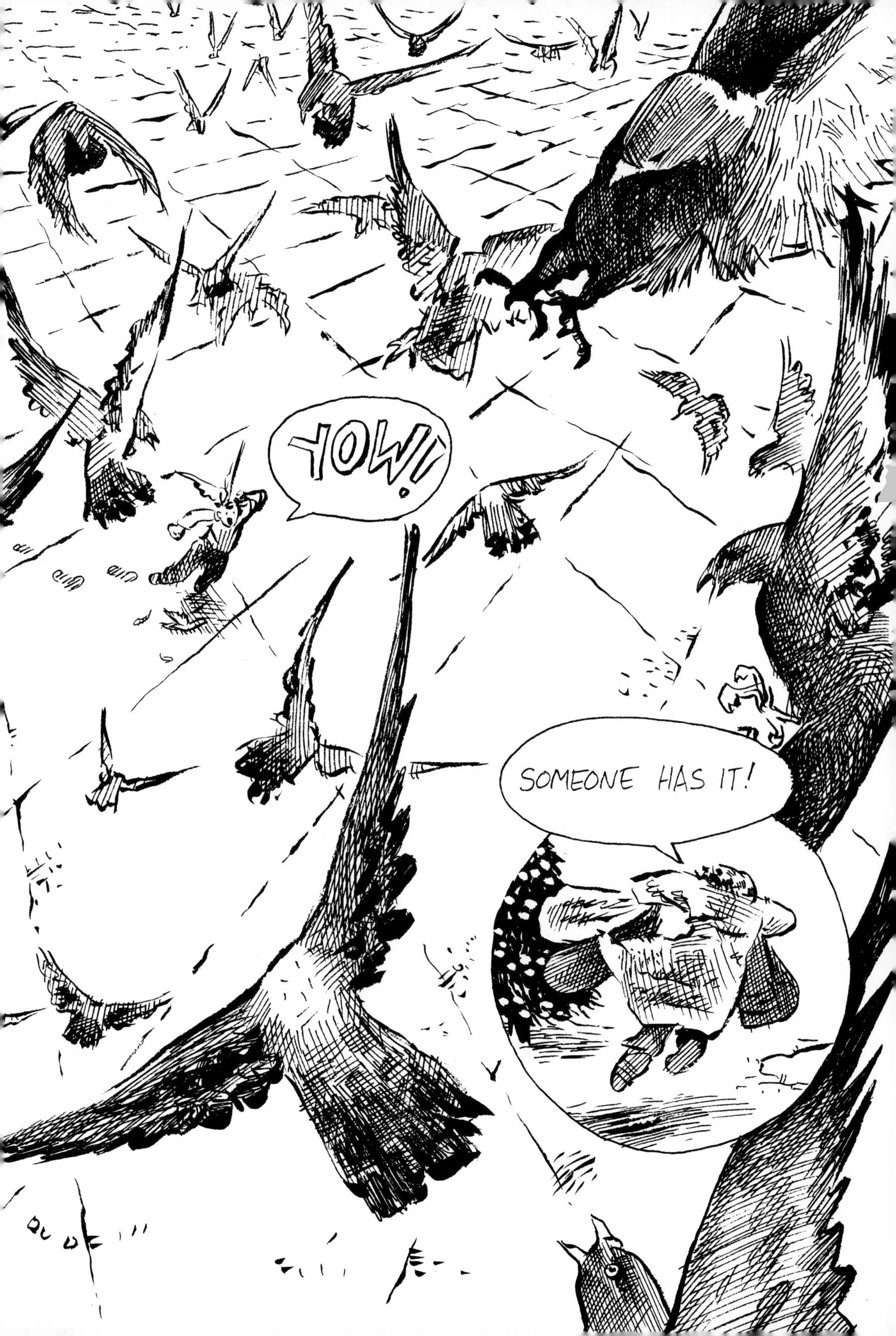
YOW!
SOMEONE HAS IT!

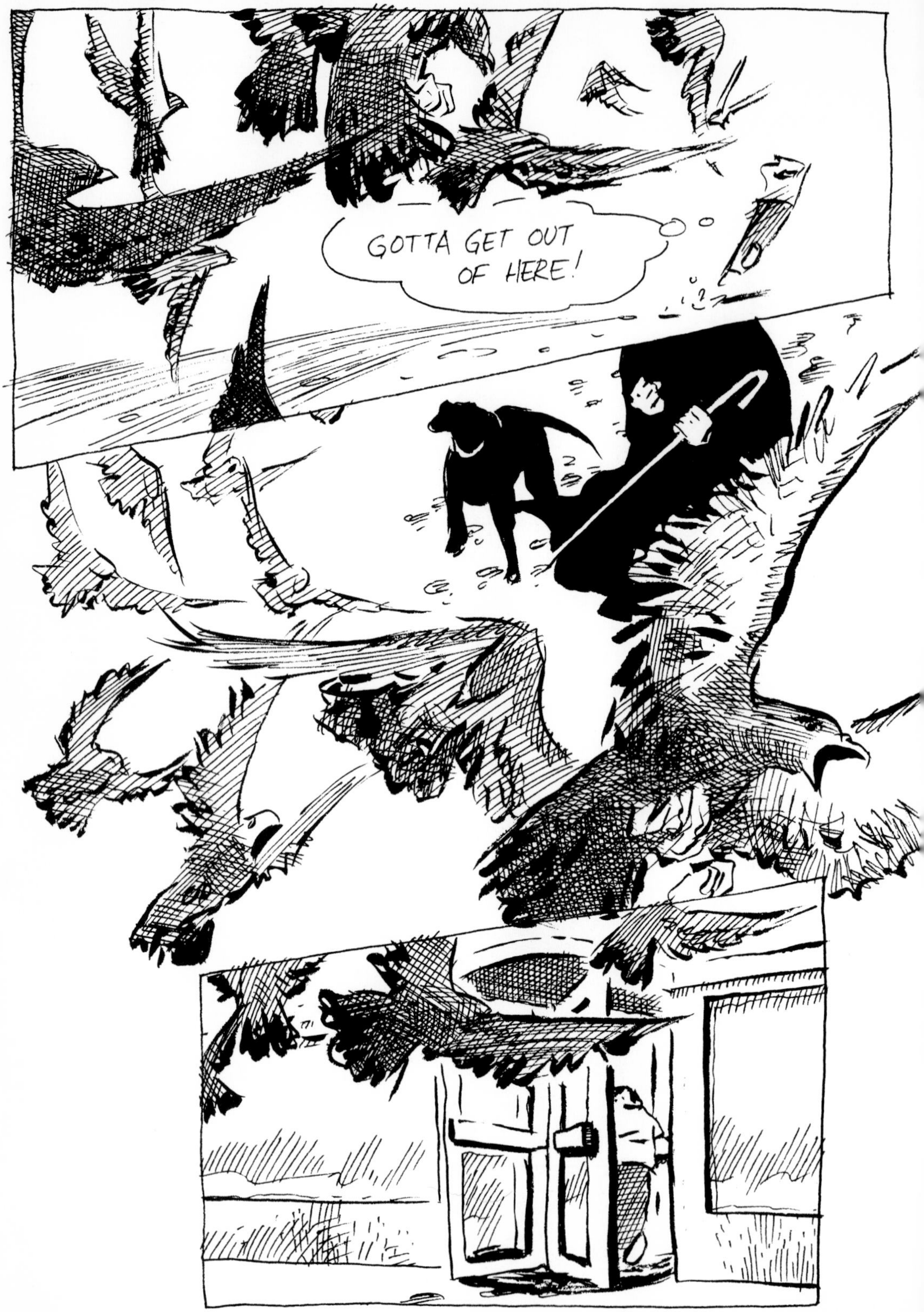
GOTTA GET OUT OF HERE!

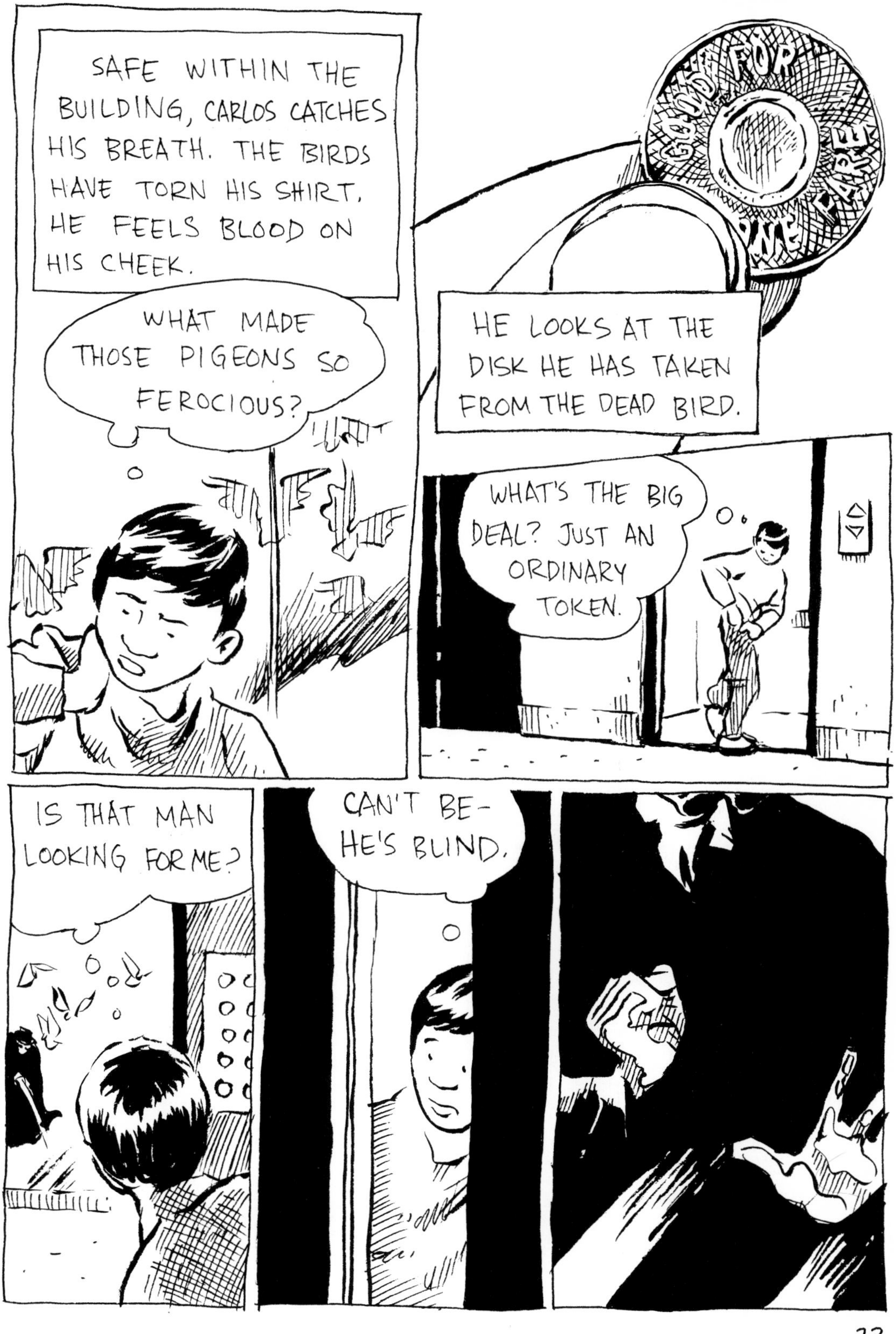
SAFE WITHIN THE BUILDING, CARLOS CATCHES HIS BREATH. THE BIRDS HAVE TORN HIS SHIRT. HE FEELS BLOOD ON HIS CHEEK.
WHAT MADE THOSE PIGEONS SO FEROCIOUS?
GOOD FOR ONE FARE
HE LOOKS AT THE DISK HE HAS TAKEN FROM THE DEAD BIRD.
WHAT'S THE BIG DEAL? JUST AN ORDINARY TOKEN.
IS THAT MAN LOOKING FOR ME?
CAN'T BE- HE'S BLIND.

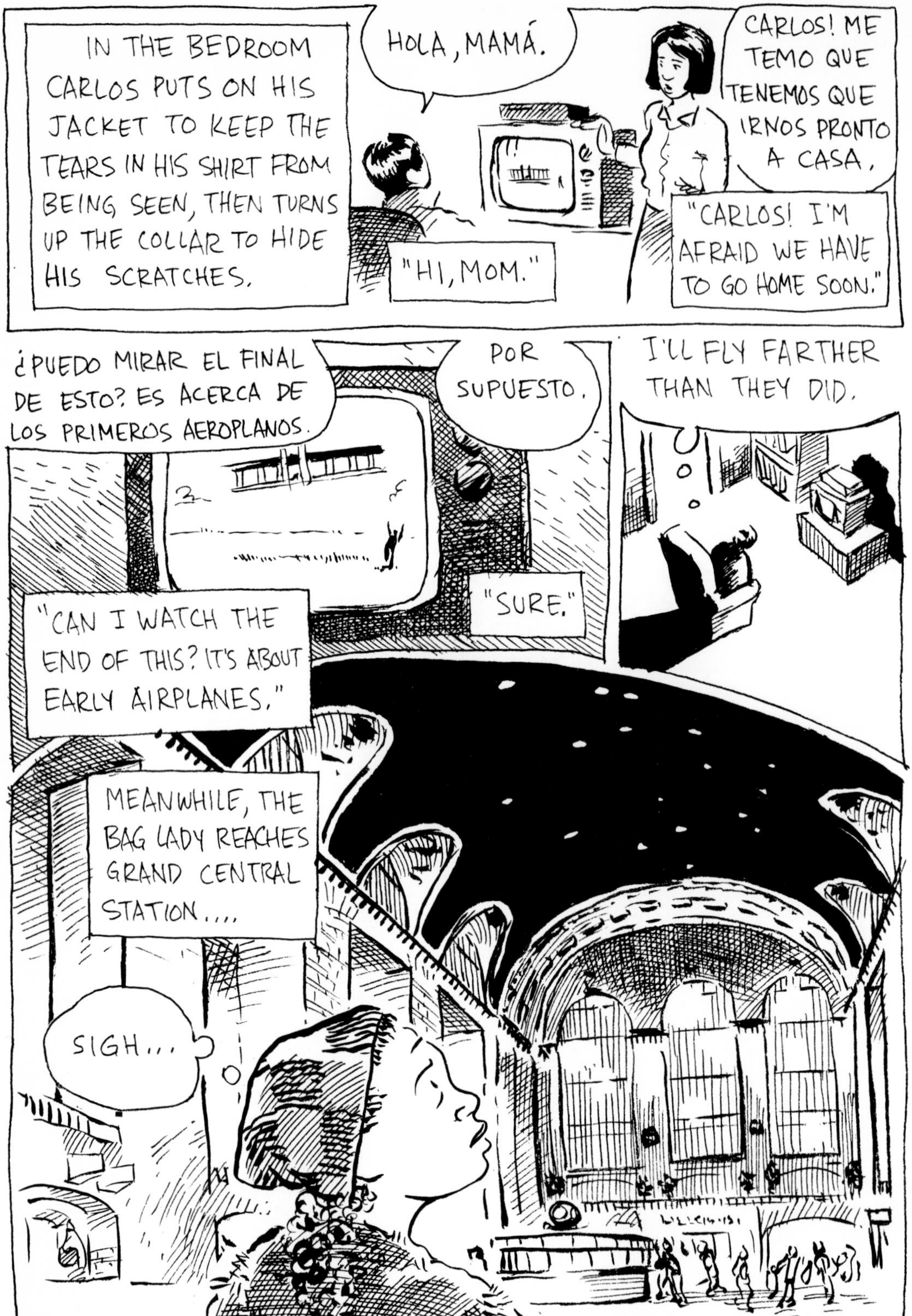
IN THE BEDROOM CARLOS PUTS ON HIS JACKET TO KEEP THE TEARS IN HIS SHIRT FROM BEING SEEN, THEN TURNS UP THE COLLAR TO HIDE HIS SCRATCHES.
HOLA, MAMÁ.
"HI, MOM."
CARLOS! ME TEMO QUE TENEMOS QUE IRNOS PRONTO A CASA.
"CARLOS! I'M AFRAID WE HAVE TO GO HOME SOON."
¿PUEDO MIRAR EL FINAL DE ESTO? ES ACERCA DE LOS PRIMEROS AEROPLANOS.
"CAN I WATCH THE END OF THIS? IT'S ABOUT EARLY AIRPLANES."
POR SUPUESTO.
"SURE."
I'LL FLY FARTHER THAN THEY DID.
MEANWHILE, THE BAG LADY REACHES GRAND CENTRAL STATION....
SIGH...

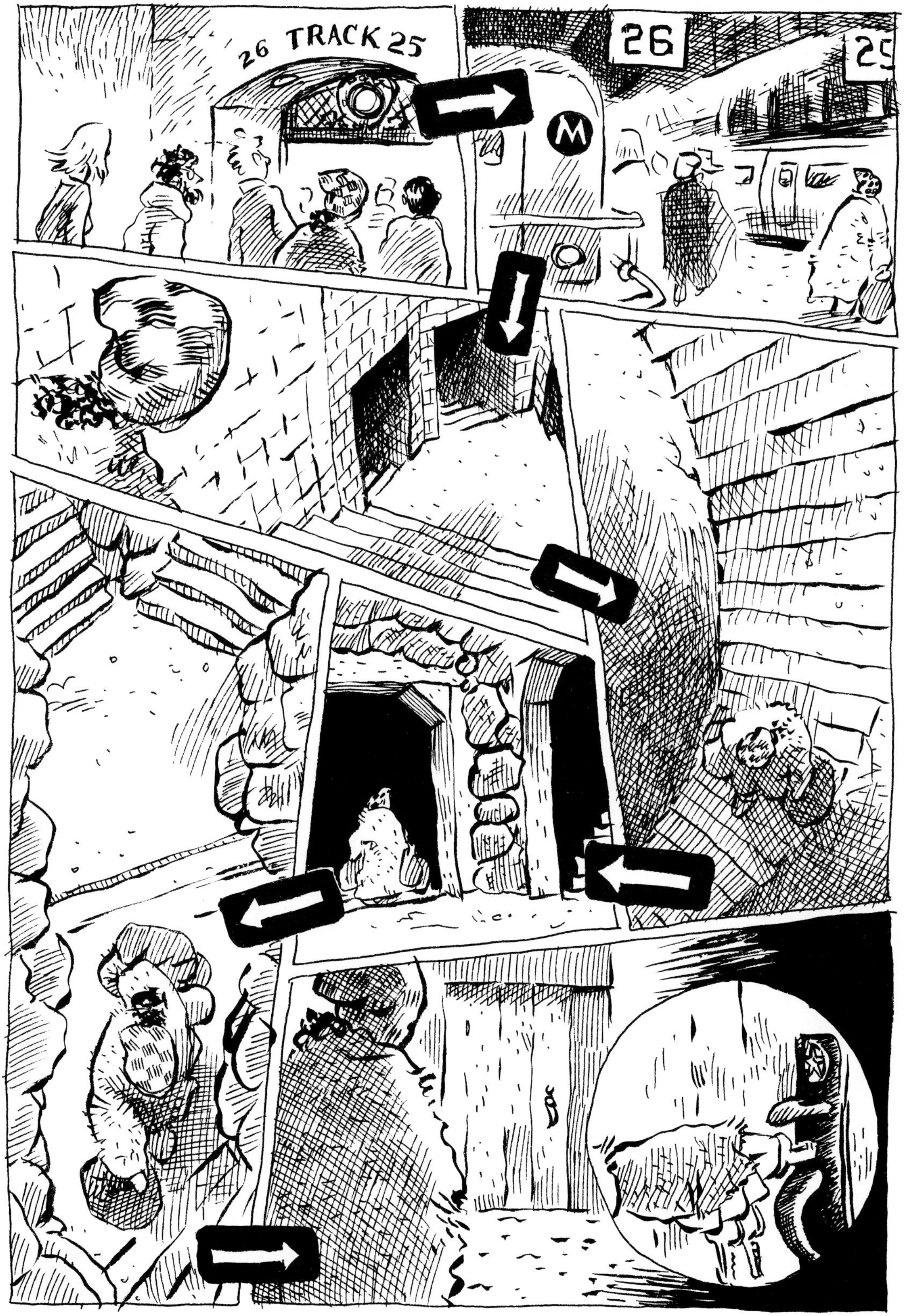
26 TRACK 25
26
25
M

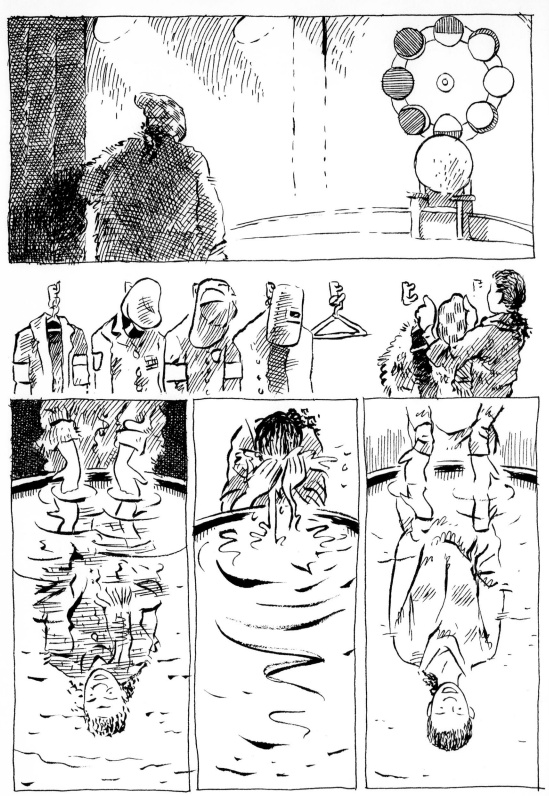

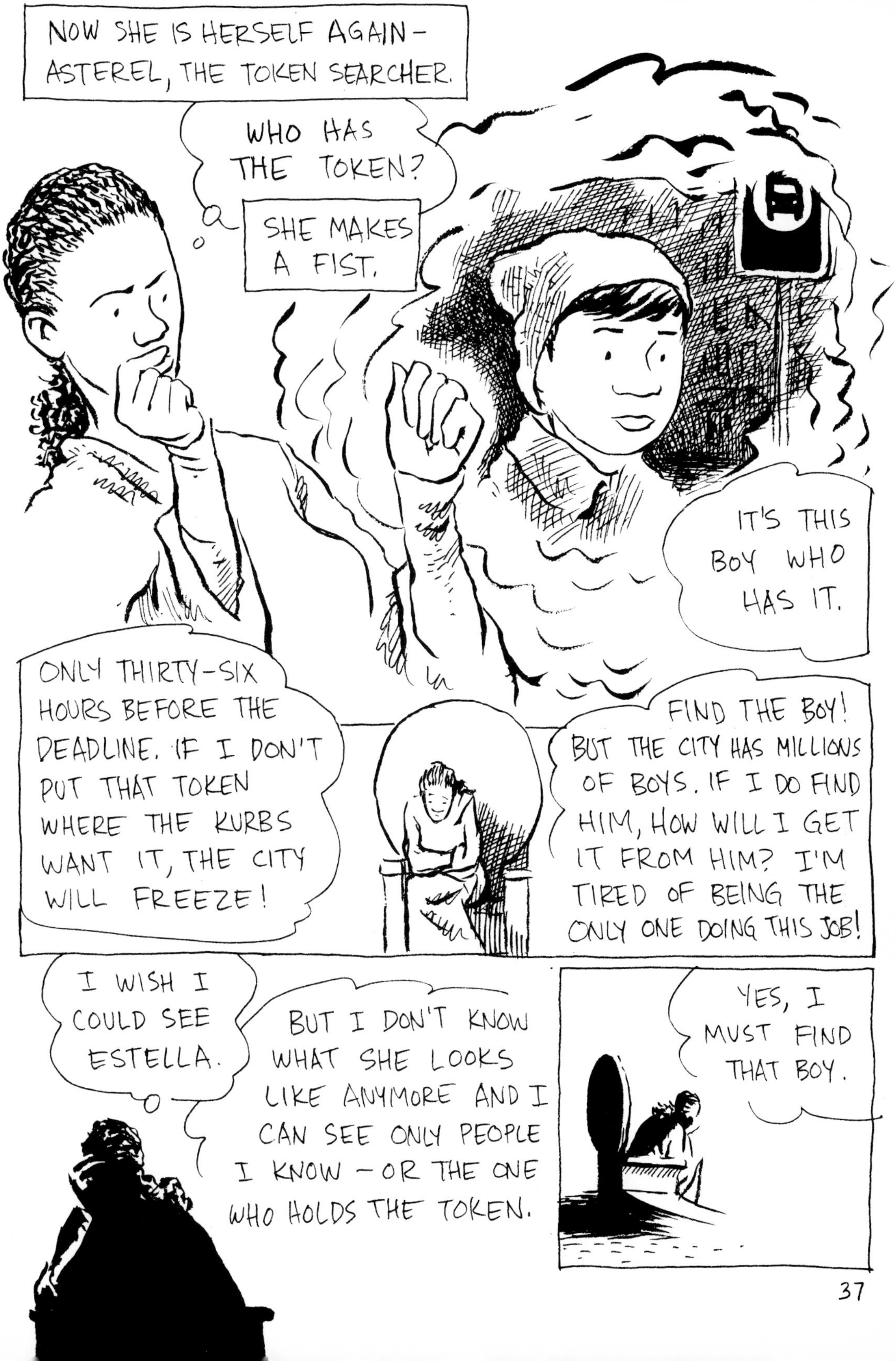
NOW SHE IS HERSELF AGAIN - ASTEREL, THE TOKEN SEARCHER.
WHO HAS THE TOKEN?
SHE MAKES A FIST.
IT'S THIS BOY WHO HAS IT.
ONLY THIRTY-SIX HOURS BEFORE THE DEADLINE. IF I DON'T PUT THAT TOKEN WHERE THE KURBS WANT IT, THE CITY WILL FREEZE!
FIND THE BOY! BUT THE CITY HAS MILLIONS OF BOYS. IF I DO FIND HIM, HOW WILL I GET IT FROM HIM? I'M TIRED OF BEING THE ONLY ONE DOING THIS JOB!
I WISH I COULD SEE ESTELLA.
BUT I DON'T KNOW WHAT SHE LOOKS LIKE ANYMORE AND I CAN SEE ONLY PEOPLE I KNOW - OR THE ONE WHO HOLDS THE TOKEN.
YES, I MUST FIND THAT BOY.

IN A LUMBERING CITY BUS...
CARLOS AND HIS MOTHER SIT IN
THE BACK ROW. AS HIS MOTHER DOZES,
CARLOS REACHES INTO HIS POCKET
AND PULLS THE TOKEN OUT, CURLING
HIS FINGERS OVER IT.

O'Leary's

PHNOM PENH
CAMBODIAN CUIS.

STARTLED BY THE SUDDEN LIGHT, CARLOS
SHOVES THE TOKEN BACK INTO HIS POCKET.
IT BECOMES DARK AGAIN.

YAWN!
MUST BE
TIRED.

CARLOS SLEEPS.

UNSEEN BY THE BOY...

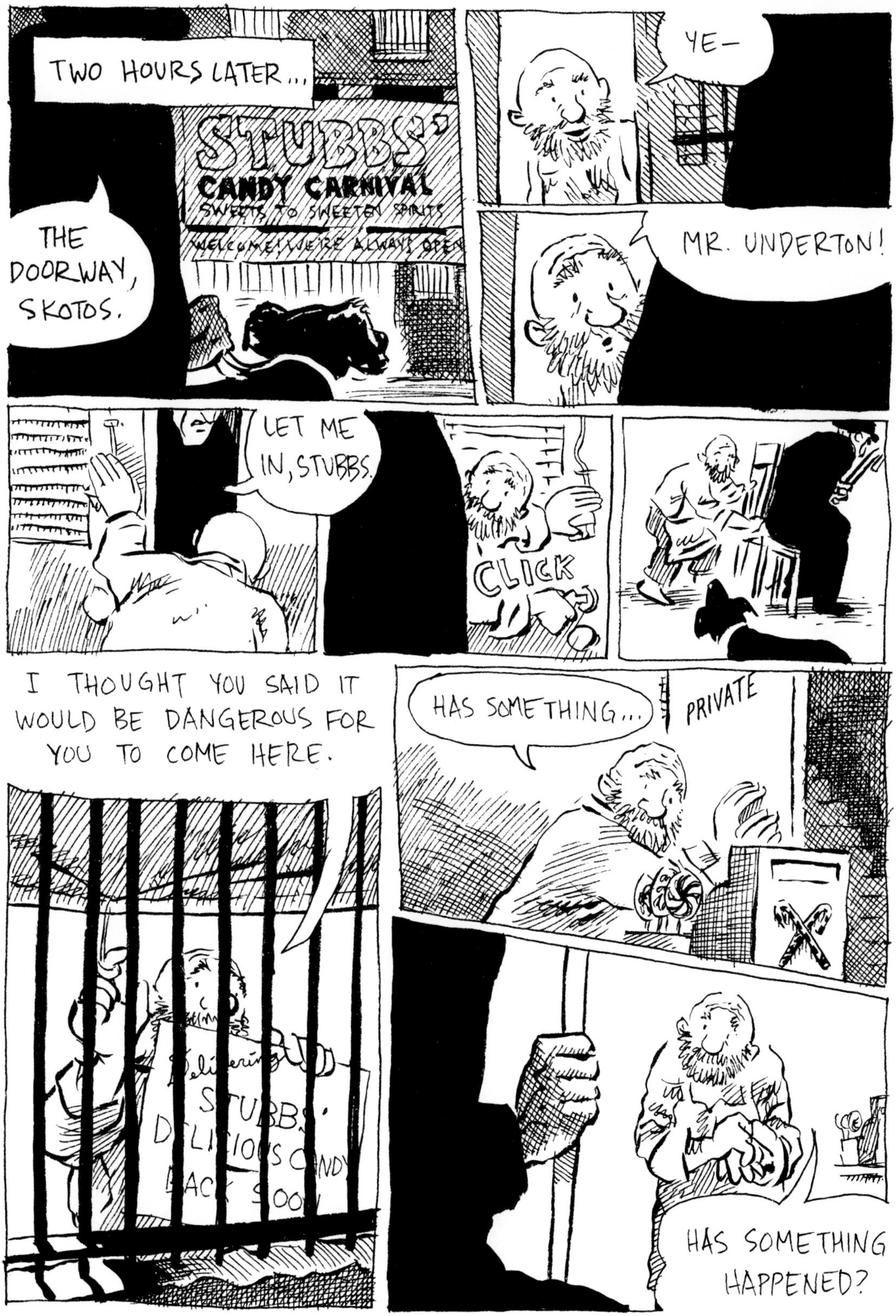

TWO HOURS LATER...
STUBBS'
CANDY CARNIVAL
SWEETS TO SWEETEN SPIRITS
WELCOME! WE'RE ALWAYS OPEN
THE DOORWAY, SKOTOS.
YE—
MR. UNDERTON!
LET ME IN, STUBBS.
CLICK
I THOUGHT YOU SAID IT WOULD BE DANGEROUS FOR YOU TO COME HERE.
HAS SOMETHING...
PRIVATE
HAS SOMETHING HAPPENED?

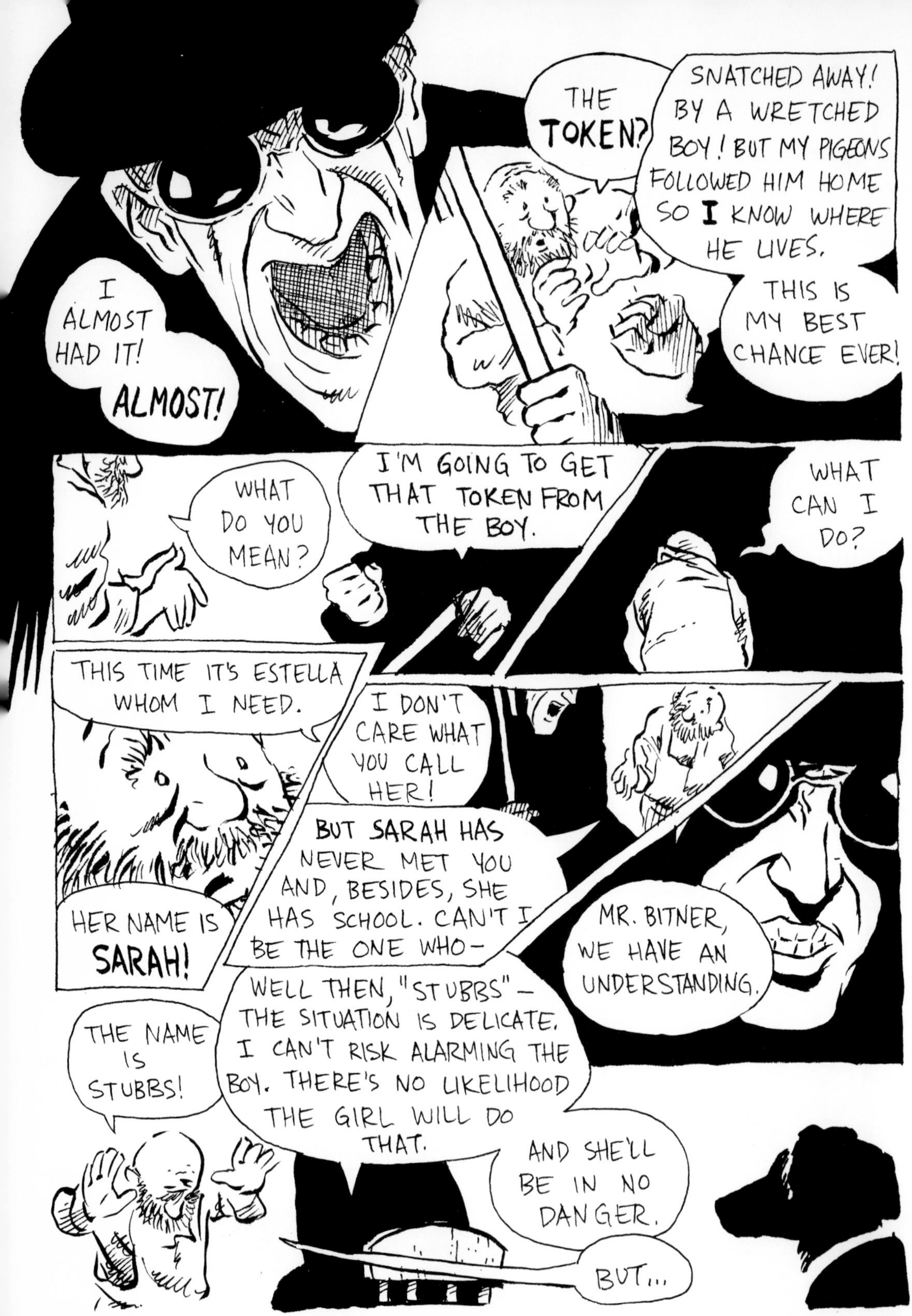
I ALMOST HAD IT! ALMOST!
THE TOKEN?
SNATCHED AWAY! BY A WRETCHED BOY! BUT MY PIGEONS FOLLOWED HIM HOME SO I KNOW WHERE HE LIVES.
THIS IS MY BEST CHANCE EVER!
WHAT DO YOU MEAN?
I'M GOING TO GET THAT TOKEN FROM THE BOY.
WHAT CAN I DO?
THIS TIME IT'S ESTELLA WHOM I NEED.
HER NAME IS SARAH!
I DON'T CARE WHAT YOU CALL HER!
BUT SARAH HAS NEVER MET YOU AND, BESIDES, SHE HAS SCHOOL. CAN'T I BE THE ONE WHO-
MR. BITNER, WE HAVE AN UNDERSTANDING.
THE NAME IS STUBBS!
WELL THEN, "STUBBS" - THE SITUATION IS DELICATE. I CAN'T RISK ALARMING THE BOY. THERE'S NO LIKELIHOOD THE GIRL WILL DO THAT.
AND SHE'LL BE IN NO DANGER.
BUT...

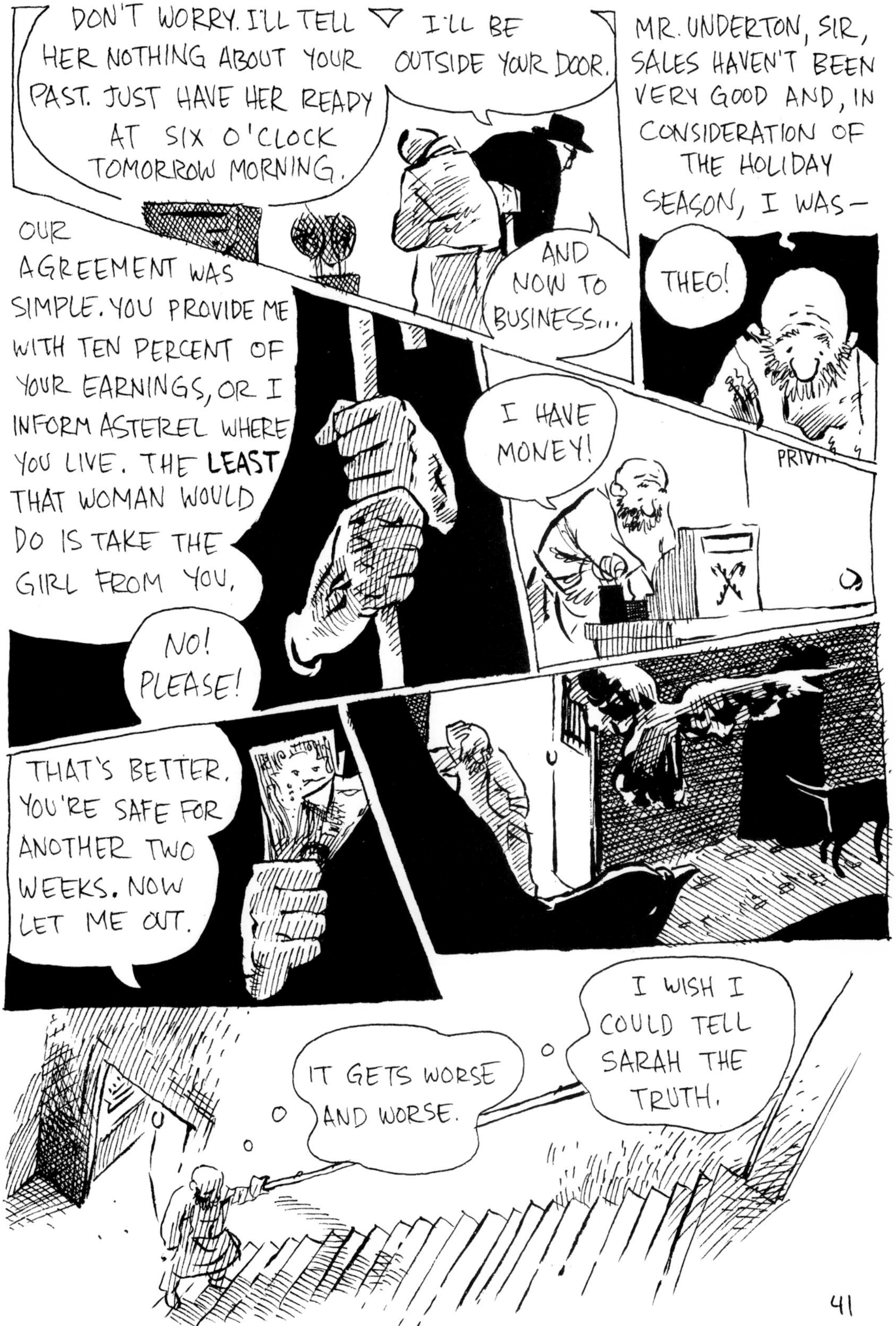
DON'T WORRY. I'LL TELL HER NOTHING ABOUT YOUR PAST. JUST HAVE HER READY AT SIX O'CLOCK TOMORROW MORNING.
I'LL BE OUTSIDE YOUR DOOR.
MR. UNDERTON, SIR, SALES HAVEN'T BEEN VERY GOOD AND, IN CONSIDERATION OF THE HOLIDAY SEASON, I WAS—
THEO!
AND NOW TO BUSINESS...
OUR AGREEMENT WAS SIMPLE. YOU PROVIDE ME WITH TEN PERCENT OF YOUR EARNINGS, OR I INFORM ASTEREL WHERE YOU LIVE. THE **LEAST** THAT WOMAN WOULD DO IS TAKE THE GIRL FROM YOU.
I HAVE MONEY!
PRIV
NO! PLEASE!
THAT'S BETTER. YOU'RE SAFE FOR ANOTHER TWO WEEKS. NOW LET ME OUT.
IT GETS WORSE AND WORSE.
I WISH I COULD TELL SARAH THE TRUTH.

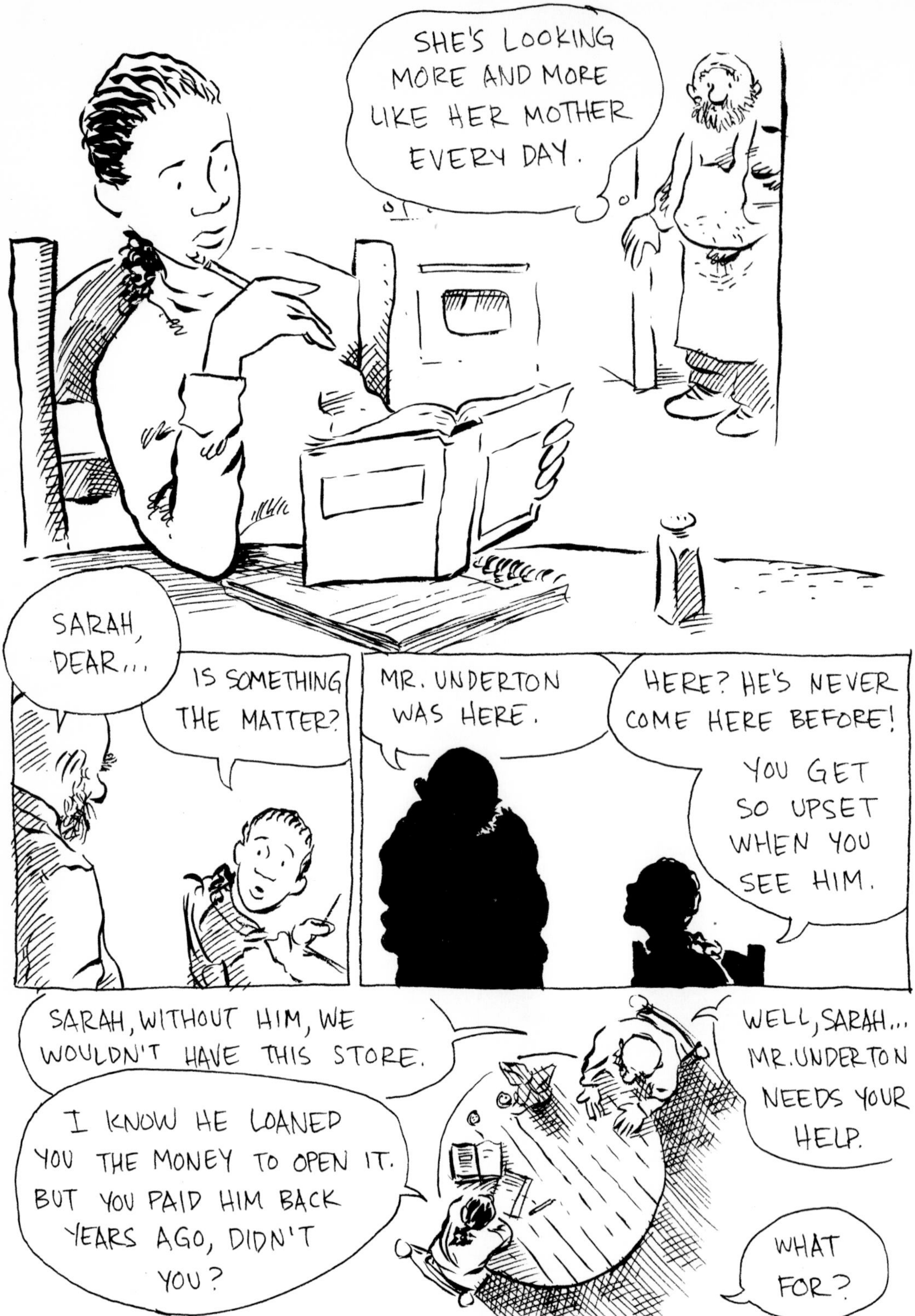

SHE'S LOOKING MORE AND MORE LIKE HER MOTHER EVERY DAY.
SARAH, DEAR...
IS SOMETHING THE MATTER?
MR. UNDERTON WAS HERE.
HERE? HE'S NEVER COME HERE BEFORE!
YOU GET SO UPSET WHEN YOU SEE HIM.
SARAH, WITHOUT HIM, WE WOULDN'T HAVE THIS STORE.
I KNOW HE LOANED YOU THE MONEY TO OPEN IT. BUT YOU PAID HIM BACK YEARS AGO, DIDN'T YOU?
WELL, SARAH... MR. UNDERTON NEEDS YOUR HELP.
WHAT FOR?

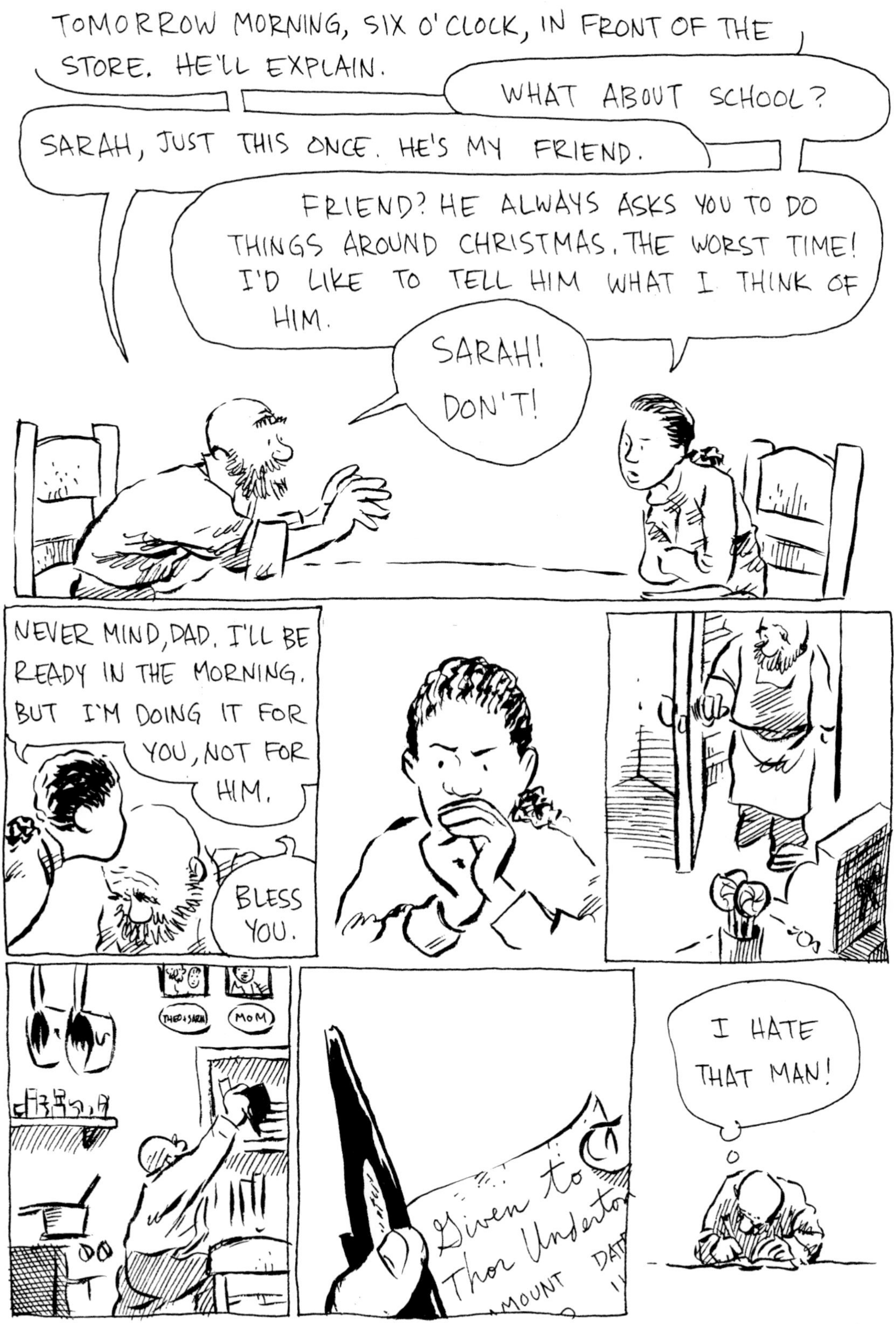
TOMORROW MORNING, SIX O'CLOCK, IN FRONT OF THE STORE. HE'LL EXPLAIN.
WHAT ABOUT SCHOOL?
SARAH, JUST THIS ONCE. HE'S MY FRIEND.
FRIEND? HE ALWAYS ASKS YOU TO DO THINGS AROUND CHRISTMAS. THE WORST TIME! I'D LIKE TO TELL HIM WHAT I THINK OF HIM.
SARAH! DON'T!
NEVER MIND, DAD. I'LL BE READY IN THE MORNING. BUT I'M DOING IT FOR YOU, NOT FOR HIM.
BLESS YOU.
THEO + SARAH
MOM
Given to
Thor Underton
AMOUNT
I HATE THAT MAN!

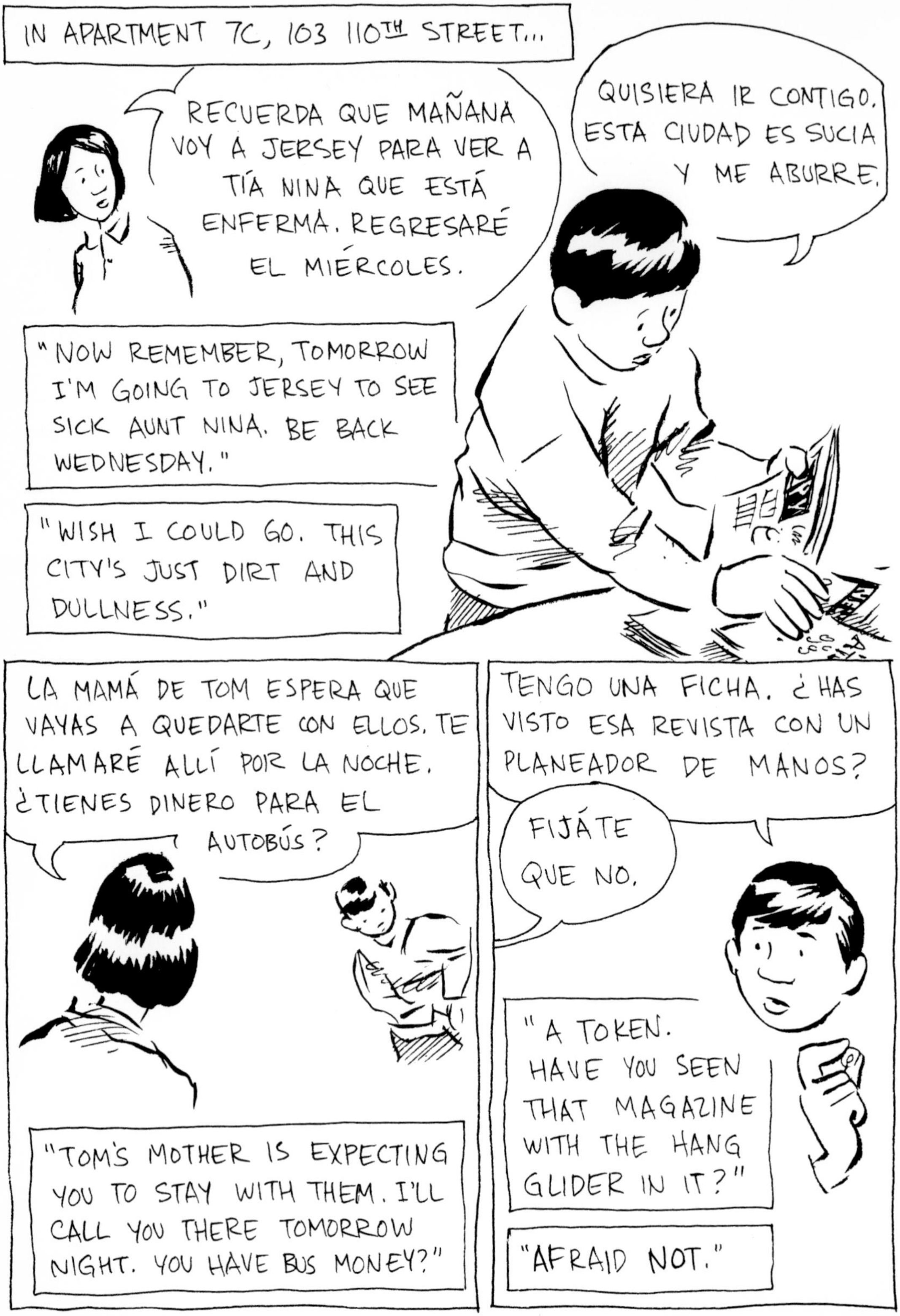
IN APARTMENT 7C, 103 110TH STREET...
RECUERDA QUE MAÑANA VOY A JERSEY PARA VER A TÍA NINA QUE ESTÁ ENFERMA. REGRESARÉ EL MIÉRCOLES.
QUISIERA IR CONTIGO. ESTA CIUDAD ES SUCIA Y ME ABURRE.
"NOW REMEMBER, TOMORROW I'M GOING TO JERSEY TO SEE SICK AUNT NINA. BE BACK WEDNESDAY."
"WISH I COULD GO. THIS CITY'S JUST DIRT AND DULLNESS."
LA MAMÁ DE TOM ESPERA QUE VAYAS A QUEDARTE CON ELLOS. TE LLAMARÉ ALLÍ POR LA NOCHE. ¿TIENES DINERO PARA EL AUTOBÚS?
"TOM'S MOTHER IS EXPECTING YOU TO STAY WITH THEM. I'LL CALL YOU THERE TOMORROW NIGHT. YOU HAVE BUS MONEY?"
TENGO UNA FICHA. ¿HAS VISTO ESA REVISTA CON UN PLANEADOR DE MANOS?
FIJÁTE QUE NO.
"A TOKEN. HAVE YOU SEEN THAT MAGAZINE WITH THE HANG GLIDER IN IT?"
"AFRAID NOT."

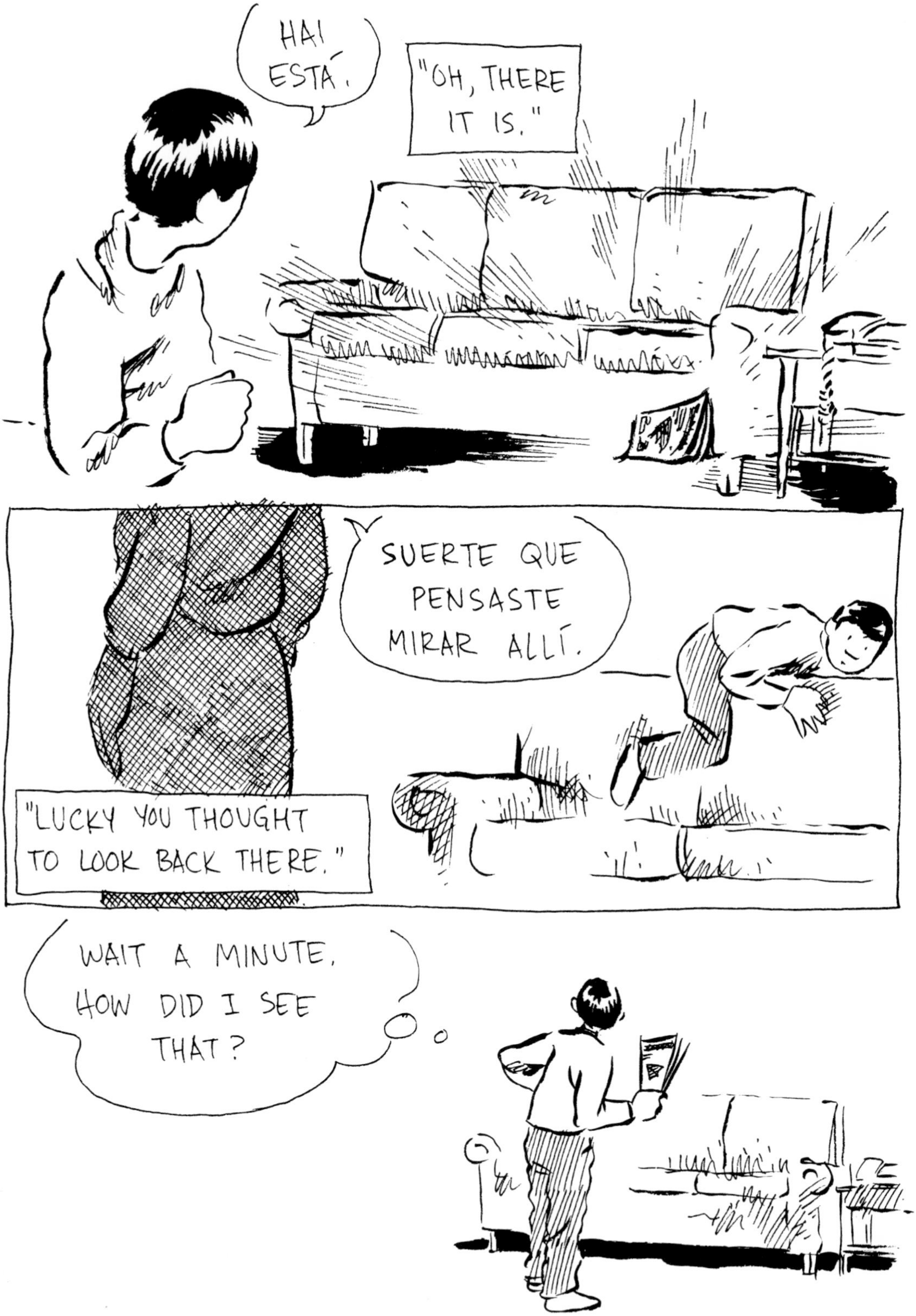
HAI ESTÁ.
"OH, THERE IT IS."
SUERTE QUE PENSASTE MIRAR ALLÍ.
"LUCKY YOU THOUGHT TO LOOK BACK THERE."
WAIT A MINUTE. HOW DID I SEE THAT?

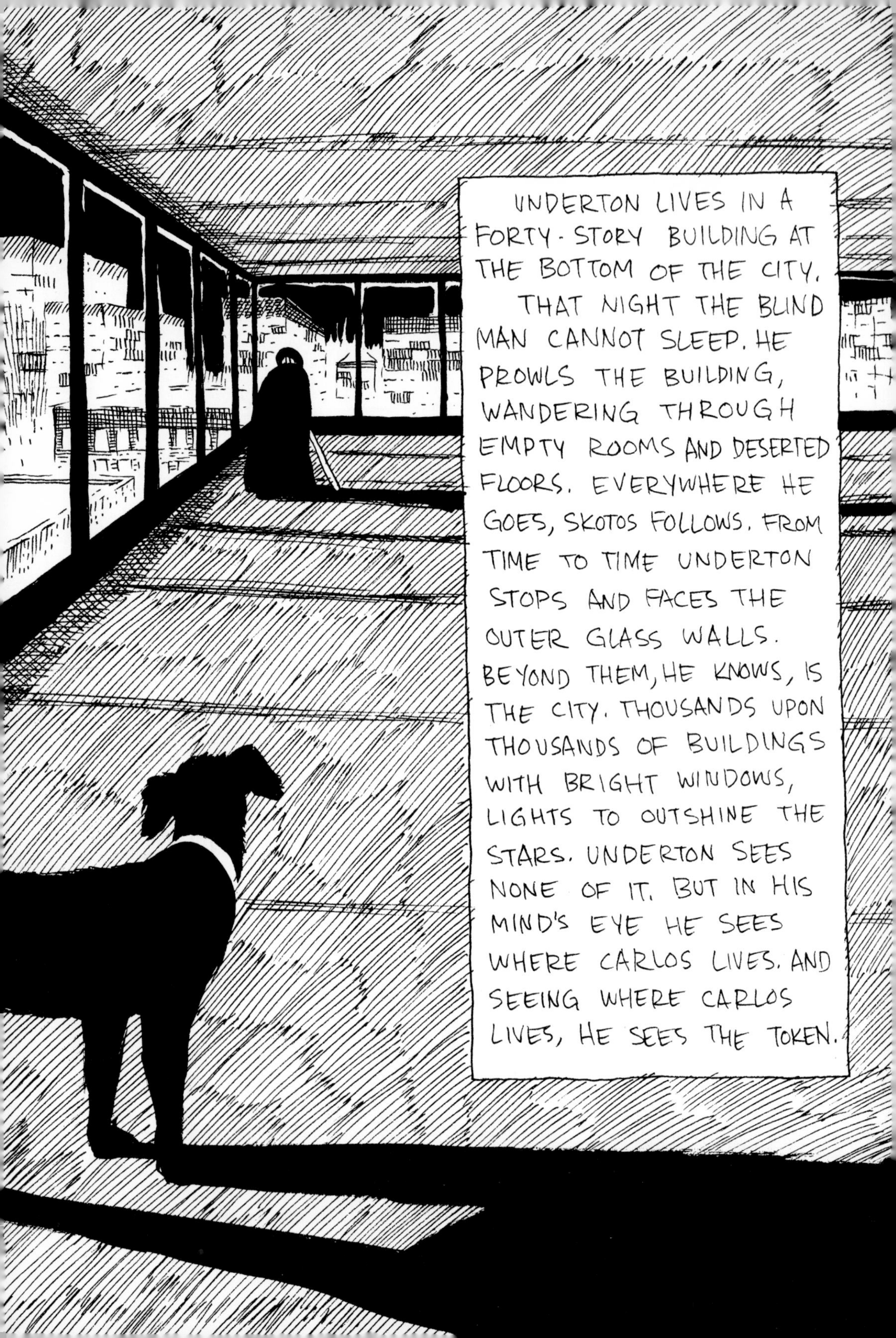
UNDERTON LIVES IN A FORTY-STORY BUILDING AT THE BOTTOM OF THE CITY. THAT NIGHT THE BLIND MAN CANNOT SLEEP. HE PROWLS THE BUILDING, WANDERING THROUGH EMPTY ROOMS AND DESERTED FLOORS. EVERYWHERE HE GOES, SKOTOS FOLLOWS. FROM TIME TO TIME UNDERTON STOPS AND FACES THE OUTER GLASS WALLS. BEYOND THEM, HE KNOWS, IS THE CITY. THOUSANDS UPON THOUSANDS OF BUILDINGS WITH BRIGHT WINDOWS, LIGHTS TO OUTSHINE THE STARS. UNDERTON SEES NONE OF IT. BUT IN HIS MIND'S EYE HE SEES WHERE CARLOS LIVES. AND SEEING WHERE CARLOS LIVES, HE SEES THE TOKEN.

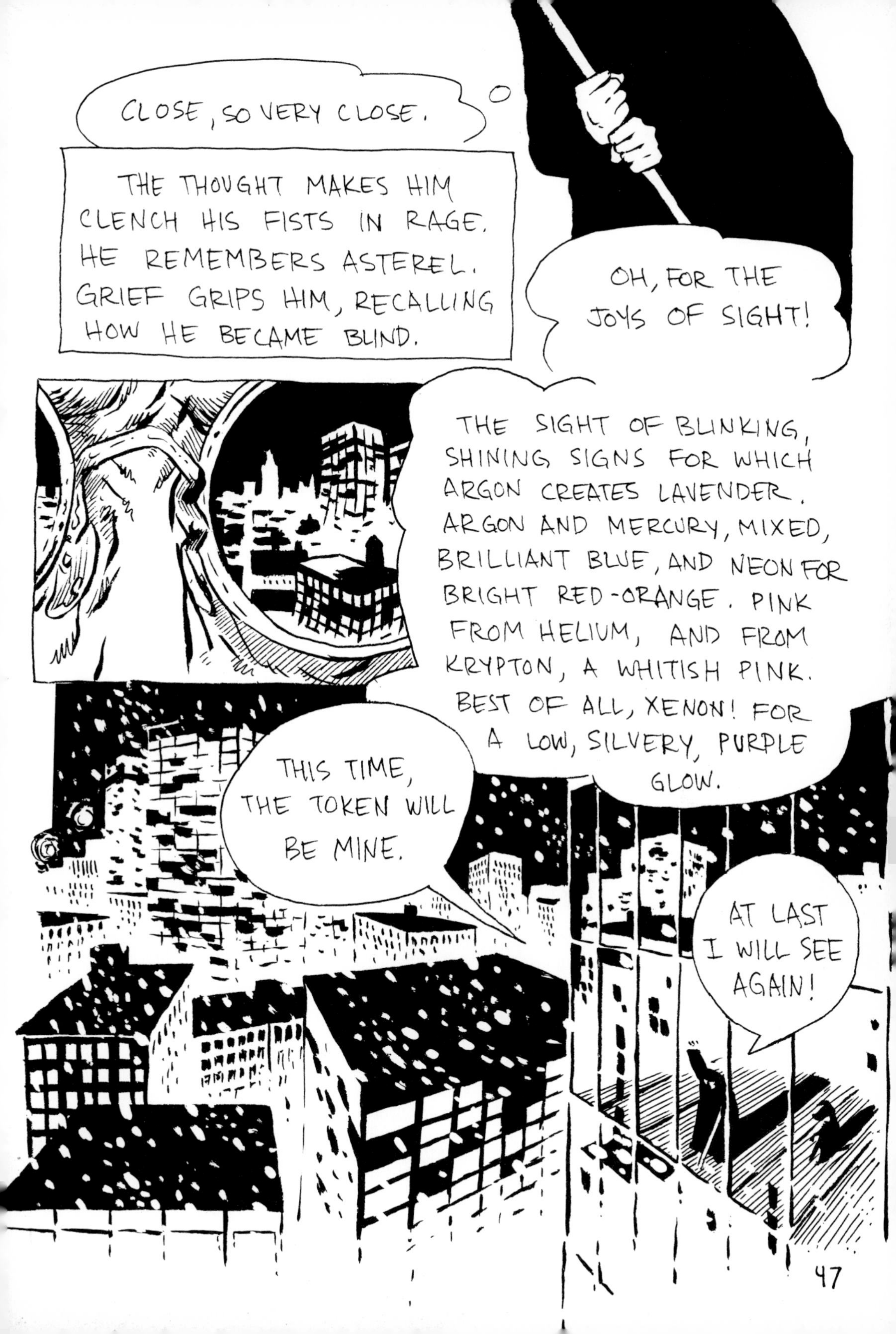
CLOSE, SO VERY CLOSE.
THE THOUGHT MAKES HIM CLENCH HIS FISTS IN RAGE. HE REMEMBERS ASTEREL. GRIEF GRIPS HIM, RECALLING HOW HE BECAME BLIND.
OH, FOR THE JOYS OF SIGHT!
THE SIGHT OF BLINKING, SHINING SIGNS FOR WHICH ARGON CREATES LAVENDER. ARGON AND MERCURY, MIXED, BRILLIANT BLUE, AND NEON FOR BRIGHT RED-ORANGE. PINK FROM HELIUM, AND FROM KRYPTON, A WHITISH PINK. BEST OF ALL, XENON! FOR A LOW, SILVERY, PURPLE GLOW.
THIS TIME, THE TOKEN WILL BE MINE.
AT LAST I WILL SEE AGAIN!

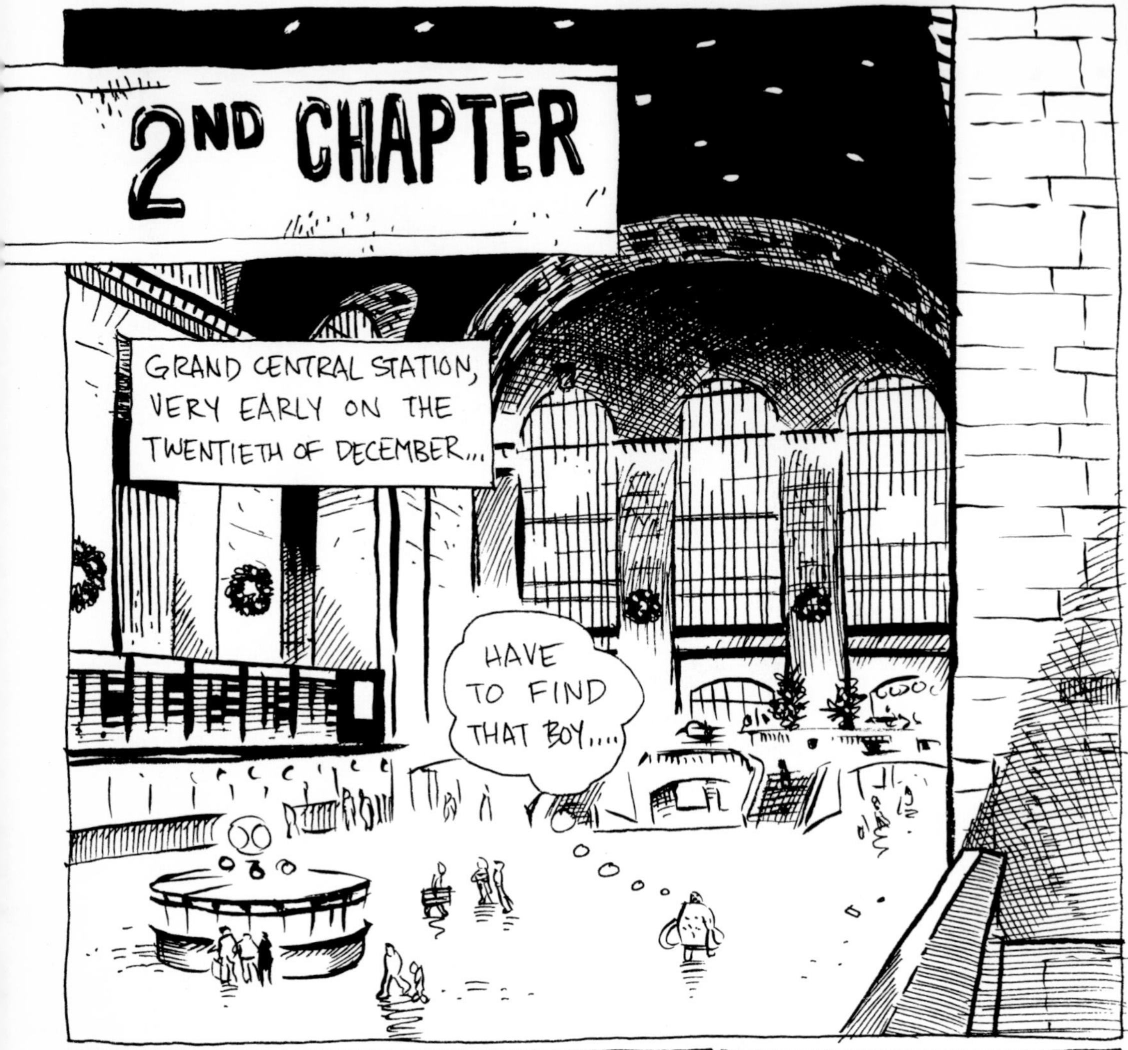
2ND CHAPTER
GRAND CENTRAL STATION, VERY EARLY ON THE TWENTIETH OF DECEMBER...
HAVE TO FIND THAT BOY....

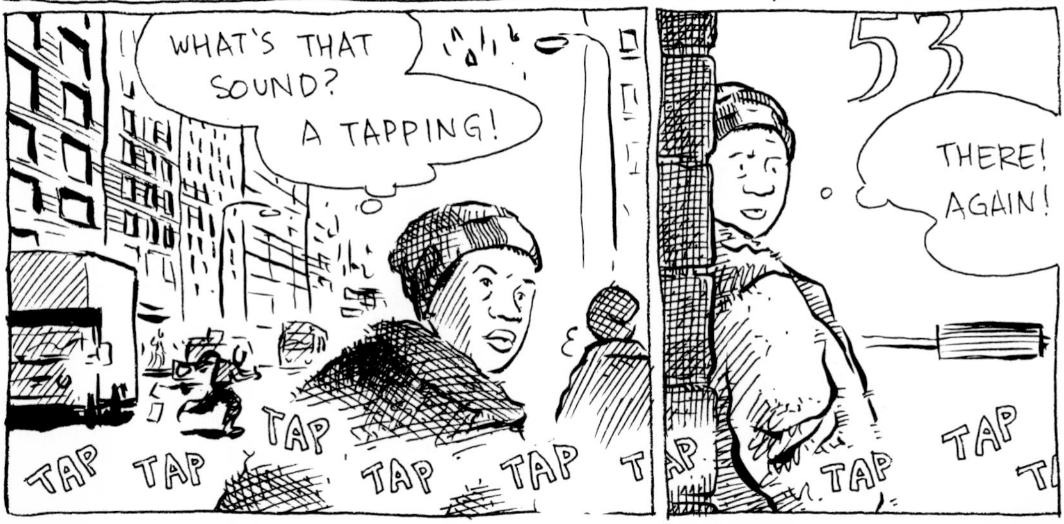
WHAT'S THAT SOUND? A TAPPING!
TAP TAP TAP TAP TAP
53
THERE! AGAIN!
TAP TAP TAP

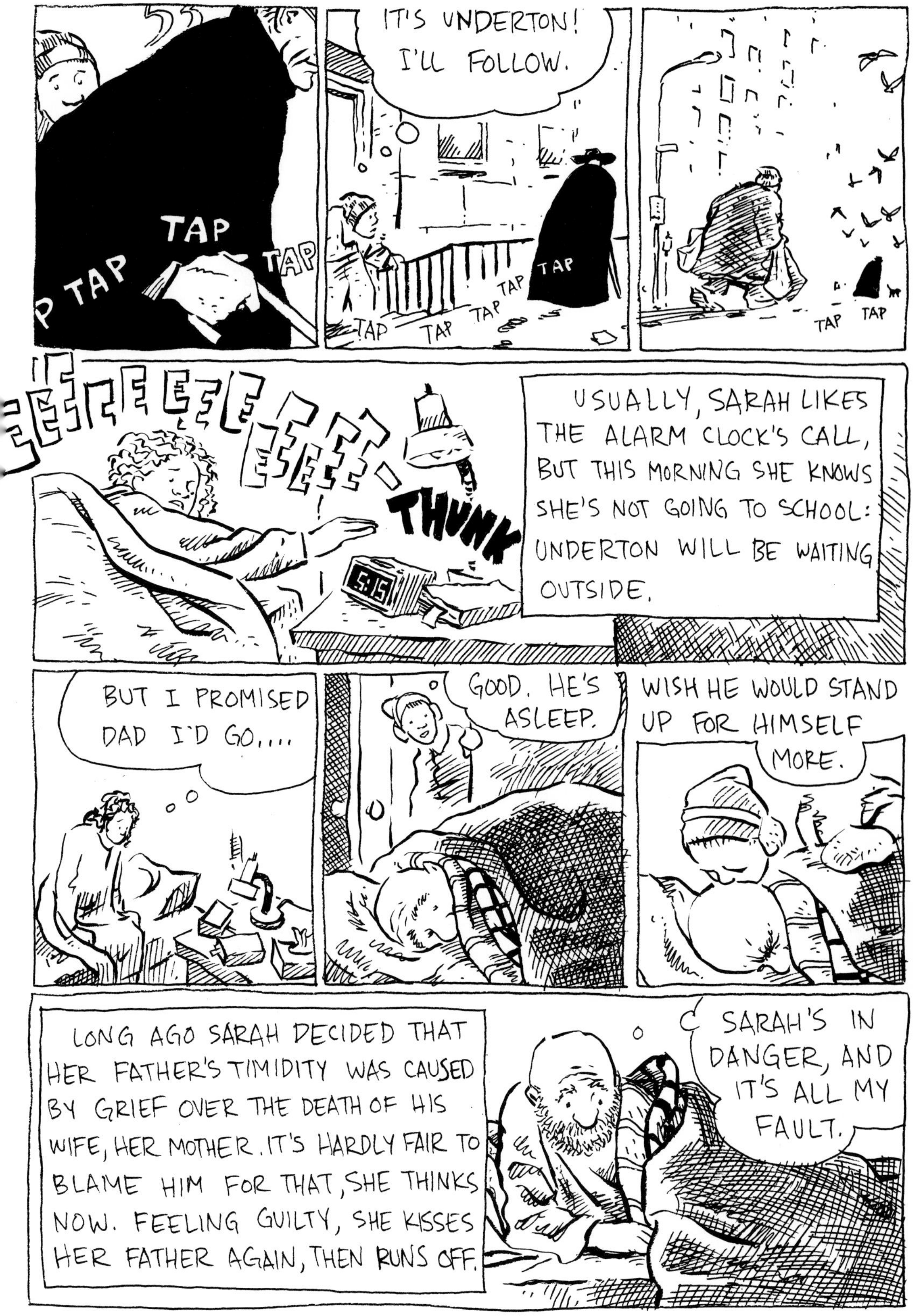
TAP TAP TAP
IT'S UNDERTON! I'LL FOLLOW.
TAP TAP TAP TAP TAP
TAP TAP
EEEEREEEE EEEEEEEE
THUNK
USUALLY, SARAH LIKES THE ALARM CLOCK'S CALL, BUT THIS MORNING SHE KNOWS SHE'S NOT GOING TO SCHOOL: UNDERTON WILL BE WAITING OUTSIDE.
BUT I PROMISED DAD I'D GO....
GOOD. HE'S ASLEEP.
WISH HE WOULD STAND UP FOR HIMSELF MORE.
LONG AGO SARAH DECIDED THAT HER FATHER'S TIMIDITY WAS CAUSED BY GRIEF OVER THE DEATH OF HIS WIFE, HER MOTHER. IT'S HARDLY FAIR TO BLAME HIM FOR THAT, SHE THINKS NOW. FEELING GUILTY, SHE KISSES HER FATHER AGAIN, THEN RUNS OFF.
SARAH'S IN DANGER, AND IT'S ALL MY FAULT.

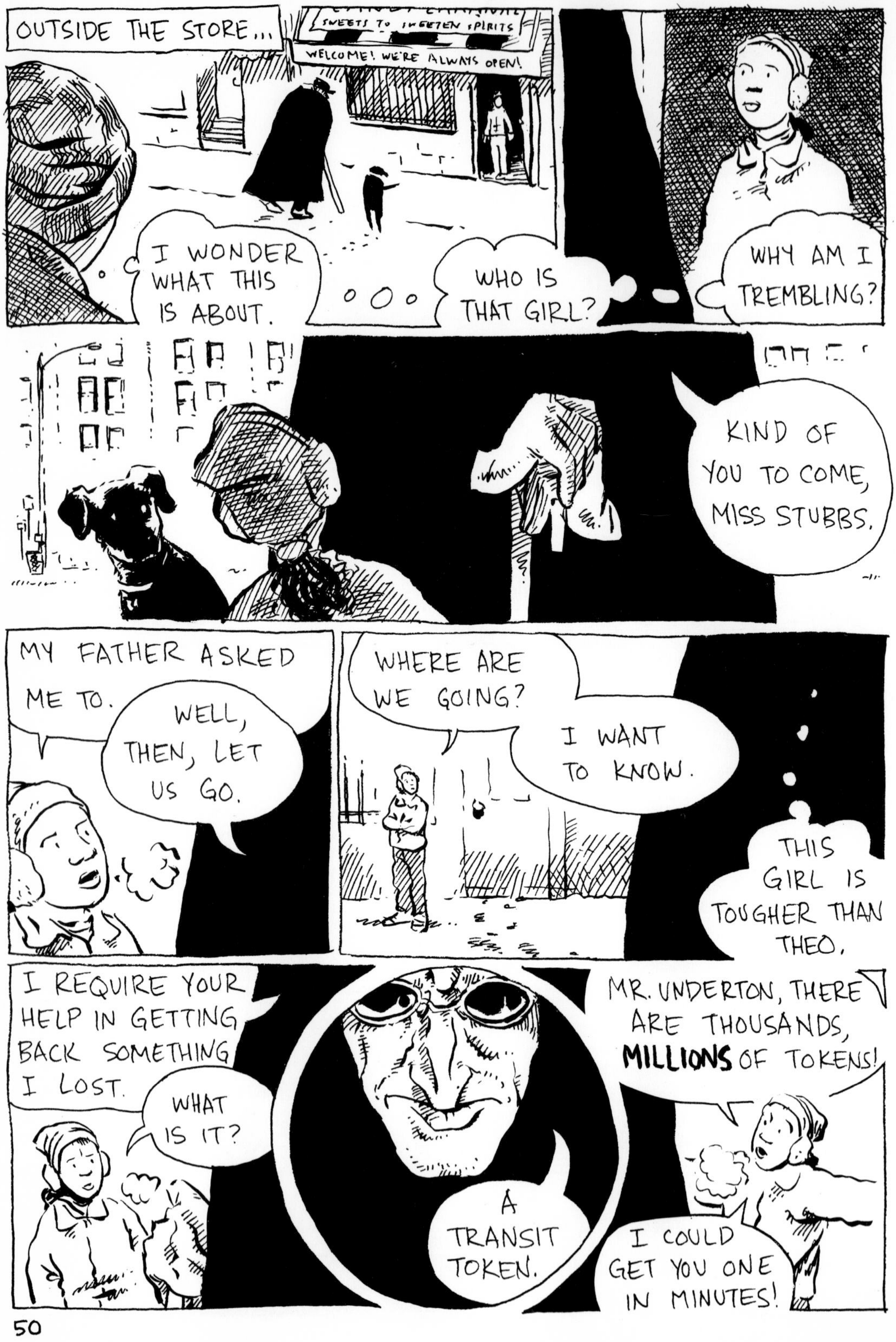
OUTSIDE THE STORE...
SWEETS TO SWEETEN SPIRITS
WELCOME! WE'RE ALWAYS OPEN!
I WONDER WHAT THIS IS ABOUT.
WHO IS THAT GIRL?
WHY AM I TREMBLING?
KIND OF YOU TO COME, MISS STUBBS.
MY FATHER ASKED ME TO.
WELL, THEN, LET US GO.
WHERE ARE WE GOING?
I WANT TO KNOW.
THIS GIRL IS TOUGHER THAN THEO.
I REQUIRE YOUR HELP IN GETTING BACK SOMETHING I LOST.
WHAT IS IT?
A TRANSIT TOKEN.
MR. UNDERTON, THERE ARE THOUSANDS, **MILLIONS** OF TOKENS!
I COULD GET YOU ONE IN MINUTES!

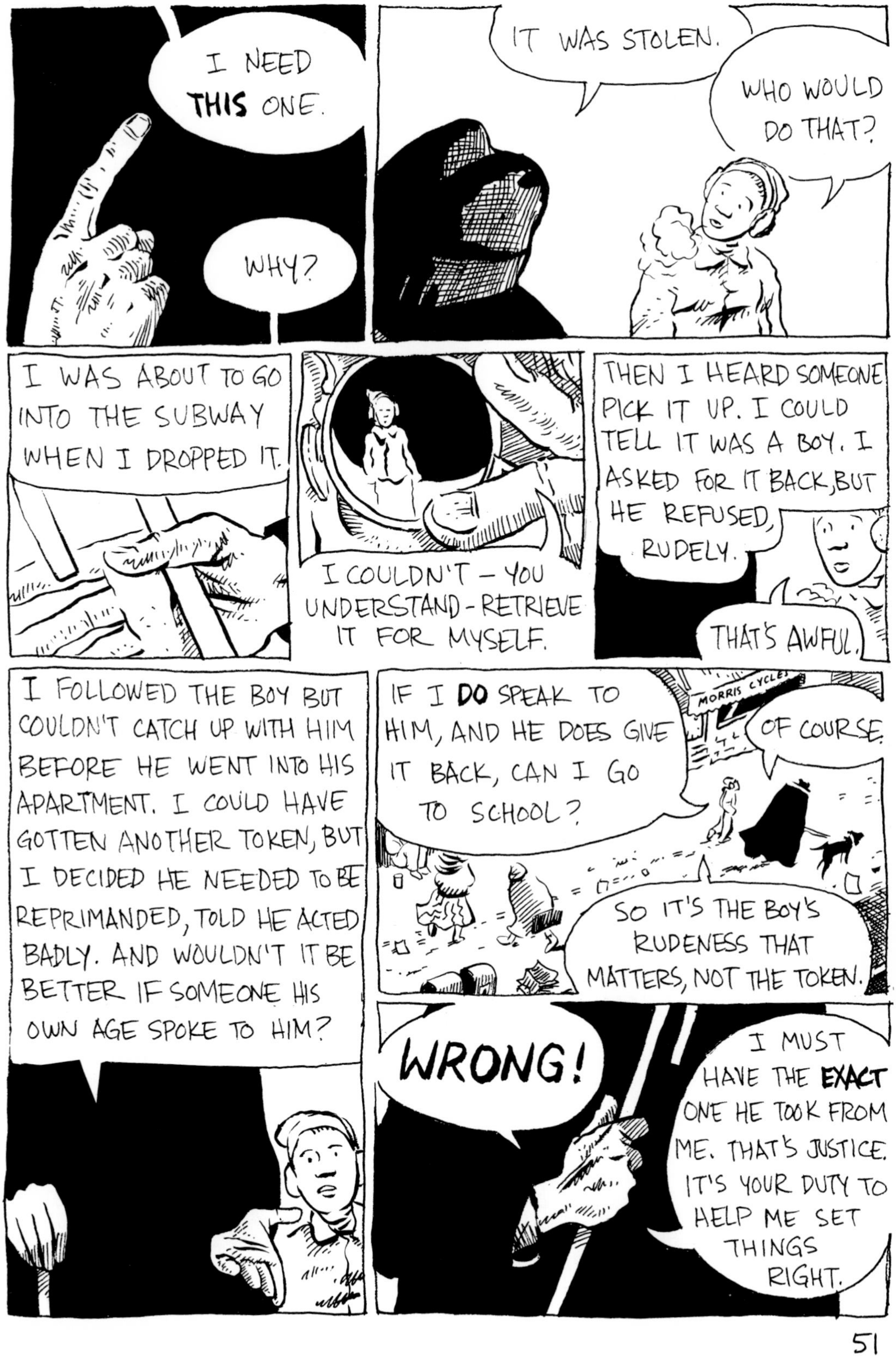
I NEED **THIS** ONE.
WHY?
IT WAS STOLEN.
WHO WOULD DO THAT?
I WAS ABOUT TO GO INTO THE SUBWAY WHEN I DROPPED IT.
I COULDN'T – YOU UNDERSTAND – RETRIEVE IT FOR MYSELF.
THEN I HEARD SOMEONE PICK IT UP. I COULD TELL IT WAS A BOY. I ASKED FOR IT BACK, BUT HE REFUSED, RUDELY.
THAT'S AWFUL.
I FOLLOWED THE BOY BUT COULDN'T CATCH UP WITH HIM BEFORE HE WENT INTO HIS APARTMENT. I COULD HAVE GOTTEN ANOTHER TOKEN, BUT I DECIDED HE NEEDED TO BE REPRIMANDED, TOLD HE ACTED BADLY. AND WOULDN'T IT BE BETTER IF SOMEONE HIS OWN AGE SPOKE TO HIM?
IF I **DO** SPEAK TO HIM, AND HE DOES GIVE IT BACK, CAN I GO TO SCHOOL?
MORRIS CYCLE
OF COURSE.
SO IT'S THE BOY'S RUDENESS THAT MATTERS, NOT THE TOKEN.
WRONG!
I MUST HAVE THE **EXACT** ONE HE TOOK FROM ME. THAT'S JUSTICE. IT'S YOUR DUTY TO HELP ME SET THINGS RIGHT.

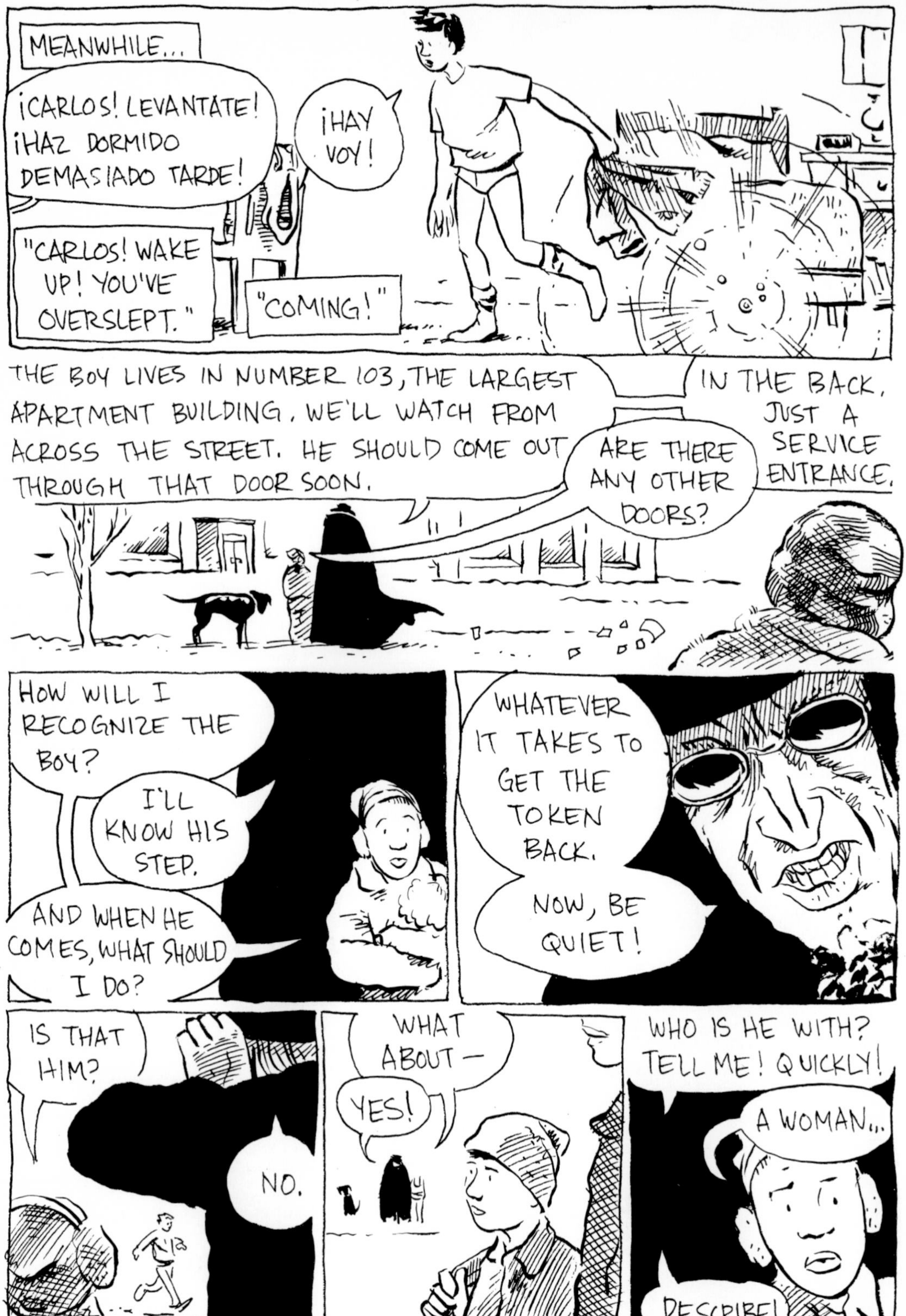
MEANWHILE...
¡CARLOS! LEVANTATE! ¡HAZ DORMIDO DEMASIADO TARDE!
"CARLOS! WAKE UP! YOU'VE OVERSLEPT."
¡HAY VOY!
"COMING!"
THE BOY LIVES IN NUMBER 103, THE LARGEST APARTMENT BUILDING. WE'LL WATCH FROM ACROSS THE STREET. HE SHOULD COME OUT THROUGH THAT DOOR SOON.
ARE THERE ANY OTHER DOORS?
IN THE BACK, JUST A SERVICE ENTRANCE.
HOW WILL I RECOGNIZE THE BOY?
I'LL KNOW HIS STEP.
AND WHEN HE COMES, WHAT SHOULD I DO?
WHATEVER IT TAKES TO GET THE TOKEN BACK.
NOW, BE QUIET!
IS THAT HIM?
NO.
WHAT ABOUT—
YES!
WHO IS HE WITH? TELL ME! QUICKLY!
A WOMAN...
DESCRIBE!

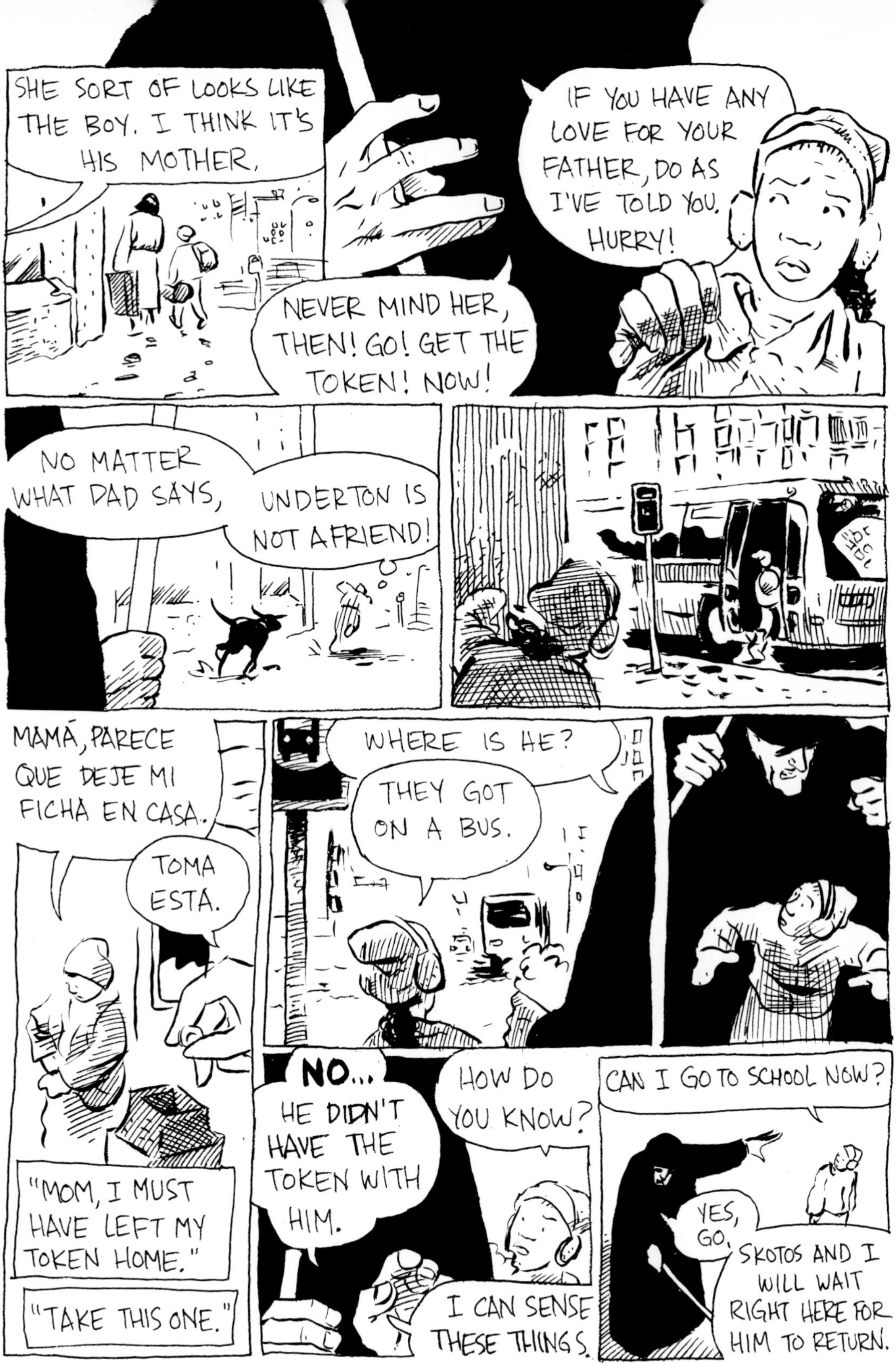
SHE SORT OF LOOKS LIKE THE BOY. I THINK IT'S HIS MOTHER.
IF YOU HAVE ANY LOVE FOR YOUR FATHER, DO AS I'VE TOLD YOU. HURRY!
NEVER MIND HER, THEN! GO! GET THE TOKEN! NOW!
NO MATTER WHAT DAD SAYS,
UNDERTON IS NOT A FRIEND!
MAMÁ, PARECE QUE DEJE MI FICHA EN CASA.
TOMA ESTA.
"MOM, I MUST HAVE LEFT MY TOKEN HOME."
"TAKE THIS ONE."
WHERE IS HE?
THEY GOT ON A BUS.
NO... HE DIDN'T HAVE THE TOKEN WITH HIM.
HOW DO YOU KNOW?
I CAN SENSE THESE THINGS.
CAN I GO TO SCHOOL NOW?
YES, GO.
SKOTOS AND I WILL WAIT RIGHT HERE FOR HIM TO RETURN.

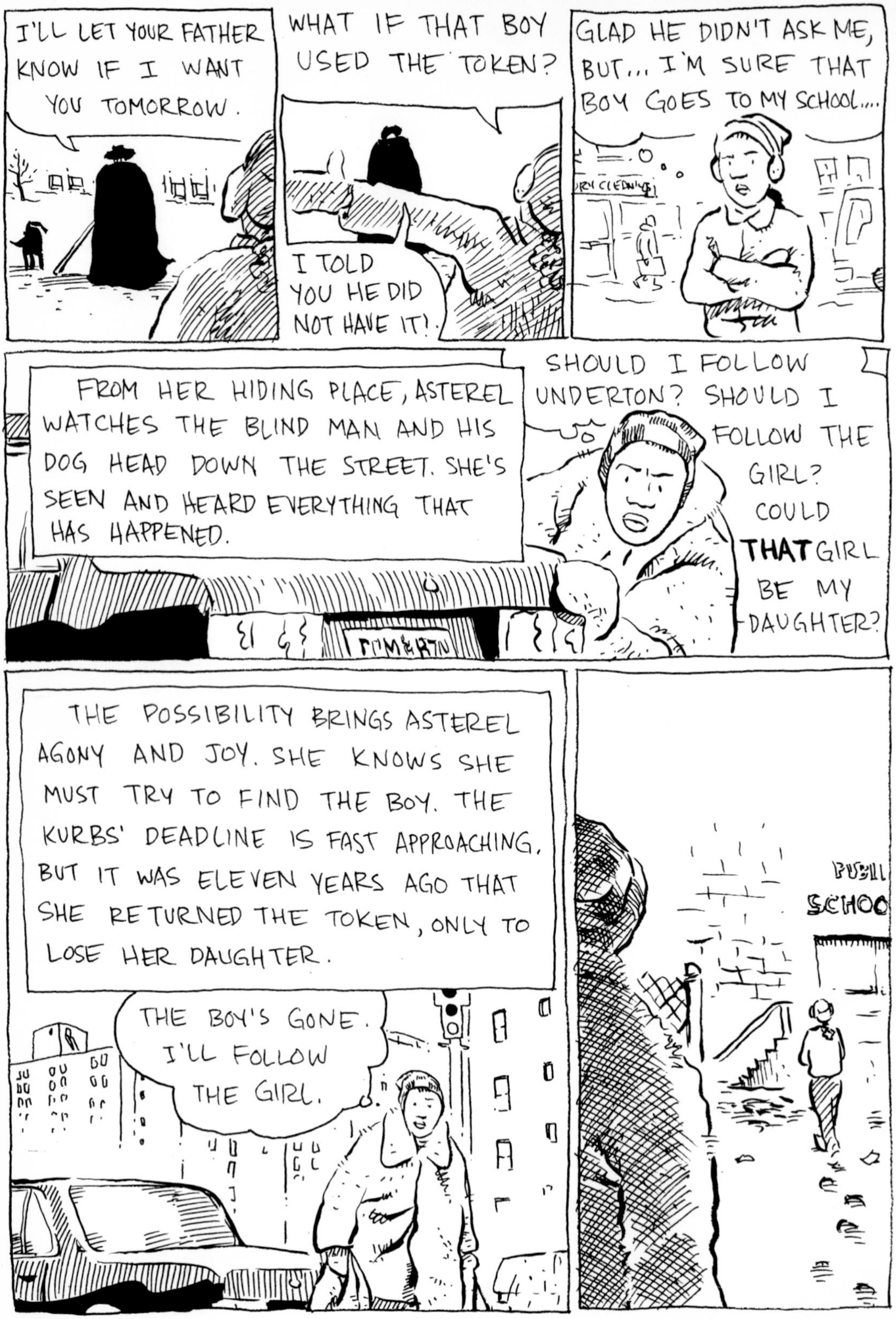
I'LL LET YOUR FATHER KNOW IF I WANT YOU TOMORROW.
WHAT IF THAT BOY USED THE TOKEN?
I TOLD YOU HE DID NOT HAVE IT!
GLAD HE DIDN'T ASK ME, BUT... I'M SURE THAT BOY GOES TO MY SCHOOL....
FROM HER HIDING PLACE, ASTEREL WATCHES THE BLIND MAN AND HIS DOG HEAD DOWN THE STREET. SHE'S SEEN AND HEARD EVERYTHING THAT HAS HAPPENED.
SHOULD I FOLLOW UNDERTON? SHOULD I FOLLOW THE GIRL? COULD **THAT** GIRL BE MY DAUGHTER?
THE POSSIBILITY BRINGS ASTEREL AGONY AND JOY. SHE KNOWS SHE MUST TRY TO FIND THE BOY. THE KURBS' DEADLINE IS FAST APPROACHING. BUT IT WAS ELEVEN YEARS AGO THAT SHE RETURNED THE TOKEN, ONLY TO LOSE HER DAUGHTER.
THE BOY'S GONE. I'LL FOLLOW THE GIRL.
SCHOO

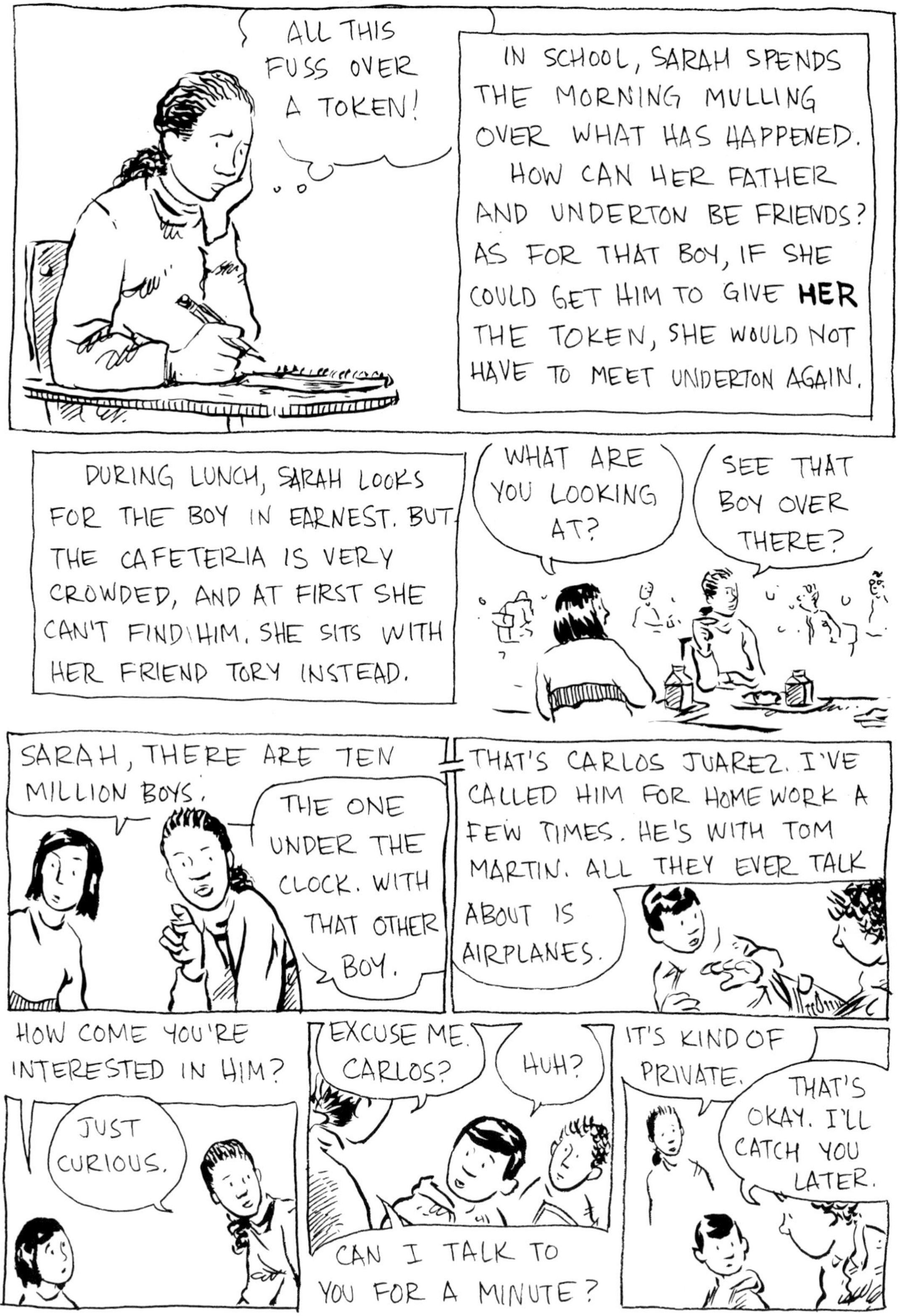
ALL THIS FUSS OVER A TOKEN!
IN SCHOOL, SARAH SPENDS THE MORNING MULLING OVER WHAT HAS HAPPENED. HOW CAN HER FATHER AND UNDERTON BE FRIENDS? AS FOR THAT BOY, IF SHE COULD GET HIM TO GIVE **HER** THE TOKEN, SHE WOULD NOT HAVE TO MEET UNDERTON AGAIN.
DURING LUNCH, SARAH LOOKS FOR THE BOY IN EARNEST. BUT THE CAFETERIA IS VERY CROWDED, AND AT FIRST SHE CAN'T FIND HIM. SHE SITS WITH HER FRIEND TORY INSTEAD.
WHAT ARE YOU LOOKING AT?
SEE THAT BOY OVER THERE?
SARAH, THERE ARE TEN MILLION BOYS.
THE ONE UNDER THE CLOCK. WITH THAT OTHER BOY.
THAT'S CARLOS JUAREZ. I'VE CALLED HIM FOR HOMEWORK A FEW TIMES. HE'S WITH TOM MARTIN. ALL THEY EVER TALK ABOUT IS AIRPLANES.
HOW COME YOU'RE INTERESTED IN HIM?
JUST CURIOUS.
EXCUSE ME. CARLOS?
HUH?
CAN I TALK TO YOU FOR A MINUTE?
IT'S KIND OF PRIVATE.
THAT'S OKAY. I'LL CATCH YOU LATER.

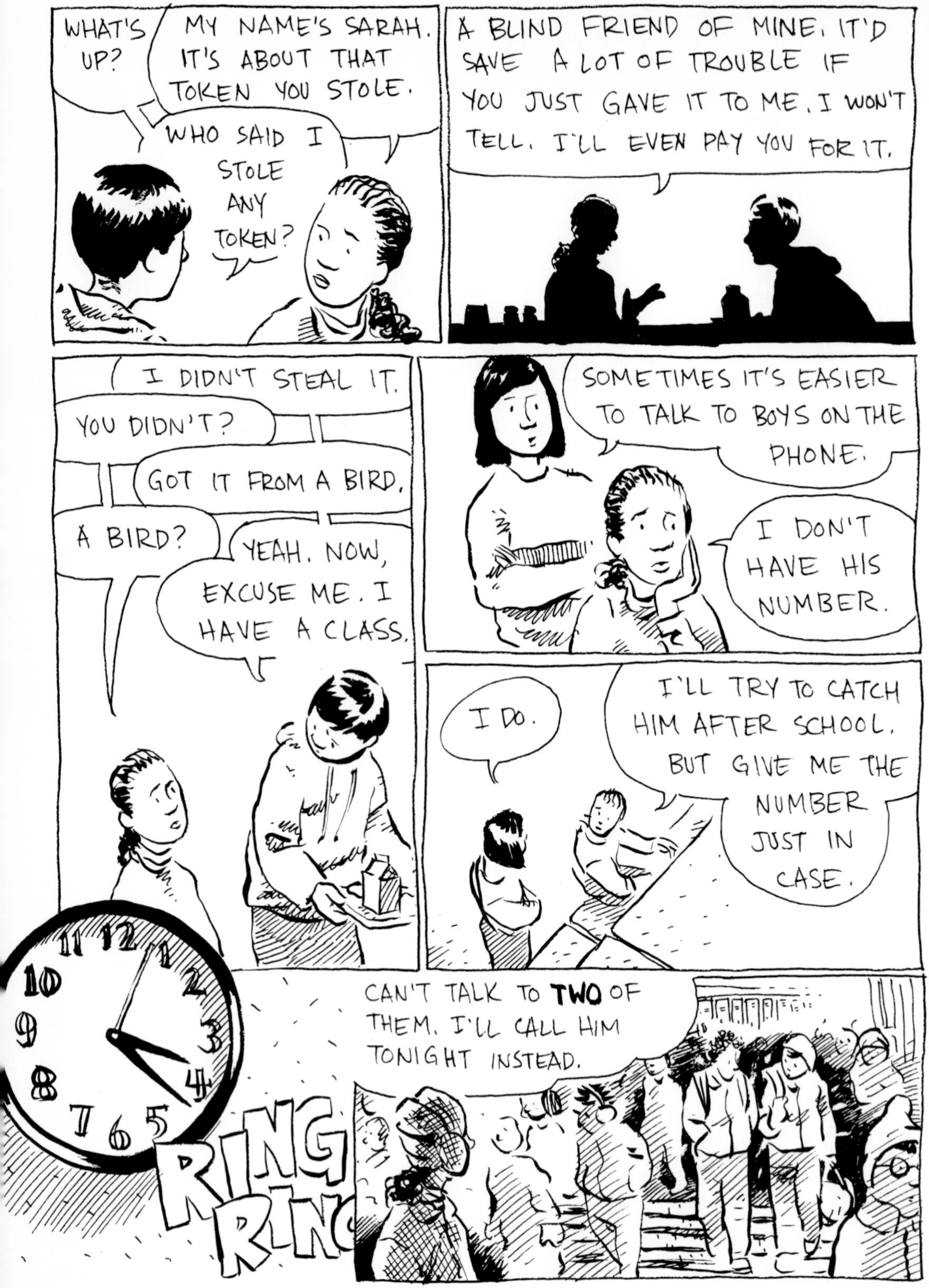
WHAT'S UP?
MY NAME'S SARAH. IT'S ABOUT THAT TOKEN YOU STOLE.
WHO SAID I STOLE ANY TOKEN?
A BLIND FRIEND OF MINE. IT'D SAVE A LOT OF TROUBLE IF YOU JUST GAVE IT TO ME. I WON'T TELL. I'LL EVEN PAY YOU FOR IT.
I DIDN'T STEAL IT.
YOU DIDN'T?
GOT IT FROM A BIRD.
A BIRD?
YEAH. NOW, EXCUSE ME. I HAVE A CLASS.
SOMETIMES IT'S EASIER TO TALK TO BOYS ON THE PHONE.
I DON'T HAVE HIS NUMBER.
I DO.
I'LL TRY TO CATCH HIM AFTER SCHOOL. BUT GIVE ME THE NUMBER JUST IN CASE.
CAN'T TALK TO **TWO** OF THEM. I'LL CALL HIM TONIGHT INSTEAD.
RING RING

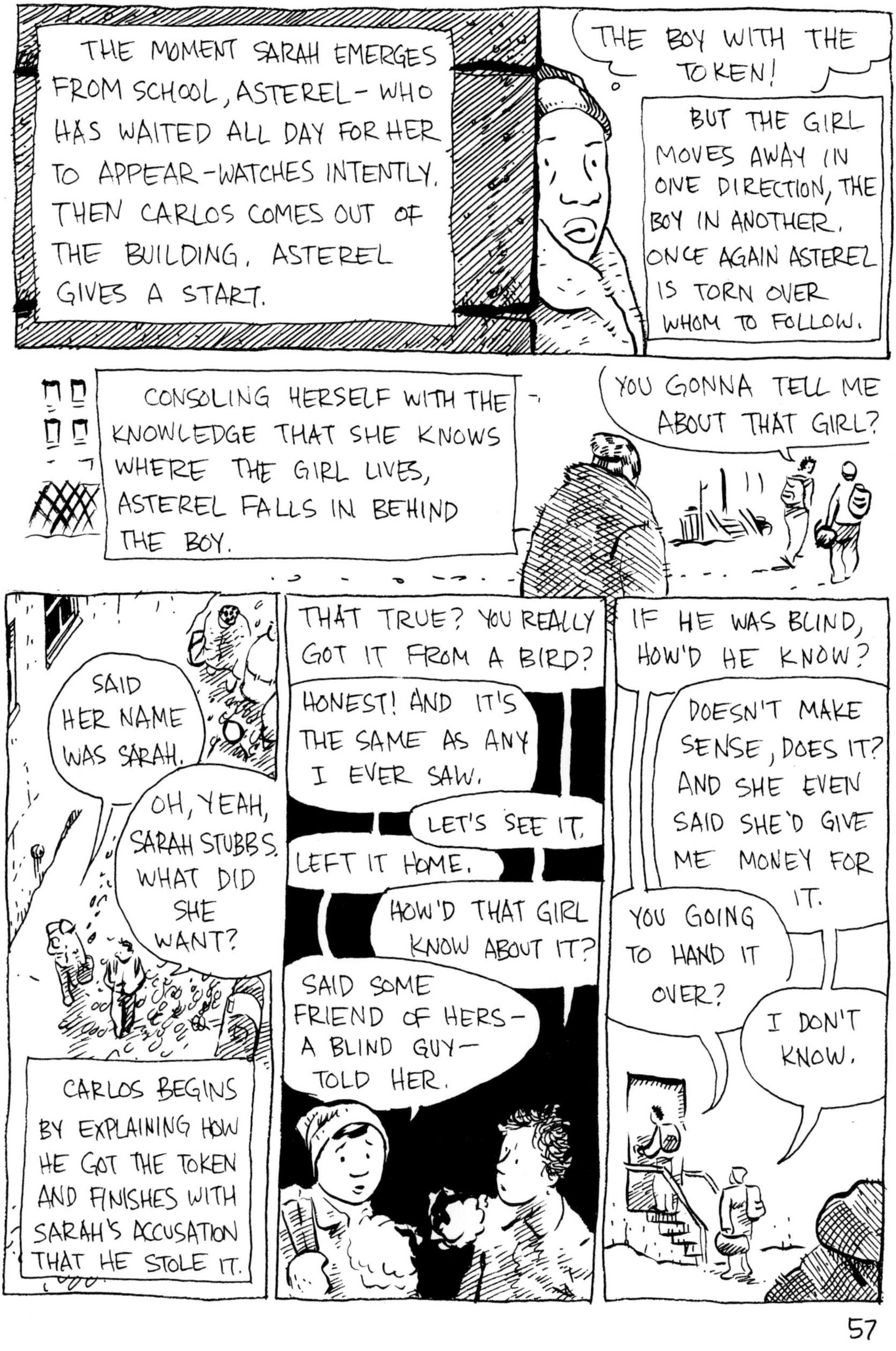
THE MOMENT SARAH EMERGES FROM SCHOOL, ASTEREL - WHO HAS WAITED ALL DAY FOR HER TO APPEAR - WATCHES INTENTLY. THEN CARLOS COMES OUT OF THE BUILDING. ASTEREL GIVES A START.
THE BOY WITH THE TOKEN!
BUT THE GIRL MOVES AWAY IN ONE DIRECTION, THE BOY IN ANOTHER. ONCE AGAIN ASTEREL IS TORN OVER WHOM TO FOLLOW.
CONSOLING HERSELF WITH THE KNOWLEDGE THAT SHE KNOWS WHERE THE GIRL LIVES, ASTEREL FALLS IN BEHIND THE BOY.
YOU GONNA TELL ME ABOUT THAT GIRL?
SAID HER NAME WAS SARAH.
OH, YEAH, SARAH STUBBS. WHAT DID SHE WANT?
CARLOS BEGINS BY EXPLAINING HOW HE GOT THE TOKEN AND FINISHES WITH SARAH'S ACCUSATION THAT HE STOLE IT.
THAT TRUE? YOU REALLY GOT IT FROM A BIRD?
HONEST! AND IT'S THE SAME AS ANY I EVER SAW.
LET'S SEE IT.
LEFT IT HOME.
HOW'D THAT GIRL KNOW ABOUT IT?
SAID SOME FRIEND OF HERS - A BLIND GUY - TOLD HER.
IF HE WAS BLIND, HOW'D HE KNOW?
DOESN'T MAKE SENSE, DOES IT? AND SHE EVEN SAID SHE'D GIVE ME MONEY FOR IT.
YOU GOING TO HAND IT OVER?
I DON'T KNOW.

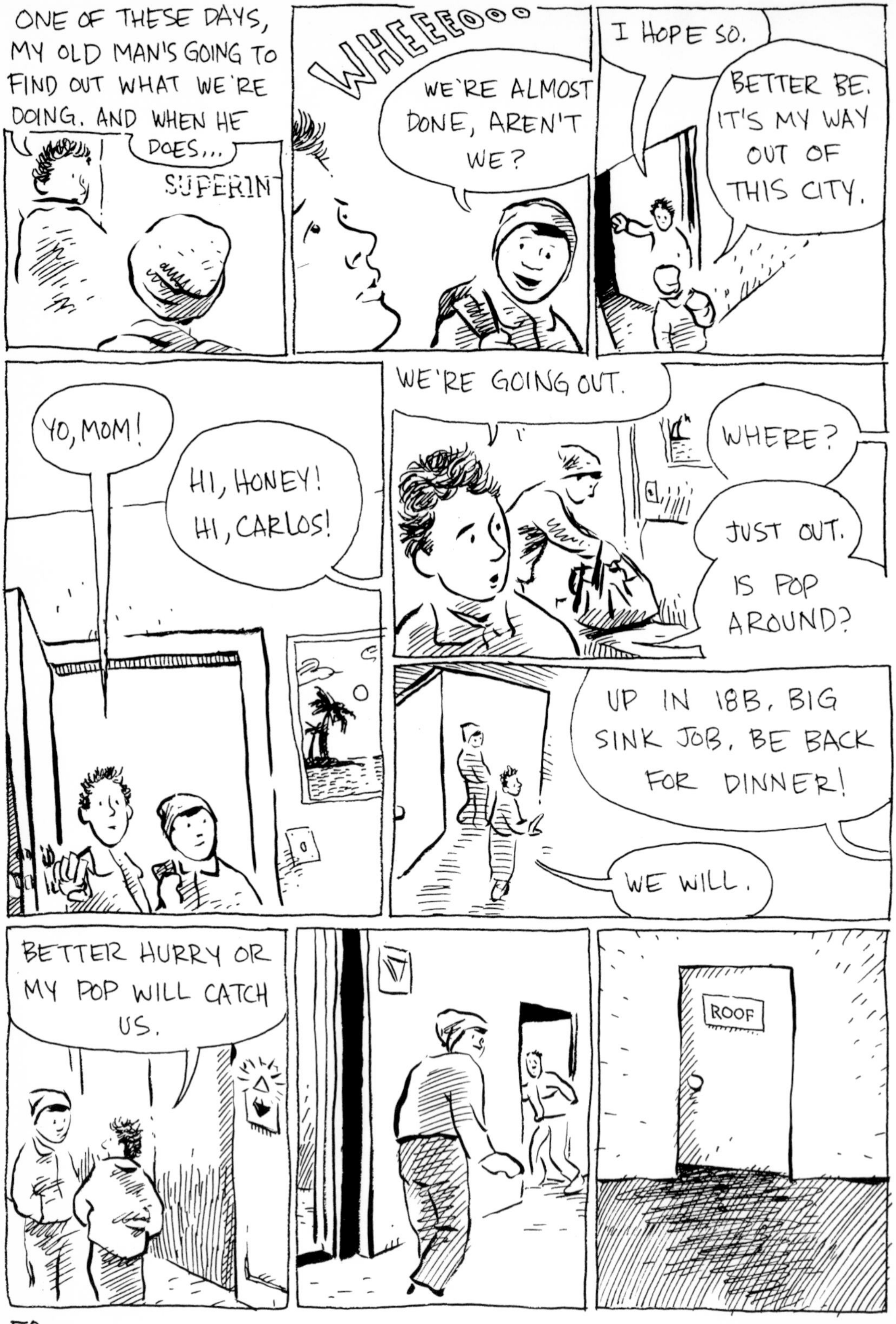
ONE OF THESE DAYS, MY OLD MAN'S GOING TO FIND OUT WHAT WE'RE DOING. AND WHEN HE DOES,...
SUPERINT
WHEEEEOOOO
WE'RE ALMOST DONE, AREN'T WE?
I HOPE SO.
BETTER BE. IT'S MY WAY OUT OF THIS CITY.
YO, MOM!
HI, HONEY! HI, CARLOS!
WE'RE GOING OUT.
WHERE?
JUST OUT.
IS POP AROUND?
UP IN 18B. BIG SINK JOB. BE BACK FOR DINNER!
WE WILL.
BETTER HURRY OR MY POP WILL CATCH US.
ROOF

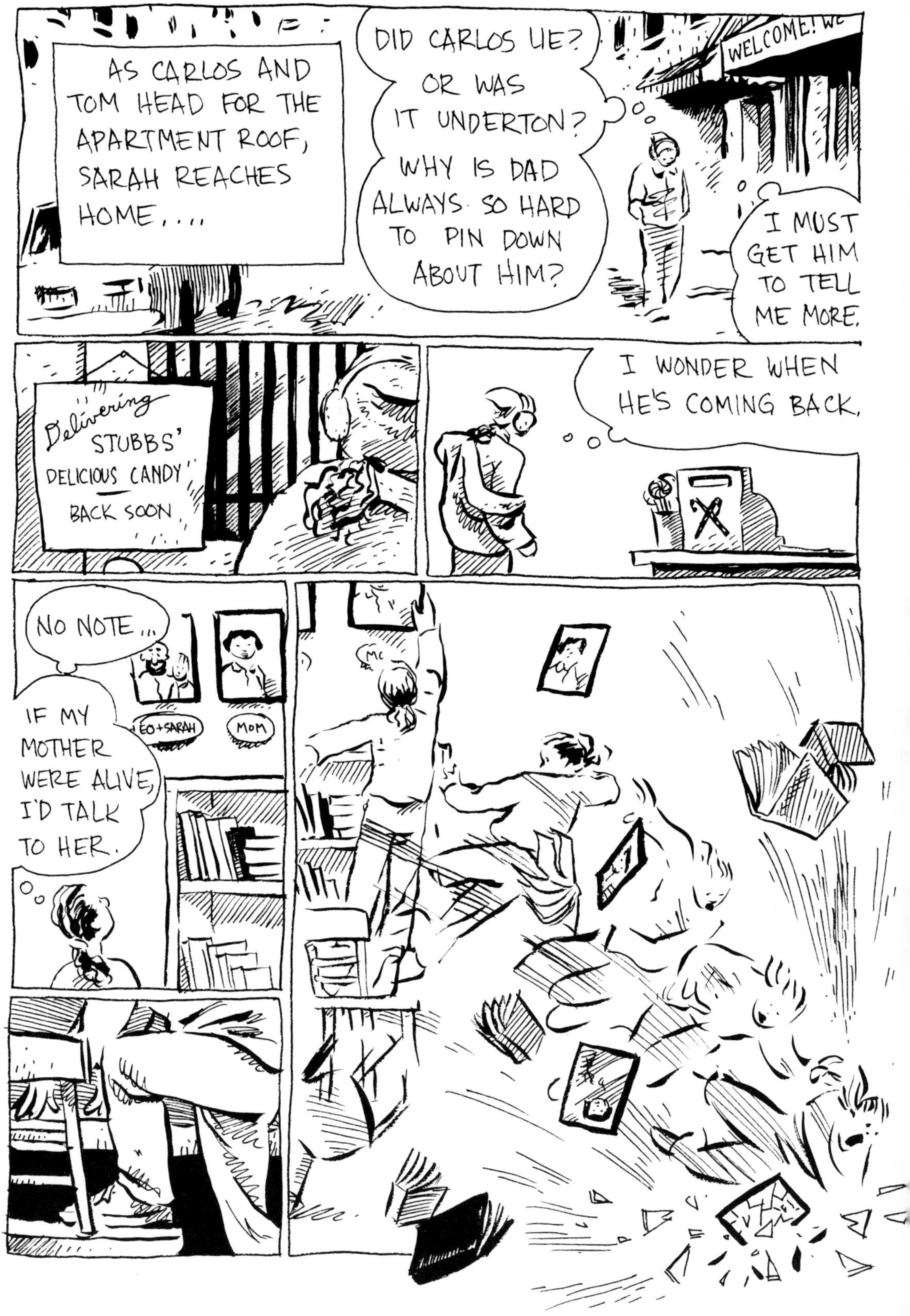
AS CARLOS AND TOM HEAD FOR THE APARTMENT ROOF, SARAH REACHES HOME,...
DID CARLOS LIE? OR WAS IT UNDERTON? WHY IS DAD ALWAYS SO HARD TO PIN DOWN ABOUT HIM?
WELCOME!
I MUST GET HIM TO TELL ME MORE.
Delivering STUBBS' DELICIOUS CANDY BACK SOON
I WONDER WHEN HE'S COMING BACK.
NO NOTE...
IF MY MOTHER WERE ALIVE, I'D TALK TO HER.
MOM

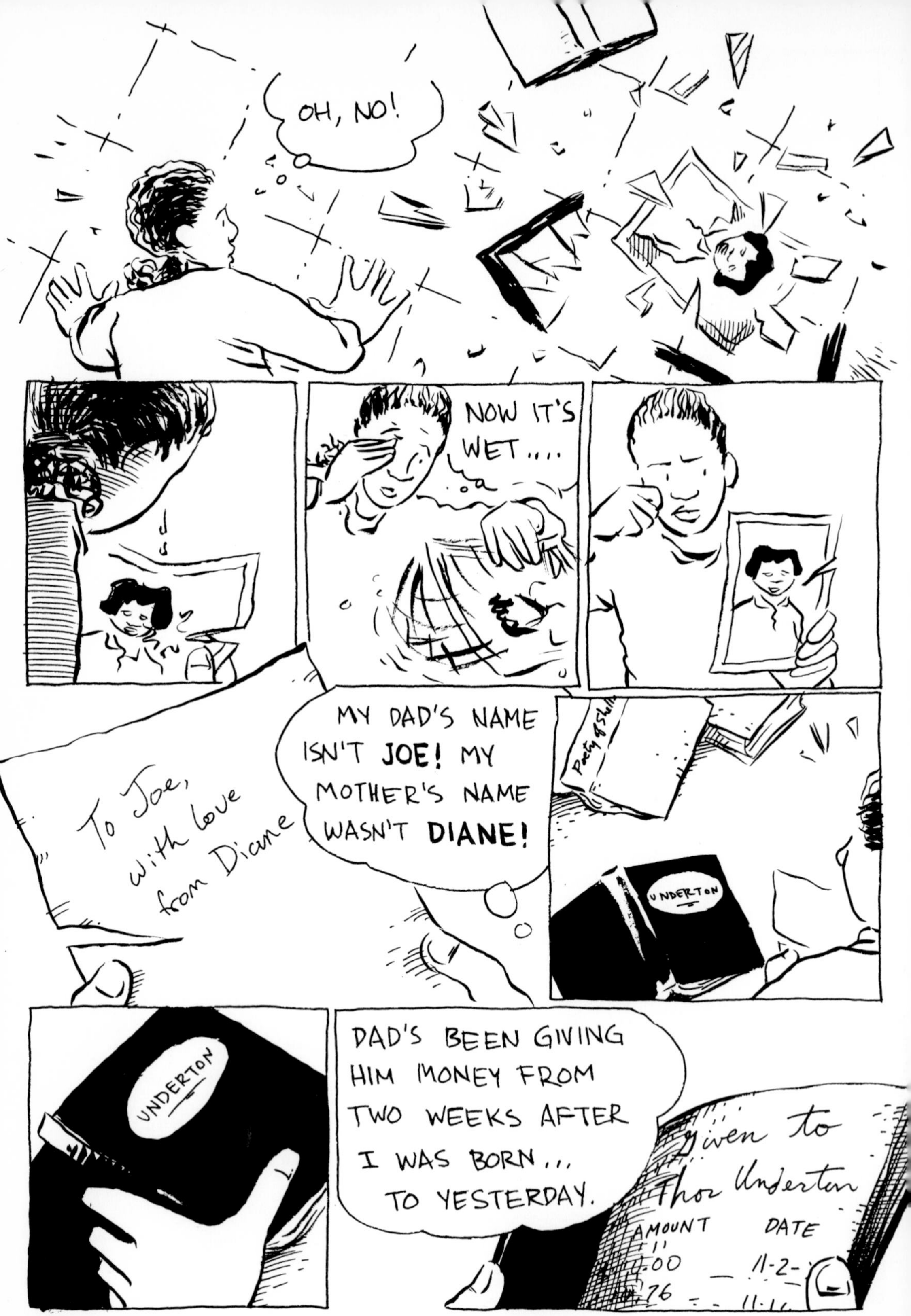
OH, NO!
NOW IT'S WET....
To Joe, with love from Diane
MY DAD'S NAME ISN'T **JOE!** MY MOTHER'S NAME WASN'T **DIANE!**
UNDERTON
UNDERTON
DAD'S BEEN GIVING HIM MONEY FROM TWO WEEKS AFTER I WAS BORN... TO YESTERDAY.
Thos Underton
AMOUNT
DATE

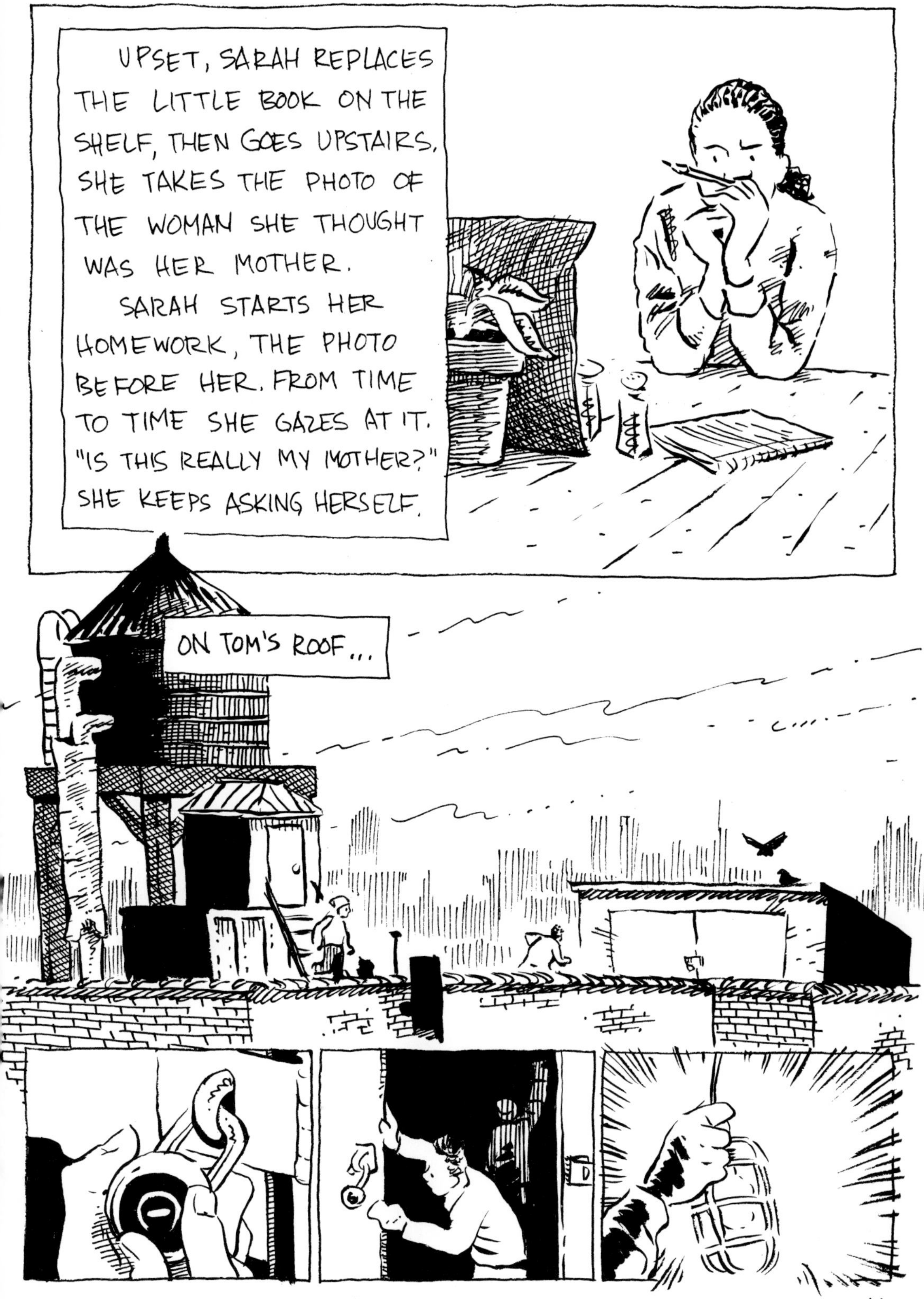
UPSET, SARAH REPLACES THE LITTLE BOOK ON THE SHELF, THEN GOES UPSTAIRS. SHE TAKES THE PHOTO OF THE WOMAN SHE THOUGHT WAS HER MOTHER.
SARAH STARTS HER HOMEWORK, THE PHOTO BEFORE HER. FROM TIME TO TIME SHE GAZES AT IT. "IS THIS REALLY MY MOTHER?" SHE KEEPS ASKING HERSELF.
ON TOM'S ROOF...

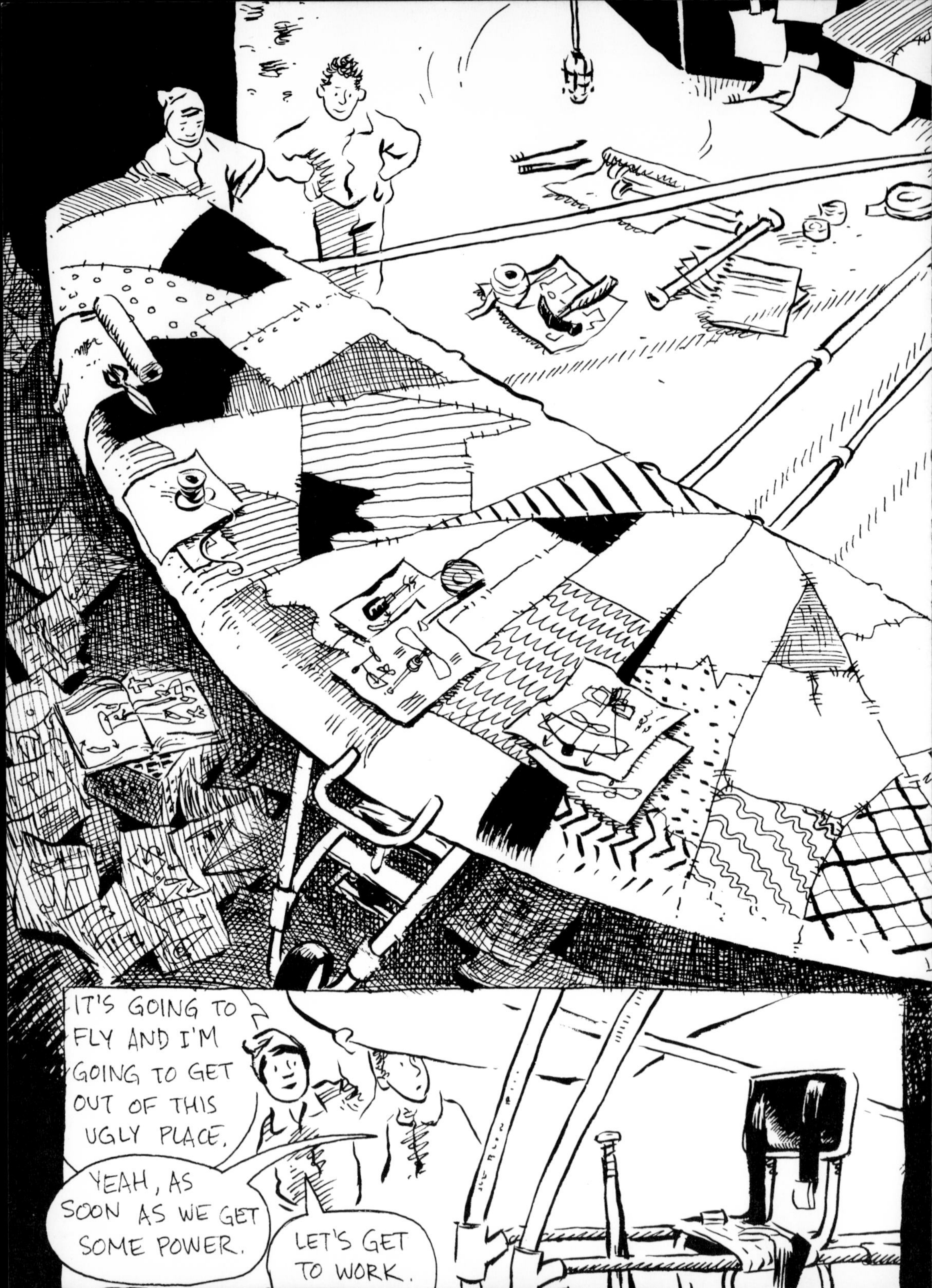
IT'S GOING TO FLY AND I'M GOING TO GET OUT OF THIS UGLY PLACE.
YEAH, AS SOON AS WE GET SOME POWER.
LET'S GET TO WORK.

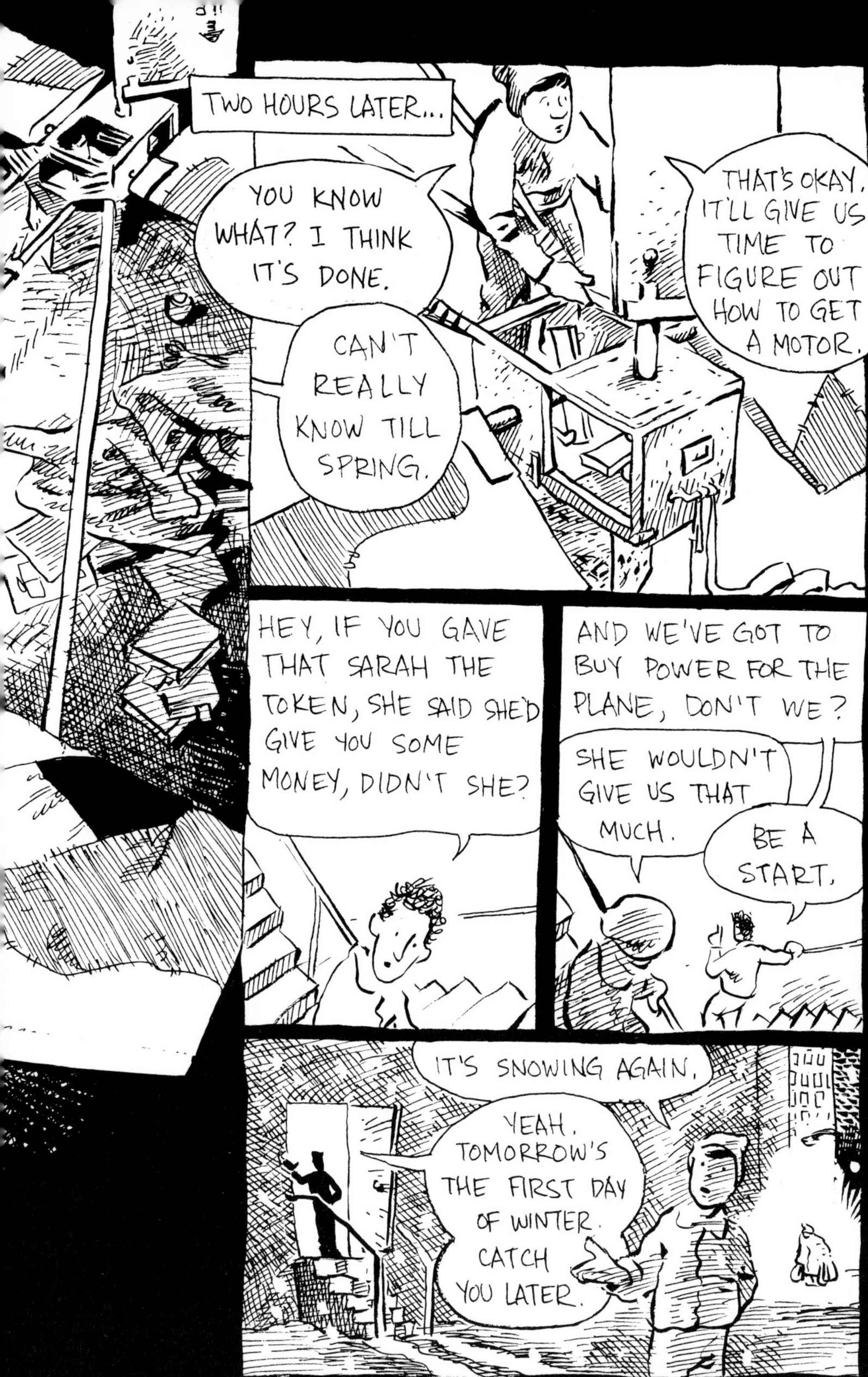

TWO HOURS LATER...
YOU KNOW WHAT? I THINK IT'S DONE.
CAN'T REALLY KNOW TILL SPRING.
THAT'S OKAY. IT'LL GIVE US TIME TO FIGURE OUT HOW TO GET A MOTOR.
HEY, IF YOU GAVE THAT SARAH THE TOKEN, SHE SAID SHE'D GIVE YOU SOME MONEY, DIDN'T SHE?
AND WE'VE GOT TO BUY POWER FOR THE PLANE, DON'T WE?
SHE WOULDN'T GIVE US THAT MUCH.
BE A START.
IT'S SNOWING AGAIN.
YEAH. TOMORROW'S THE FIRST DAY OF WINTER. CATCH YOU LATER.

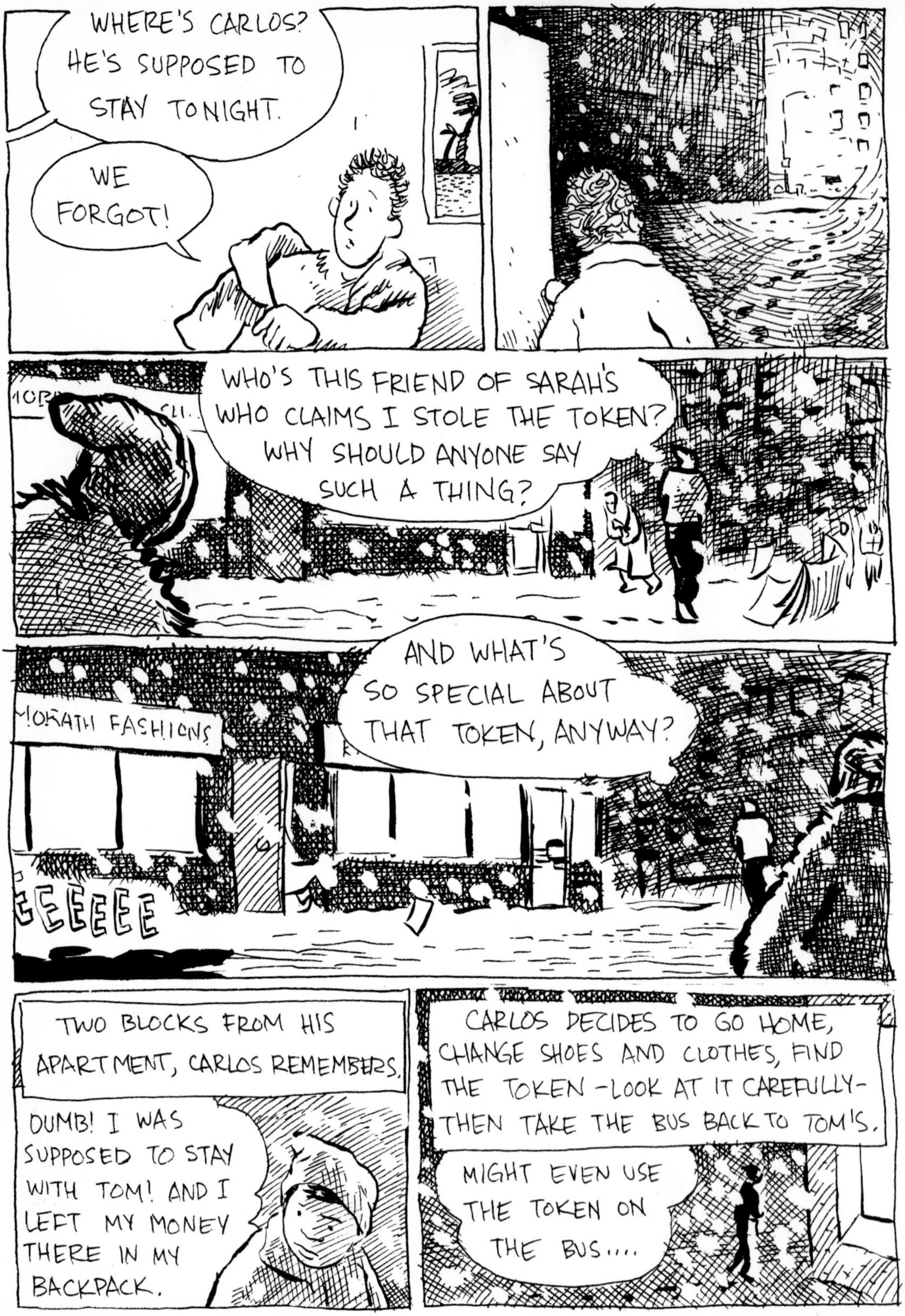
WHERE'S CARLOS? HE'S SUPPOSED TO STAY TONIGHT.
WE FORGOT!
WHO'S THIS FRIEND OF SARAH'S WHO CLAIMS I STOLE THE TOKEN? WHY SHOULD ANYONE SAY SUCH A THING?
AND WHAT'S SO SPECIAL ABOUT THAT TOKEN, ANYWAY?
TWO BLOCKS FROM HIS APARTMENT, CARLOS REMEMBERS.
DUMB! I WAS SUPPOSED TO STAY WITH TOM! AND I LEFT MY MONEY THERE IN MY BACKPACK.
CARLOS DECIDES TO GO HOME, CHANGE SHOES AND CLOTHES, FIND THE TOKEN -LOOK AT IT CAREFULLY- THEN TAKE THE BUS BACK TO TOM'S.
MIGHT EVEN USE THE TOKEN ON THE BUS....

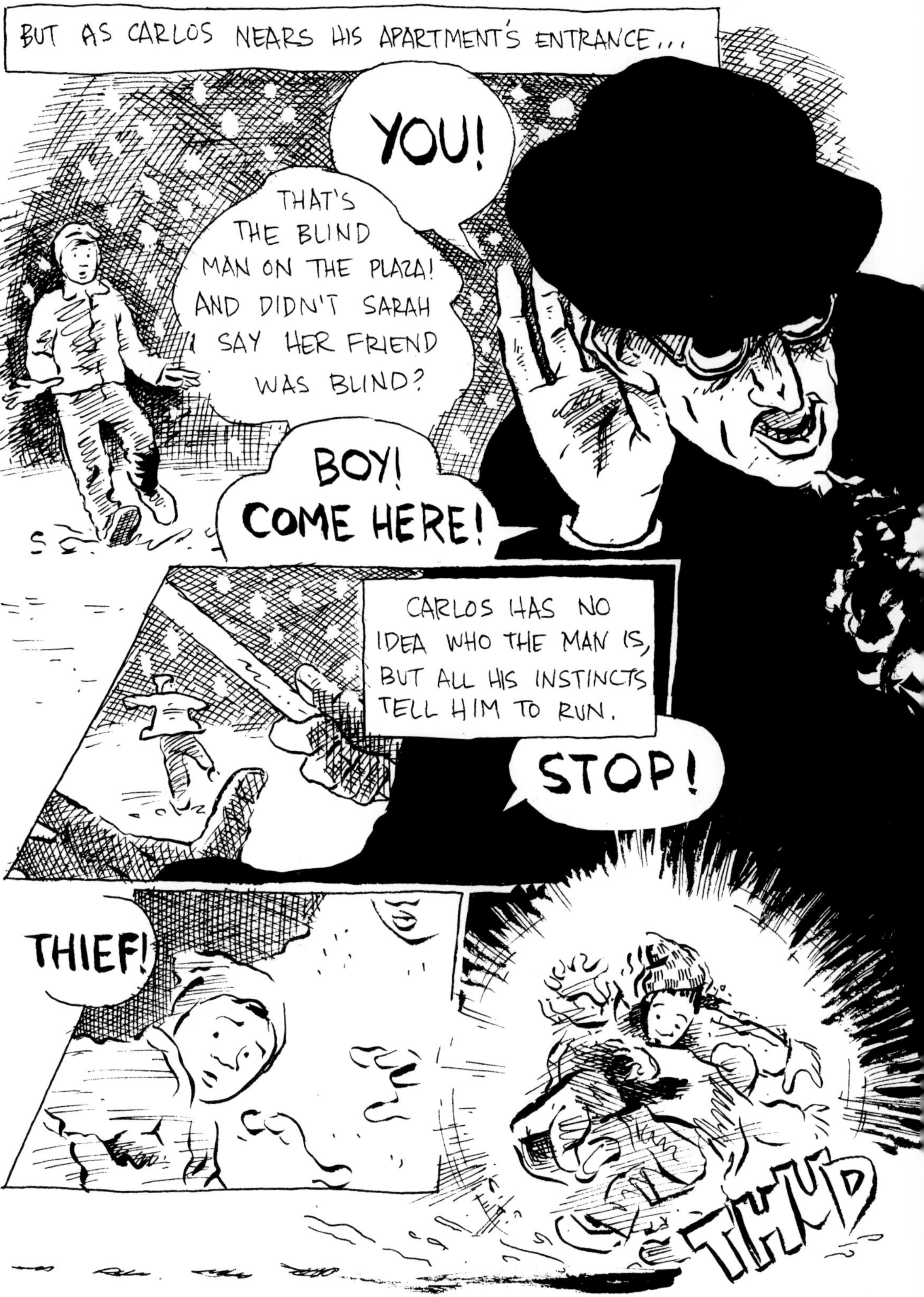
BUT AS CARLOS NEARS HIS APARTMENT'S ENTRANCE...
YOU!
THAT'S THE BLIND MAN ON THE PLAZA! AND DIDN'T SARAH SAY HER FRIEND WAS BLIND?
BOY! COME HERE!
CARLOS HAS NO IDEA WHO THE MAN IS, BUT ALL HIS INSTINCTS TELL HIM TO RUN.
STOP!
THIEF!
THUD

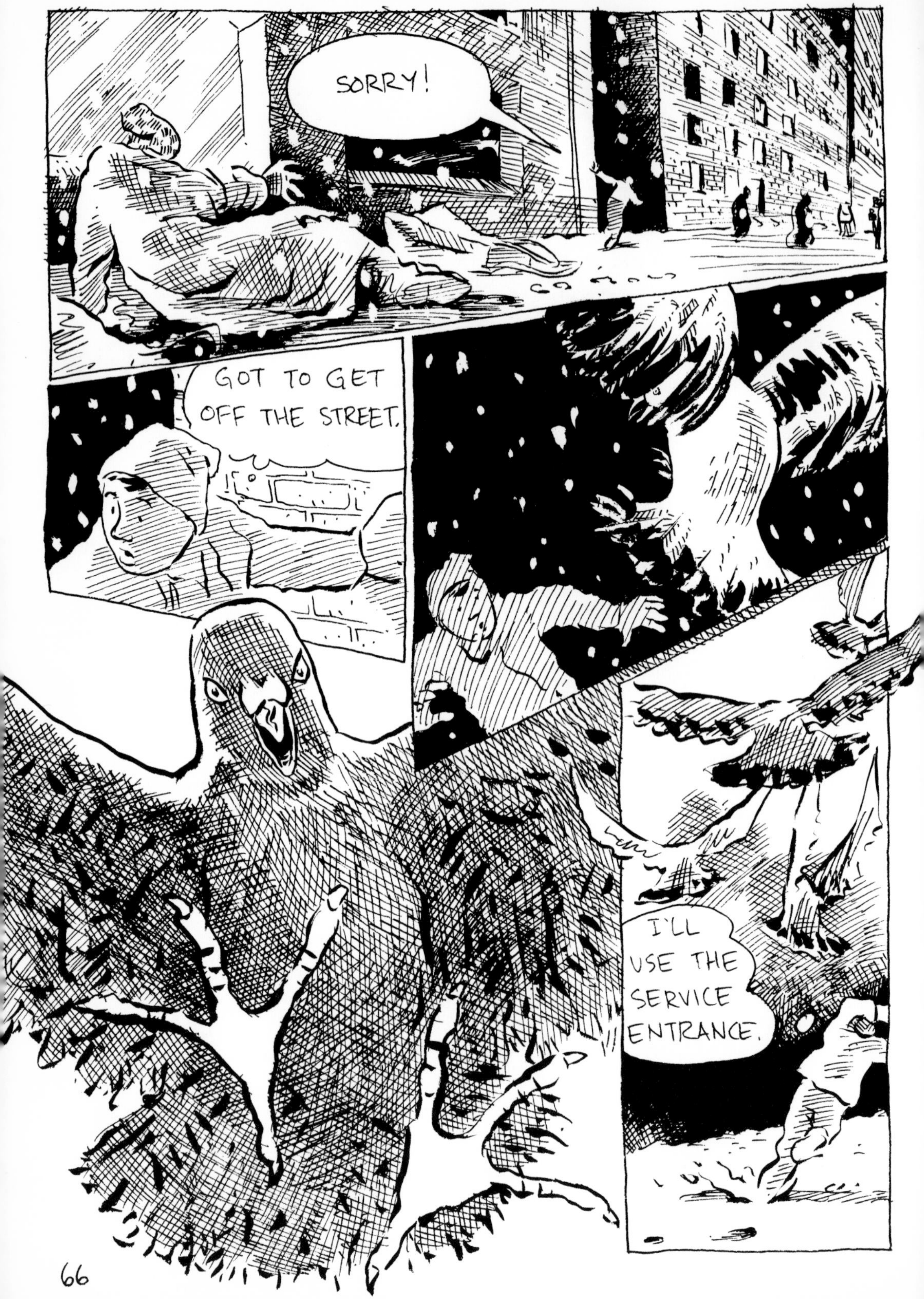
SORRY!
GOT TO GET OFF THE STREET.
I'LL USE THE SERVICE ENTRANCE.

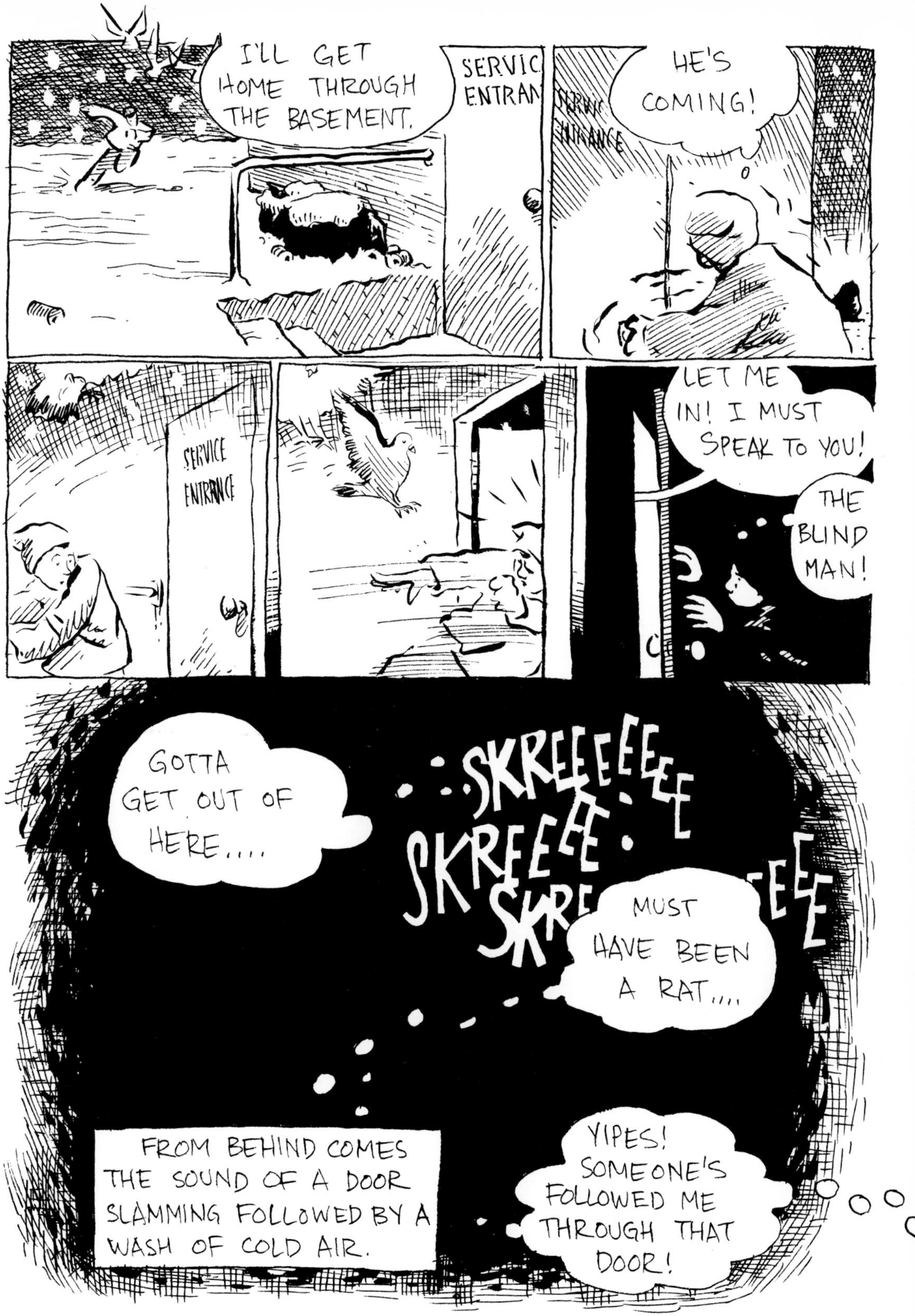
I'LL GET HOME THROUGH THE BASEMENT.
SERVIC ENTRAN
HE'S COMING!
SERVICE ENTRANCE
LET ME IN! I MUST SPEAK TO YOU!
THE BLIND MAN!
GOTTA GET OUT OF HERE....
SKREEEEEEE
SKREEEE
MUST HAVE BEEN A RAT....
FROM BEHIND COMES THE SOUND OF A DOOR SLAMMING FOLLOWED BY A WASH OF COLD AIR.
YIPES! SOMEONE'S FOLLOWED ME THROUGH THAT DOOR!

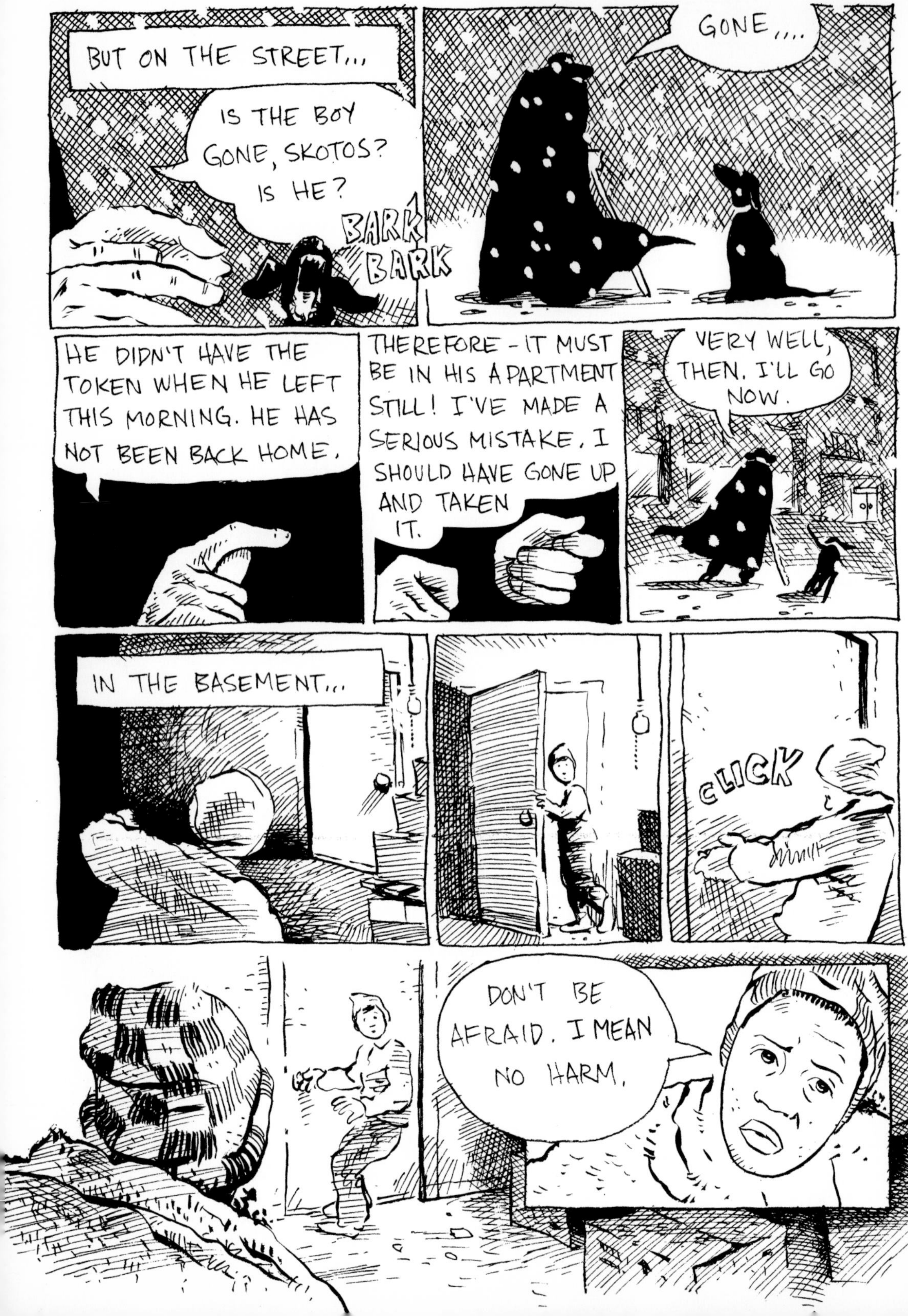
BUT ON THE STREET...
IS THE BOY GONE, SKOTOS? IS HE?
BARK BARK
GONE....
HE DIDN'T HAVE THE TOKEN WHEN HE LEFT THIS MORNING. HE HAS NOT BEEN BACK HOME.
THEREFORE - IT MUST BE IN HIS APARTMENT STILL! I'VE MADE A SERIOUS MISTAKE. I SHOULD HAVE GONE UP AND TAKEN IT.
VERY WELL, THEN. I'LL GO NOW.
IN THE BASEMENT...
CLICK
DON'T BE AFRAID. I MEAN NO HARM.

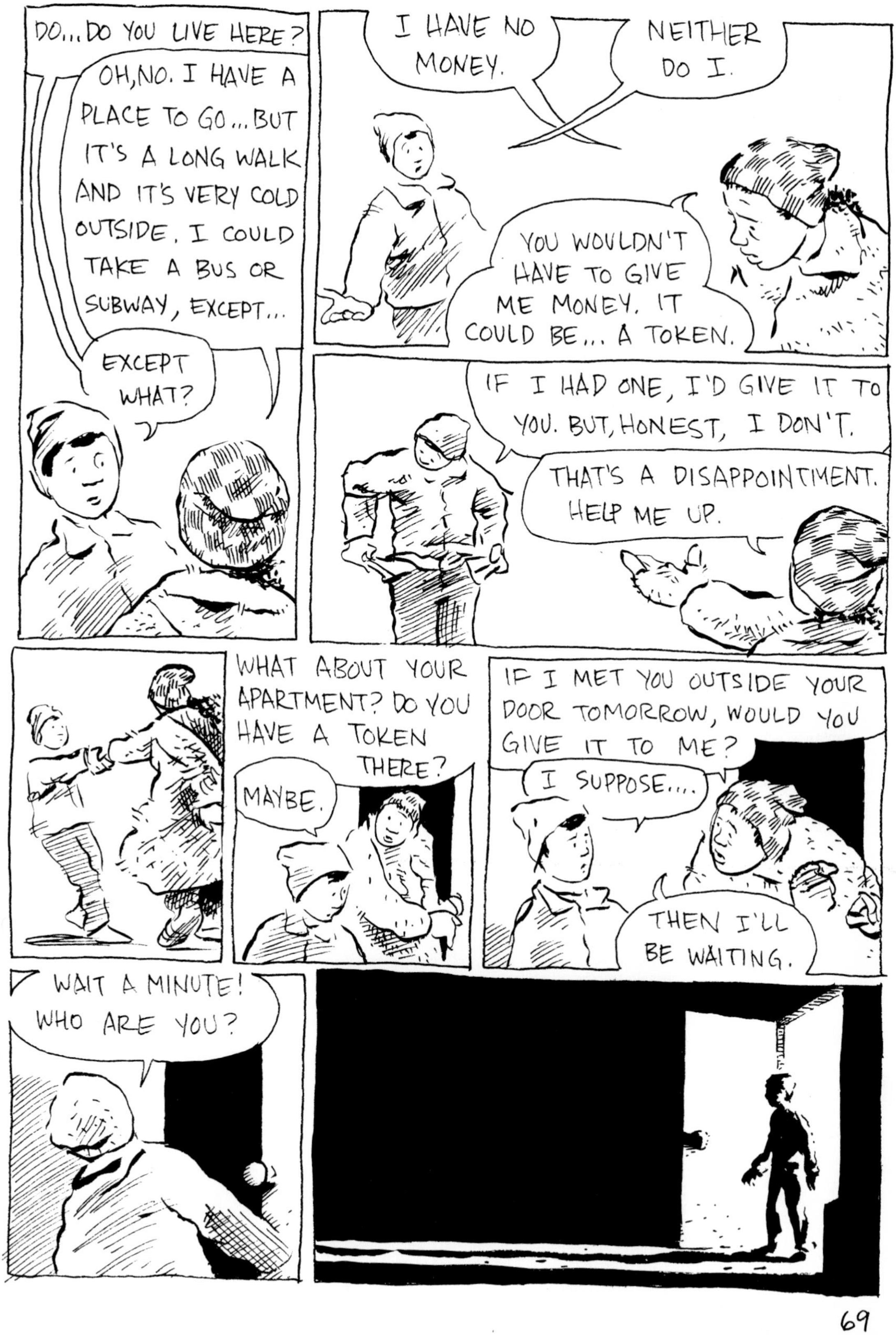
DO... DO YOU LIVE HERE?
OH, NO. I HAVE A PLACE TO GO... BUT IT'S A LONG WALK AND IT'S VERY COLD OUTSIDE. I COULD TAKE A BUS OR SUBWAY, EXCEPT...
EXCEPT WHAT?
I HAVE NO MONEY.
NEITHER DO I.
YOU WOULDN'T HAVE TO GIVE ME MONEY. IT COULD BE... A TOKEN.
IF I HAD ONE, I'D GIVE IT TO YOU. BUT, HONEST, I DON'T.
THAT'S A DISAPPOINTMENT. HELP ME UP.
WHAT ABOUT YOUR APARTMENT? DO YOU HAVE A TOKEN THERE?
MAYBE.
IF I MET YOU OUTSIDE YOUR DOOR TOMORROW, WOULD YOU GIVE IT TO ME?
I SUPPOSE....
THEN I'LL BE WAITING.
WAIT A MINUTE! WHO ARE YOU?

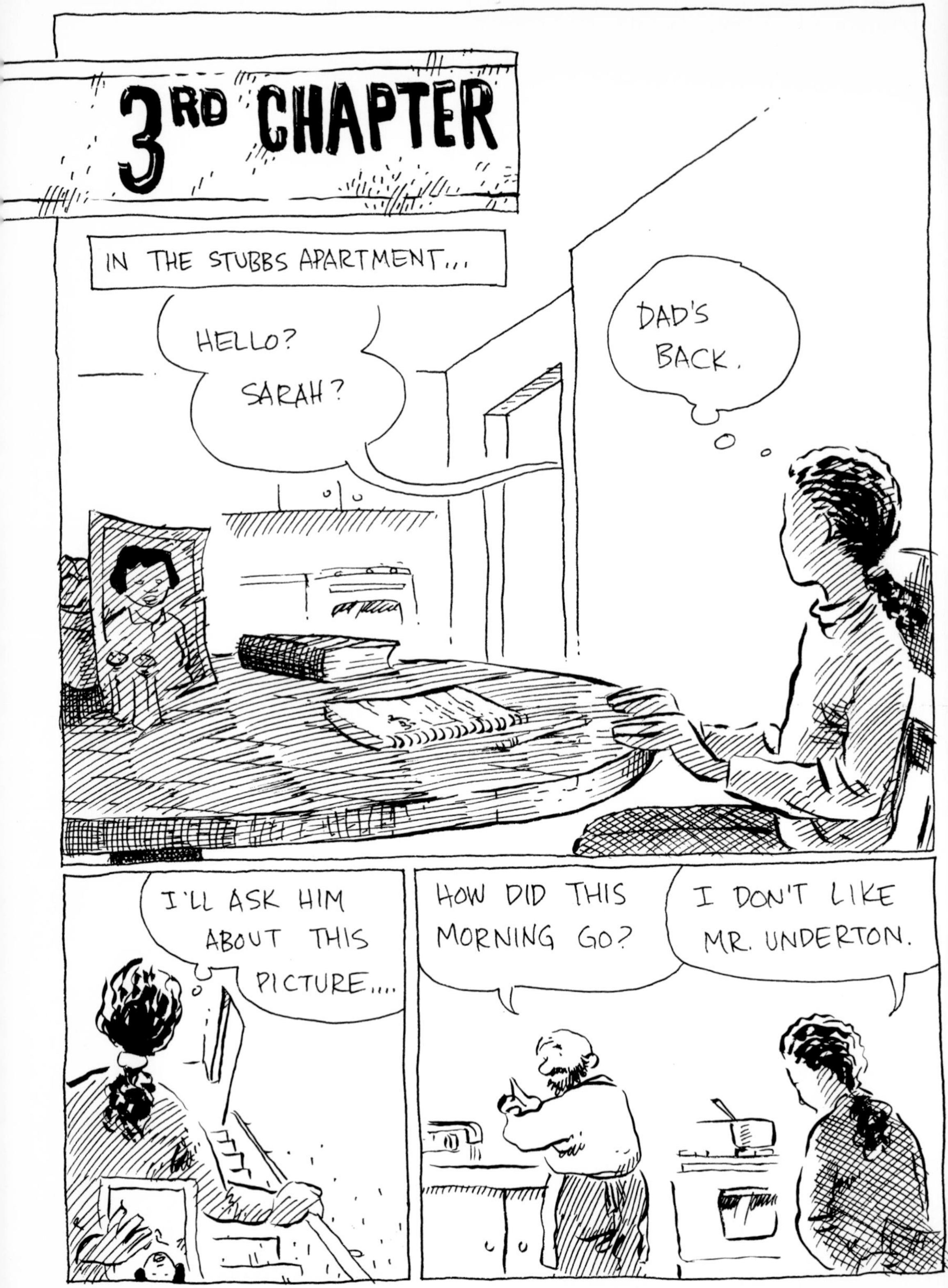
3RD CHAPTER
IN THE STUBBS APARTMENT...
HELLO? SARAH?
DAD'S BACK.
I'LL ASK HIM ABOUT THIS PICTURE....
HOW DID THIS MORNING GO?
I DON'T LIKE MR. UNDERTON.

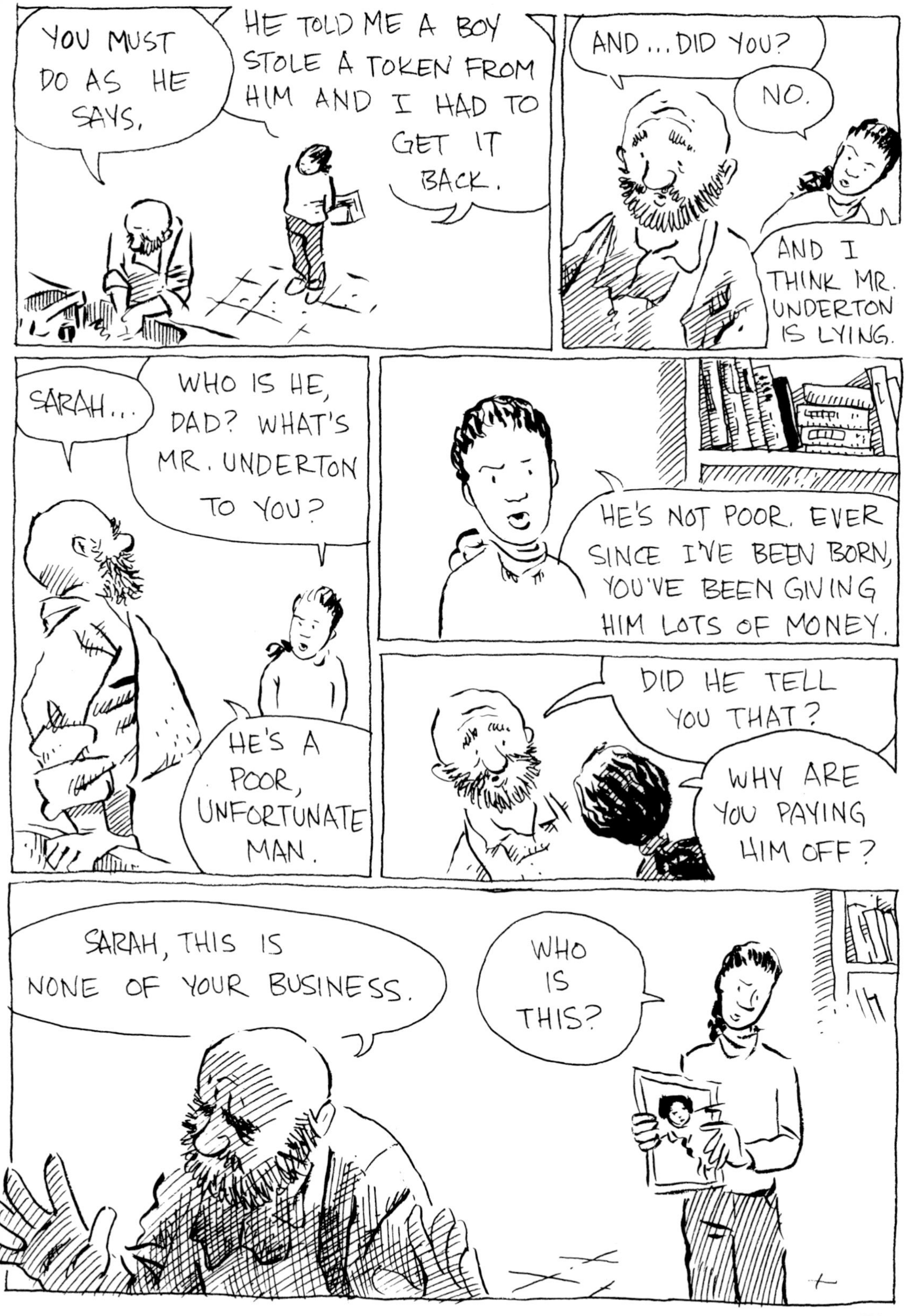
YOU MUST DO AS HE SAYS.
HE TOLD ME A BOY STOLE A TOKEN FROM HIM AND I HAD TO GET IT BACK.
AND ... DID YOU?
NO.
AND I THINK MR. UNDERTON IS LYING.
SARAH...
WHO IS HE, DAD? WHAT'S MR. UNDERTON TO YOU?
HE'S A POOR, UNFORTUNATE MAN.
HE'S NOT POOR. EVER SINCE I'VE BEEN BORN, YOU'VE BEEN GIVING HIM LOTS OF MONEY.
DID HE TELL YOU THAT?
WHY ARE YOU PAYING HIM OFF?
SARAH, THIS IS NONE OF YOUR BUSINESS.
WHO IS THIS?

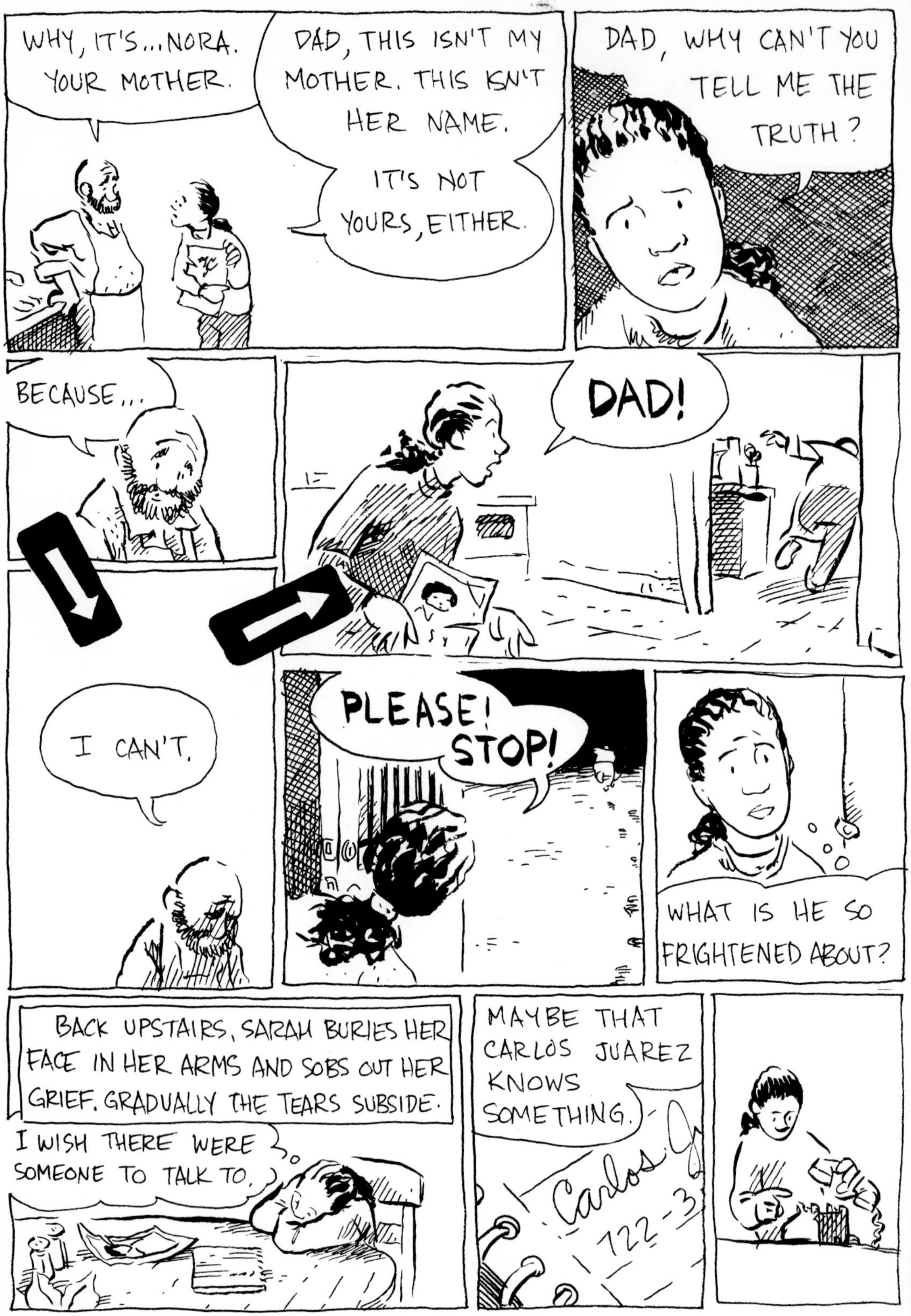
WHY, IT'S...NORA. YOUR MOTHER.
DAD, THIS ISN'T MY MOTHER. THIS ISN'T HER NAME.
IT'S NOT YOURS, EITHER.
DAD, WHY CAN'T YOU TELL ME THE TRUTH?
BECAUSE...
DAD!
I CAN'T.
PLEASE! STOP!
WHAT IS HE SO FRIGHTENED ABOUT?
BACK UPSTAIRS, SARAH BURIES HER FACE IN HER ARMS AND SOBS OUT HER GRIEF. GRADUALLY THE TEARS SUBSIDE.
I WISH THERE WERE SOMEONE TO TALK TO.
MAYBE THAT CARLOS JUAREZ KNOWS SOMETHING.
Carlos J
722-3

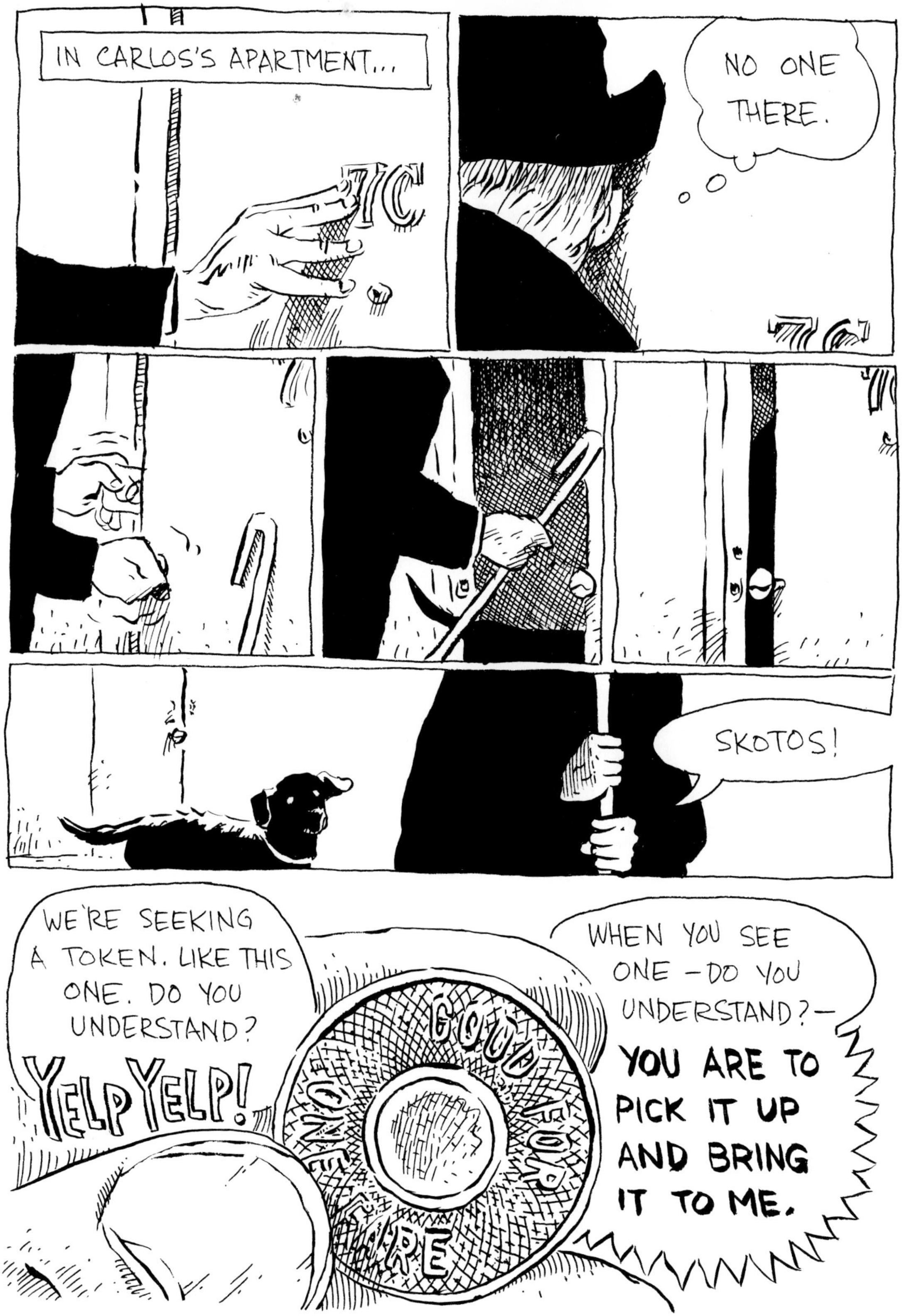
IN CARLOS'S APARTMENT...
7C
NO ONE THERE.
SKOTOS!
WE'RE SEEKING A TOKEN. LIKE THIS ONE. DO YOU UNDERSTAND?
YELP YELP!
GOOD FOR ONE FARE
WHEN YOU SEE ONE –DO YOU UNDERSTAND?–
YOU ARE TO PICK IT UP AND BRING IT TO ME.

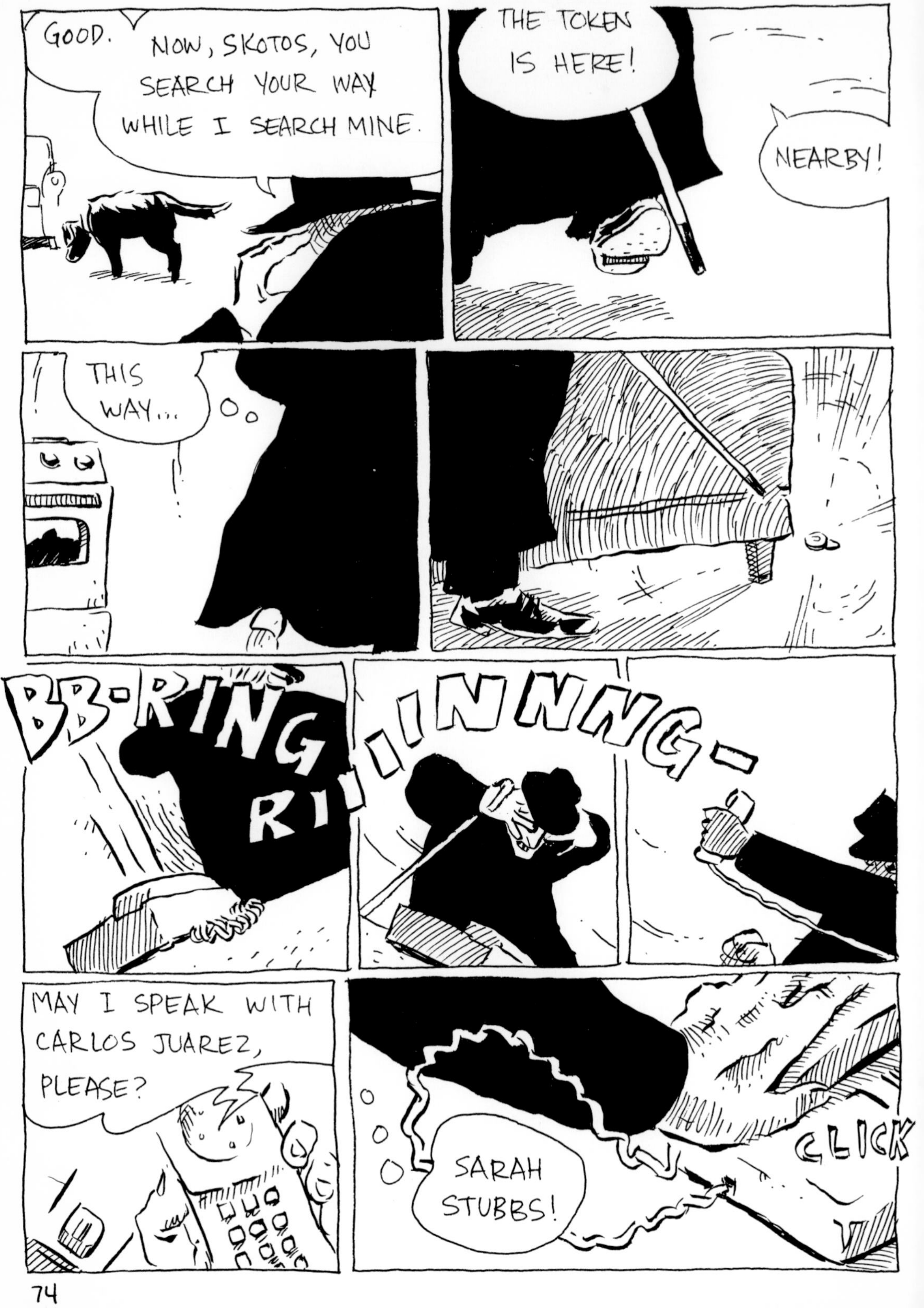
GOOD.
NOW, SKOTOS, YOU SEARCH YOUR WAY WHILE I SEARCH MINE.
THE TOKEN IS HERE!
NEARBY!
THIS WAY...
BB-RING RI--INNNG-
MAY I SPEAK WITH CARLOS JUAREZ, PLEASE?
SARAH STUBBS!
CLICK

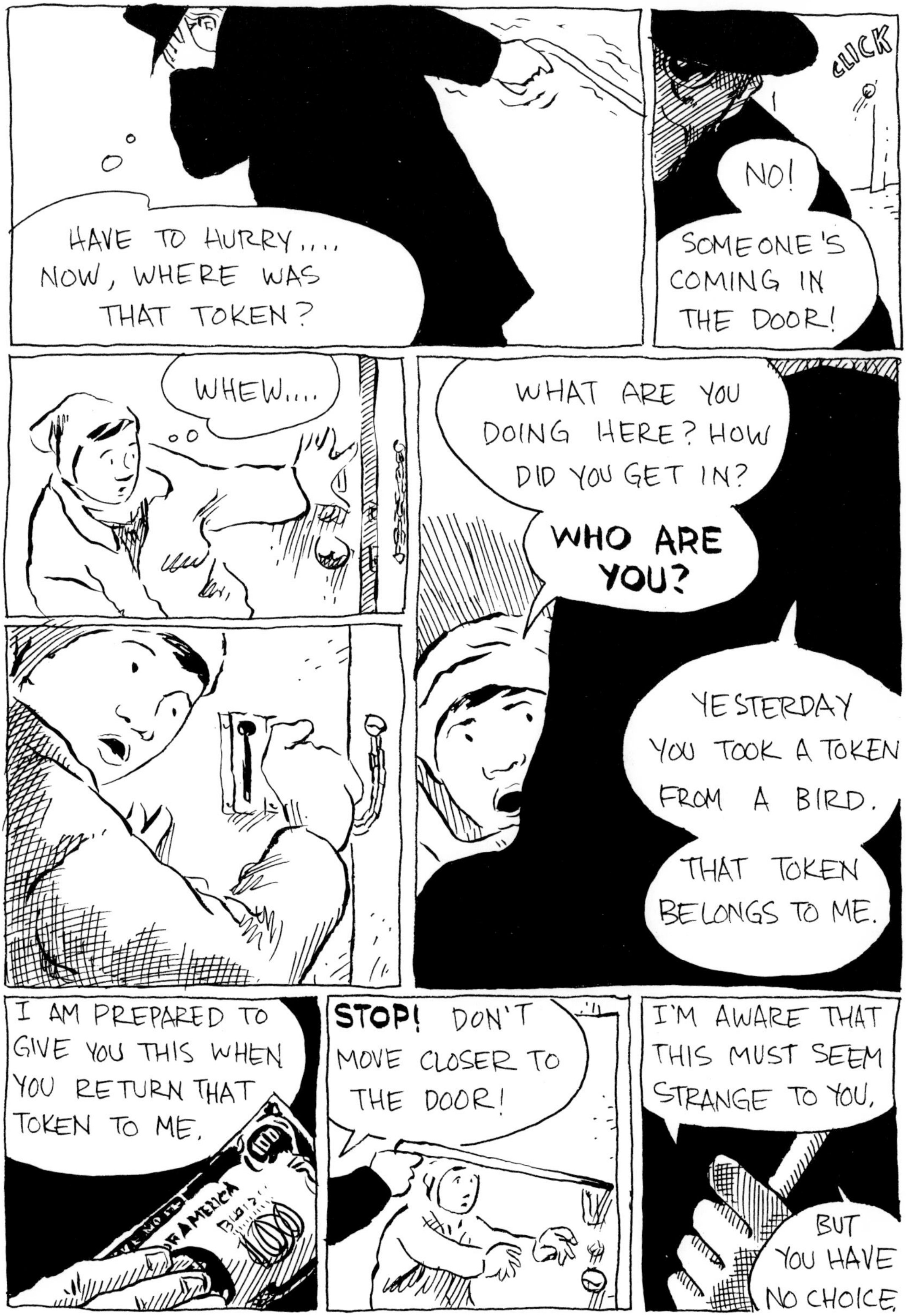
HAVE TO HURRY.... NOW, WHERE WAS THAT TOKEN?
CLICK
NO!
SOMEONE'S COMING IN THE DOOR!
WHEW....
WHAT ARE YOU DOING HERE? HOW DID YOU GET IN?
WHO ARE YOU?
YESTERDAY YOU TOOK A TOKEN FROM A BIRD.
THAT TOKEN BELONGS TO ME.
I AM PREPARED TO GIVE YOU THIS WHEN YOU RETURN THAT TOKEN TO ME.
STOP! DON'T MOVE CLOSER TO THE DOOR!
I'M AWARE THAT THIS MUST SEEM STRANGE TO YOU.
BUT YOU HAVE NO CHOICE.

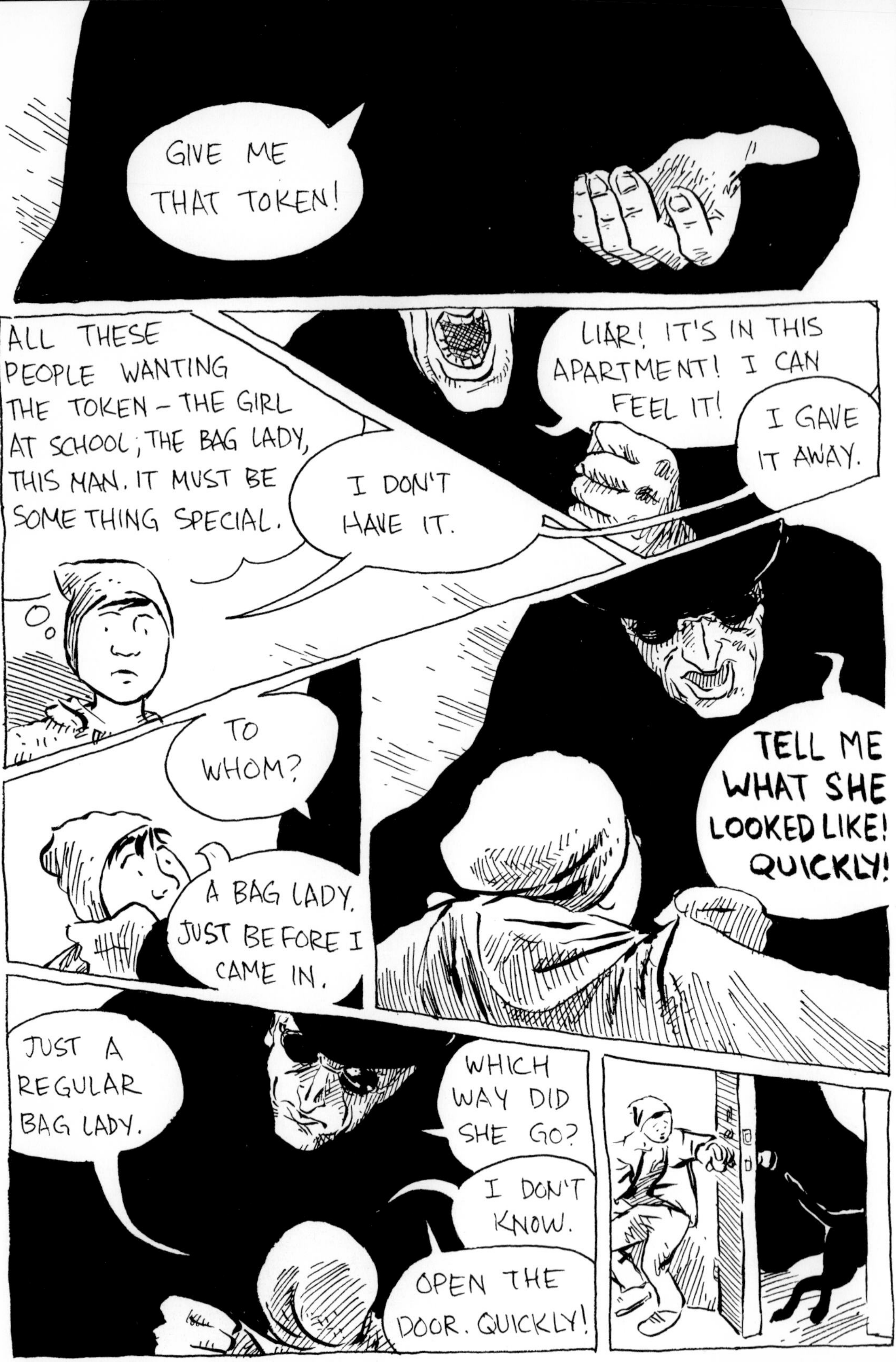
GIVE ME THAT TOKEN!
ALL THESE PEOPLE WANTING THE TOKEN – THE GIRL AT SCHOOL; THE BAG LADY, THIS MAN. IT MUST BE SOMETHING SPECIAL.
I DON'T HAVE IT.
LIAR! IT'S IN THIS APARTMENT! I CAN FEEL IT!
I GAVE IT AWAY.
TO WHOM?
A BAG LADY. JUST BEFORE I CAME IN.
TELL ME WHAT SHE LOOKED LIKE! QUICKLY!
JUST A REGULAR BAG LADY.
WHICH WAY DID SHE GO?
I DON'T KNOW.
OPEN THE DOOR. QUICKLY!

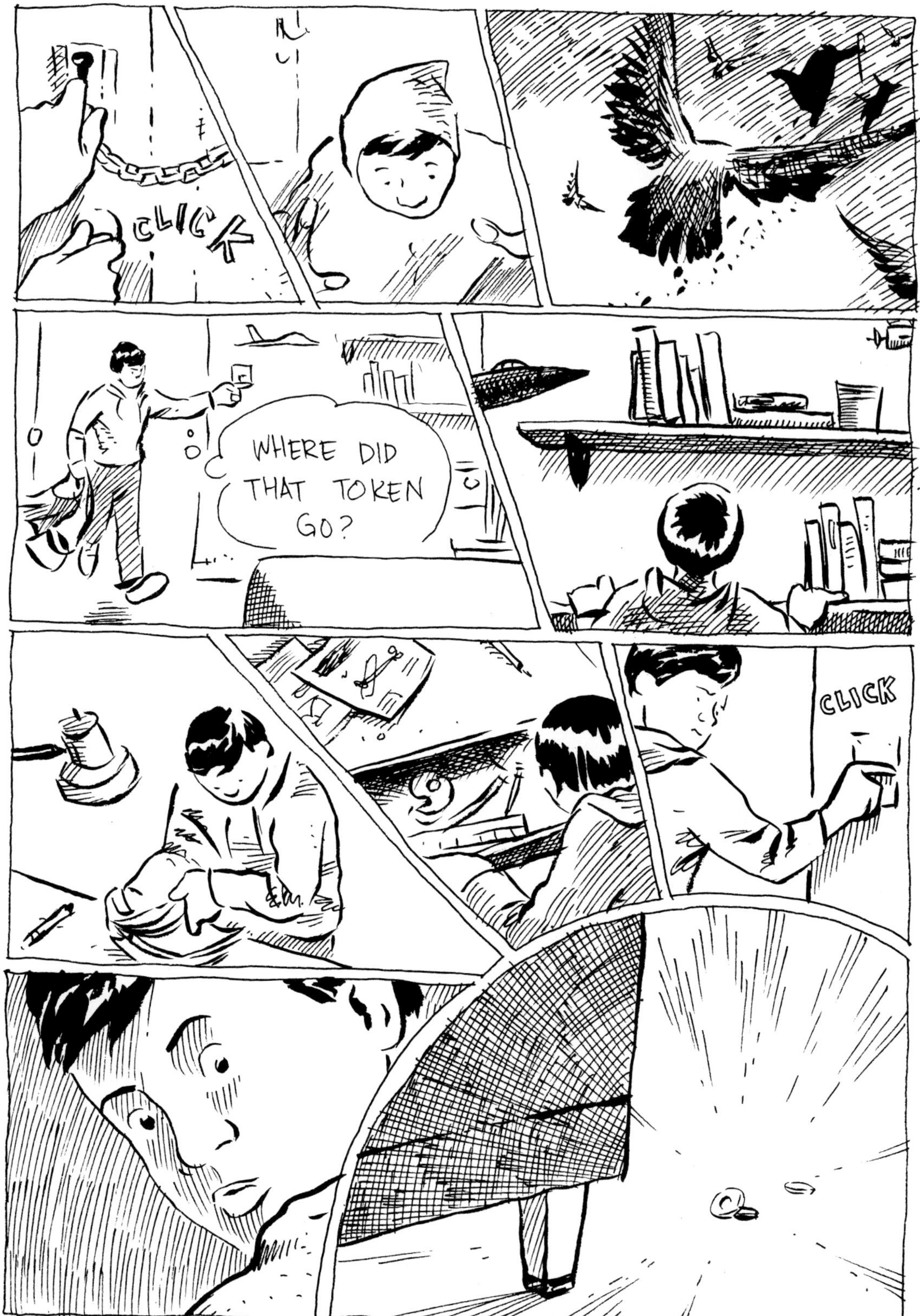
CLICK
WHERE DID THAT TOKEN GO?
CLICK

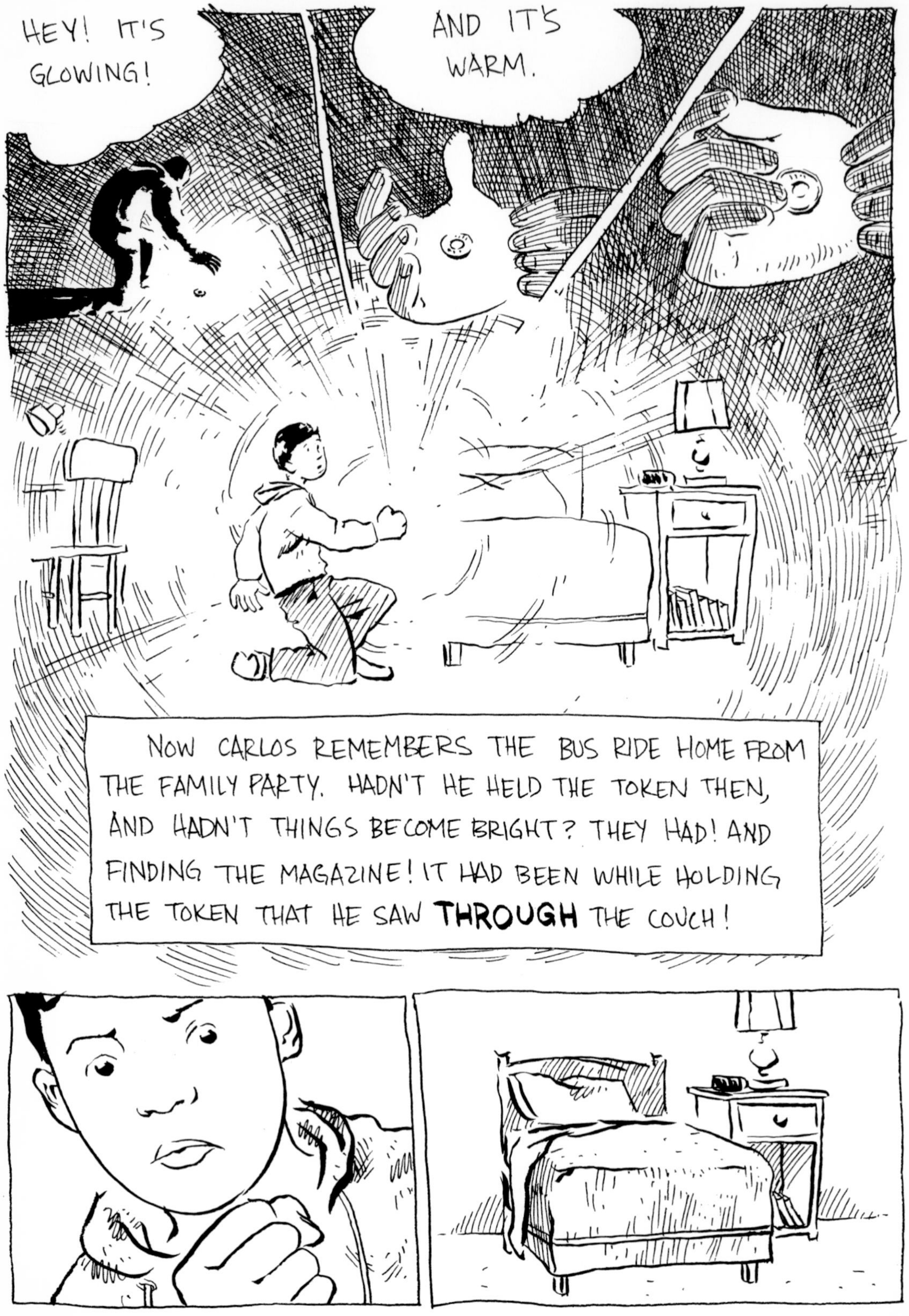
HEY! IT'S GLOWING!
AND IT'S WARM.
NOW CARLOS REMEMBERS THE BUS RIDE HOME FROM THE FAMILY PARTY. HADN'T HE HELD THE TOKEN THEN, AND HADN'T THINGS BECOME BRIGHT? THEY HAD! AND FINDING THE MAGAZINE! IT HAD BEEN WHILE HOLDING THE TOKEN THAT HE SAW **THROUGH** THE COUCH!

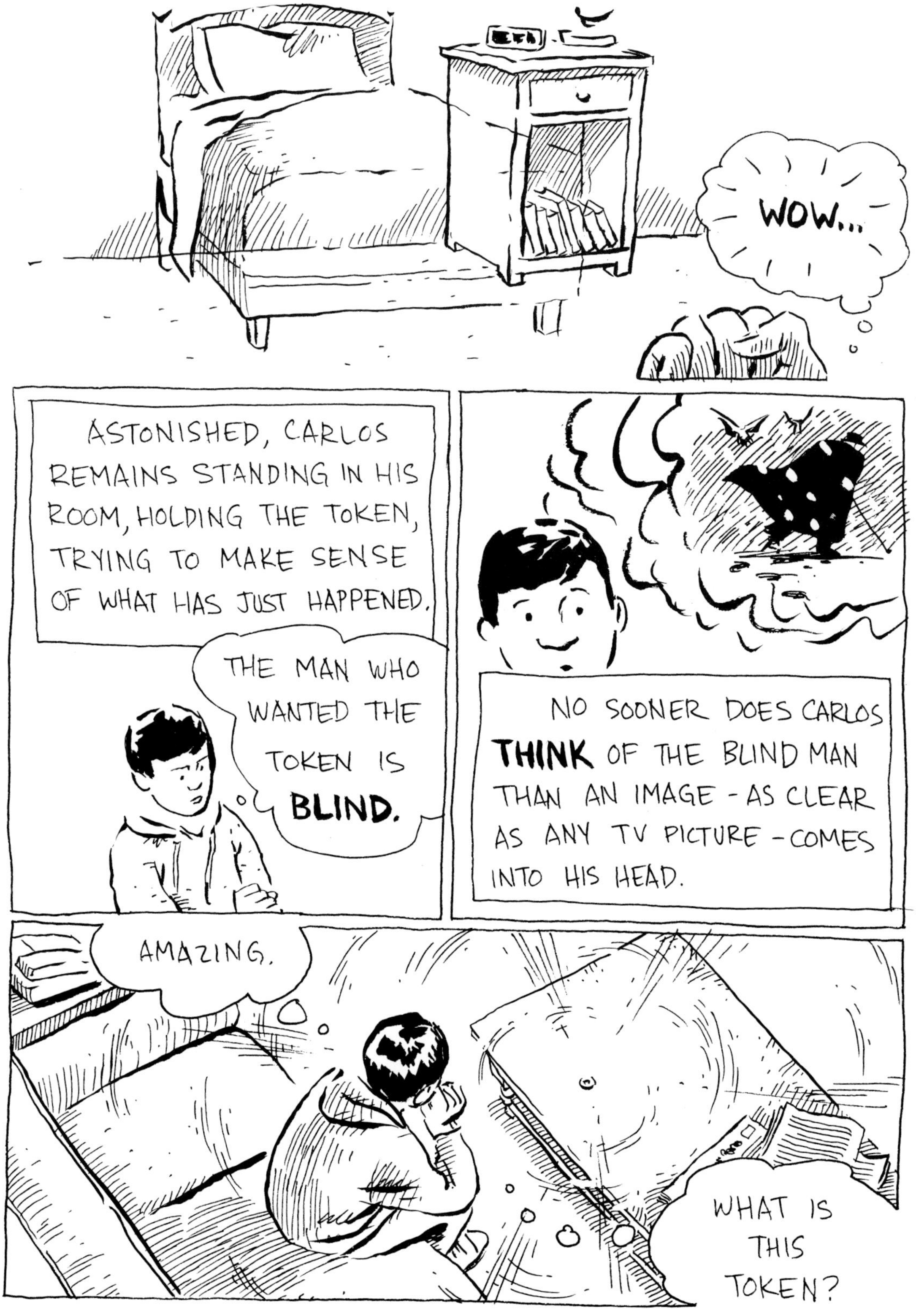

WOW...
ASTONISHED, CARLOS REMAINS STANDING IN HIS ROOM, HOLDING THE TOKEN, TRYING TO MAKE SENSE OF WHAT HAS JUST HAPPENED.
THE MAN WHO WANTED THE TOKEN IS **BLIND.**
NO SOONER DOES CARLOS **THINK** OF THE BLIND MAN THAN AN IMAGE - AS CLEAR AS ANY TV PICTURE - COMES INTO HIS HEAD.
AMAZING.
WHAT IS THIS TOKEN?

4TH CHAPTER

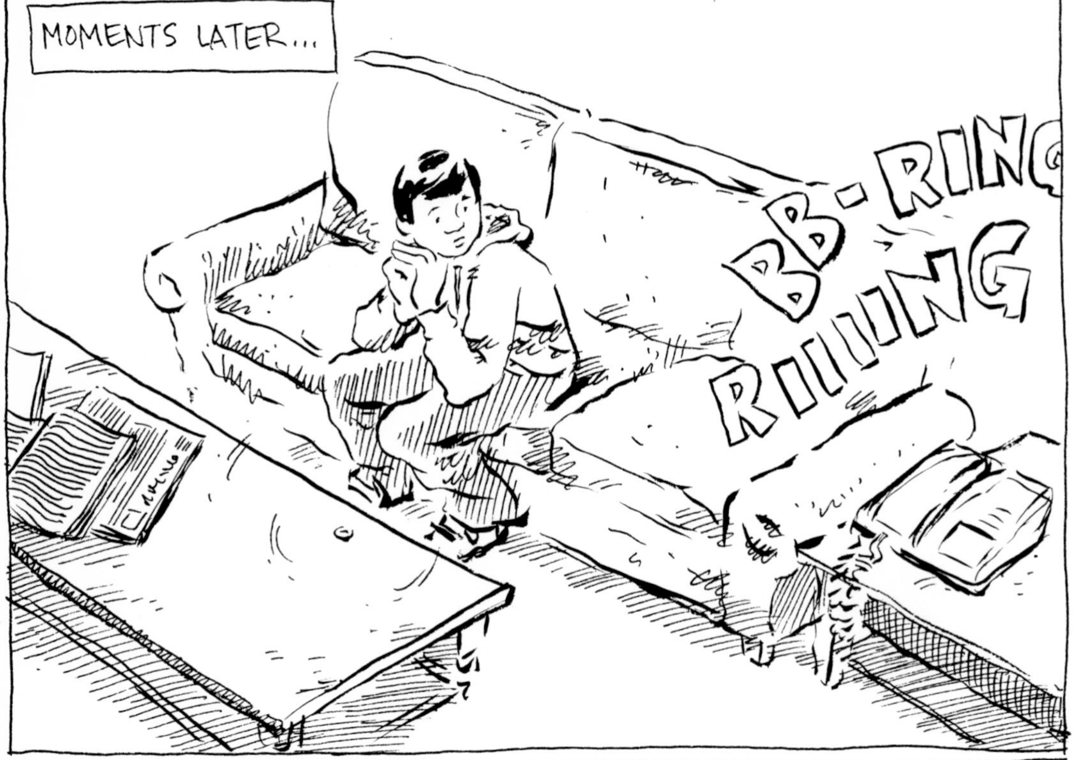

MOMENTS LATER...
BB-RING RIIIING

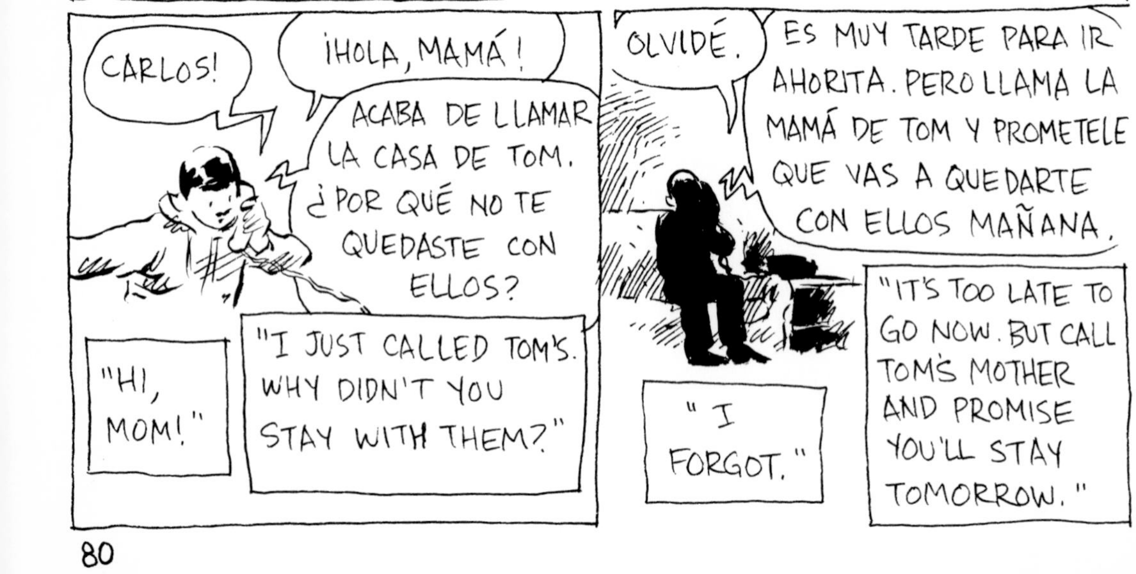

CARLOS!
¡HOLA, MAMÁ!
ACABA DE LLAMAR LA CASA DE TOM. ¿POR QUÉ NO TE QUEDASTE CON ELLOS?
"HI, MOM!"
"I JUST CALLED TOM'S. WHY DIDN'T YOU STAY WITH THEM?"
OLVIDÉ.
ES MUY TARDE PARA IR AHORITA. PERO LLAMA LA MAMÁ DE TOM Y PROMETELE QUE VAS A QUEDARTE CON ELLOS MAÑANA.
"I FORGOT."
"IT'S TOO LATE TO GO NOW. BUT CALL TOM'S MOTHER AND PROMISE YOU'LL STAY TOMORROW."

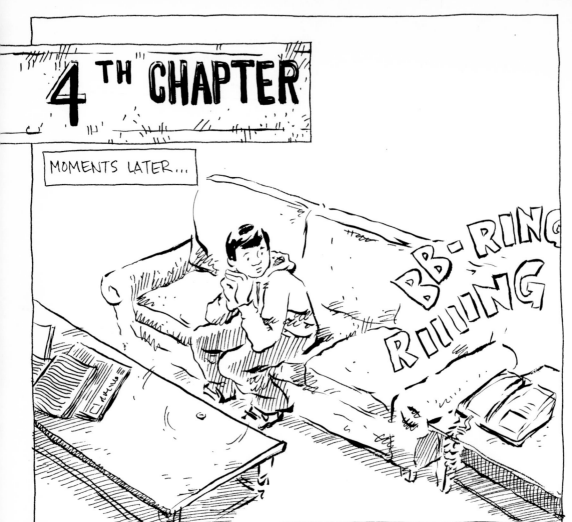

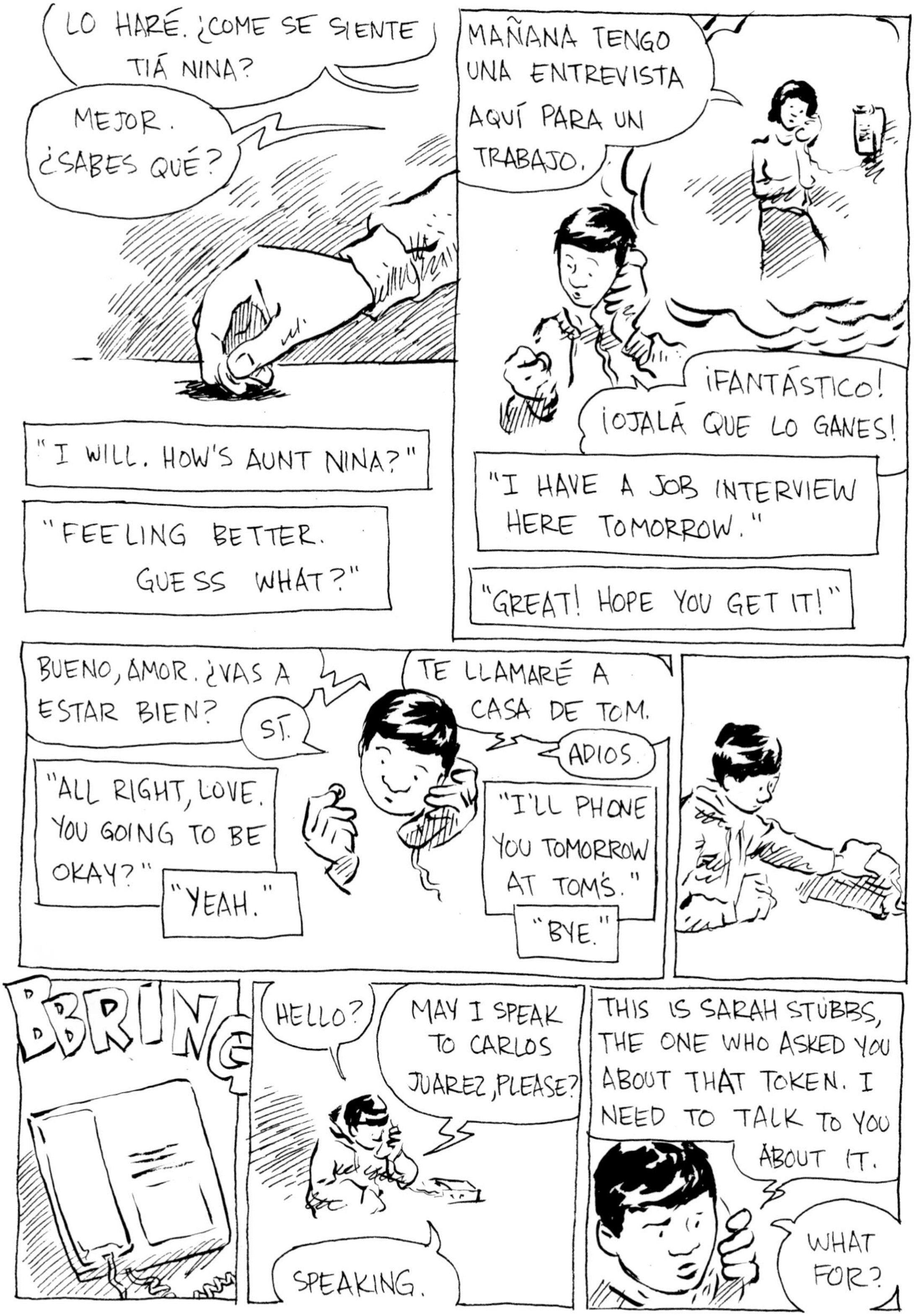
LO HARÉ. ¿COME SE SIENTE TIÁ NINA?
MEJOR. ¿SABES QUÉ?
"I WILL. HOW'S AUNT NINA?"
"FEELING BETTER. GUESS WHAT?"
MAÑANA TENGO UNA ENTREVISTA AQUÍ PARA UN TRABAJO.
¡FANTÁSTICO! ¡OJALÁ QUE LO GANES!
"I HAVE A JOB INTERVIEW HERE TOMORROW."
"GREAT! HOPE YOU GET IT!"
BUENO, AMOR. ¿VAS A ESTAR BIEN?
SÍ.
TE LLAMARÉ A CASA DE TOM.
ADIOS.
"ALL RIGHT, LOVE. YOU GOING TO BE OKAY?"
"YEAH."
"I'LL PHONE YOU TOMORROW AT TOM'S."
"BYE."
BBRING
HELLO?
MAY I SPEAK TO CARLOS JUAREZ, PLEASE?
SPEAKING.
THIS IS SARAH STUBBS, THE ONE WHO ASKED YOU ABOUT THAT TOKEN. I NEED TO TALK TO YOU ABOUT IT.
WHAT FOR?

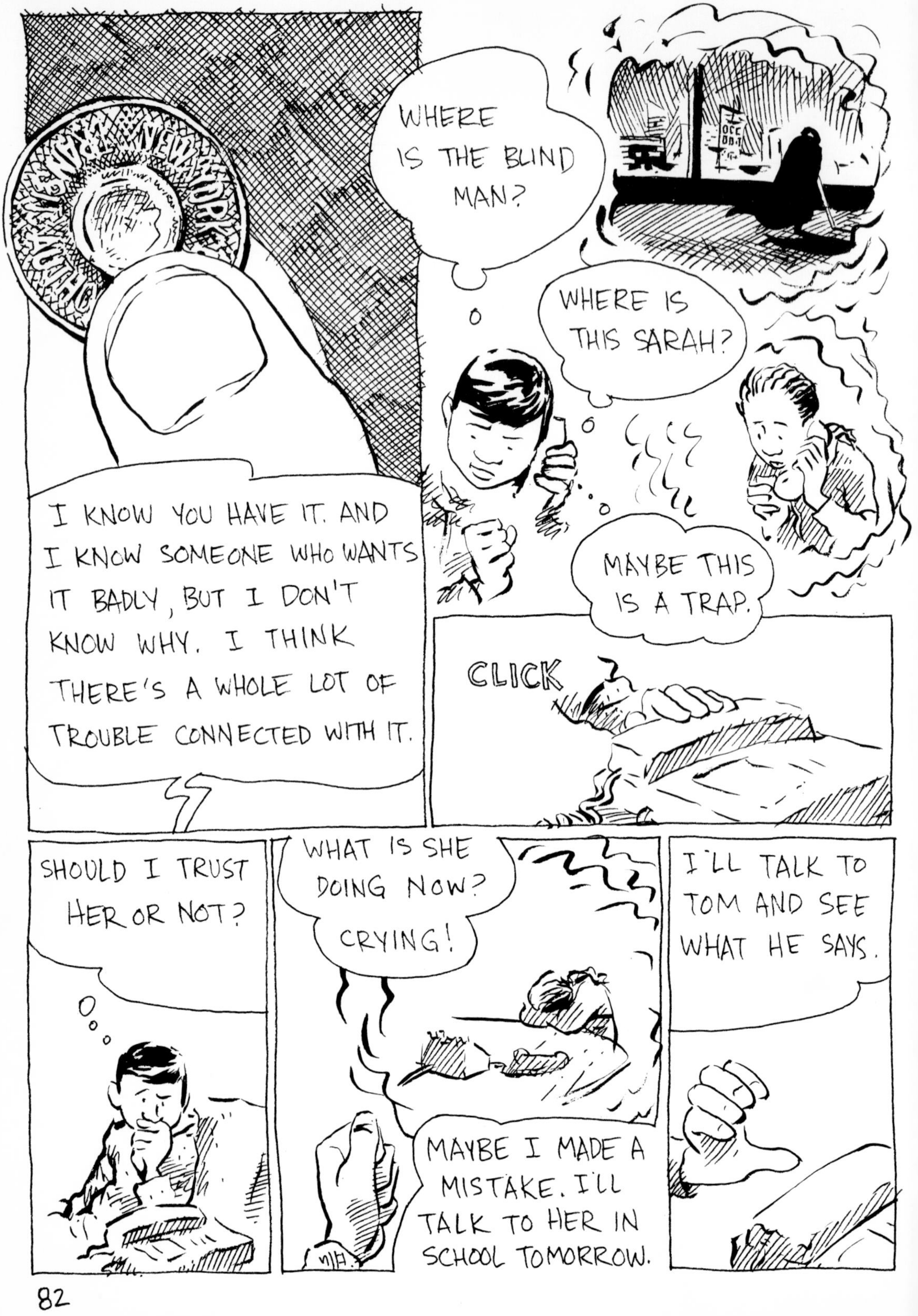
WHERE IS THE BLIND MAN?
WHERE IS THIS SARAH?
MAYBE THIS IS A TRAP.
I KNOW YOU HAVE IT. AND I KNOW SOMEONE WHO WANTS IT BADLY, BUT I DON'T KNOW WHY. I THINK THERE'S A WHOLE LOT OF TROUBLE CONNECTED WITH IT.
CLICK
SHOULD I TRUST HER OR NOT?
WHAT IS SHE DOING NOW? CRYING!
MAYBE I MADE A MISTAKE. I'LL TALK TO HER IN SCHOOL TOMORROW.
I'LL TALK TO TOM AND SEE WHAT HE SAYS.

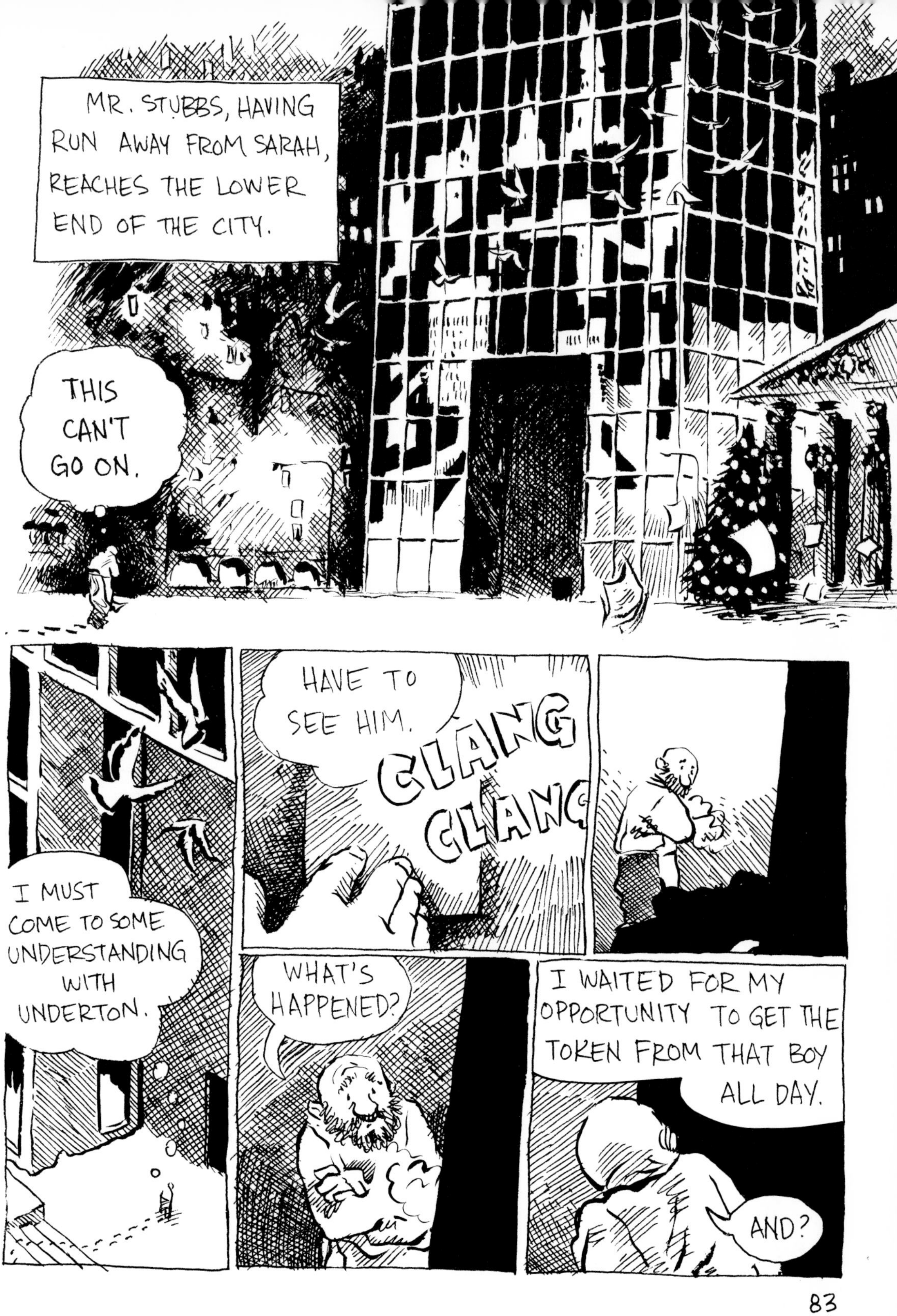
MR. STUBBS, HAVING RUN AWAY FROM SARAH, REACHES THE LOWER END OF THE CITY.
THIS CAN'T GO ON.
I MUST COME TO SOME UNDERSTANDING WITH UNDERTON.
HAVE TO SEE HIM.
CLANG
CLANG
WHAT'S HAPPENED?
I WAITED FOR MY OPPORTUNITY TO GET THE TOKEN FROM THAT BOY ALL DAY.
AND?

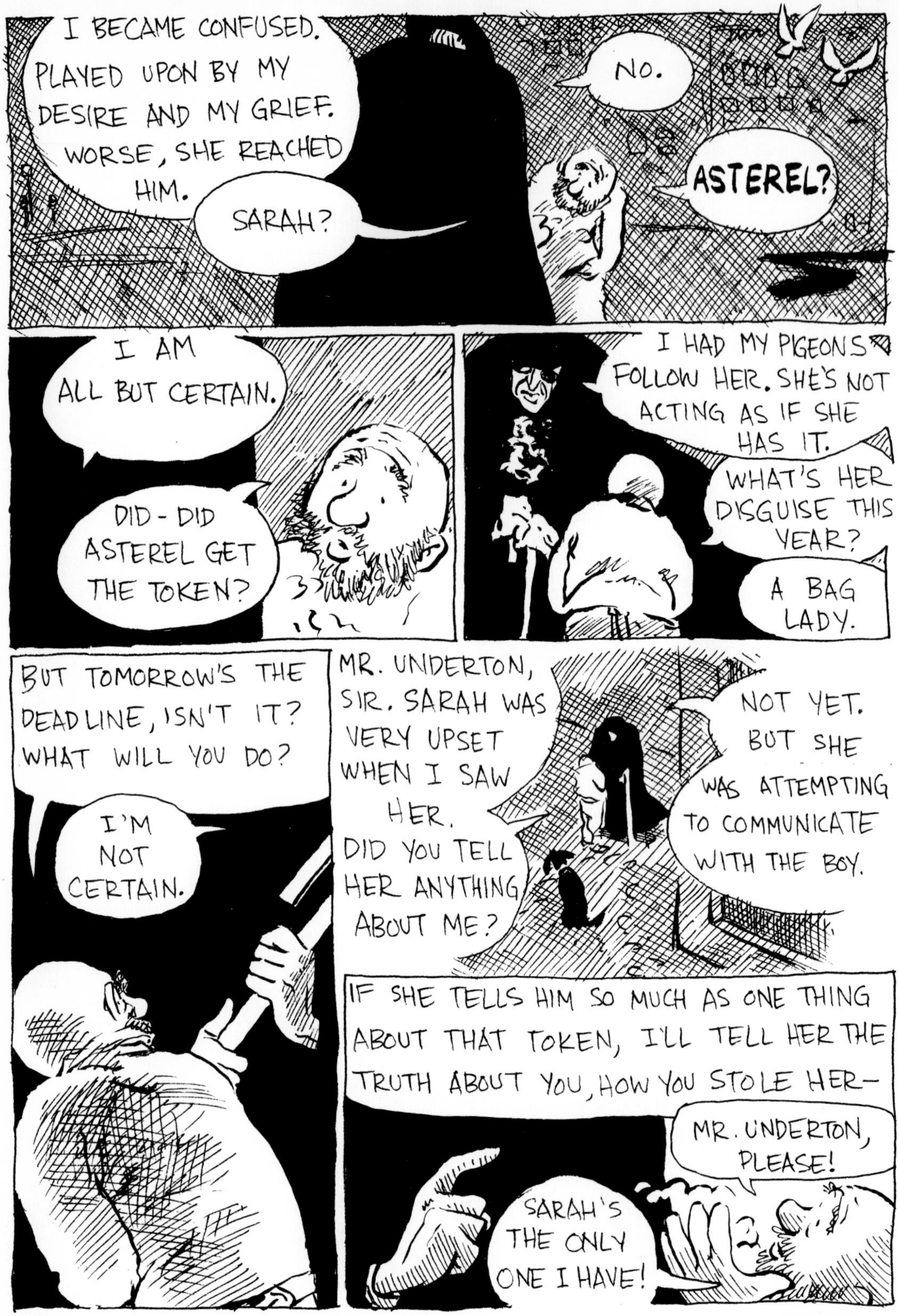
I BECAME CONFUSED. PLAYED UPON BY MY DESIRE AND MY GRIEF. WORSE, SHE REACHED HIM.
SARAH?
NO.
ASTEREL?
I AM ALL BUT CERTAIN.
DID - DID ASTEREL GET THE TOKEN?
I HAD MY PIGEONS FOLLOW HER. SHE'S NOT ACTING AS IF SHE HAS IT.
WHAT'S HER DISGUISE THIS YEAR?
A BAG LADY.
BUT TOMORROW'S THE DEADLINE, ISN'T IT? WHAT WILL YOU DO?
I'M NOT CERTAIN.
MR. UNDERTON, SIR. SARAH WAS VERY UPSET WHEN I SAW HER. DID YOU TELL HER ANYTHING ABOUT ME?
NOT YET. BUT SHE WAS ATTEMPTING TO COMMUNICATE WITH THE BOY.
IF SHE TELLS HIM SO MUCH AS ONE THING ABOUT THAT TOKEN, I'LL TELL HER THE TRUTH ABOUT YOU, HOW YOU STOLE HER—
MR. UNDERTON, PLEASE!
SARAH'S THE ONLY ONE I HAVE!

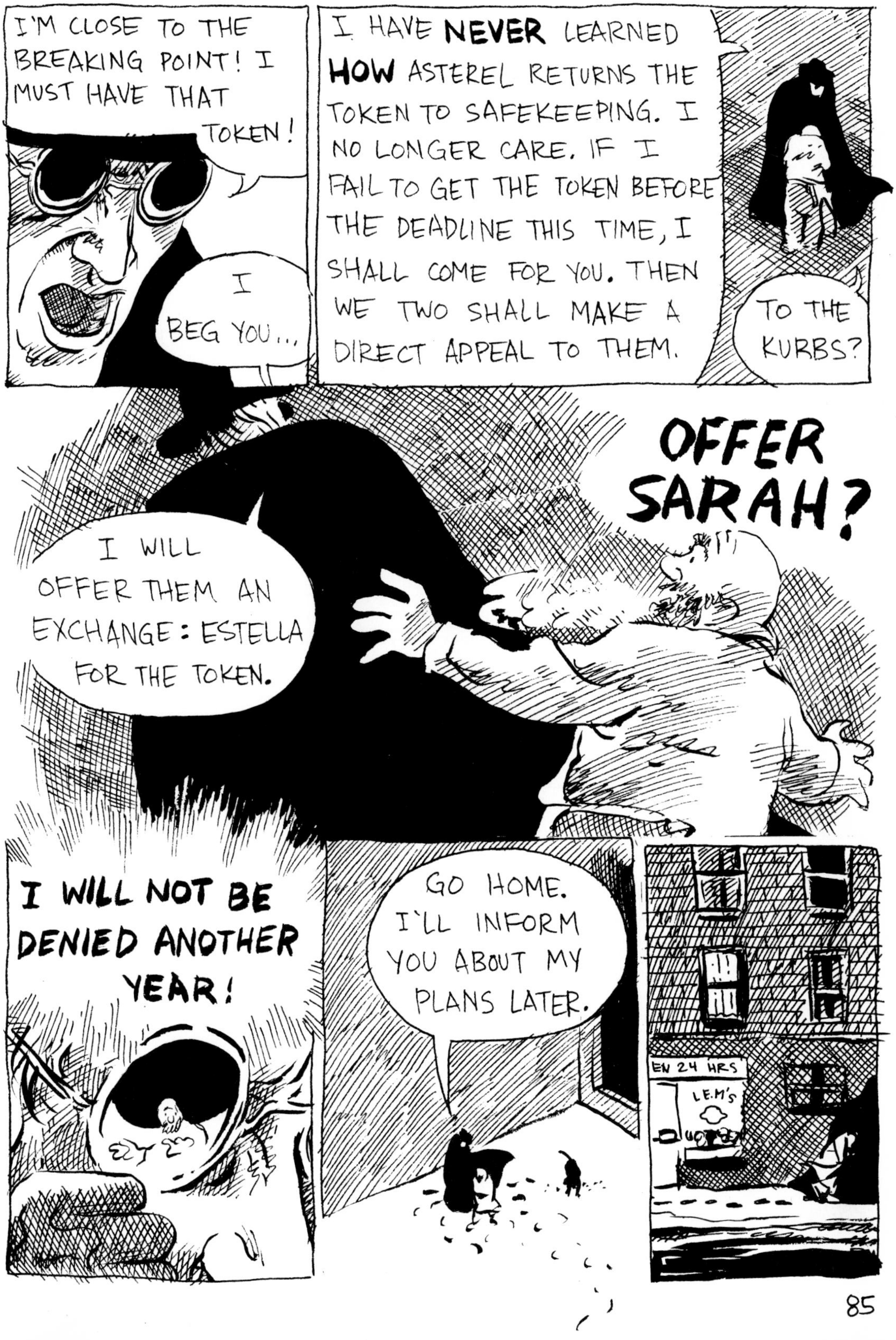

I'M CLOSE TO THE BREAKING POINT! I MUST HAVE THAT TOKEN!
I BEG YOU...
I HAVE NEVER LEARNED HOW ASTEREL RETURNS THE TOKEN TO SAFEKEEPING. I NO LONGER CARE. IF I FAIL TO GET THE TOKEN BEFORE THE DEADLINE THIS TIME, I SHALL COME FOR YOU. THEN WE TWO SHALL MAKE A DIRECT APPEAL TO THEM.
TO THE KURBS?
I WILL OFFER THEM AN EXCHANGE: ESTELLA FOR THE TOKEN.
OFFER SARAH?
I WILL NOT BE DENIED ANOTHER YEAR!
GO HOME. I'LL INFORM YOU ABOUT MY PLANS LATER.
EN 24 HRS
LE.M'S

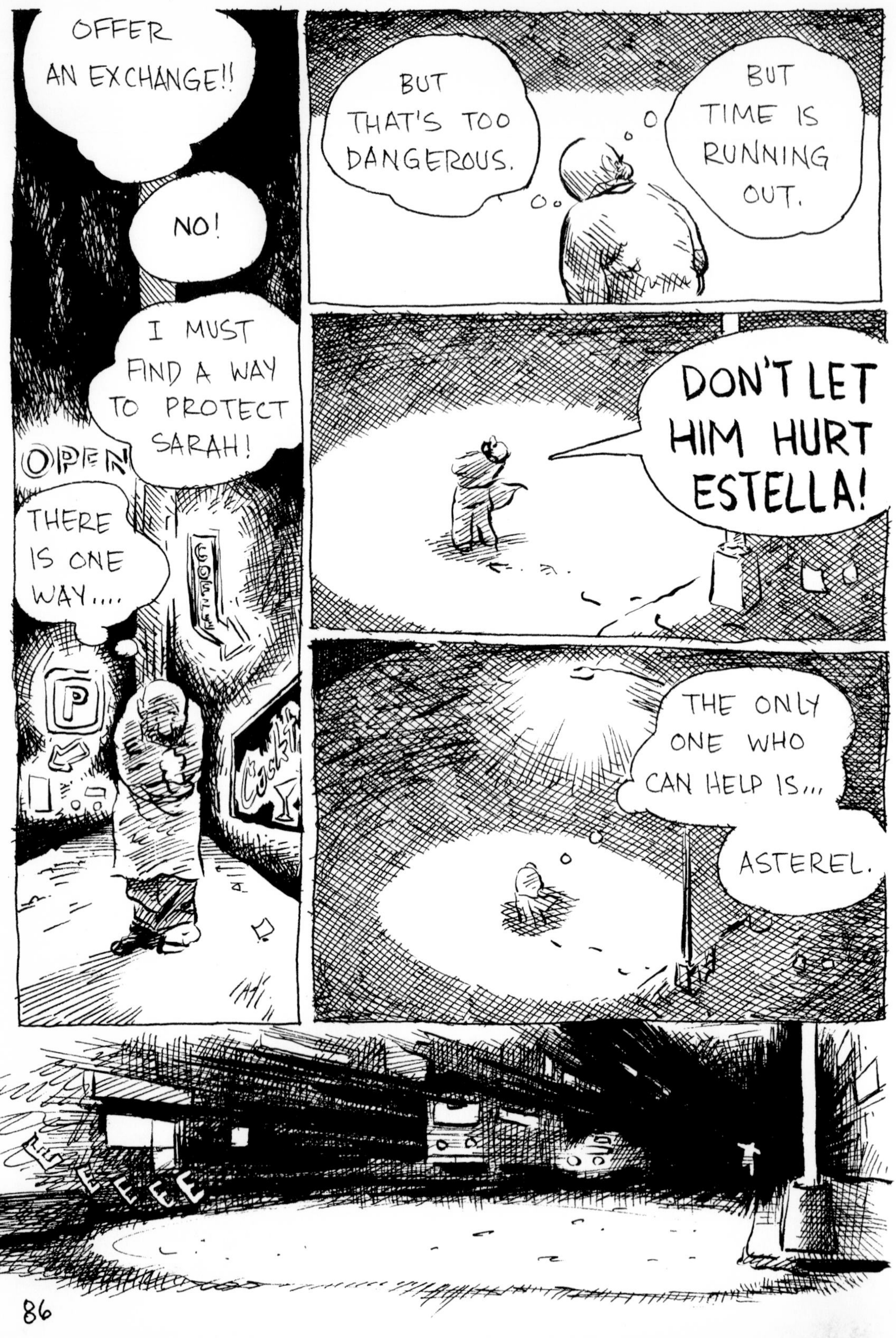
OFFER AN EXCHANGE!!
NO!
I MUST FIND A WAY TO PROTECT SARAH!
OPEN
THERE IS ONE WAY....
COFFEE
P
BUT THAT'S TOO DANGEROUS.
BUT TIME IS RUNNING OUT.
DON'T LET HIM HURT ESTELLA!
THE ONLY ONE WHO CAN HELP IS...
ASTEREL.
EEEEE

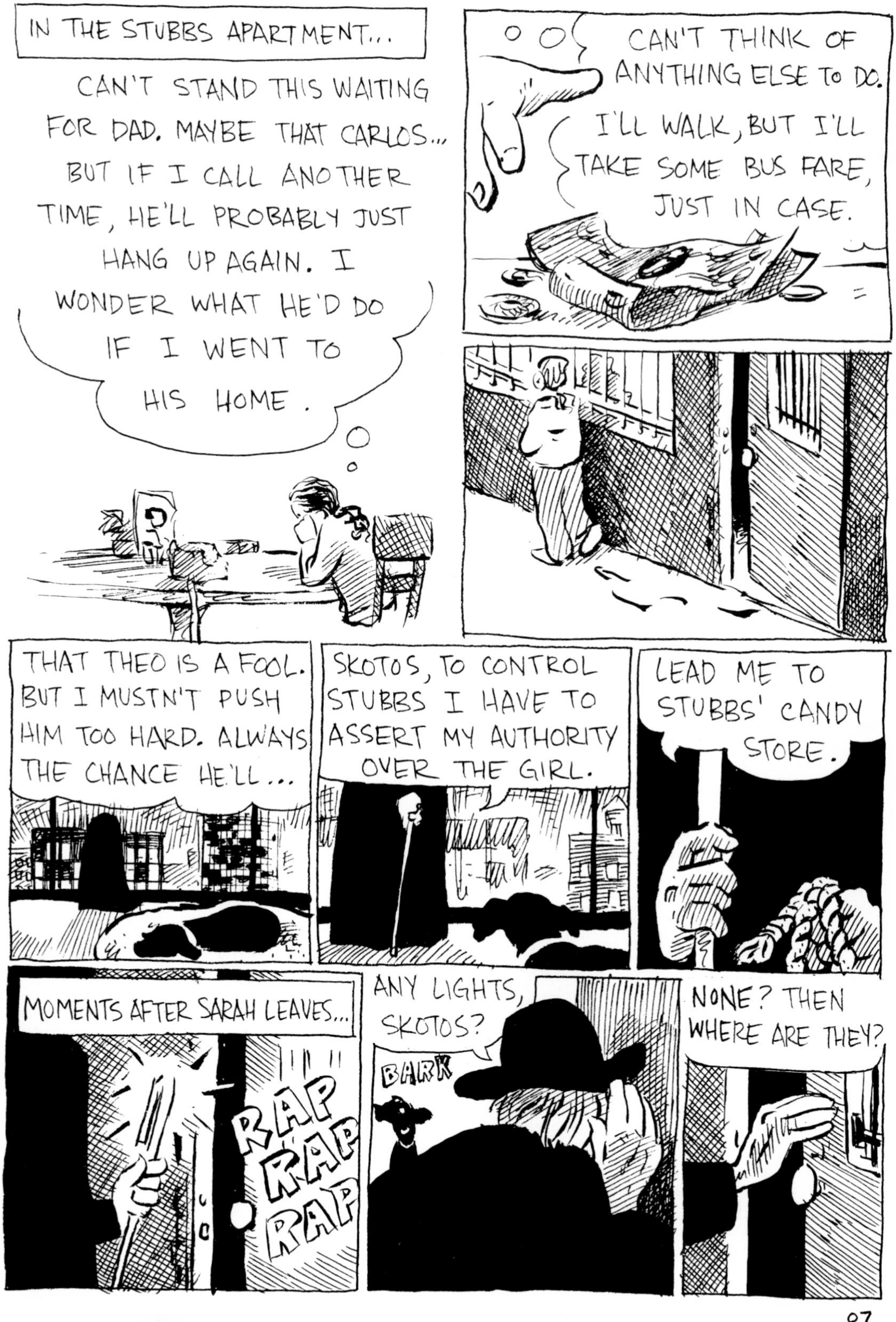
IN THE STUBBS APARTMENT...
CAN'T STAND THIS WAITING FOR DAD. MAYBE THAT CARLOS... BUT IF I CALL ANOTHER TIME, HE'LL PROBABLY JUST HANG UP AGAIN. I WONDER WHAT HE'D DO IF I WENT TO HIS HOME.
CAN'T THINK OF ANYTHING ELSE TO DO.
I'LL WALK, BUT I'LL TAKE SOME BUS FARE, JUST IN CASE.
THAT THEO IS A FOOL. BUT I MUSTN'T PUSH HIM TOO HARD. ALWAYS THE CHANCE HE'LL...
SKOTOS, TO CONTROL STUBBS I HAVE TO ASSERT MY AUTHORITY OVER THE GIRL.
LEAD ME TO STUBBS' CANDY STORE.
MOMENTS AFTER SARAH LEAVES...
RAP RAP RAP
ANY LIGHTS, SKOTOS?
BARK
NONE? THEN WHERE ARE THEY?

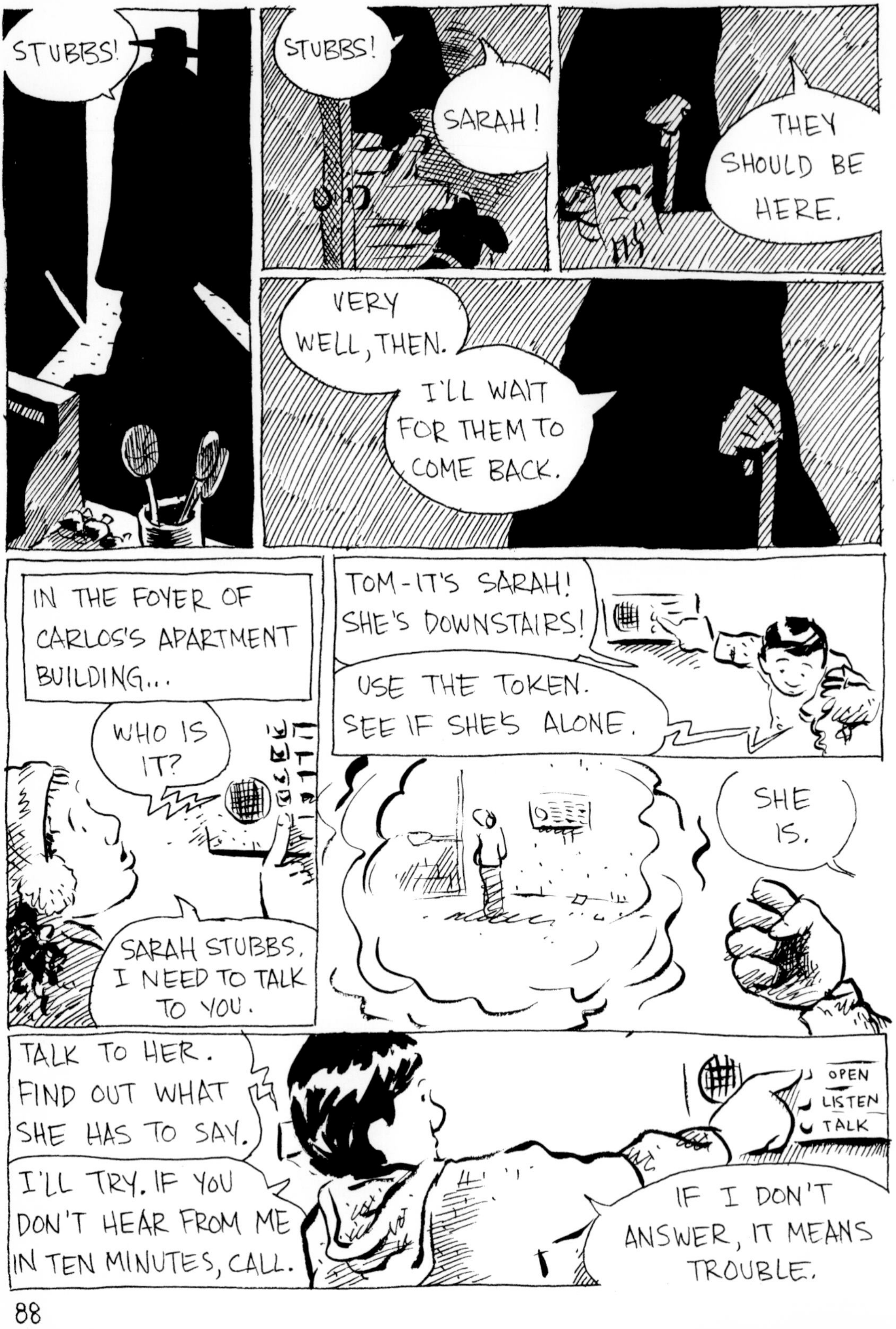

STUBBS!
STUBBS!
SARAH!
THEY SHOULD BE HERE.
VERY WELL, THEN.
I'LL WAIT FOR THEM TO COME BACK.
IN THE FOYER OF CARLOS'S APARTMENT BUILDING...
WHO IS IT?
SARAH STUBBS. I NEED TO TALK TO YOU.
TOM-IT'S SARAH! SHE'S DOWNSTAIRS!
USE THE TOKEN. SEE IF SHE'S ALONE.
SHE IS.
TALK TO HER. FIND OUT WHAT SHE HAS TO SAY.
OPEN
LISTEN
TALK
I'LL TRY. IF YOU DON'T HEAR FROM ME IN TEN MINUTES, CALL.
IF I DON'T ANSWER, IT MEANS TROUBLE.

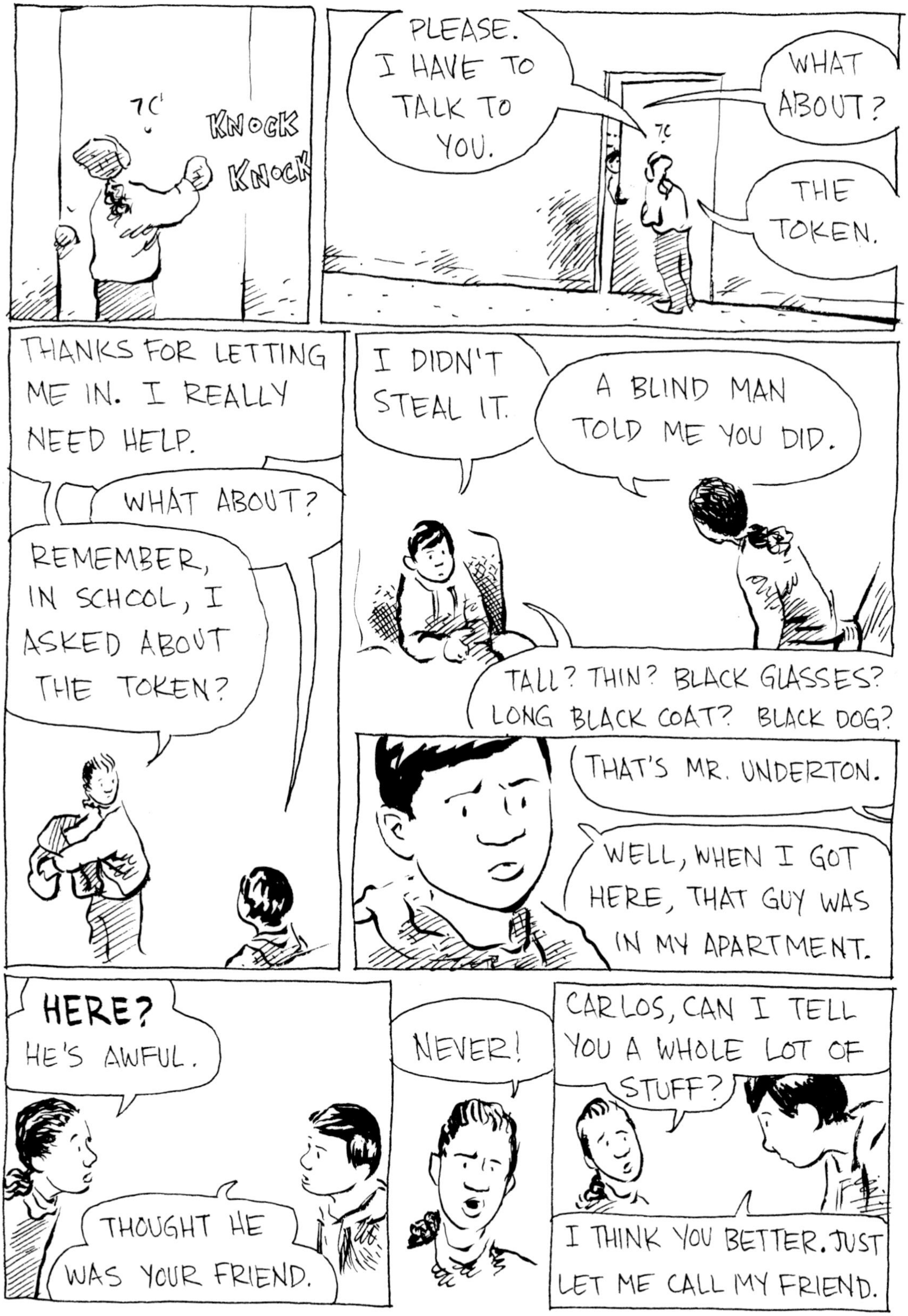
?!
KNOCK
KNOCK
PLEASE. I HAVE TO TALK TO YOU.
?!
WHAT ABOUT?
THE TOKEN.
THANKS FOR LETTING ME IN. I REALLY NEED HELP.
WHAT ABOUT?
REMEMBER, IN SCHOOL, I ASKED ABOUT THE TOKEN?
I DIDN'T STEAL IT.
A BLIND MAN TOLD ME YOU DID.
TALL? THIN? BLACK GLASSES? LONG BLACK COAT? BLACK DOG?
THAT'S MR. UNDERTON.
WELL, WHEN I GOT HERE, THAT GUY WAS IN MY APARTMENT.
HERE? HE'S AWFUL.
THOUGHT HE WAS YOUR FRIEND.
NEVER!
CARLOS, CAN I TELL YOU A WHOLE LOT OF STUFF?
I THINK YOU BETTER. JUST LET ME CALL MY FRIEND.

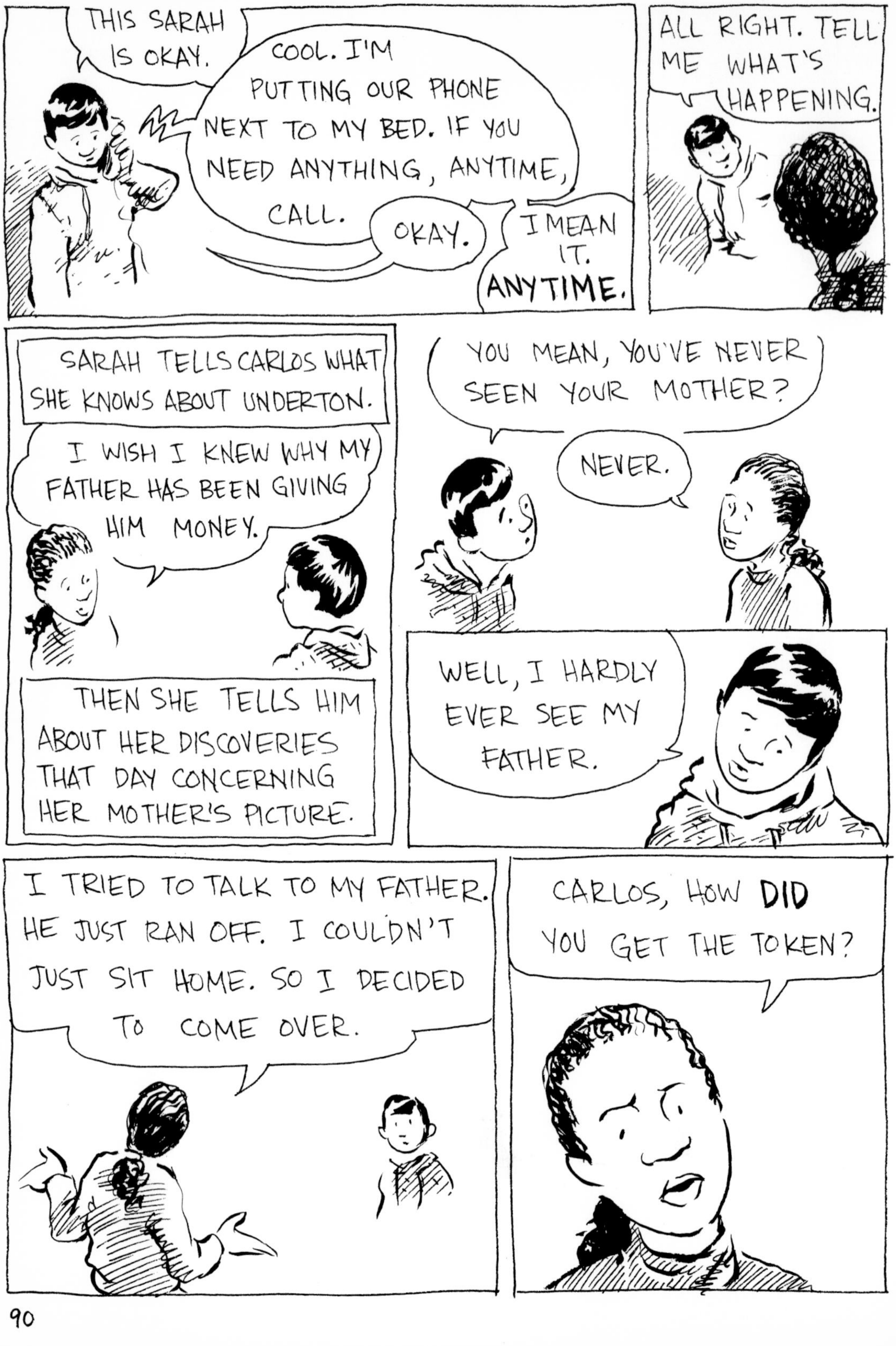
THIS SARAH IS OKAY.
COOL. I'M PUTTING OUR PHONE NEXT TO MY BED. IF YOU NEED ANYTHING, ANYTIME, CALL.
OKAY.
I MEAN IT. **ANYTIME.**
ALL RIGHT. TELL ME WHAT'S HAPPENING.
SARAH TELLS CARLOS WHAT SHE KNOWS ABOUT UNDERTON.
I WISH I KNEW WHY MY FATHER HAS BEEN GIVING HIM MONEY.
THEN SHE TELLS HIM ABOUT HER DISCOVERIES THAT DAY CONCERNING HER MOTHER'S PICTURE.
YOU MEAN, YOU'VE NEVER SEEN YOUR MOTHER?
NEVER.
WELL, I HARDLY EVER SEE MY FATHER.
I TRIED TO TALK TO MY FATHER. HE JUST RAN OFF. I COULDN'T JUST SIT HOME. SO I DECIDED TO COME OVER.
CARLOS, HOW **DID** YOU GET THE TOKEN?

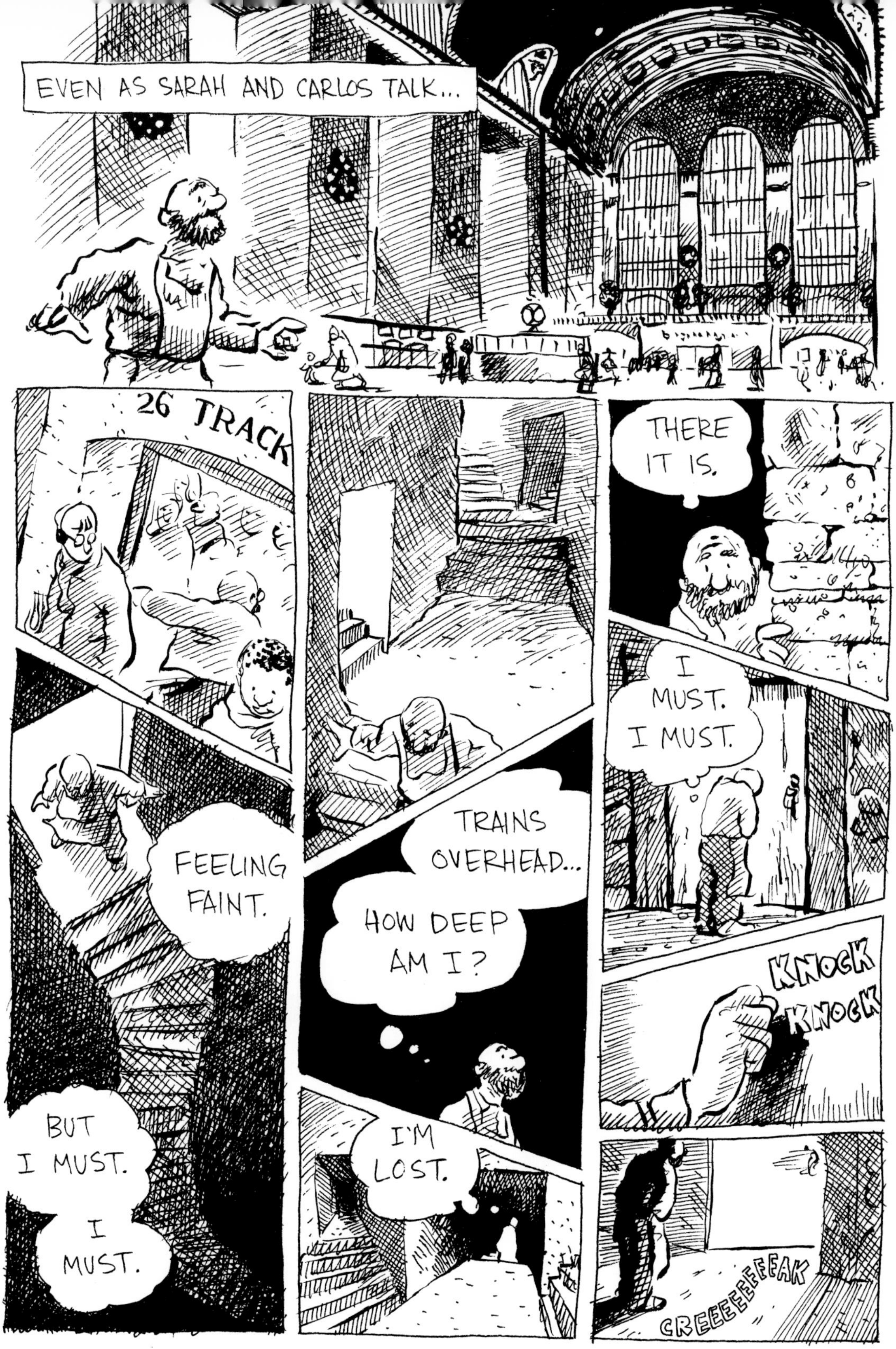
EVEN AS SARAH AND CARLOS TALK...
26 TRACK
FEELING FAINT.
BUT I MUST.
I MUST.
TRAINS OVERHEAD...
HOW DEEP AM I?
I'M LOST.
THERE IT IS.
I MUST. I MUST.
KNOCK KNOCK
CREEEEEEEEAK

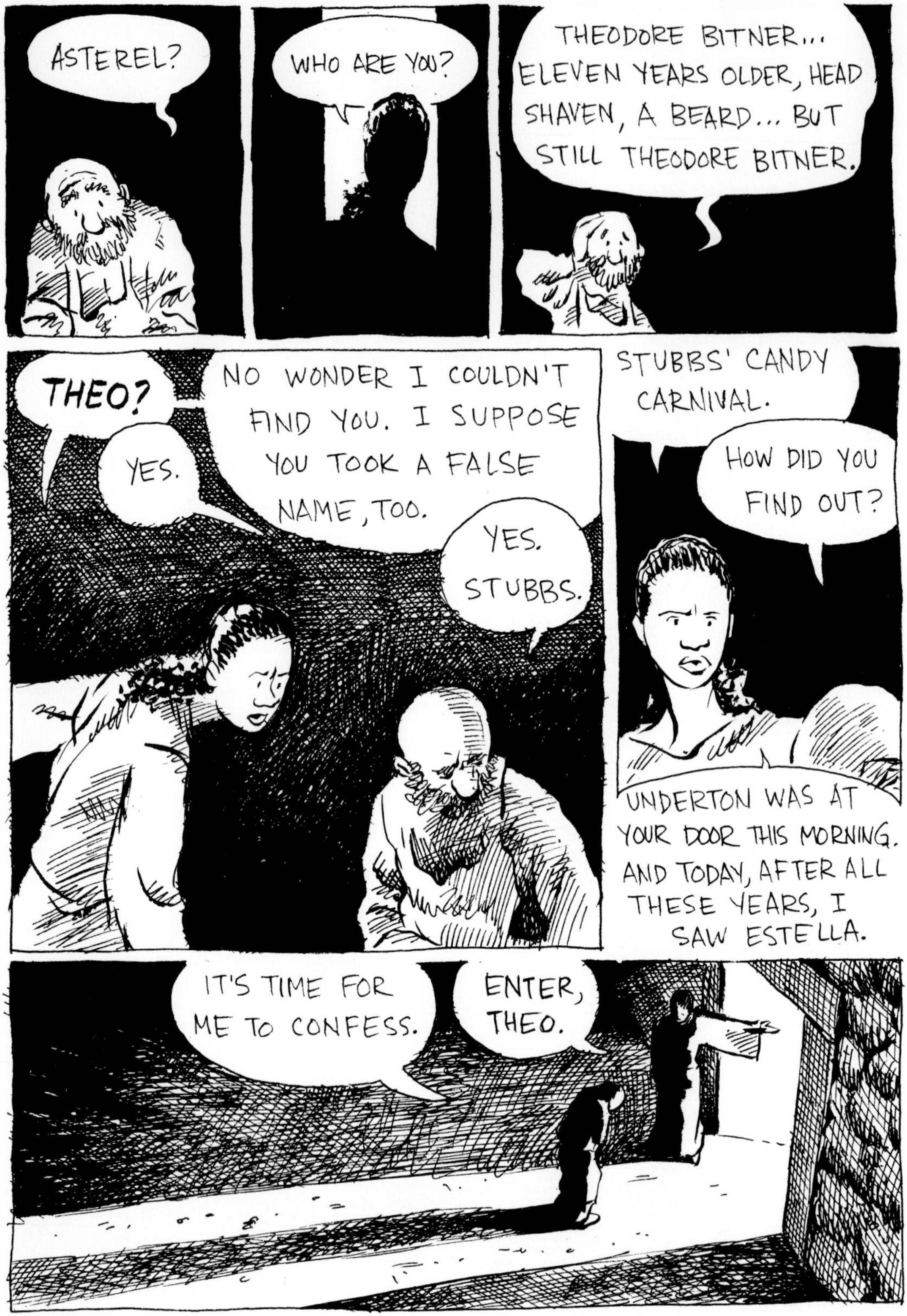
ASTEREL?
WHO ARE YOU?
THEODORE BITNER... ELEVEN YEARS OLDER, HEAD SHAVEN, A BEARD... BUT STILL THEODORE BITNER.
THEO?
YES.
NO WONDER I COULDN'T FIND YOU. I SUPPOSE YOU TOOK A FALSE NAME, TOO.
YES. STUBBS.
STUBBS' CANDY CARNIVAL.
HOW DID YOU FIND OUT?
UNDERTON WAS AT YOUR DOOR THIS MORNING. AND TODAY, AFTER ALL THESE YEARS, I SAW ESTELLA.
IT'S TIME FOR ME TO CONFESS.
ENTER, THEO.

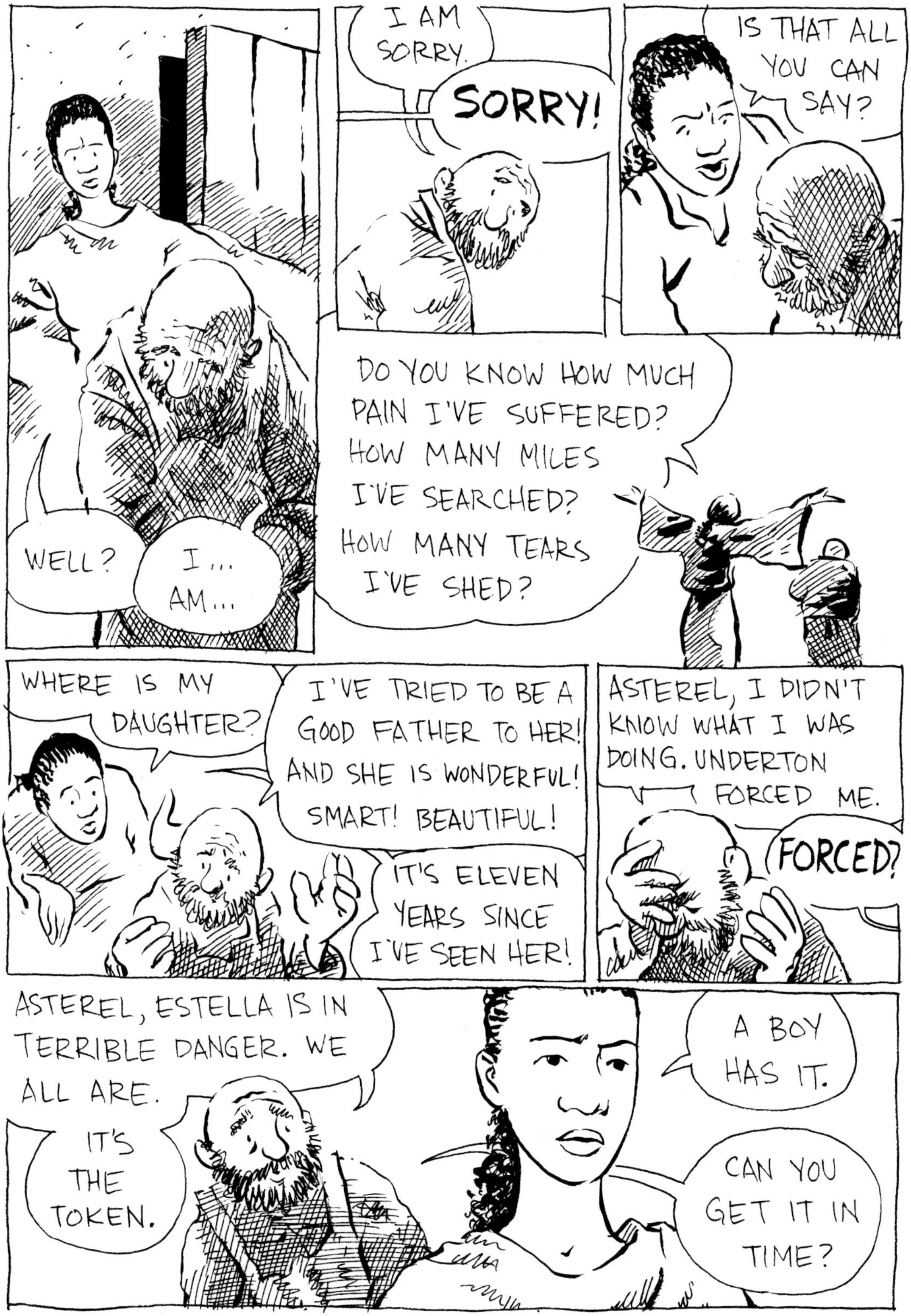
WELL?
I... AM...
I AM SORRY.
SORRY!
IS THAT ALL YOU CAN SAY?
DO YOU KNOW HOW MUCH PAIN I'VE SUFFERED? HOW MANY MILES I'VE SEARCHED? HOW MANY TEARS I'VE SHED?
WHERE IS MY DAUGHTER?
I'VE TRIED TO BE A GOOD FATHER TO HER! AND SHE IS WONDERFUL! SMART! BEAUTIFUL!
IT'S ELEVEN YEARS SINCE I'VE SEEN HER!
ASTEREL, I DIDN'T KNOW WHAT I WAS DOING. UNDERTON FORCED ME.
FORCED?
ASTEREL, ESTELLA IS IN TERRIBLE DANGER. WE ALL ARE.
IT'S THE TOKEN.
A BOY HAS IT.
CAN YOU GET IT IN TIME?

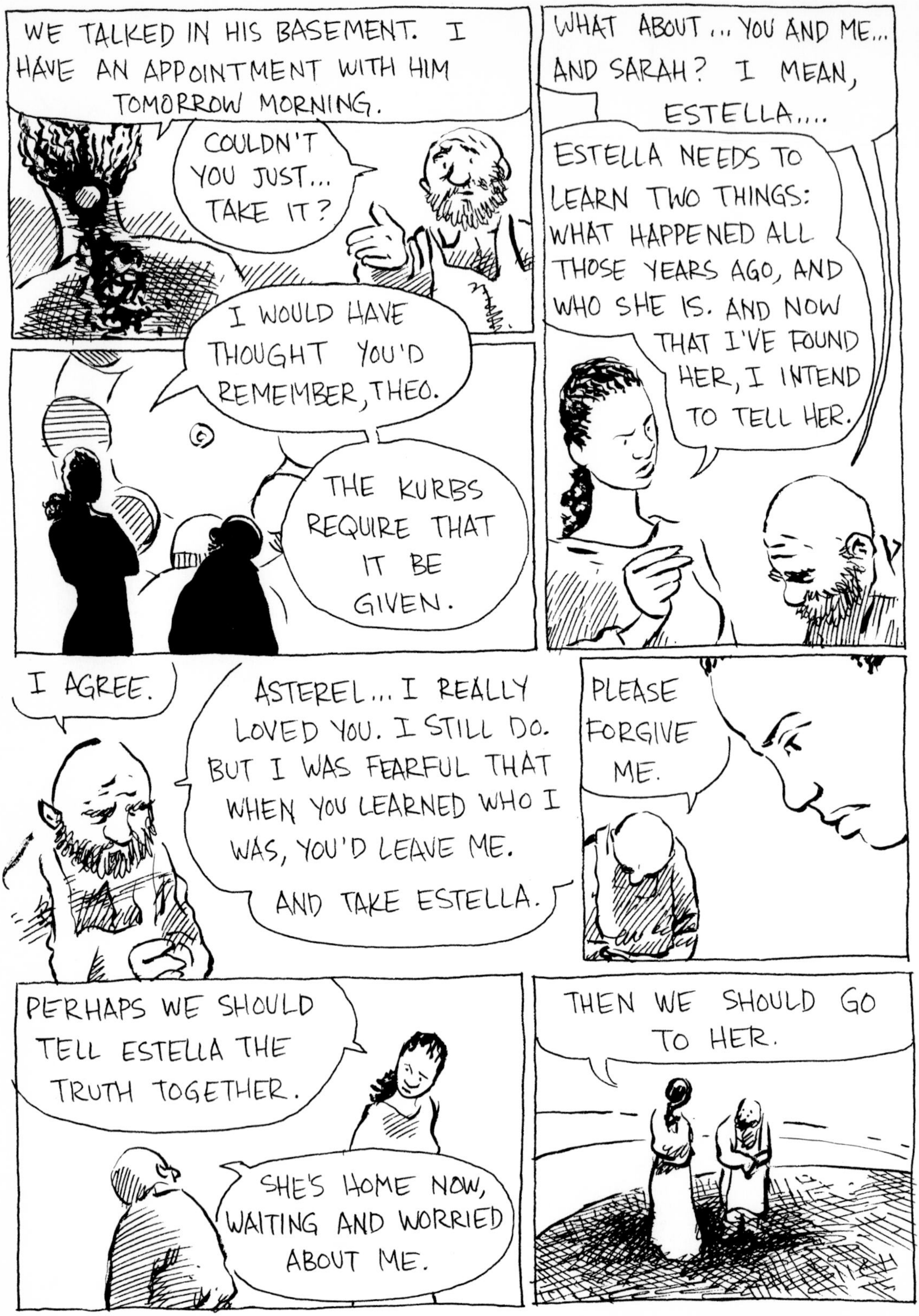
WE TALKED IN HIS BASEMENT. I HAVE AN APPOINTMENT WITH HIM TOMORROW MORNING.
COULDN'T YOU JUST... TAKE IT?
I WOULD HAVE THOUGHT YOU'D REMEMBER, THEO.
THE KURBS REQUIRE THAT IT BE GIVEN.
WHAT ABOUT... YOU AND ME... AND SARAH? I MEAN, ESTELLA....
ESTELLA NEEDS TO LEARN TWO THINGS: WHAT HAPPENED ALL THOSE YEARS AGO, AND WHO SHE IS. AND NOW THAT I'VE FOUND HER, I INTEND TO TELL HER.
I AGREE.
ASTEREL... I REALLY LOVED YOU. I STILL DO. BUT I WAS FEARFUL THAT WHEN YOU LEARNED WHO I WAS, YOU'D LEAVE ME.
AND TAKE ESTELLA.
PLEASE FORGIVE ME.
PERHAPS WE SHOULD TELL ESTELLA THE TRUTH TOGETHER.
SHE'S HOME NOW, WAITING AND WORRIED ABOUT ME.
THEN WE SHOULD GO TO HER.

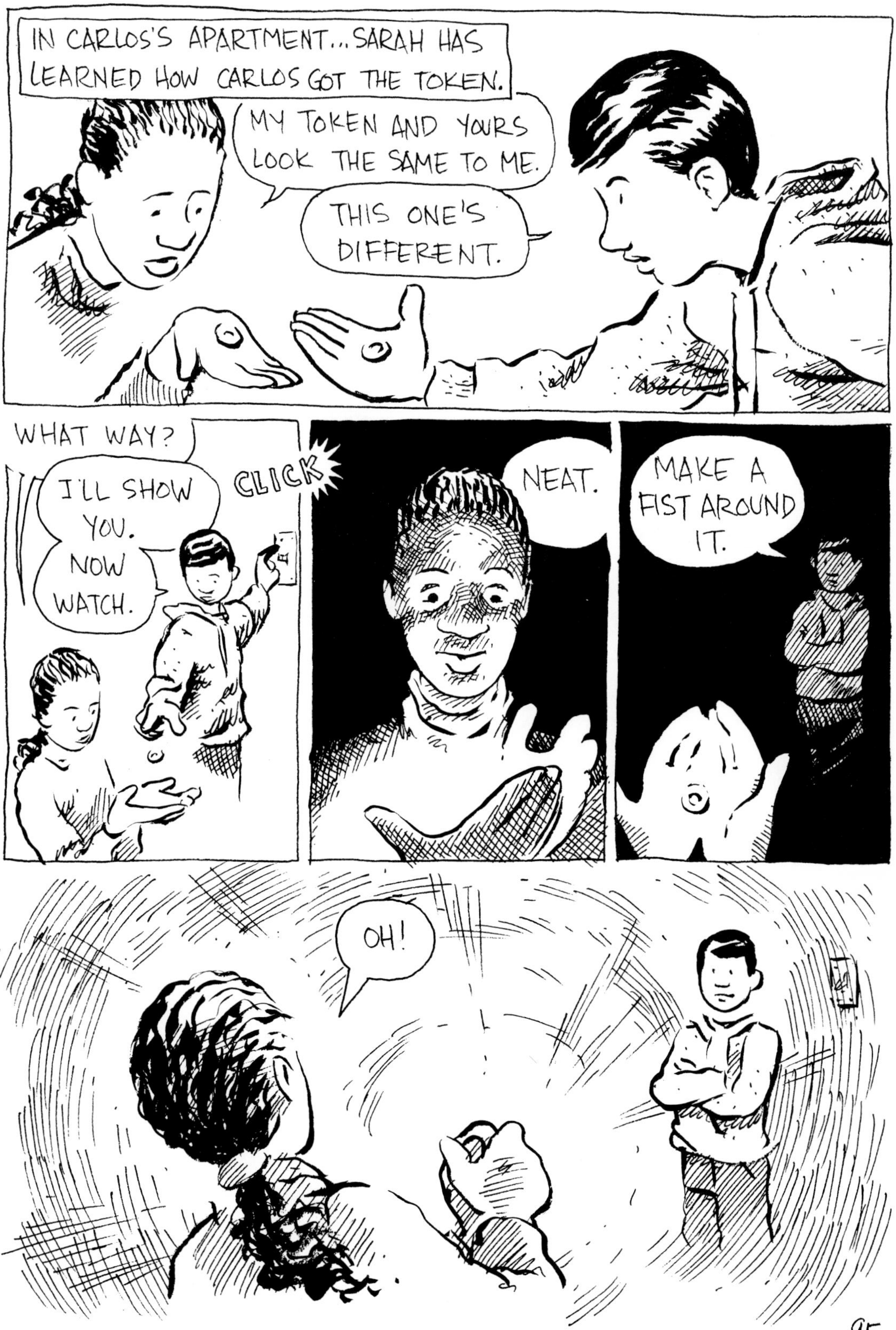
IN CARLOS'S APARTMENT... SARAH HAS LEARNED HOW CARLOS GOT THE TOKEN.
MY TOKEN AND YOURS LOOK THE SAME TO ME.
THIS ONE'S DIFFERENT.
WHAT WAY?
I'LL SHOW YOU.
NOW WATCH.
CLICK
NEAT.
MAKE A FIST AROUND IT.
OH!

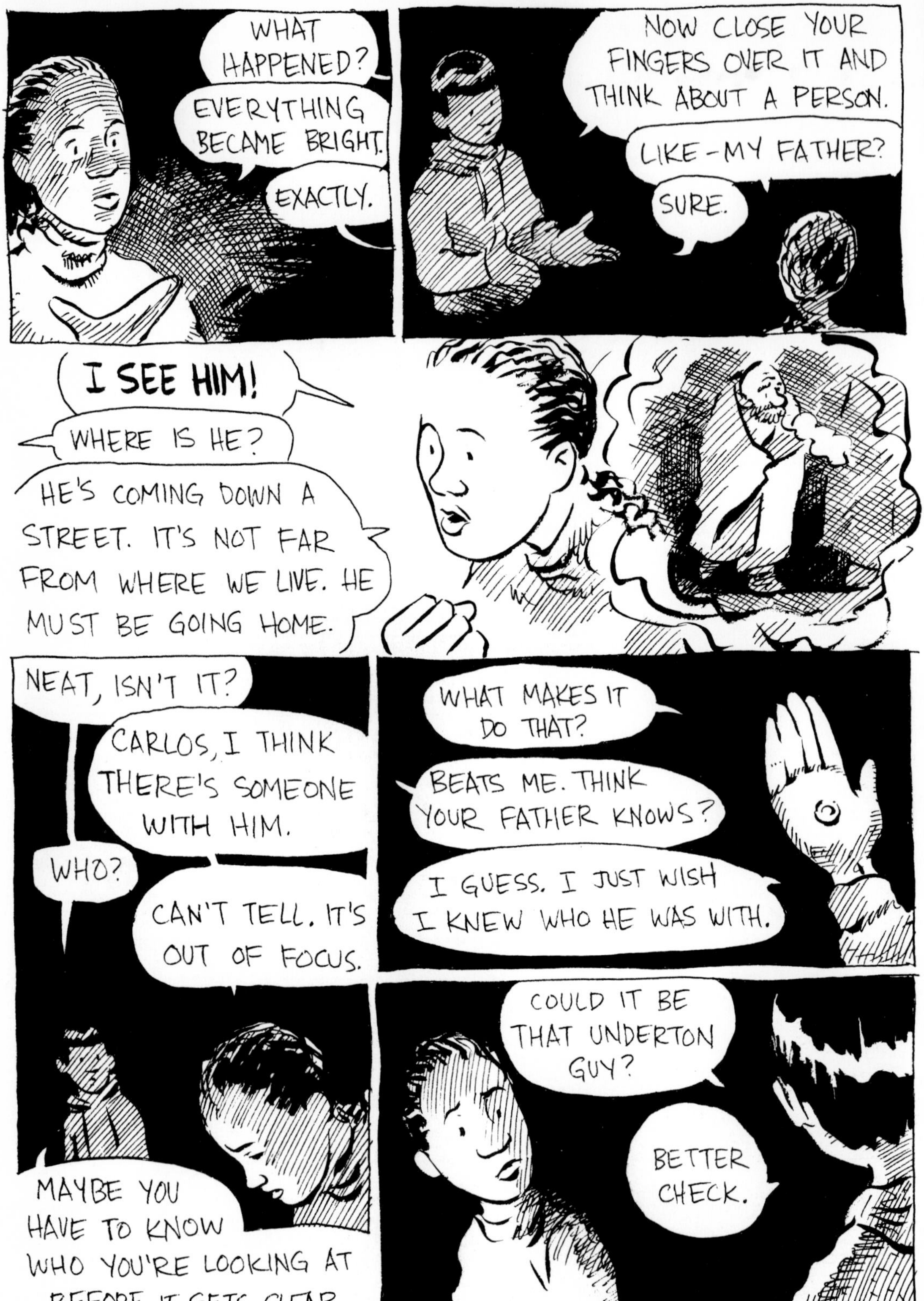
WHAT HAPPENED?
EVERYTHING BECAME BRIGHT.
EXACTLY.
NOW CLOSE YOUR FINGERS OVER IT AND THINK ABOUT A PERSON.
LIKE-MY FATHER?
SURE.
I SEE HIM!
WHERE IS HE?
HE'S COMING DOWN A STREET. IT'S NOT FAR FROM WHERE WE LIVE. HE MUST BE GOING HOME.
NEAT, ISN'T IT?
CARLOS, I THINK THERE'S SOMEONE WITH HIM.
WHO?
CAN'T TELL. IT'S OUT OF FOCUS.
WHAT MAKES IT DO THAT?
BEATS ME. THINK YOUR FATHER KNOWS?
I GUESS. I JUST WISH I KNEW WHO HE WAS WITH.
MAYBE YOU HAVE TO KNOW WHO YOU'RE LOOKING AT BEFORE IT GETS CLEAR.
COULD IT BE THAT UNDERTON GUY?
BETTER CHECK.

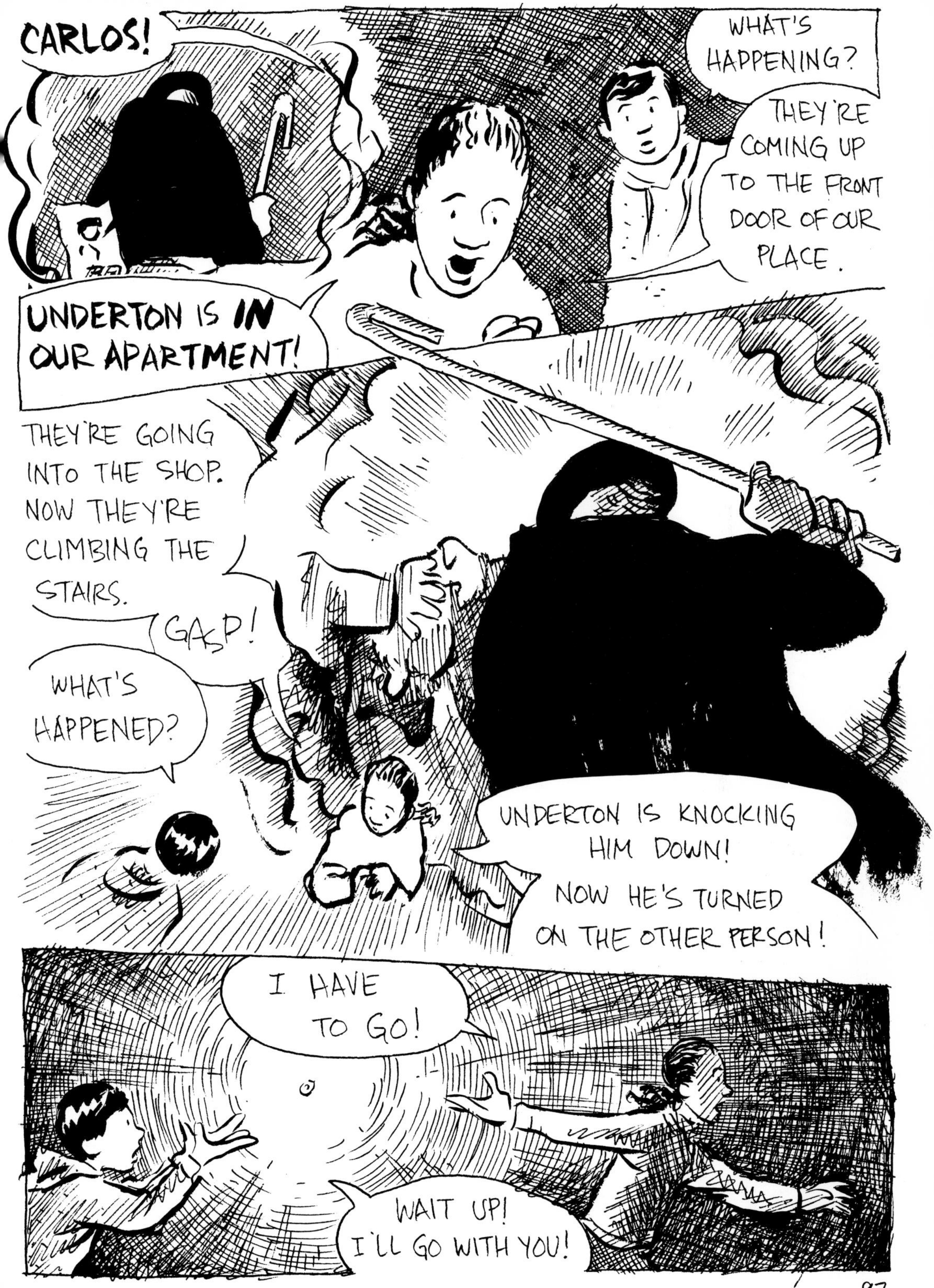
CARLOS!
WHAT'S HAPPENING?
THEY'RE COMING UP TO THE FRONT DOOR OF OUR PLACE.
UNDERTON IS IN OUR APARTMENT!
THEY'RE GOING INTO THE SHOP. NOW THEY'RE CLIMBING THE STAIRS.
GASP!
WHAT'S HAPPENED?
UNDERTON IS KNOCKING HIM DOWN!
NOW HE'S TURNED ON THE OTHER PERSON!
I HAVE TO GO!
WAIT UP! I'LL GO WITH YOU!

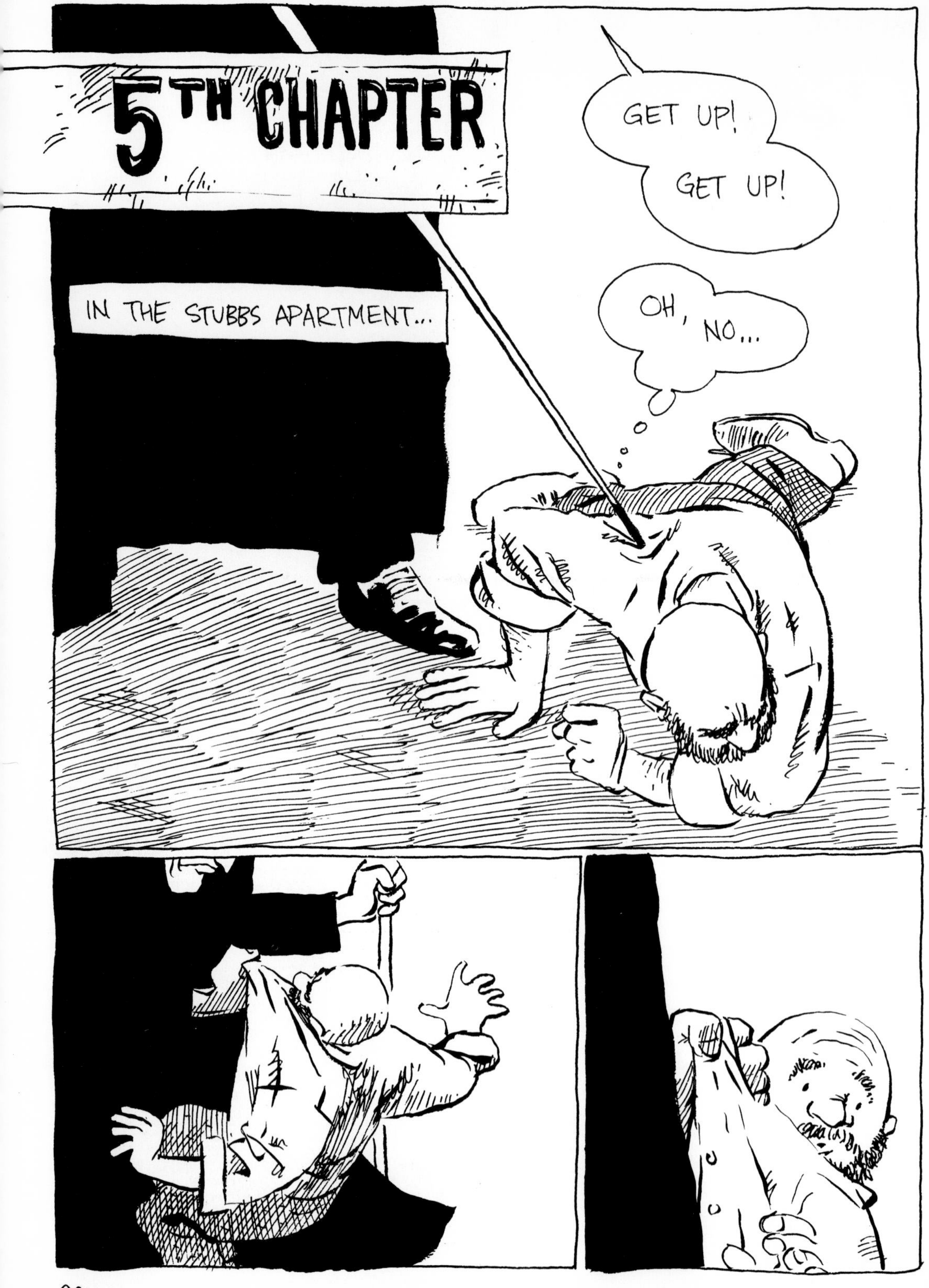
5TH CHAPTER
IN THE STUBBS APARTMENT...
GET UP!
GET UP!
OH, NO...

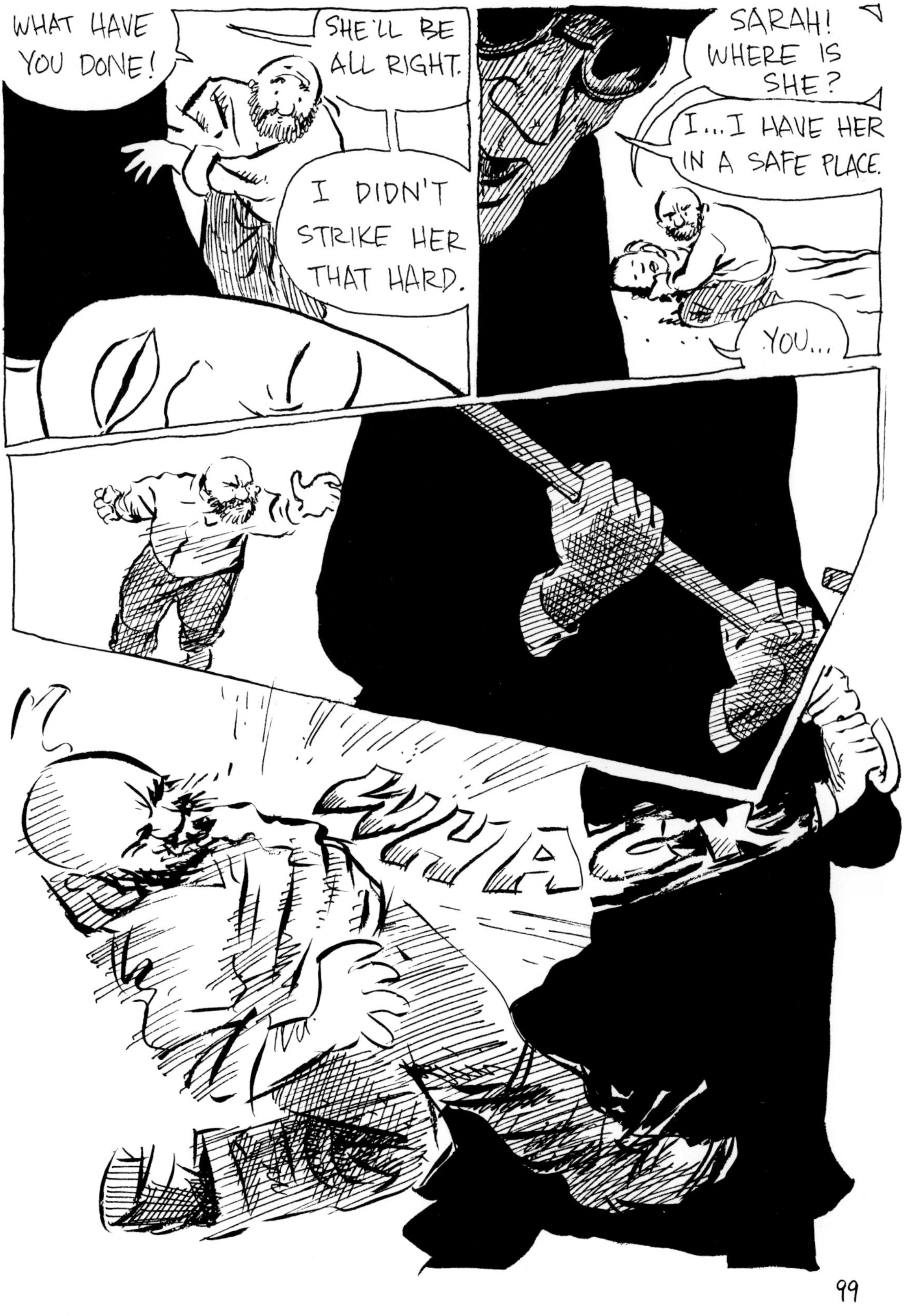
WHAT HAVE YOU DONE!
SHE'LL BE ALL RIGHT.
I DIDN'T STRIKE HER THAT HARD.
SARAH! WHERE IS SHE?
I...I HAVE HER IN A SAFE PLACE.
YOU...
WHACK

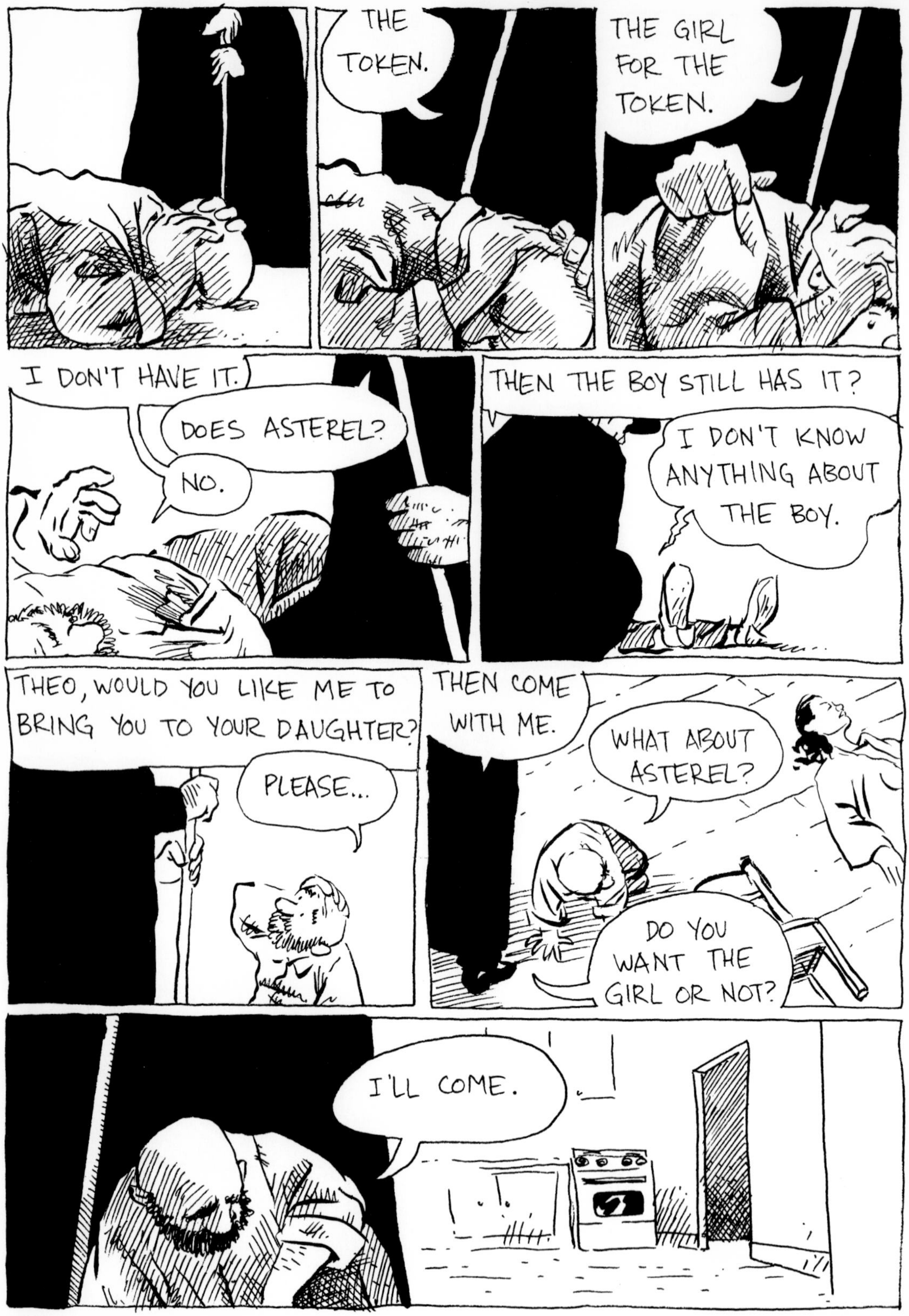
THE TOKEN.
THE GIRL FOR THE TOKEN.
I DON'T HAVE IT.
DOES ASTEREL?
NO.
THEN THE BOY STILL HAS IT?
I DON'T KNOW ANYTHING ABOUT THE BOY.
THEO, WOULD YOU LIKE ME TO BRING YOU TO YOUR DAUGHTER?
PLEASE...
THEN COME WITH ME.
WHAT ABOUT ASTEREL?
DO YOU WANT THE GIRL OR NOT?
I'LL COME.

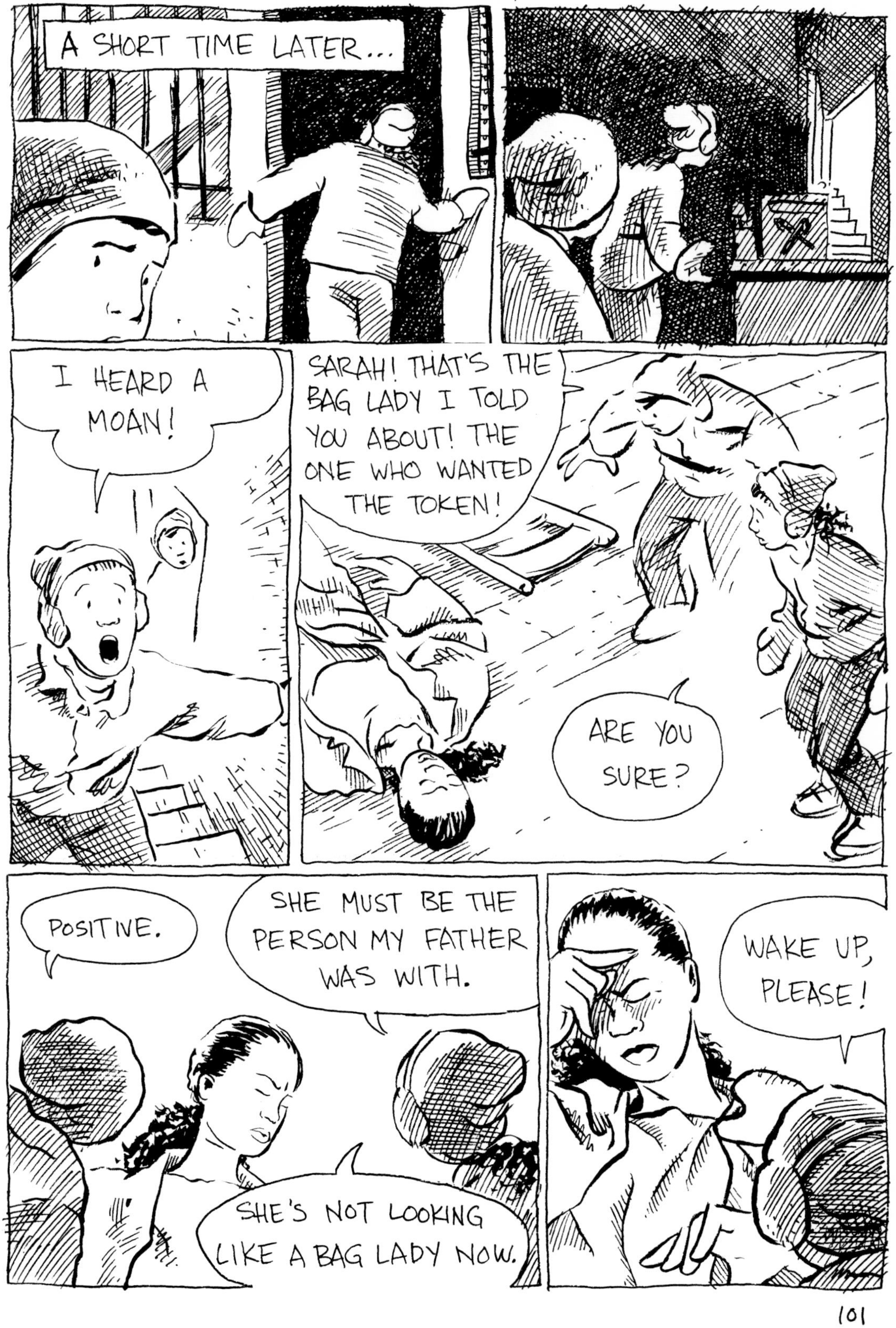
A SHORT TIME LATER...
I HEARD A MOAN!
SARAH! THAT'S THE BAG LADY I TOLD YOU ABOUT! THE ONE WHO WANTED THE TOKEN!
ARE YOU SURE?
POSITIVE.
SHE MUST BE THE PERSON MY FATHER WAS WITH.
SHE'S NOT LOOKING LIKE A BAG LADY NOW.
WAKE UP, PLEASE!

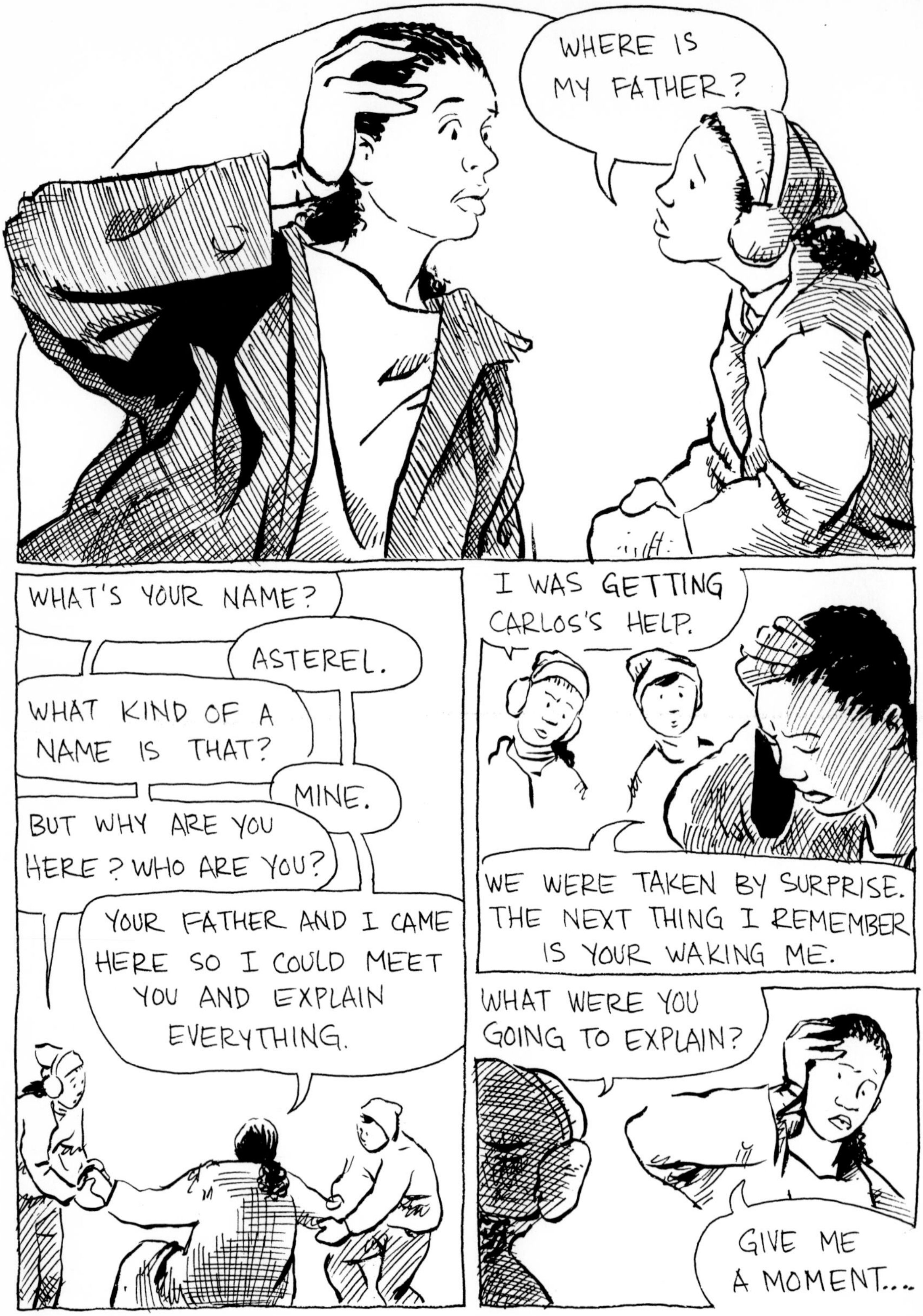
WHERE IS MY FATHER?
WHAT'S YOUR NAME?
ASTEREL.
WHAT KIND OF A NAME IS THAT?
MINE.
BUT WHY ARE YOU HERE? WHO ARE YOU?
YOUR FATHER AND I CAME HERE SO I COULD MEET YOU AND EXPLAIN EVERYTHING.
I WAS GETTING CARLOS'S HELP.
WE WERE TAKEN BY SURPRISE. THE NEXT THING I REMEMBER IS YOUR WAKING ME.
WHAT WERE YOU GOING TO EXPLAIN?
GIVE ME A MOMENT....

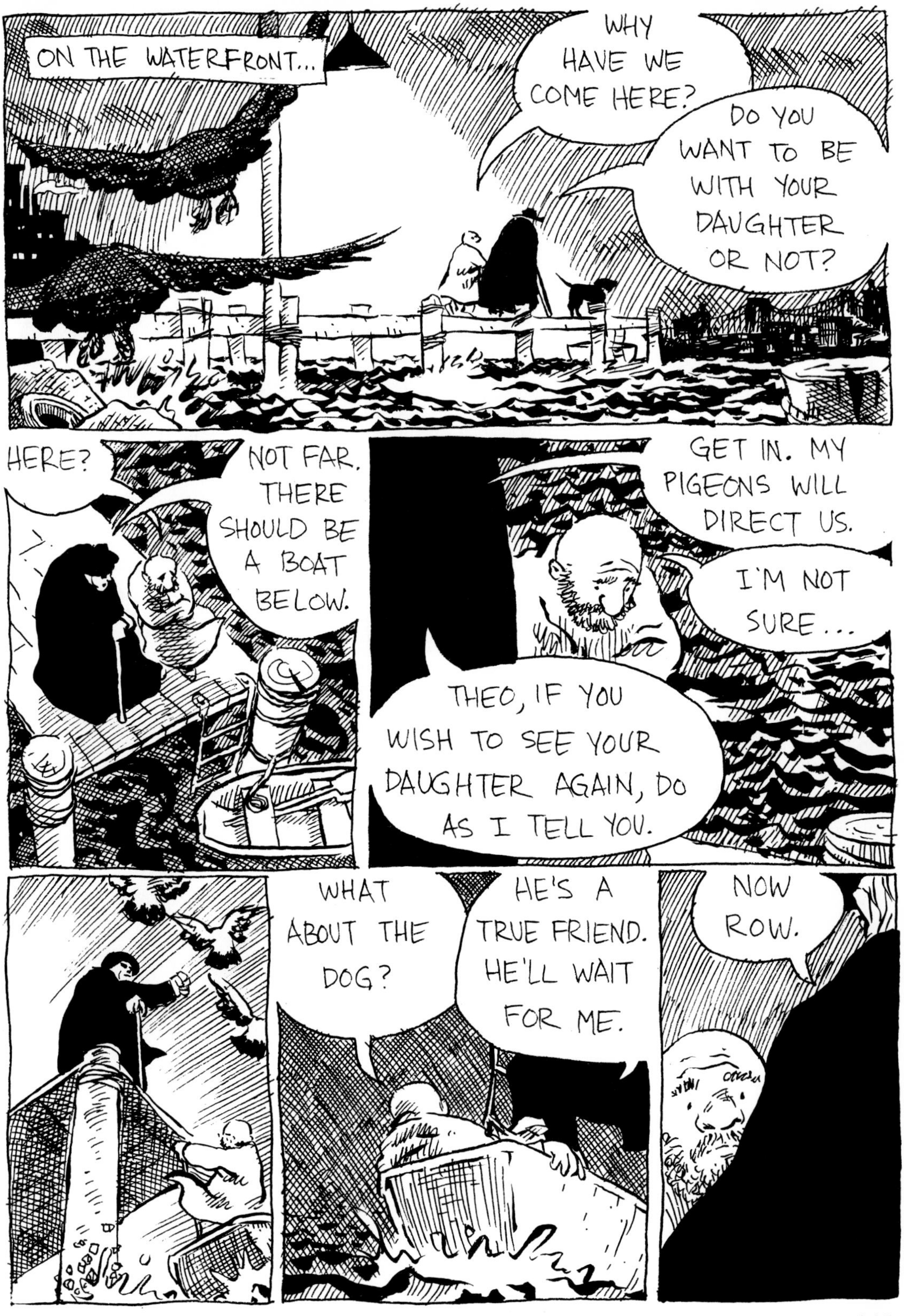
ON THE WATERFRONT...
WHY HAVE WE COME HERE?
DO YOU WANT TO BE WITH YOUR DAUGHTER OR NOT?
HERE?
NOT FAR. THERE SHOULD BE A BOAT BELOW.
GET IN. MY PIGEONS WILL DIRECT US.
I'M NOT SURE...
THEO, IF YOU WISH TO SEE YOUR DAUGHTER AGAIN, DO AS I TELL YOU.
WHAT ABOUT THE DOG?
HE'S A TRUE FRIEND. HE'LL WAIT FOR ME.
NOW ROW.

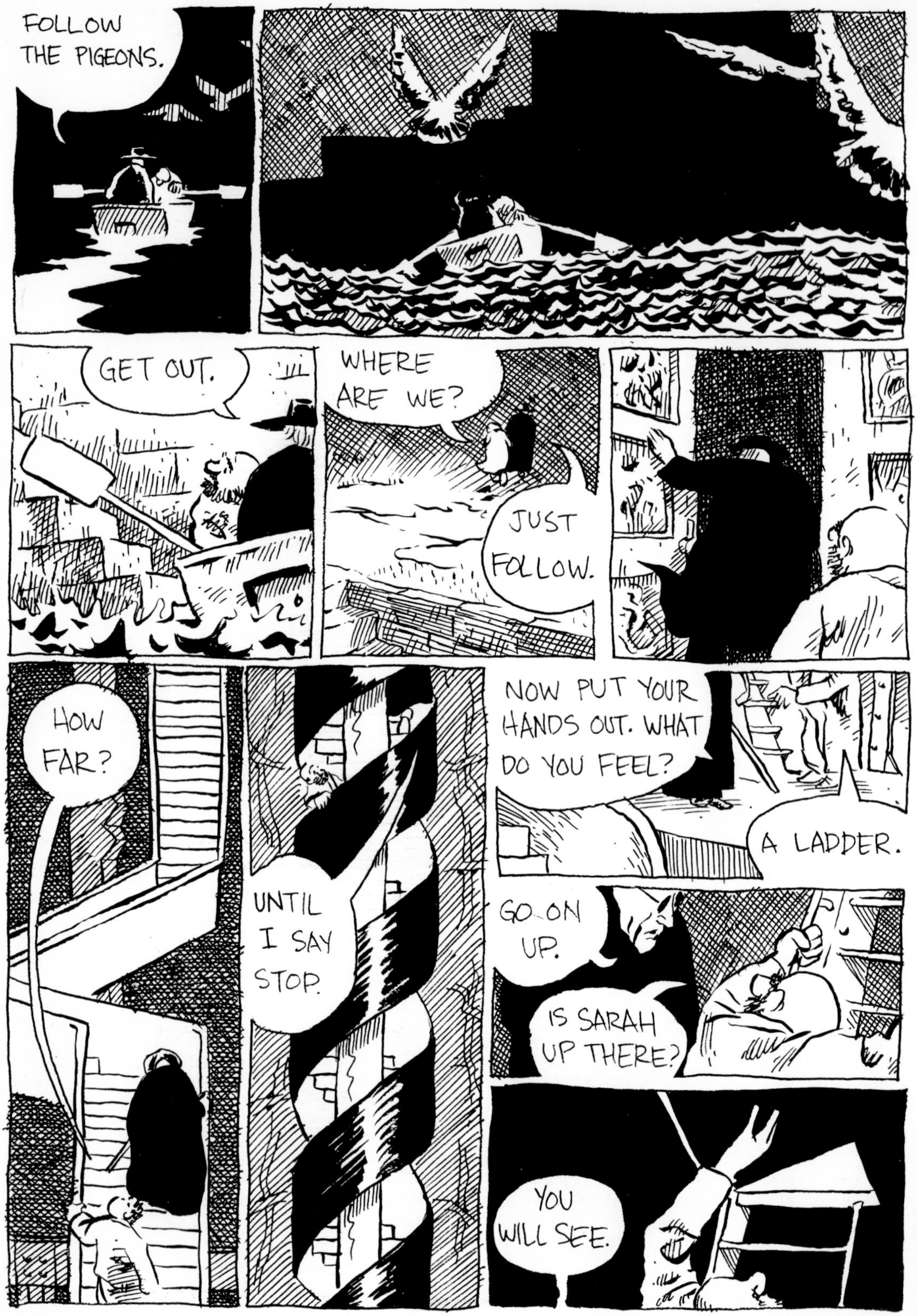
FOLLOW THE PIGEONS.
GET OUT.
WHERE ARE WE?
JUST FOLLOW.
HOW FAR?
UNTIL I SAY STOP.
NOW PUT YOUR HANDS OUT. WHAT DO YOU FEEL?
A LADDER.
GO ON UP.
IS SARAH UP THERE?
YOU WILL SEE.

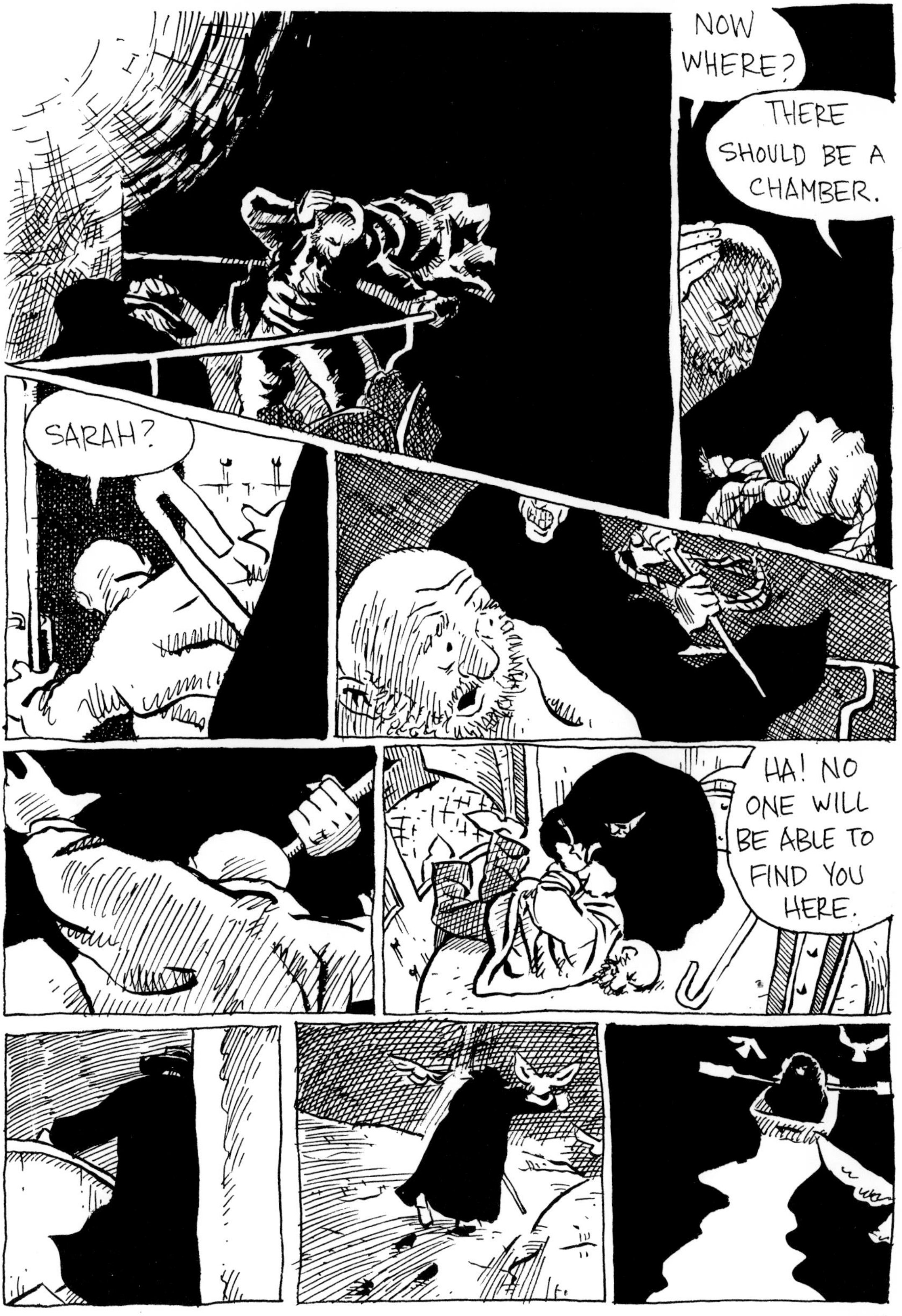
NOW WHERE?
THERE SHOULD BE A CHAMBER.
SARAH?
HA! NO ONE WILL BE ABLE TO FIND YOU HERE.

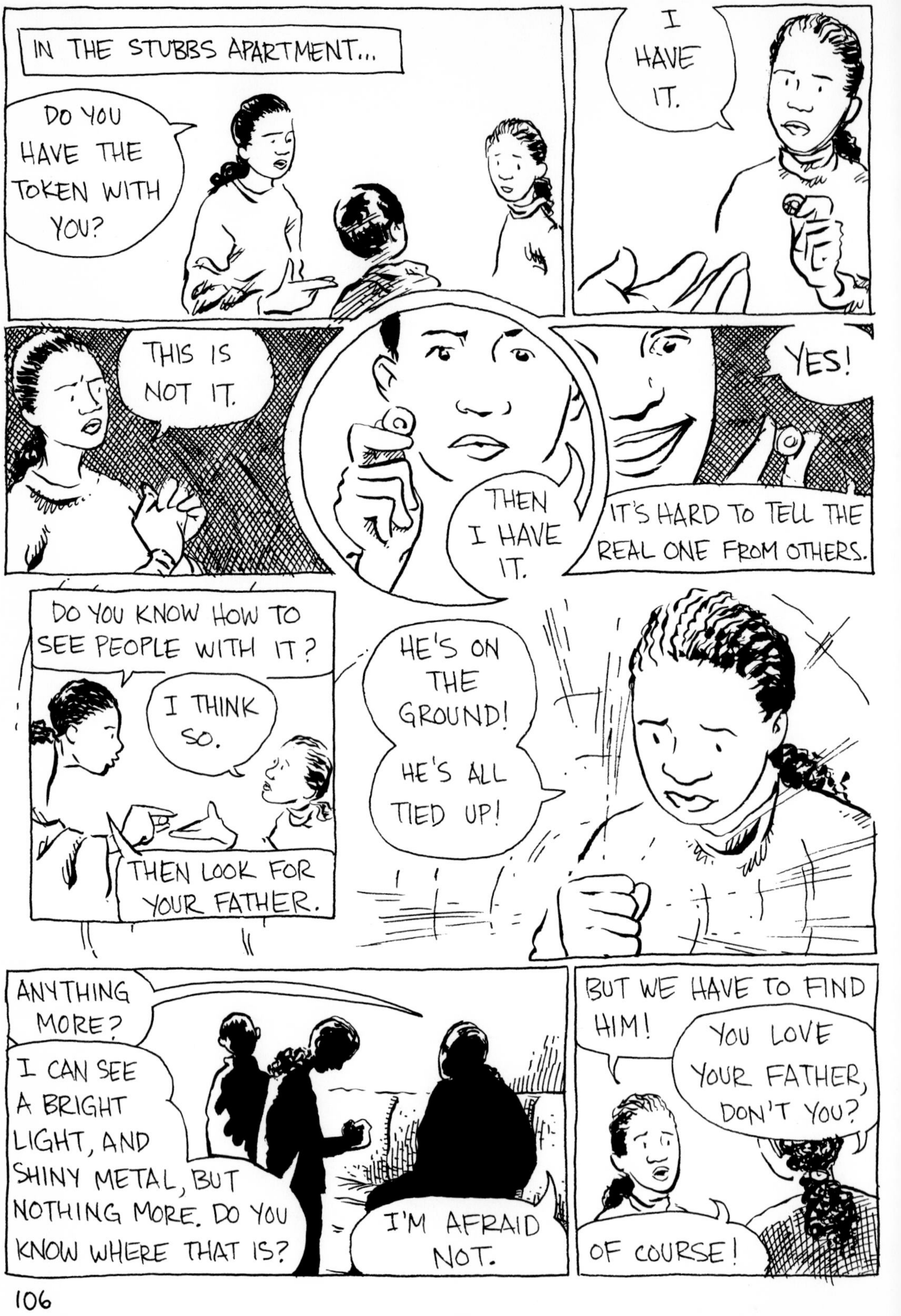
IN THE STUBBS APARTMENT...
DO YOU HAVE THE TOKEN WITH YOU?
I HAVE IT.
THIS IS NOT IT.
THEN I HAVE IT.
YES!
IT'S HARD TO TELL THE REAL ONE FROM OTHERS.
DO YOU KNOW HOW TO SEE PEOPLE WITH IT?
I THINK SO.
THEN LOOK FOR YOUR FATHER.
HE'S ON THE GROUND!
HE'S ALL TIED UP!
ANYTHING MORE?
I CAN SEE A BRIGHT LIGHT, AND SHINY METAL, BUT NOTHING MORE. DO YOU KNOW WHERE THAT IS?
I'M AFRAID NOT.
BUT WE HAVE TO FIND HIM!
YOU LOVE YOUR FATHER, DON'T YOU?
OF COURSE!

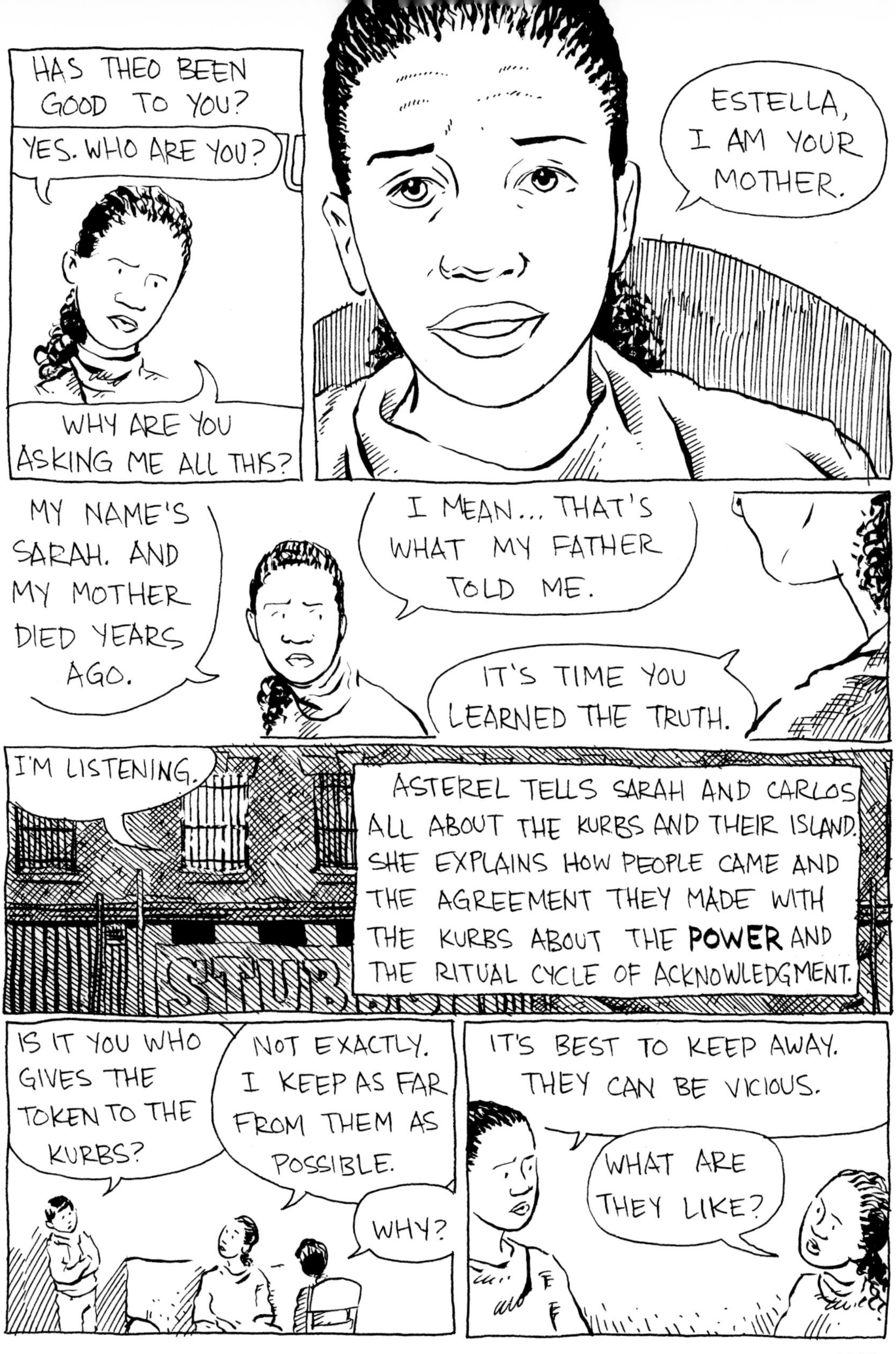
HAS THEO BEEN GOOD TO YOU?
YES. WHO ARE YOU?
WHY ARE YOU ASKING ME ALL THIS?
ESTELLA, I AM YOUR MOTHER.
MY NAME'S SARAH. AND MY MOTHER DIED YEARS AGO.
I MEAN... THAT'S WHAT MY FATHER TOLD ME.
IT'S TIME YOU LEARNED THE TRUTH.
I'M LISTENING.
ASTEREL TELLS SARAH AND CARLOS ALL ABOUT THE KURBS AND THEIR ISLAND. SHE EXPLAINS HOW PEOPLE CAME AND THE AGREEMENT THEY MADE WITH THE KURBS ABOUT THE **POWER** AND THE RITUAL CYCLE OF ACKNOWLEDGMENT.
IS IT YOU WHO GIVES THE TOKEN TO THE KURBS?
NOT EXACTLY. I KEEP AS FAR FROM THEM AS POSSIBLE.
WHY?
IT'S BEST TO KEEP AWAY. THEY CAN BE VICIOUS.
WHAT ARE THEY LIKE?

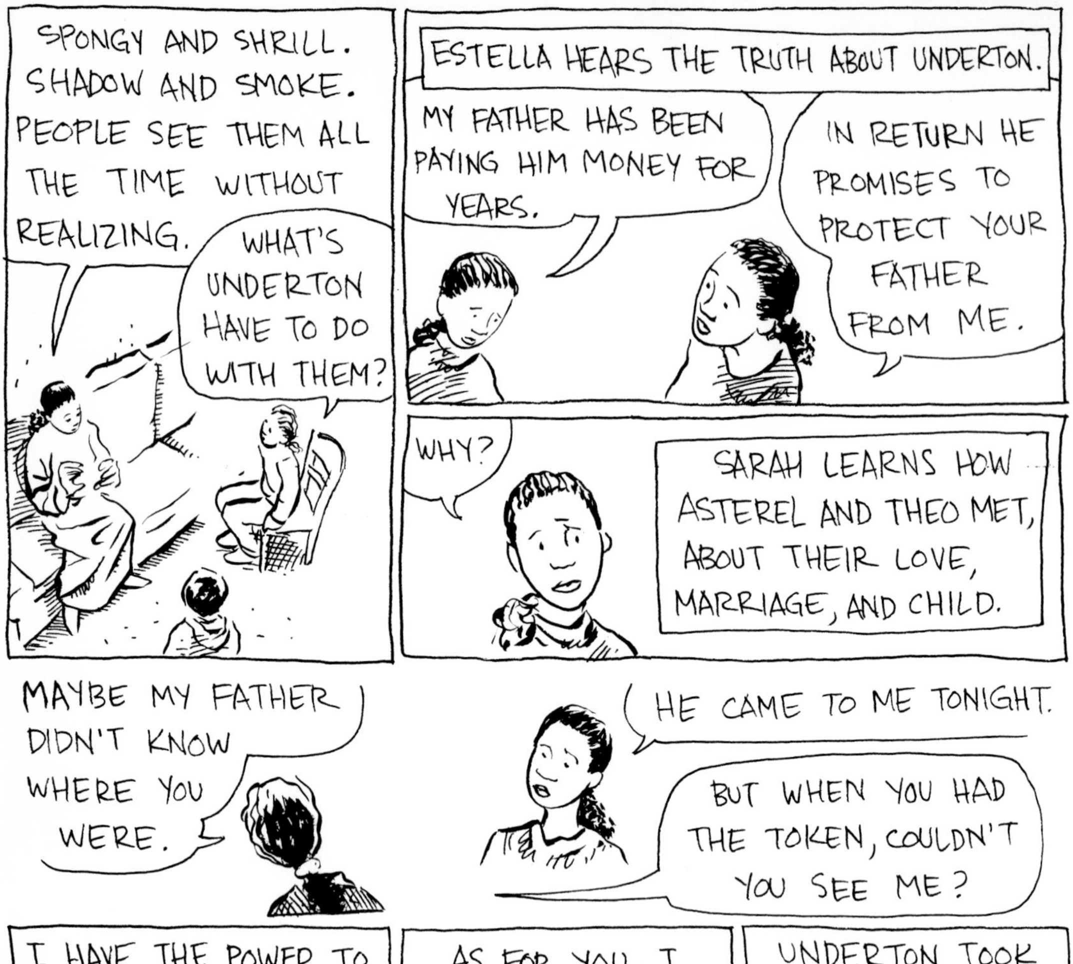
SPONGY AND SHRILL. SHADOW AND SMOKE. PEOPLE SEE THEM ALL THE TIME WITHOUT REALIZING.
WHAT'S UNDERTON HAVE TO DO WITH THEM?
ESTELLA HEARS THE TRUTH ABOUT UNDERTON.
MY FATHER HAS BEEN PAYING HIM MONEY FOR YEARS.
IN RETURN HE PROMISES TO PROTECT YOUR FATHER FROM ME.
WHY?
SARAH LEARNS HOW ASTEREL AND THEO MET, ABOUT THEIR LOVE, MARRIAGE, AND CHILD.
MAYBE MY FATHER DIDN'T KNOW WHERE YOU WERE.
HE CAME TO ME TONIGHT.
BUT WHEN YOU HAD THE TOKEN, COULDN'T YOU SEE ME?
I HAVE THE POWER TO SEE WHO HAS THE TOKEN. TO SEE ANYONE ELSE, I MUST KNOW EXACTLY WHAT THEY LOOK LIKE. YOUR FATHER TOOK ON A DISGUISE TO PREVENT MY SEEING HIM.
AS FOR YOU, I LOOKED FOR YOU EVERYWHERE I WENT. BUT THE TWO-DAY-OLD BABY I KNEW NO LONGER EXISTS, DOES SHE?
UNDERTON TOOK CARE NEVER TO COME HERE. THIS MORNING HE DID, AND WHEN I FOLLOWED HIM I SAW YOU FOR THE FIRST TIME.

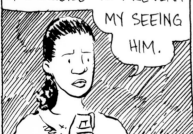

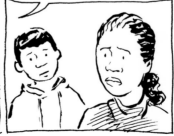

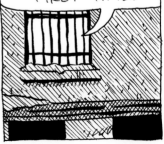

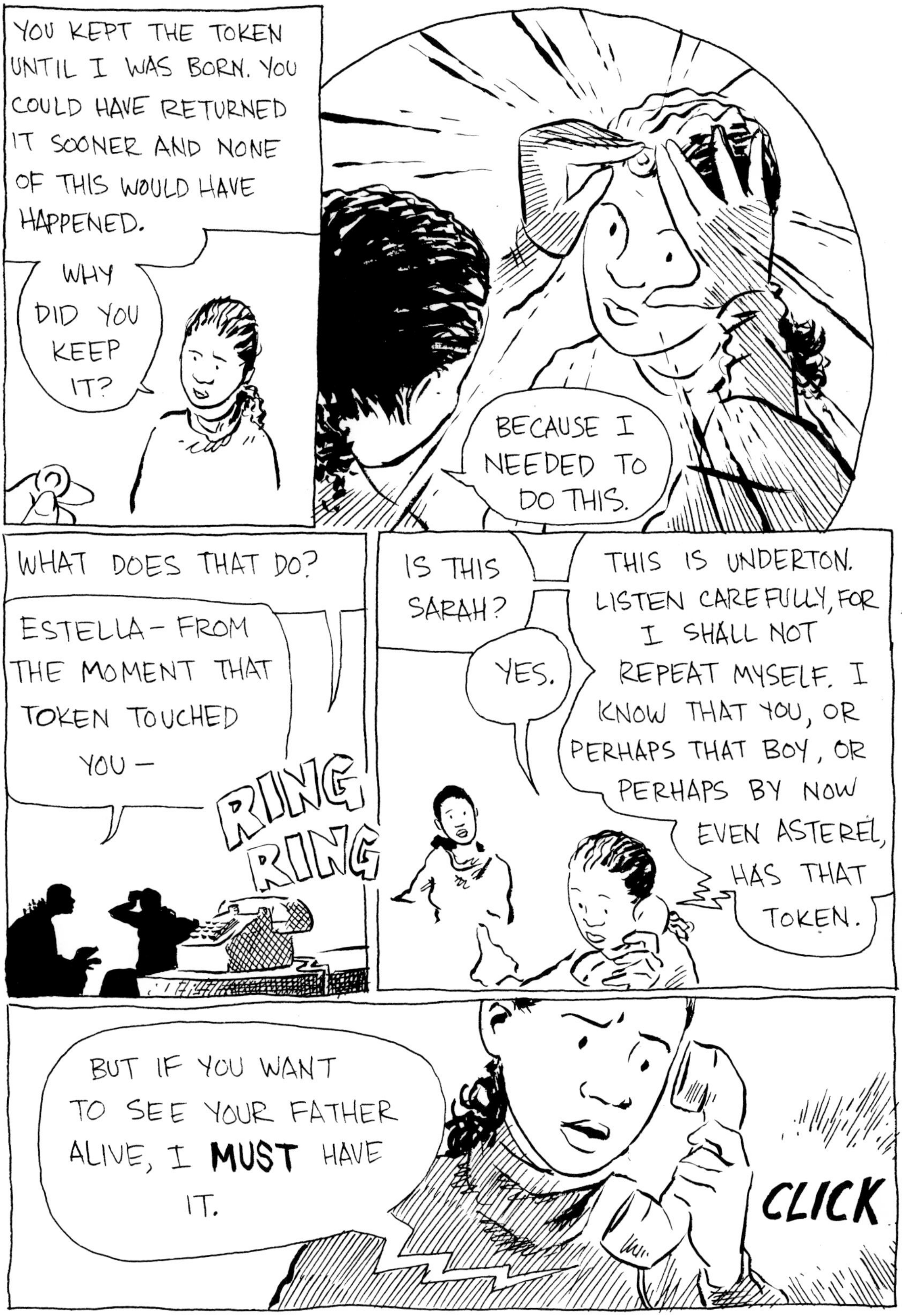
YOU KEPT THE TOKEN UNTIL I WAS BORN. YOU COULD HAVE RETURNED IT SOONER AND NONE OF THIS WOULD HAVE HAPPENED.
WHY DID YOU KEEP IT?
BECAUSE I NEEDED TO DO THIS.
WHAT DOES THAT DO?
ESTELLA- FROM THE MOMENT THAT TOKEN TOUCHED YOU -
RING RING
IS THIS SARAH?
YES.
THIS IS UNDERTON. LISTEN CAREFULLY, FOR I SHALL NOT REPEAT MYSELF. I KNOW THAT YOU, OR PERHAPS THAT BOY, OR PERHAPS BY NOW EVEN ASTEREL, HAS THAT TOKEN.
BUT IF YOU WANT TO SEE YOUR FATHER ALIVE, I **MUST** HAVE IT.
CLICK

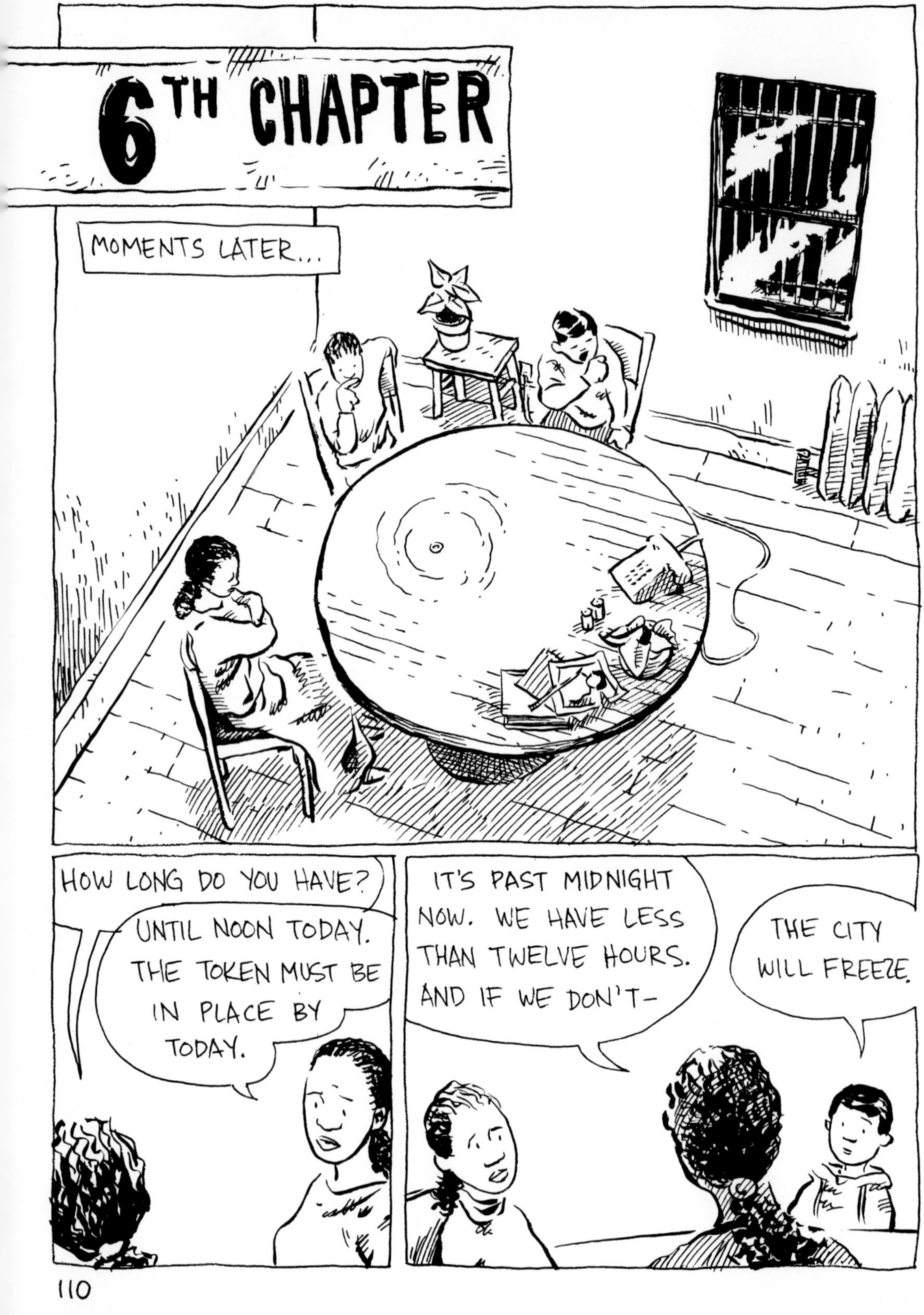
6TH CHAPTER
MOMENTS LATER...
HOW LONG DO YOU HAVE?
UNTIL NOON TODAY. THE TOKEN MUST BE IN PLACE BY TODAY.
IT'S PAST MIDNIGHT NOW. WE HAVE LESS THAN TWELVE HOURS. AND IF WE DON'T-
THE CITY WILL FREEZE.

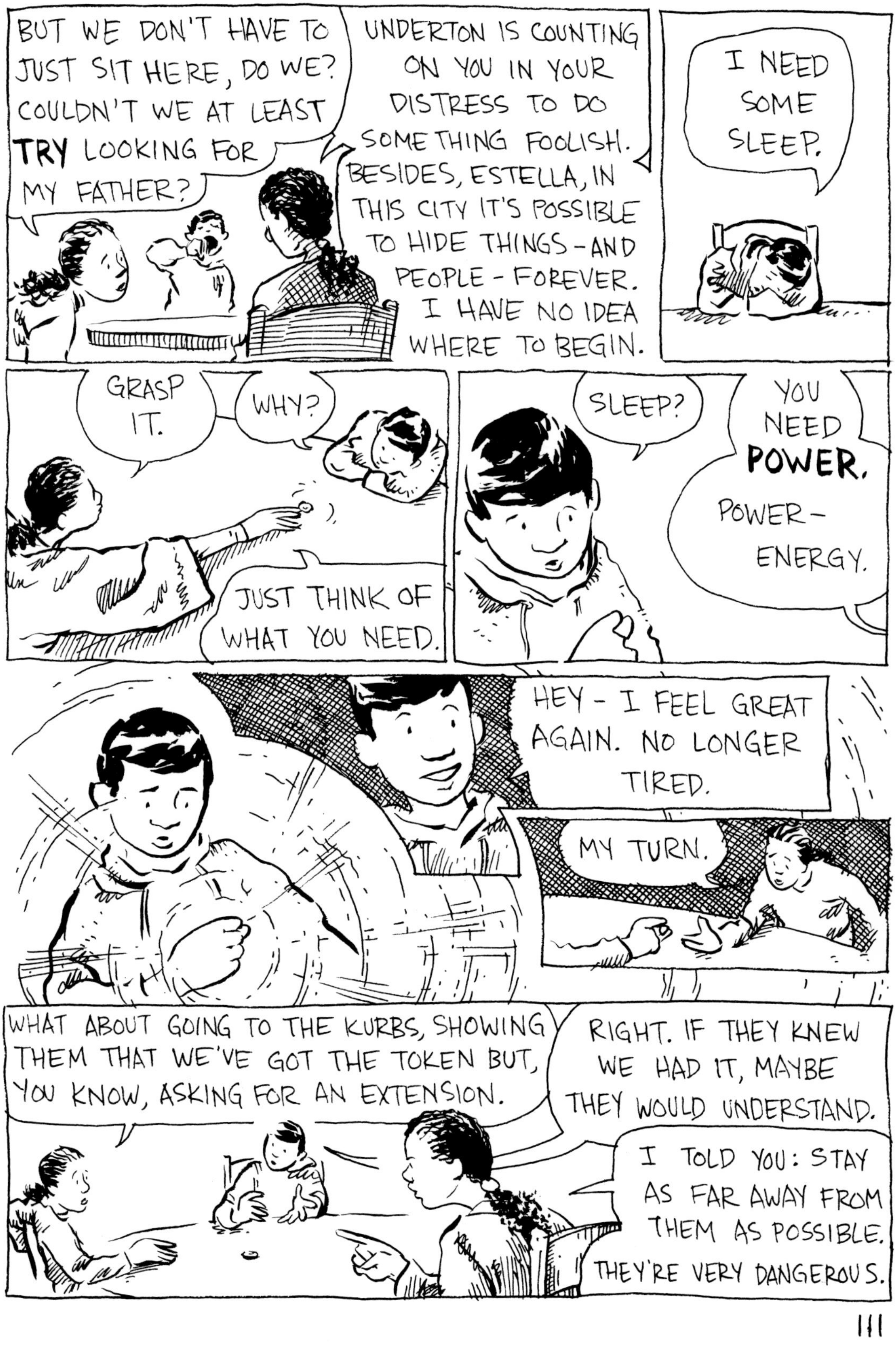

BUT WE DON'T HAVE TO JUST SIT HERE, DO WE? COULDN'T WE AT LEAST **TRY** LOOKING FOR MY FATHER?
UNDERTON IS COUNTING ON YOU IN YOUR DISTRESS TO DO SOMETHING FOOLISH. BESIDES, ESTELLA, IN THIS CITY IT'S POSSIBLE TO HIDE THINGS - AND PEOPLE - FOREVER. I HAVE NO IDEA WHERE TO BEGIN.
I NEED SOME SLEEP.
GRASP IT.
WHY?
JUST THINK OF WHAT YOU NEED.
SLEEP?
YOU NEED **POWER.** POWER - ENERGY.
HEY - I FEEL GREAT AGAIN. NO LONGER TIRED.
MY TURN.
WHAT ABOUT GOING TO THE KURBS, SHOWING THEM THAT WE'VE GOT THE TOKEN BUT, YOU KNOW, ASKING FOR AN EXTENSION.
RIGHT. IF THEY KNEW WE HAD IT, MAYBE THEY WOULD UNDERSTAND.
I TOLD YOU: STAY AS FAR AWAY FROM THEM AS POSSIBLE. THEY'RE VERY DANGEROUS.

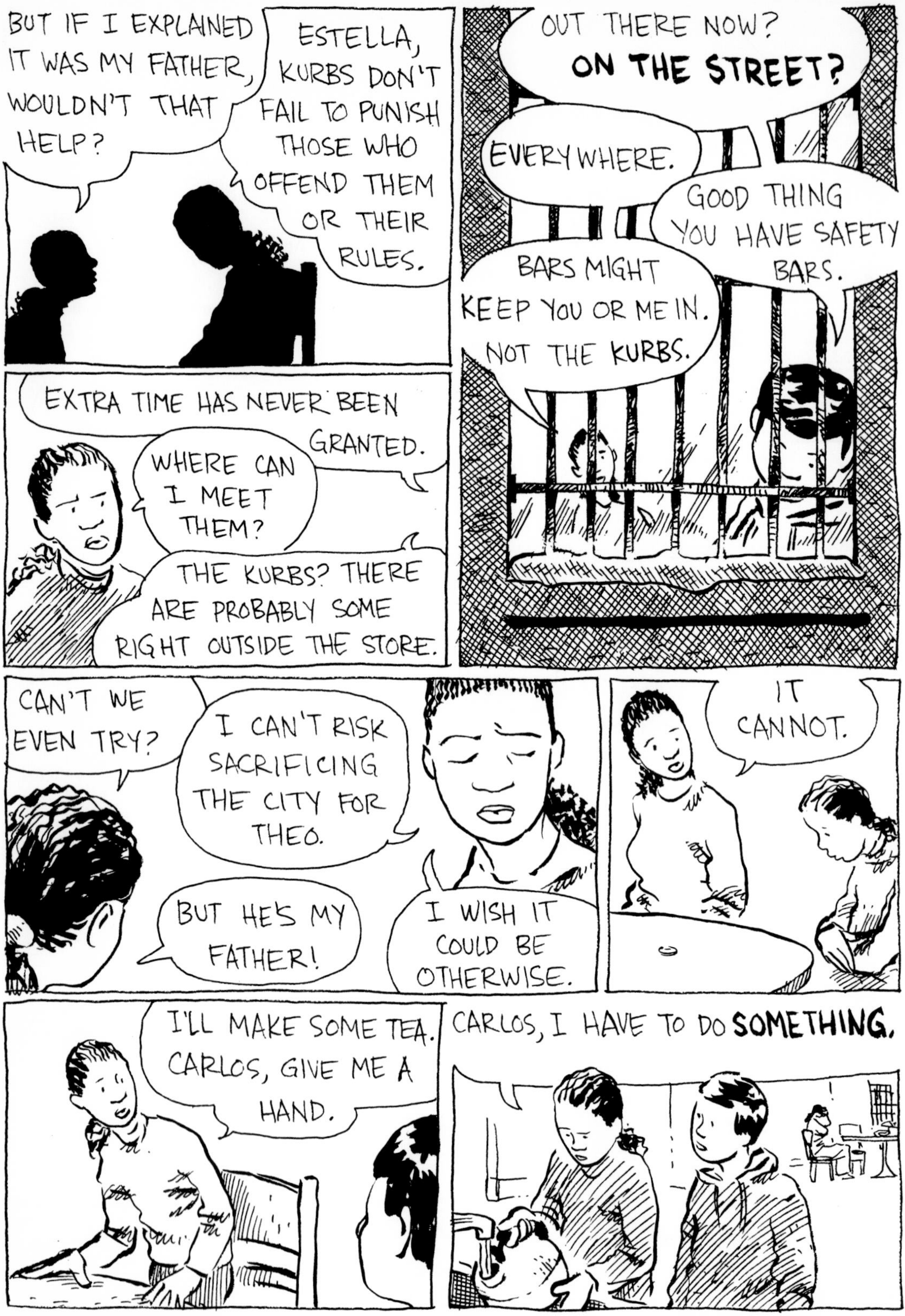

BUT IF I EXPLAINED IT WAS MY FATHER, WOULDN'T THAT HELP?
ESTELLA, KURBS DON'T FAIL TO PUNISH THOSE WHO OFFEND THEM OR THEIR RULES.
OUT THERE NOW? **ON THE STREET?**
EVERYWHERE.
GOOD THING YOU HAVE SAFETY BARS.
BARS MIGHT KEEP YOU OR ME IN. NOT THE KURBS.
EXTRA TIME HAS NEVER BEEN GRANTED.
WHERE CAN I MEET THEM?
THE KURBS? THERE ARE PROBABLY SOME RIGHT OUTSIDE THE STORE.
CAN'T WE EVEN TRY?
I CAN'T RISK SACRIFICING THE CITY FOR THEO.
BUT HE'S MY FATHER!
I WISH IT COULD BE OTHERWISE.
IT CANNOT.
I'LL MAKE SOME TEA. CARLOS, GIVE ME A HAND.
CARLOS, I HAVE TO DO **SOMETHING.**

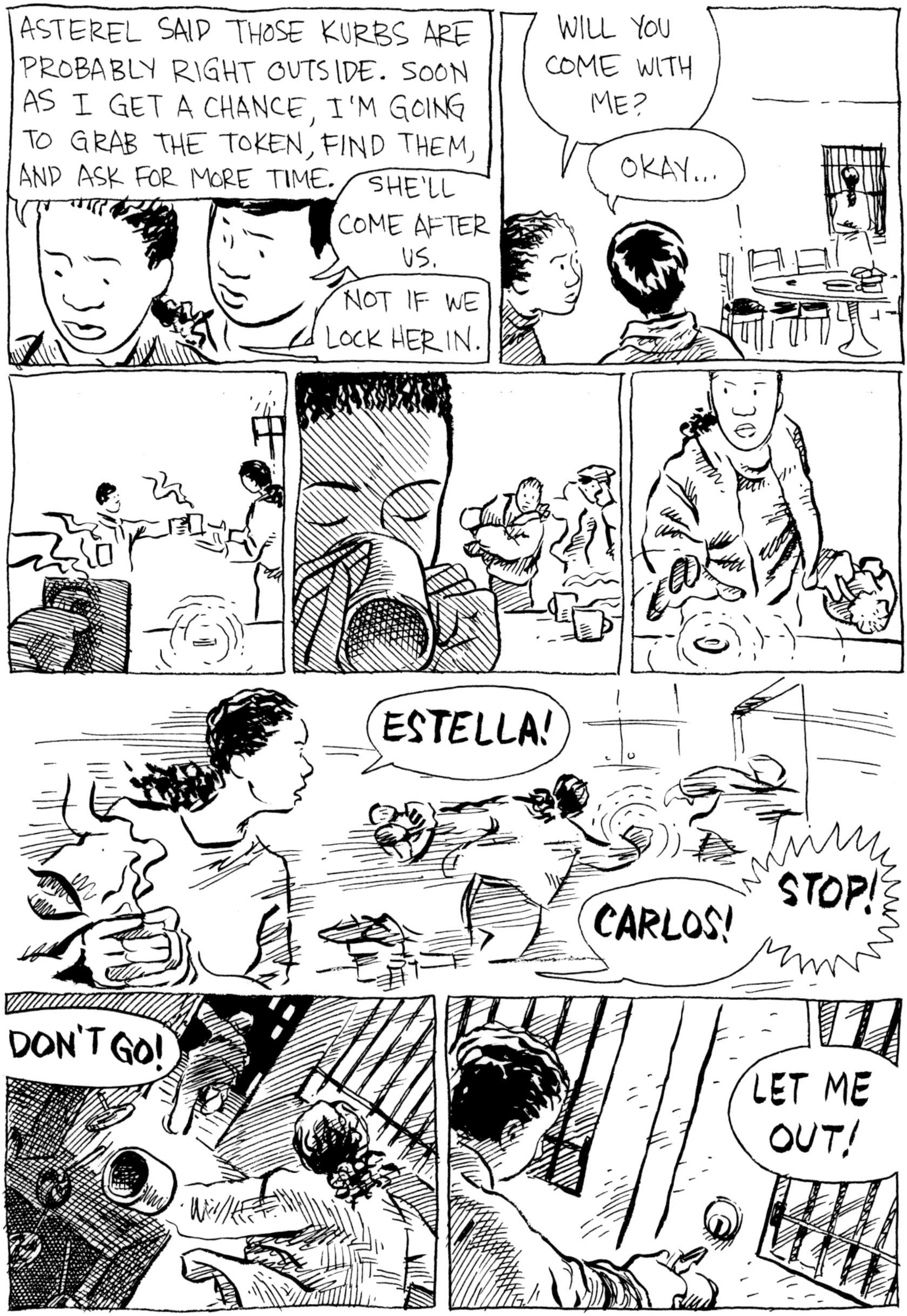

ASTEREL SAID THOSE KURBS ARE PROBABLY RIGHT OUTSIDE. SOON AS I GET A CHANCE, I'M GOING TO GRAB THE TOKEN, FIND THEM, AND ASK FOR MORE TIME.
SHE'LL COME AFTER US.
NOT IF WE LOCK HER IN.
WILL YOU COME WITH ME?
OKAY...
ESTELLA!
CARLOS!
STOP!
DON'T GO!
LET ME OUT!

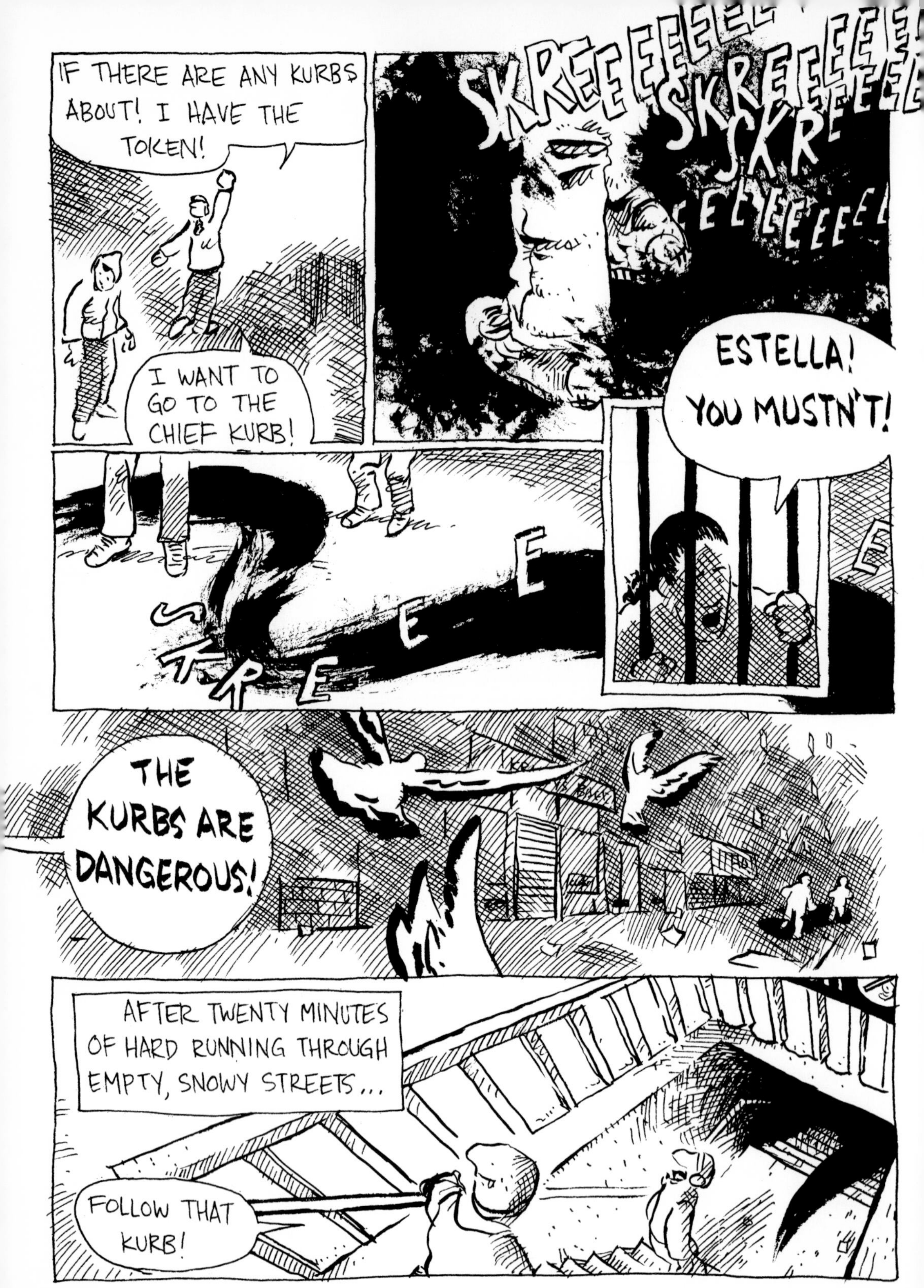
IF THERE ARE ANY KURBS ABOUT! I HAVE THE TOKEN!
I WANT TO GO TO THE CHIEF KURB!
SKREEEEEEE! SKREEEEEEE! SKREEEEEEE!
ESTELLA! YOU MUSTN'T!
SKREEEE
THE KURBS ARE DANGEROUS!
AFTER TWENTY MINUTES OF HARD RUNNING THROUGH EMPTY, SNOWY STREETS...
FOLLOW THAT KURB!

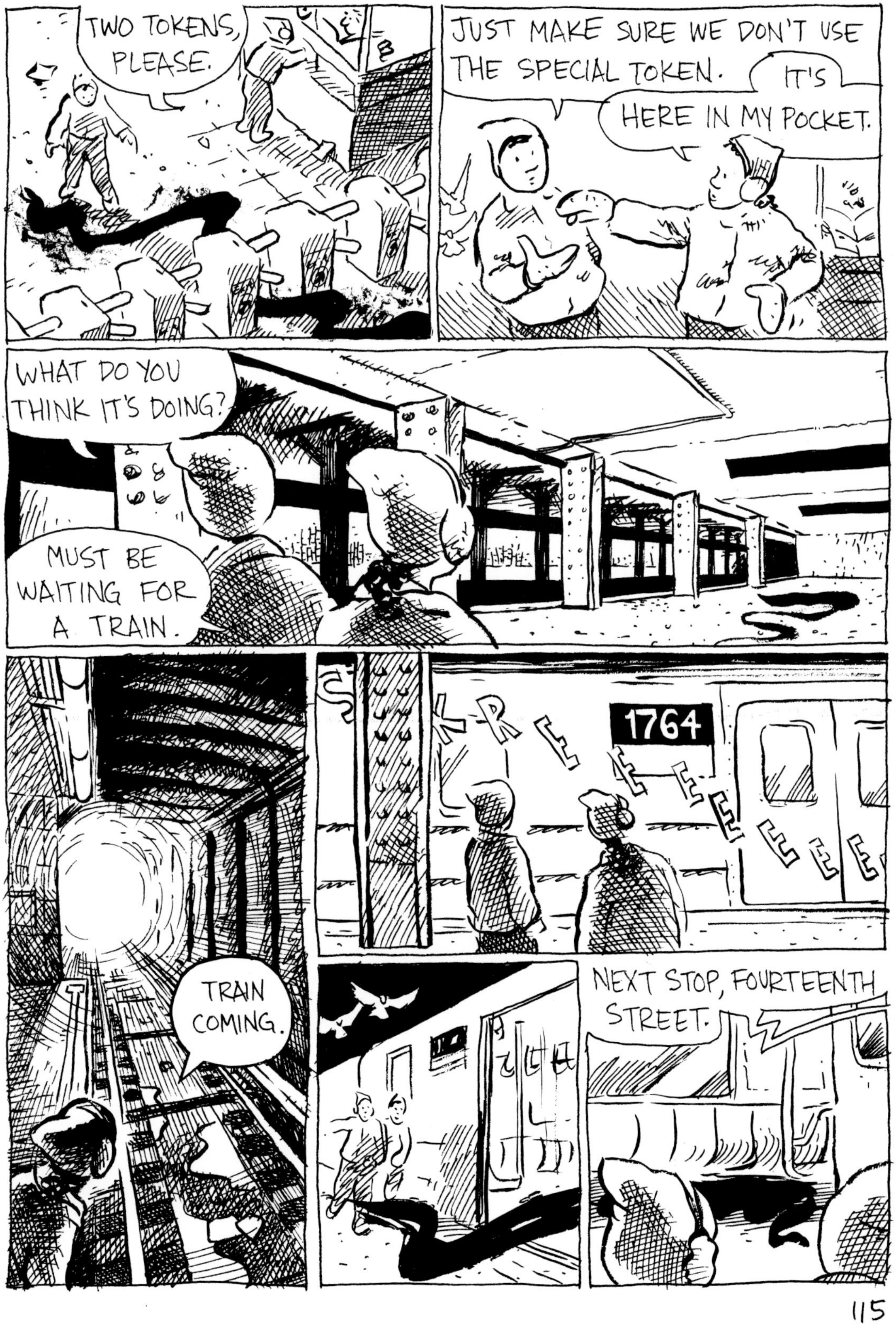
TWO TOKENS, PLEASE.
JUST MAKE SURE WE DON'T USE THE SPECIAL TOKEN.
IT'S HERE IN MY POCKET.
WHAT DO YOU THINK IT'S DOING?
MUST BE WAITING FOR A TRAIN.
TRAIN COMING.
SKREEEEEEEEE
1764
NEXT STOP, FOURTEENTH STREET.

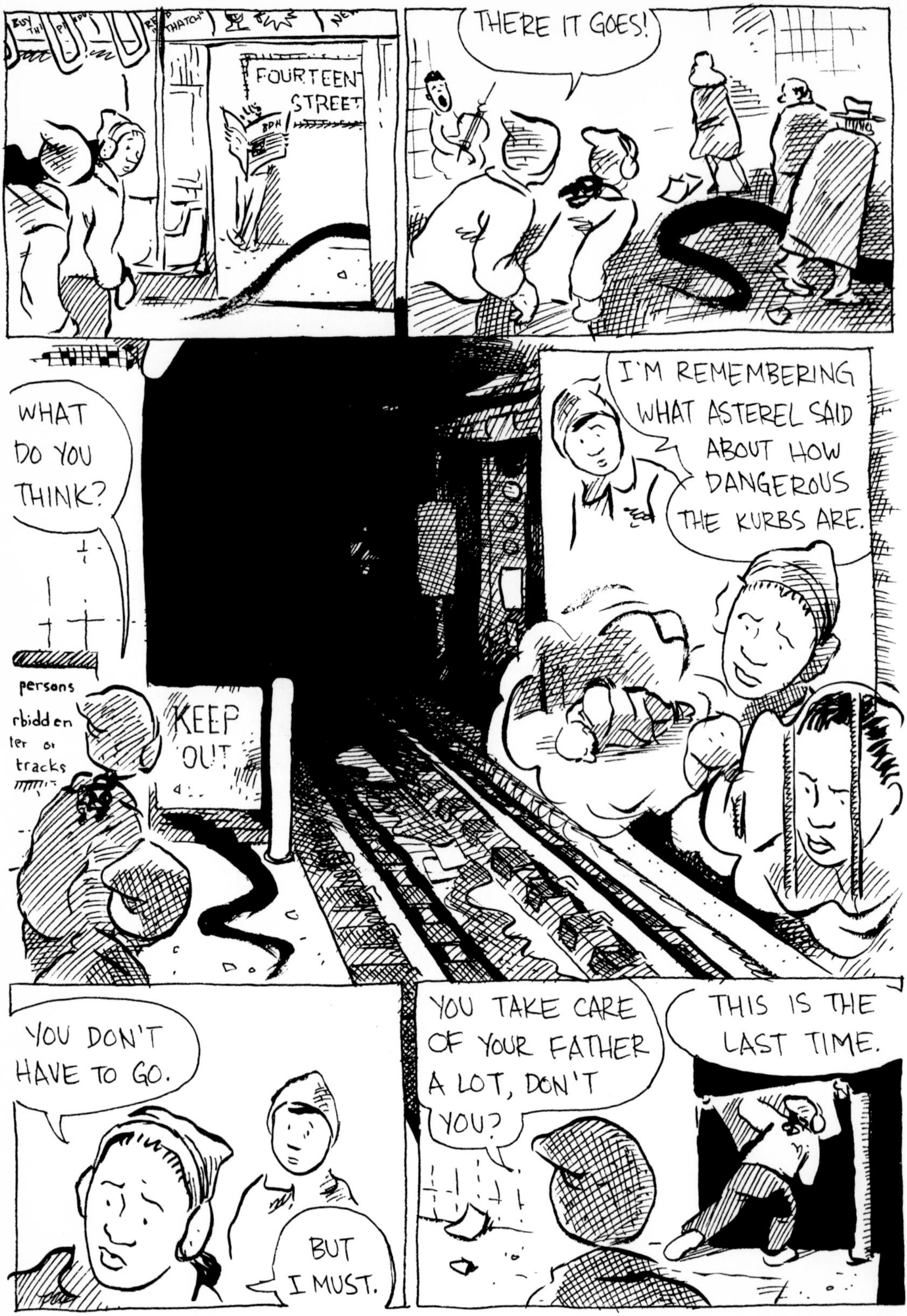
FOURTEEN STREET
THERE IT GOES!
WHAT DO YOU THINK?
I'M REMEMBERING WHAT ASTEREL SAID ABOUT HOW DANGEROUS THE KURBS ARE.
persons
rbidden
ter on
tracks
KEEP OUT
YOU DON'T HAVE TO GO.
BUT I MUST.
YOU TAKE CARE OF YOUR FATHER A LOT, DON'T YOU?
THIS IS THE LAST TIME.

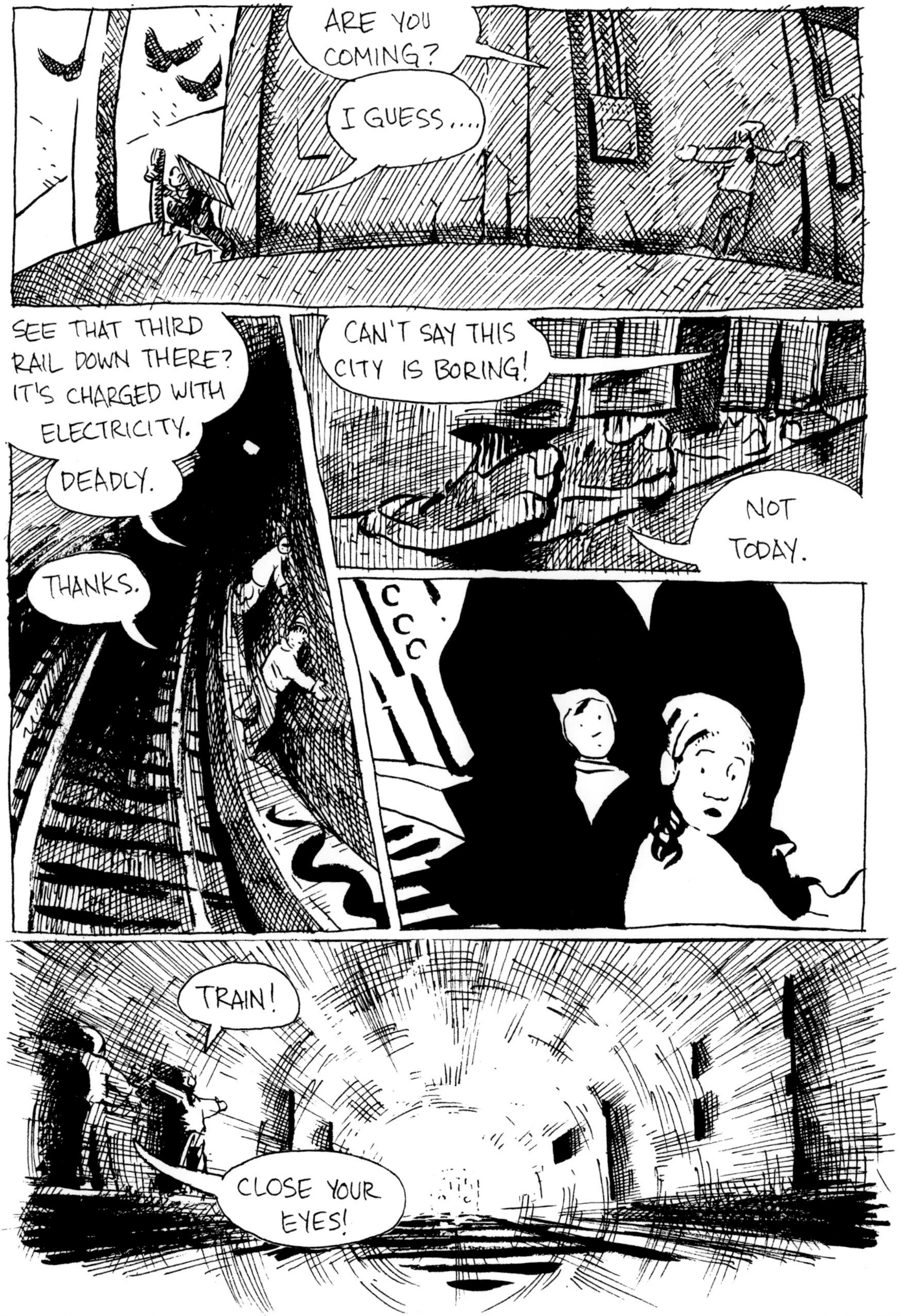
ARE YOU COMING?
I GUESS....
SEE THAT THIRD RAIL DOWN THERE? IT'S CHARGED WITH ELECTRICITY.
DEADLY.
THANKS.
CAN'T SAY THIS CITY IS BORING!
NOT TODAY.
TRAIN!
CLOSE YOUR EYES!

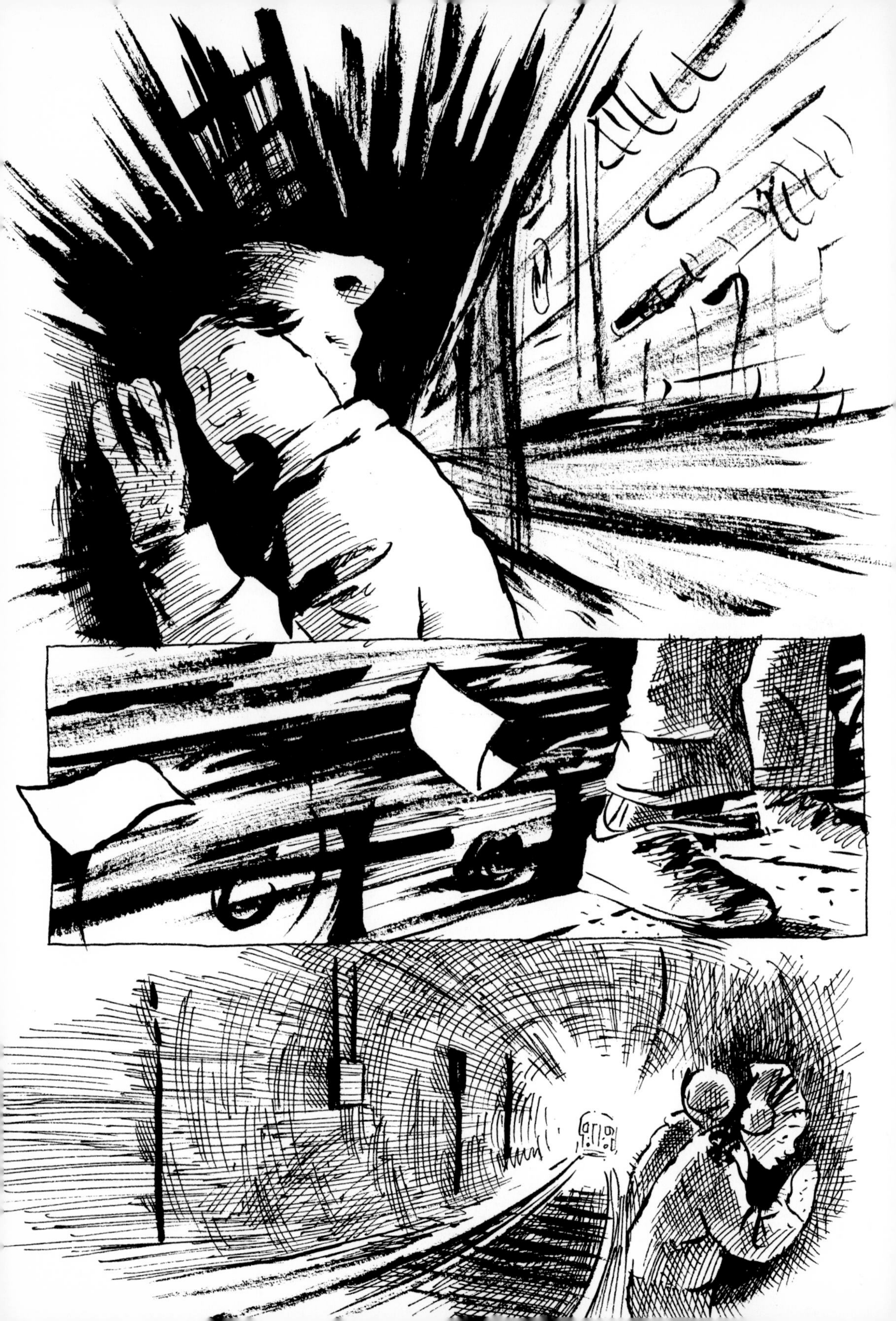

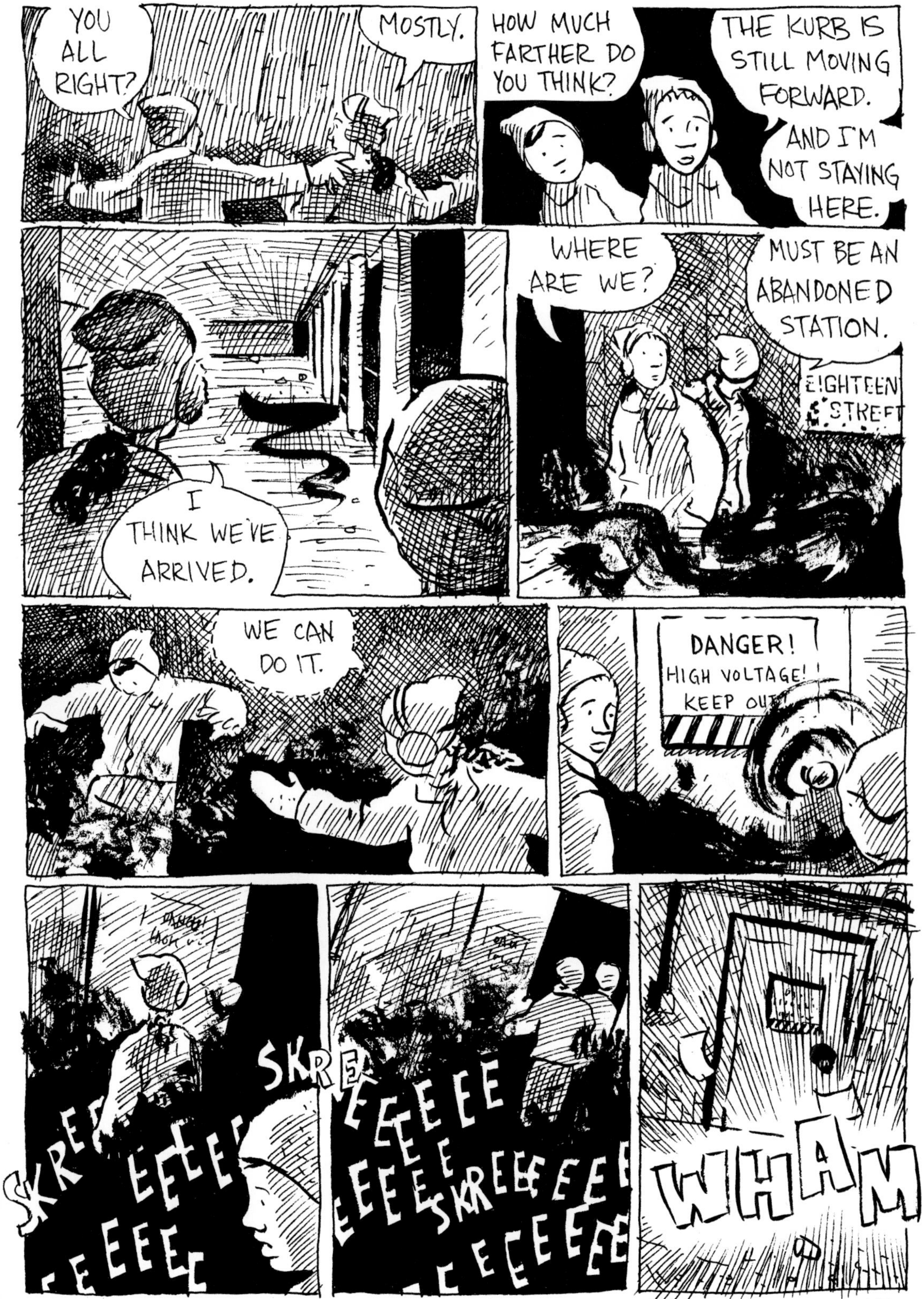
YOU ALL RIGHT?
MOSTLY.
HOW MUCH FARTHER DO YOU THINK?
THE KURB IS STILL MOVING FORWARD.
AND I'M NOT STAYING HERE.
I THINK WE'VE ARRIVED.
WHERE ARE WE?
MUST BE AN ABANDONED STATION.
EIGHTEEN
STREET
WE CAN DO IT.
DANGER!
HIGH VOLTAGE!
KEEP OUT
SKREEEEEEEEE
SKREEEEEEEEEEE
SKREEEEEEEEEEE
WHAM

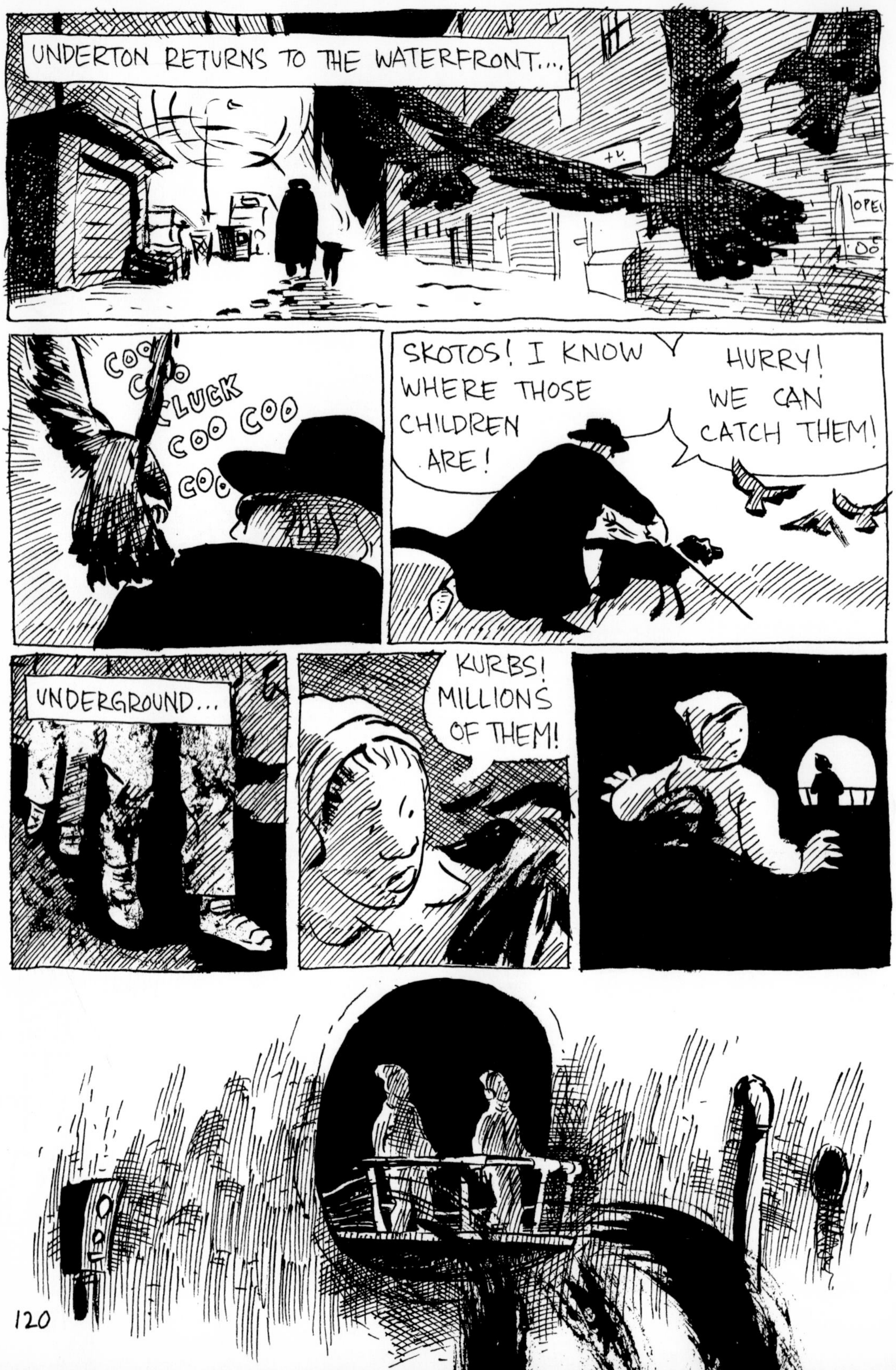
UNDERTON RETURNS TO THE WATERFRONT....
COO COO CLUCK COO COO COO
SKOTOS! I KNOW WHERE THOSE CHILDREN ARE!
HURRY! WE CAN CATCH THEM!
UNDERGROUND...
KURBS! MILLIONS OF THEM!

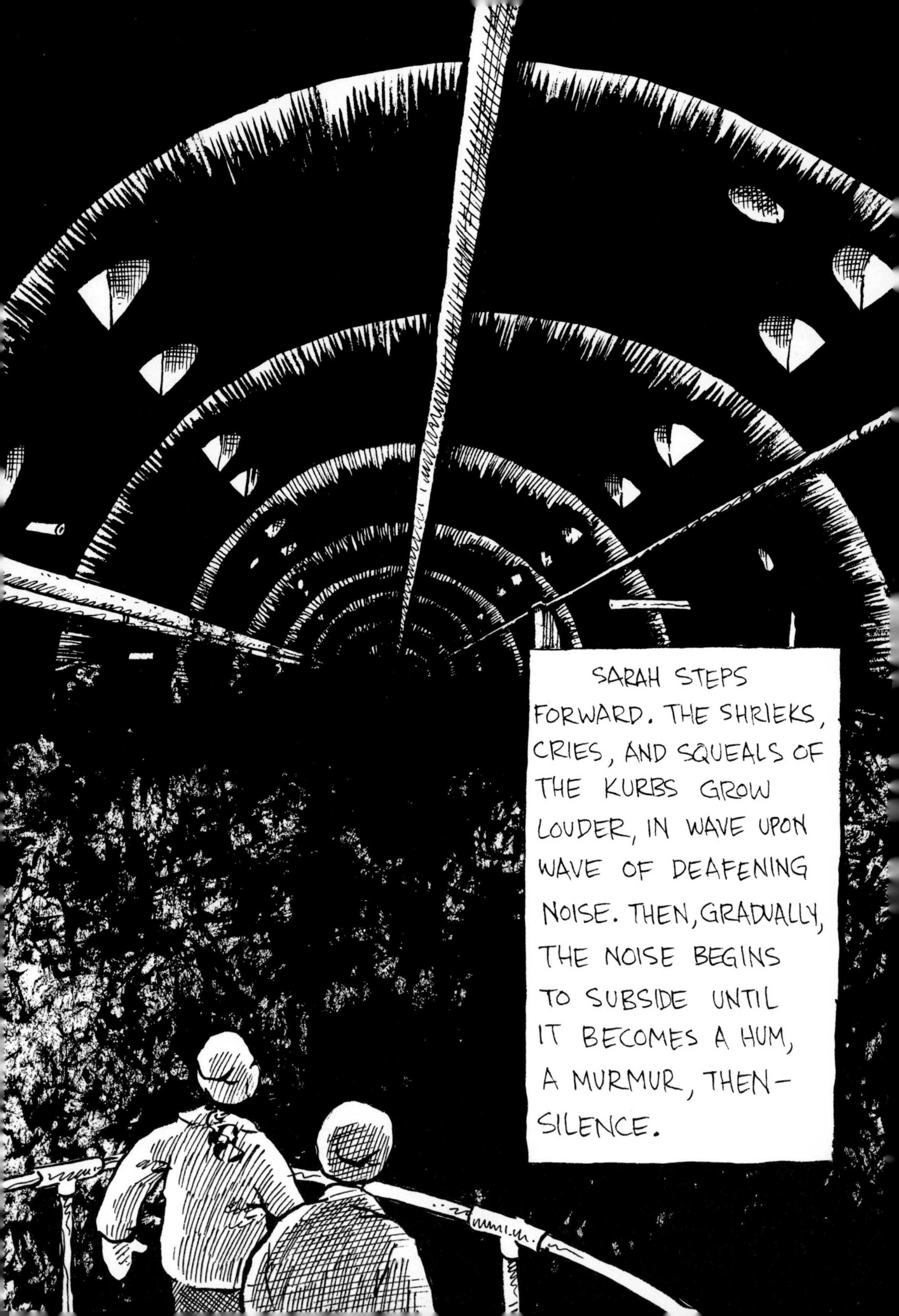
SARAH STEPS FORWARD. THE SHRIEKS, CRIES, AND SQUEALS OF THE KURBS GROW LOUDER, IN WAVE UPON WAVE OF DEAFENING NOISE. THEN, GRADUALLY, THE NOISE BEGINS TO SUBSIDE UNTIL IT BECOMES A HUM, A MURMUR, THEN– SILENCE.

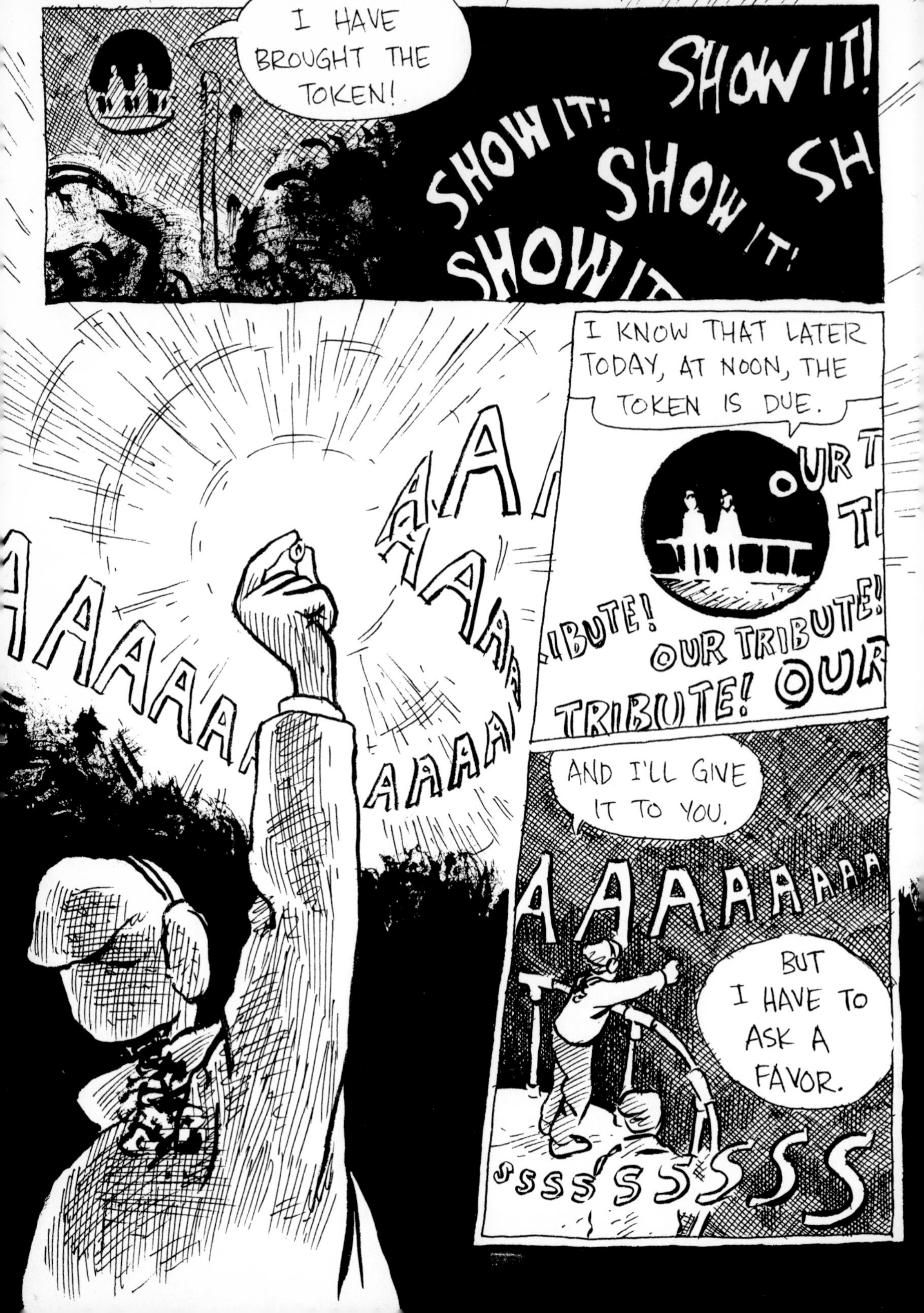
I HAVE BROUGHT THE TOKEN!
SHOW IT! SHOW IT! SHOW IT! SHOW IT! SH
AAAAAAAAAAAA
I KNOW THAT LATER TODAY, AT NOON, THE TOKEN IS DUE.
OUR TRIBUTE! OUR TRIBUTE! OUR TRIBUTE! OUR
AND I'LL GIVE IT TO YOU.
AAAAAAAA
BUT I HAVE TO ASK A FAVOR.
SSSSSSSSSS

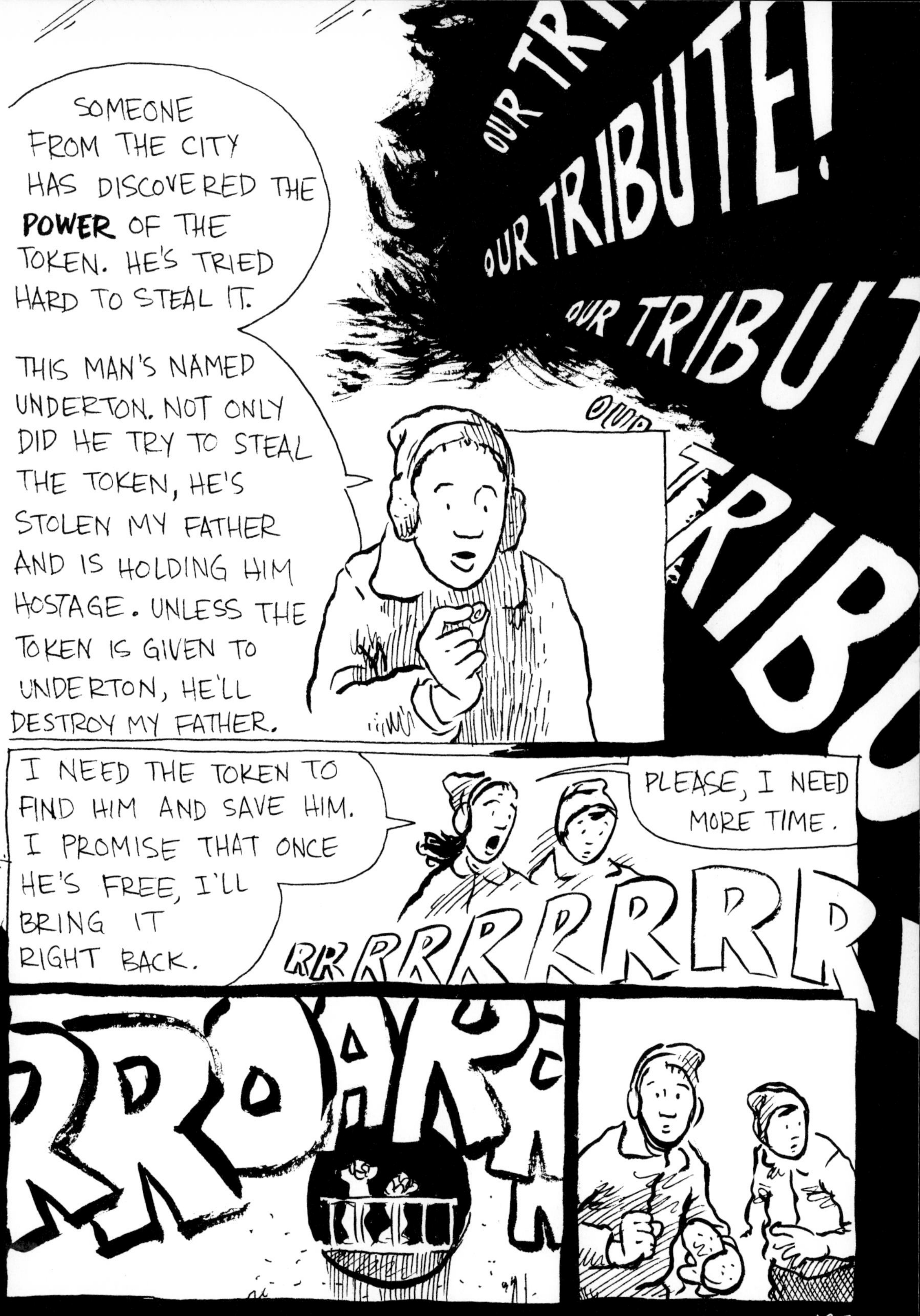

OUR TRIBUTE! OUR TRIBUTE! OUR TRIBU OUR TRIBU
SOMEONE FROM THE CITY HAS DISCOVERED THE **POWER** OF THE TOKEN. HE'S TRIED HARD TO STEAL IT.
THIS MAN'S NAMED UNDERTON. NOT ONLY DID HE TRY TO STEAL THE TOKEN, HE'S STOLEN MY FATHER AND IS HOLDING HIM HOSTAGE. UNLESS THE TOKEN IS GIVEN TO UNDERTON, HE'LL DESTROY MY FATHER.
I NEED THE TOKEN TO FIND HIM AND SAVE HIM. I PROMISE THAT ONCE HE'S FREE, I'LL BRING IT RIGHT BACK.
PLEASE, I NEED MORE TIME.
RRRRRRRRRRR
RROAR

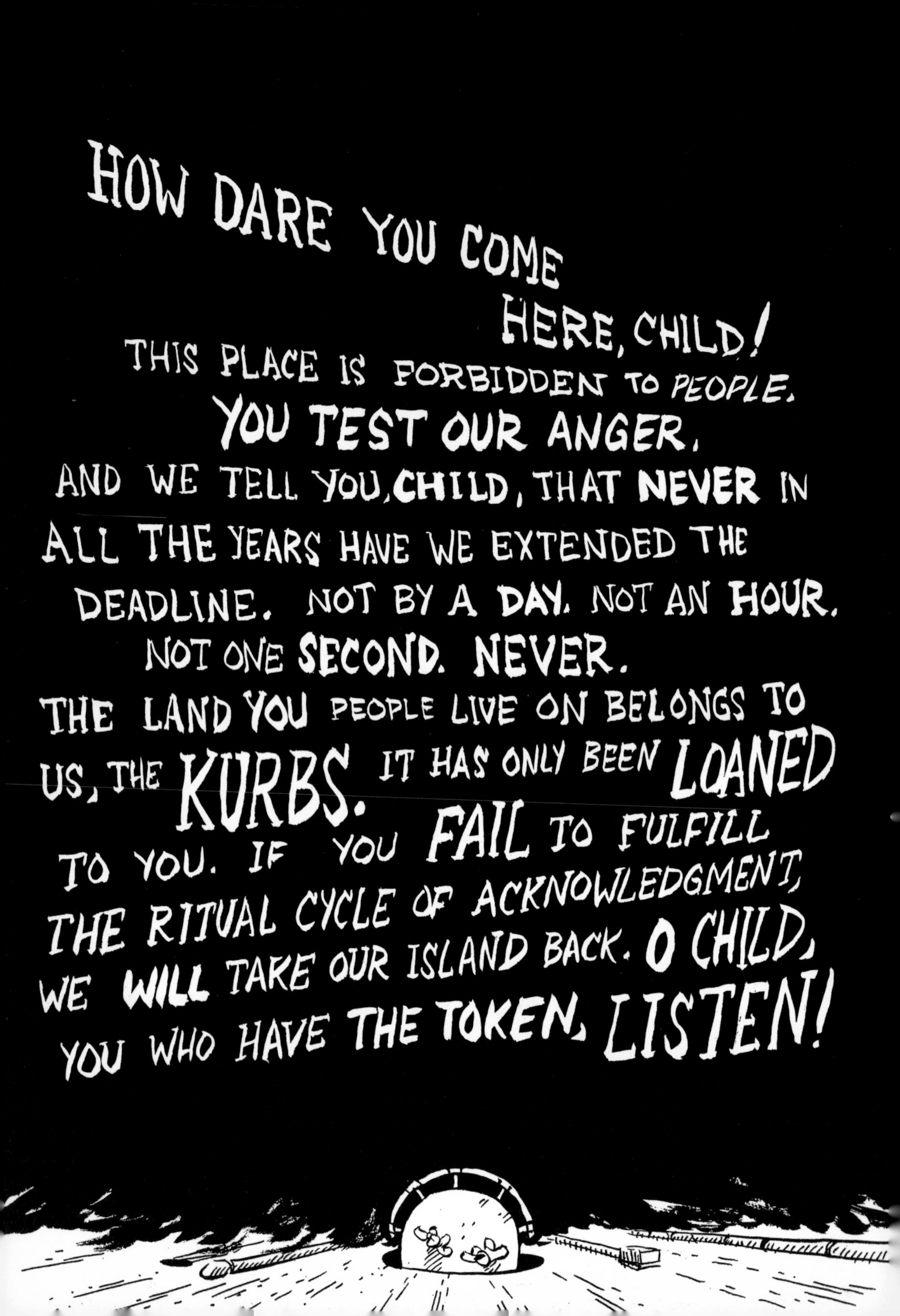
HOW DARE YOU COME HERE, CHILD!
THIS PLACE IS FORBIDDEN TO PEOPLE.
YOU TEST OUR ANGER.
AND WE TELL YOU, CHILD, THAT NEVER IN ALL THE YEARS HAVE WE EXTENDED THE DEADLINE. NOT BY A DAY. NOT AN HOUR. NOT ONE SECOND. NEVER.
THE LAND YOU PEOPLE LIVE ON BELONGS TO US, THE KURBS. IT HAS ONLY BEEN LOANED TO YOU. IF YOU FAIL TO FULFILL THE RITUAL CYCLE OF ACKNOWLEDGMENT, WE WILL TAKE OUR ISLAND BACK. O CHILD, YOU WHO HAVE THE TOKEN, LISTEN!

THE RITUAL INSISTS THE TOKEN SHALL BE IN ITS REQUIRED PLACE OF SAFEKEEPING BY THE TWENTY-FIRST DAY OF DECEMBER, AT THE STROKE OF NOON, OR YOU PEOPLE SHALL SUFFER THE CONSEQUENCES! THE DEADLINE IS TODAY! **BE WARNED!**

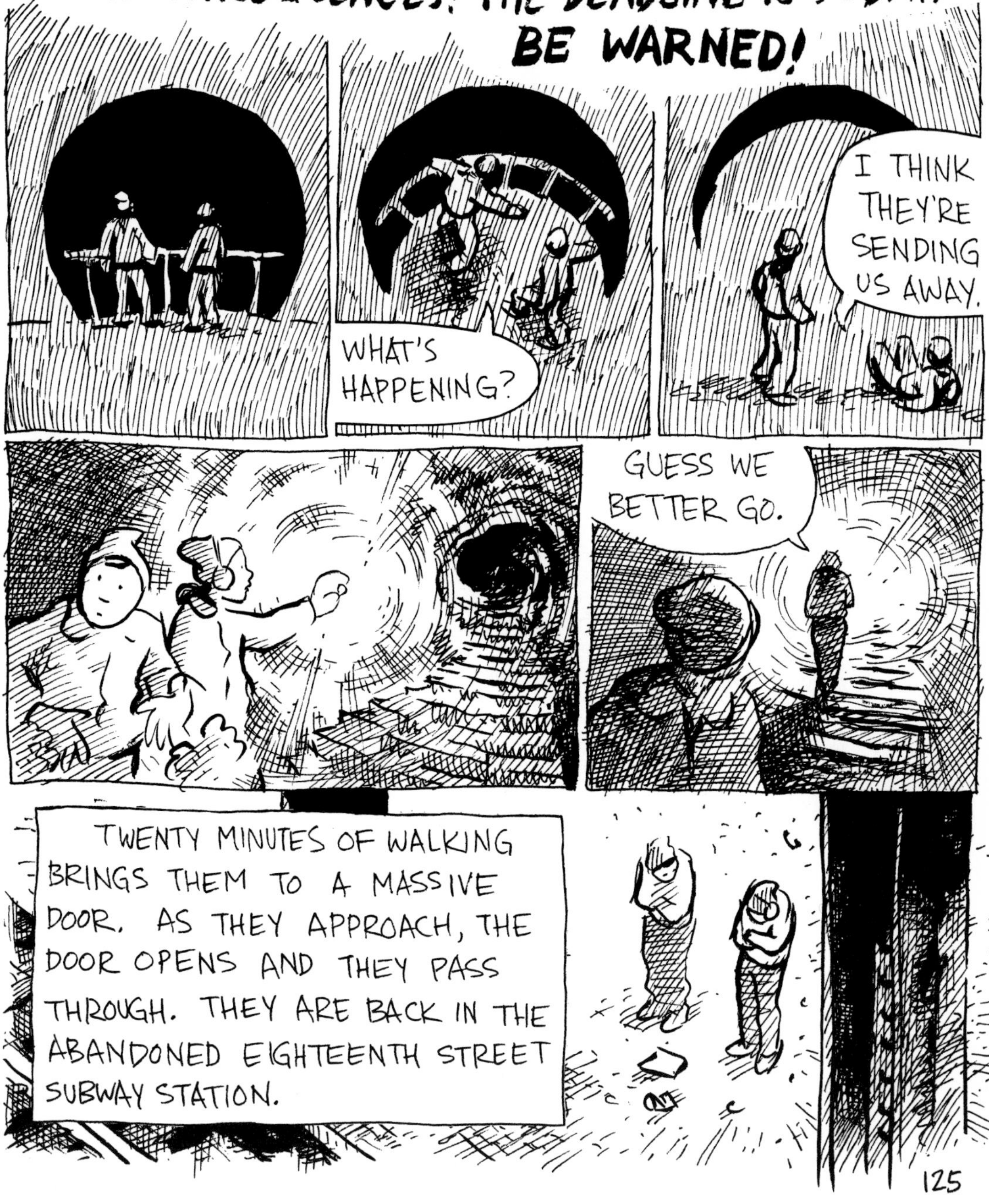
WHAT'S HAPPENING?
I THINK THEY'RE SENDING US AWAY.
GUESS WE BETTER GO.
TWENTY MINUTES OF WALKING BRINGS THEM TO A MASSIVE DOOR. AS THEY APPROACH, THE DOOR OPENS AND THEY PASS THROUGH. THEY ARE BACK IN THE ABANDONED EIGHTEENTH STREET SUBWAY STATION.

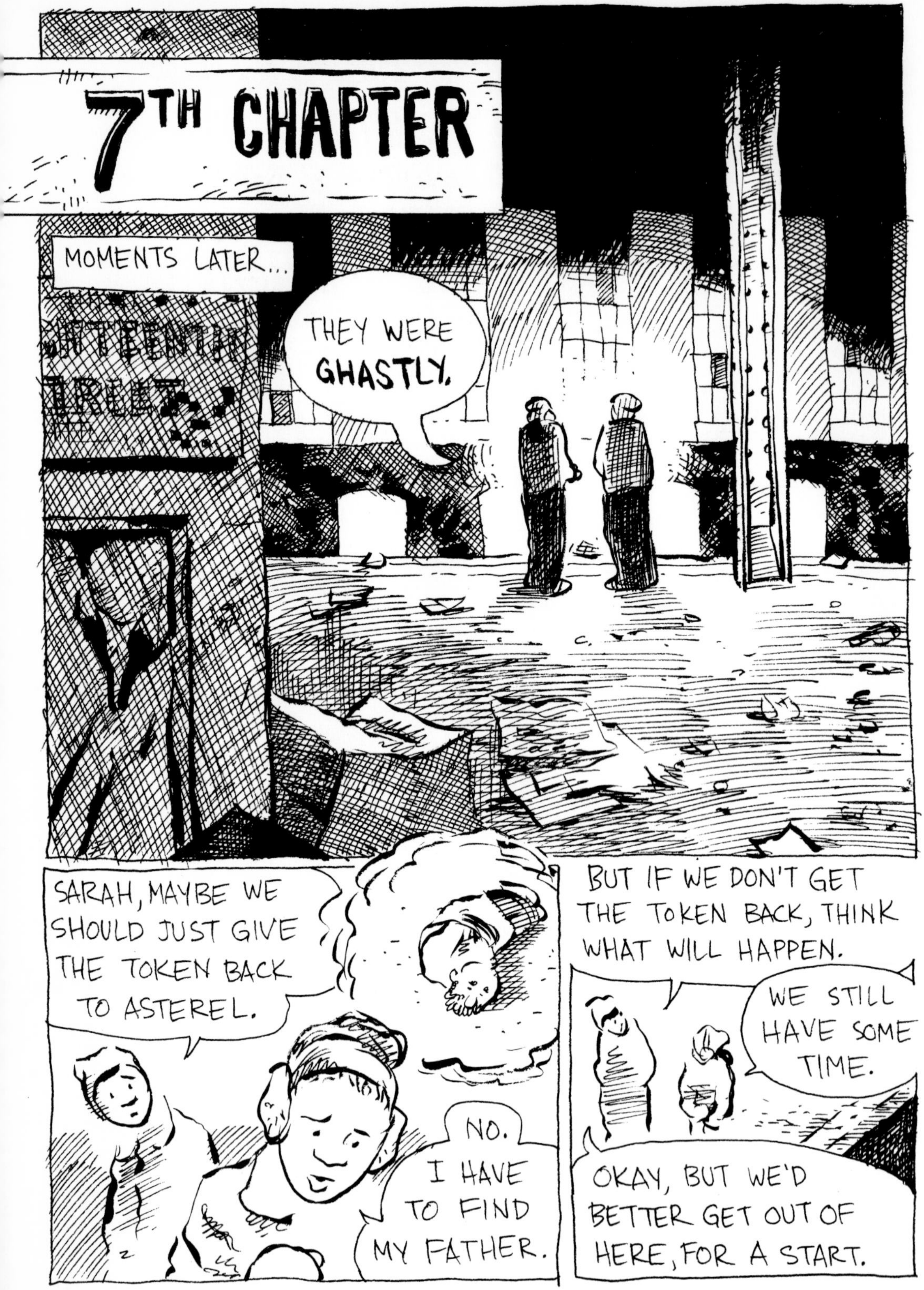
7TH CHAPTER
MOMENTS LATER...
THEY WERE GHASTLY.
SARAH, MAYBE WE SHOULD JUST GIVE THE TOKEN BACK TO ASTEREL.
NO. I HAVE TO FIND MY FATHER.
BUT IF WE DON'T GET THE TOKEN BACK, THINK WHAT WILL HAPPEN.
WE STILL HAVE SOME TIME.
OKAY, BUT WE'D BETTER GET OUT OF HERE, FOR A START.

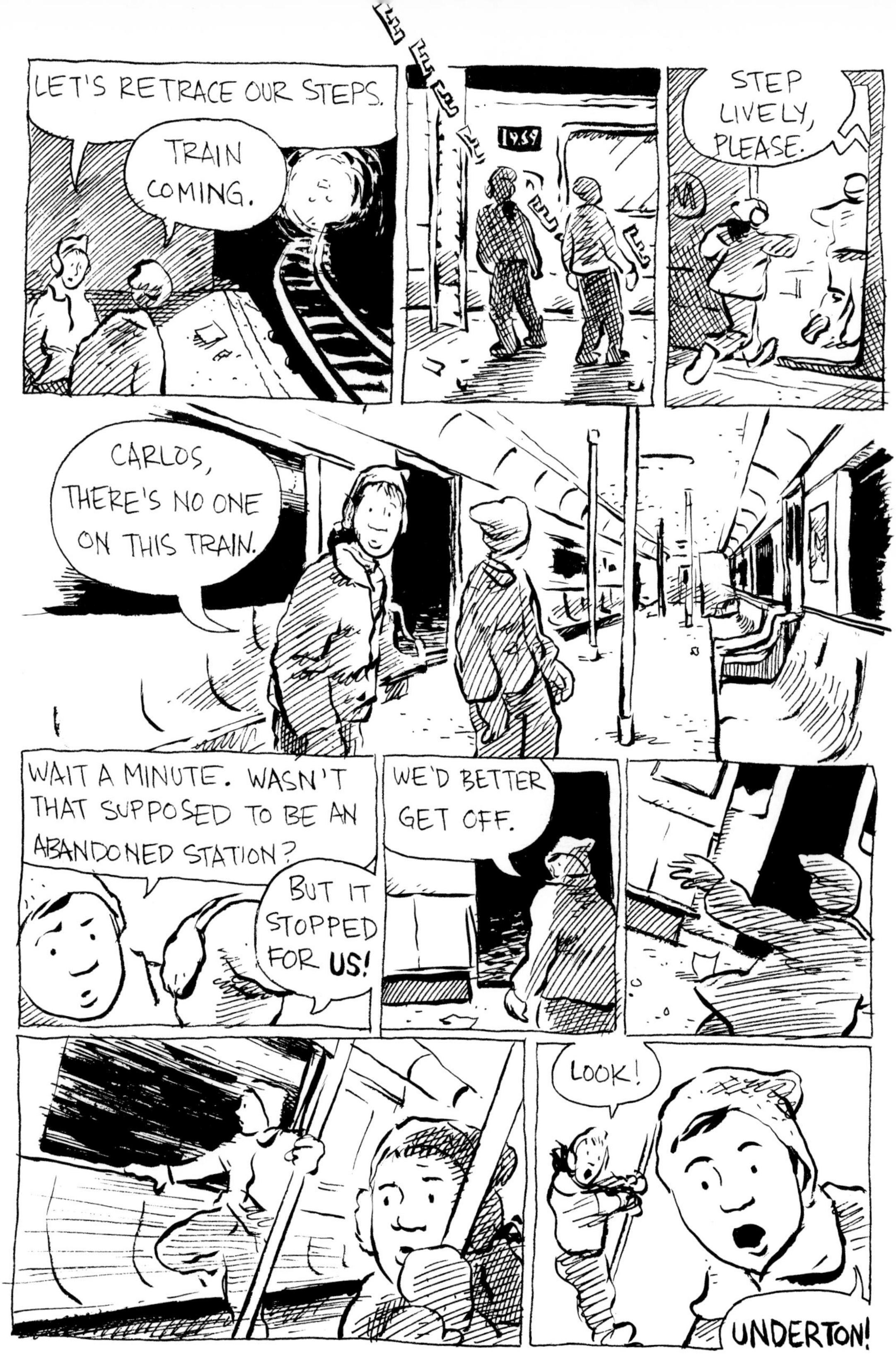
LET'S RETRACE OUR STEPS.
TRAIN COMING.
1959
STEP LIVELY, PLEASE.
CARLOS, THERE'S NO ONE ON THIS TRAIN.
WAIT A MINUTE. WASN'T THAT SUPPOSED TO BE AN ABANDONED STATION?
BUT IT STOPPED FOR US!
WE'D BETTER GET OFF.
LOOK!
UNDERTON!

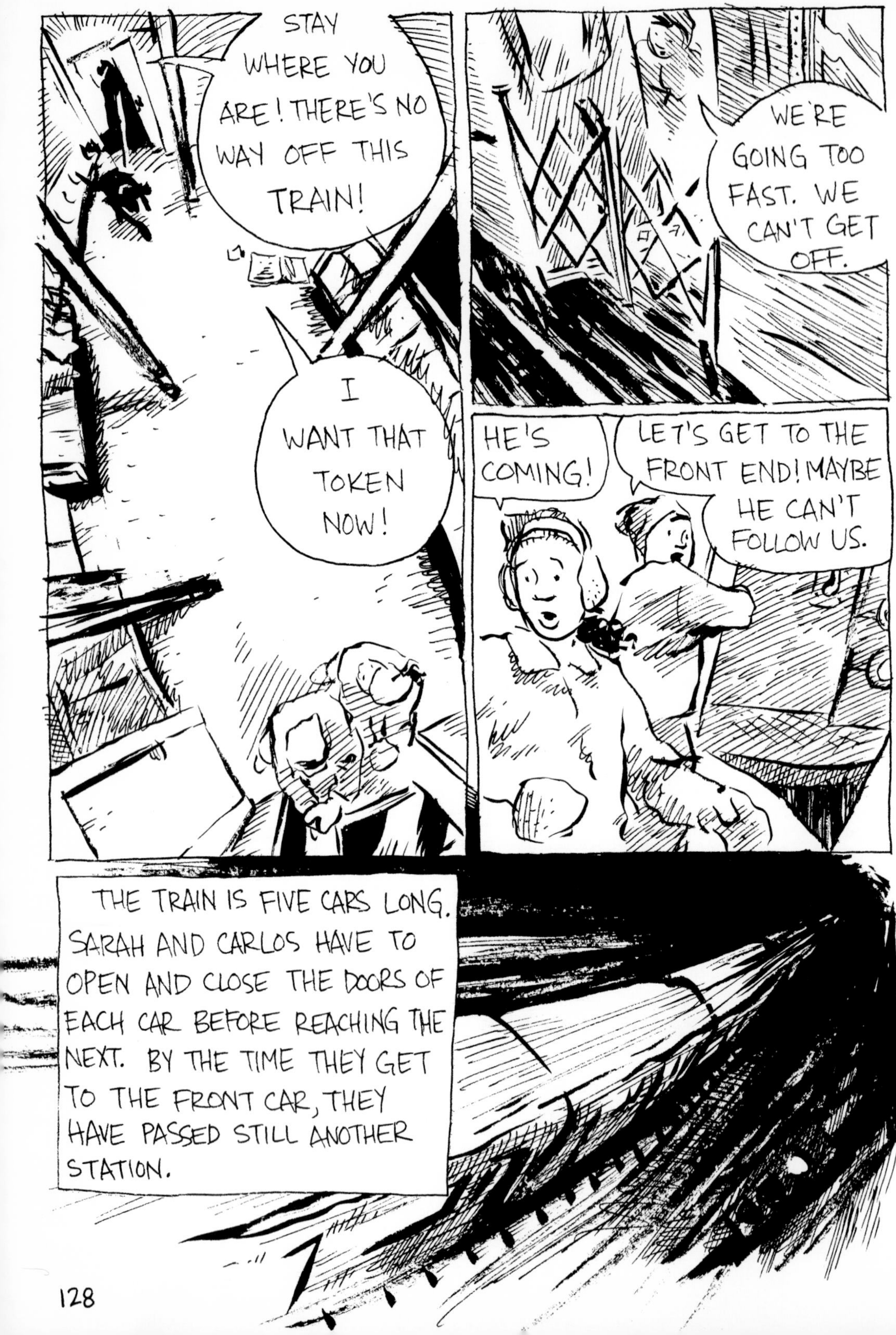

STAY WHERE YOU ARE! THERE'S NO WAY OFF THIS TRAIN!
I WANT THAT TOKEN NOW!
WE'RE GOING TOO FAST. WE CAN'T GET OFF.
HE'S COMING!
LET'S GET TO THE FRONT END! MAYBE HE CAN'T FOLLOW US.
THE TRAIN IS FIVE CARS LONG. SARAH AND CARLOS HAVE TO OPEN AND CLOSE THE DOORS OF EACH CAR BEFORE REACHING THE NEXT. BY THE TIME THEY GET TO THE FRONT CAR, THEY HAVE PASSED STILL ANOTHER STATION.

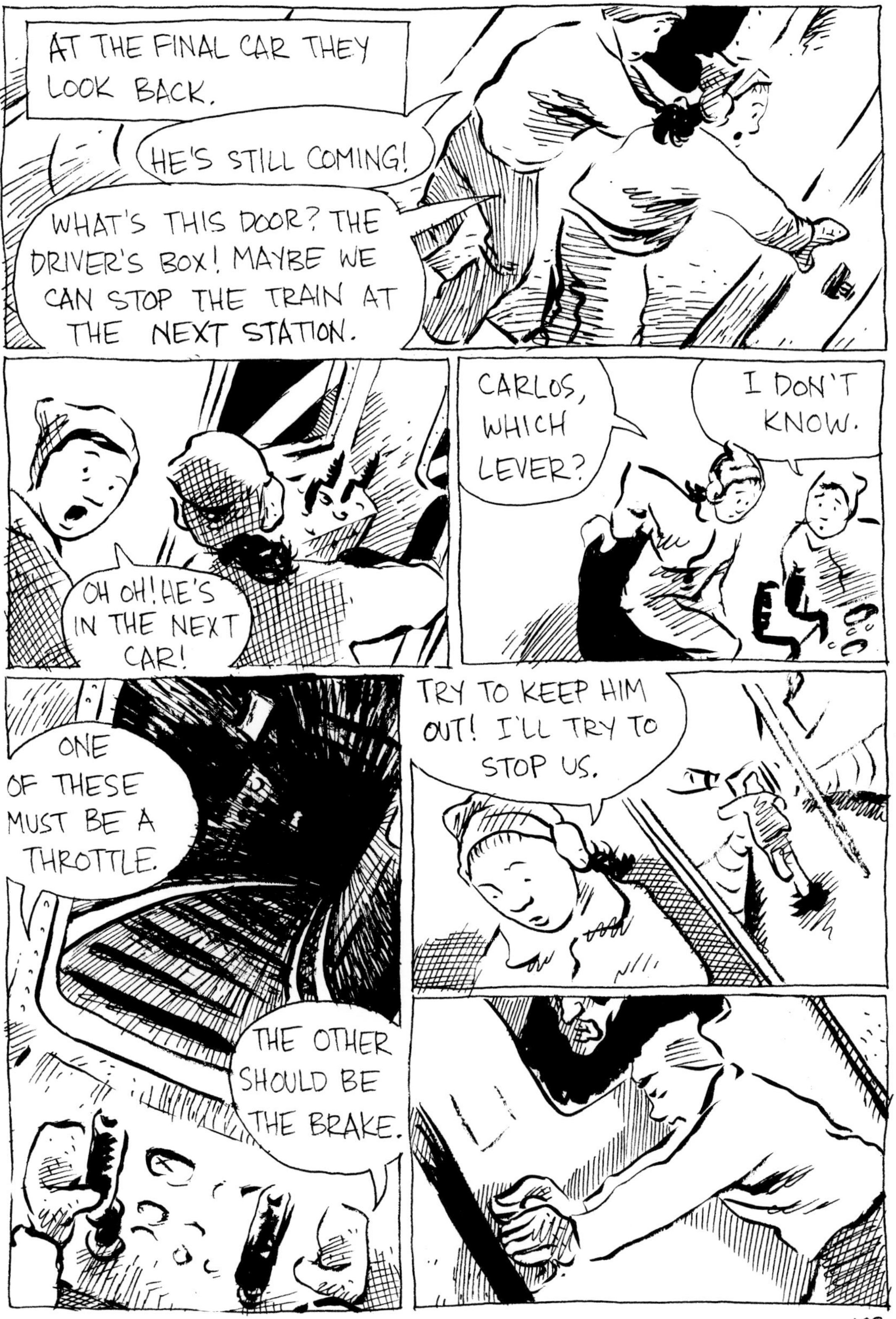

AT THE FINAL CAR THEY LOOK BACK.
HE'S STILL COMING!
WHAT'S THIS DOOR? THE DRIVER'S BOX! MAYBE WE CAN STOP THE TRAIN AT THE NEXT STATION.
OH OH! HE'S IN THE NEXT CAR!
CARLOS, WHICH LEVER?
I DON'T KNOW.
ONE OF THESE MUST BE A THROTTLE.
THE OTHER SHOULD BE THE BRAKE.
TRY TO KEEP HIM OUT! I'LL TRY TO STOP US.

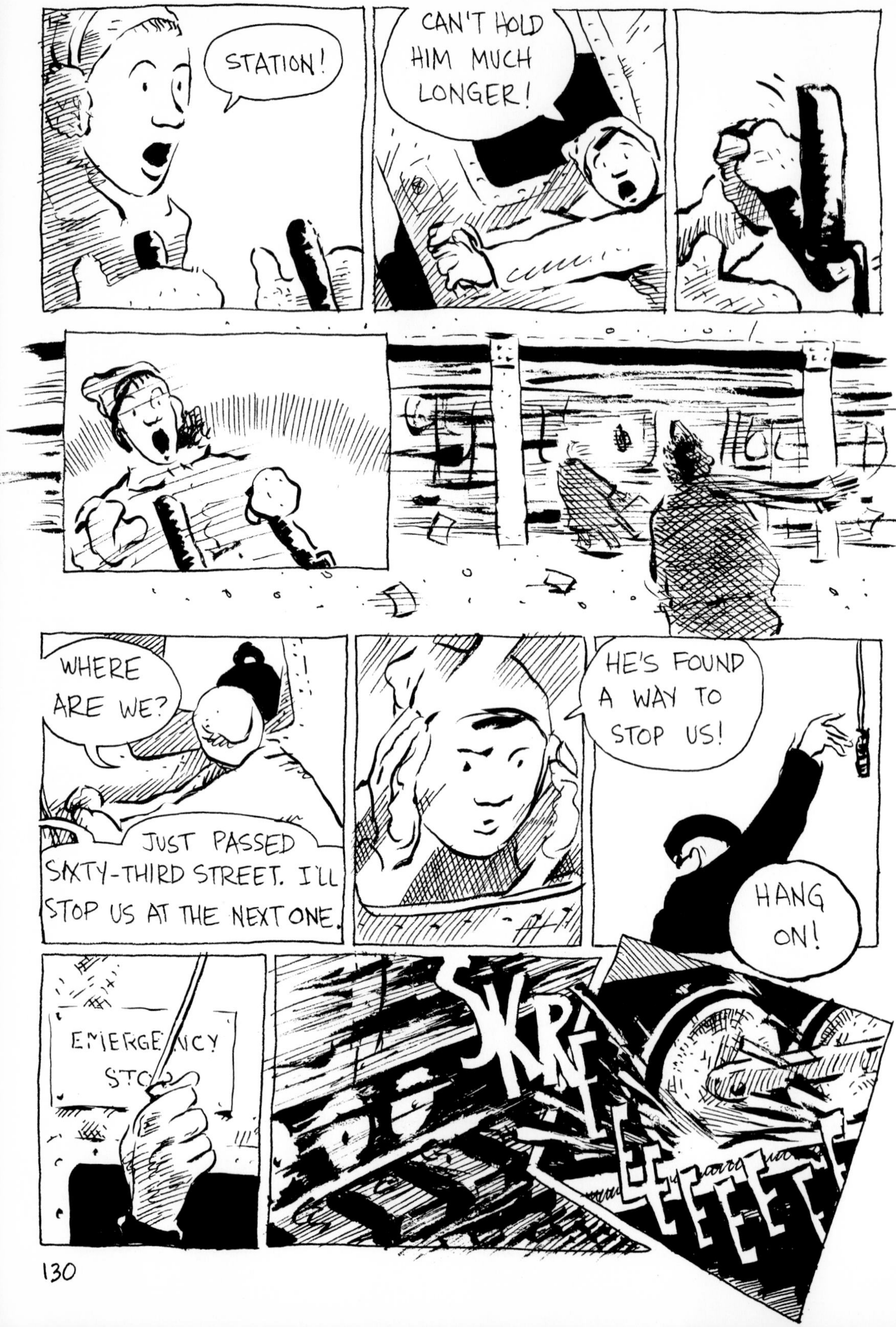
STATION!
CAN'T HOLD HIM MUCH LONGER!
WHERE ARE WE?
JUST PASSED SIXTY-THIRD STREET. I'LL STOP US AT THE NEXT ONE.
HE'S FOUND A WAY TO STOP US!
HANG ON!
EMERGENCY STOP
SKREEEEEEE

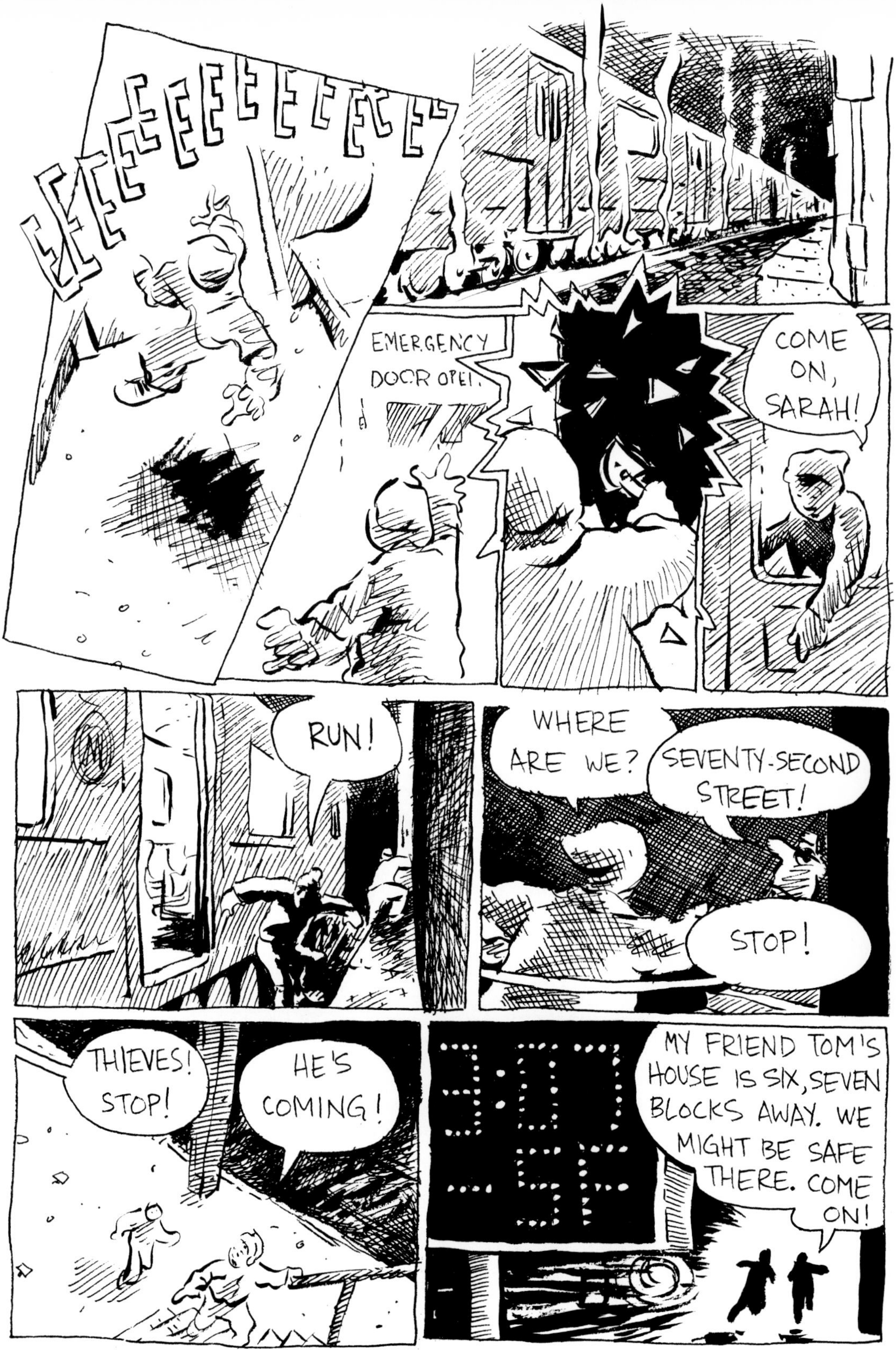
EMERGENCY DOOR OPE
COME ON, SARAH!
RUN!
WHERE ARE WE?
SEVENTY-SECOND STREET!
STOP!
THIEVES! STOP!
HE'S COMING!
MY FRIEND TOM'S HOUSE IS SIX, SEVEN BLOCKS AWAY. WE MIGHT BE SAFE THERE. COME ON!

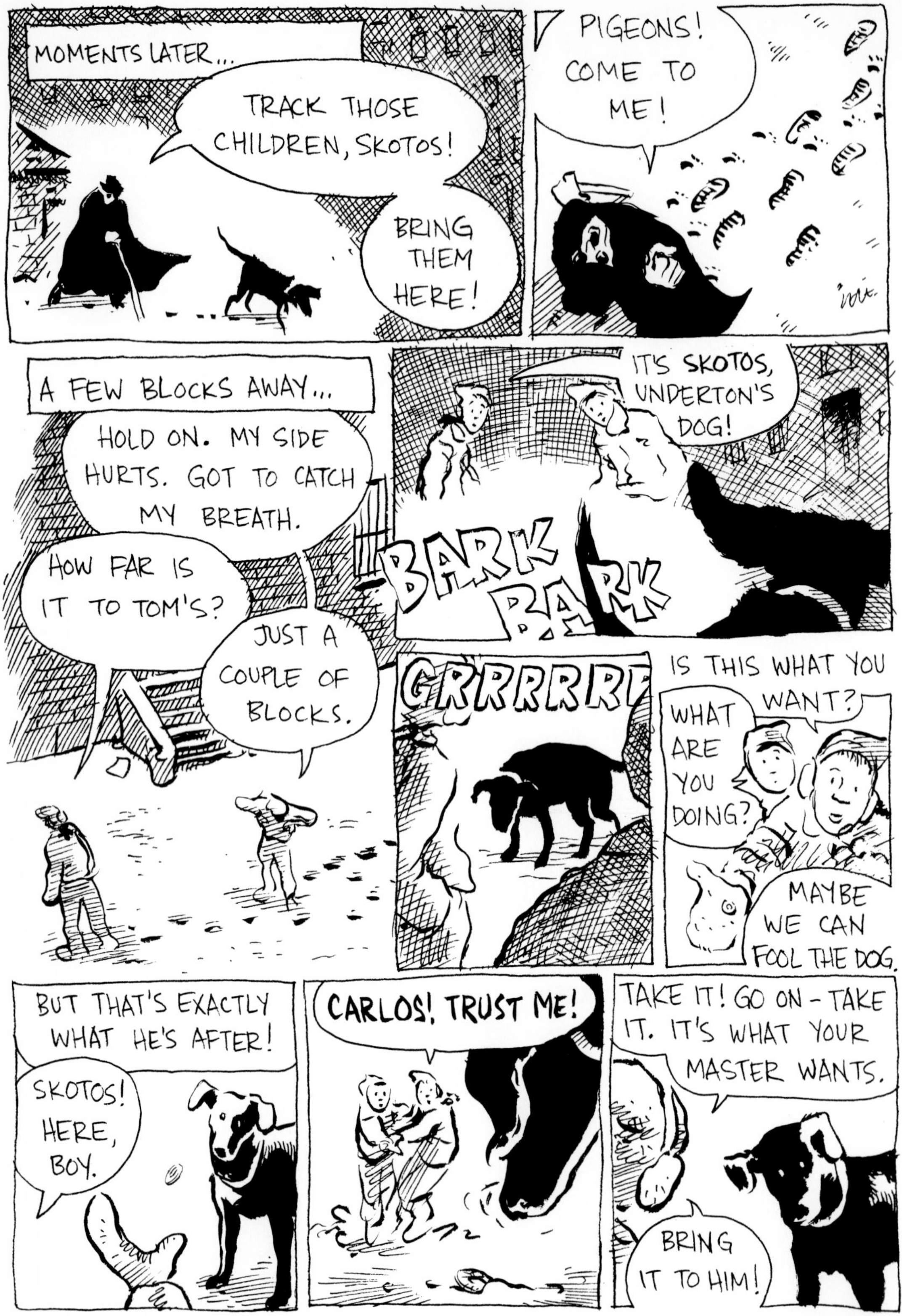
MOMENTS LATER...
TRACK THOSE CHILDREN, SKOTOS!
BRING THEM HERE!
PIGEONS! COME TO ME!
A FEW BLOCKS AWAY...
HOLD ON. MY SIDE HURTS. GOT TO CATCH MY BREATH.
HOW FAR IS IT TO TOM'S?
JUST A COUPLE OF BLOCKS.
IT'S SKOTOS, UNDERTON'S DOG!
BARK
BARK
GRRRRRR
IS THIS WHAT YOU WANT?
WHAT ARE YOU DOING?
MAYBE WE CAN FOOL THE DOG.
BUT THAT'S EXACTLY WHAT HE'S AFTER!
SKOTOS! HERE, BOY.
CARLOS! TRUST ME!
TAKE IT! GO ON - TAKE IT. IT'S WHAT YOUR MASTER WANTS.
BRING IT TO HIM!

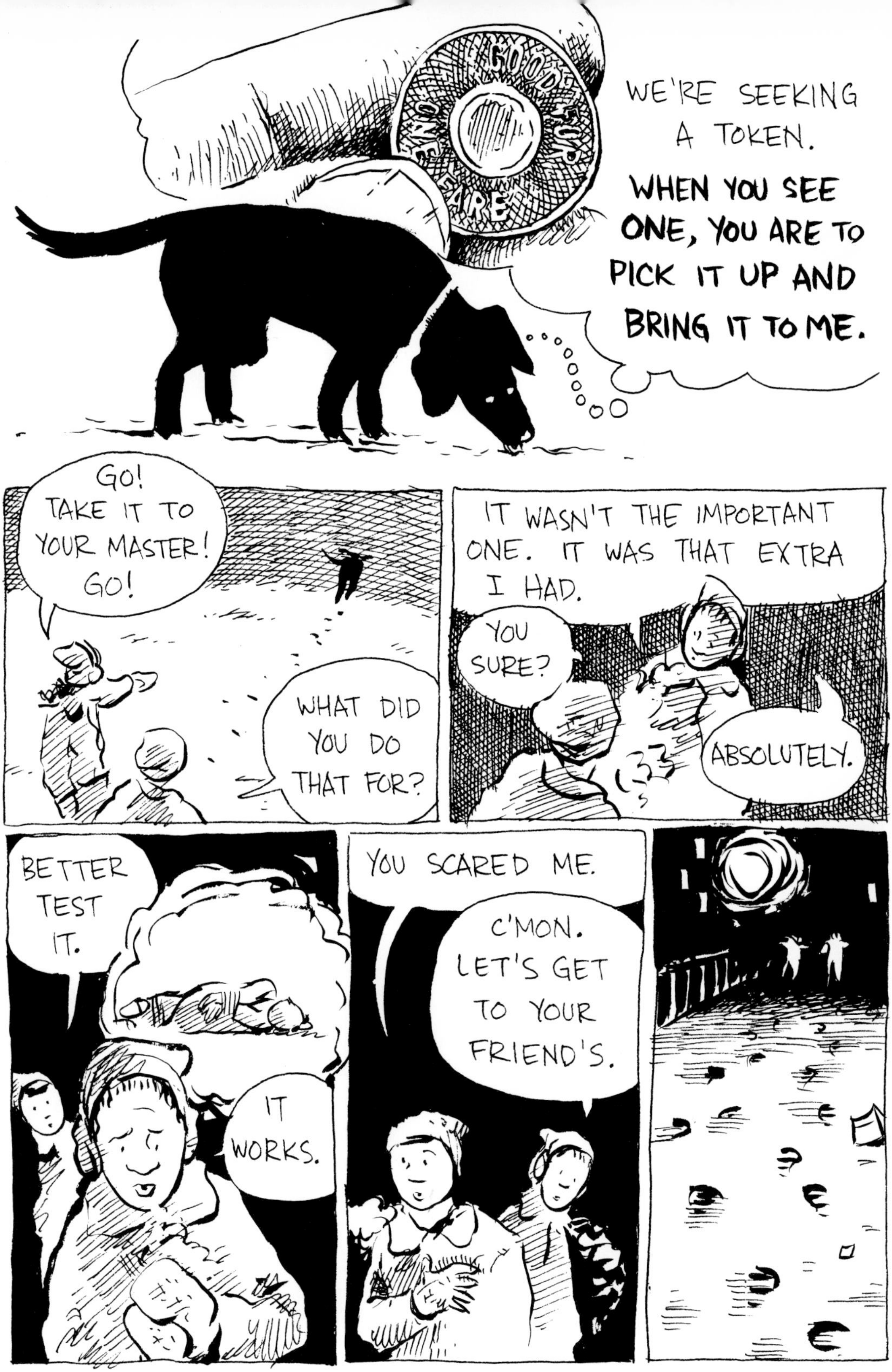
GOOD FOR ONE FARE
WE'RE SEEKING A TOKEN.
WHEN YOU SEE ONE, YOU ARE TO PICK IT UP AND BRING IT TO ME.
GO! TAKE IT TO YOUR MASTER! GO!
WHAT DID YOU DO THAT FOR?
IT WASN'T THE IMPORTANT ONE. IT WAS THAT EXTRA I HAD.
YOU SURE?
ABSOLUTELY.
BETTER TEST IT.
IT WORKS.
YOU SCARED ME.
C'MON. LET'S GET TO YOUR FRIEND'S.

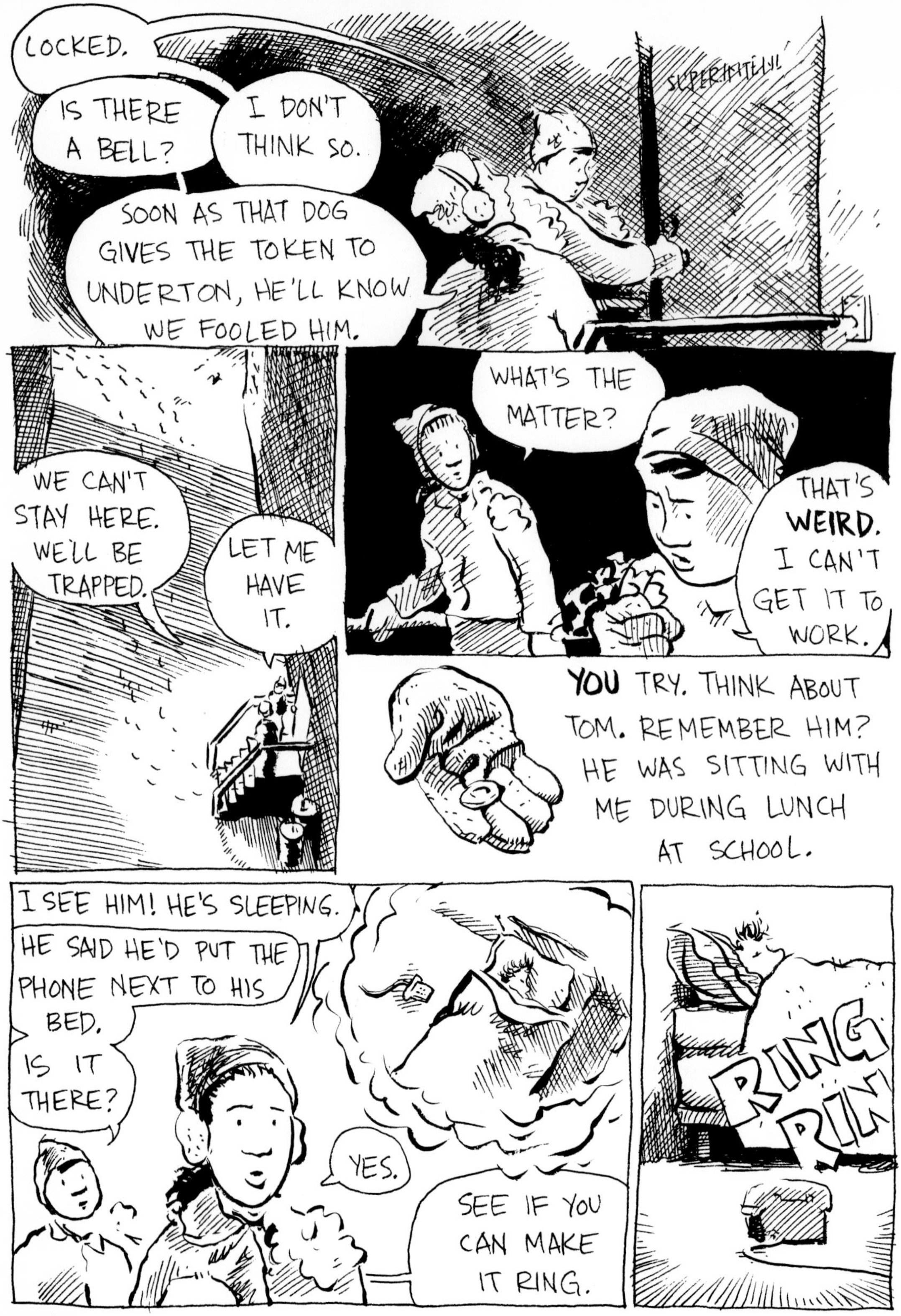
LOCKED.
IS THERE A BELL?
I DON'T THINK SO.
SOON AS THAT DOG GIVES THE TOKEN TO UNDERTON, HE'LL KNOW WE FOOLED HIM.
WE CAN'T STAY HERE. WE'LL BE TRAPPED.
LET ME HAVE IT.
WHAT'S THE MATTER?
THAT'S **WEIRD.** I CAN'T GET IT TO WORK.
YOU TRY. THINK ABOUT TOM. REMEMBER HIM? HE WAS SITTING WITH ME DURING LUNCH AT SCHOOL.
I SEE HIM! HE'S SLEEPING.
HE SAID HE'D PUT THE PHONE NEXT TO HIS BED.
IS IT THERE?
YES.
SEE IF YOU CAN MAKE IT RING.
RING
RIN

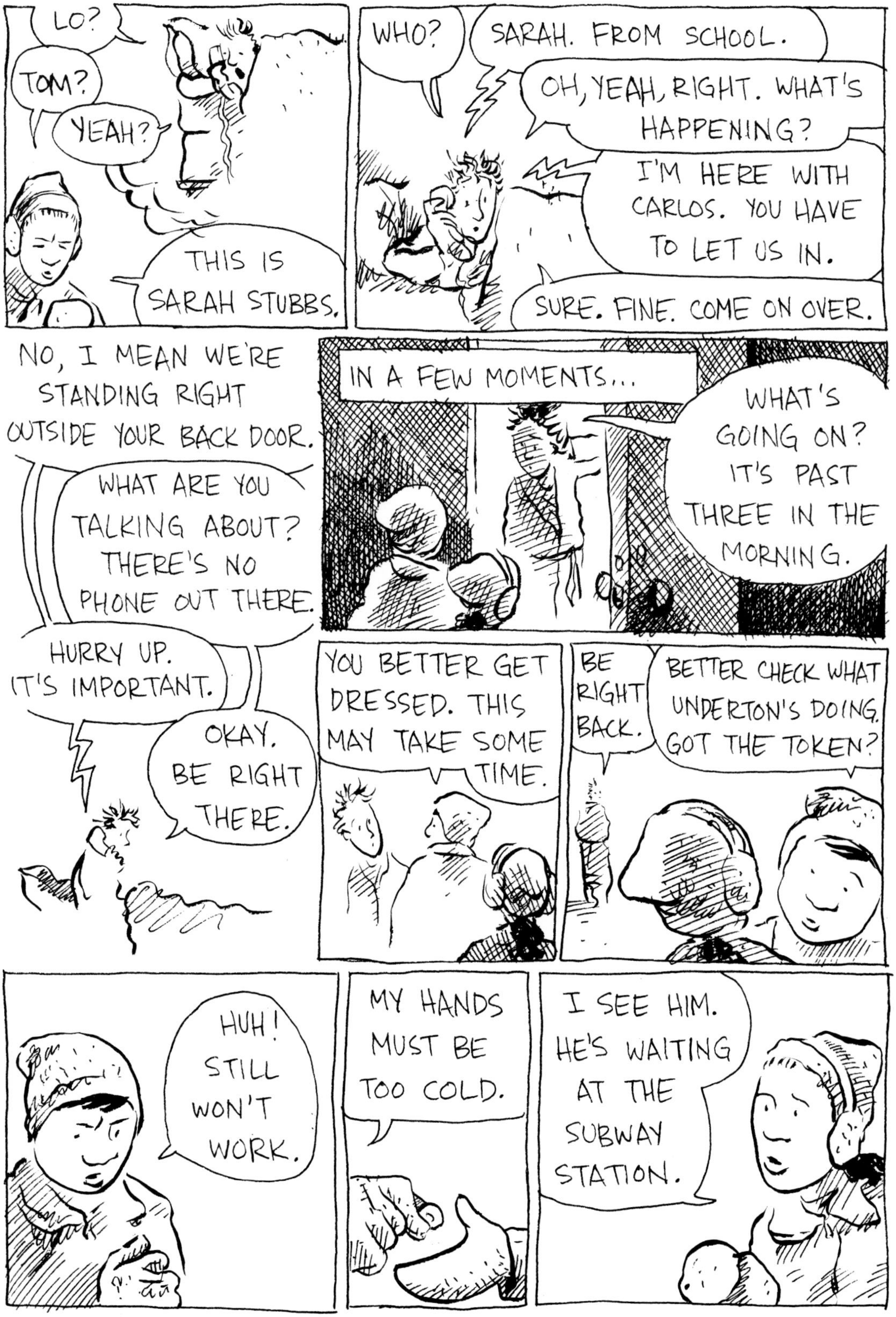
LO?
TOM?
YEAH?
THIS IS SARAH STUBBS.
WHO?
SARAH. FROM SCHOOL.
OH, YEAH, RIGHT. WHAT'S HAPPENING?
I'M HERE WITH CARLOS. YOU HAVE TO LET US IN.
SURE. FINE. COME ON OVER.
NO, I MEAN WE'RE STANDING RIGHT OUTSIDE YOUR BACK DOOR.
WHAT ARE YOU TALKING ABOUT? THERE'S NO PHONE OUT THERE.
HURRY UP. IT'S IMPORTANT.
OKAY. BE RIGHT THERE.
IN A FEW MOMENTS...
WHAT'S GOING ON? IT'S PAST THREE IN THE MORNING.
YOU BETTER GET DRESSED. THIS MAY TAKE SOME TIME.
BE RIGHT BACK.
BETTER CHECK WHAT UNDERTON'S DOING. GOT THE TOKEN?
HUH! STILL WON'T WORK.
MY HANDS MUST BE TOO COLD.
I SEE HIM. HE'S WAITING AT THE SUBWAY STATION.

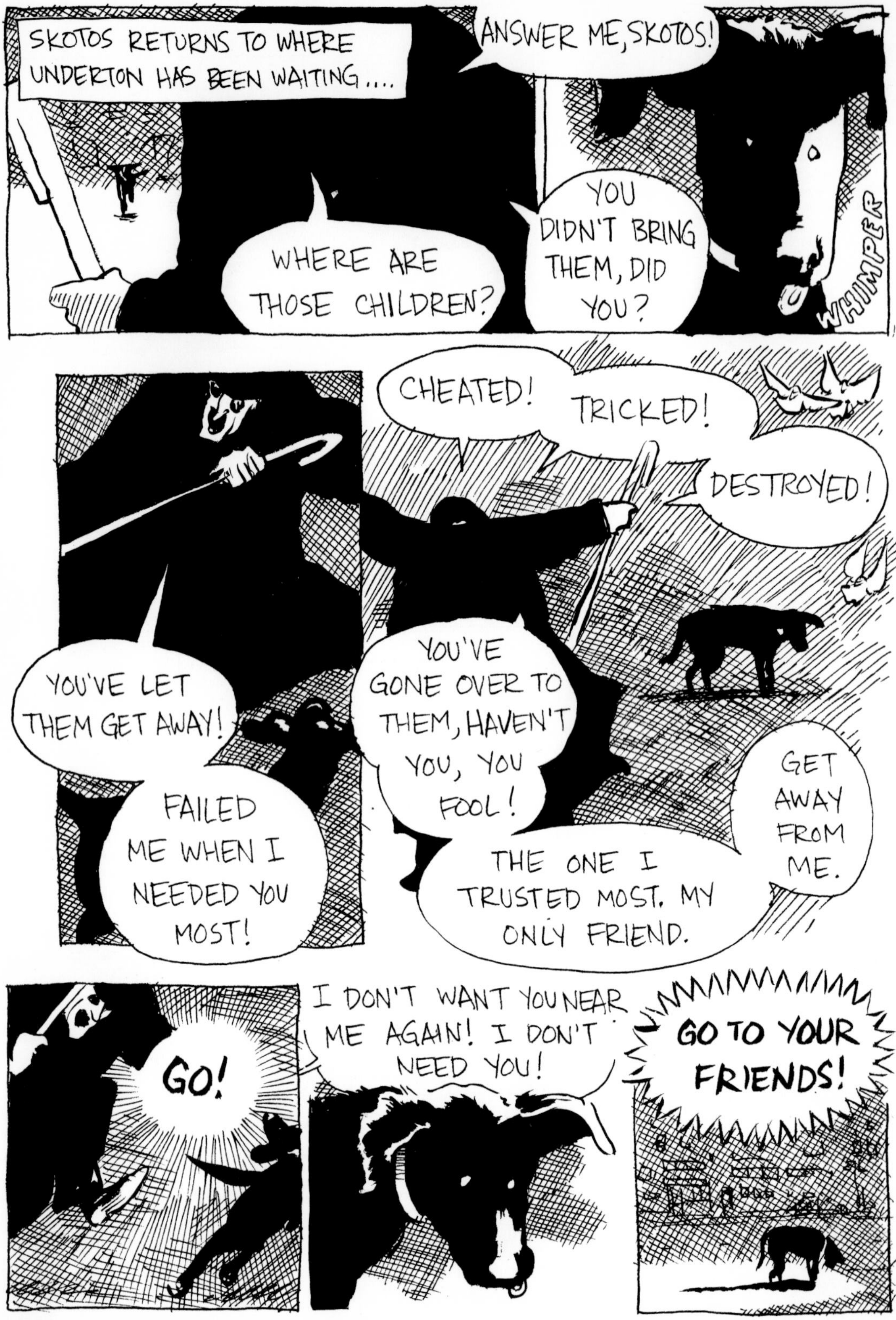
SKOTOS RETURNS TO WHERE UNDERTON HAS BEEN WAITING....
ANSWER ME, SKOTOS!
WHERE ARE THOSE CHILDREN?
YOU DIDN'T BRING THEM, DID YOU?
WHIMPER
CHEATED!
TRICKED!
DESTROYED!
YOU'VE LET THEM GET AWAY!
YOU'VE GONE OVER TO THEM, HAVEN'T YOU, YOU FOOL!
FAILED ME WHEN I NEEDED YOU MOST!
THE ONE I TRUSTED MOST. MY ONLY FRIEND.
GET AWAY FROM ME.
GO!
I DON'T WANT YOU NEAR ME AGAIN! I DON'T NEED YOU!
GO TO YOUR FRIENDS!

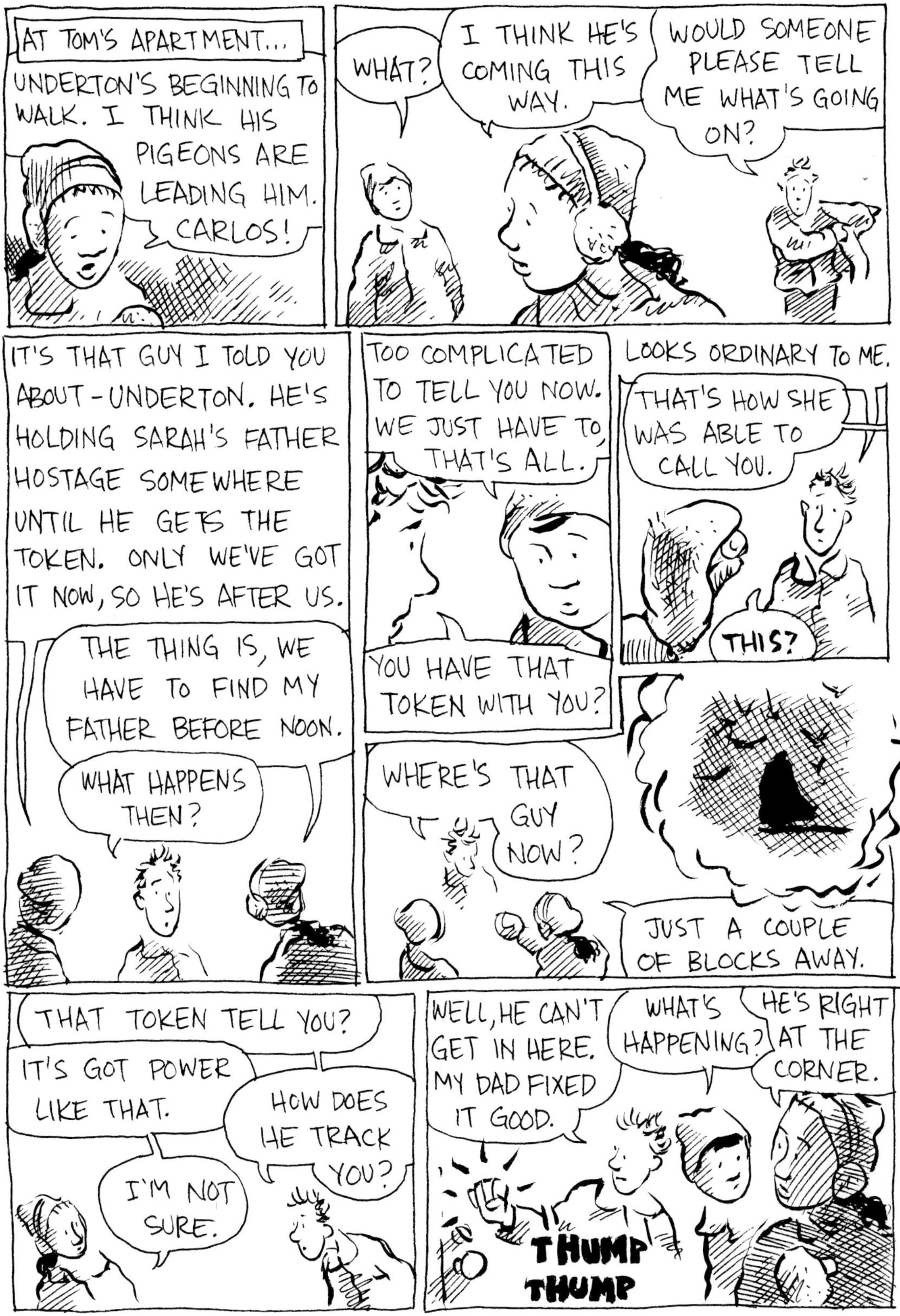
AT TOM'S APARTMENT...
UNDERTON'S BEGINNING TO WALK. I THINK HIS PIGEONS ARE LEADING HIM. CARLOS!
WHAT?
I THINK HE'S COMING THIS WAY.
WOULD SOMEONE PLEASE TELL ME WHAT'S GOING ON?
IT'S THAT GUY I TOLD YOU ABOUT-UNDERTON. HE'S HOLDING SARAH'S FATHER HOSTAGE SOMEWHERE UNTIL HE GETS THE TOKEN. ONLY WE'VE GOT IT NOW, SO HE'S AFTER US.
THE THING IS, WE HAVE TO FIND MY FATHER BEFORE NOON.
WHAT HAPPENS THEN?
TOO COMPLICATED TO TELL YOU NOW. WE JUST HAVE TO, THAT'S ALL.
YOU HAVE THAT TOKEN WITH YOU?
THIS?
LOOKS ORDINARY TO ME.
THAT'S HOW SHE WAS ABLE TO CALL YOU.
WHERE'S THAT GUY NOW?
JUST A COUPLE OF BLOCKS AWAY.
HOW DOES HE TRACK YOU?
I'M NOT SURE.
THAT TOKEN TELL YOU?
IT'S GOT POWER LIKE THAT.
WELL, HE CAN'T GET IN HERE. MY DAD FIXED IT GOOD.
WHAT'S HAPPENING?
HE'S RIGHT AT THE CORNER.
THUMP
THUMP

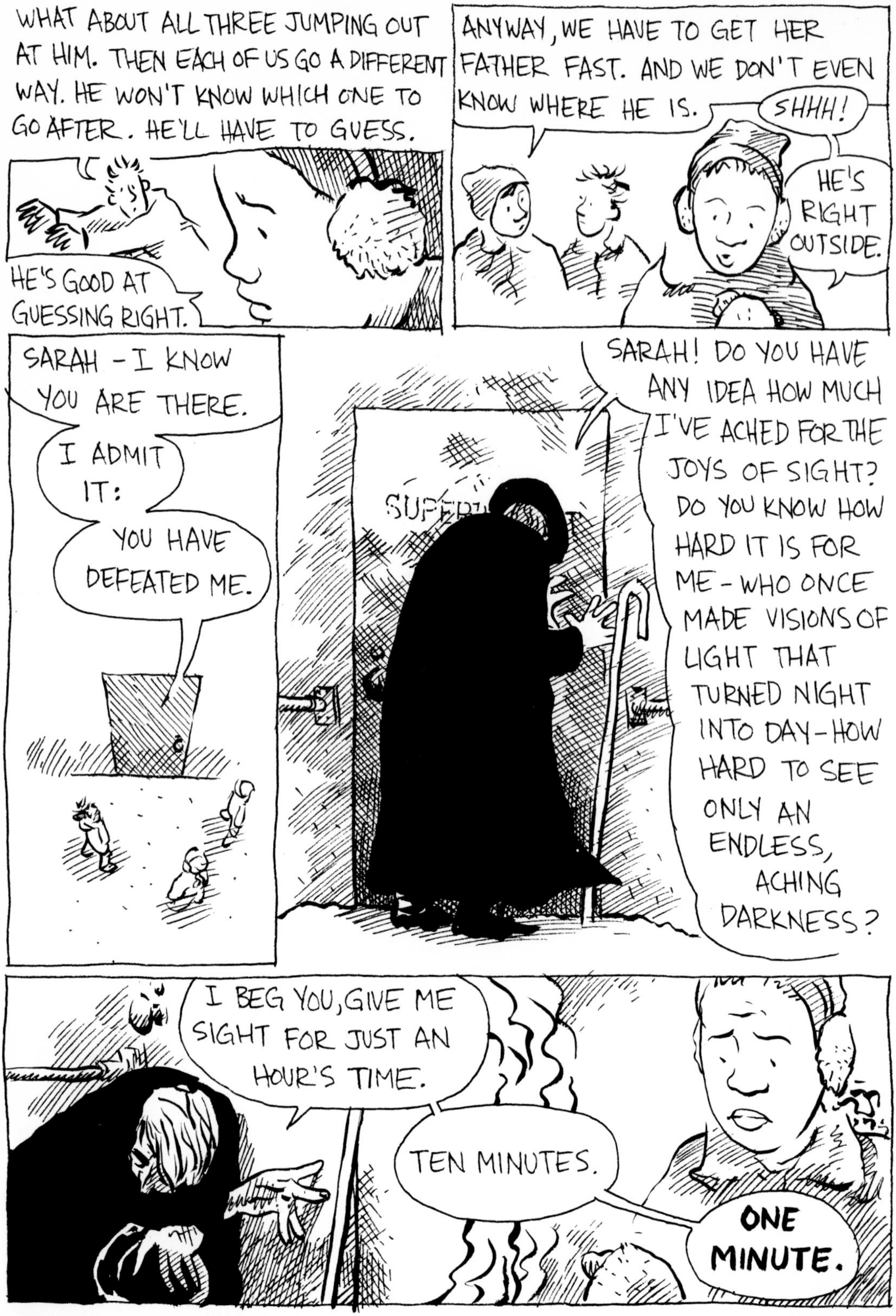
WHAT ABOUT ALL THREE JUMPING OUT AT HIM. THEN EACH OF US GO A DIFFERENT WAY. HE WON'T KNOW WHICH ONE TO GO AFTER. HE'LL HAVE TO GUESS.
HE'S GOOD AT GUESSING RIGHT.
ANYWAY, WE HAVE TO GET HER FATHER FAST. AND WE DON'T EVEN KNOW WHERE HE IS.
SHHH!
HE'S RIGHT OUTSIDE.
SARAH - I KNOW YOU ARE THERE.
I ADMIT IT:
YOU HAVE DEFEATED ME.
SARAH! DO YOU HAVE ANY IDEA HOW MUCH I'VE ACHED FOR THE JOYS OF SIGHT? DO YOU KNOW HOW HARD IT IS FOR ME - WHO ONCE MADE VISIONS OF LIGHT THAT TURNED NIGHT INTO DAY - HOW HARD TO SEE ONLY AN ENDLESS, ACHING DARKNESS?
I BEG YOU, GIVE ME SIGHT FOR JUST AN HOUR'S TIME.
TEN MINUTES.
ONE MINUTE.

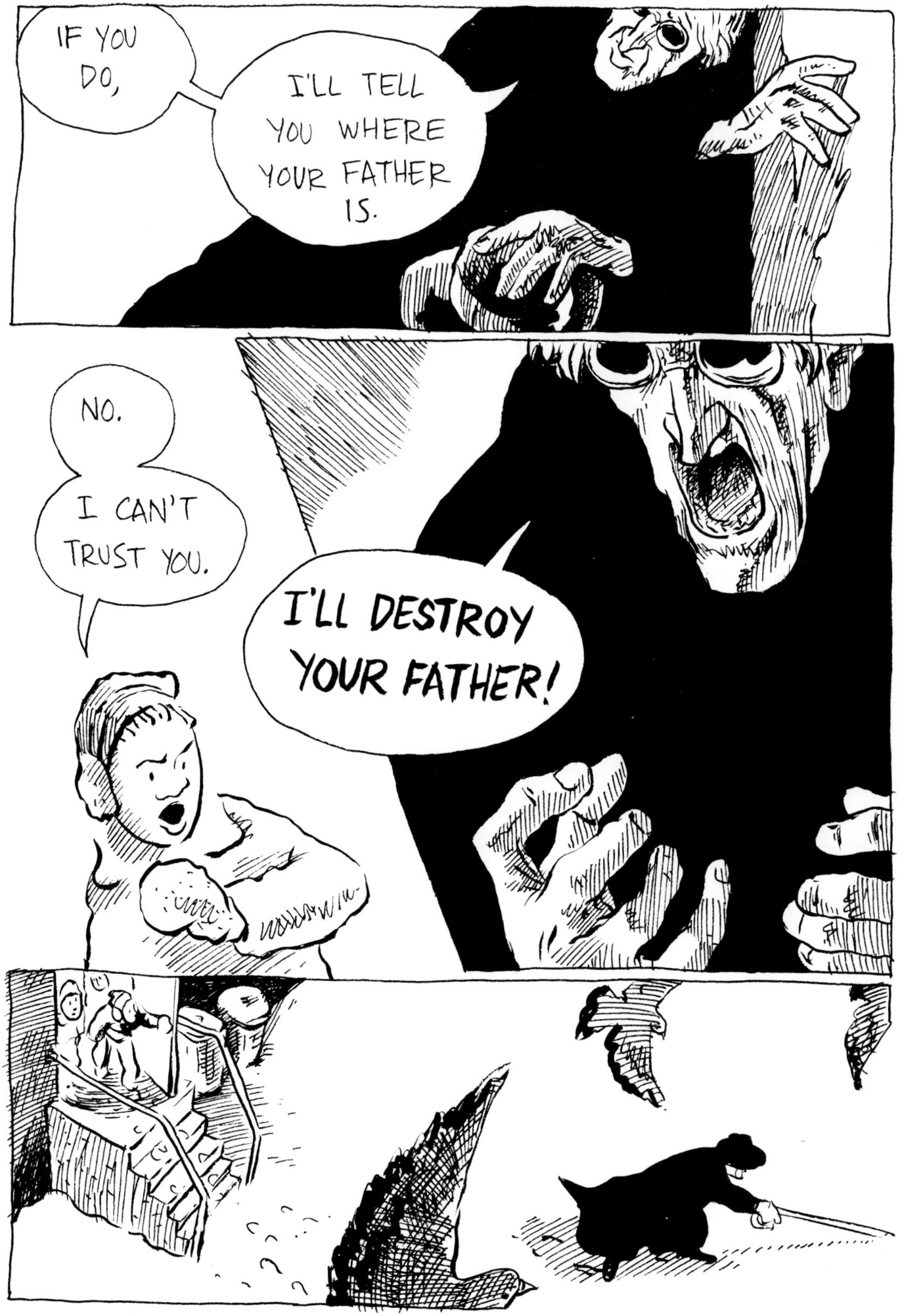
IF YOU DO,
I'LL TELL YOU WHERE YOUR FATHER IS.
NO.
I CAN'T TRUST YOU.
I'LL DESTROY YOUR FATHER!

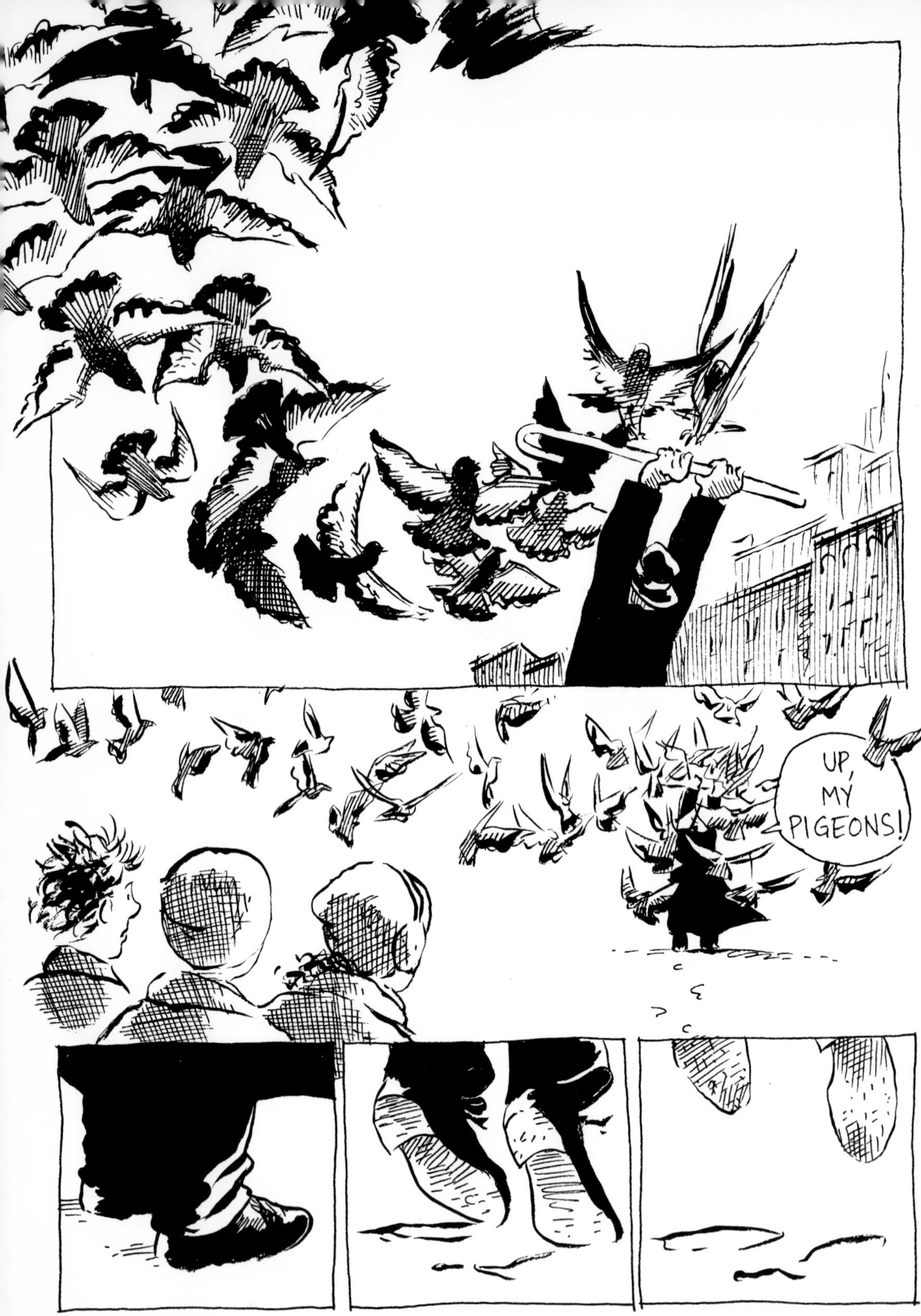
UP, MY PIGEONS!

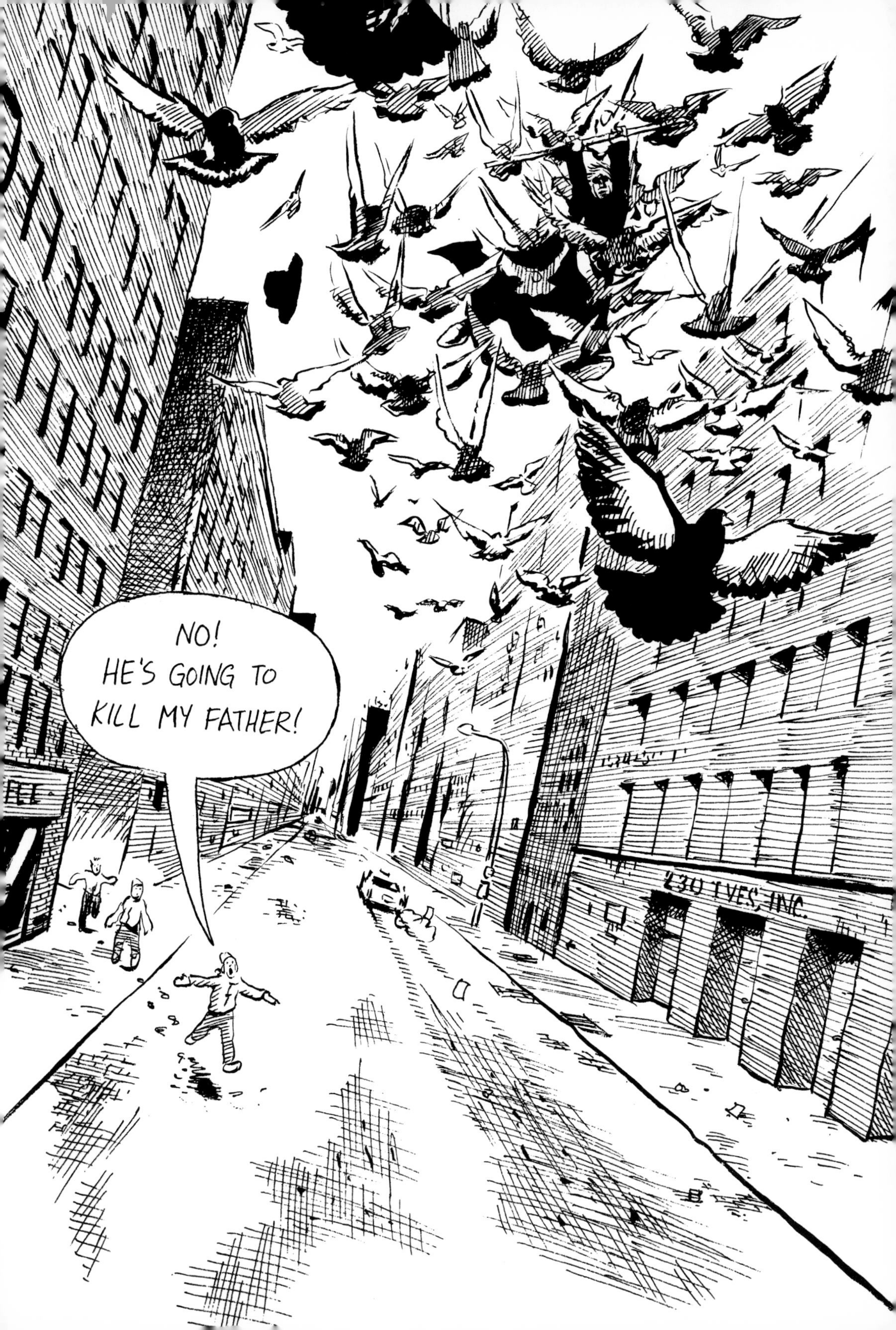
NO!
HE'S GOING TO
KILL MY FATHER!
230 IVES, INC.

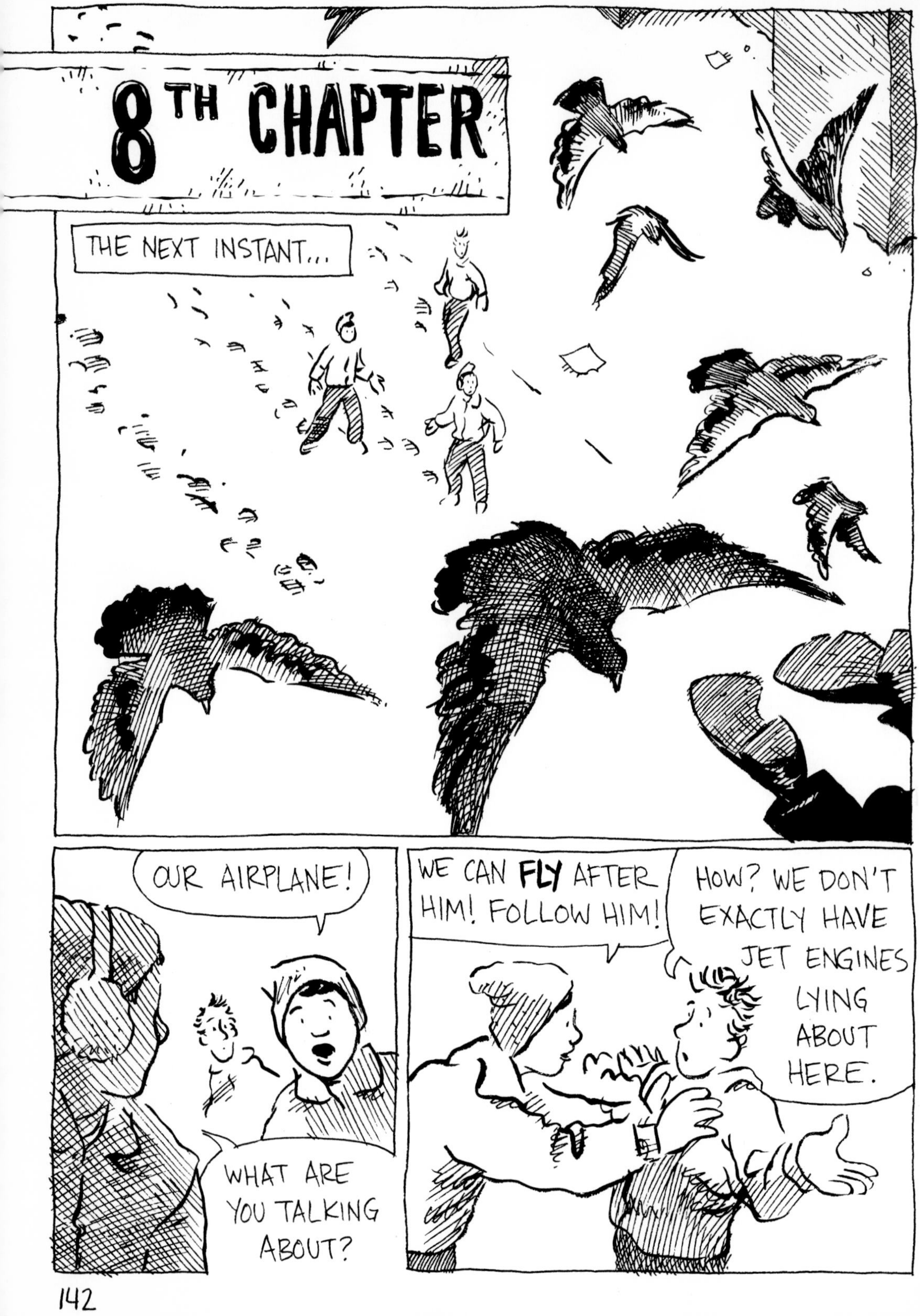
8TH CHAPTER
THE NEXT INSTANT...
OUR AIRPLANE!
WHAT ARE YOU TALKING ABOUT?
WE CAN **FLY** AFTER HIM! FOLLOW HIM!
HOW? WE DON'T EXACTLY HAVE JET ENGINES LYING ABOUT HERE.

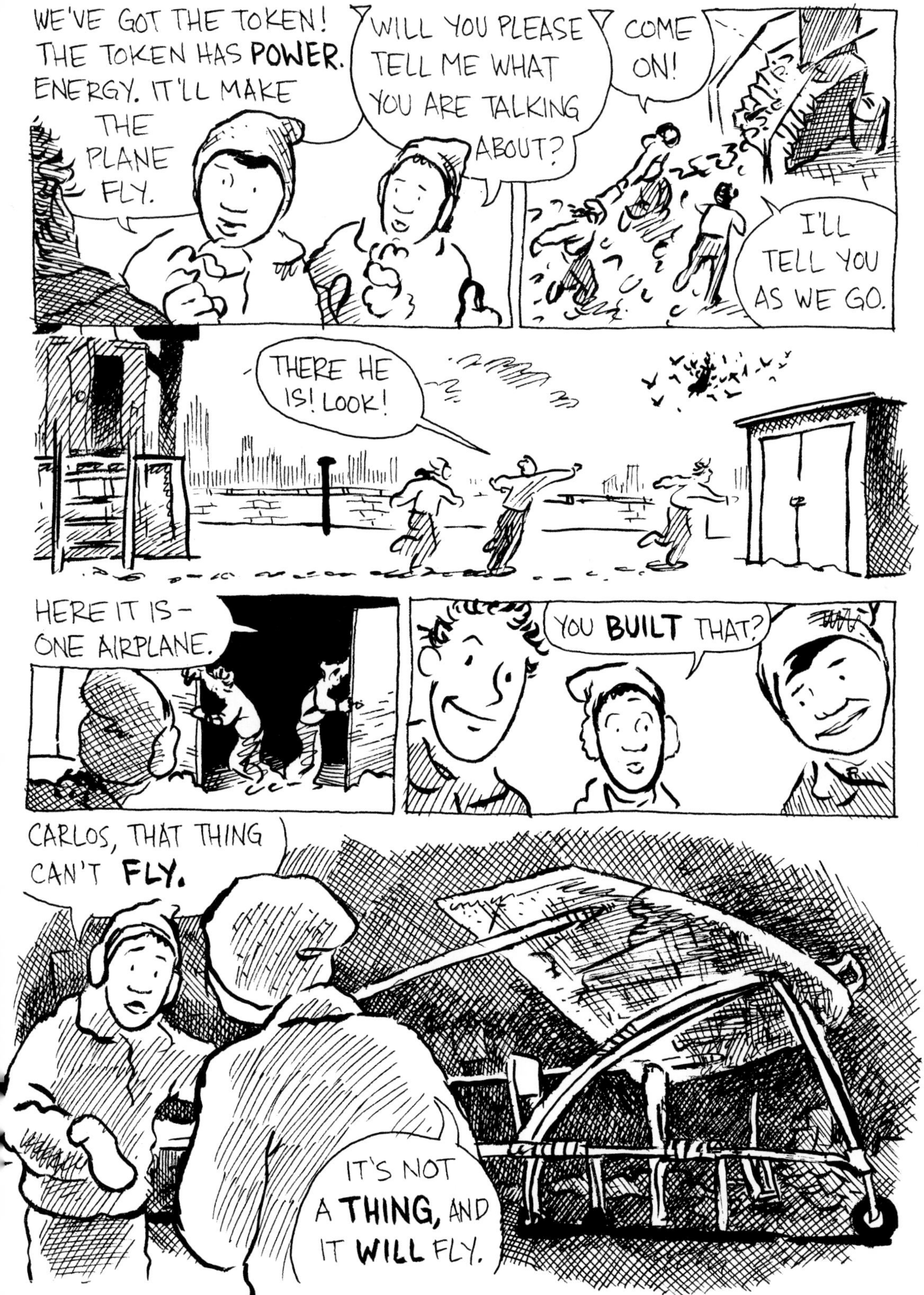
WE'VE GOT THE TOKEN! THE TOKEN HAS **POWER.** ENERGY. IT'LL MAKE THE PLANE FLY.
WILL YOU PLEASE TELL ME WHAT YOU ARE TALKING ABOUT?
COME ON!
I'LL TELL YOU AS WE GO.
THERE HE IS! LOOK!
HERE IT IS— ONE AIRPLANE.
YOU **BUILT** THAT?
CARLOS, THAT THING CAN'T **FLY.**
IT'S NOT A **THING,** AND IT **WILL** FLY.

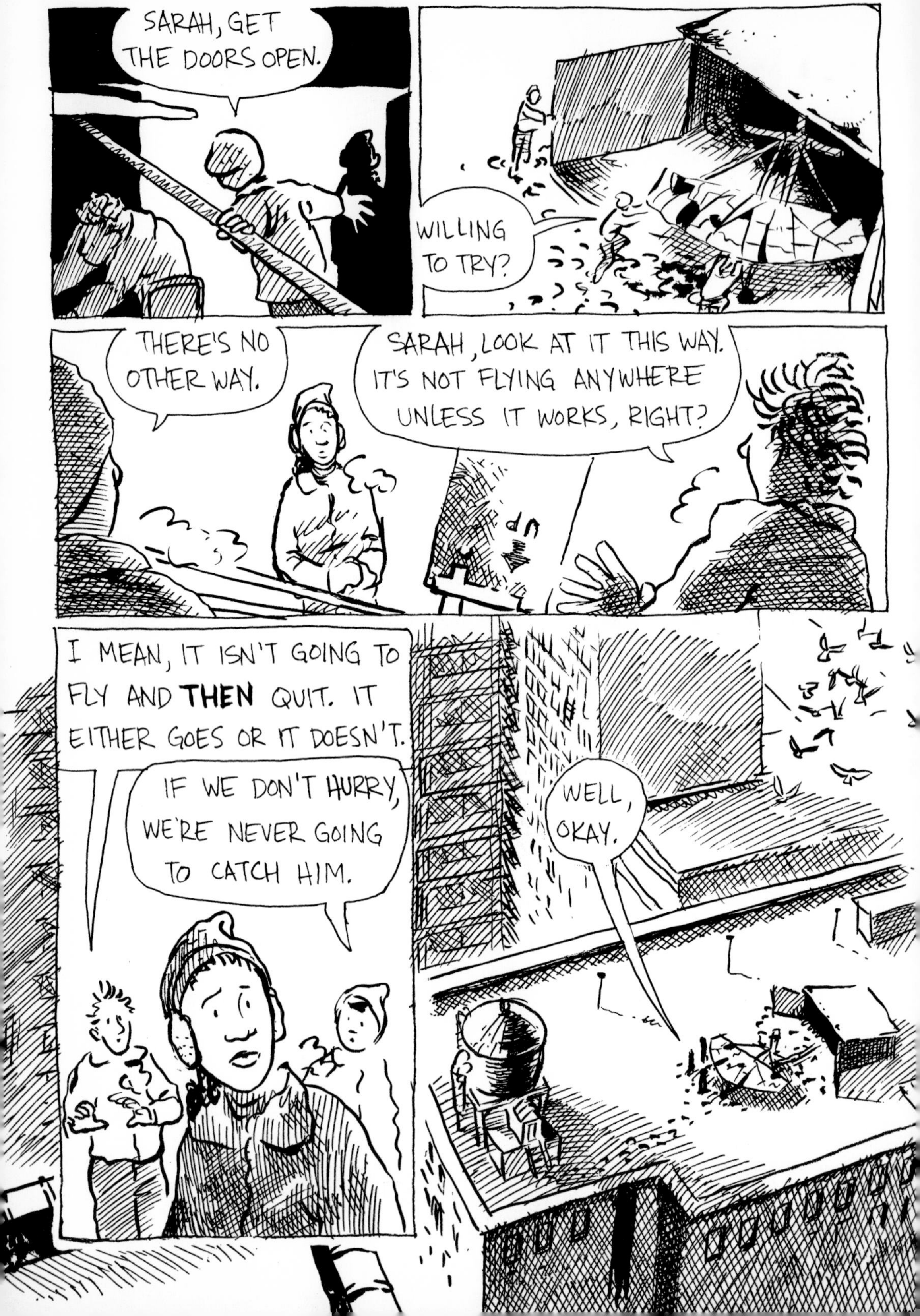

SARAH, GET THE DOORS OPEN.
WILLING TO TRY?
THERE'S NO OTHER WAY.
SARAH, LOOK AT IT THIS WAY. IT'S NOT FLYING ANYWHERE UNLESS IT WORKS, RIGHT?
I MEAN, IT ISN'T GOING TO FLY AND **THEN** QUIT. IT EITHER GOES OR IT DOESN'T.
IF WE DON'T HURRY, WE'RE NEVER GOING TO CATCH HIM.
WELL, OKAY.

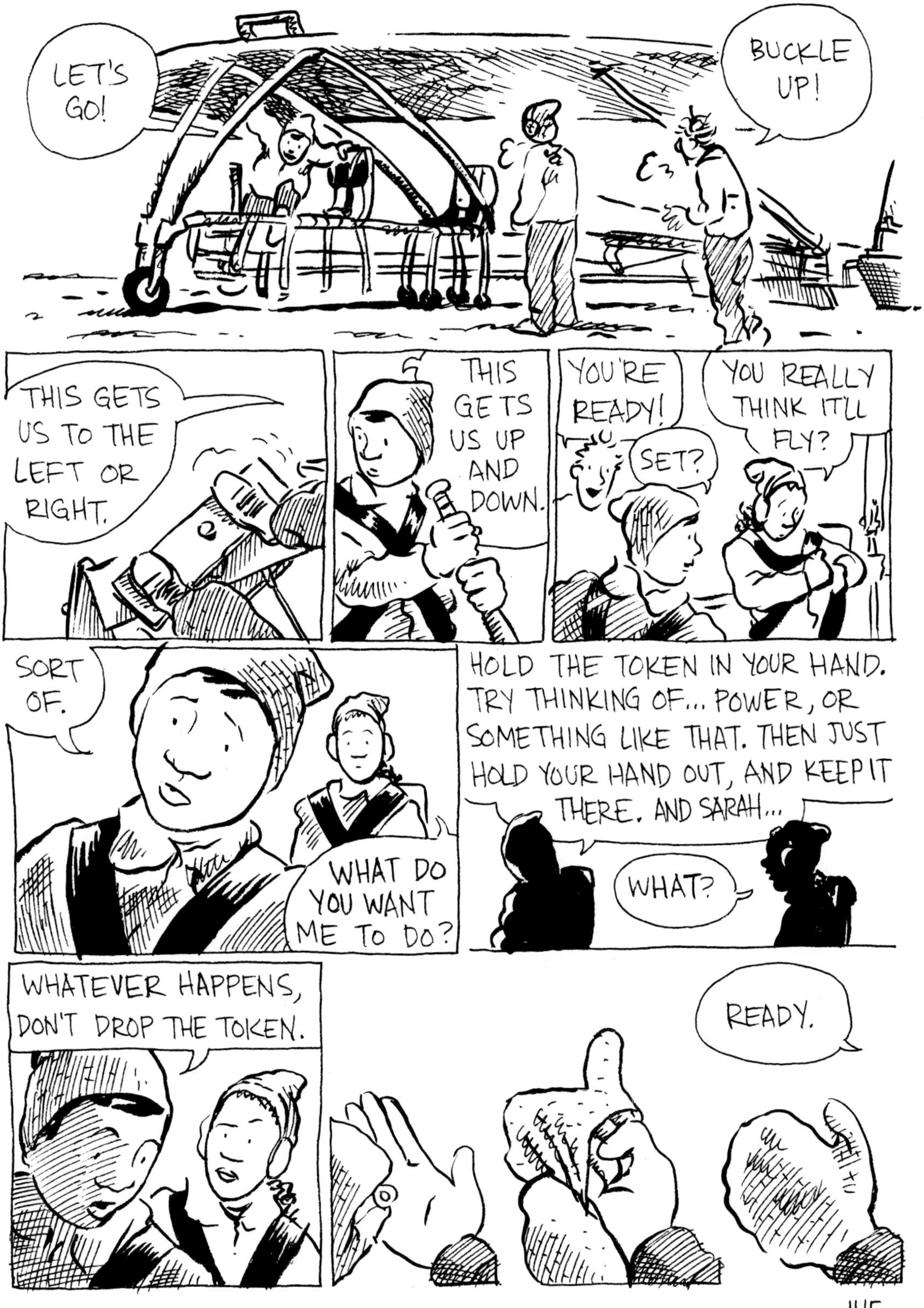
LET'S GO!
BUCKLE UP!
THIS GETS US TO THE LEFT OR RIGHT.
THIS GETS US UP AND DOWN.
YOU'RE READY!
SET?
YOU REALLY THINK IT'LL FLY?
SORT OF.
WHAT DO YOU WANT ME TO DO?
HOLD THE TOKEN IN YOUR HAND. TRY THINKING OF... POWER, OR SOMETHING LIKE THAT. THEN JUST HOLD YOUR HAND OUT, AND KEEP IT THERE. AND SARAH...
WHAT?
WHATEVER HAPPENS, DON'T DROP THE TOKEN.
READY.

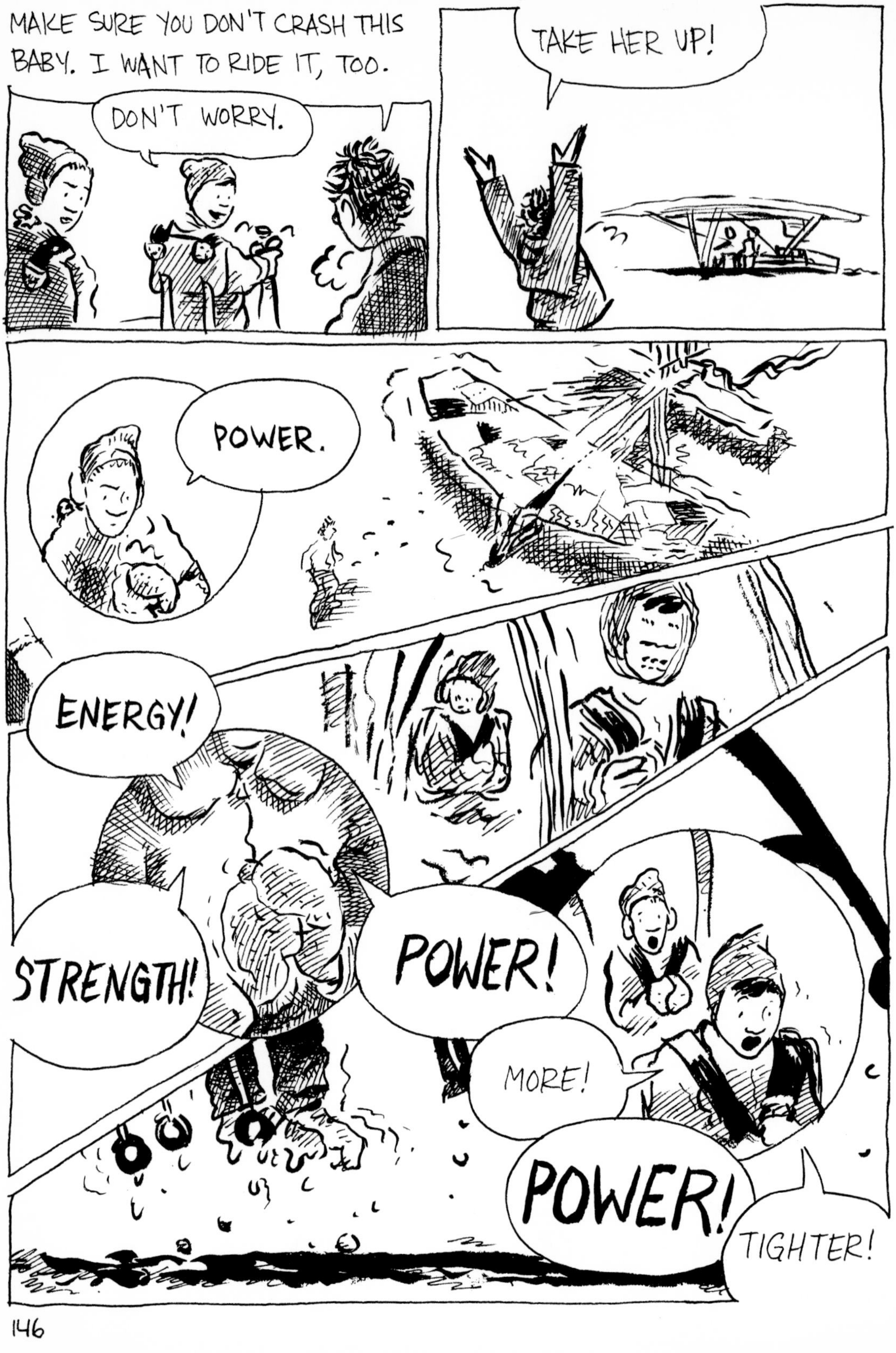
MAKE SURE YOU DON'T CRASH THIS BABY. I WANT TO RIDE IT, TOO.
DON'T WORRY.
TAKE HER UP!
POWER.
ENERGY!
STRENGTH!
POWER!
MORE!
POWER!
TIGHTER!

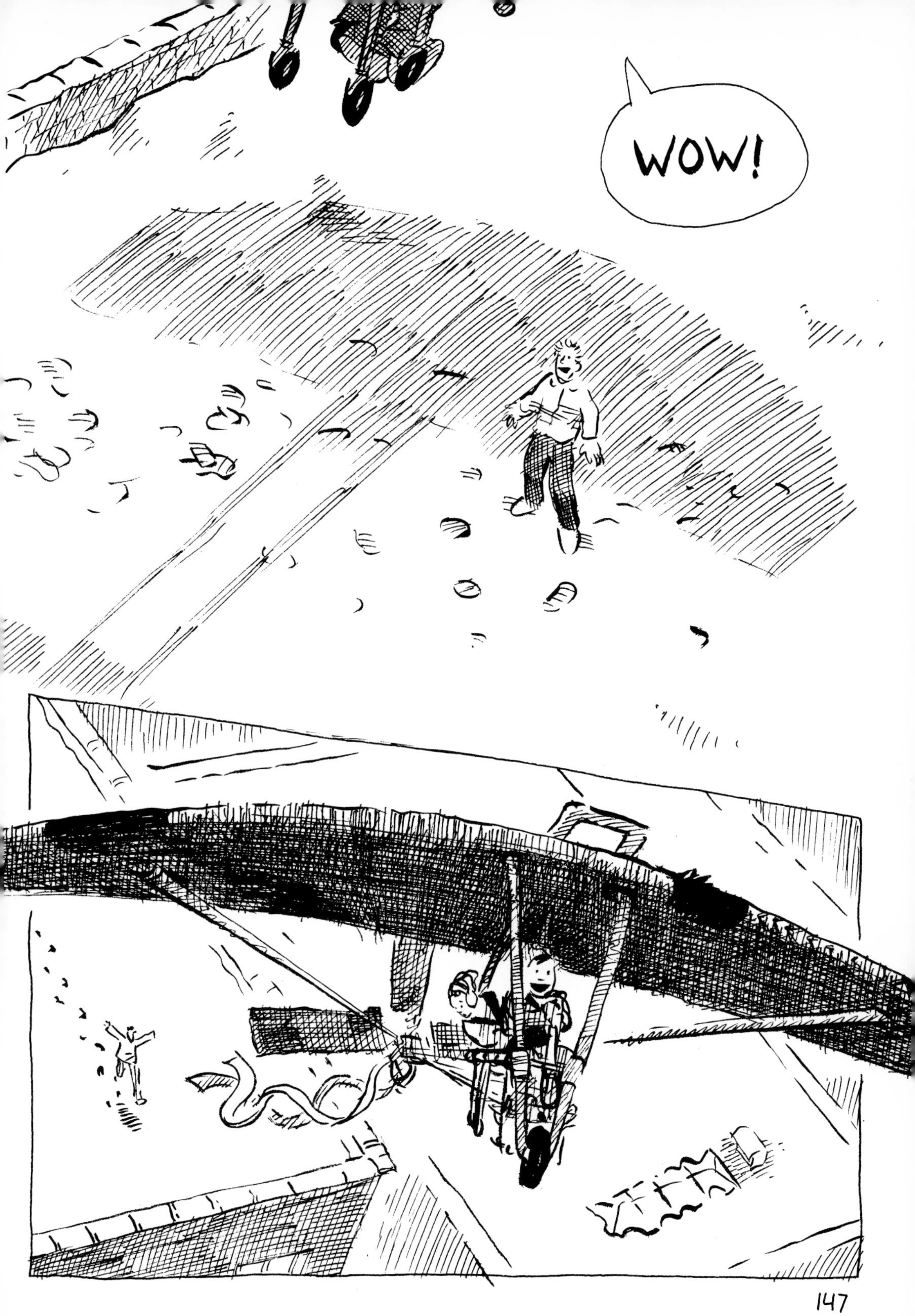
WOW!

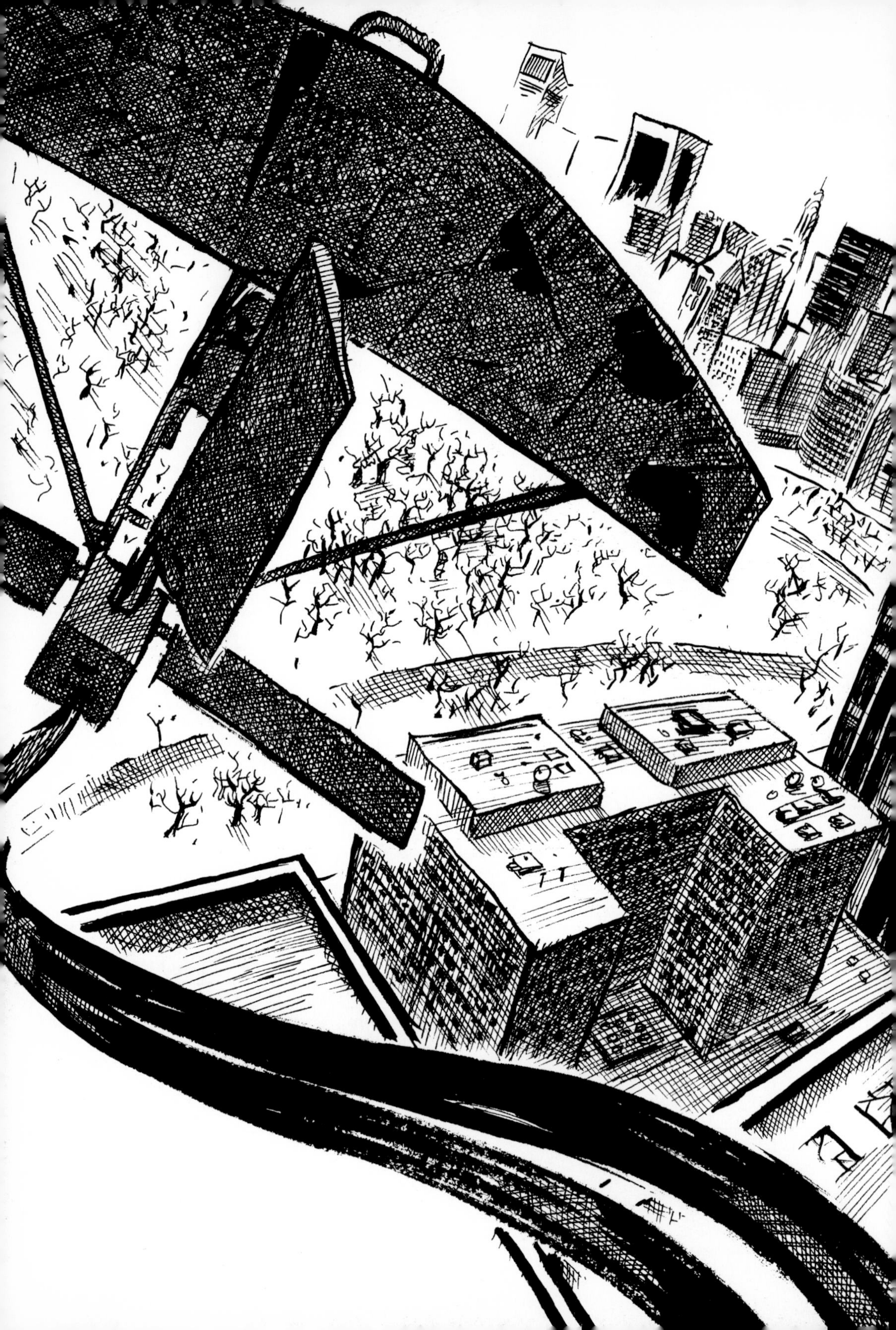

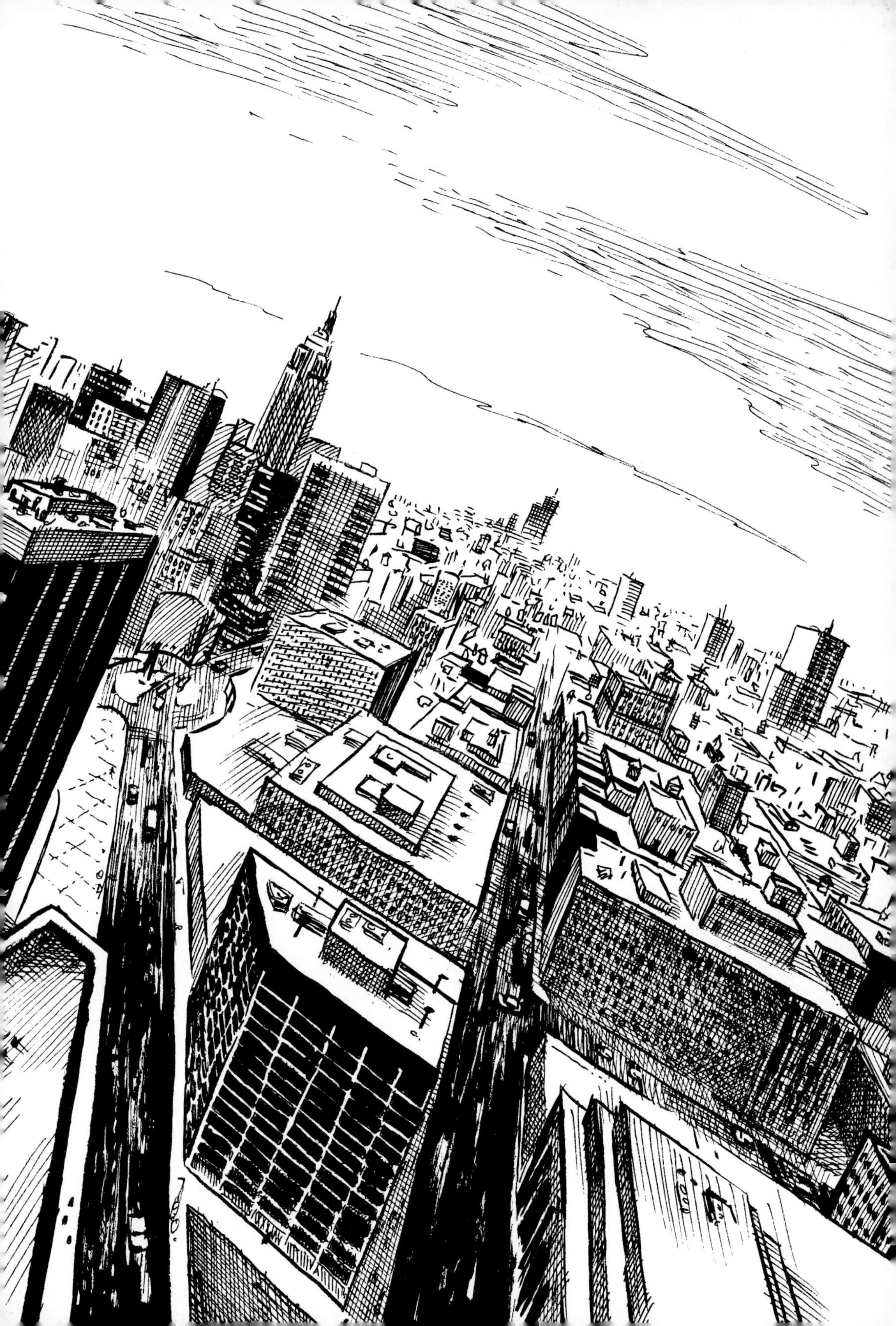

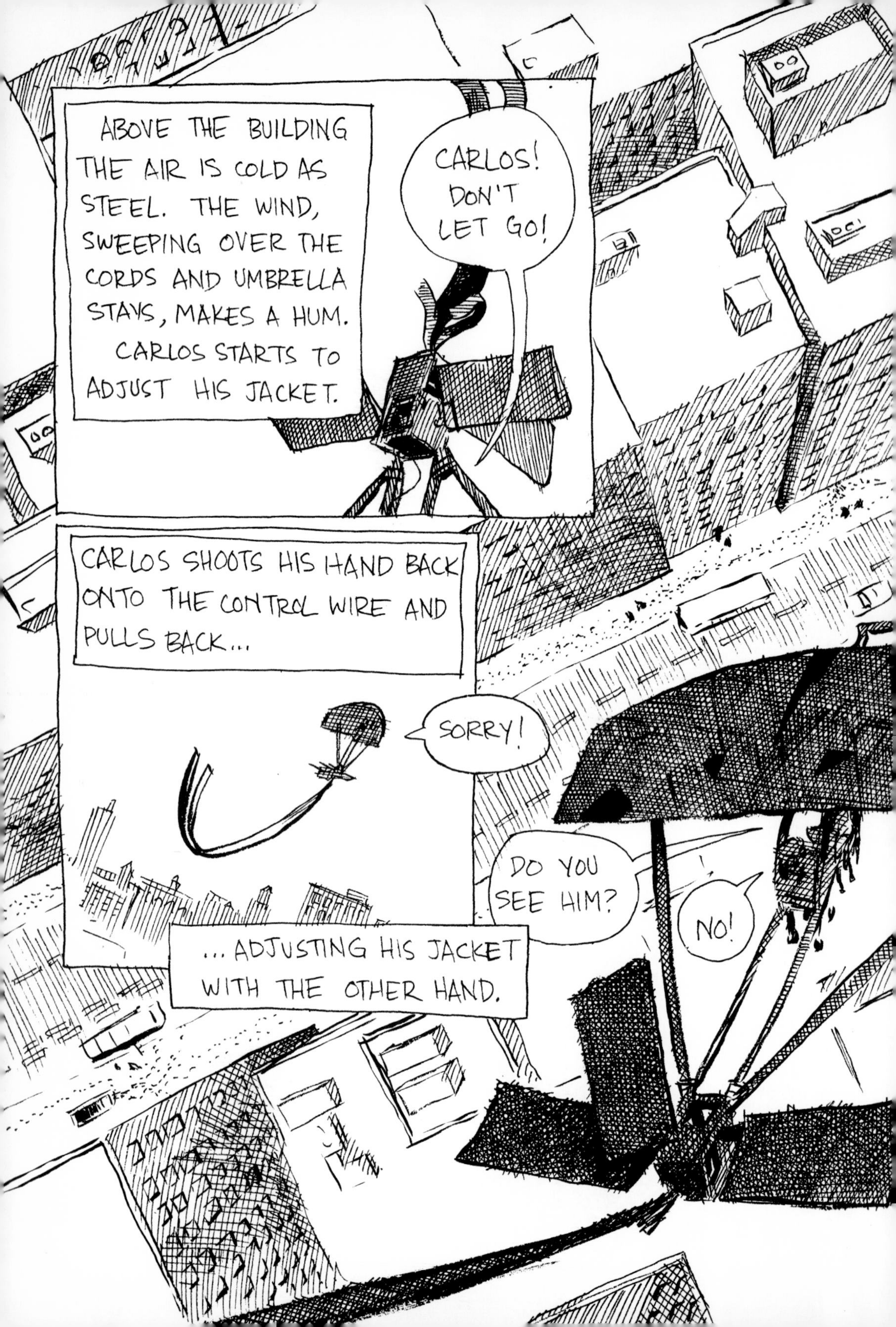
ABOVE THE BUILDING THE AIR IS COLD AS STEEL. THE WIND, SWEEPING OVER THE CORDS AND UMBRELLA STAYS, MAKES A HUM. CARLOS STARTS TO ADJUST HIS JACKET.
CARLOS! DON'T LET GO!
CARLOS SHOOTS HIS HAND BACK ONTO THE CONTROL WIRE AND PULLS BACK...
SORRY!
...ADJUSTING HIS JACKET WITH THE OTHER HAND.
DO YOU SEE HIM?
NO!

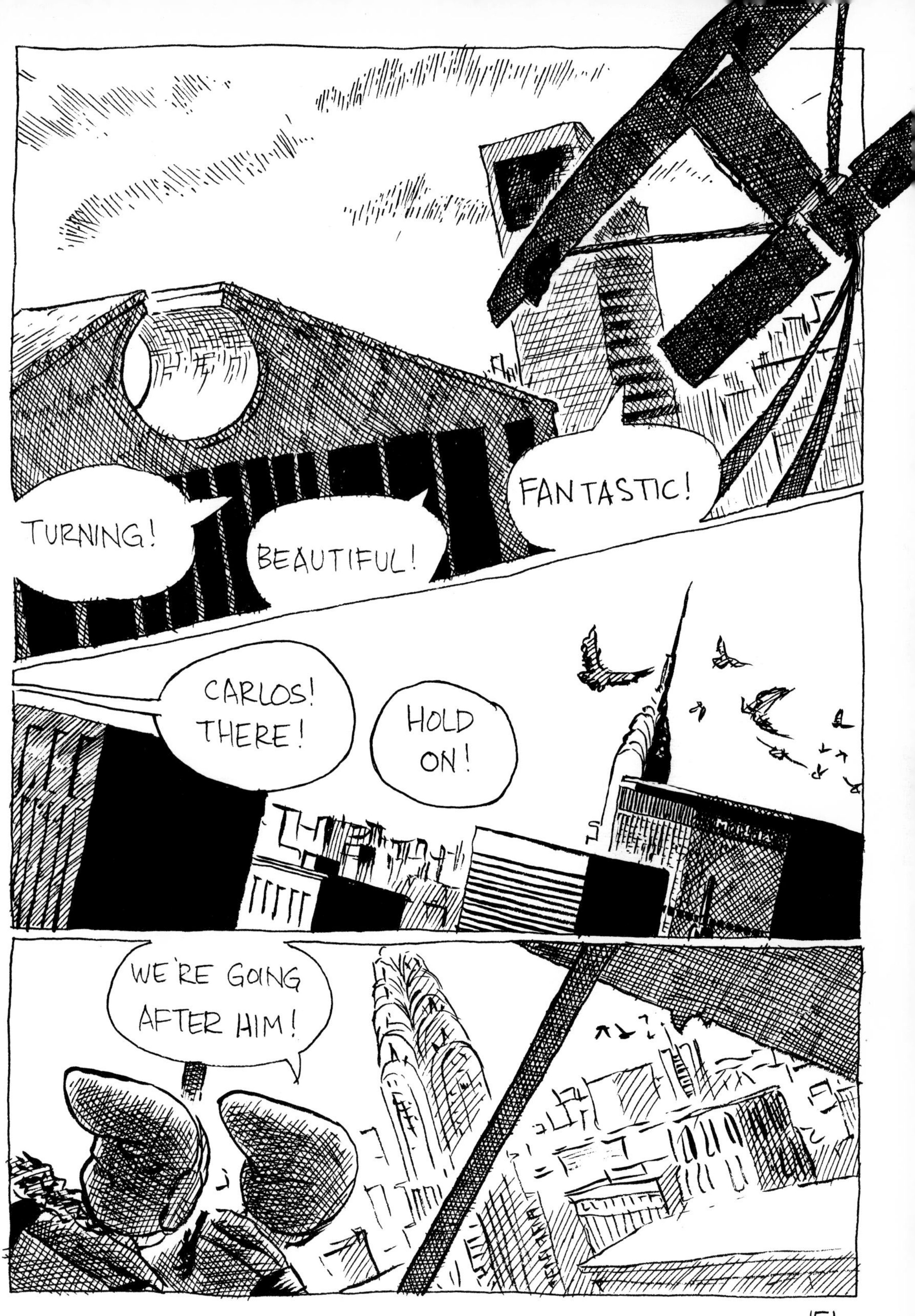
TURNING!
BEAUTIFUL!
FANTASTIC!
CARLOS! THERE!
HOLD ON!
WE'RE GOING AFTER HIM!

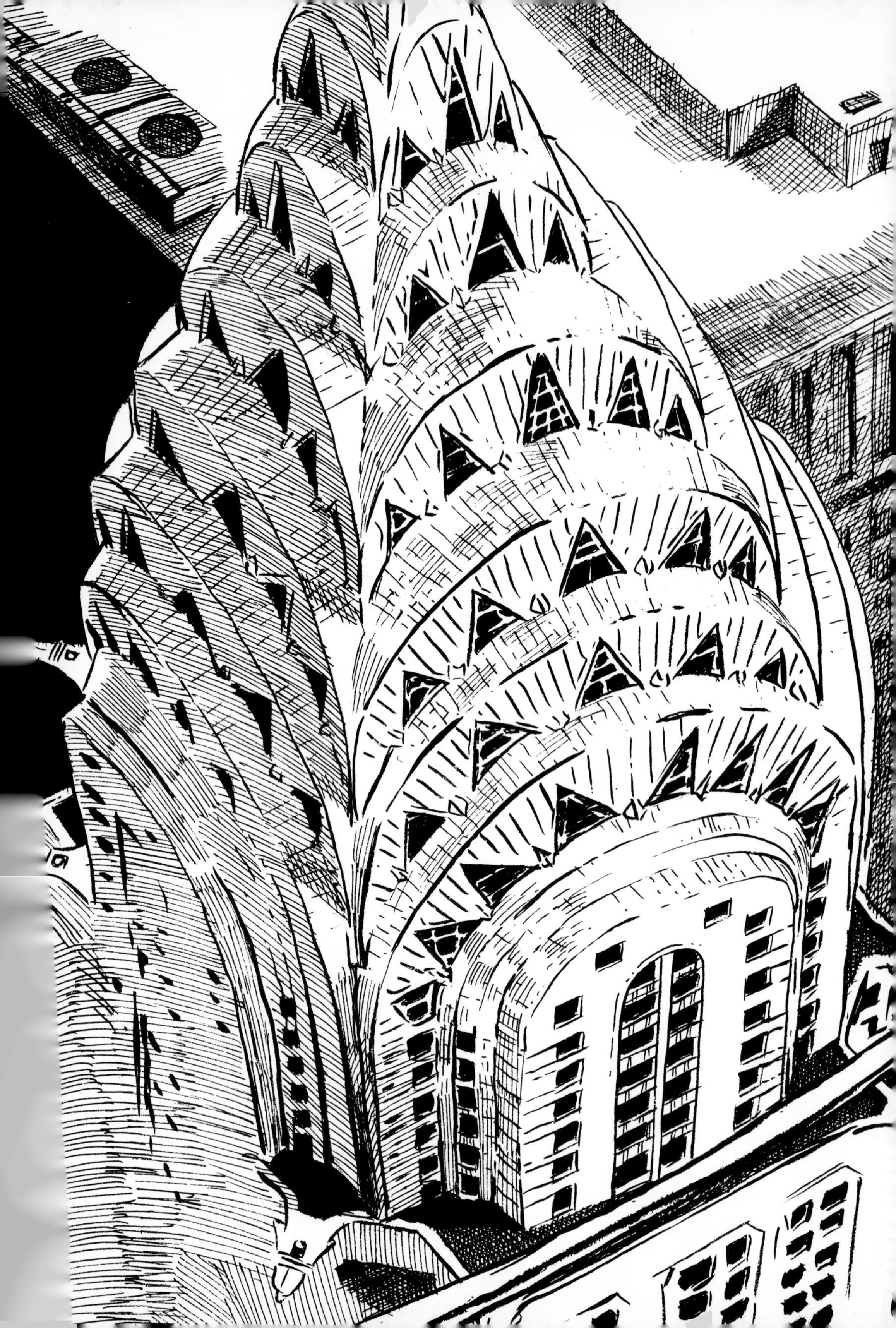

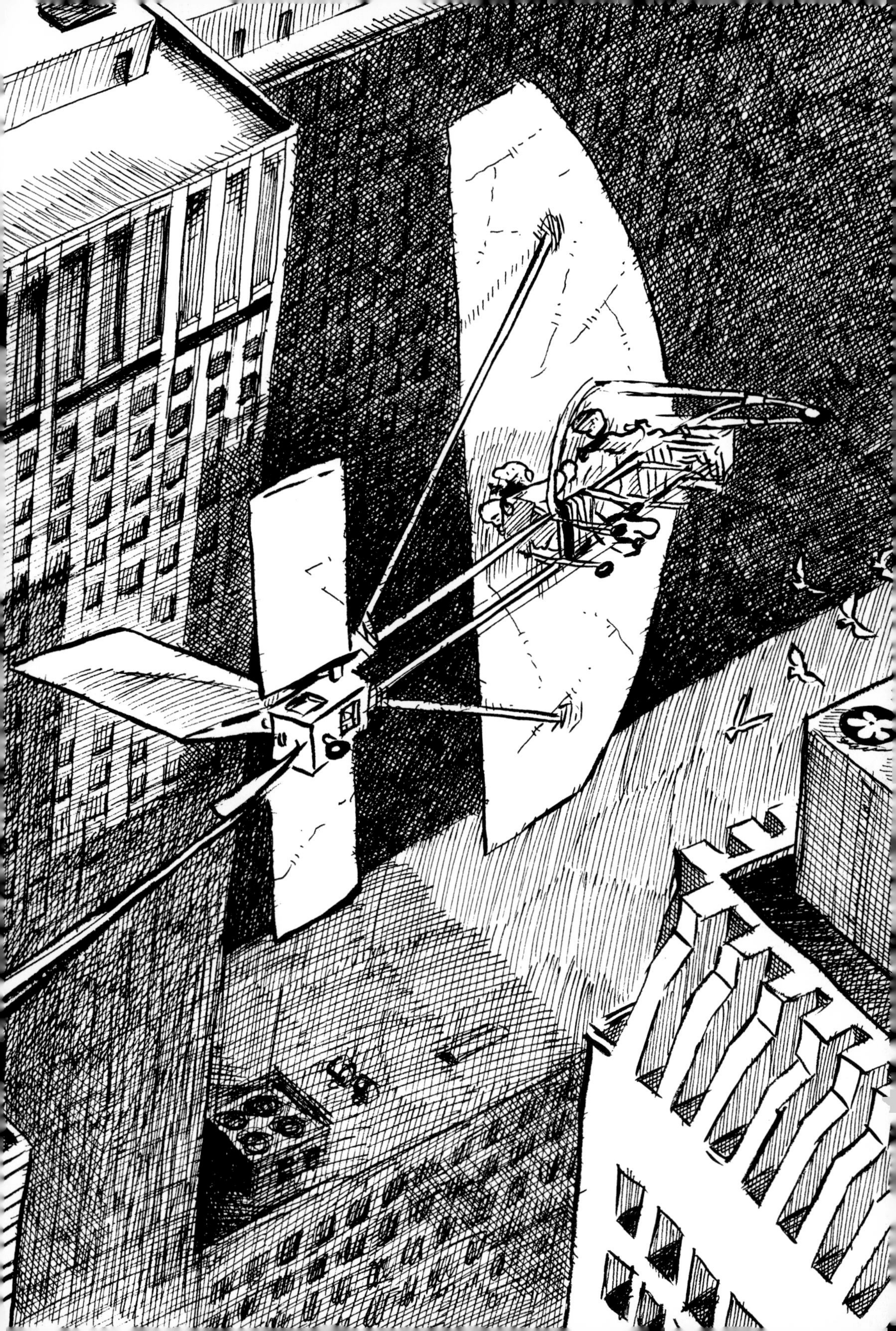

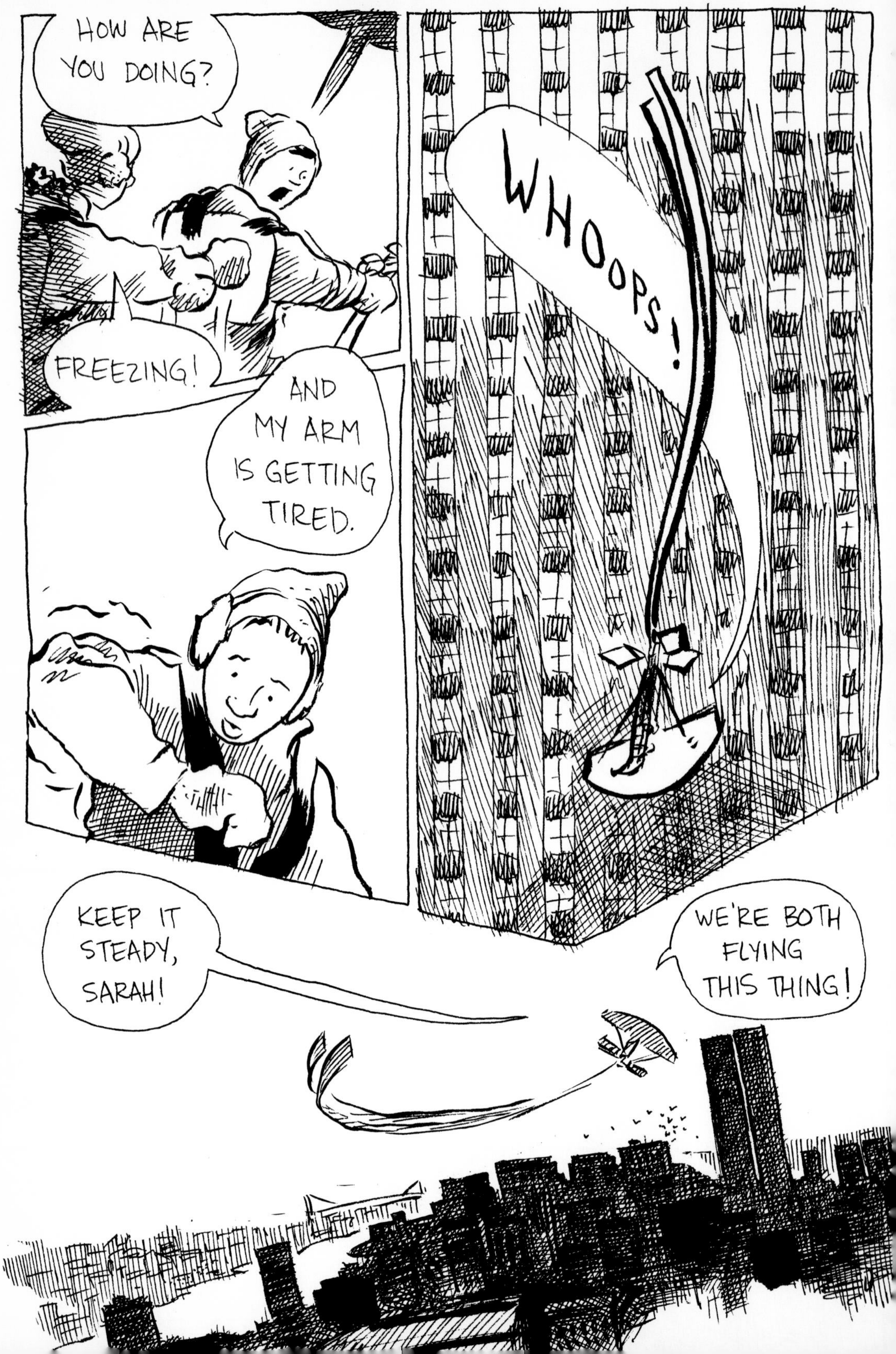
HOW ARE YOU DOING?
FREEZING!
AND MY ARM IS GETTING TIRED.
WHOOPS!
KEEP IT STEADY, SARAH!
WE'RE BOTH FLYING THIS THING!

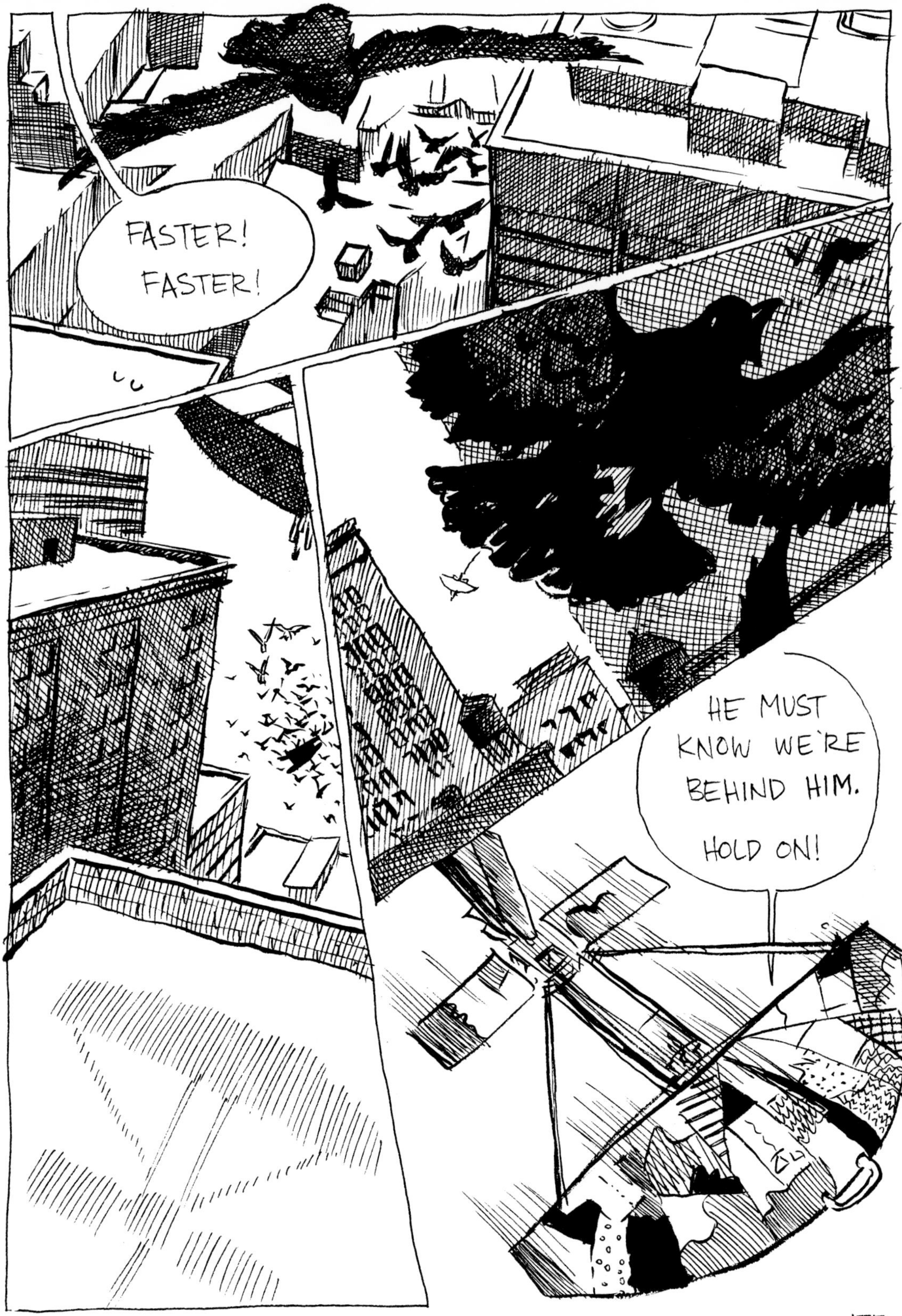
FASTER! FASTER!
HE MUST KNOW WE'RE BEHIND HIM.
HOLD ON!

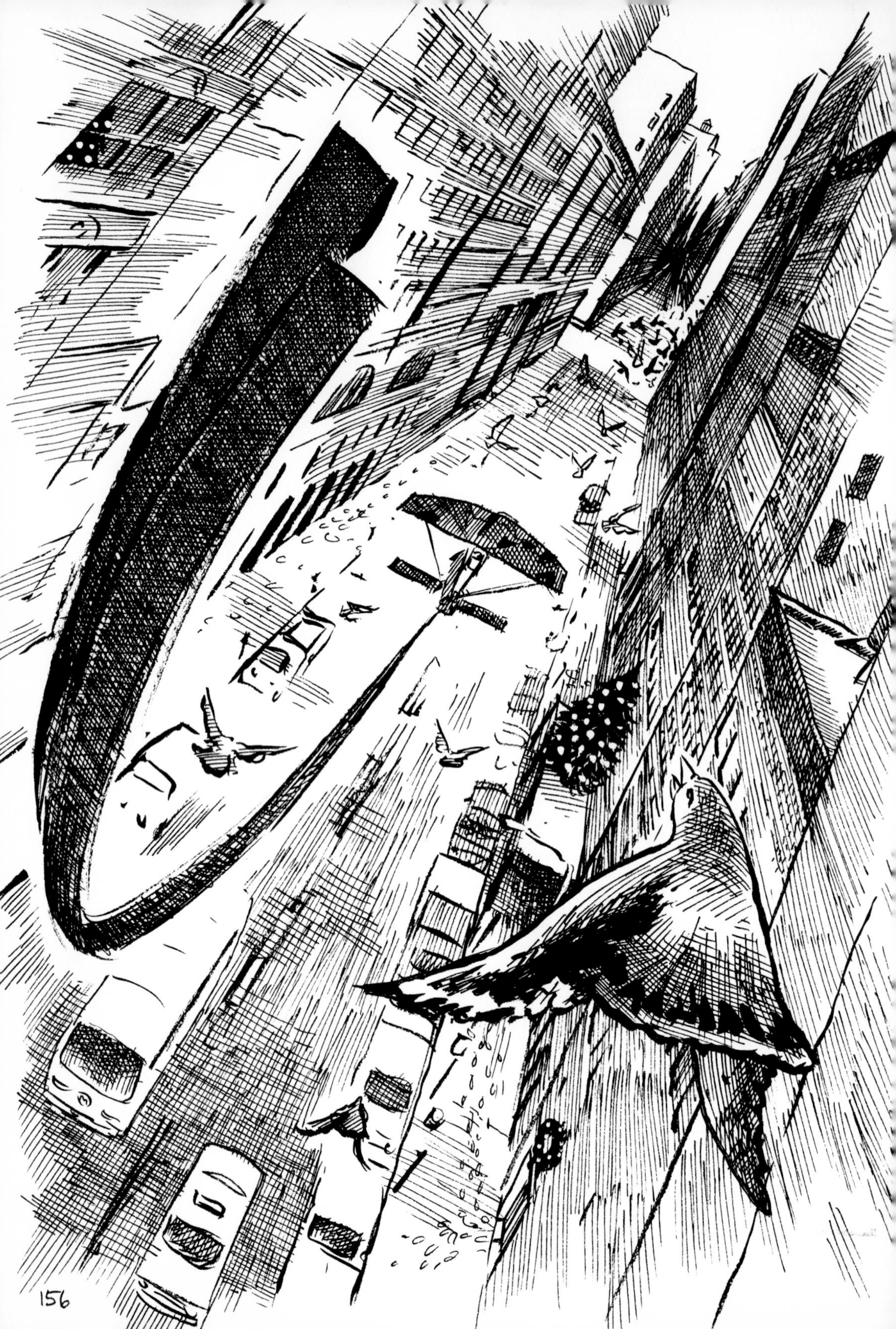

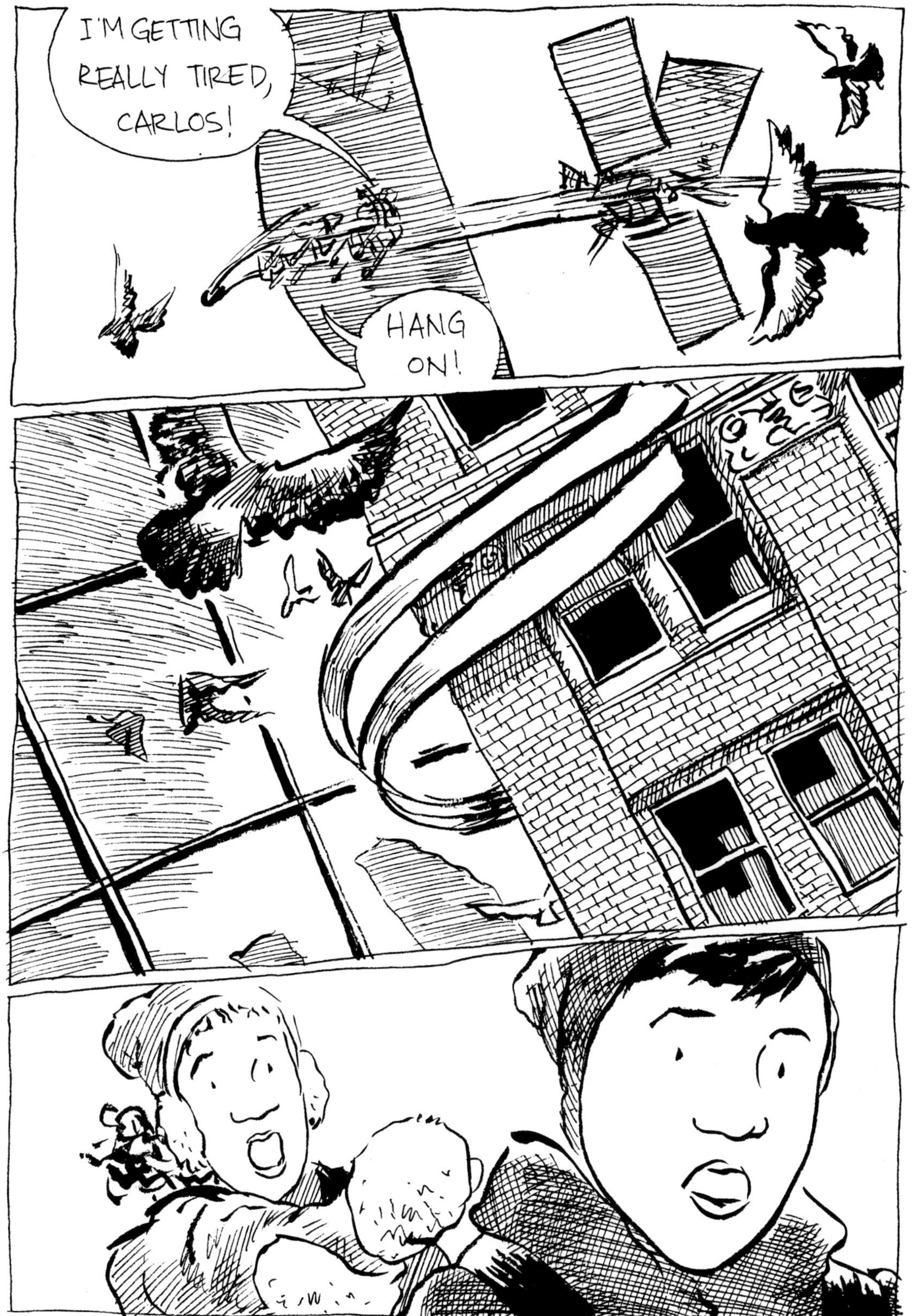
I'M GETTING REALLY TIRED, CARLOS!
HANG ON!

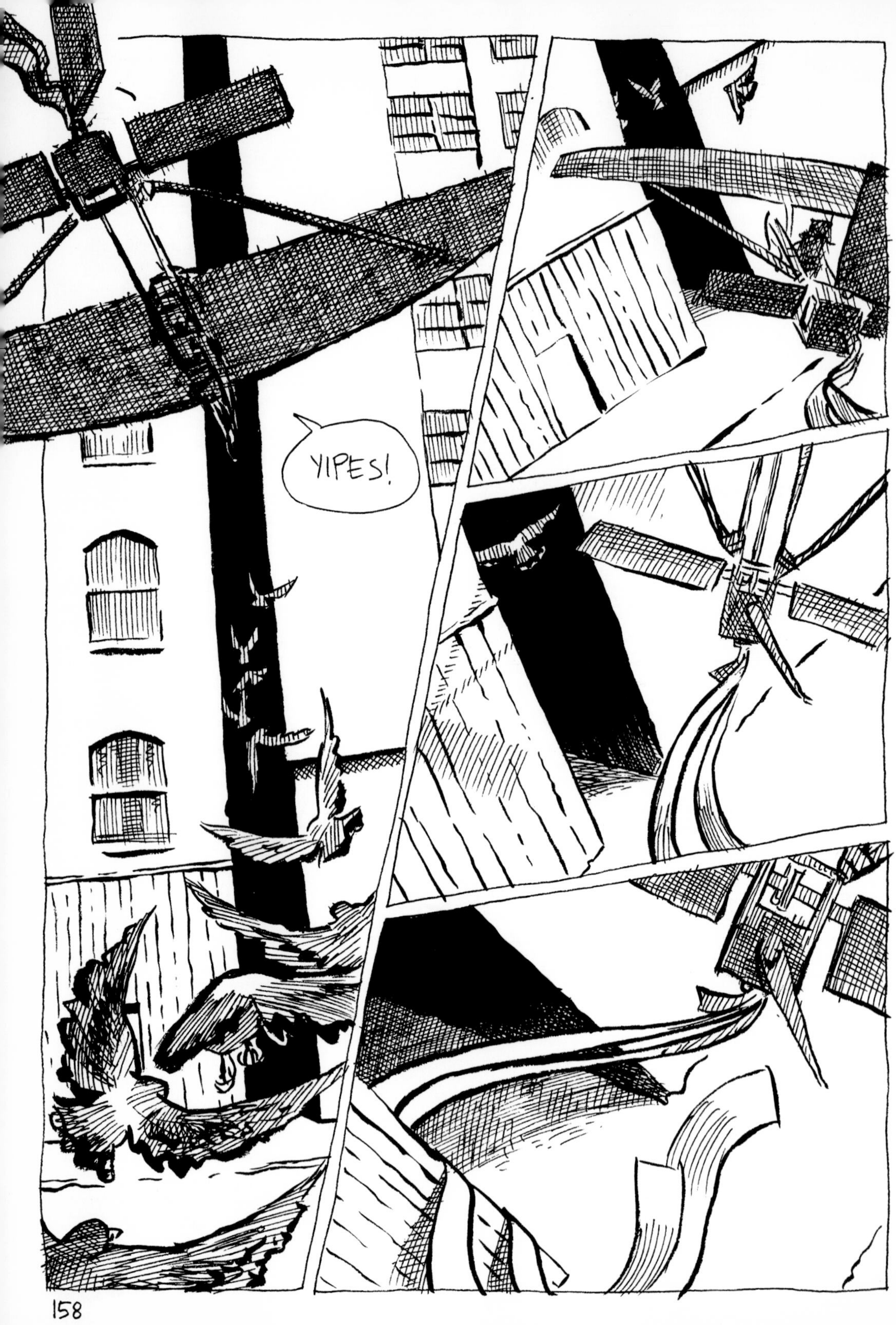
YIPES!

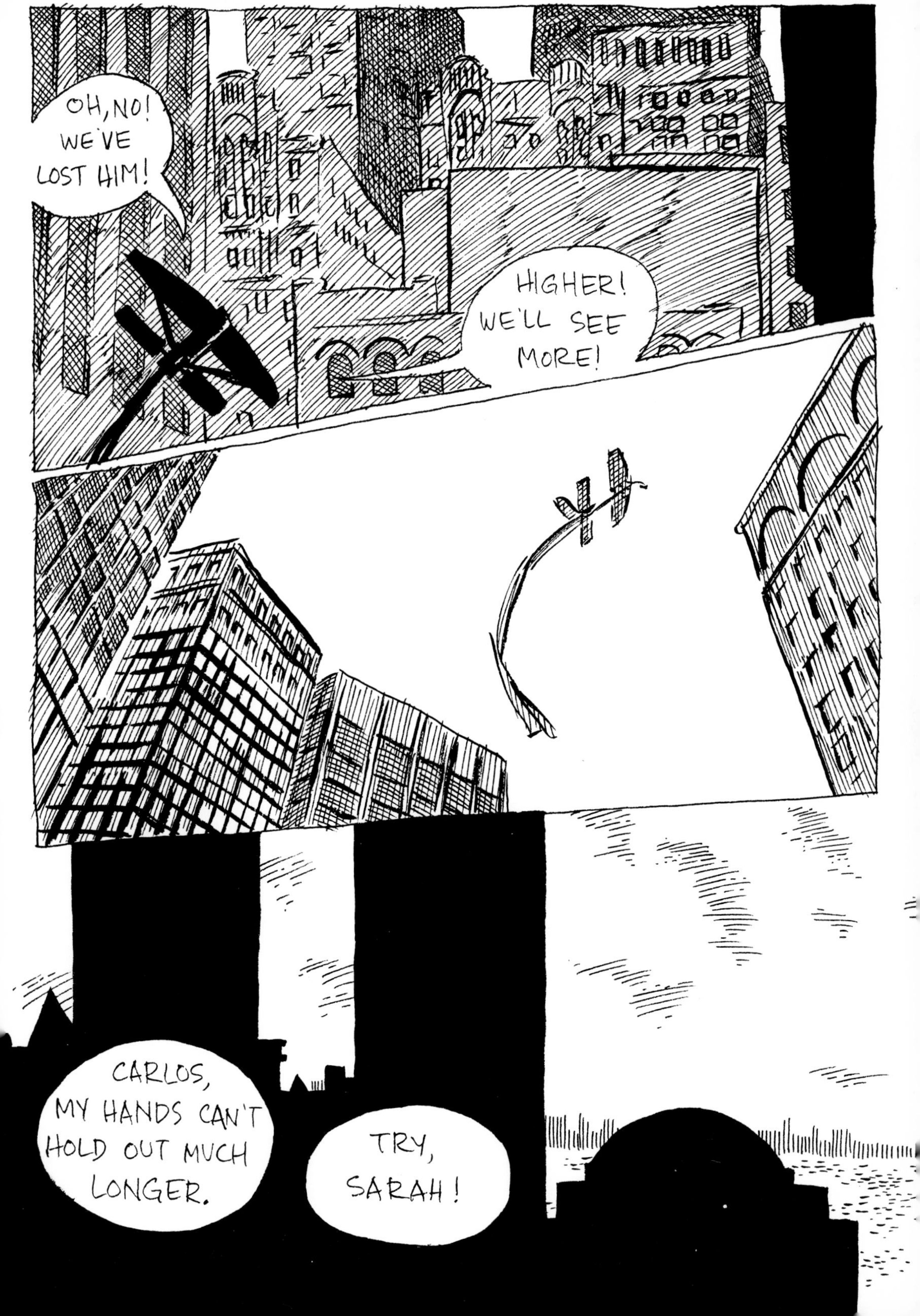
OH, NO! WE'VE LOST HIM!
HIGHER! WE'LL SEE MORE!
CARLOS, MY HANDS CAN'T HOLD OUT MUCH LONGER.
TRY, SARAH!

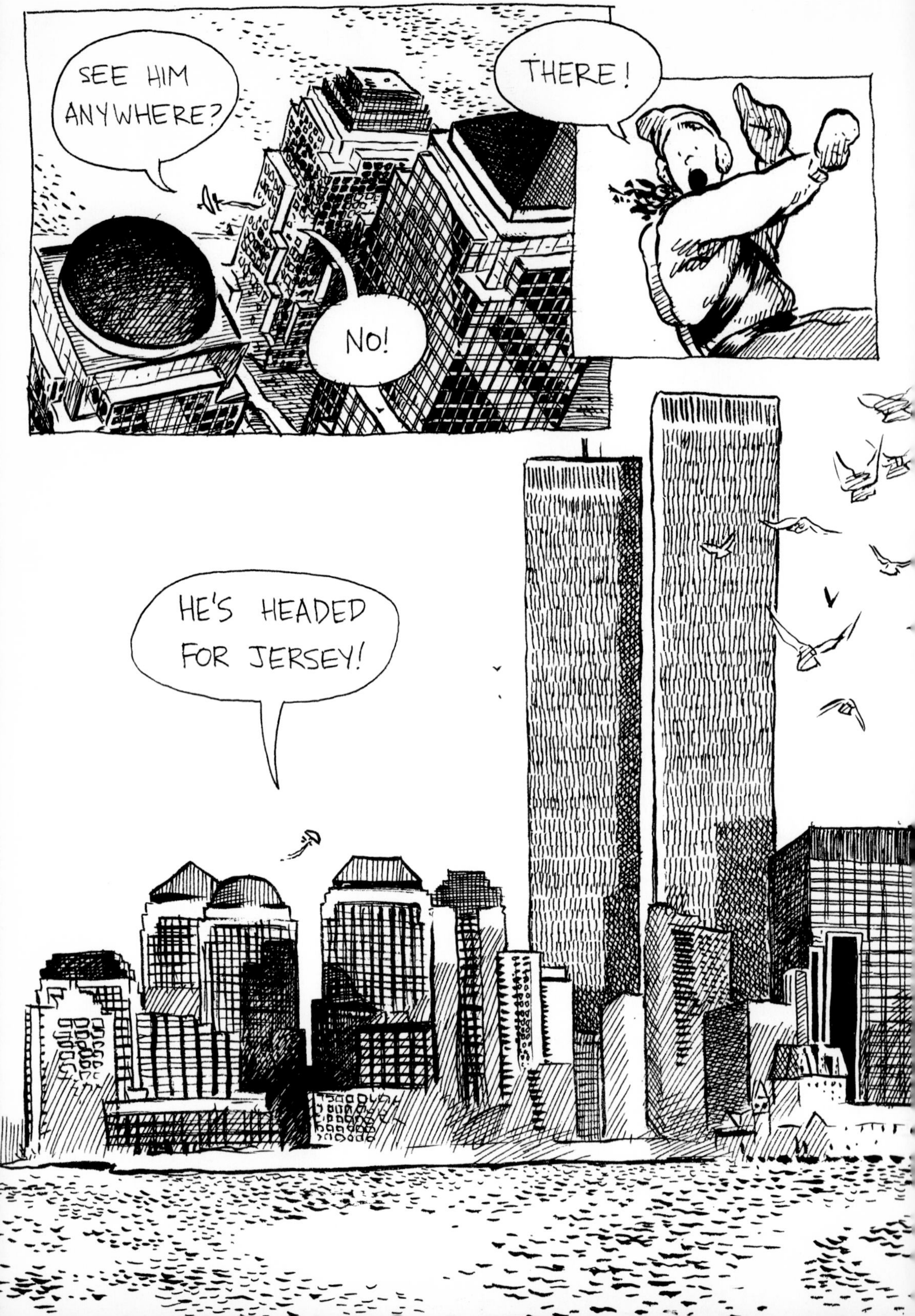
SEE HIM ANYWHERE?
NO!
THERE!
HE'S HEADED FOR JERSEY!

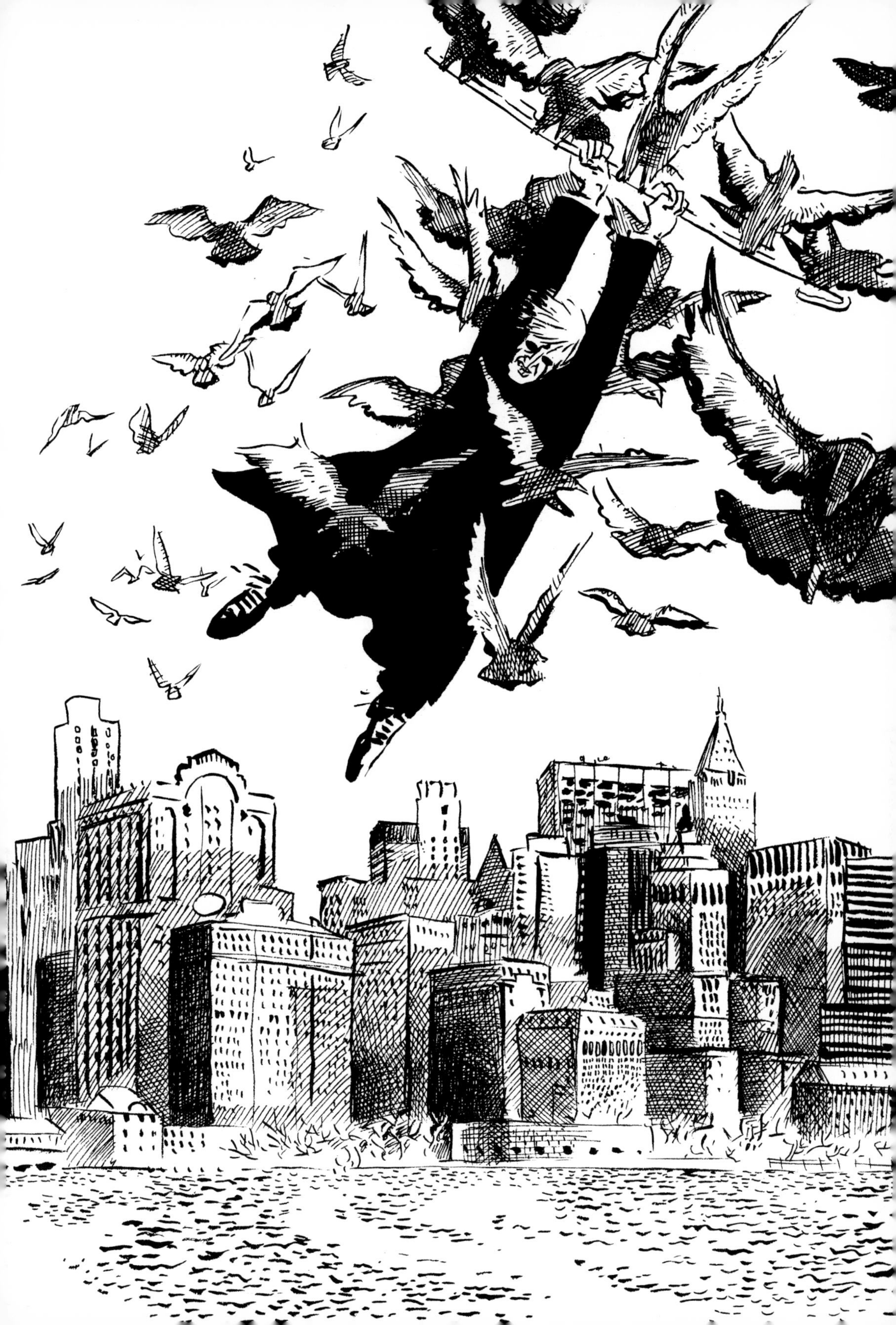

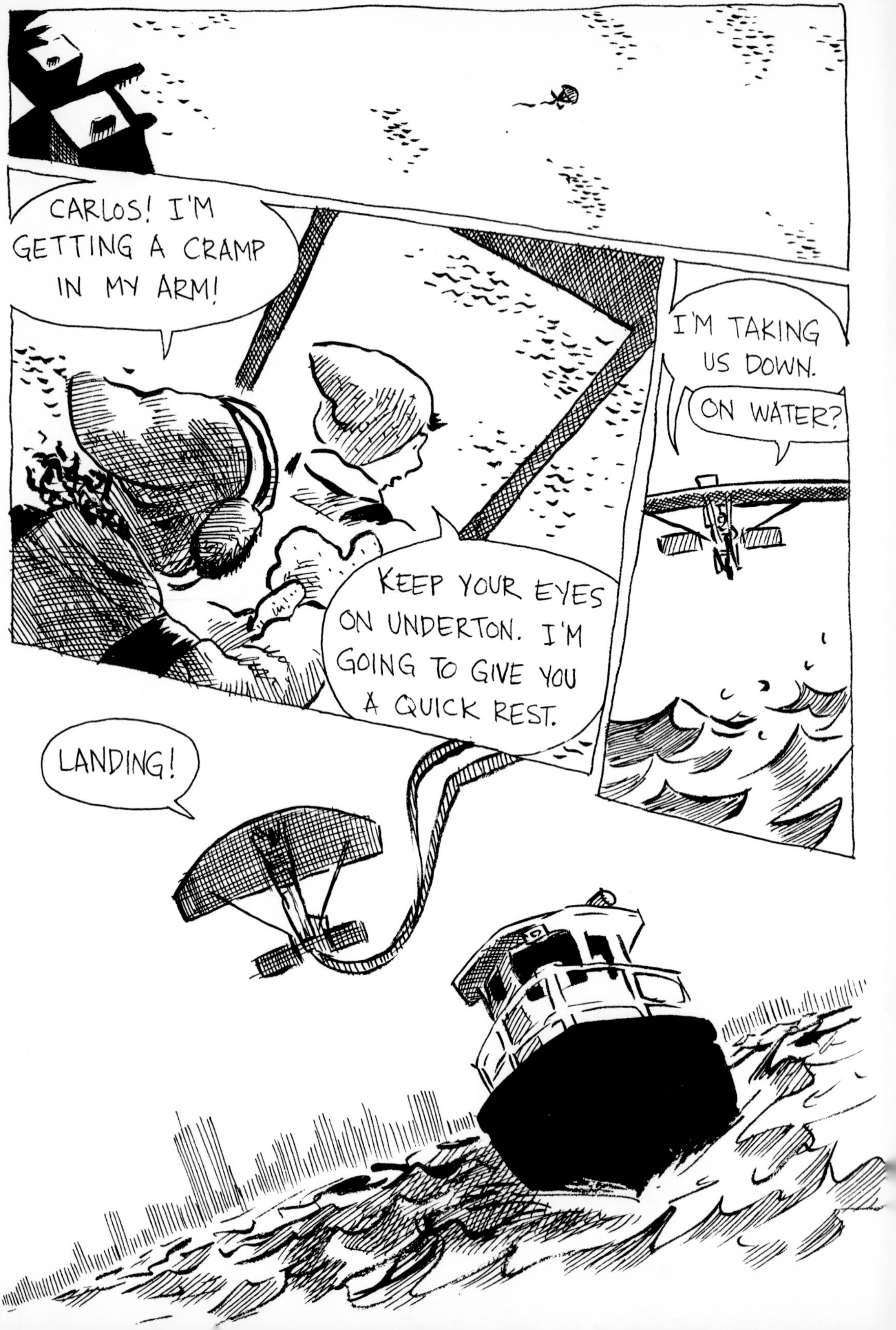
CARLOS! I'M GETTING A CRAMP IN MY ARM!
KEEP YOUR EYES ON UNDERTON. I'M GOING TO GIVE YOU A QUICK REST.
I'M TAKING US DOWN.
ON WATER?
LANDING!

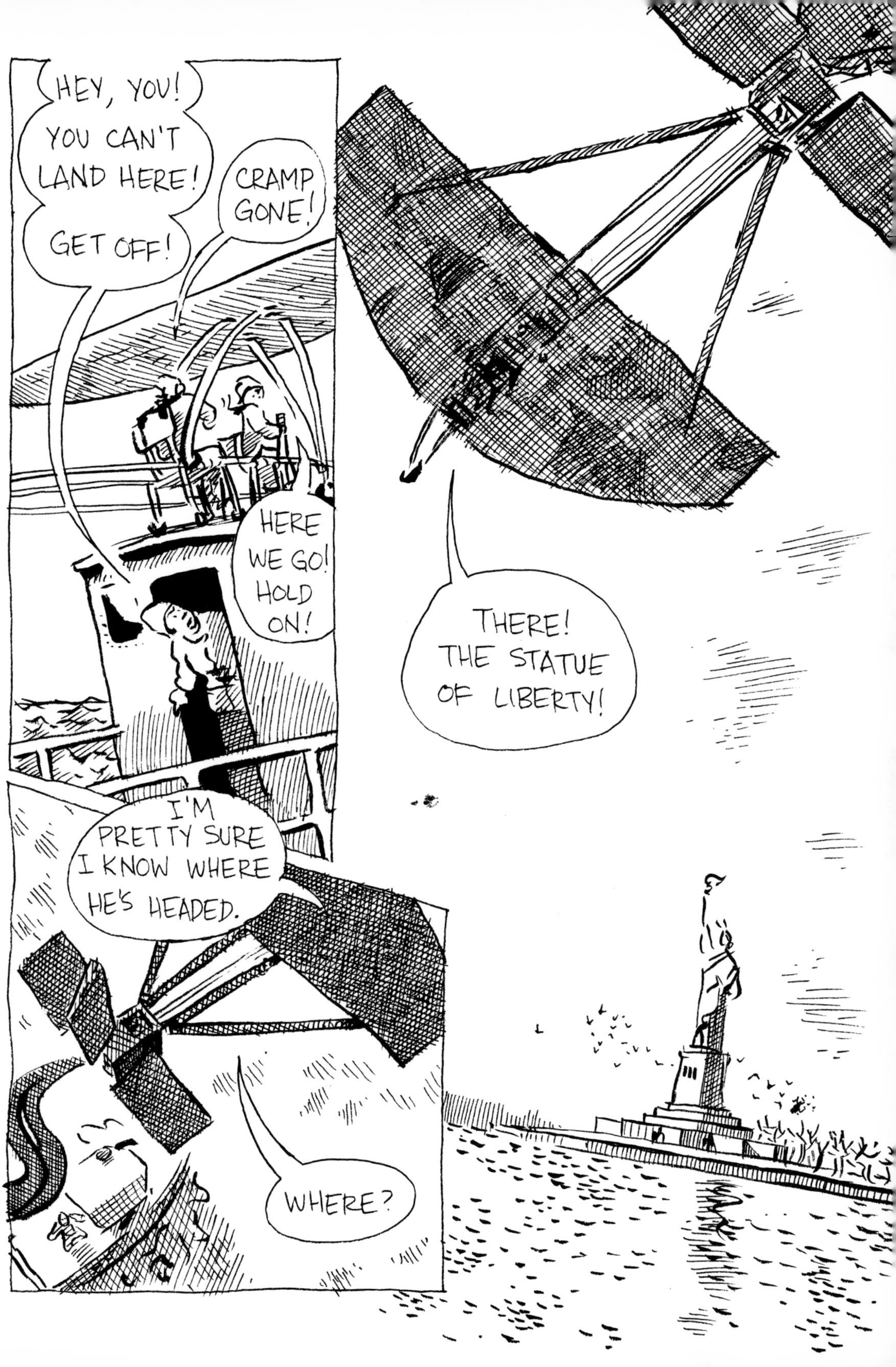
HEY, YOU! YOU CAN'T LAND HERE! GET OFF!
CRAMP GONE!
HERE WE GO! HOLD ON!
I'M PRETTY SURE I KNOW WHERE HE'S HEADED.
WHERE?
THERE! THE STATUE OF LIBERTY!

9TH CHAPTER

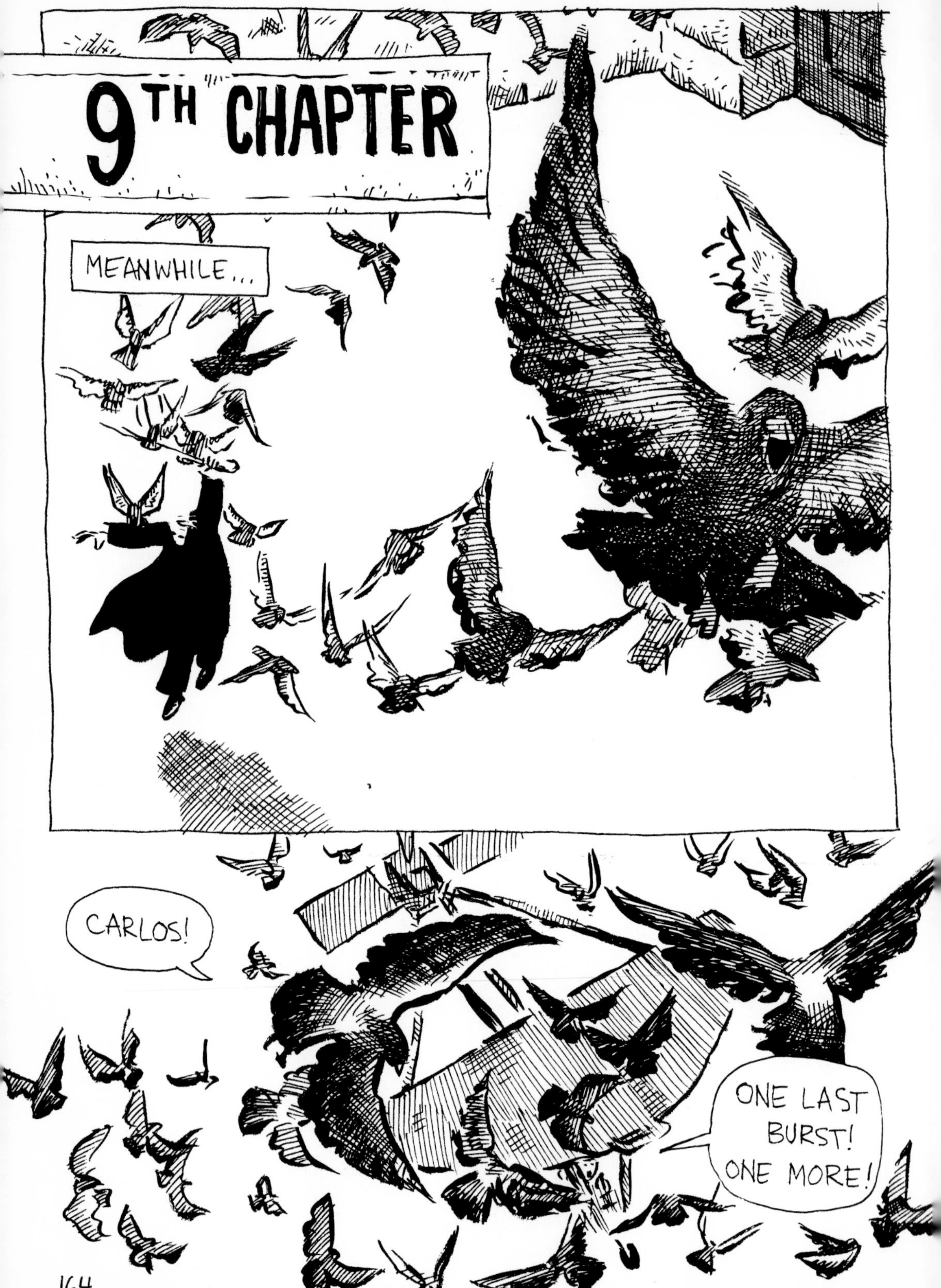
MEANWHILE...
CARLOS!
ONE LAST BURST! ONE MORE!

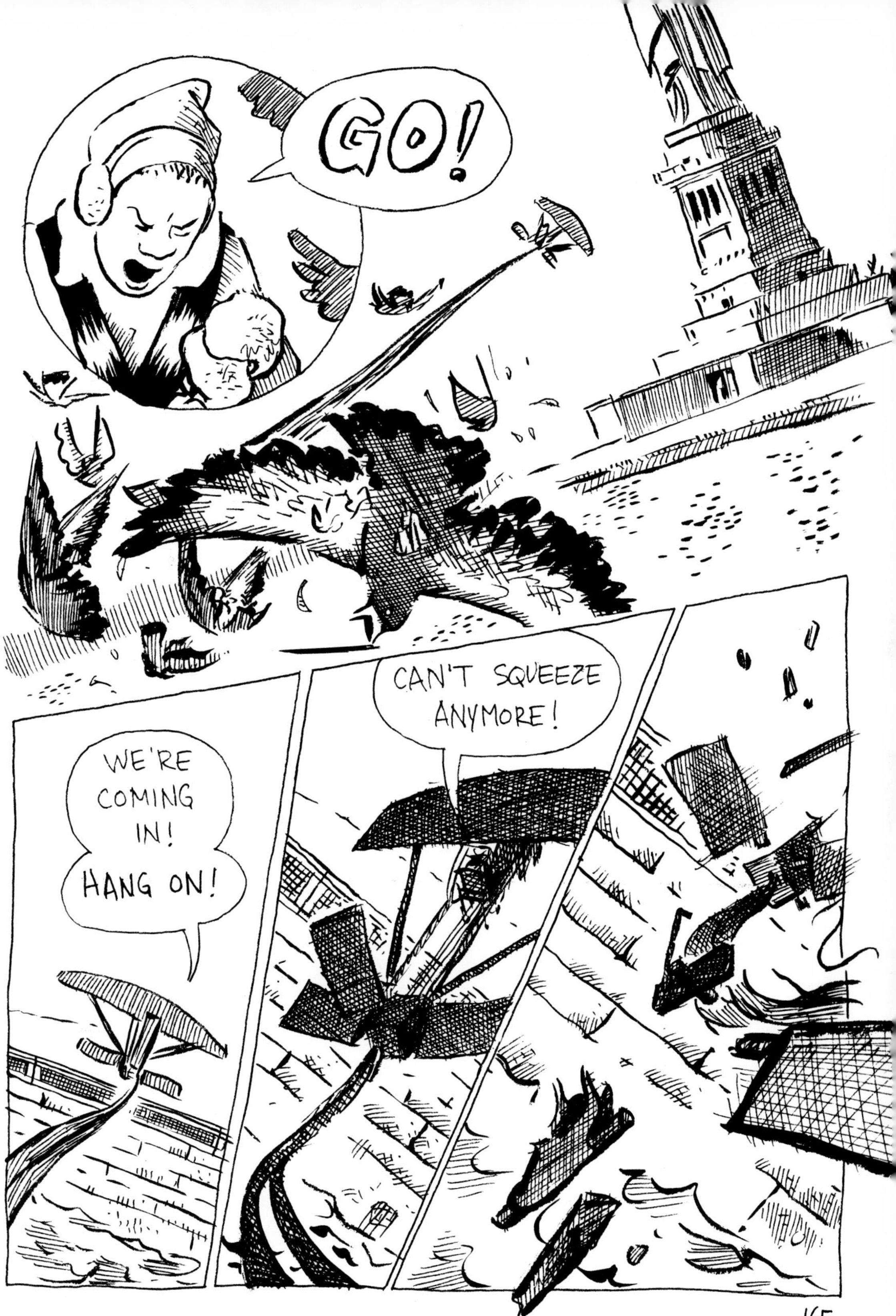
GO!
WE'RE COMING IN! HANG ON!
CAN'T SQUEEZE ANYMORE!

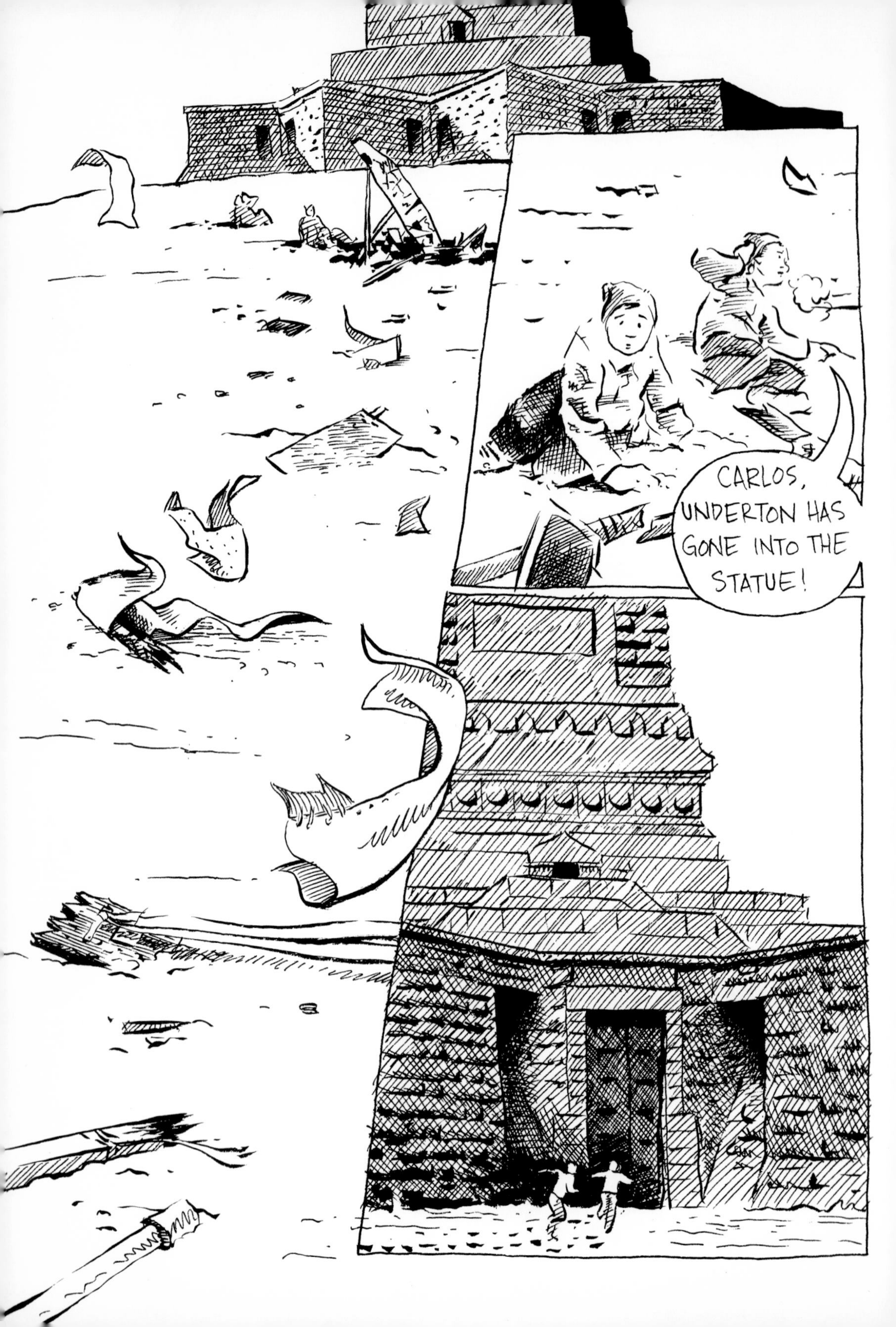
CARLOS, UNDERTON HAS GONE INTO THE STATUE!

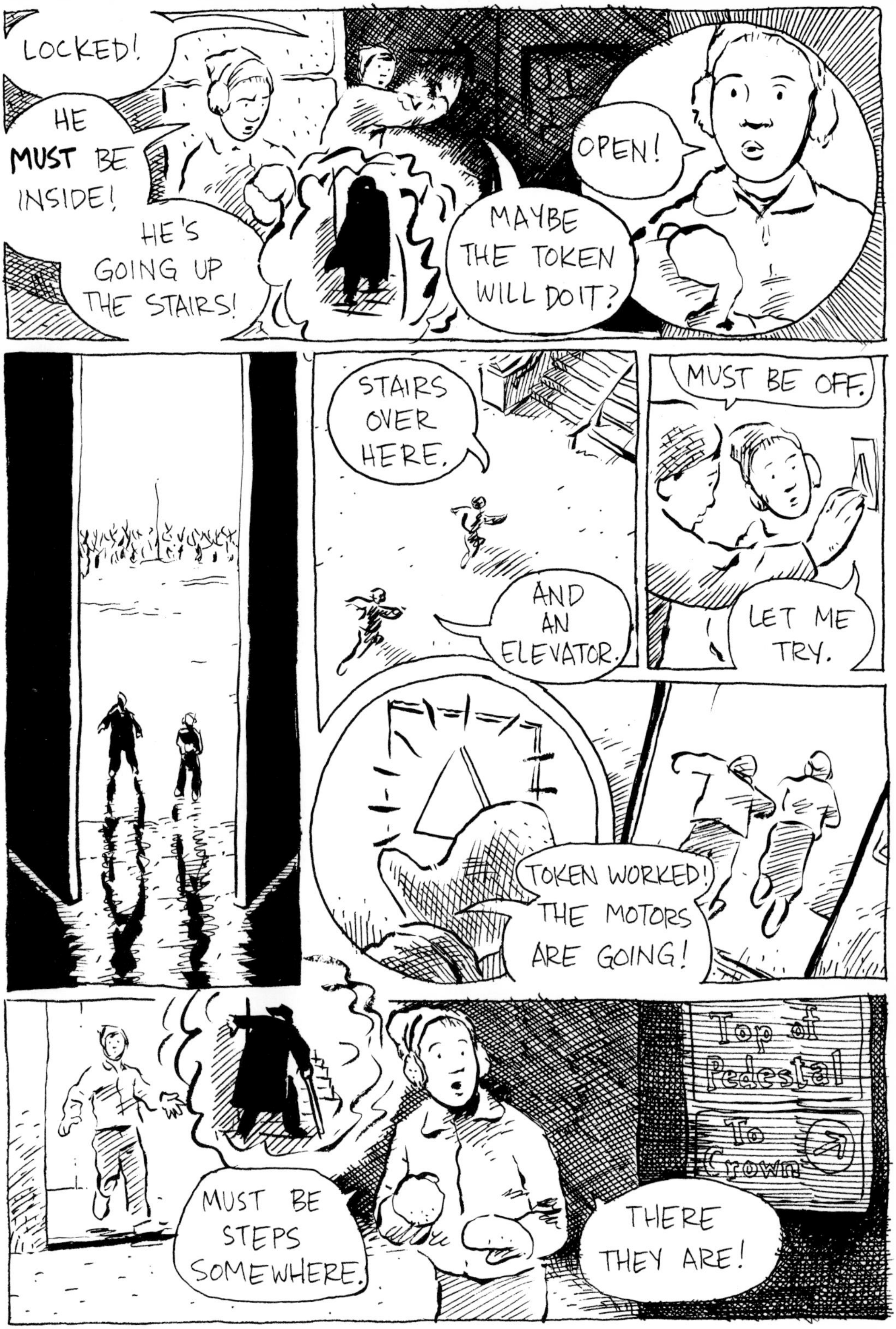
LOCKED!
HE MUST BE INSIDE!
HE'S GOING UP THE STAIRS!
MAYBE THE TOKEN WILL DO IT?
OPEN!
STAIRS OVER HERE.
AND AN ELEVATOR.
MUST BE OFF.
LET ME TRY.
TOKEN WORKED! THE MOTORS ARE GOING!
MUST BE STEPS SOMEWHERE.
THERE THEY ARE!
Top of Pedestal
To Crown

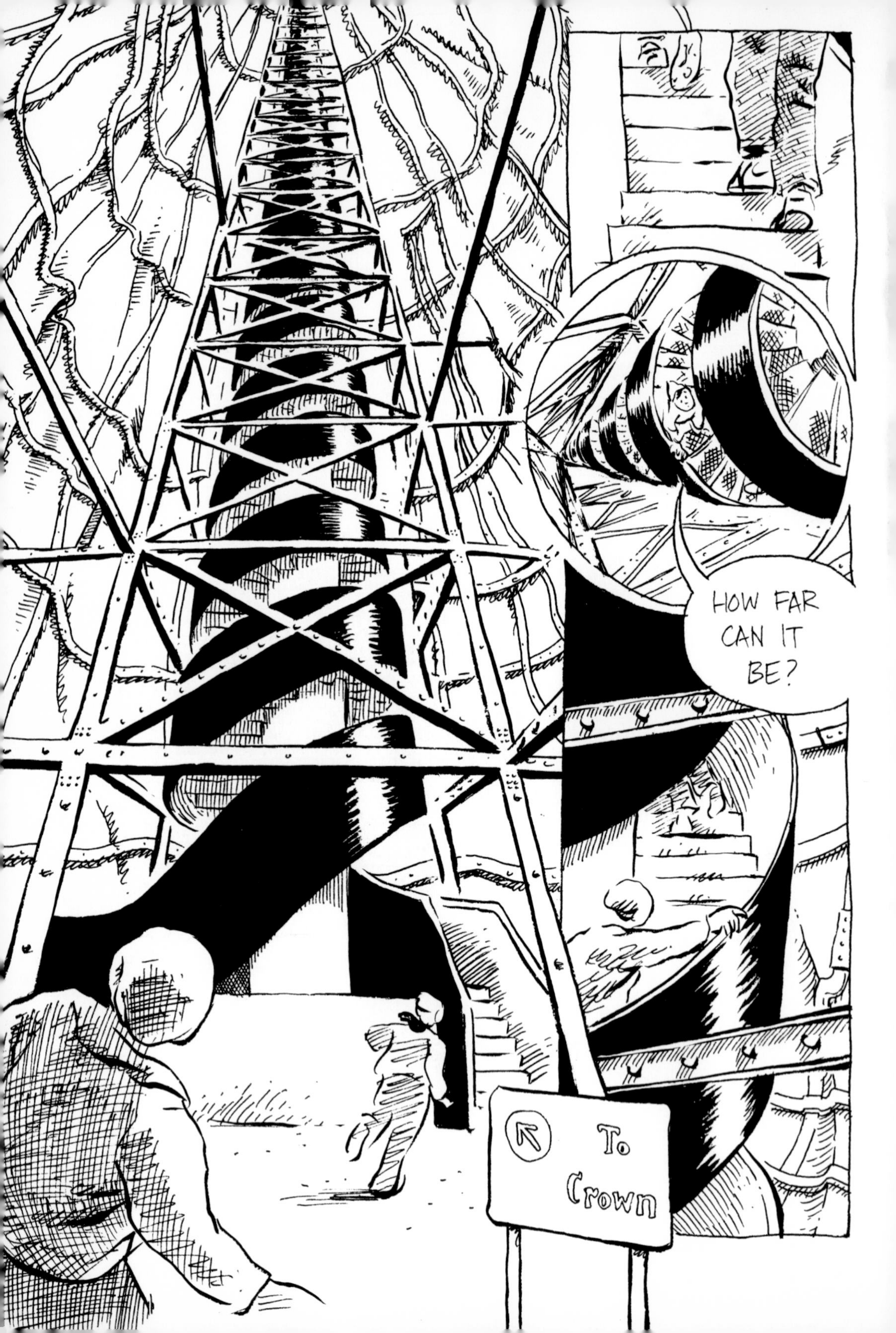
HOW FAR CAN IT BE?
To Crown

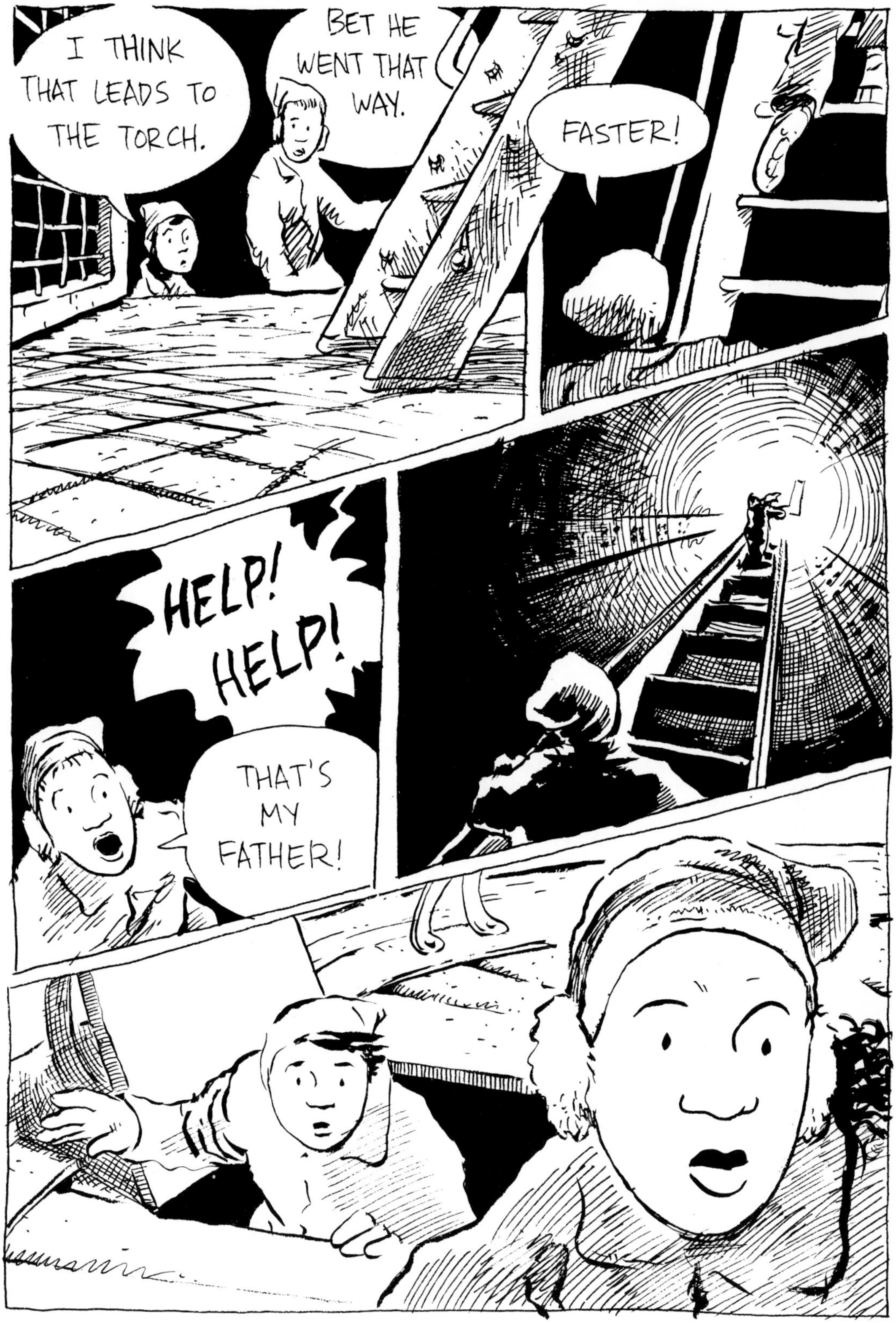
I THINK THAT LEADS TO THE TORCH.
BET HE WENT THAT WAY.
FASTER!
HELP! HELP!
THAT'S MY FATHER!

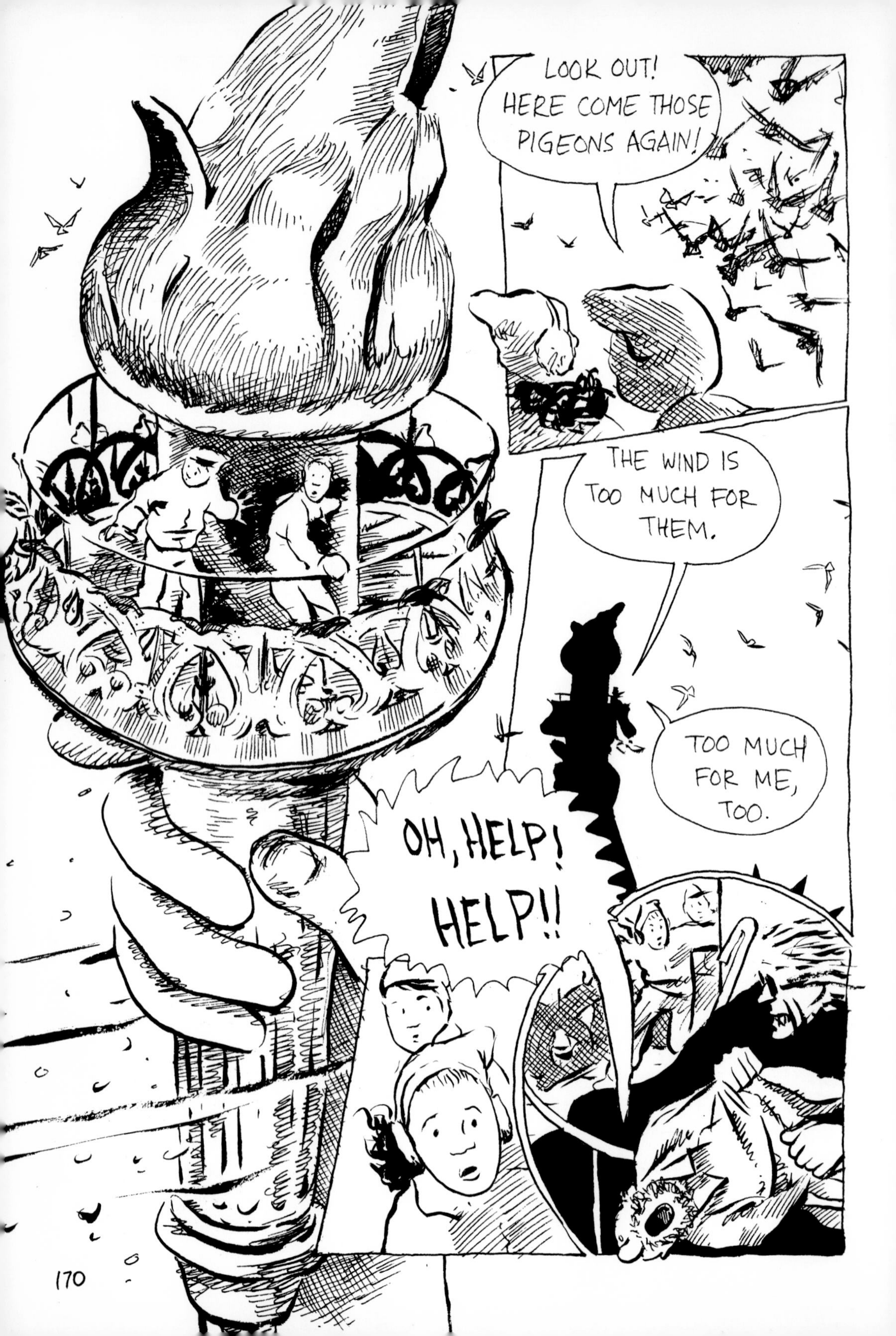
LOOK OUT! HERE COME THOSE PIGEONS AGAIN!
THE WIND IS TOO MUCH FOR THEM.
TOO MUCH FOR ME, TOO.
OH, HELP! HELP!!

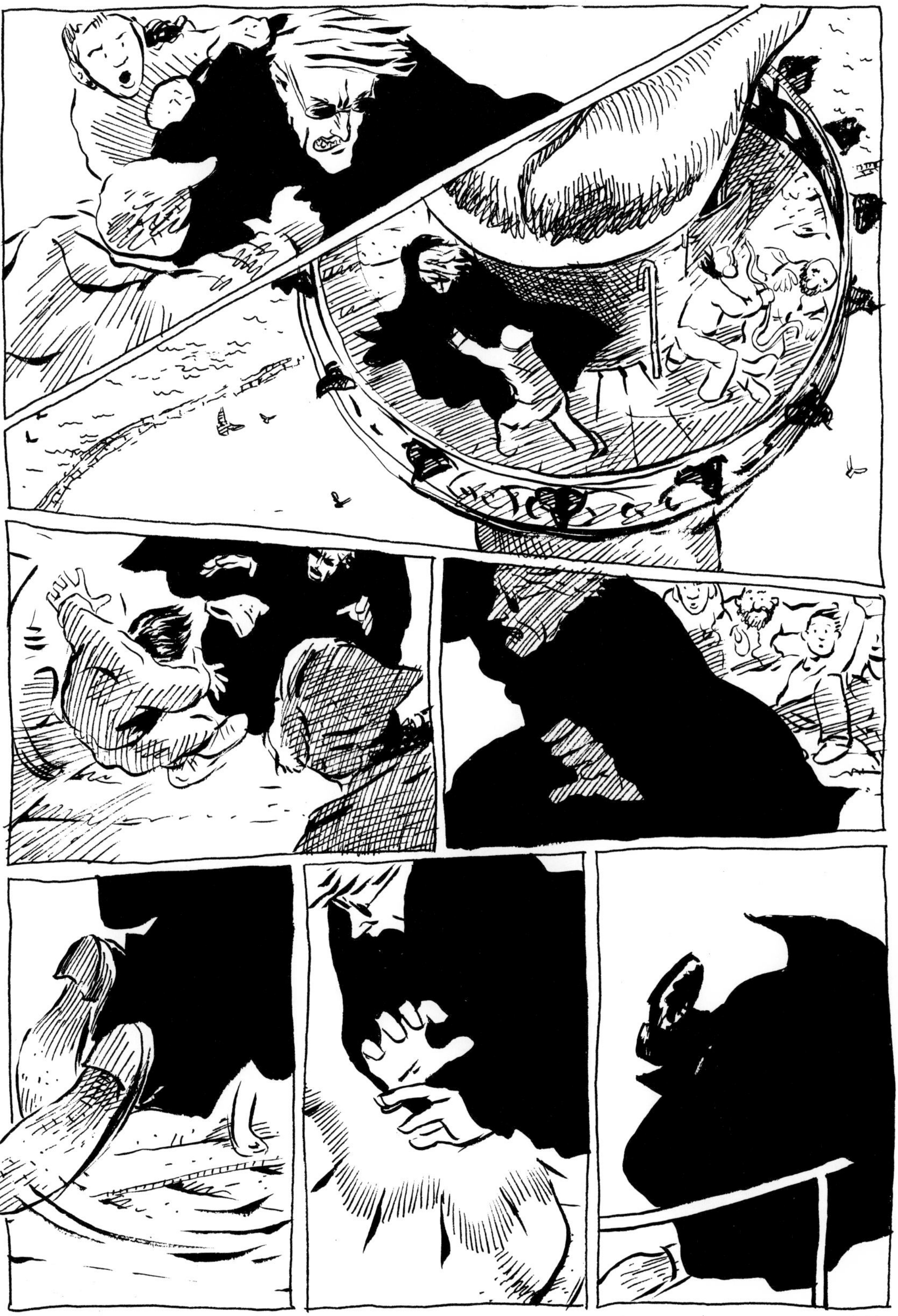

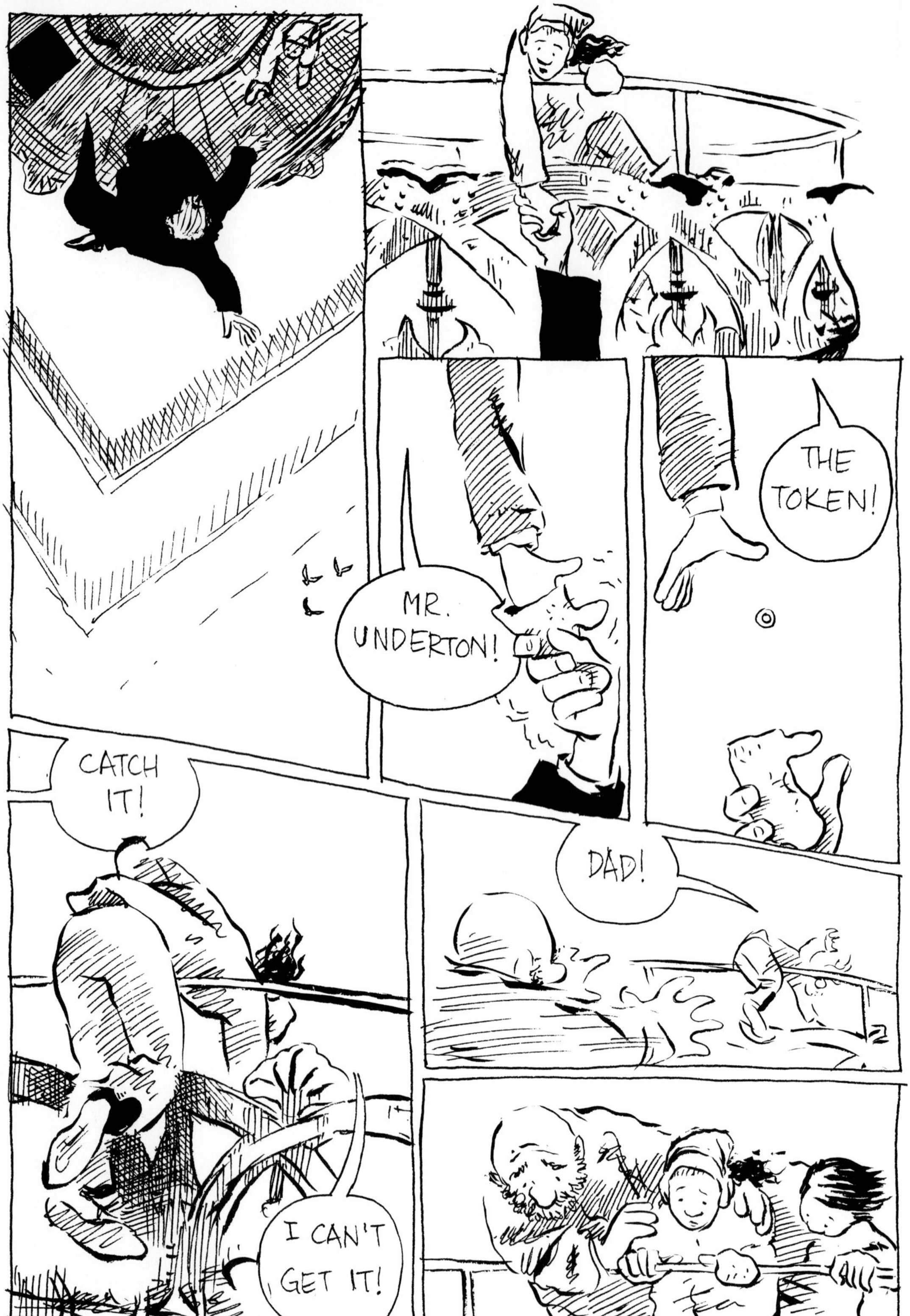
MR. UNDERTON!
THE TOKEN!
CATCH IT!
DAD!
I CAN'T GET IT!

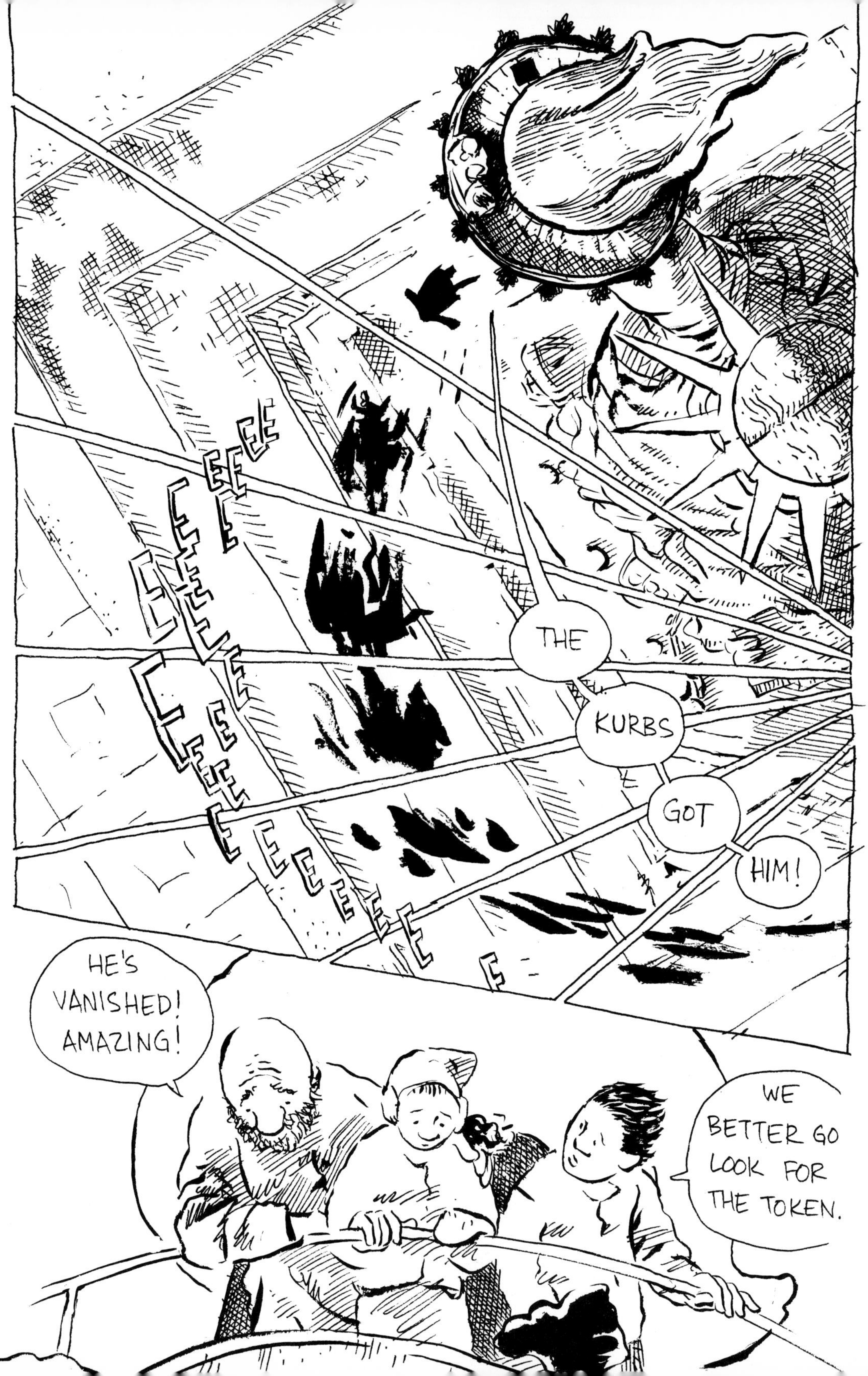
THE
KURBS
GOT
HIM!
HE'S VANISHED! AMAZING!
WE BETTER GO LOOK FOR THE TOKEN.

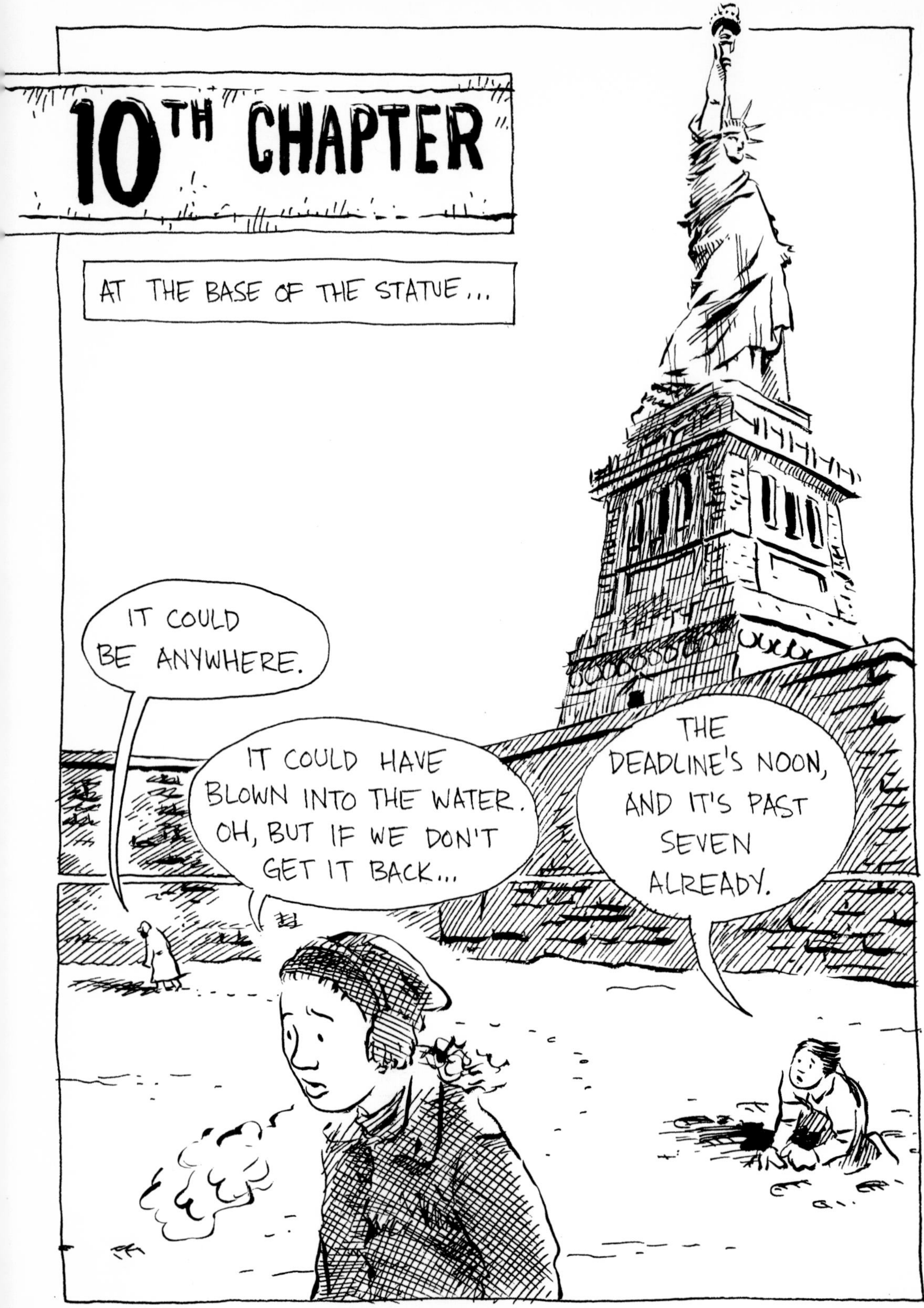
10TH CHAPTER
AT THE BASE OF THE STATUE...
IT COULD BE ANYWHERE.
IT COULD HAVE BLOWN INTO THE WATER. OH, BUT IF WE DON'T GET IT BACK...
THE DEADLINE'S NOON, AND IT'S PAST SEVEN ALREADY.

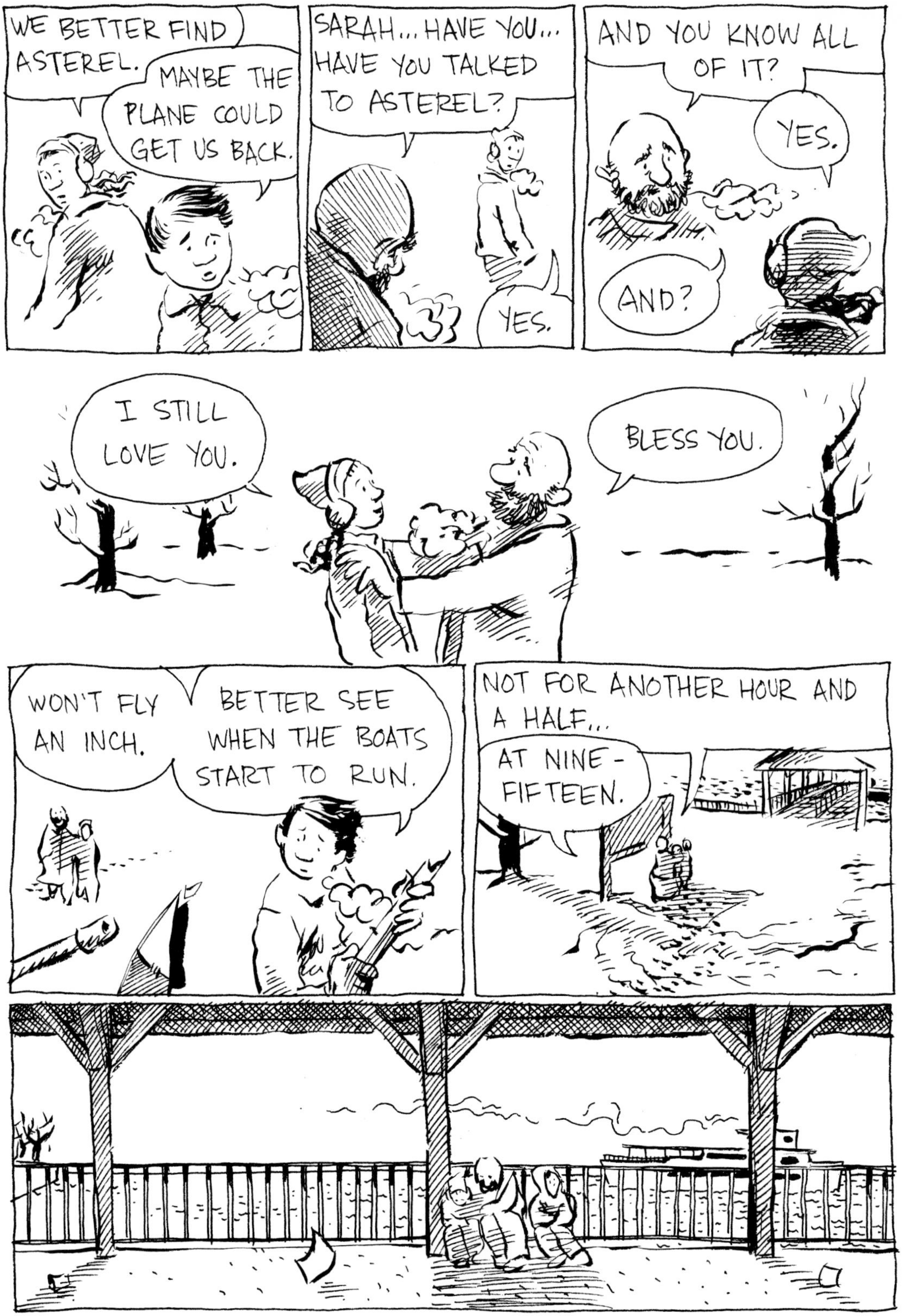
WE BETTER FIND ASTEREL.
MAYBE THE PLANE COULD GET US BACK.
SARAH... HAVE YOU... HAVE YOU TALKED TO ASTEREL?
YES.
AND YOU KNOW ALL OF IT?
YES.
AND?
I STILL LOVE YOU.
BLESS YOU.
WON'T FLY AN INCH.
BETTER SEE WHEN THE BOATS START TO RUN.
NOT FOR ANOTHER HOUR AND A HALF...
AT NINE-FIFTEEN.

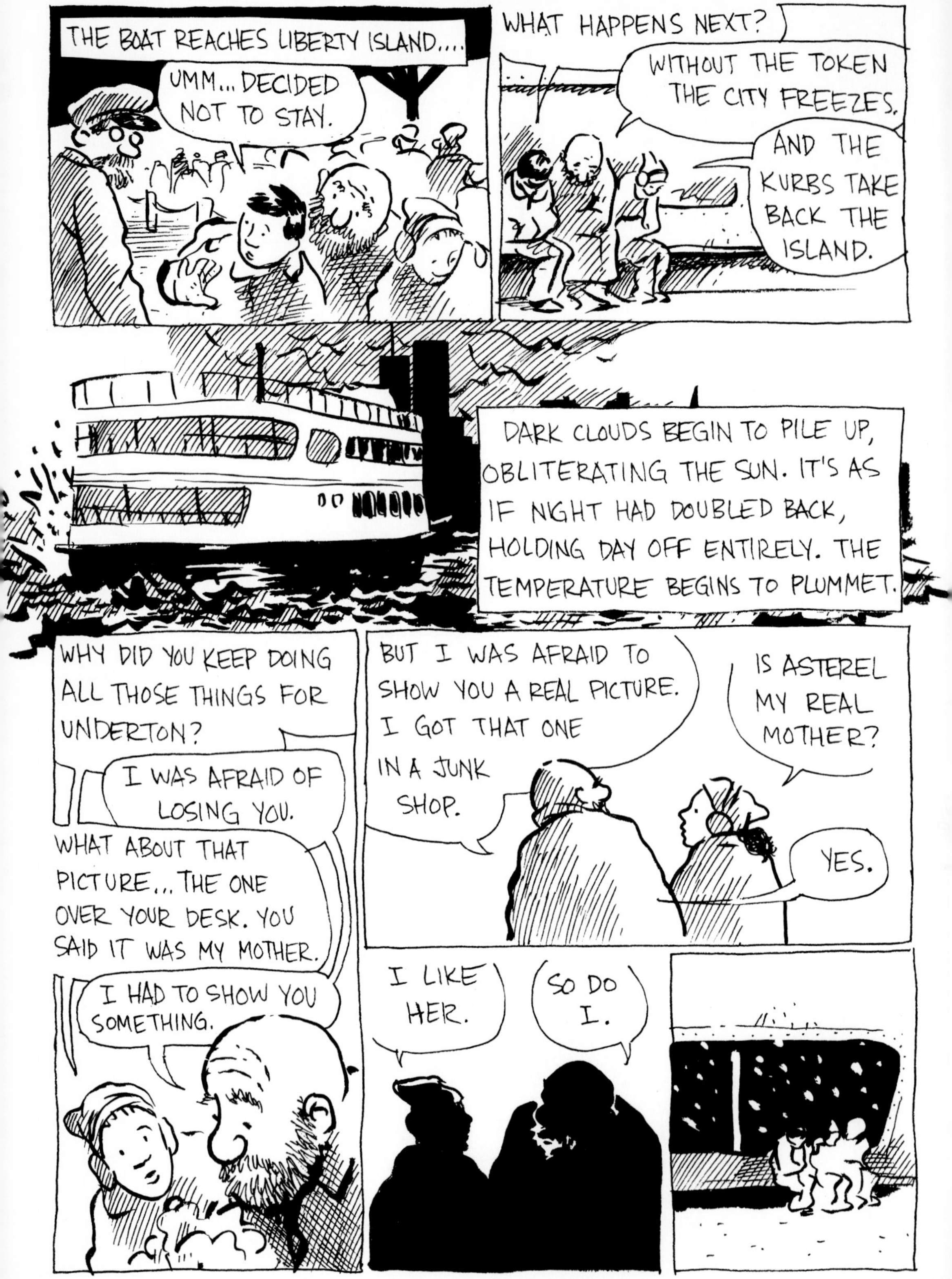

THE BOAT REACHES LIBERTY ISLAND....
UMM... DECIDED NOT TO STAY.
WHAT HAPPENS NEXT?
WITHOUT THE TOKEN THE CITY FREEZES.
AND THE KURBS TAKE BACK THE ISLAND.
DARK CLOUDS BEGIN TO PILE UP, OBLITERATING THE SUN. IT'S AS IF NIGHT HAD DOUBLED BACK, HOLDING DAY OFF ENTIRELY. THE TEMPERATURE BEGINS TO PLUMMET.
WHY DID YOU KEEP DOING ALL THOSE THINGS FOR UNDERTON?
I WAS AFRAID OF LOSING YOU.
WHAT ABOUT THAT PICTURE... THE ONE OVER YOUR DESK. YOU SAID IT WAS MY MOTHER.
I HAD TO SHOW YOU SOMETHING.
BUT I WAS AFRAID TO SHOW YOU A REAL PICTURE. I GOT THAT ONE IN A JUNK SHOP.
IS ASTEREL MY REAL MOTHER?
YES.
I LIKE HER.
SO DO I.

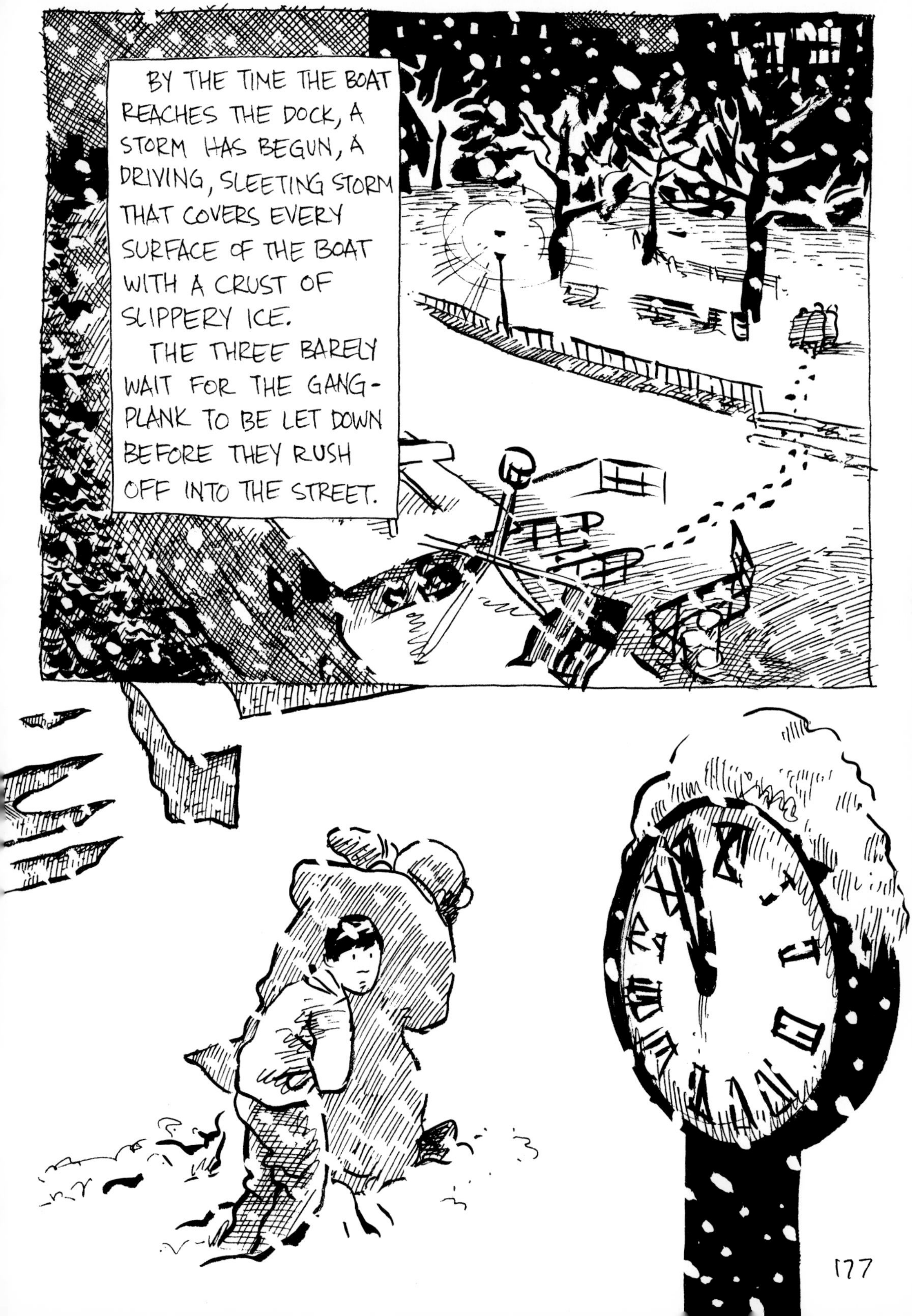
BY THE TIME THE BOAT REACHES THE DOCK, A STORM HAS BEGUN, A DRIVING, SLEETING STORM THAT COVERS EVERY SURFACE OF THE BOAT WITH A CRUST OF SLIPPERY ICE.
THE THREE BARELY WAIT FOR THE GANG-PLANK TO BE LET DOWN BEFORE THEY RUSH OFF INTO THE STREET.
TEP
TEP

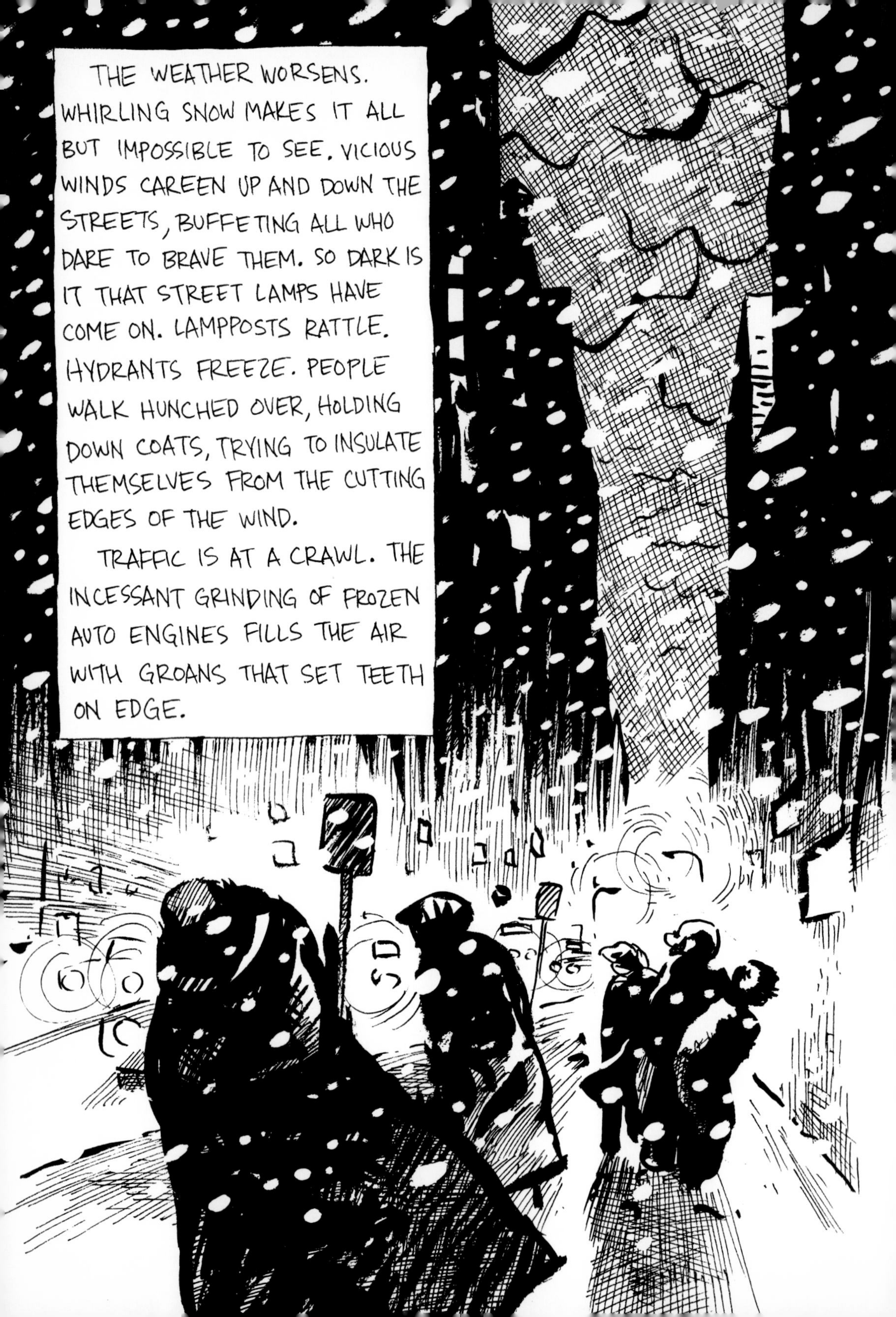
THE WEATHER WORSENS. WHIRLING SNOW MAKES IT ALL BUT IMPOSSIBLE TO SEE. VICIOUS WINDS CAREEN UP AND DOWN THE STREETS, BUFFETING ALL WHO DARE TO BRAVE THEM. SO DARK IS IT THAT STREET LAMPS HAVE COME ON. LAMPPOSTS RATTLE. HYDRANTS FREEZE. PEOPLE WALK HUNCHED OVER, HOLDING DOWN COATS, TRYING TO INSULATE THEMSELVES FROM THE CUTTING EDGES OF THE WIND.
TRAFFIC IS AT A CRAWL. THE INCESSANT GRINDING OF FROZEN AUTO ENGINES FILLS THE AIR WITH GROANS THAT SET TEETH ON EDGE.

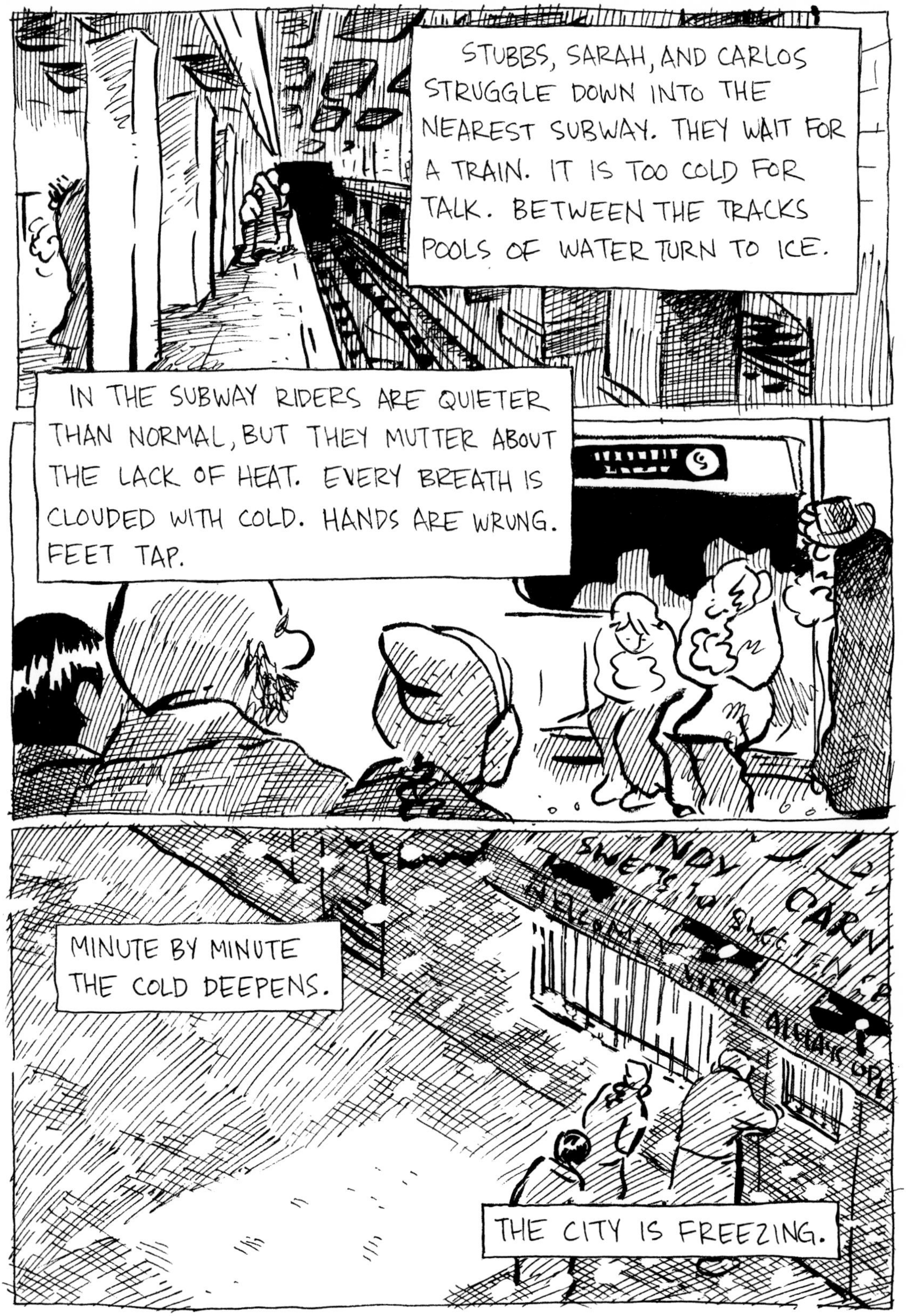
STUBBS, SARAH, AND CARLOS STRUGGLE DOWN INTO THE NEAREST SUBWAY. THEY WAIT FOR A TRAIN. IT IS TOO COLD FOR TALK. BETWEEN THE TRACKS POOLS OF WATER TURN TO ICE.
IN THE SUBWAY RIDERS ARE QUIETER THAN NORMAL, BUT THEY MUTTER ABOUT THE LACK OF HEAT. EVERY BREATH IS CLOUDED WITH COLD. HANDS ARE WRUNG. FEET TAP.
MINUTE BY MINUTE THE COLD DEEPENS.
THE CITY IS FREEZING.

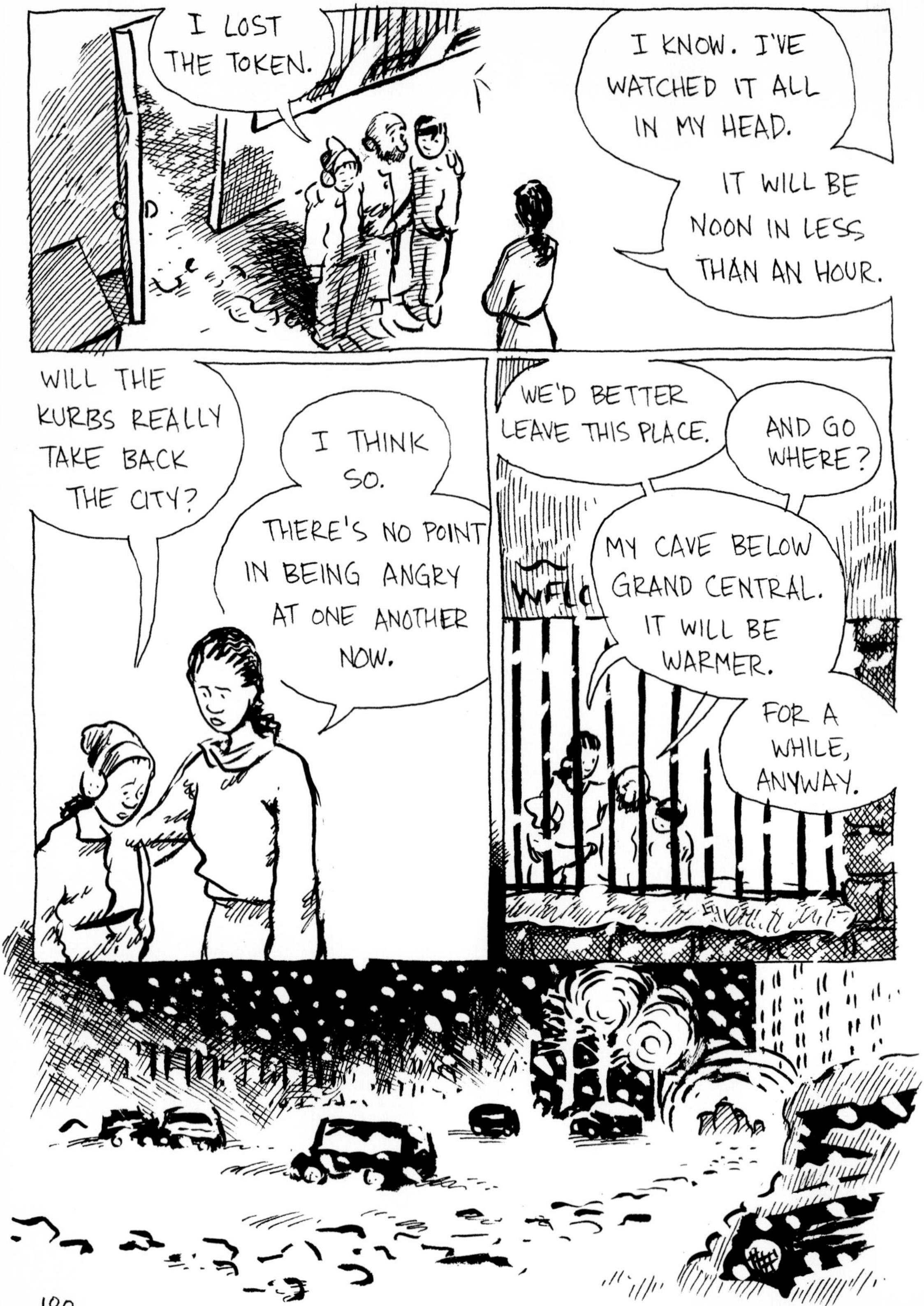
I LOST THE TOKEN.
I KNOW. I'VE WATCHED IT ALL IN MY HEAD.
IT WILL BE NOON IN LESS THAN AN HOUR.
WILL THE KURBS REALLY TAKE BACK THE CITY?
I THINK SO.
THERE'S NO POINT IN BEING ANGRY AT ONE ANOTHER NOW.
WE'D BETTER LEAVE THIS PLACE.
AND GO WHERE?
MY CAVE BELOW GRAND CENTRAL. IT WILL BE WARMER.
FOR A WHILE, ANYWAY.

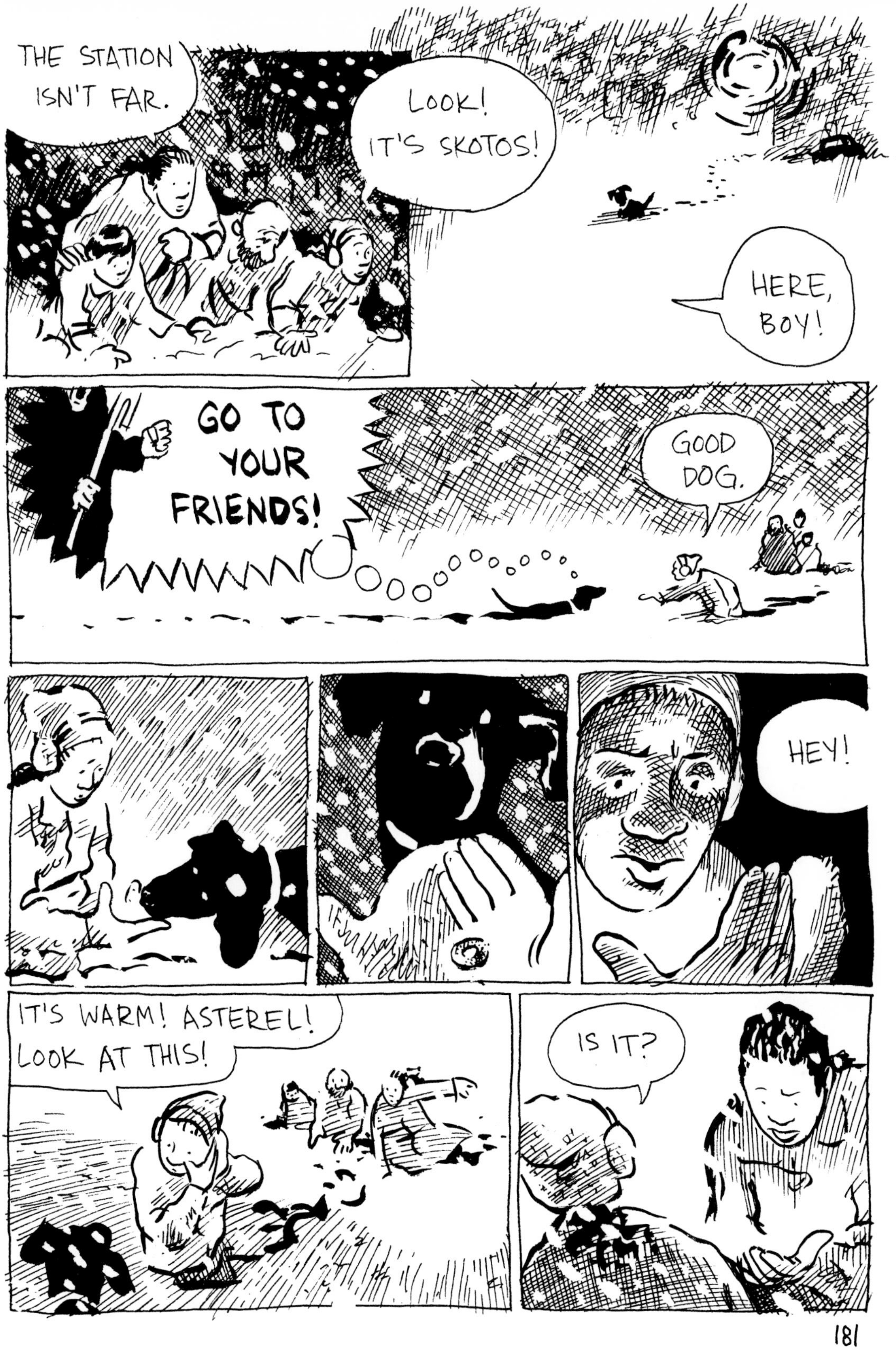
THE STATION ISN'T FAR.
LOOK! IT'S SKOTOS!
HERE, BOY!
GO TO YOUR FRIENDS!
GOOD DOG.
HEY!
IT'S WARM! ASTEREL! LOOK AT THIS!
IS IT?

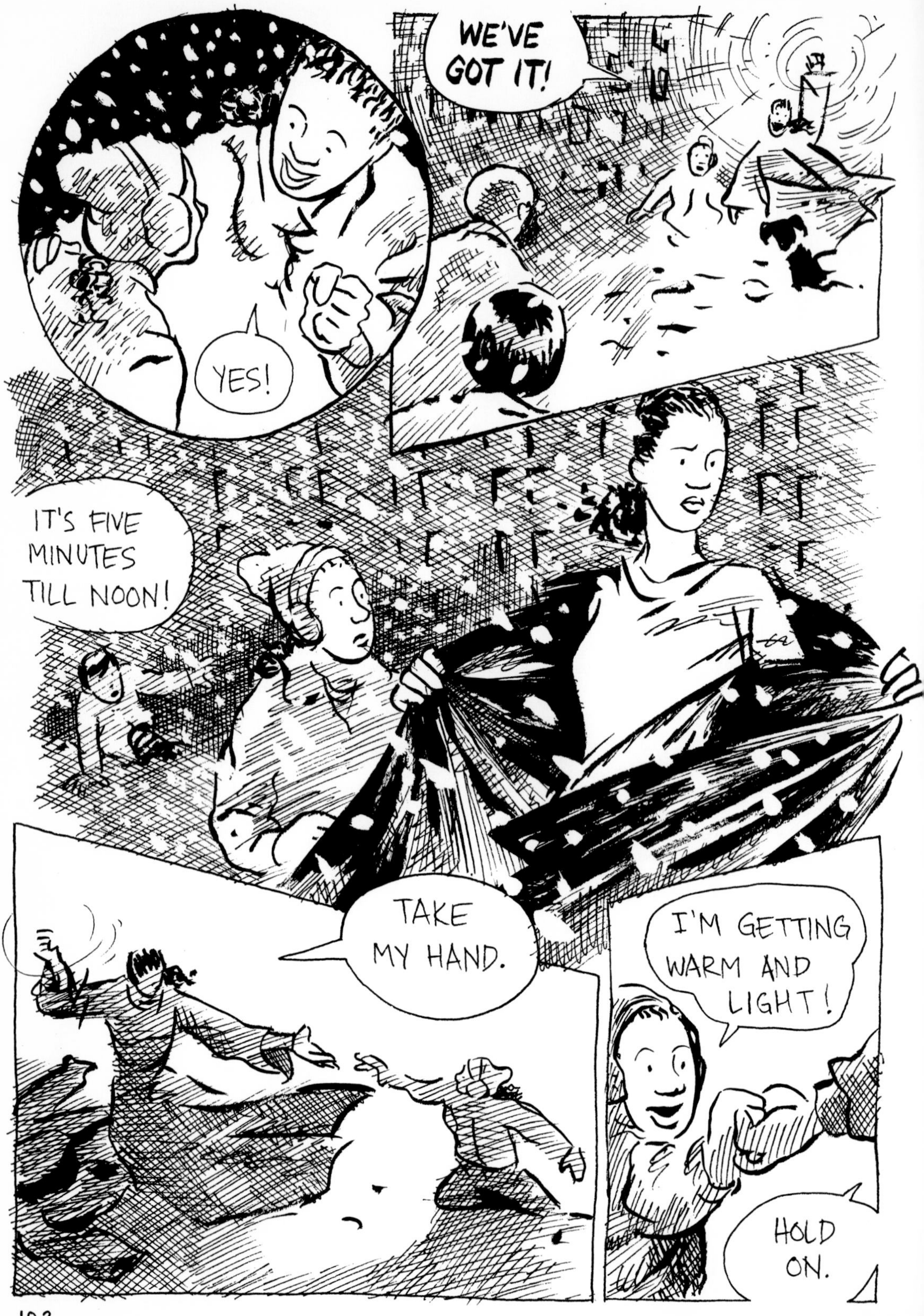
WE'VE GOT IT!
YES!
IT'S FIVE MINUTES TILL NOON!
TAKE MY HAND.
I'M GETTING WARM AND LIGHT!
HOLD ON.

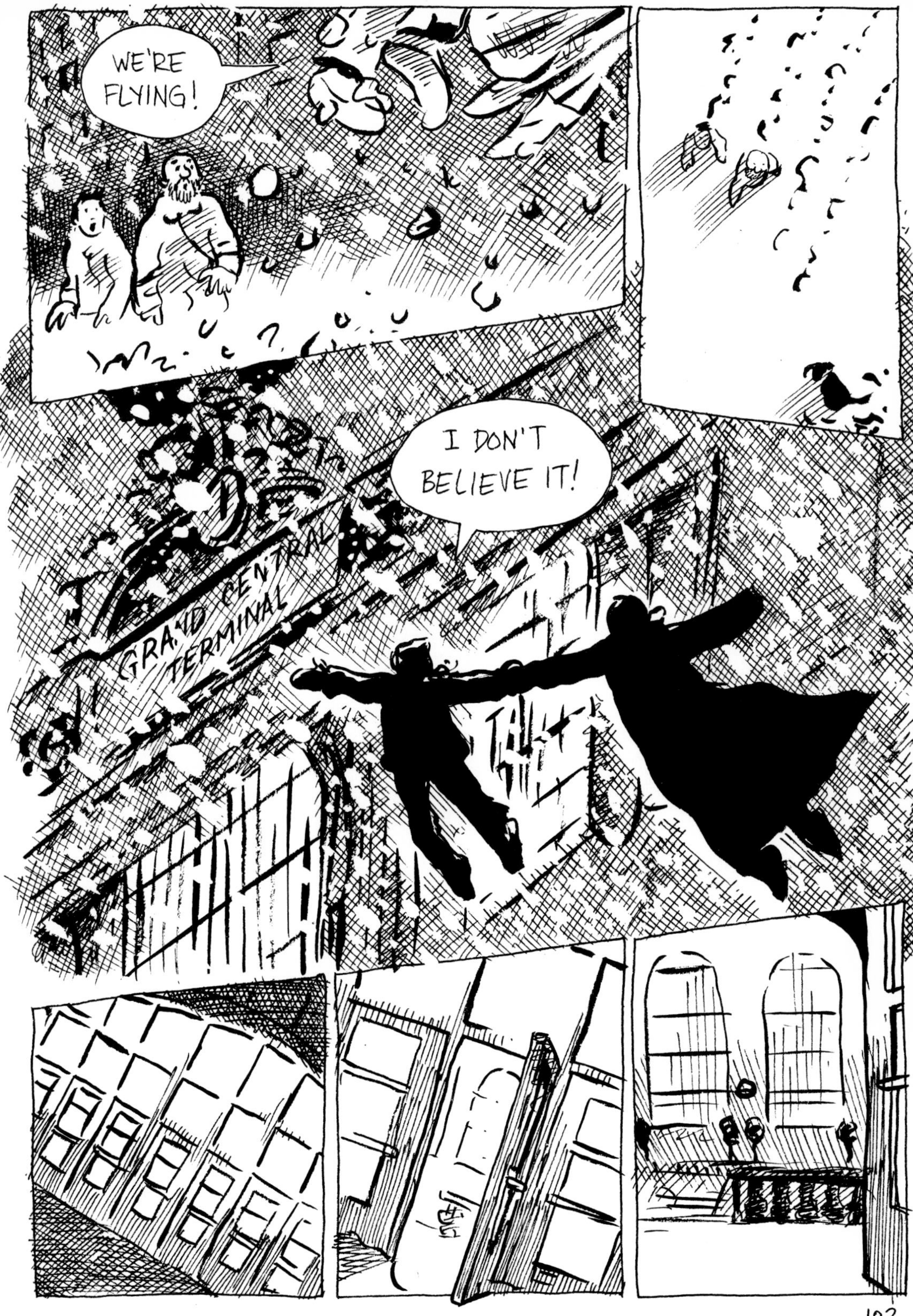
WE'RE FLYING!
I DON'T BELIEVE IT!
GRAND CENTRAL TERMINAL

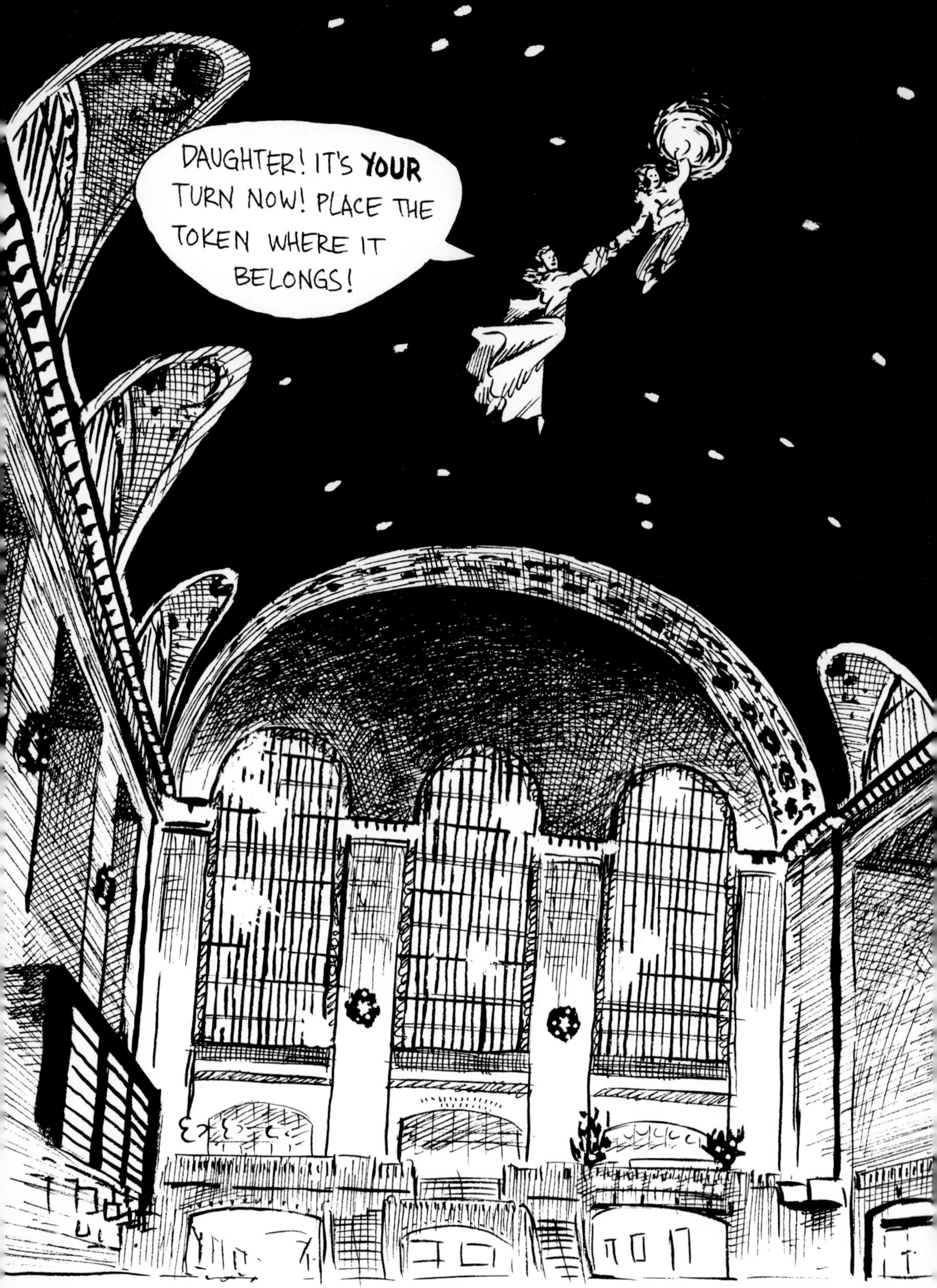
DAUGHTER! IT'S **YOUR** TURN NOW! PLACE THE TOKEN WHERE IT BELONGS!

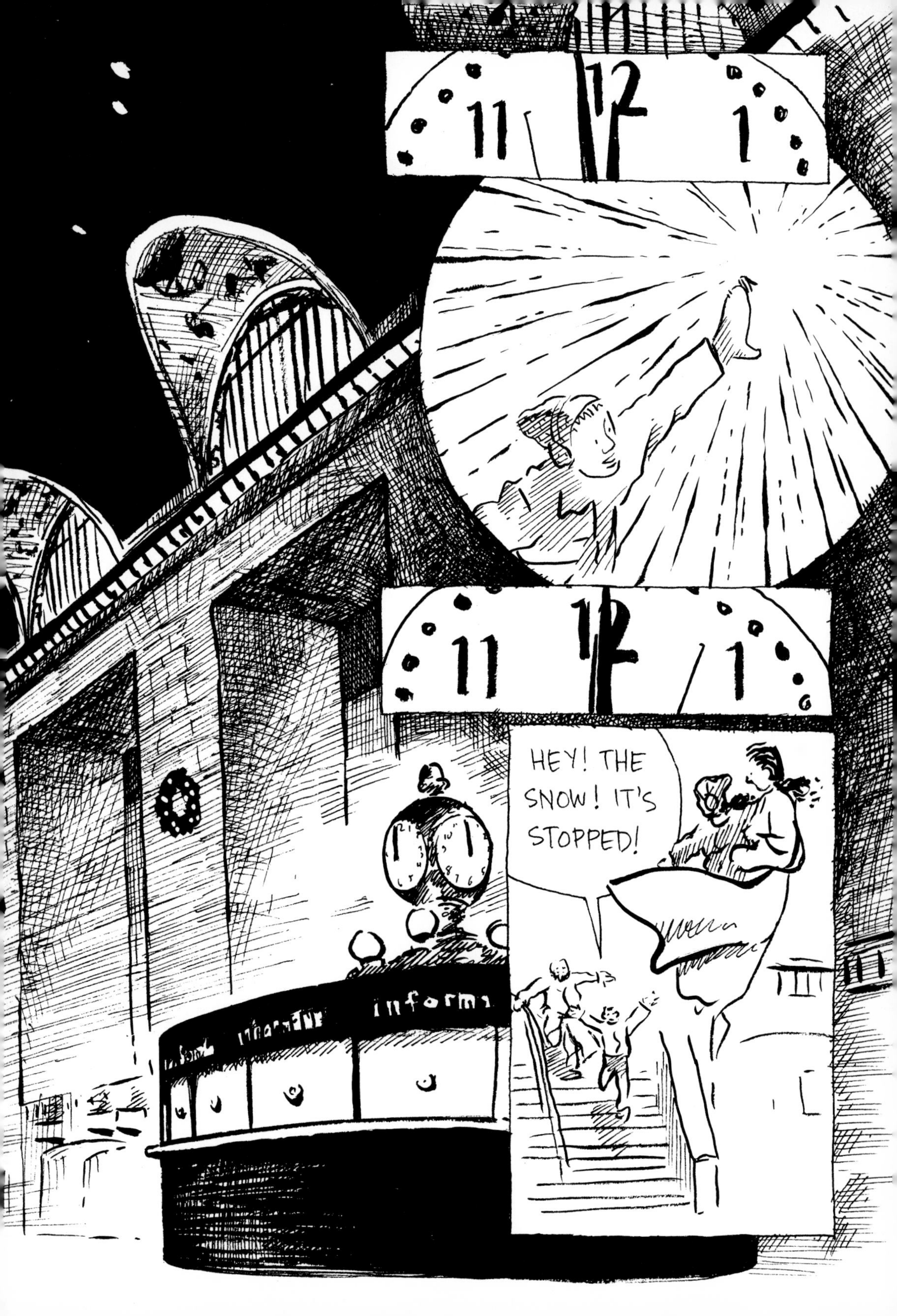
HEY! THE SNOW! IT'S STOPPED!

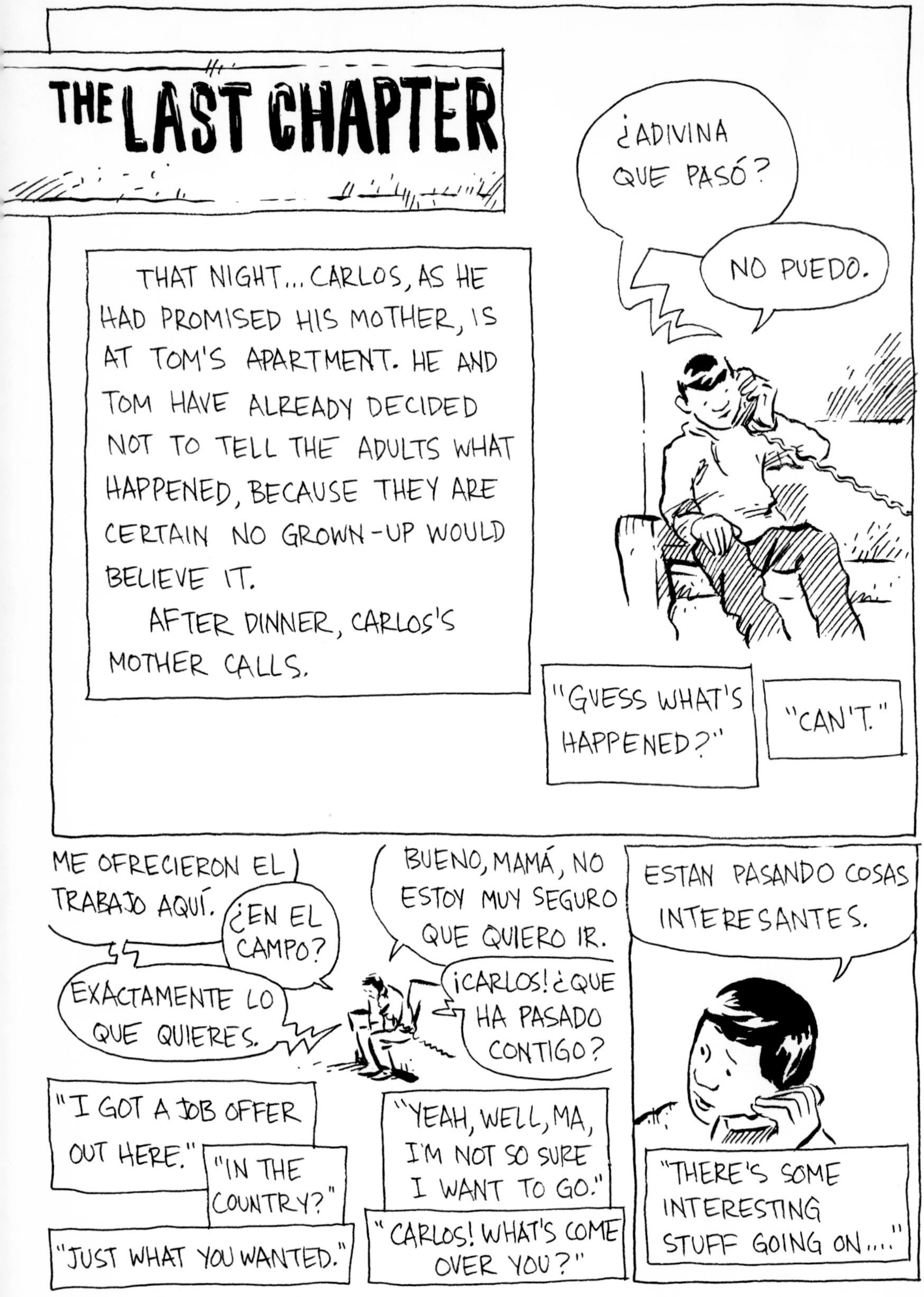
THE LAST CHAPTER
THAT NIGHT... CARLOS, AS HE HAD PROMISED HIS MOTHER, IS AT TOM'S APARTMENT. HE AND TOM HAVE ALREADY DECIDED NOT TO TELL THE ADULTS WHAT HAPPENED, BECAUSE THEY ARE CERTAIN NO GROWN-UP WOULD BELIEVE IT.
AFTER DINNER, CARLOS'S MOTHER CALLS.
¿ADIVINA QUE PASÓ?
NO PUEDO.
"GUESS WHAT'S HAPPENED?"
"CAN'T."
ME OFRECIERON EL TRABAJO AQUÍ.
¿EN EL CAMPO?
EXACTAMENTE LO QUE QUIERES.
"I GOT A JOB OFFER OUT HERE."
"IN THE COUNTRY?"
"JUST WHAT YOU WANTED."
BUENO, MAMÁ, NO ESTOY MUY SEGURO QUE QUIERO IR.
¡CARLOS! ¿QUE HA PASADO CONTIGO?
"YEAH, WELL, MA, I'M NOT SO SURE I WANT TO GO."
"CARLOS! WHAT'S COME OVER YOU?"
ESTAN PASANDO COSAS INTERESANTES.
"THERE'S SOME INTERESTING STUFF GOING ON...."

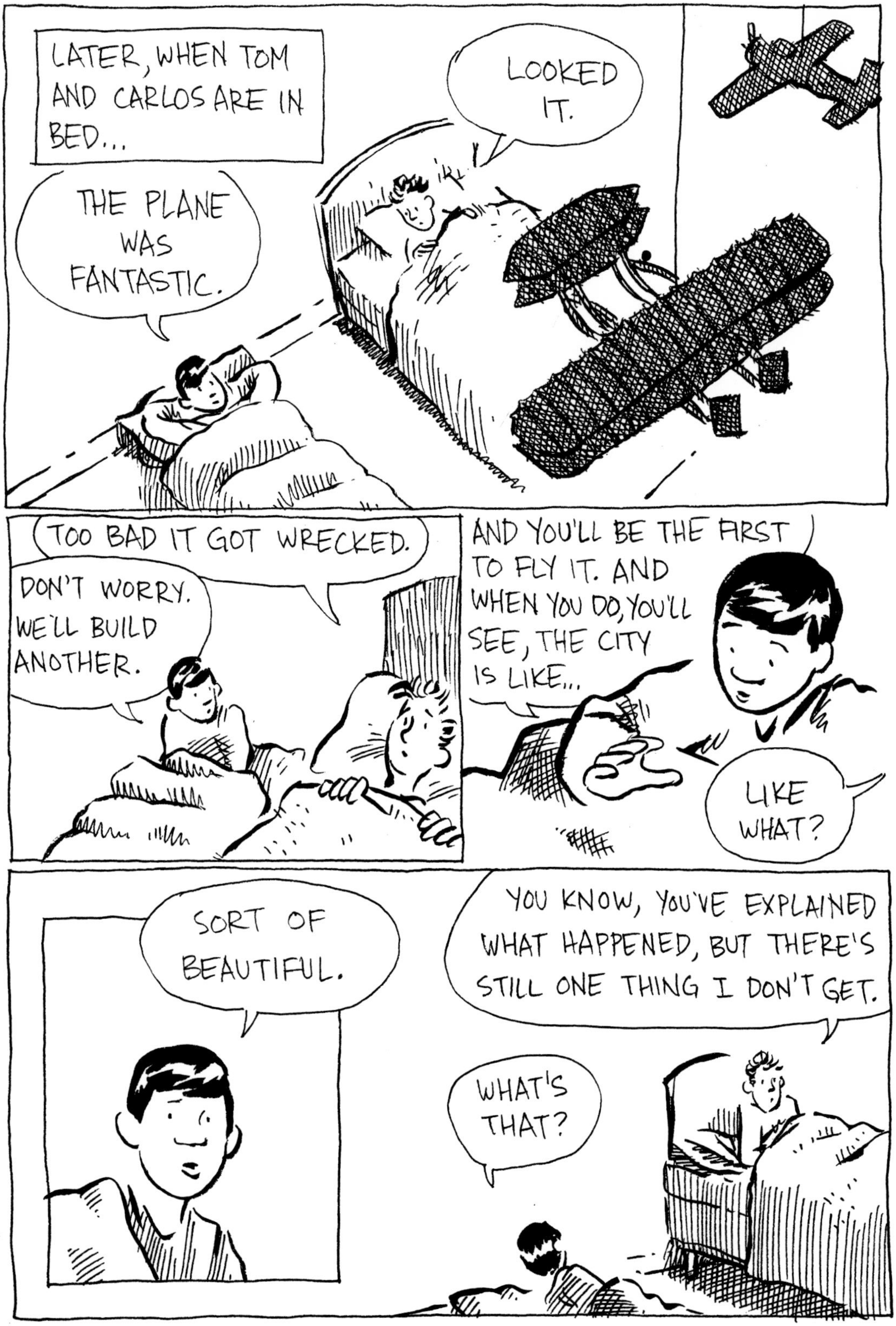
LATER, WHEN TOM AND CARLOS ARE IN BED...
THE PLANE WAS FANTASTIC.
LOOKED IT.
TOO BAD IT GOT WRECKED.
DON'T WORRY. WE'LL BUILD ANOTHER.
AND YOU'LL BE THE FIRST TO FLY IT. AND WHEN YOU DO, YOU'LL SEE, THE CITY IS LIKE...
LIKE WHAT?
SORT OF BEAUTIFUL.
YOU KNOW, YOU'VE EXPLAINED WHAT HAPPENED, BUT THERE'S STILL ONE THING I DON'T GET.
WHAT'S THAT?

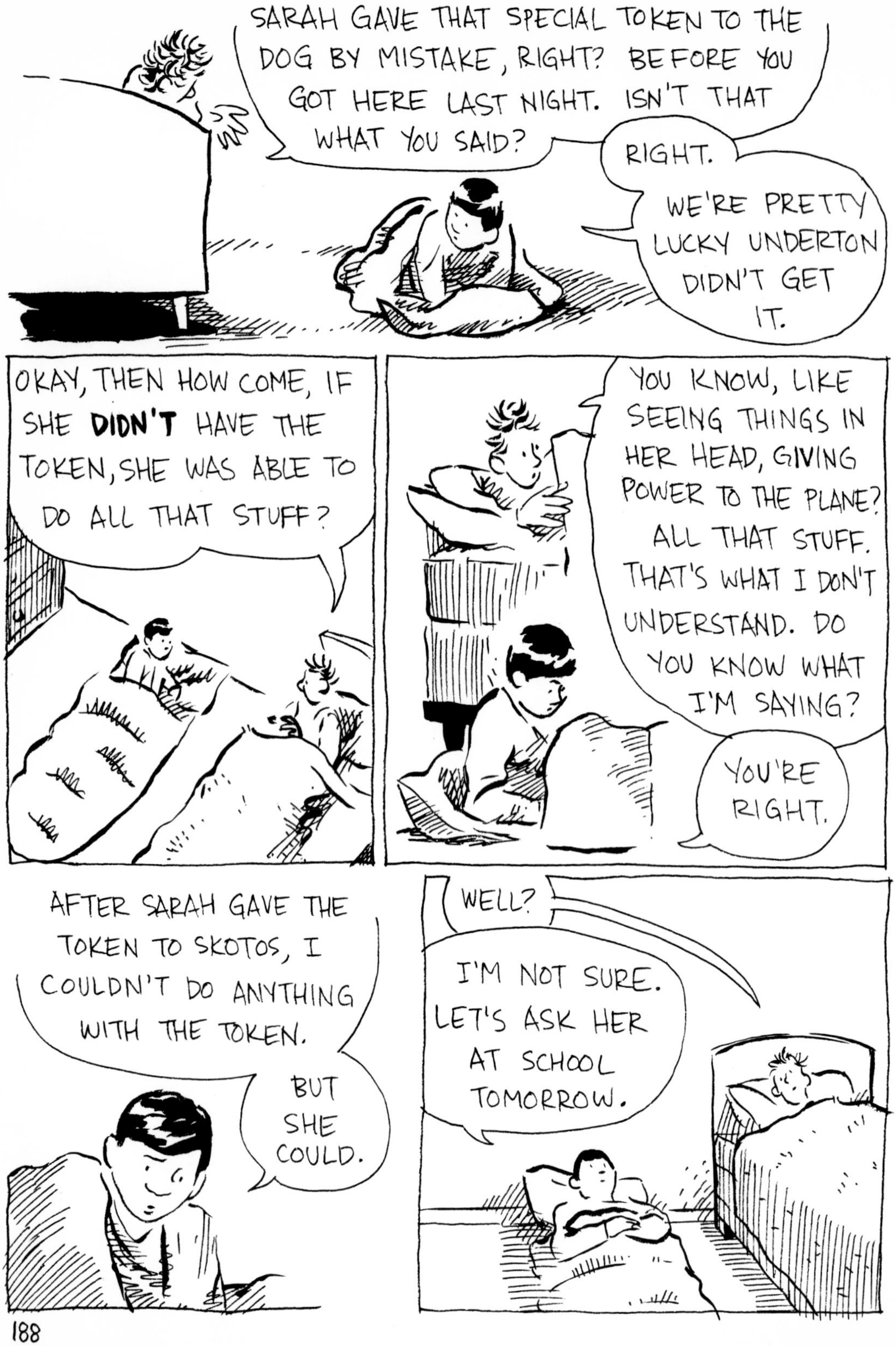
SARAH GAVE THAT SPECIAL TOKEN TO THE DOG BY MISTAKE, RIGHT? BEFORE YOU GOT HERE LAST NIGHT. ISN'T THAT WHAT YOU SAID?
RIGHT.
WE'RE PRETTY LUCKY UNDERTON DIDN'T GET IT.
OKAY, THEN HOW COME, IF SHE DIDN'T HAVE THE TOKEN, SHE WAS ABLE TO DO ALL THAT STUFF?
YOU KNOW, LIKE SEEING THINGS IN HER HEAD, GIVING POWER TO THE PLANE? ALL THAT STUFF. THAT'S WHAT I DON'T UNDERSTAND. DO YOU KNOW WHAT I'M SAYING?
YOU'RE RIGHT.
AFTER SARAH GAVE THE TOKEN TO SKOTOS, I COULDN'T DO ANYTHING WITH THE TOKEN.
BUT SHE COULD.
WELL?
I'M NOT SURE. LET'S ASK HER AT SCHOOL TOMORROW.

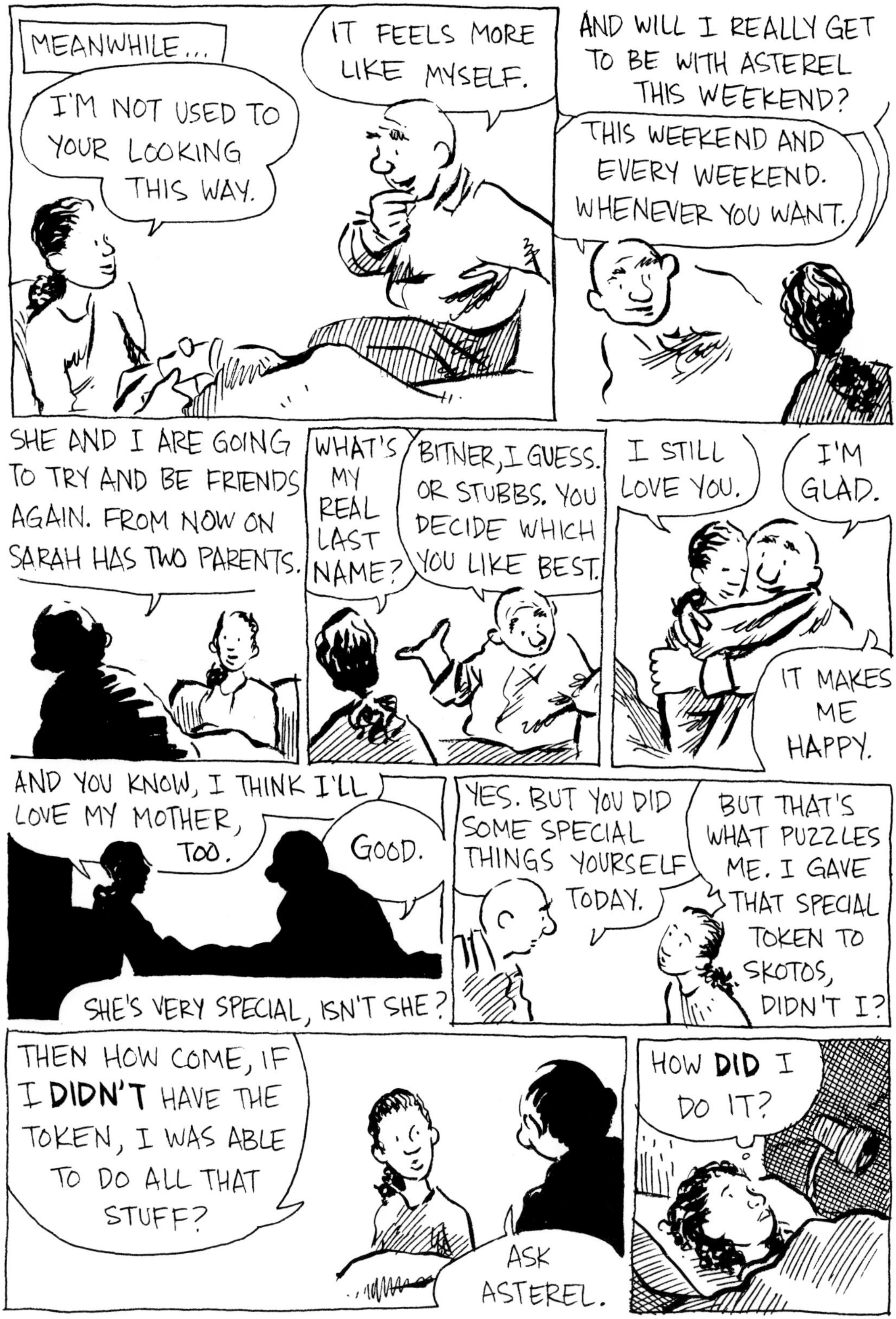
MEANWHILE...
I'M NOT USED TO YOUR LOOKING THIS WAY.
IT FEELS MORE LIKE MYSELF.
AND WILL I REALLY GET TO BE WITH ASTEREL THIS WEEKEND?
THIS WEEKEND AND EVERY WEEKEND. WHENEVER YOU WANT.
SHE AND I ARE GOING TO TRY AND BE FRIENDS AGAIN. FROM NOW ON SARAH HAS TWO PARENTS.
WHAT'S MY REAL LAST NAME?
BITNER, I GUESS. OR STUBBS. YOU DECIDE WHICH YOU LIKE BEST.
I STILL LOVE YOU.
I'M GLAD.
IT MAKES ME HAPPY.
AND YOU KNOW, I THINK I'LL LOVE MY MOTHER, TOO.
GOOD.
SHE'S VERY SPECIAL, ISN'T SHE?
YES. BUT YOU DID SOME SPECIAL THINGS YOURSELF TODAY.
BUT THAT'S WHAT PUZZLES ME. I GAVE THAT SPECIAL TOKEN TO SKOTOS, DIDN'T I?
THEN HOW COME, IF I **DIDN'T** HAVE THE TOKEN, I WAS ABLE TO DO ALL THAT STUFF?
ASK ASTEREL.
HOW **DID** I DO IT?

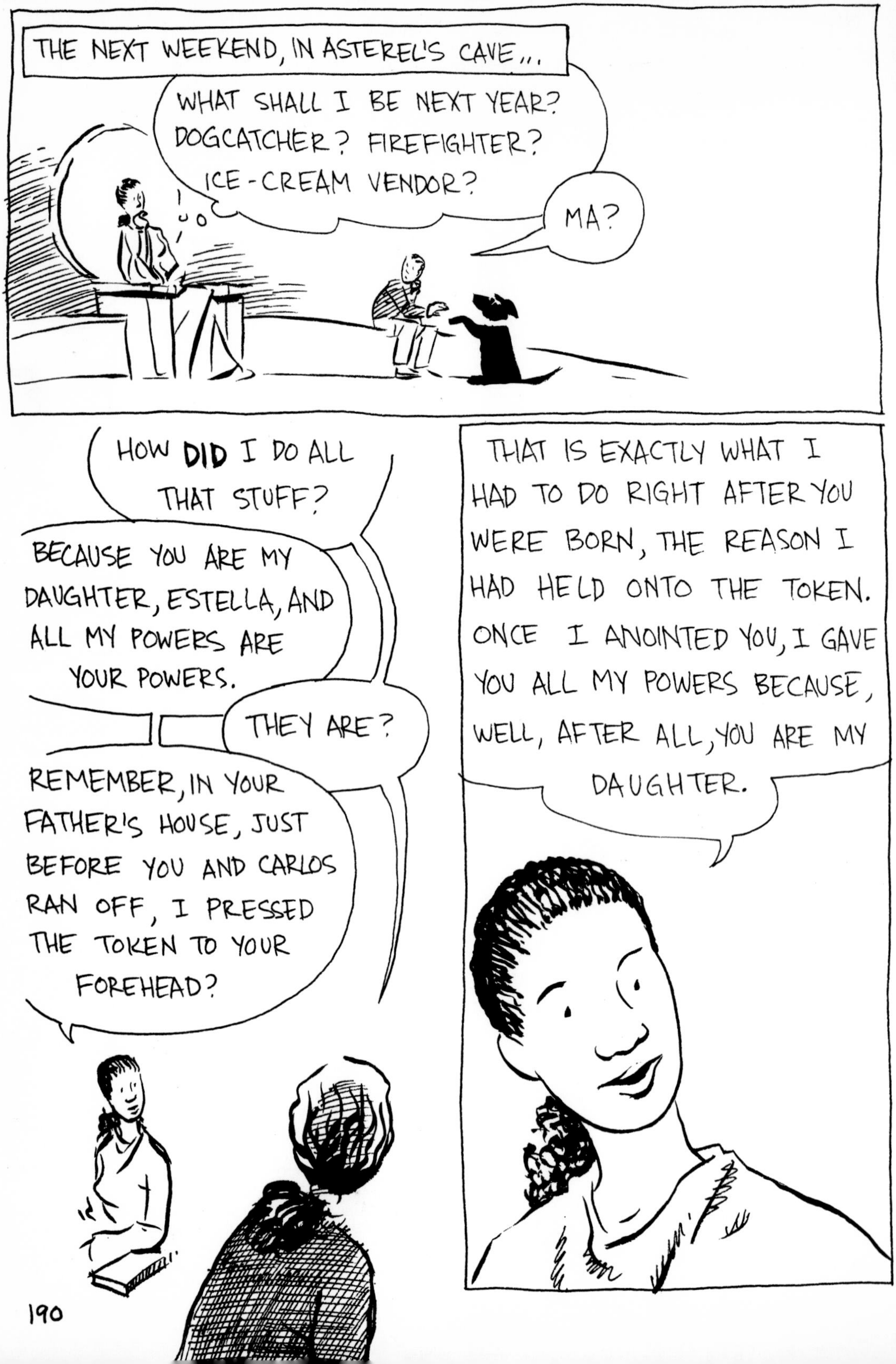
THE NEXT WEEKEND, IN ASTEREL'S CAVE...
WHAT SHALL I BE NEXT YEAR? DOGCATCHER? FIREFIGHTER? ICE-CREAM VENDOR?
MA?
HOW **DID** I DO ALL THAT STUFF?
BECAUSE YOU ARE MY DAUGHTER, ESTELLA, AND ALL MY POWERS ARE YOUR POWERS.
THEY ARE?
REMEMBER, IN YOUR FATHER'S HOUSE, JUST BEFORE YOU AND CARLOS RAN OFF, I PRESSED THE TOKEN TO YOUR FOREHEAD?
THAT IS EXACTLY WHAT I HAD TO DO RIGHT AFTER YOU WERE BORN, THE REASON I HAD HELD ONTO THE TOKEN. ONCE I ANOINTED YOU, I GAVE YOU ALL MY POWERS BECAUSE, WELL, AFTER ALL, YOU ARE MY DAUGHTER.

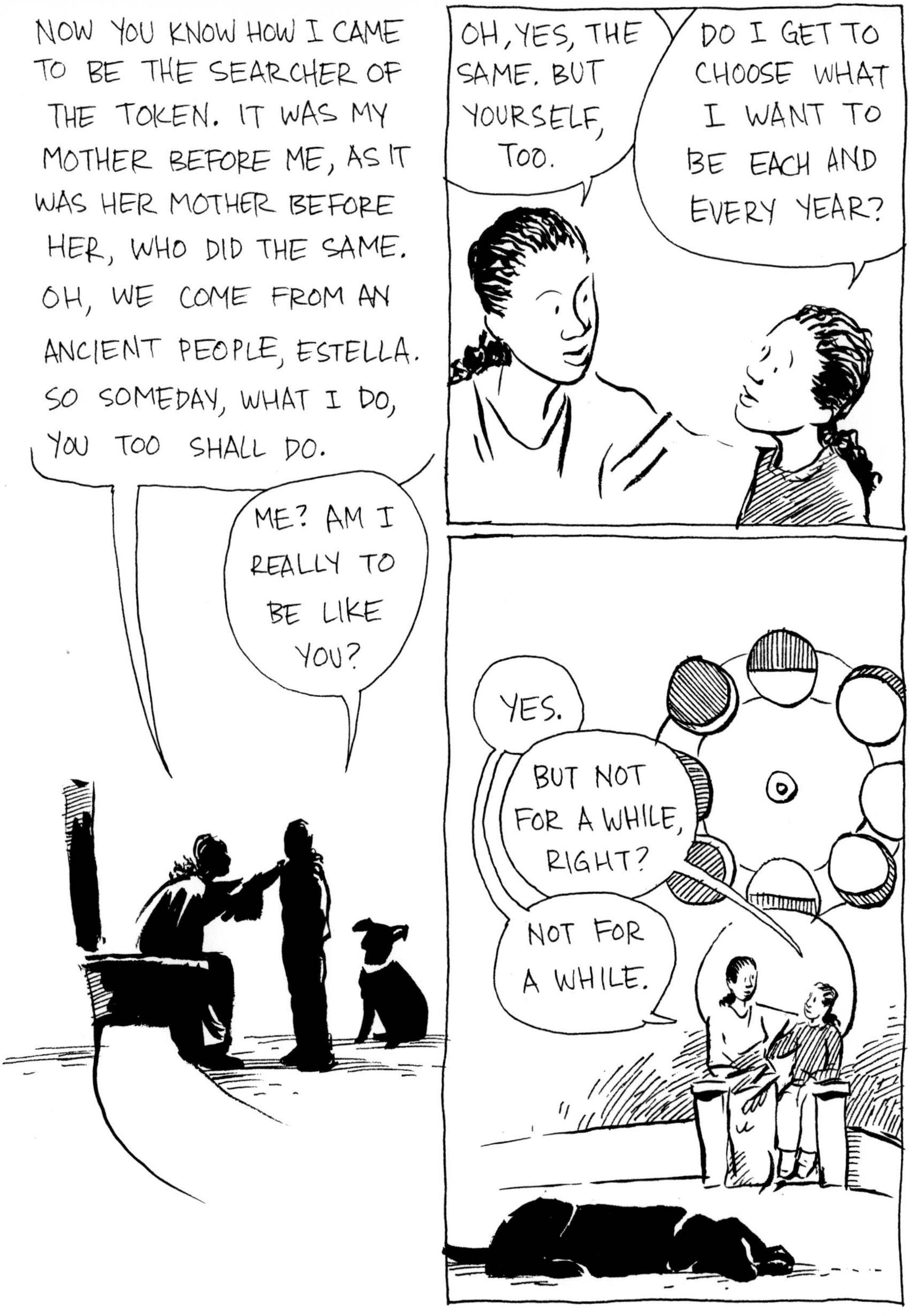
NOW YOU KNOW HOW I CAME TO BE THE SEARCHER OF THE TOKEN. IT WAS MY MOTHER BEFORE ME, AS IT WAS HER MOTHER BEFORE HER, WHO DID THE SAME. OH, WE COME FROM AN ANCIENT PEOPLE, ESTELLA. SO SOMEDAY, WHAT I DO, YOU TOO SHALL DO.
ME? AM I REALLY TO BE LIKE YOU?
OH, YES, THE SAME. BUT YOURSELF, TOO.
DO I GET TO CHOOSE WHAT I WANT TO BE EACH AND EVERY YEAR?
YES.
BUT NOT FOR A WHILE, RIGHT?
NOT FOR A WHILE.

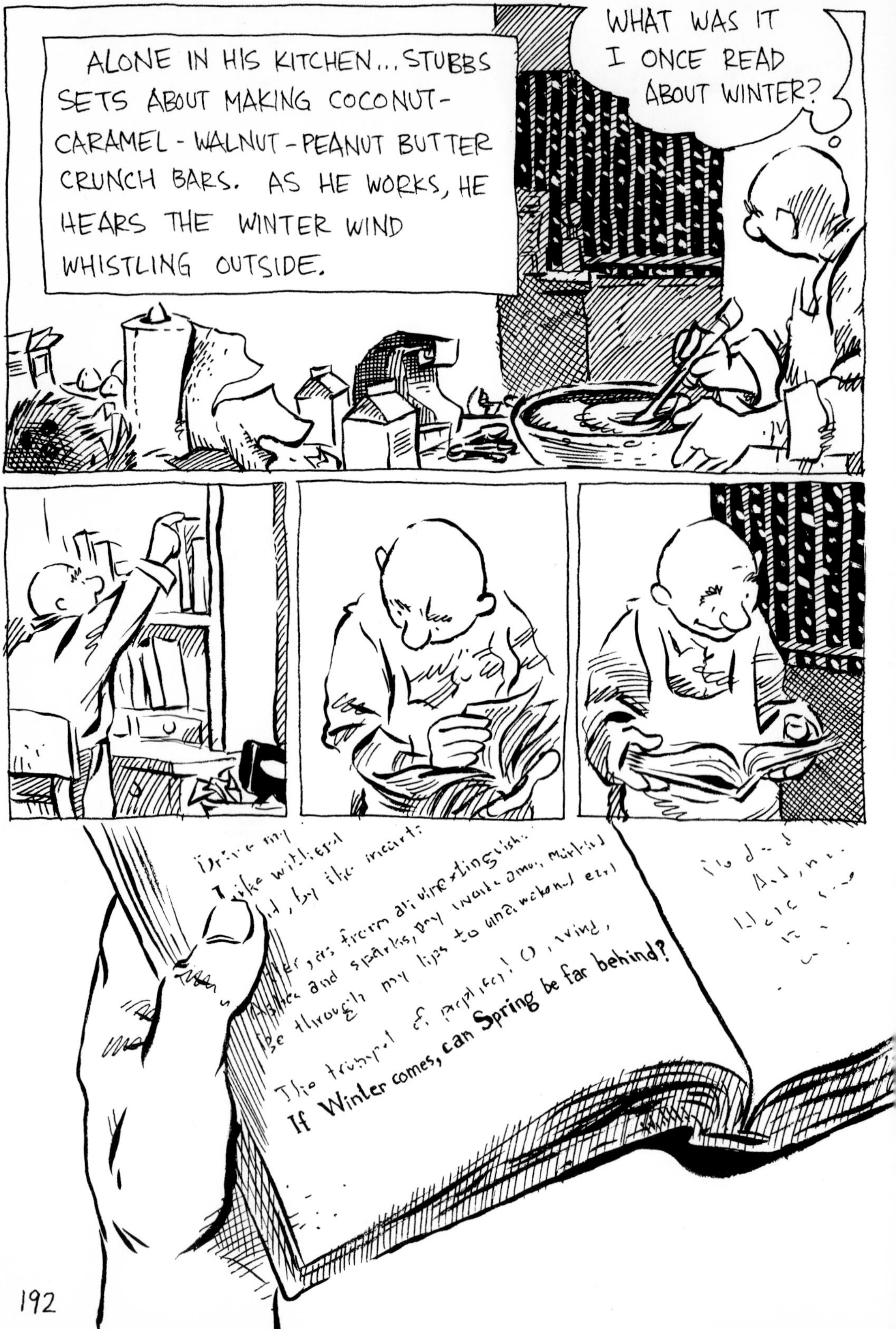
ALONE IN HIS KITCHEN... STUBBS SETS ABOUT MAKING COCONUT-CARAMEL-WALNUT-PEANUT BUTTER CRUNCH BARS. AS HE WORKS, HE HEARS THE WINTER WIND WHISTLING OUTSIDE.
WHAT WAS IT I ONCE READ ABOUT WINTER?
If Winter comes, can Spring be far behind?

Giant Soup

CONTENTS

Ready to Read

School Publications Branch
Department of Education Wellington 1984

One Thursday morning....

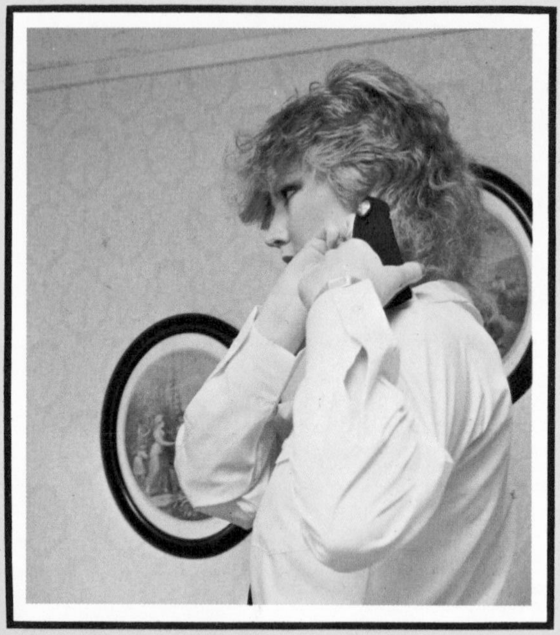

Leigh Coddington
is a traffic officer.
These photographs
show what she did on duty
one Thursday morning.

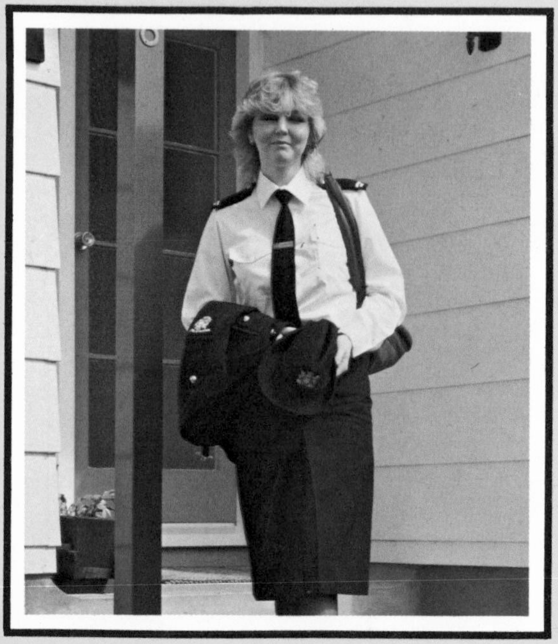

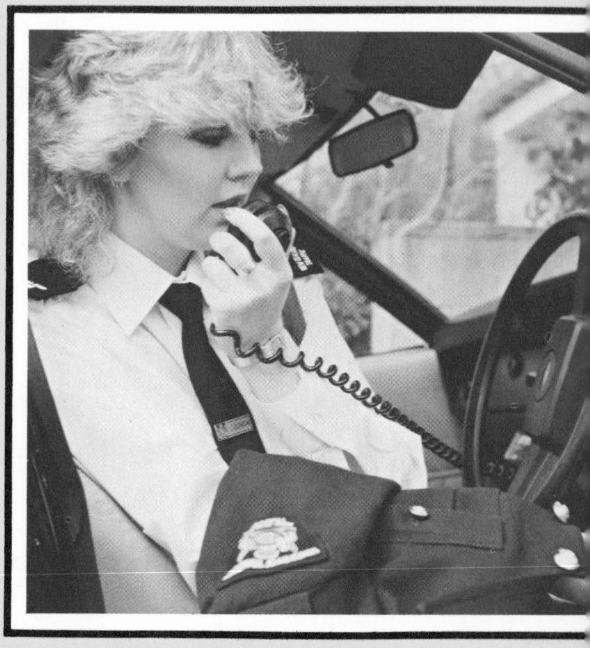

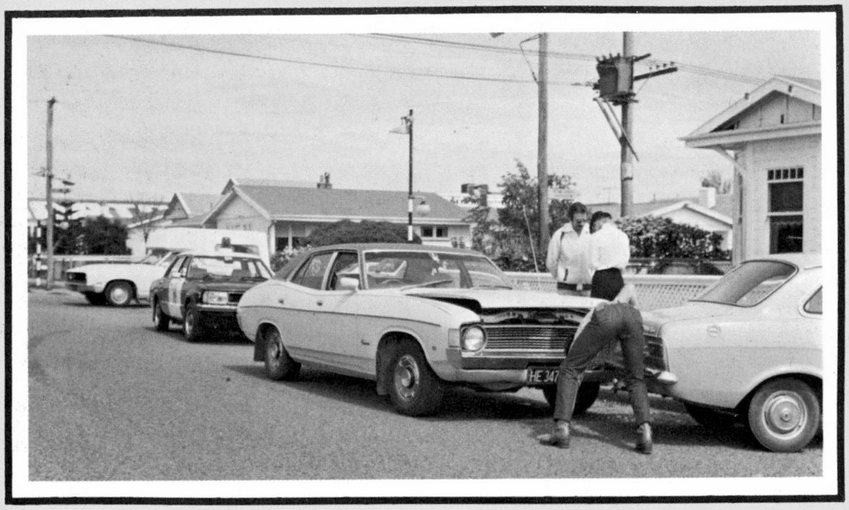

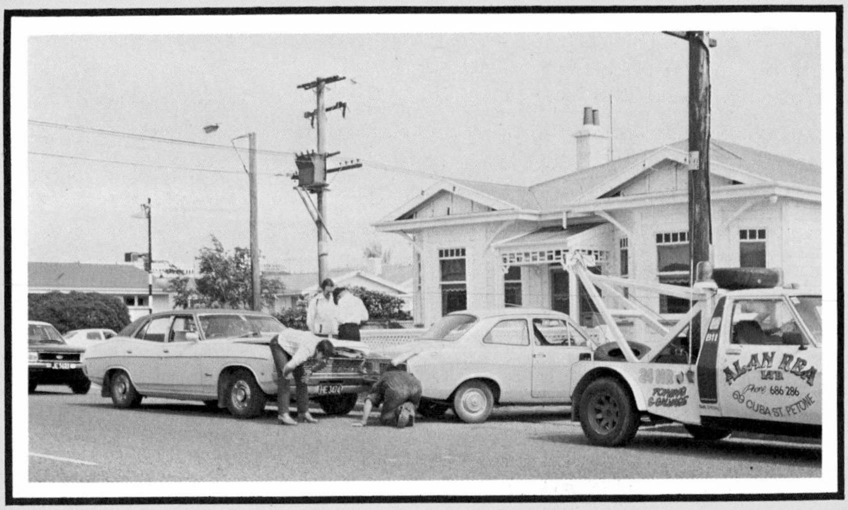
ALAN REA LTD
Phone 686 286
69 CUBA ST. PETONE

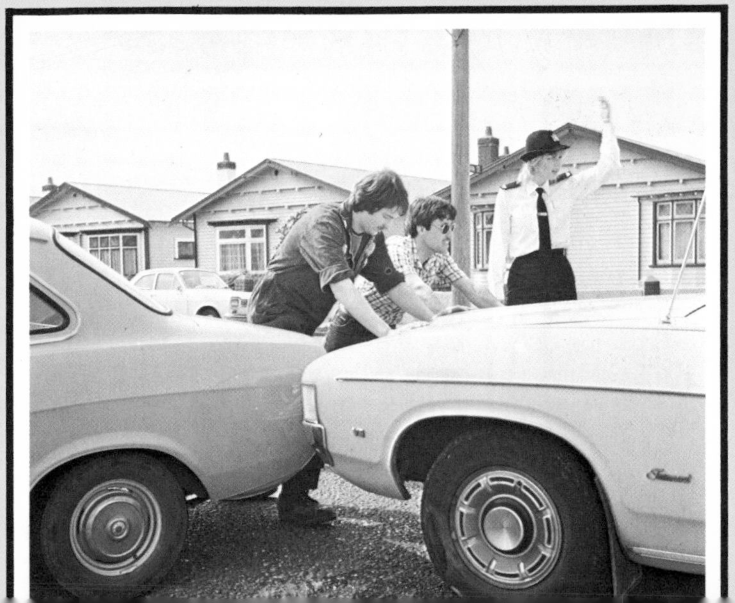

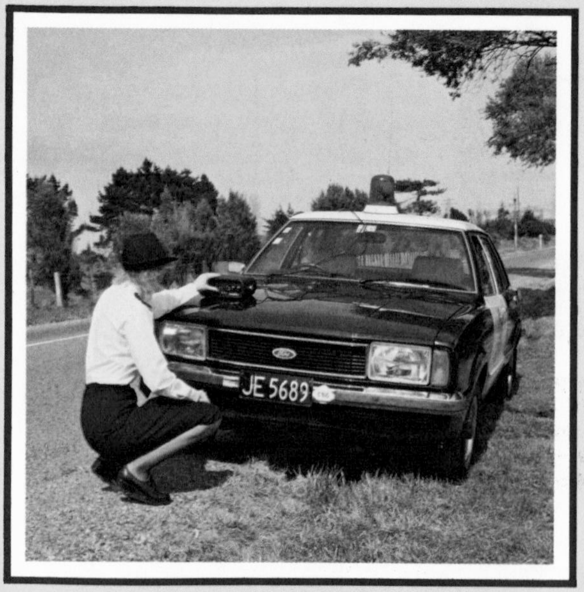
JE 5689

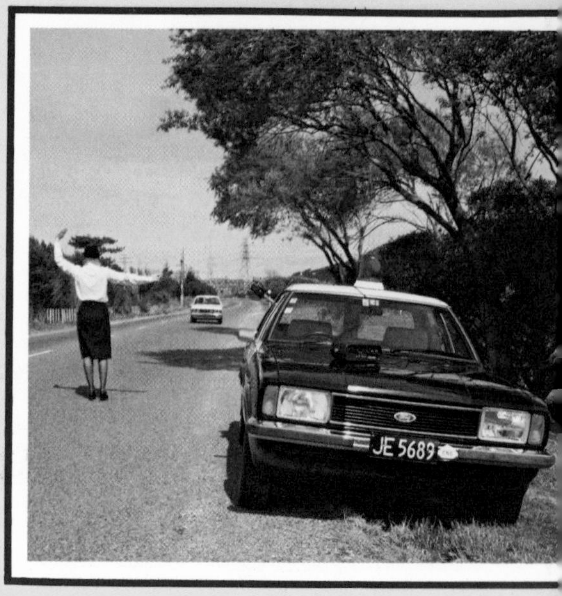
JE 5689

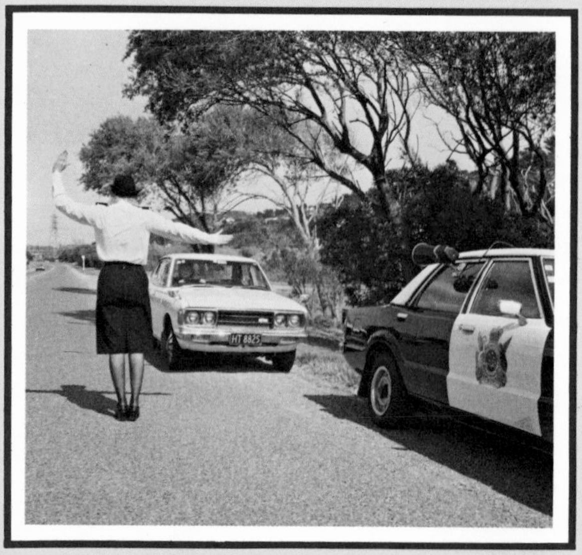
HT 8825

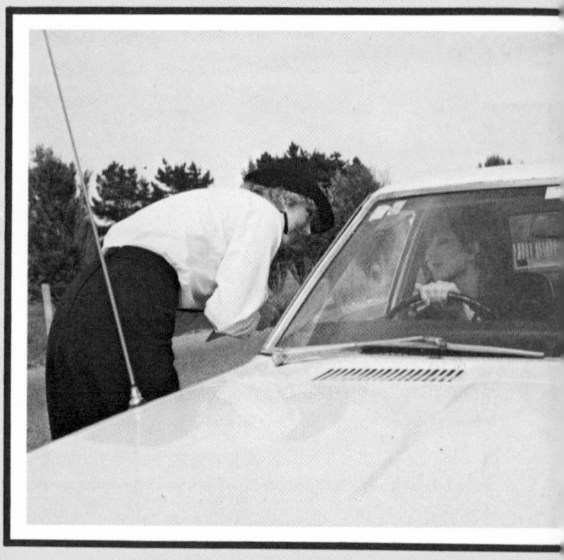

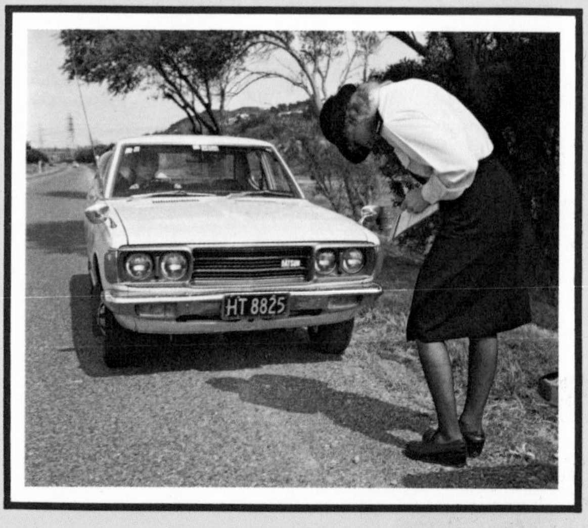
HT 8825

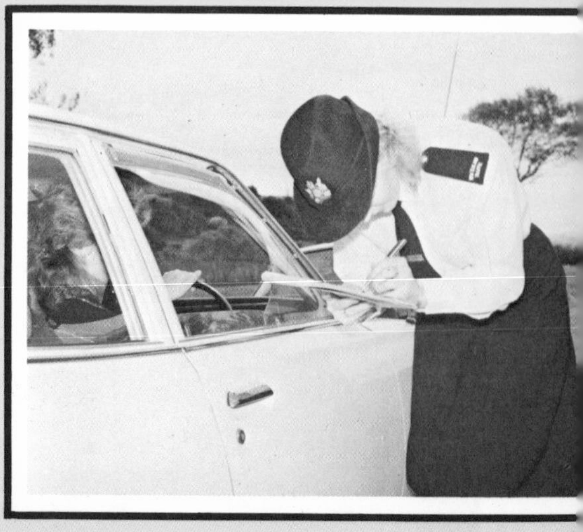

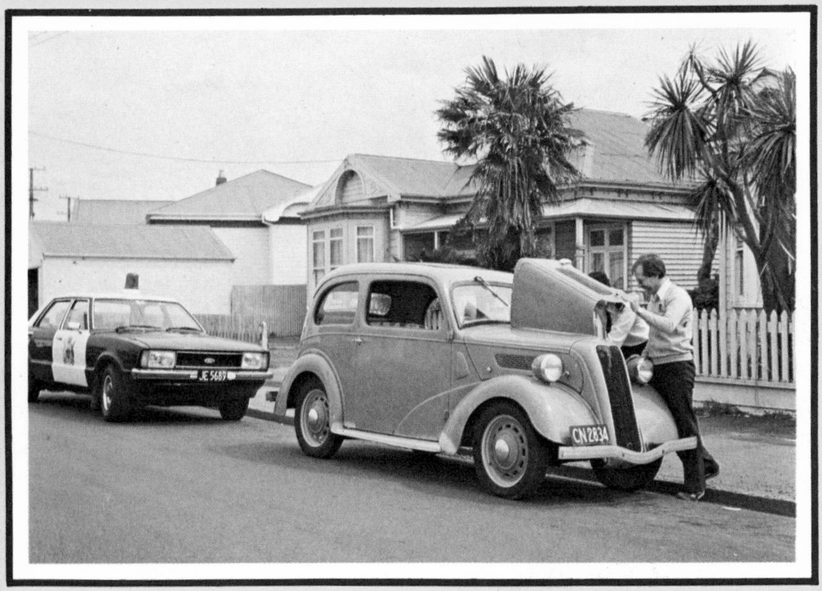
JE 5687
CN 2834

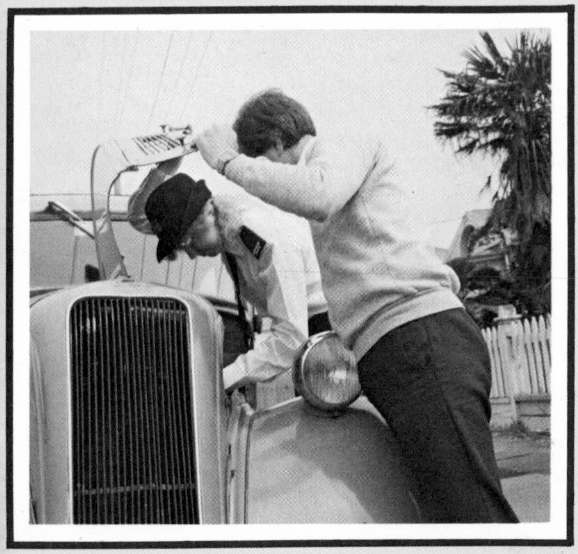

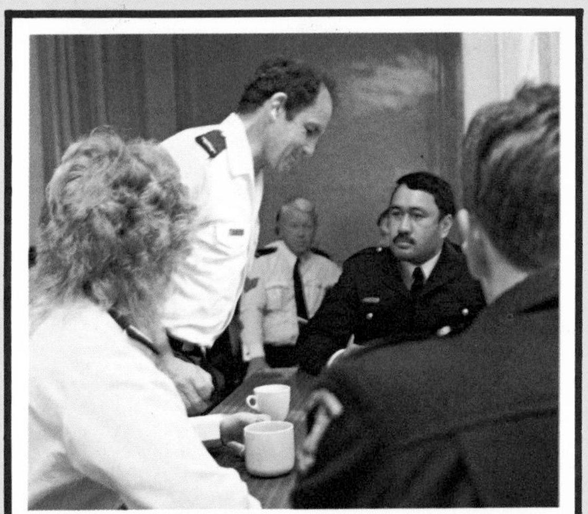

Brrrm! Brrrm!

by Margaret Mahy
pictures by Bob Kerr

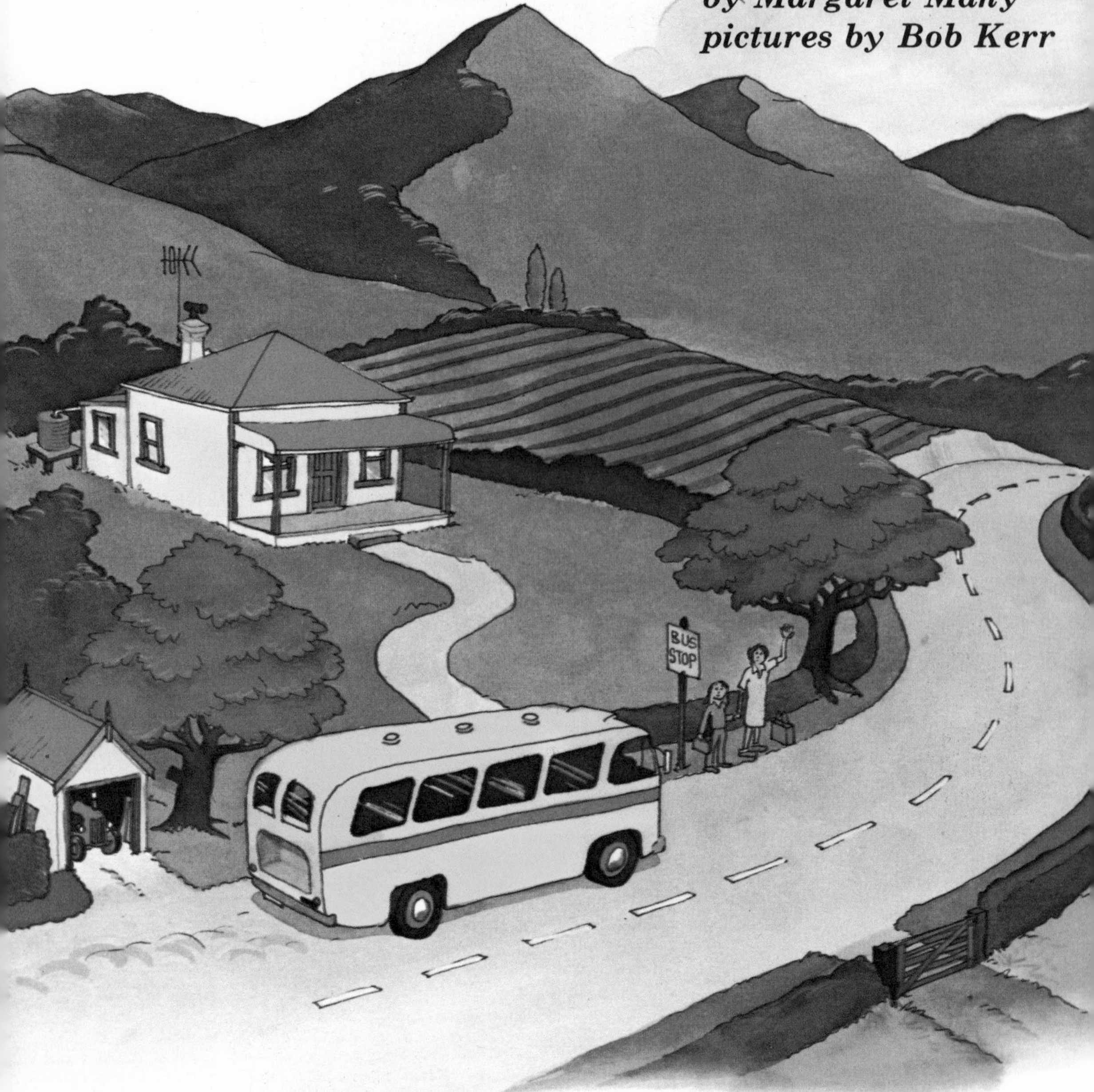

BUS STOP

Emily and her mother
were going to Auntie Annie's house.
Auntie Annie lived in town.

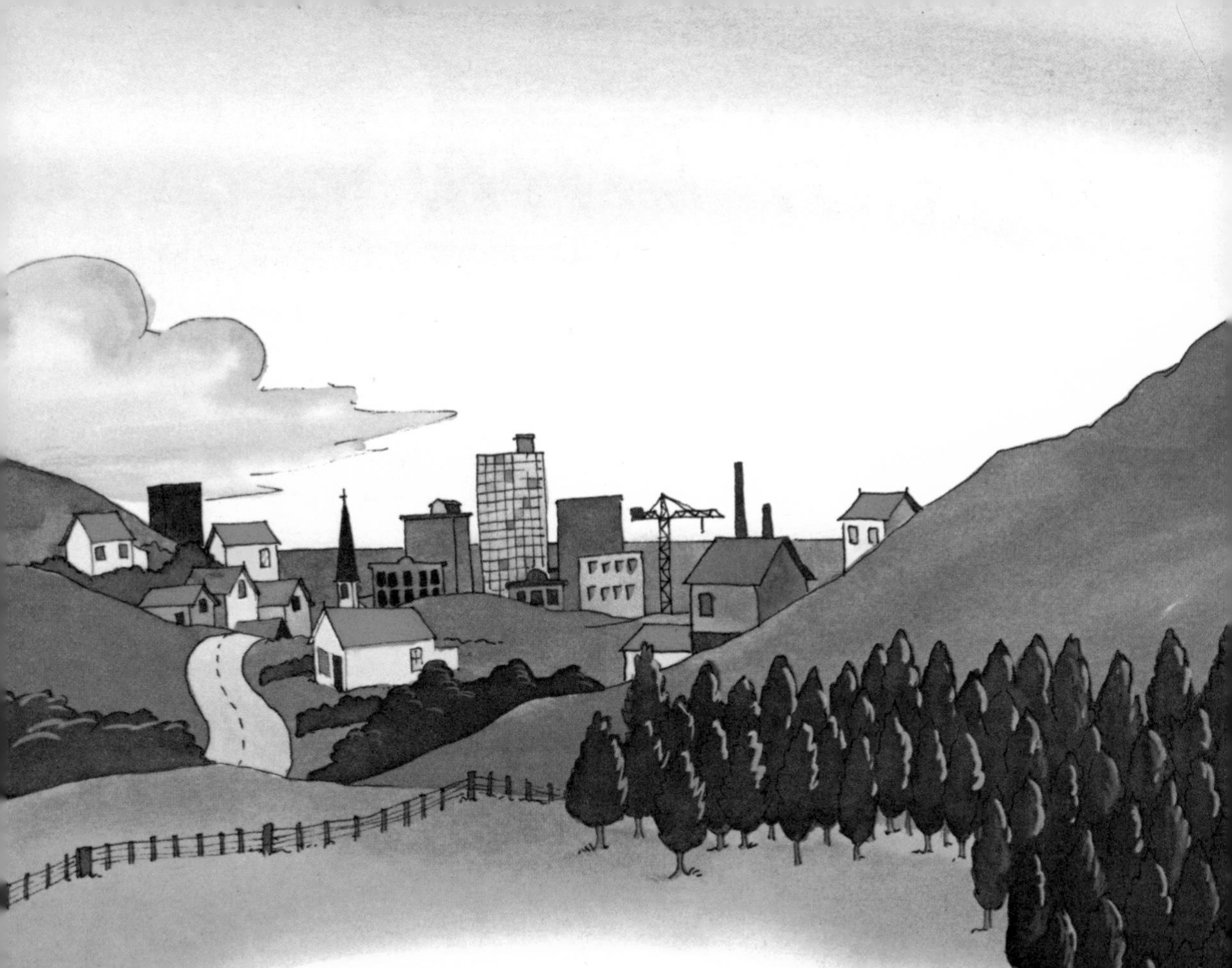

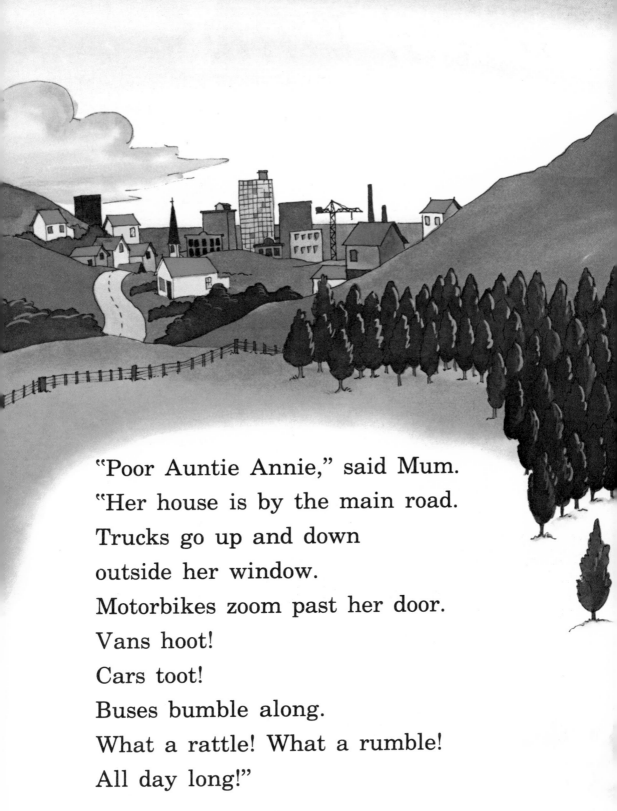

"Poor Auntie Annie," said Mum.
"Her house is by the main road.
Trucks go up and down
outside her window.
Motorbikes zoom past her door.
Vans hoot!
Cars toot!
Buses bumble along.
What a rattle! What a rumble!
All day long!"

The bus stopped outside
Auntie Annie's house.
Mum and Emily got off.
Then they had to cross
the main road.
"Stop!" said Mum.
"The traffic lights say 'Wait'.
Here come the cars!"

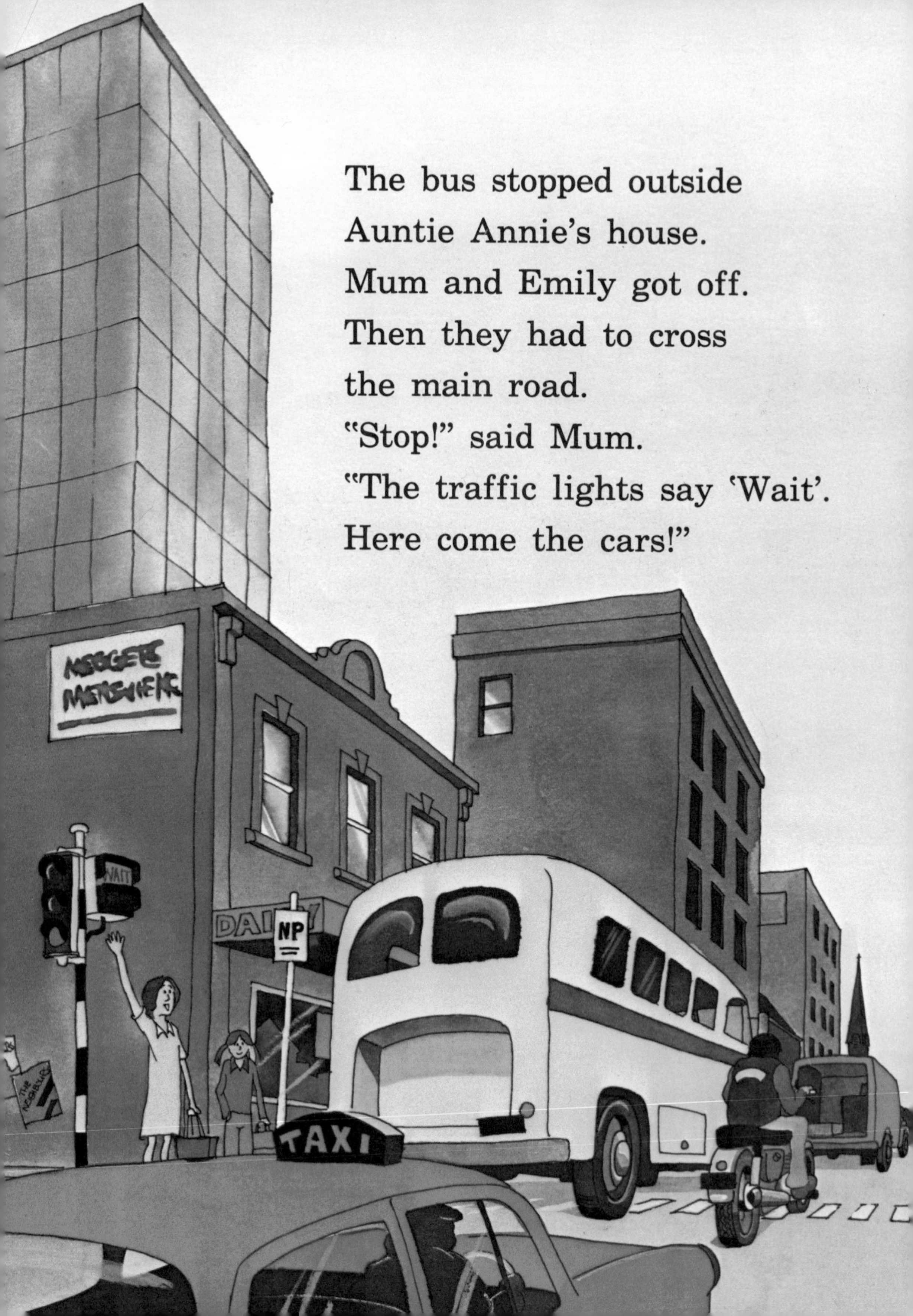
NP
TAXI

Brrrm! Brrrm!
A motorbike whizzed past.
A taxi hooted at a big truck.
Toot! Toot! Brrrm! Brrrm!
"Poor Auntie Annie," said Mum.
"It's like this all day long."

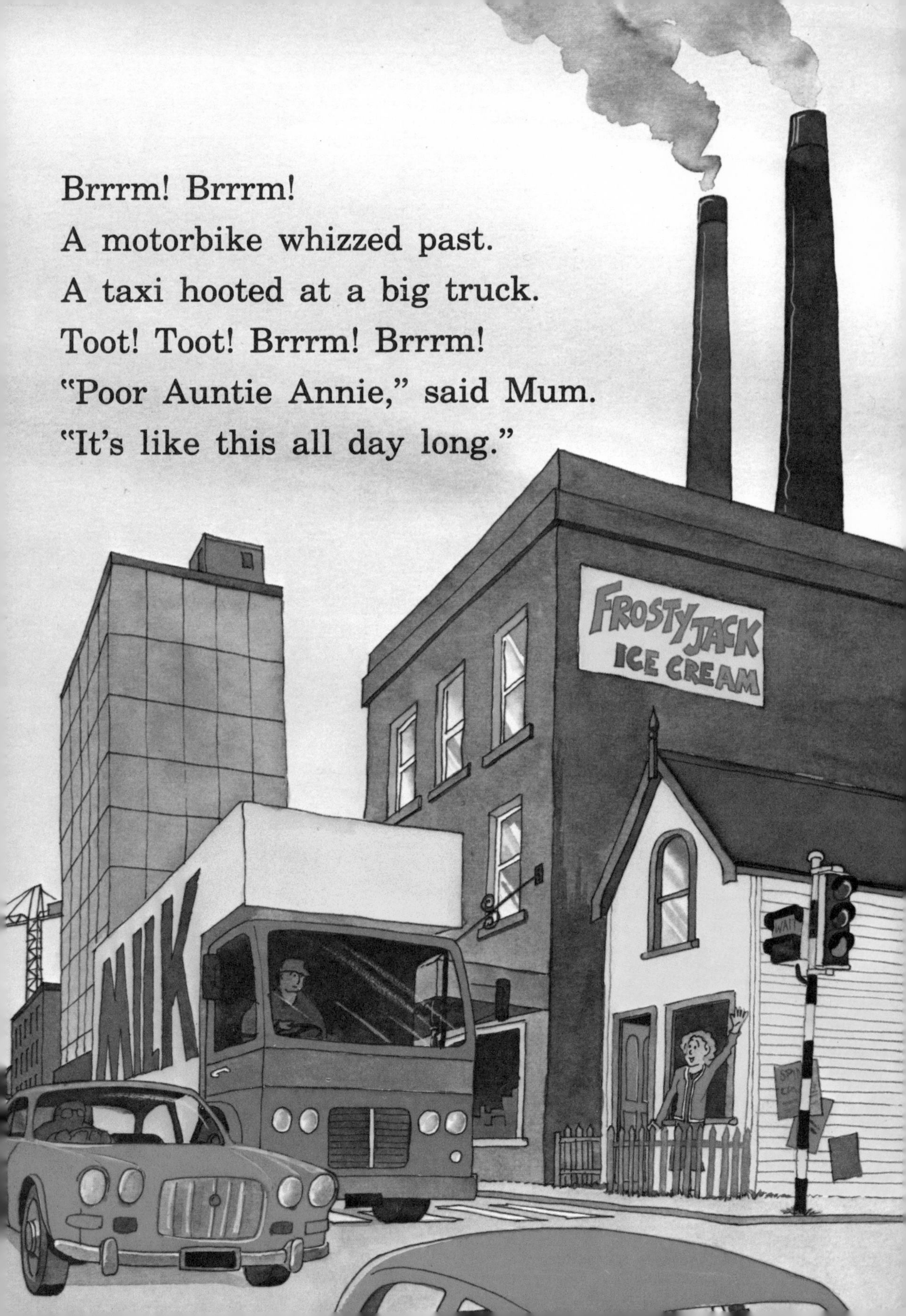
FROSTY JACK
ICE CREAM
MILK
WAIT

TOOT TOOT! BRRRM BRRRM!

Auntie Annie made them
a cup of tea.
As they talked,
trucks went up and down
the busy road.
Motorbikes zoomed past.
Vans hooted.
Cars tooted.
Buses bumbled along.
Poor Auntie Annie!
What a rattle! What a rumble!
All day long!

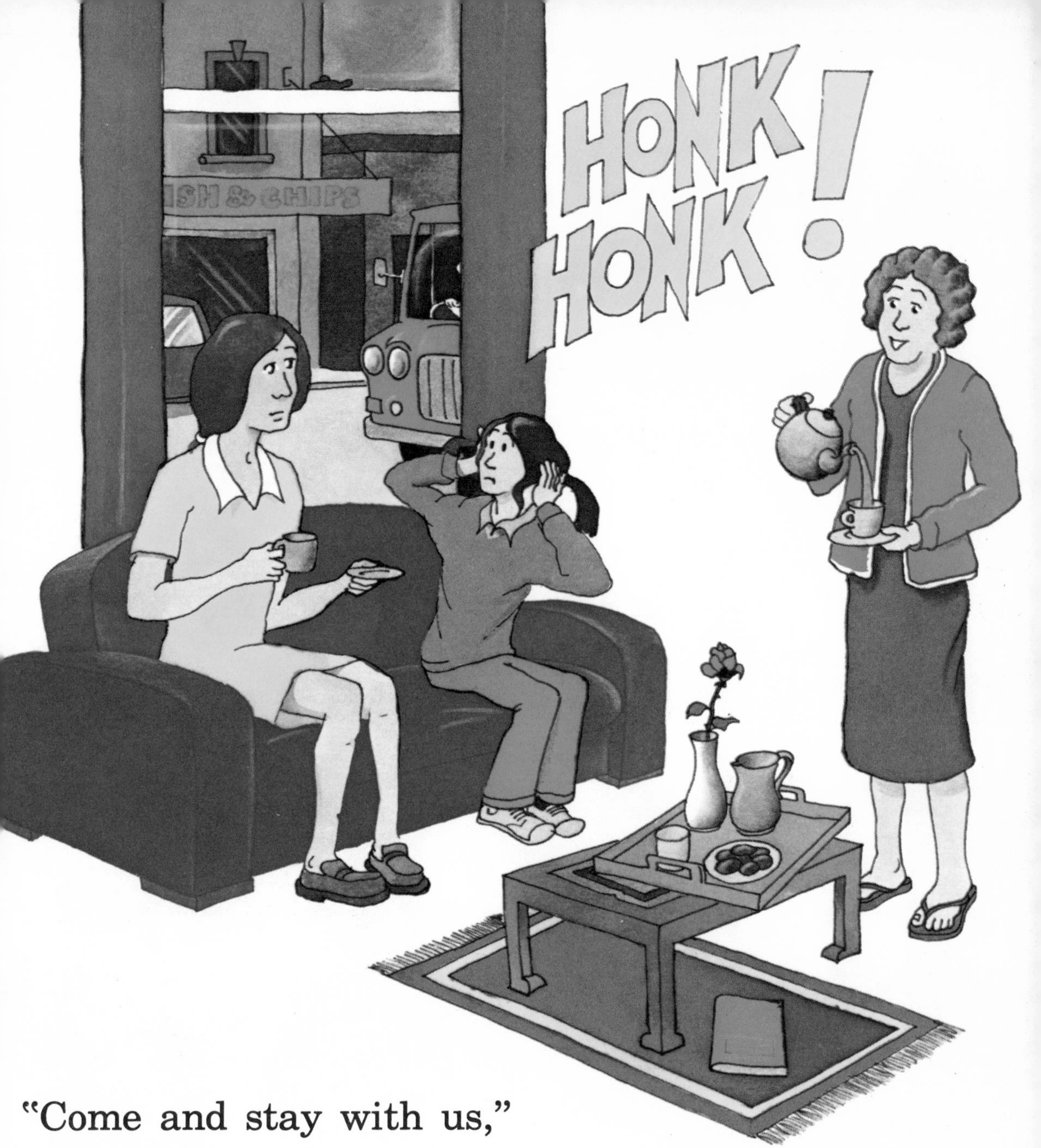
ISH & CHIPS
HONK
HONK!

"Come and stay with us,"
said Emily.
"You would like the farm.
We have cows and horses.
Our dog is called Max.
Our cat is called Punch."

"Thank you for asking me,"
said Auntie Annie.
"I like it here by my busy road.
There is so much going on.
Trucks go up and down.
Motorbikes zoom past.
Vans hoot.
Cars toot.

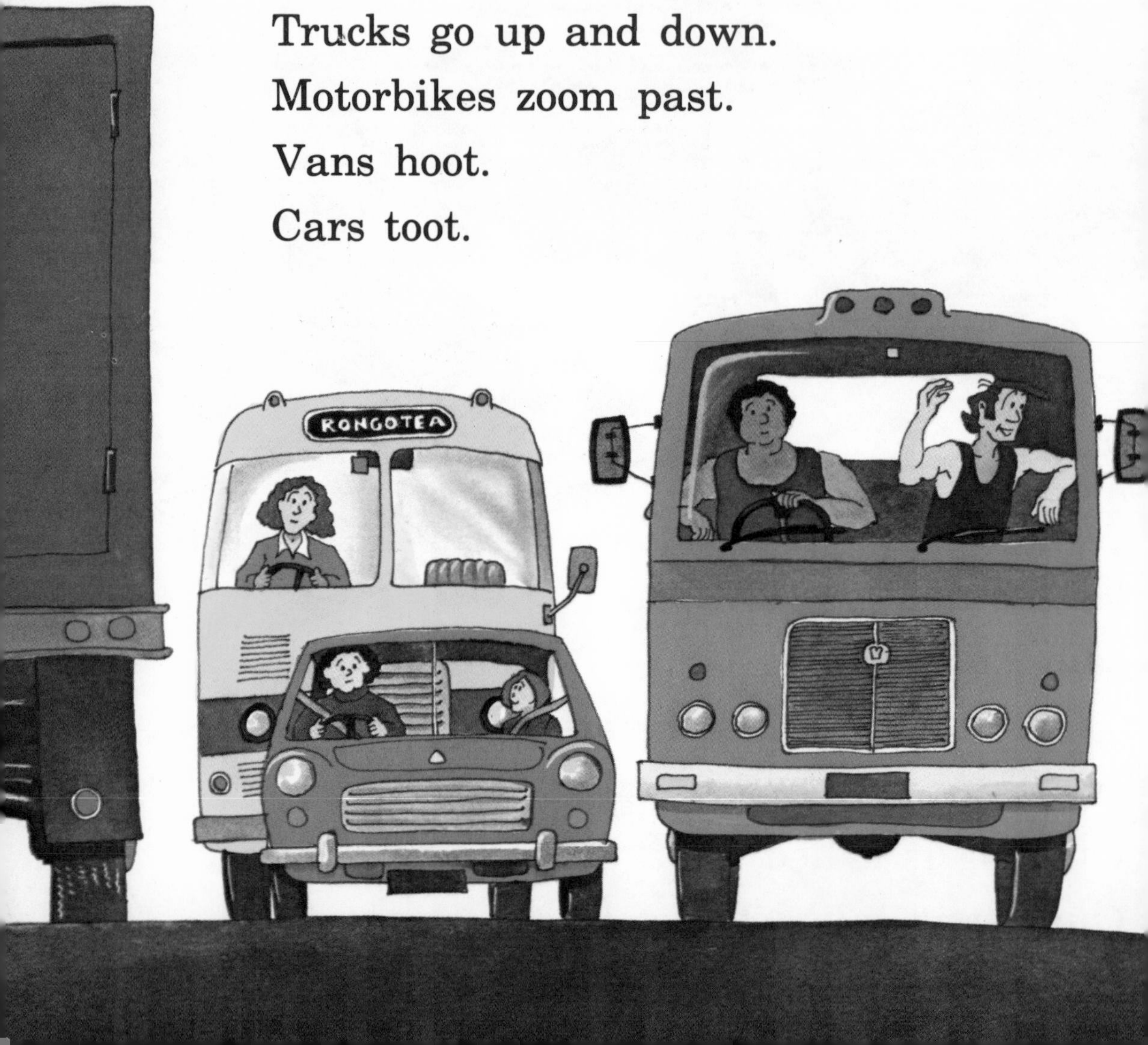
RONGOTEA

I can see people coming.
I can see people going.
A farm would be too quiet for me.
I like to see what's going on in town.
I *do* like living by the main road,
with its rattle and its rumble...
all day long."

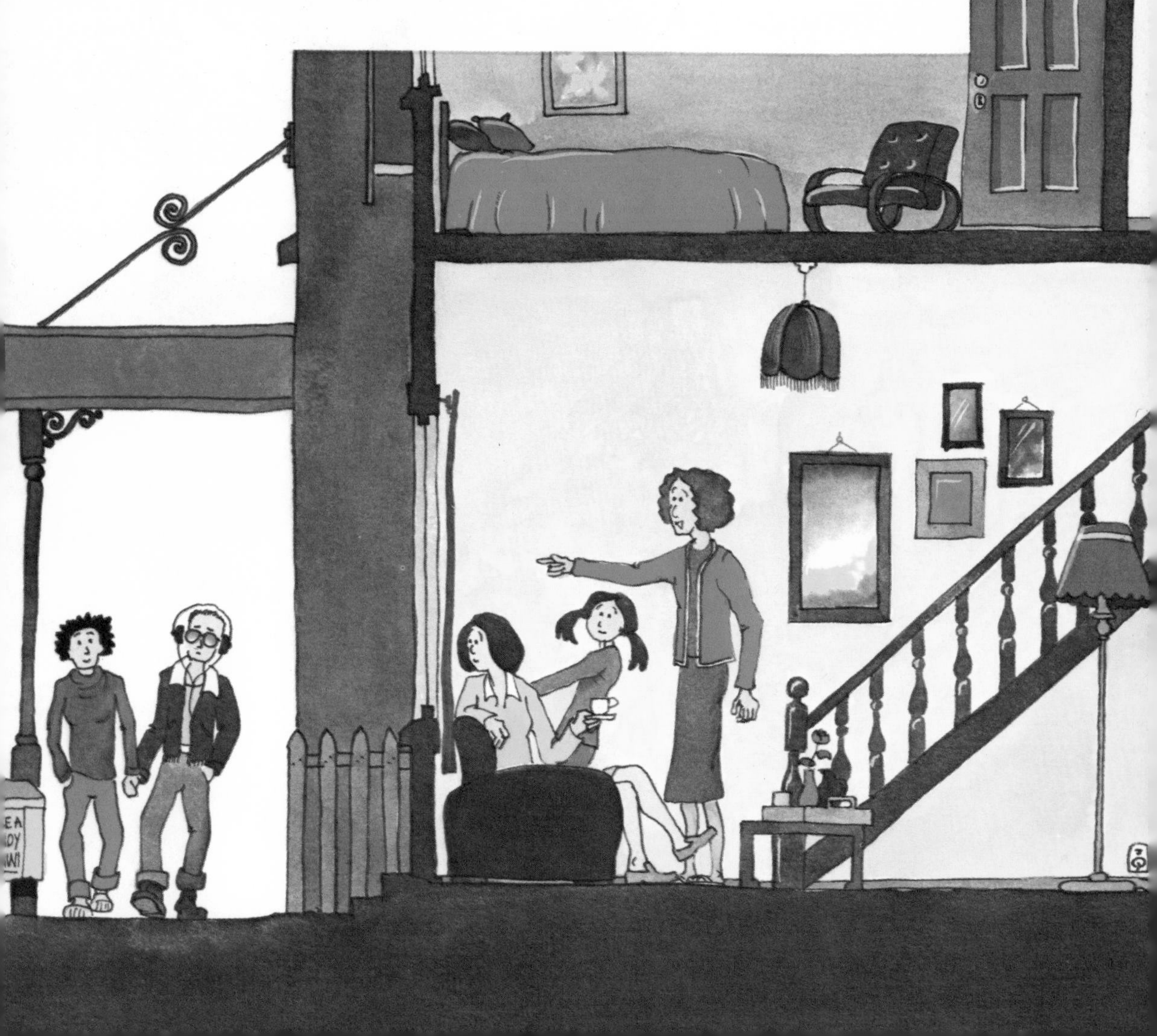

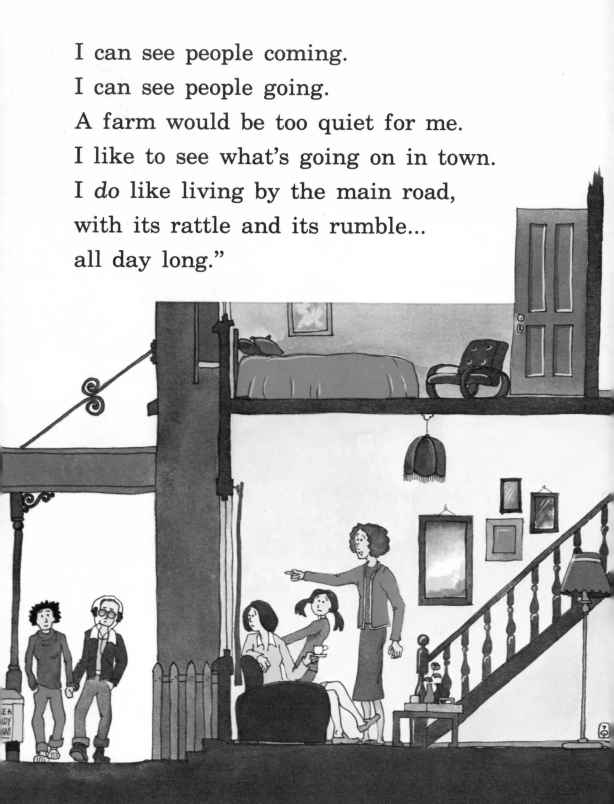

The Magpie's Tail

retold by
Valery Carrick

pictures by
Jill McDonald

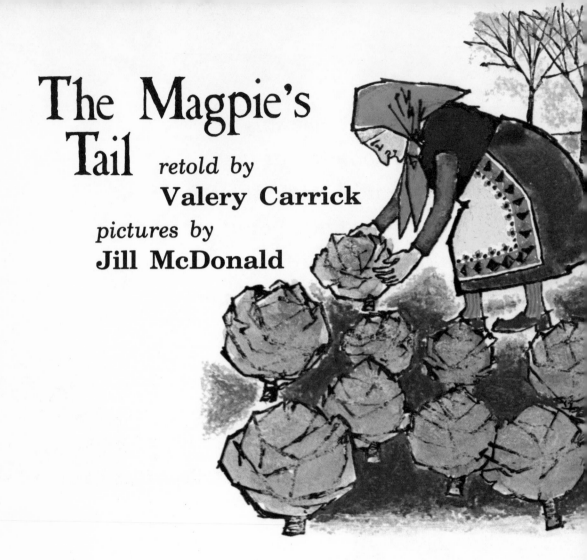

One day, an old woman
milked her cow.
Then she put the pail of milk
down on the ground,
and went to get a cabbage
from the garden.

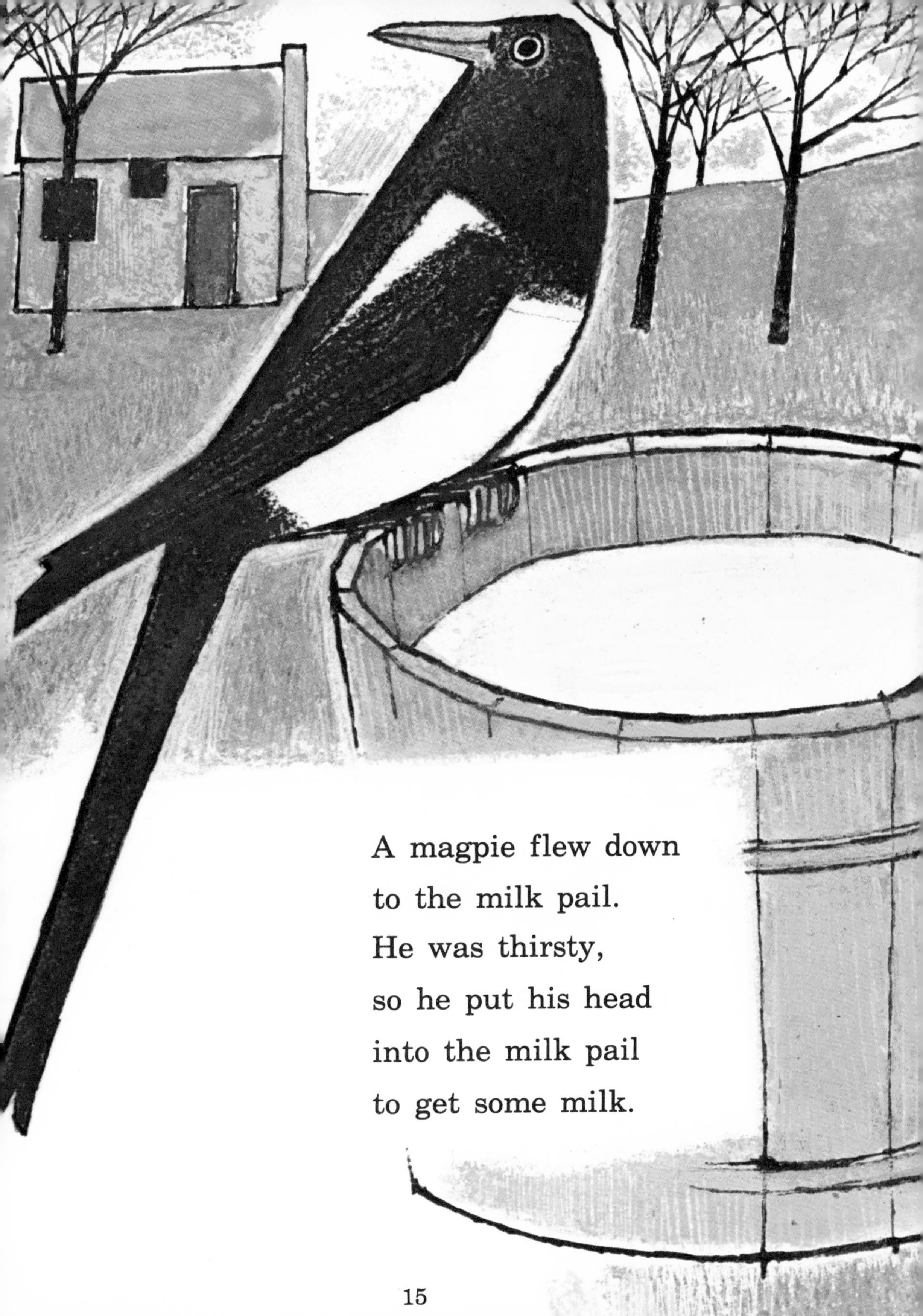

A magpie flew down
to the milk pail.
He was thirsty,
so he put his head
into the milk pail
to get some milk.

The woman came back
with a big fat cabbage.
She saw the magpie
with his head in the milk pail,
and his tail sticking out.

"Stop, you naughty magpie!"
cried the woman.
"Take your head out of my milk pail!"
But the magpie wouldn't take his head out.

So the old woman pulled
the magpie's tail.

"Stop!" cried the magpie,
and he pulled, too.

Over went the pail.
The milk ran
all over the ground.

And there was the woman
with the magpie's tail in her hand.

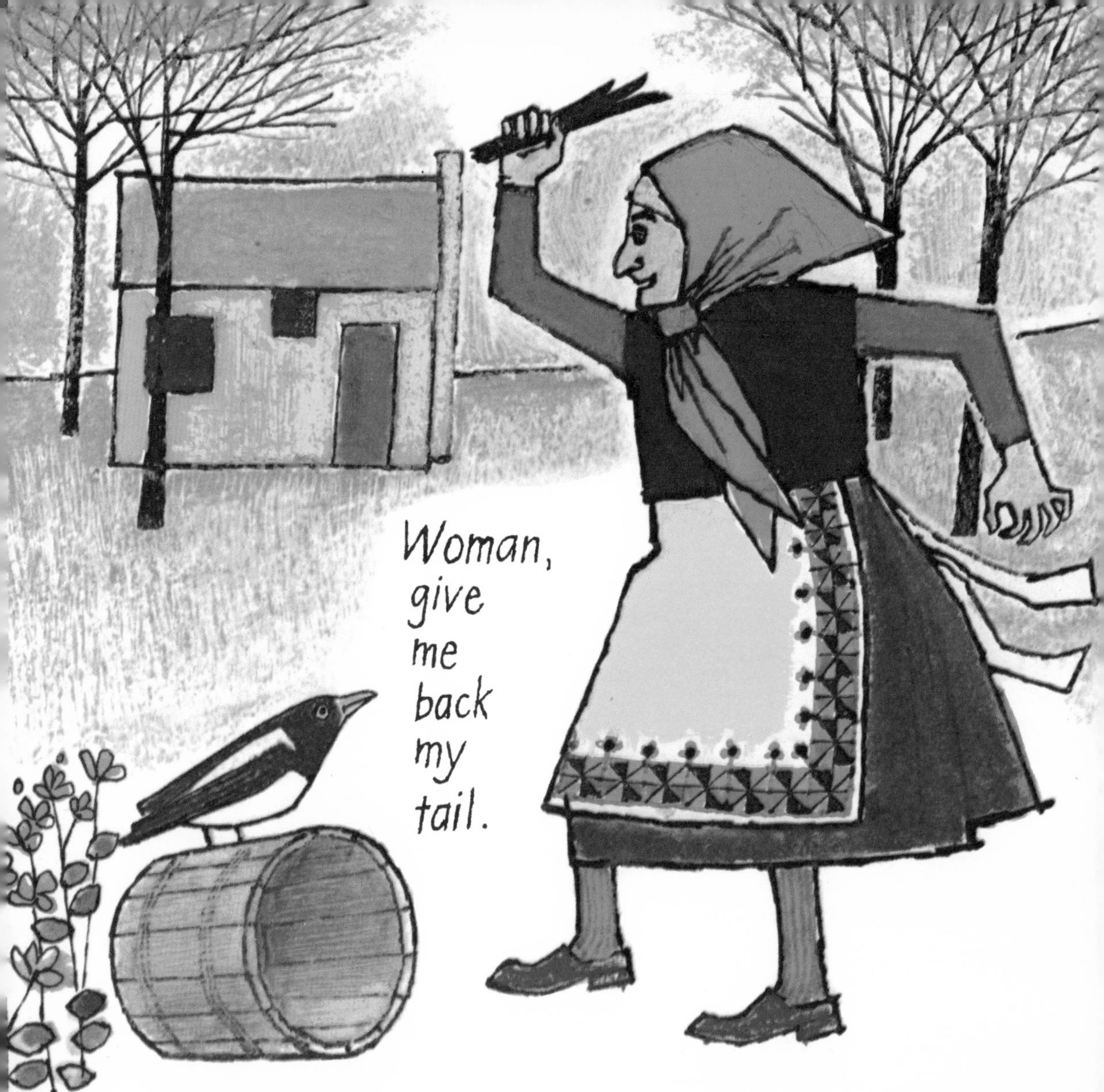
Woman, give me back my tail.

"Woman, give me back my tail!"
cried the magpie.
"I'll pin it on,
and fly back to my mother and father.
If you don't give me back my tail,
I'll eat the cabbages in your garden."

But the woman wouldn't give him back his tail.
She said, "You can eat the cabbages
from my garden,
or you can grow a new tail,
but you won't get your old tail back
if you don't get me some more milk.

The magpie went to the cow.
"Please, cow, give me some milk
for the woman," he said.
"She has pulled out my tail,
and I can't grow a new one.
If I give her some milk,
she'll give me back my old tail."

"Wait," said the cow.
"You must get me some grass,
and then I'll give you some milk."

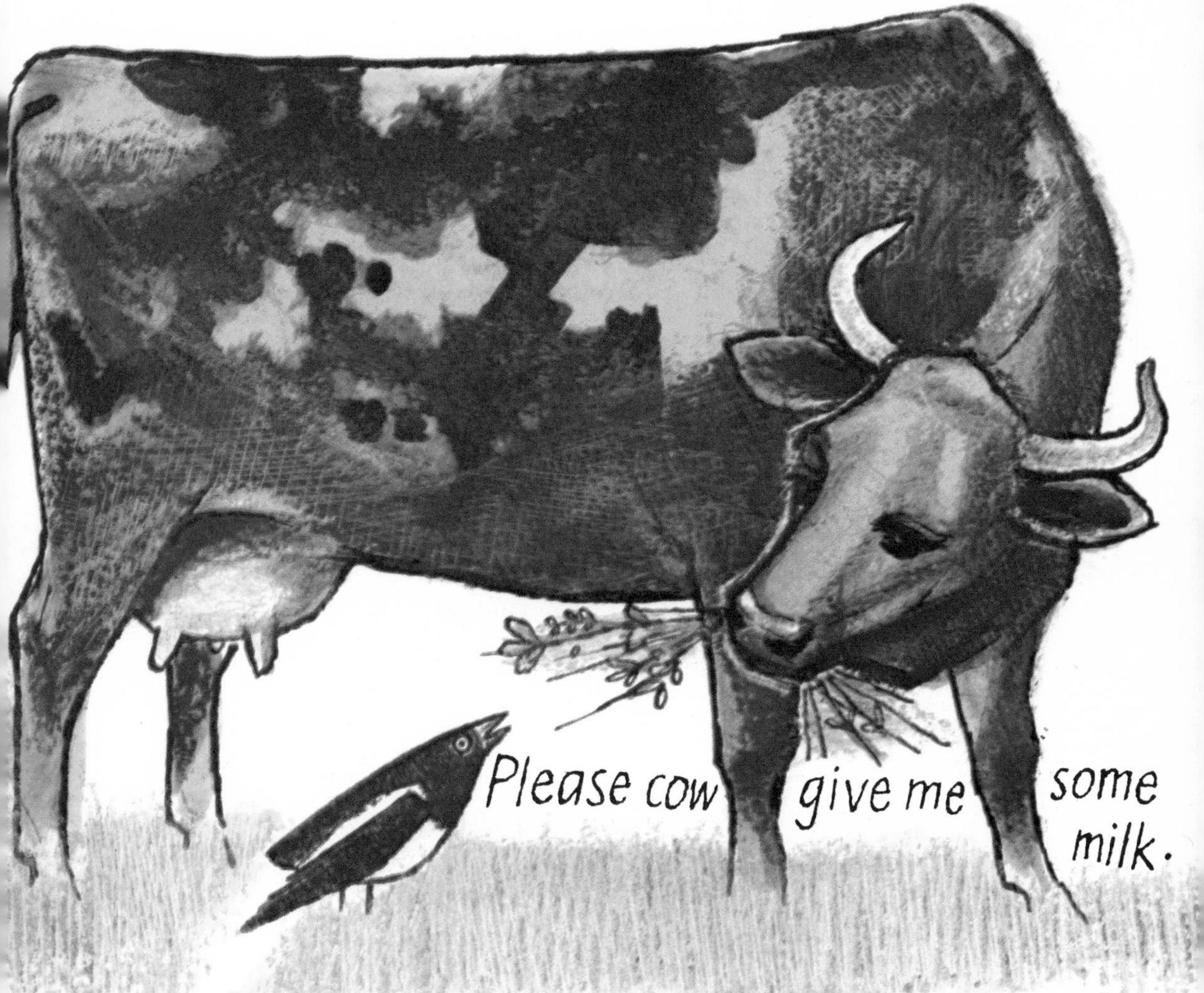
Please cow give me some milk.

So the magpie went to the paddock.
"Please, paddock, give me some grass
for the cow.
Then the cow will give me some milk
for the woman,
and the woman will give me back my tail."

"Wait," said the paddock.
"You must get me some water,
and then I'll give you some grass."

Please paddock, give me some grass for the cow.

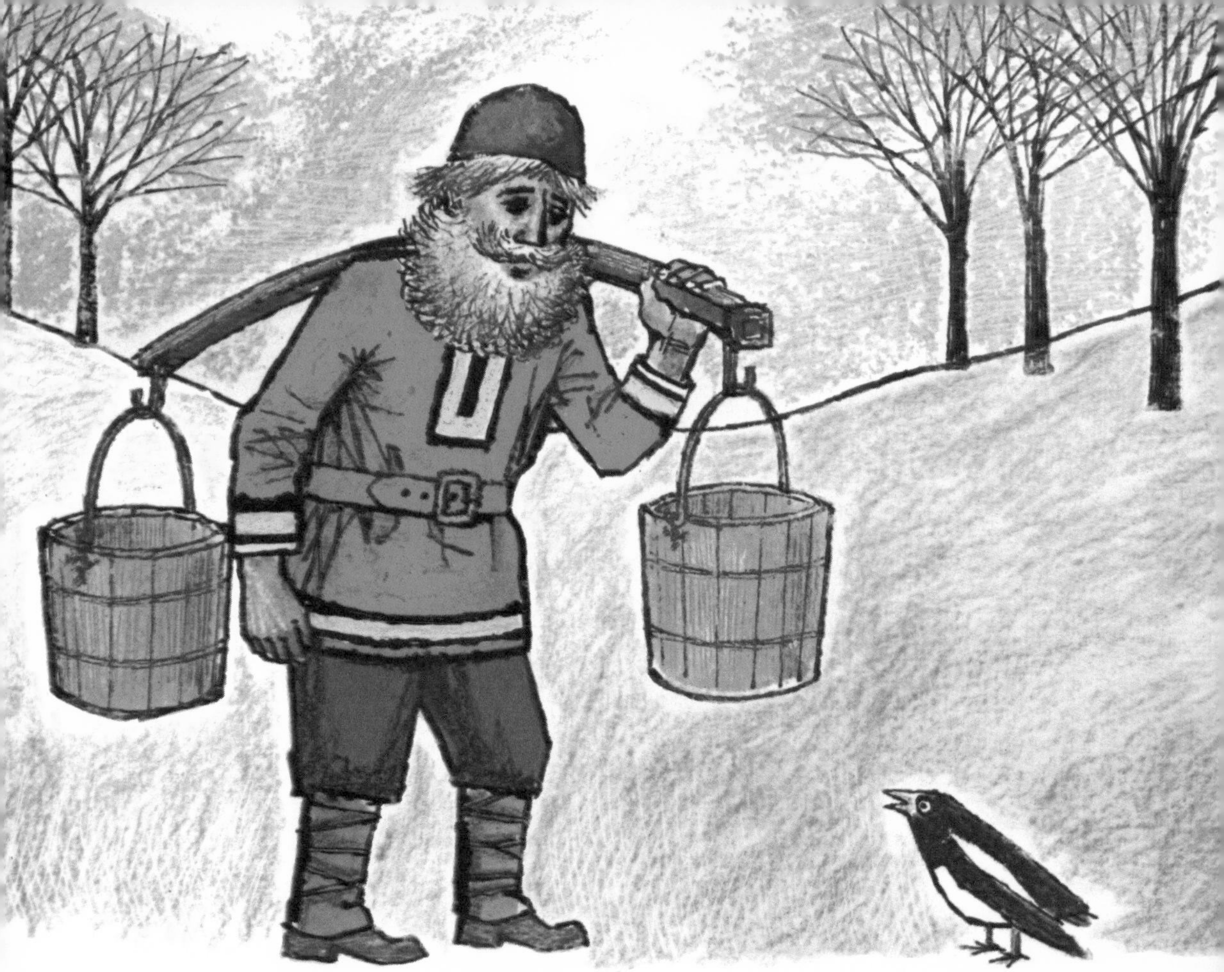

So the magpie went to the water carrier.
"Please, water carrier,
give me some water for the paddock.
Then the paddock will give me some grass
for the cow.
Then the cow will give me some milk
for the woman,
and the woman will give me back my tail."

"Wait," said the water carrier.
"You must get me an egg for my tea,
and then I'll give you some water."

So the magpie went to the hen.
"Please, hen, give me an egg
for the water carrier's tea.
Then the water carrier
will give me some water for the paddock.
Then the paddock will give me some grass
for the cow.
Then the cow will give me some milk
for the woman,
and the woman will give me back my tail.
I'll pin it on,
and fly back to my mother and father.
It's time I went home again."

"You do look funny without your tail,"
said the hen.
"I'll help you get it back."

You
do
look
funny
without
your
tail.

So the hen gave the magpie an egg,
and he took it to the water carrier.
The water carrier
gave the magpie some water,
and he took it to the paddock.
The paddock gave the magpie some grass,
and he took it to the cow.
The cow gave the magpie some milk,
and he took it to the woman.
The woman gave the magpie back his tail.
He pinned it on, and flew back
to his father and mother.

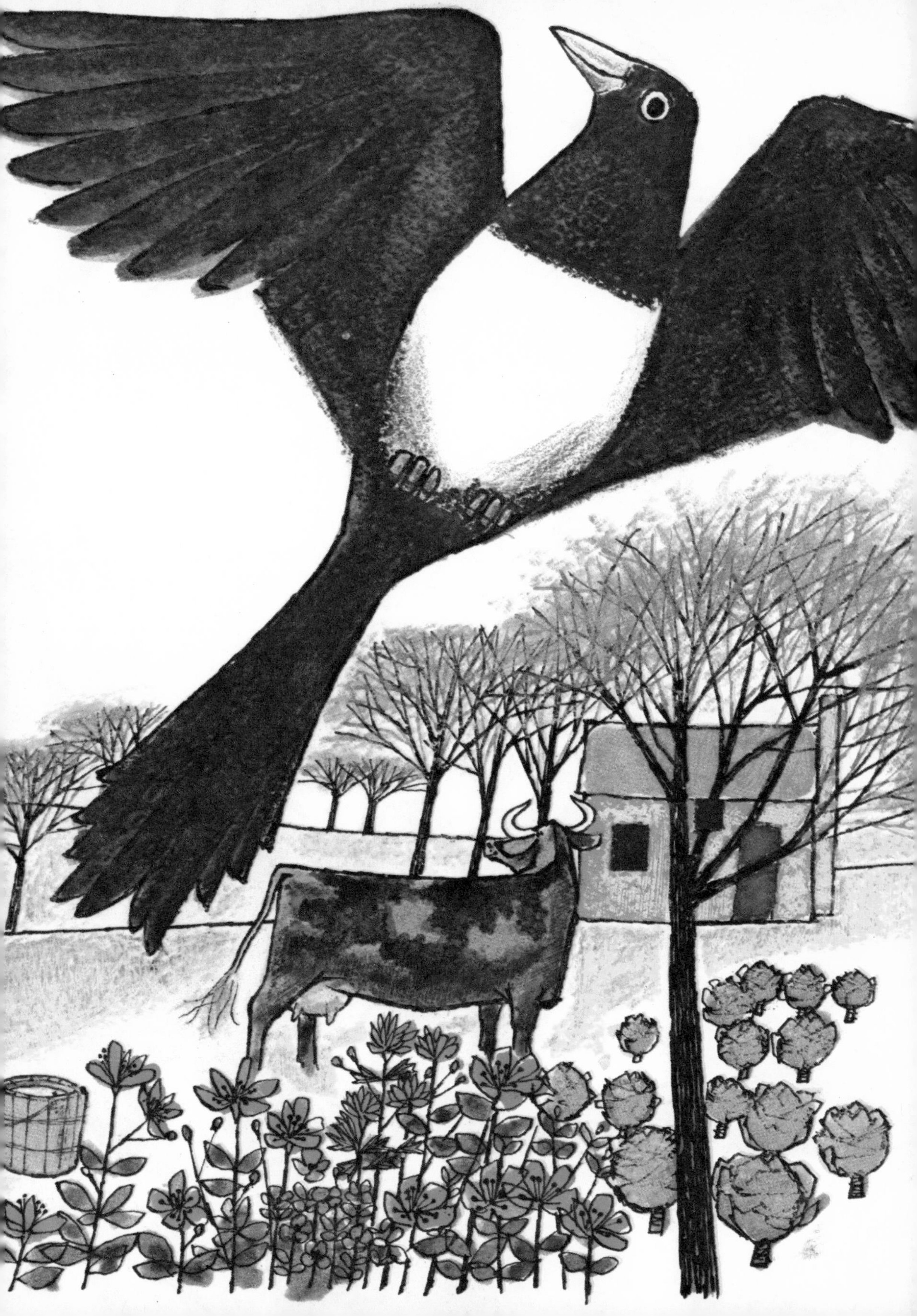

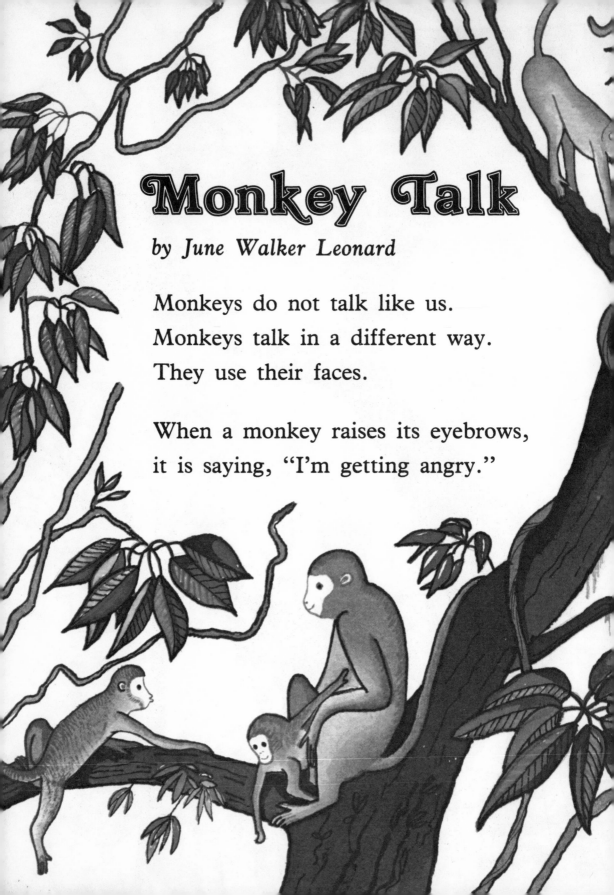

Monkey Talk

by June Walker Leonard

Monkeys do not talk like us.
Monkeys talk in a different way.
They use their faces.

When a monkey raises its eyebrows,
it is saying, "I'm getting angry."

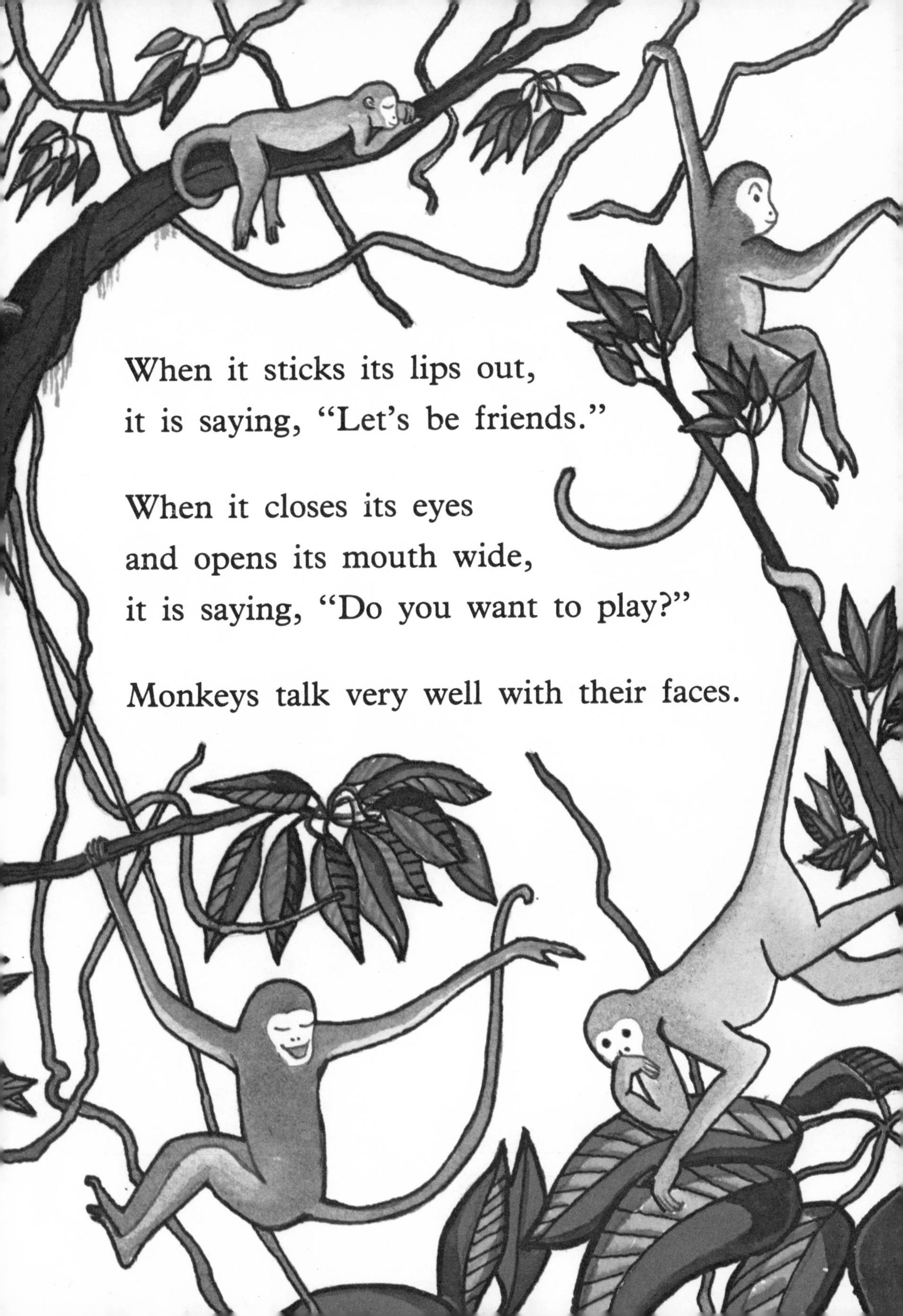

When it sticks its lips out,
it is saying, "Let's be friends."

When it closes its eyes
and opens its mouth wide,
it is saying, "Do you want to play?"

Monkeys talk very well with their faces.

Good Knee for a Cat

by Margaret Mahy
pictures by Lesley Moyes

The old cat wanted to sit on someone's knee.

"Do sit on a chair, Punch," said Mum.
"I'm too busy to have a cat sitting on my knee.
Aunt Jane and Ann are coming today."

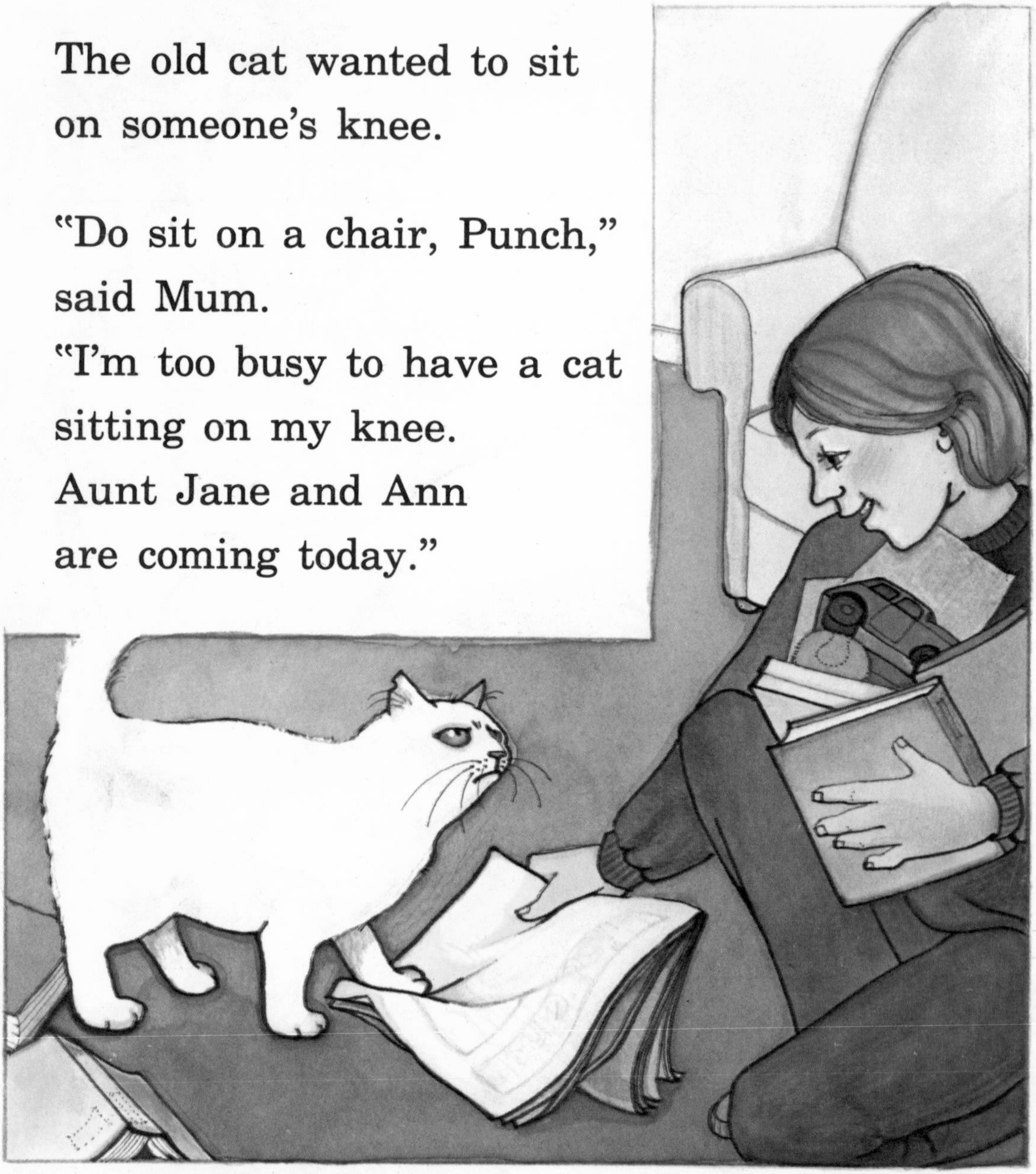

The old cat went looking
for a knee to sit on.
"Oh, Punch! Do get off!"
said Vicky.
"I have to tidy my room.
I have to clear the junk
off the floor.
Ann is coming today."

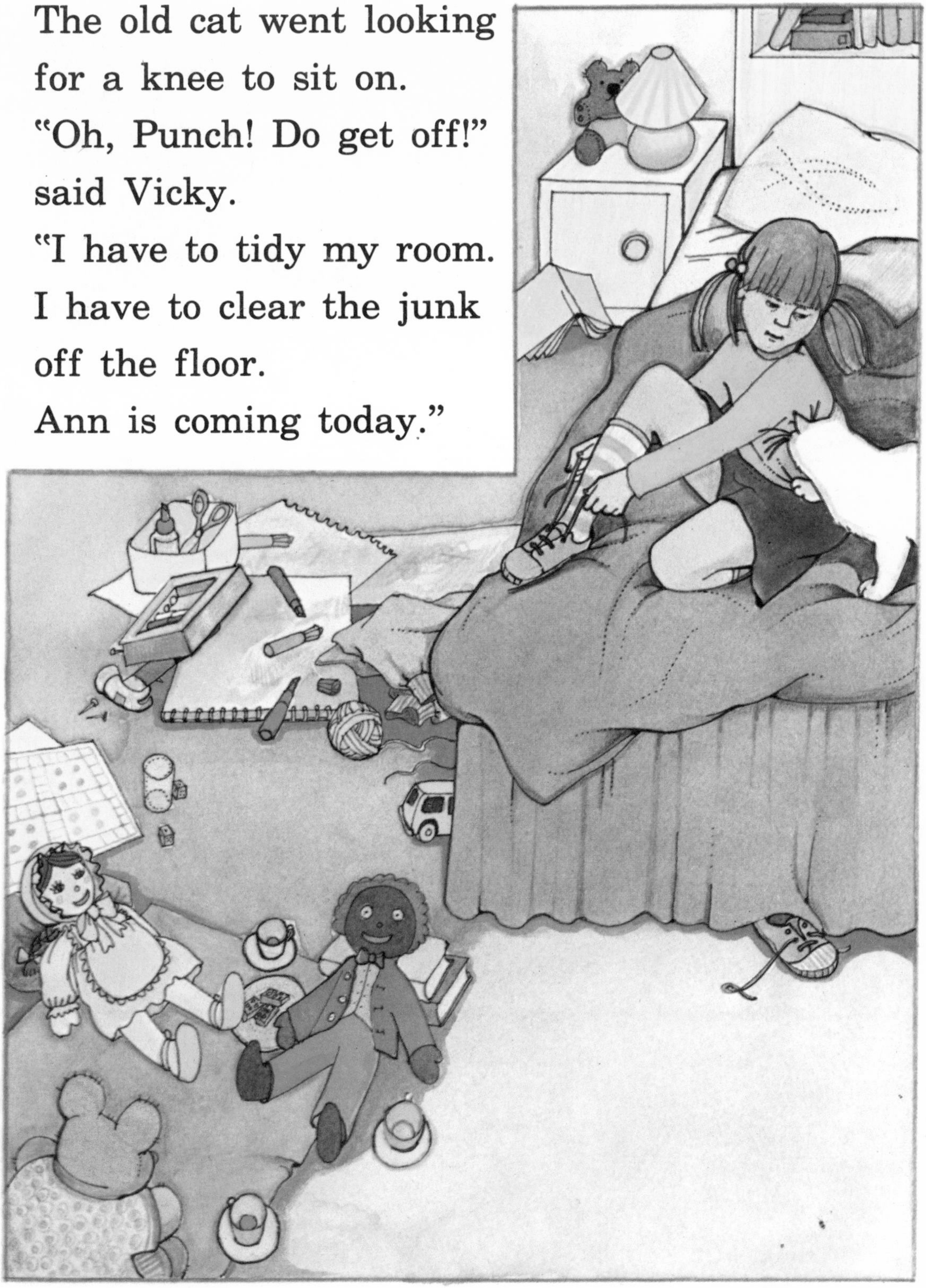

The old cat
tried to sit on Peter's knee.
Peter stood up,
and the cat fell off.
"I have to clear the junk off the path,"
Peter said.
The old cat slept on a chair,
but it was not as good as a knee.
There was no kind hand to stroke him.

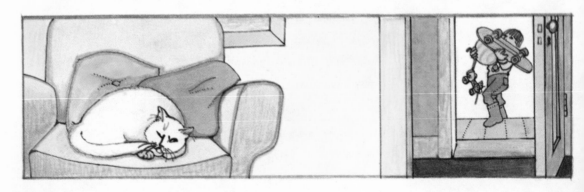

"Here's Aunt Jane and Ann!"
said Peter.
He went out to meet them.
Peter pushed Ann's wheelchair
along the path and into the house.
"How about a cup of tea?" said Mum.
"Show Ann your room, Vicky."

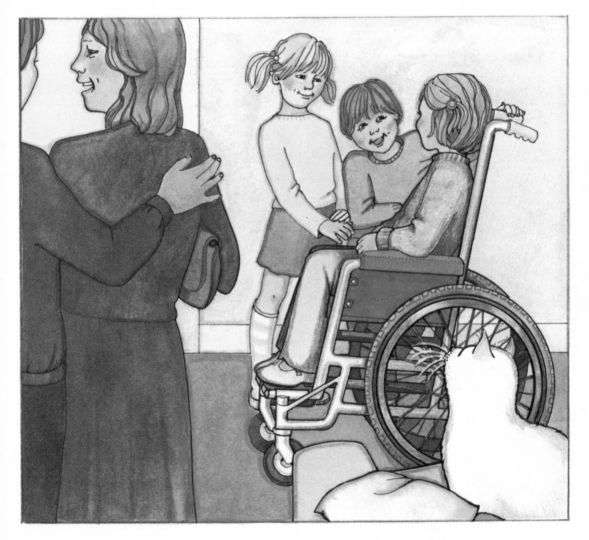

But Ann was looking at Punch.
Punch was looking at Ann.
"What a nice cat!" said Ann.
"We've got a cat, but he's very shy.
He's frightened of my chair."

The old cat got off his chair,
and came over to Ann's wheelchair.
He smelt its wheels.
Then he jumped up on Ann's knee.

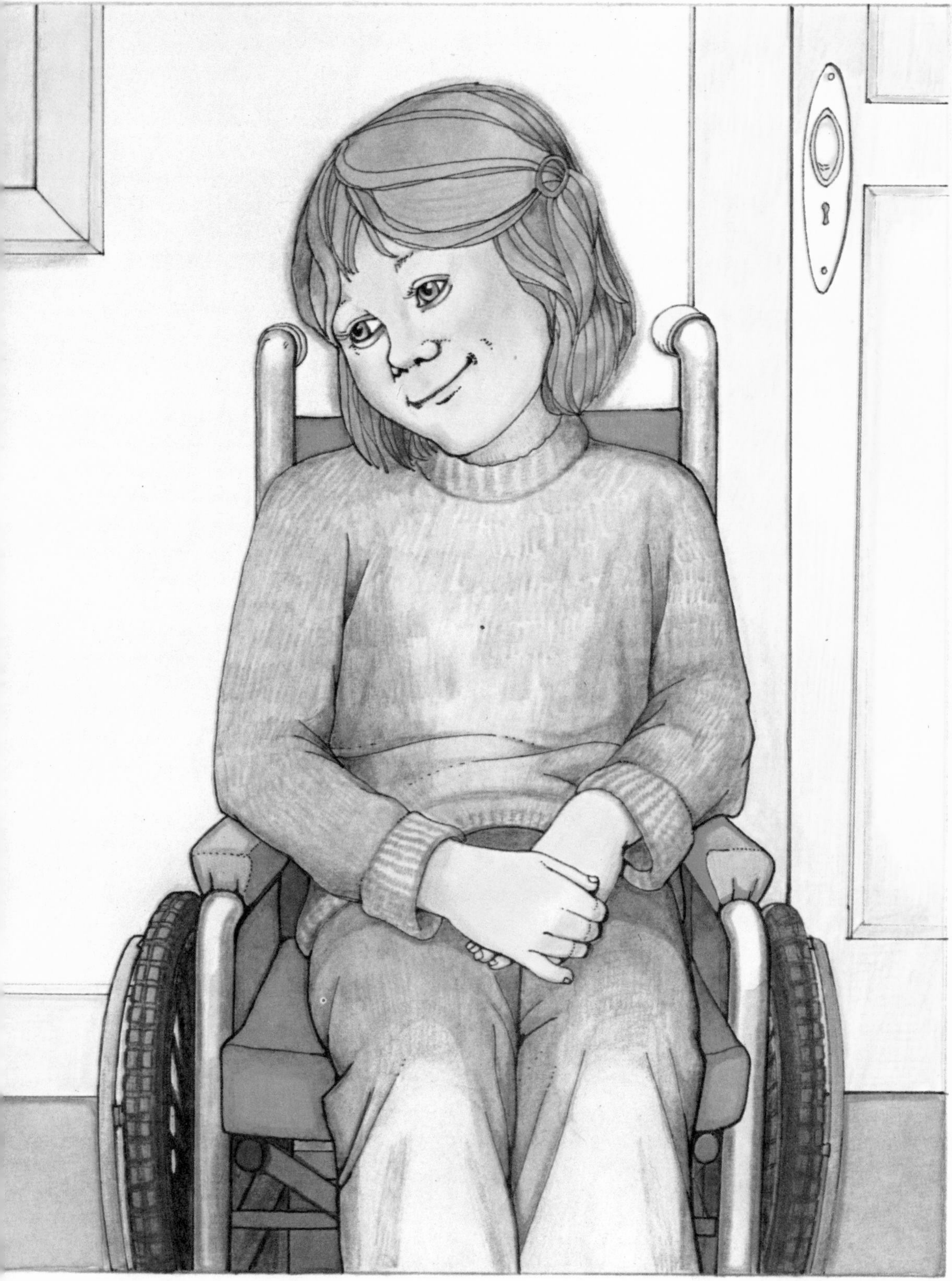

Ann stroked Punch
in just the right way.
The old cat worked his paws
up and down on her knee.
Then he curled up and went to sleep.

"He likes me," Ann said.
"He likes my knee."

Ann went around the house
with Vicky and Peter.
She talked to Mum
and told her about her school.
Then she played cards
with Vicky and Peter.

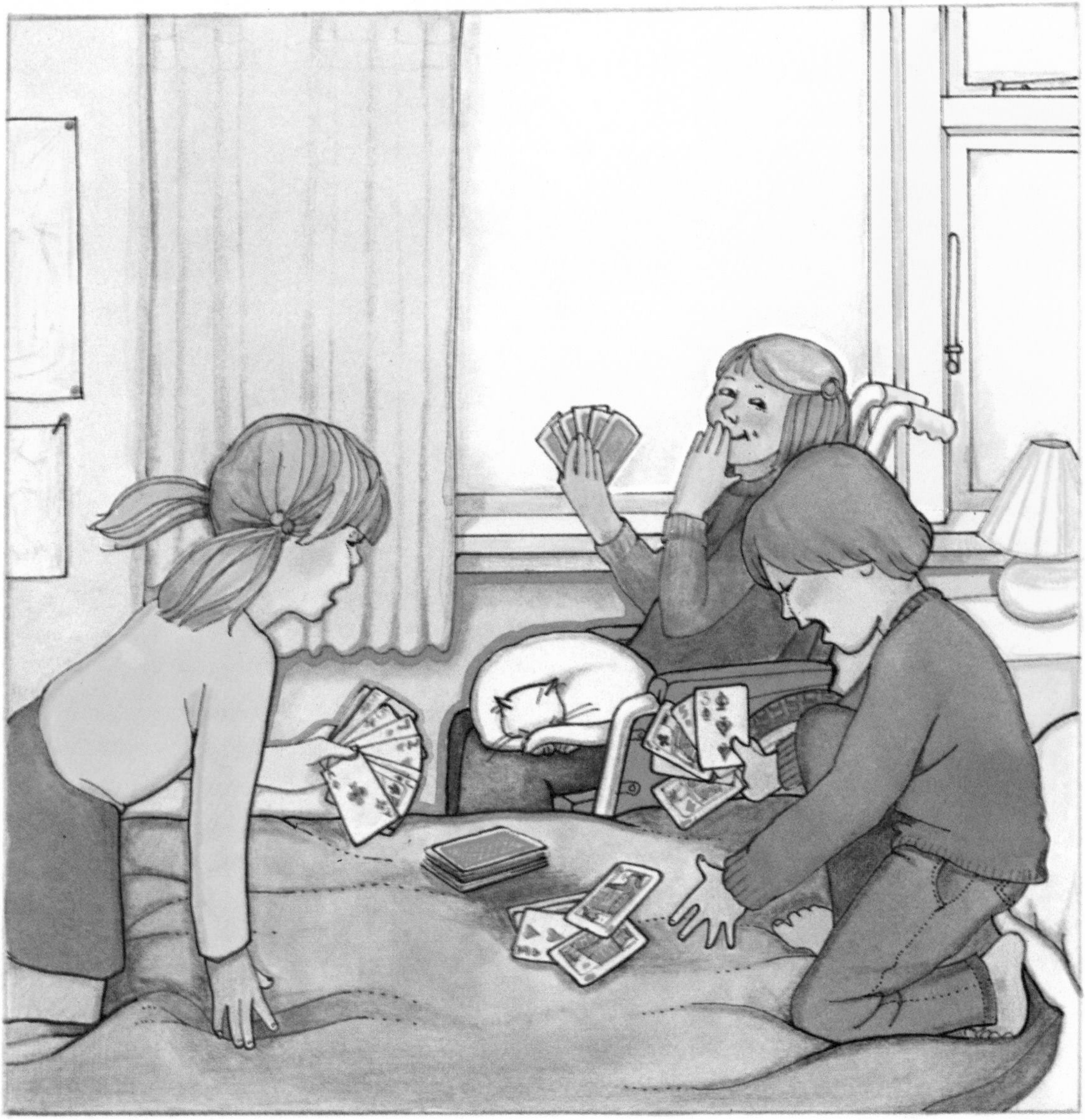

All the time, Punch slept,
curled up on Ann's knee.
"Most knees come and go,"
thought the old cat,
"but a wheelchair knee
is a treat for a cat."
And he purred himself to sleep again.

For Want of a Nail

For want of a nail
The shoe was lost,
For want of a shoe
The horse was lost,
For want of a horse
The rider was lost,
For want of a rider
The battle was lost,
For want of a battle
The kingdom was lost,
And all for the want
Of a horseshoe nail.

Traditional rhyme

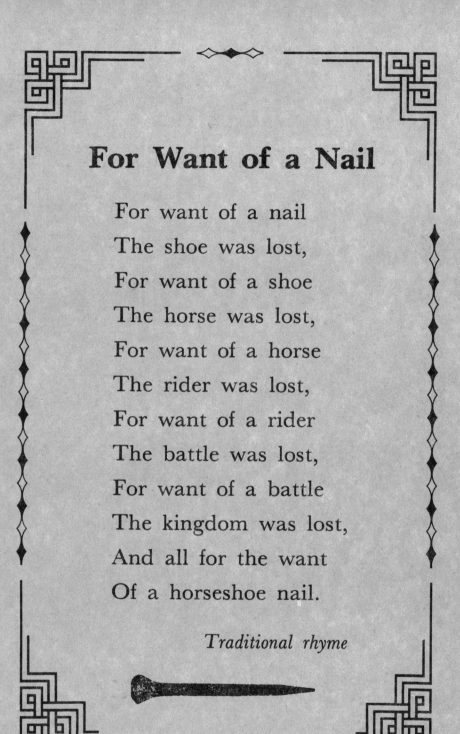

The Biggest Canoe

A story from the Pacific Islands

retold by Barbara Beveridge

pictures by Diane Perham

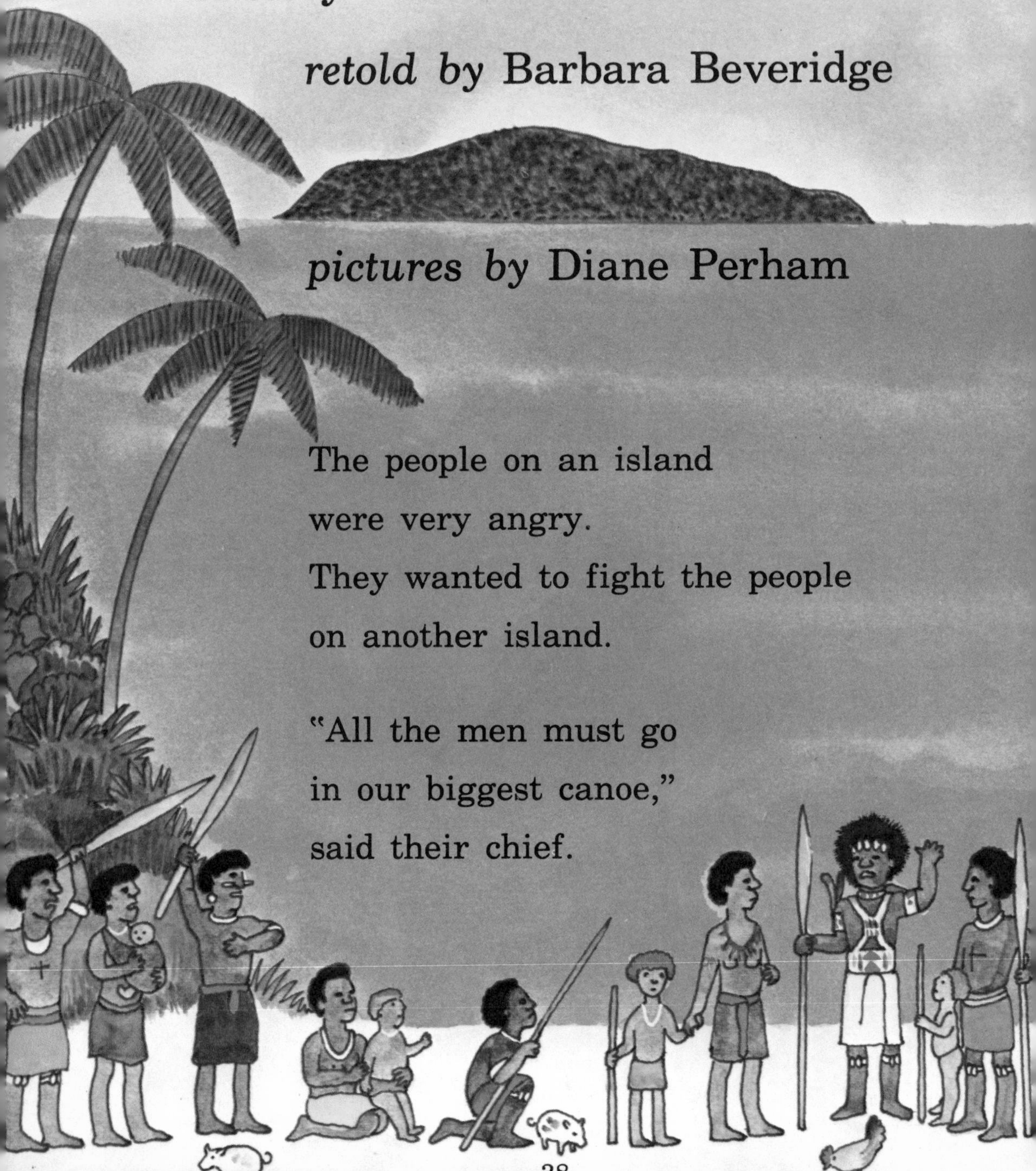

The people on an island
were very angry.
They wanted to fight the people
on another island.

"All the men must go
in our biggest canoe,"
said their chief.

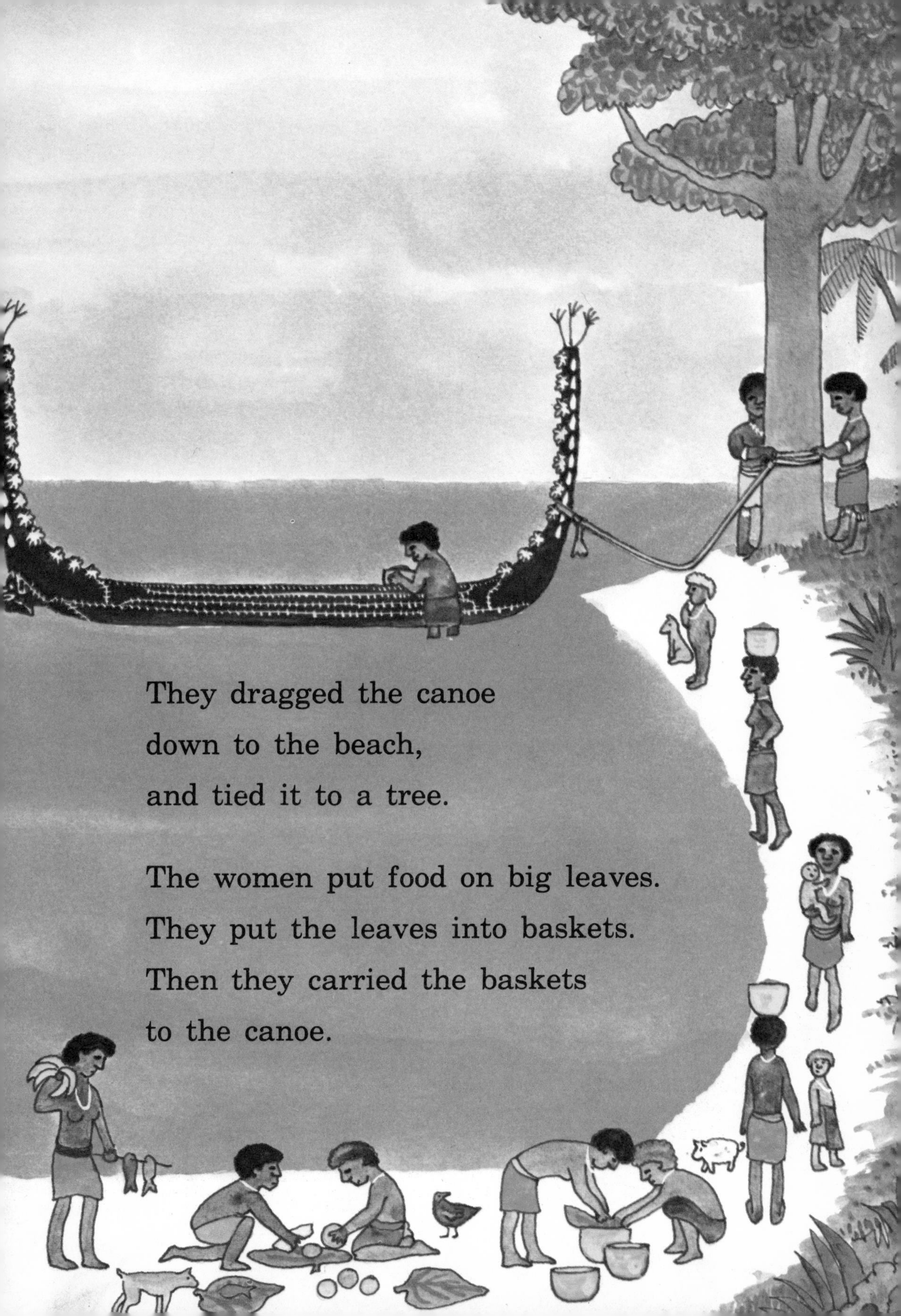

They dragged the canoe
down to the beach,
and tied it to a tree.

The women put food on big leaves.
They put the leaves into baskets.
Then they carried the baskets
to the canoe.

When it was night,
the men got into the canoe.
It was very dark.
There were no stars or moon.

The men sat in their places,
and began to paddle.
They paddled all night.

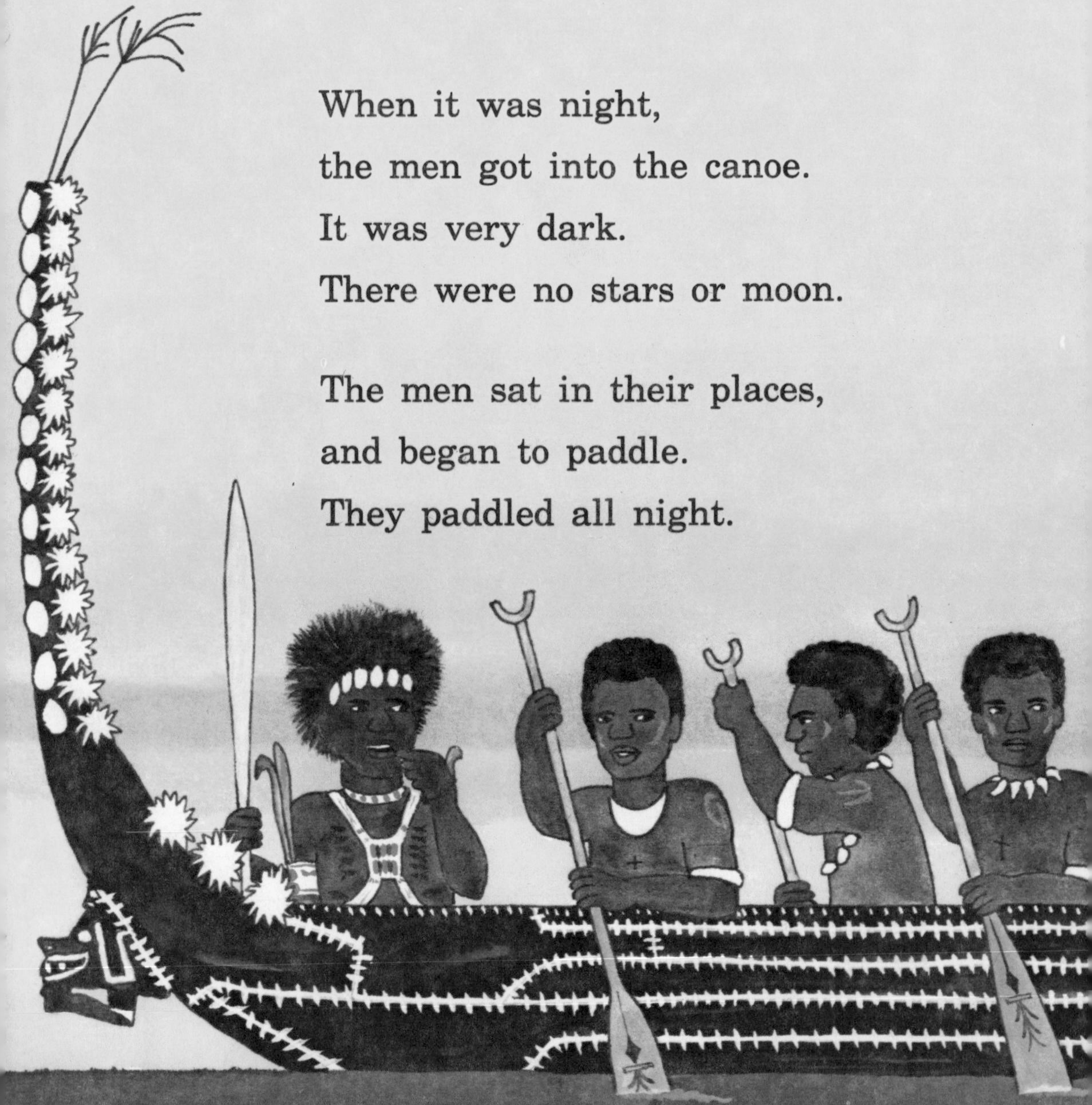

In the morning,
the sun came up.
The men looked around them.

"We haven't moved!" they said.
"We're still at our own island!"

"Oh," said their chief,
"we forgot to untie the rope.
I don't think we'll fight
those other people, now.
I think we'll just stay home."

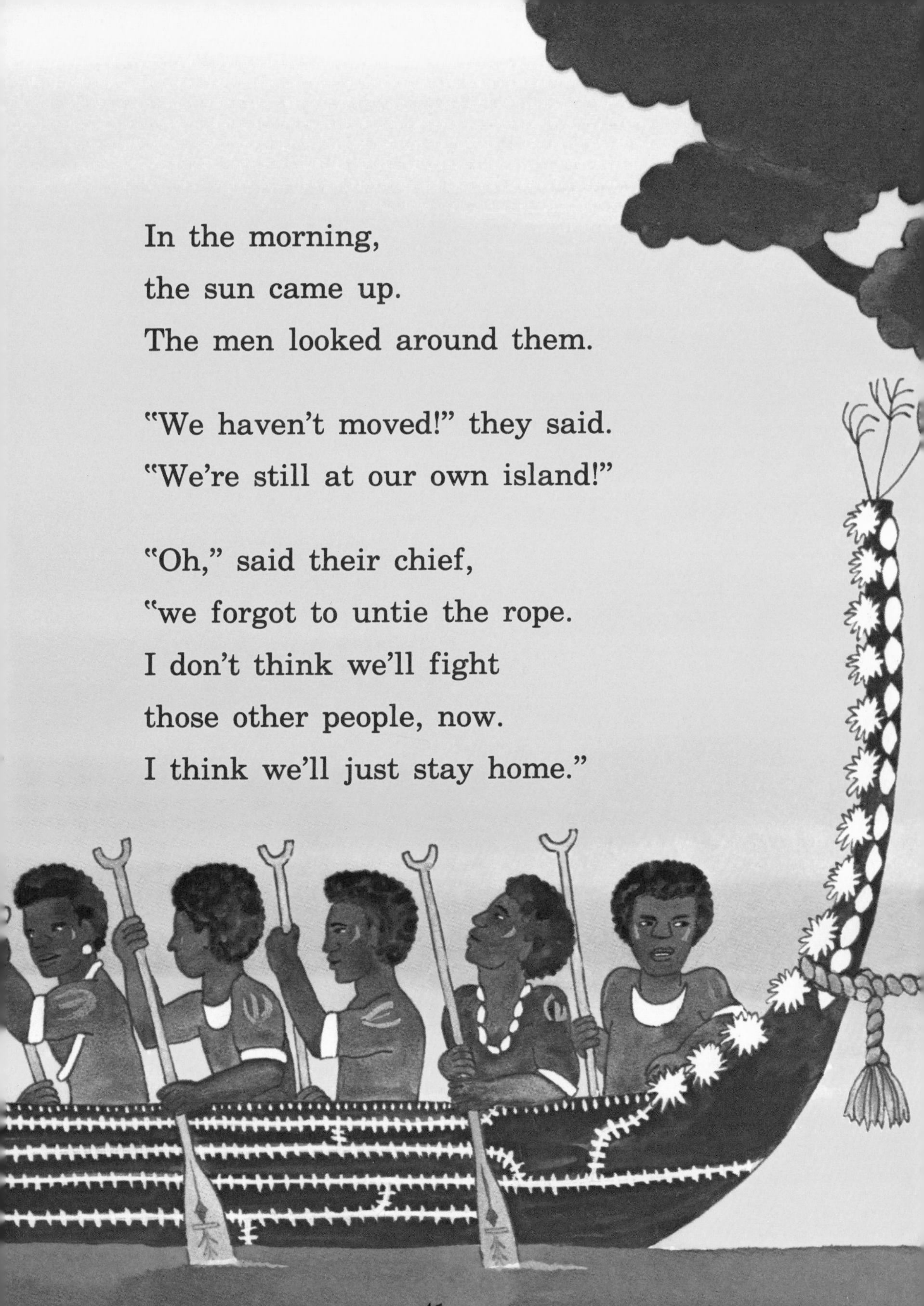

Giant Soup

by Margaret Mahy

pictures by Robyn Belton

The giant's mother
was going on a holiday.
"What shall I eat, Mum?"
asked the giant.

"Make yourself a pot of soup,"
said the giant's mother.

The giant put a big pot of water
on the stove.
He cut up a lot of onions
and put them in the water.
Then he tried it.
"This soup is no good,"
said the giant.
"It must have carrots in it."

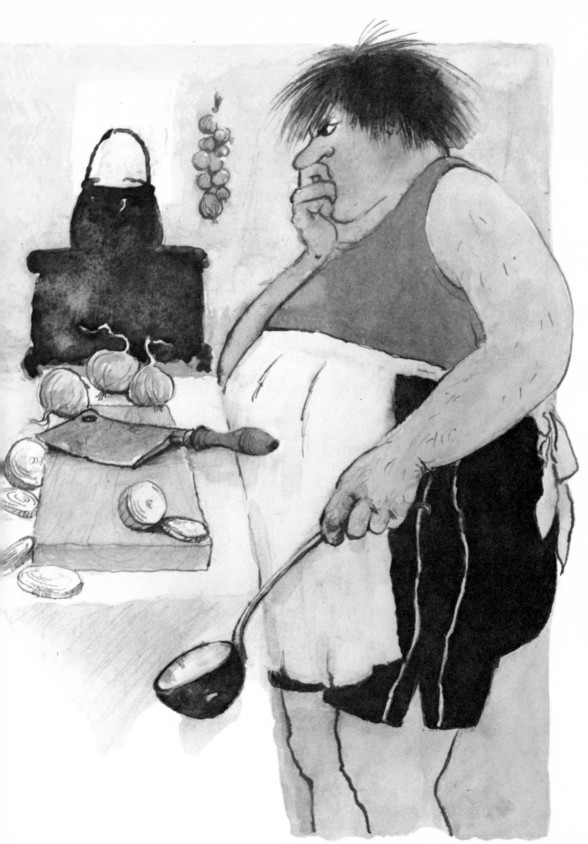

The giant went out to his garden
and got some carrots.
He put them into the soup.
Then he tried the soup again.
"This soup is no good,"
said the giant.
"It must have a beef bone in it."

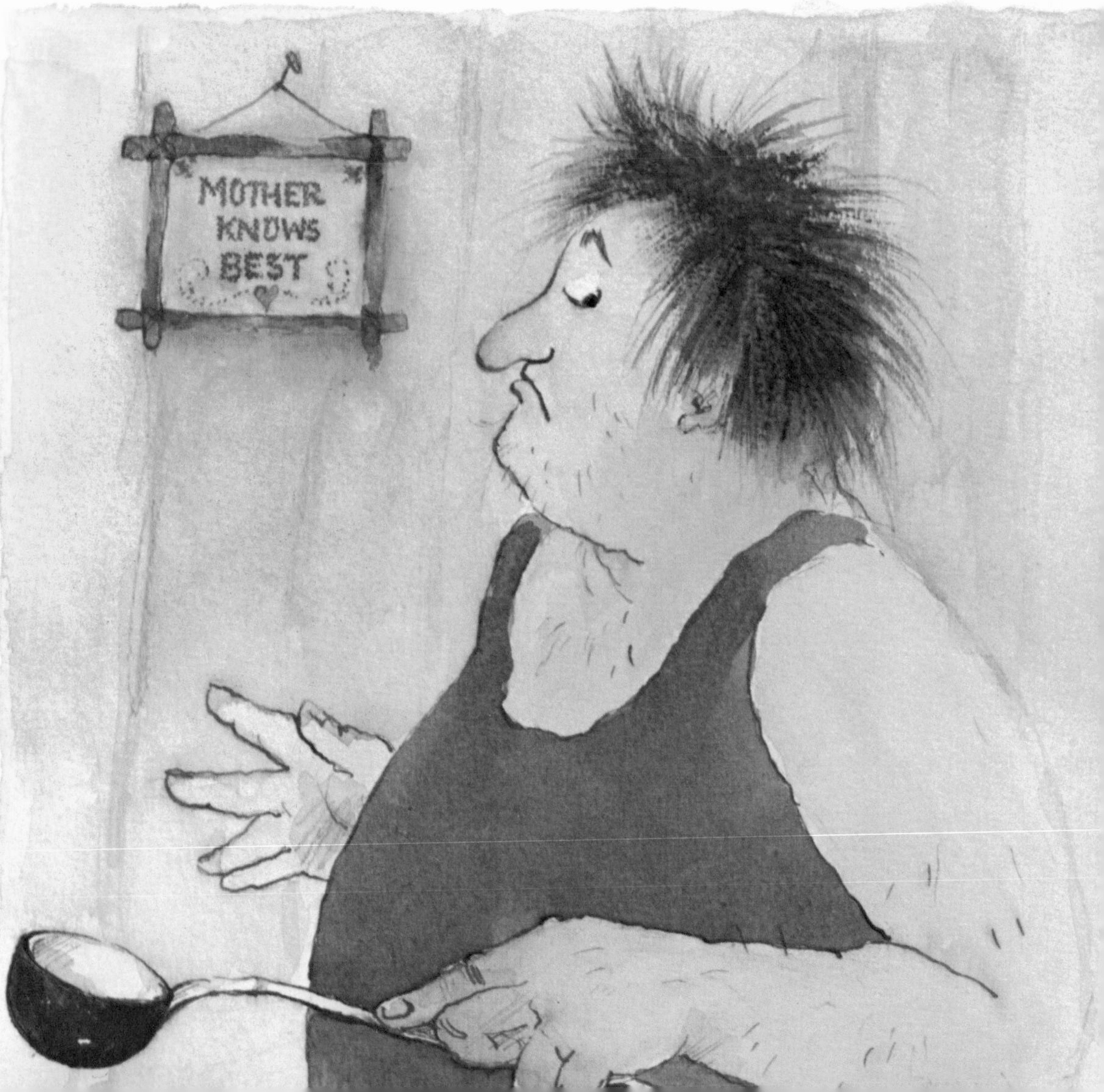
MOTHER
KNOWS
BEST

He went to his refrigerator
and got a beef bone.
He put it into the soup.
Then he tried the soup again.
"This soup is still no good,"
said the giant.
"It must have a boy in it."

He put on his giant sneakers
and ran quietly out into the world.
A boy called Jason
was walking home from school.
He was reading a book
as he walked along.
It was a cook book.

The giant came up quietly behind Jason
and caught him.
He took him home
and popped him into the big pot of soup.

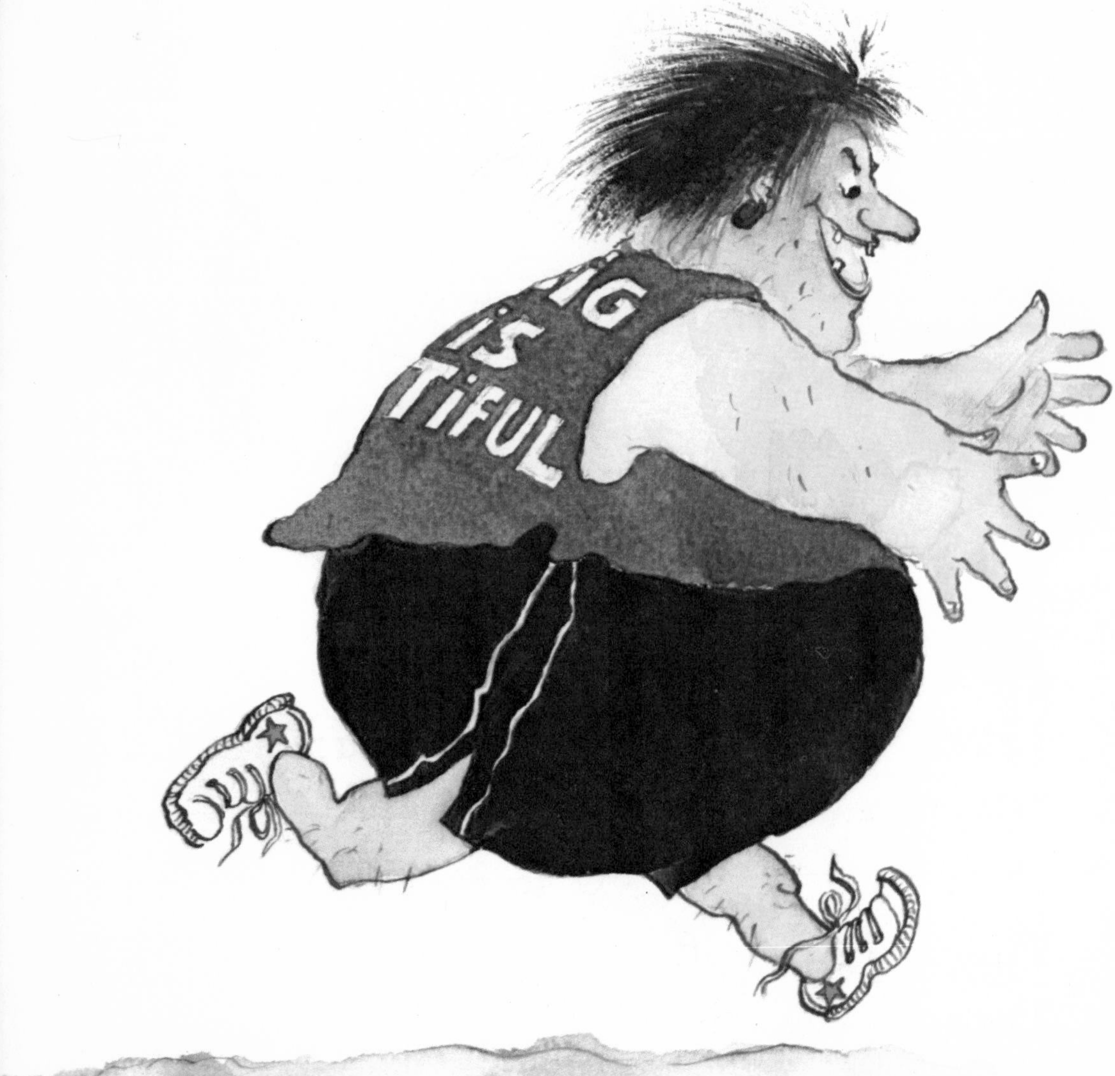

IG
IS
TIFUL

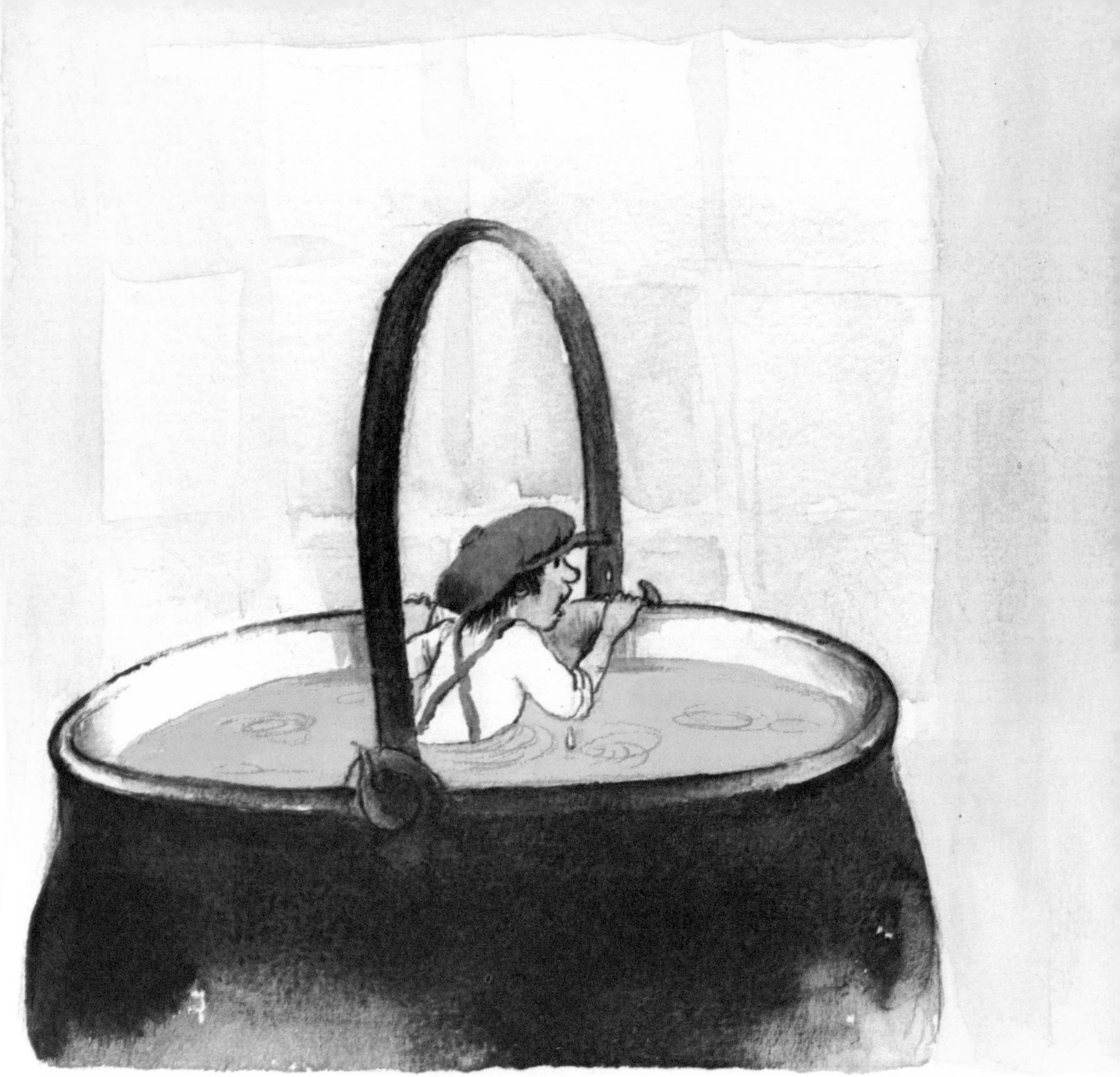

Jason swam round and round
among the bits of onion and carrot.
"Hey!" said Jason.
"You don't know how to cook.
This soup is cold.
Turn on the stove."

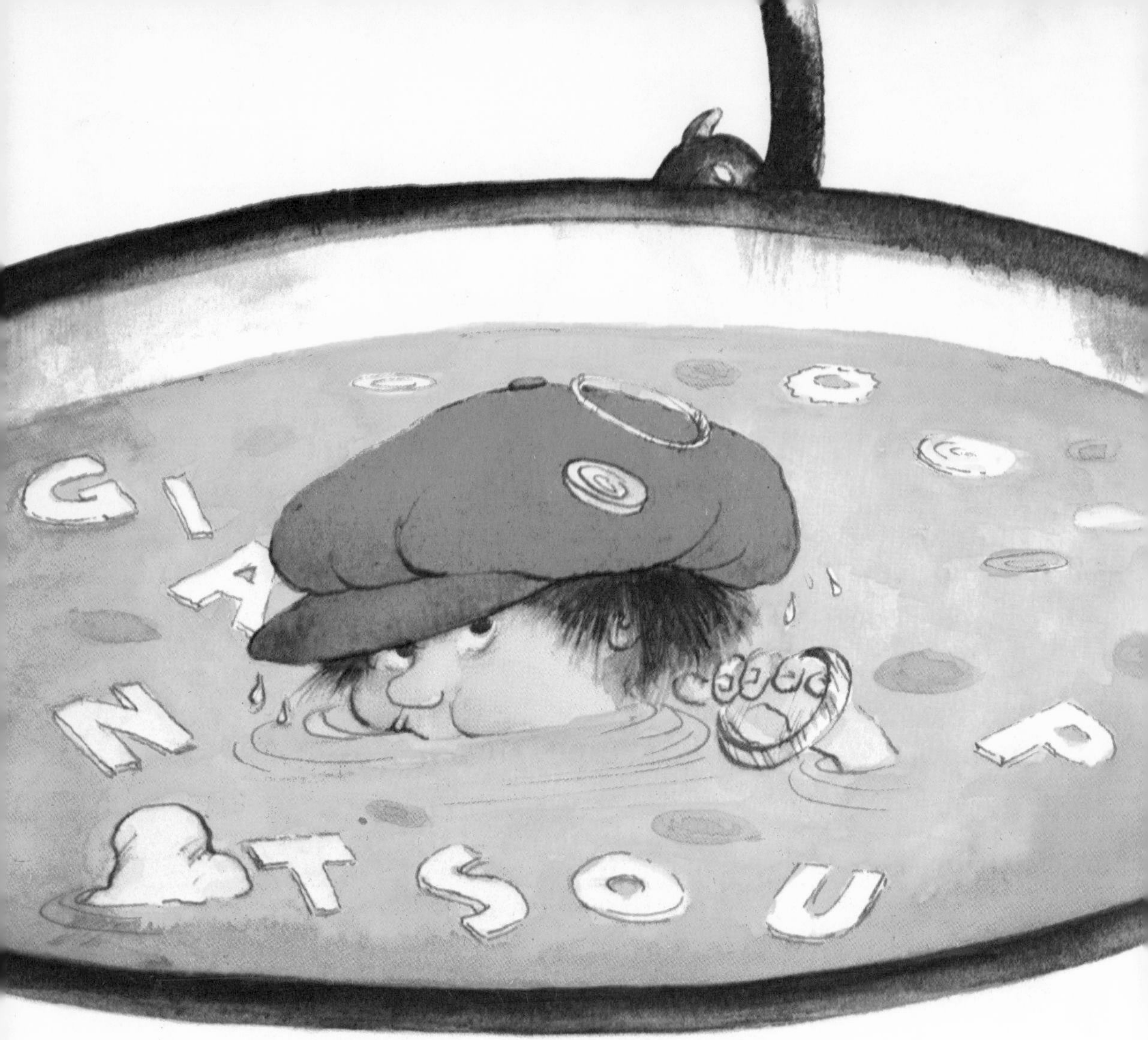

The giant turned on the stove.
Jason swam round and round.
He drank a bit of giant soup.
"Hey!" said Jason.
"There's no salt in it.
You can't make soup."
The giant put some salt in the soup.

"That's better," said Jason.
He swam round and round
and drank a bit more soup.

"Don't drink it all!"
cried the giant.

"Hey!" said Jason.
"This soup isn't right.
There's no pepper in it."

The giant put pepper in the soup.
"That's better," said Jason.
The soup was lovely and warm by now.
He swam round and round
among the bits of onion and carrot.
"What lovely soup!" said Jason.
He drank a bit more.

"You're drinking it all!
You're drinking it all!"
cried the giant.
He quickly took Jason out of the soup.
"There will be no soup left for me,"
he said.

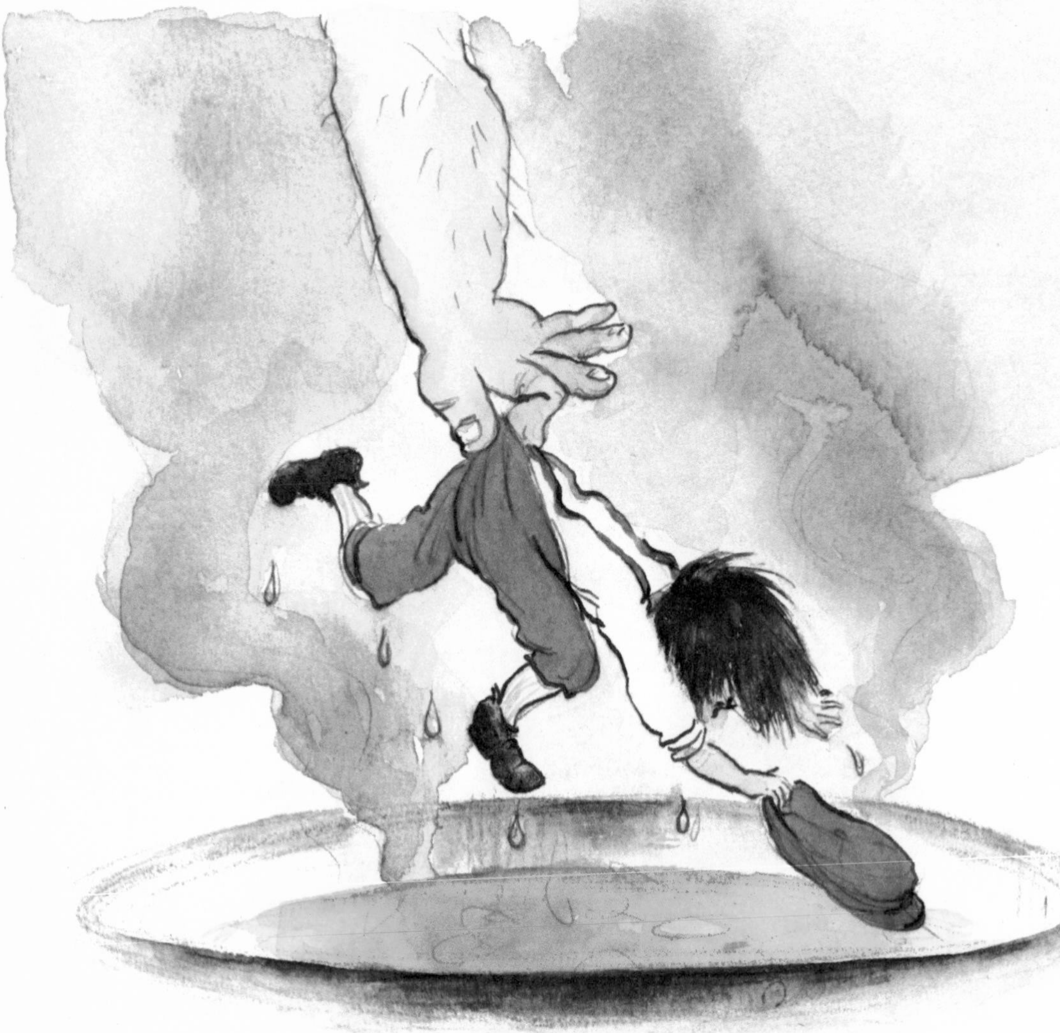

"I might as well go home, then,"
said Jason.
"I'll come in tomorrow
and see how you're getting on."

"I'm cooking a cake tomorrow,"
said the giant.

"I'd better come and help you,"
Jason said.
"And I'll bring my recipe book."

"Oh, no, no, no!
You eat too much!" cried the giant.
"Don't come back again—
ever, ever, ever!"

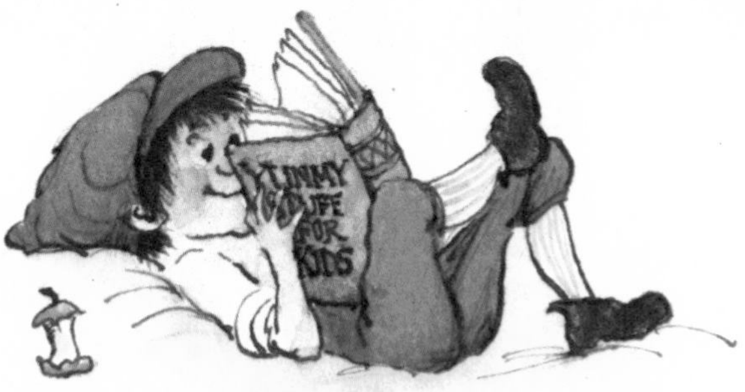
FOR

Flies Taste with their Legs

by June Walker Leonard

The fly likes to eat sweet food
like the honey on your bread.

He stands on the honey
so he can taste it.

You taste your food with your tongue,
but the fly does not have a tongue.
He tastes his food
with his feet and legs.

There are little hairs
all over his feet and legs.
These little hairs help the fly
to taste his food.

If the food tastes good,
the fly lowers his long trunk.
Then he sucks the food up
with his trunk.

Uamairangi

by **Katarina Mataira**
pictures by **Robyn Kahukiwa**

Uamairangi was hungry.

He was so hungry,

he could have eaten

a whole packet of potato chips,

a whole cake,

a whole packet of chocolate biscuits,

and a pot full of pork bones and puha.

So he went to the cupboard

and found a packet of potato chips.

But it wasn't a whole packet of potato chips—

there was only one tiny chip.

And he gobbled it up.

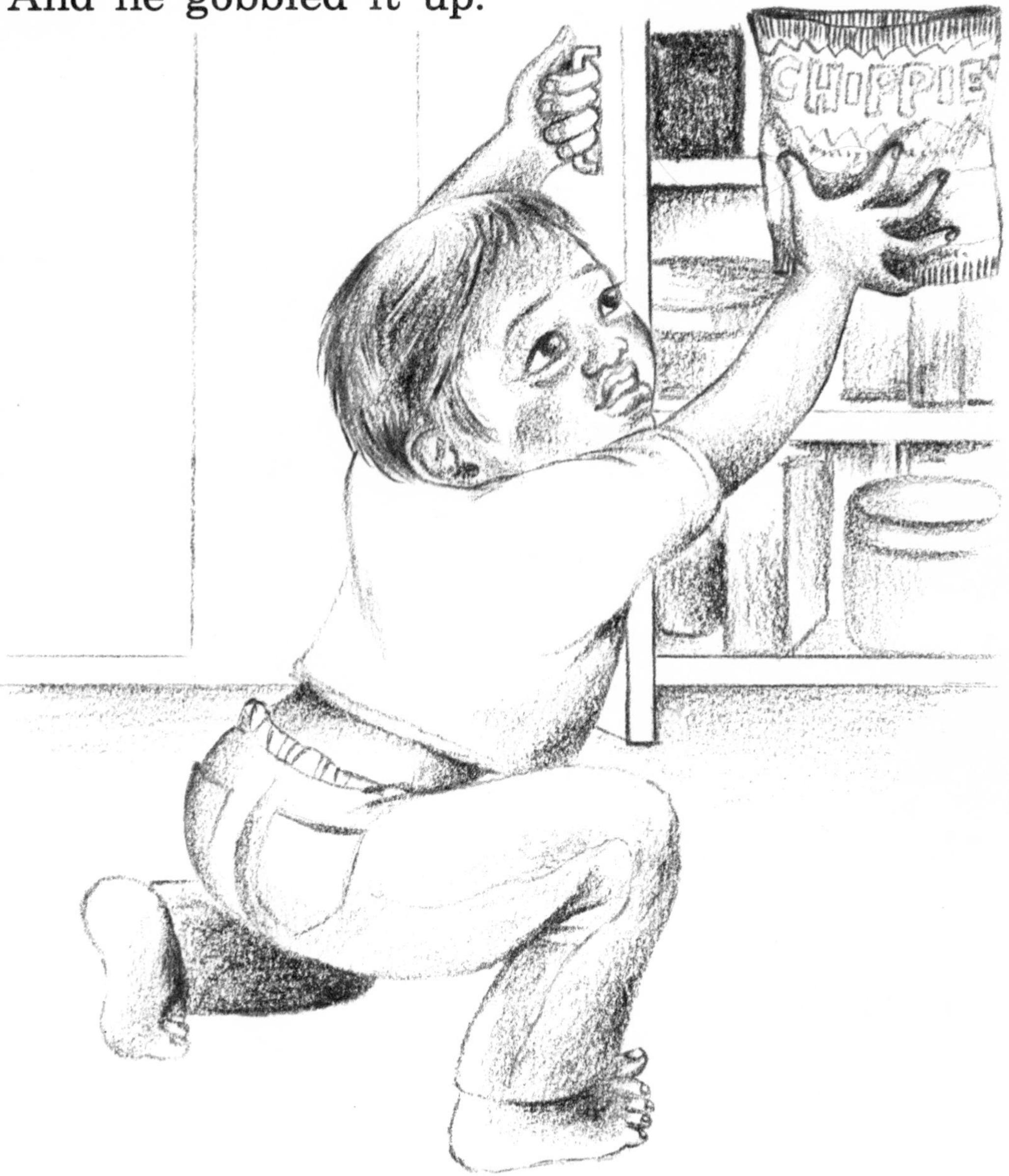
CHIPPIES

But Uamairangi was still hungry,
so he looked in the cake tin.
But there wasn't a whole cake—
there was only one tiny piece.
And he gobbled it up.

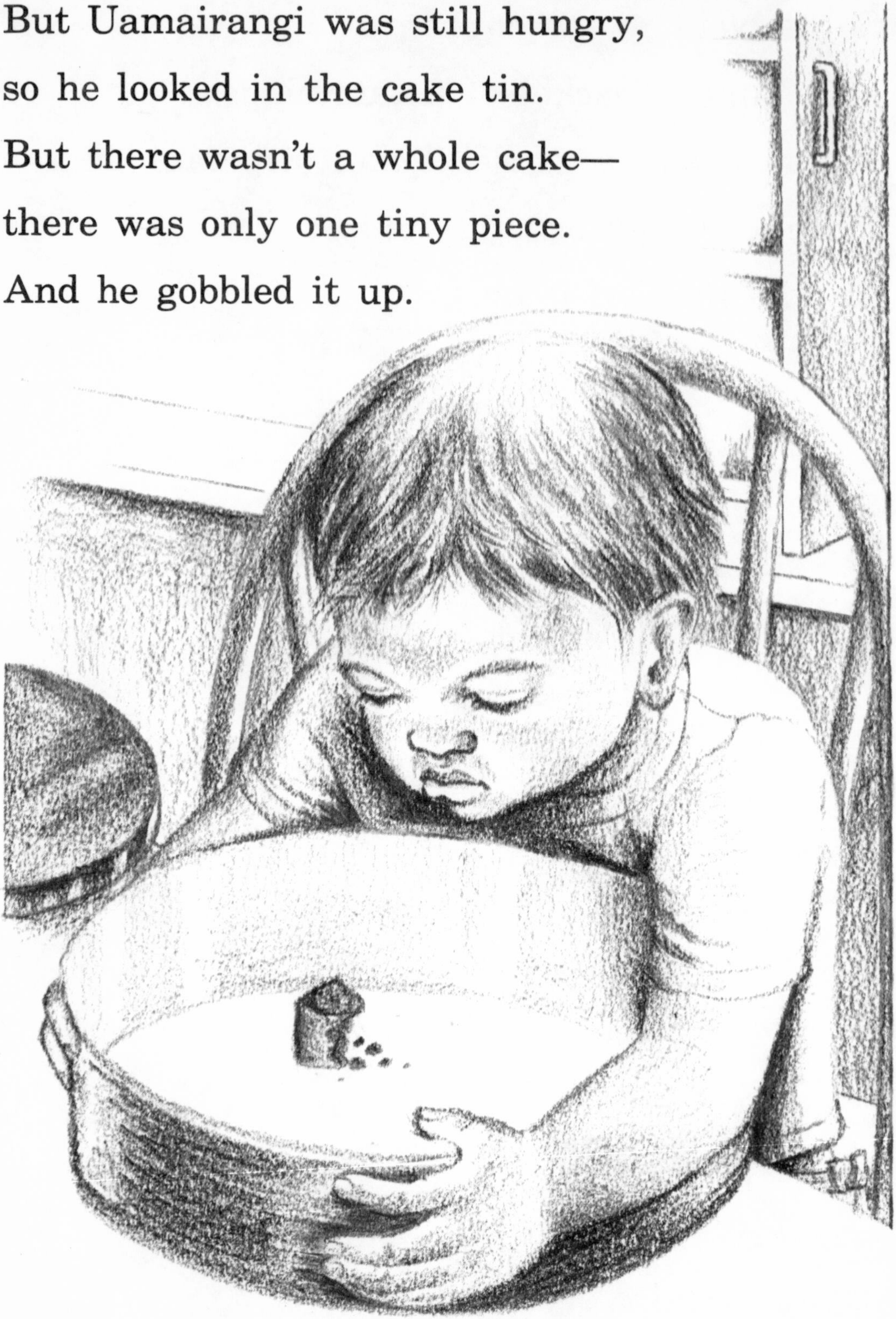

But Uamairangi was still hungry,

so he looked in the biscuit tin.

But there wasn't a whole packet of biscuits—

there was only one tiny biscuit.

And he gobbled it up.

But Uamairangi was *still* hungry,
so he looked in the pot.
But it wasn't full of pork bones and puha—
there wasn't even a little tiny bone.
The pot was empty.

Uamairangi nearly cried.

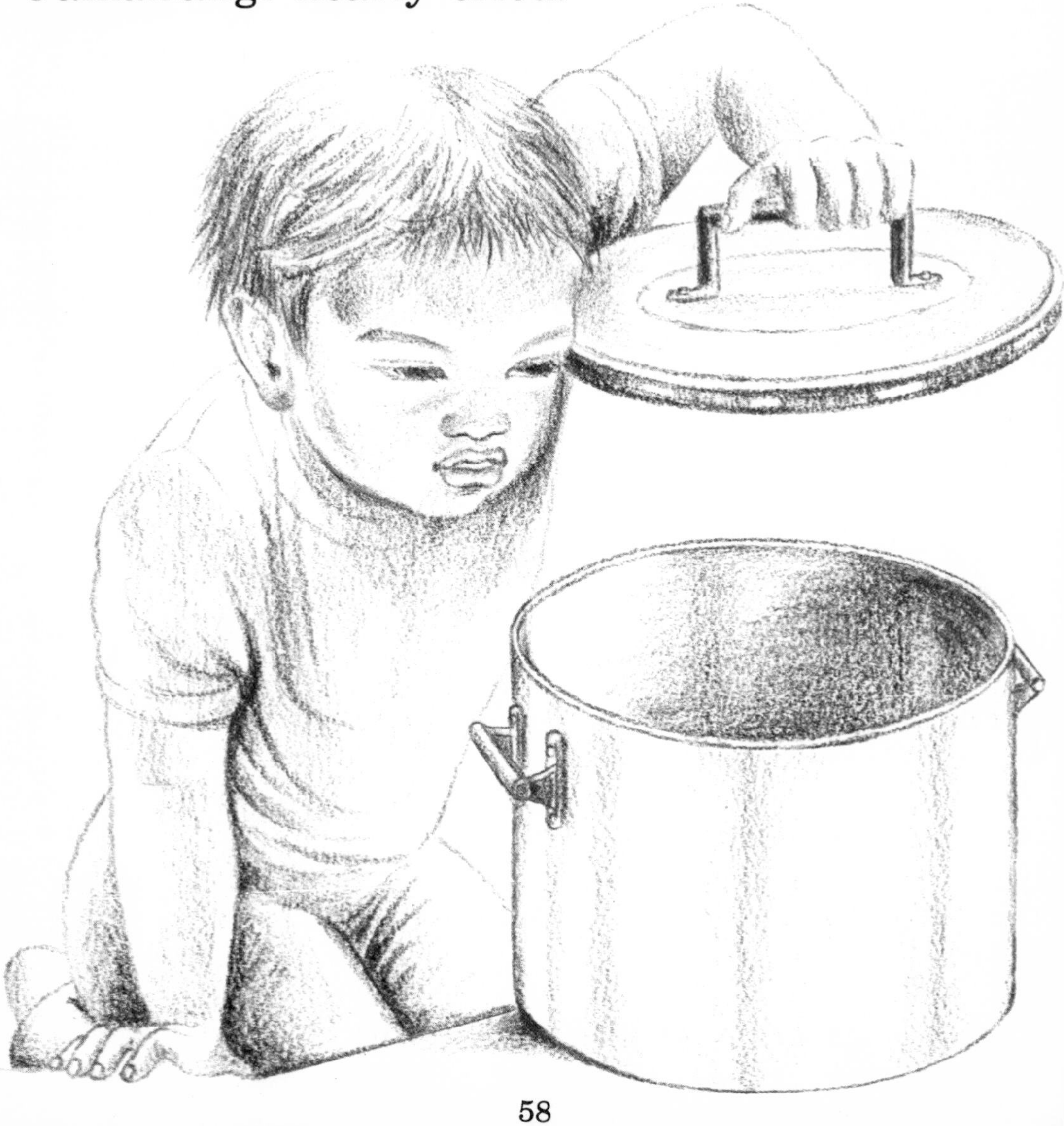

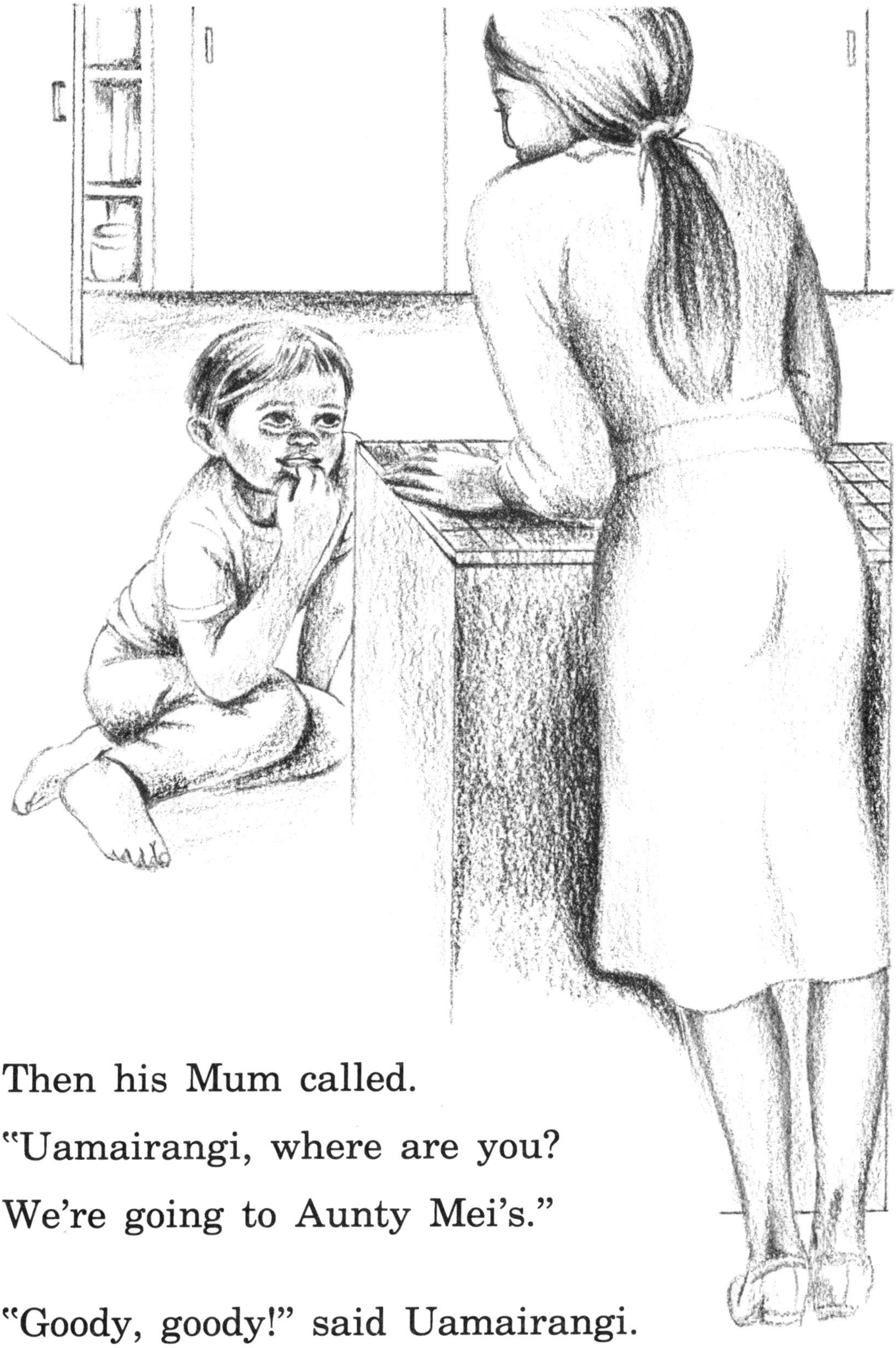

Then his Mum called.
"Uamairangi, where are you?
We're going to Aunty Mei's."

"Goody, goody!" said Uamairangi.

At Aunty Mei's,
he forgot about being hungry.

There were lots of people.
They talked and laughed.
Then Aunty Mei said,
"Haere mai ki te kai."
And they all went to the table.

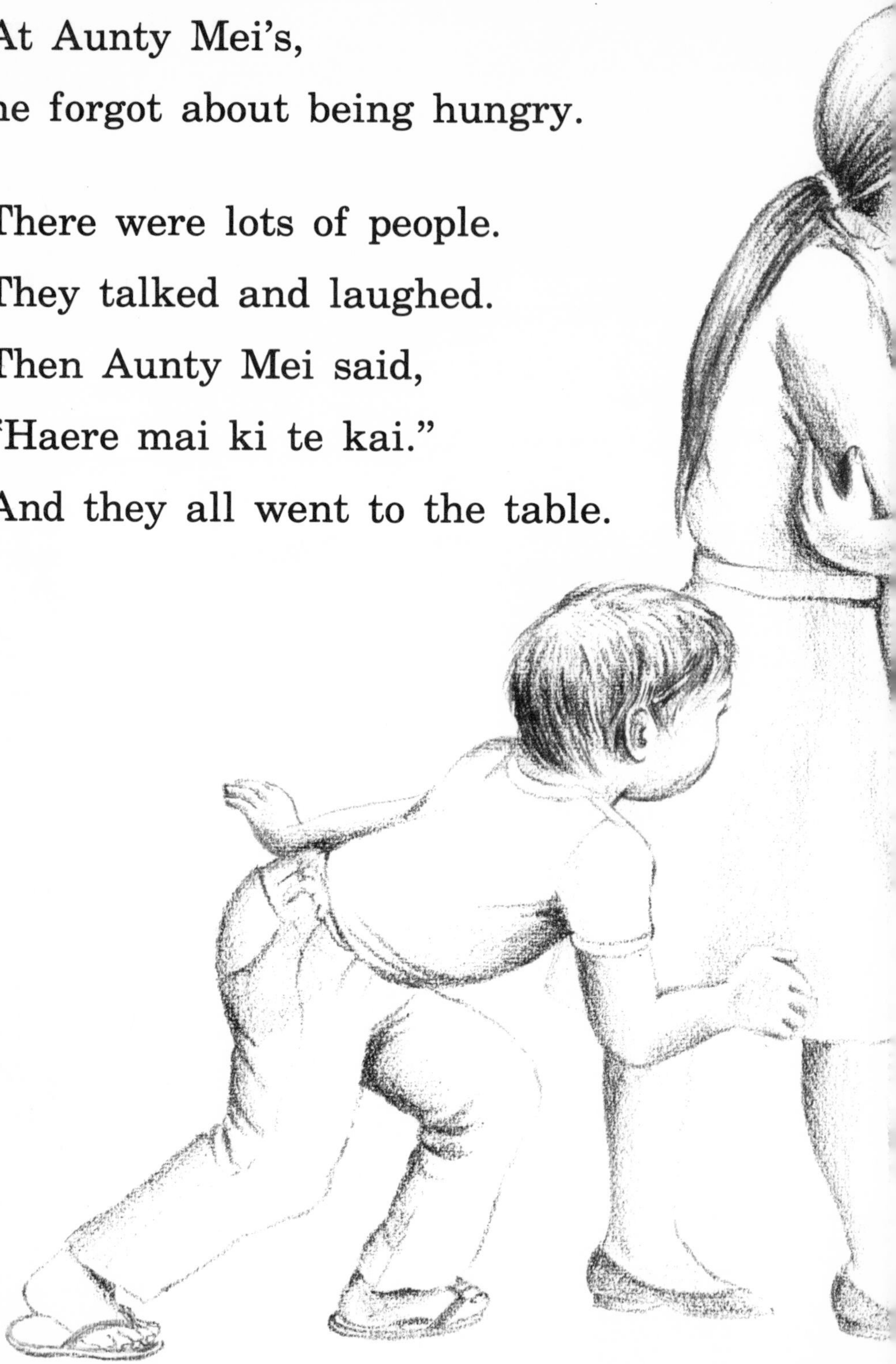

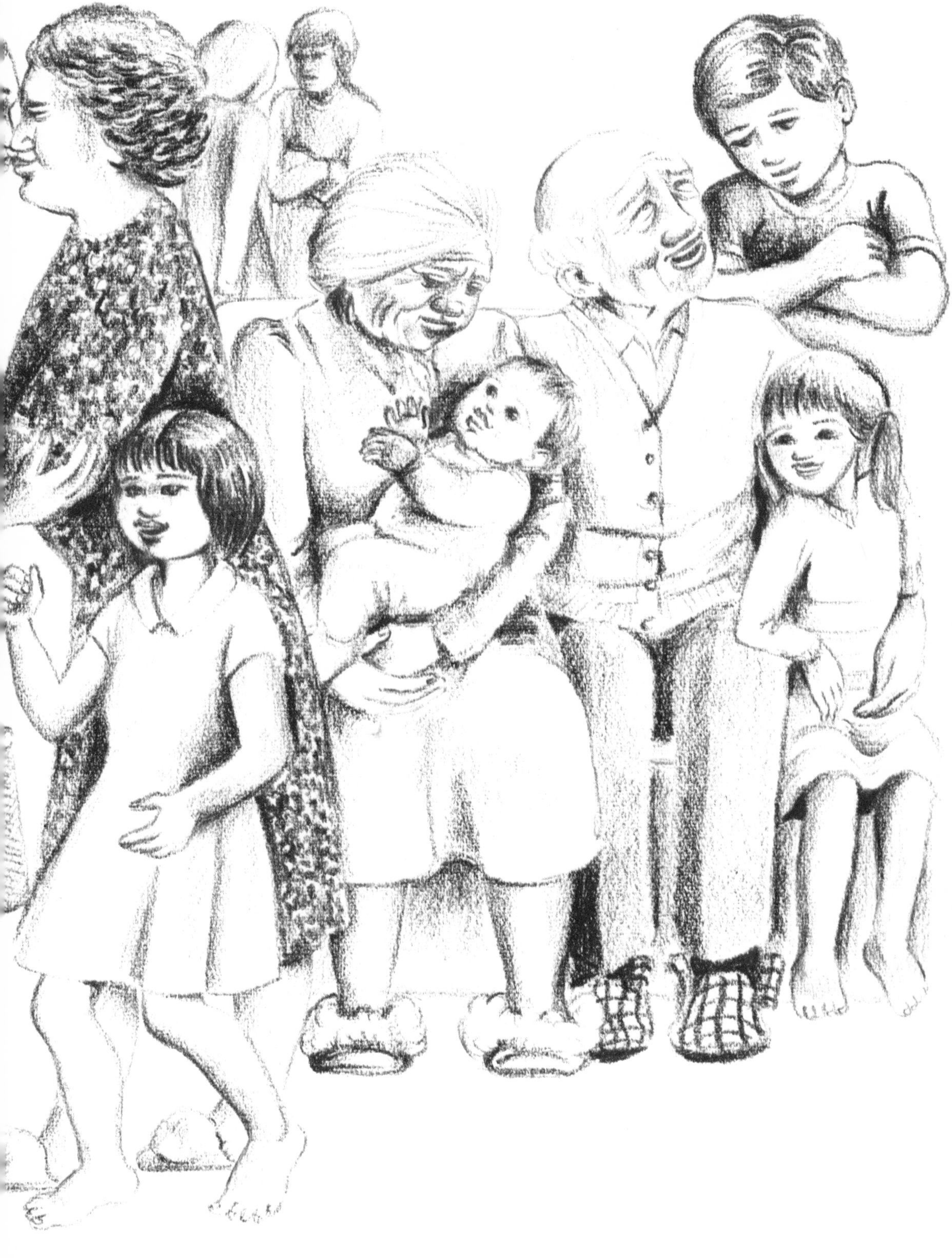

"Ooh! Ooh! Oooh!"
said Uamairangi.
There wasn't just one whole cake
on the table—
there were four.
There wasn't just one whole packet
of potato chips on the table—
there were five.
There wasn't just one whole packet
of chocolate biscuits on the table—
there were six.

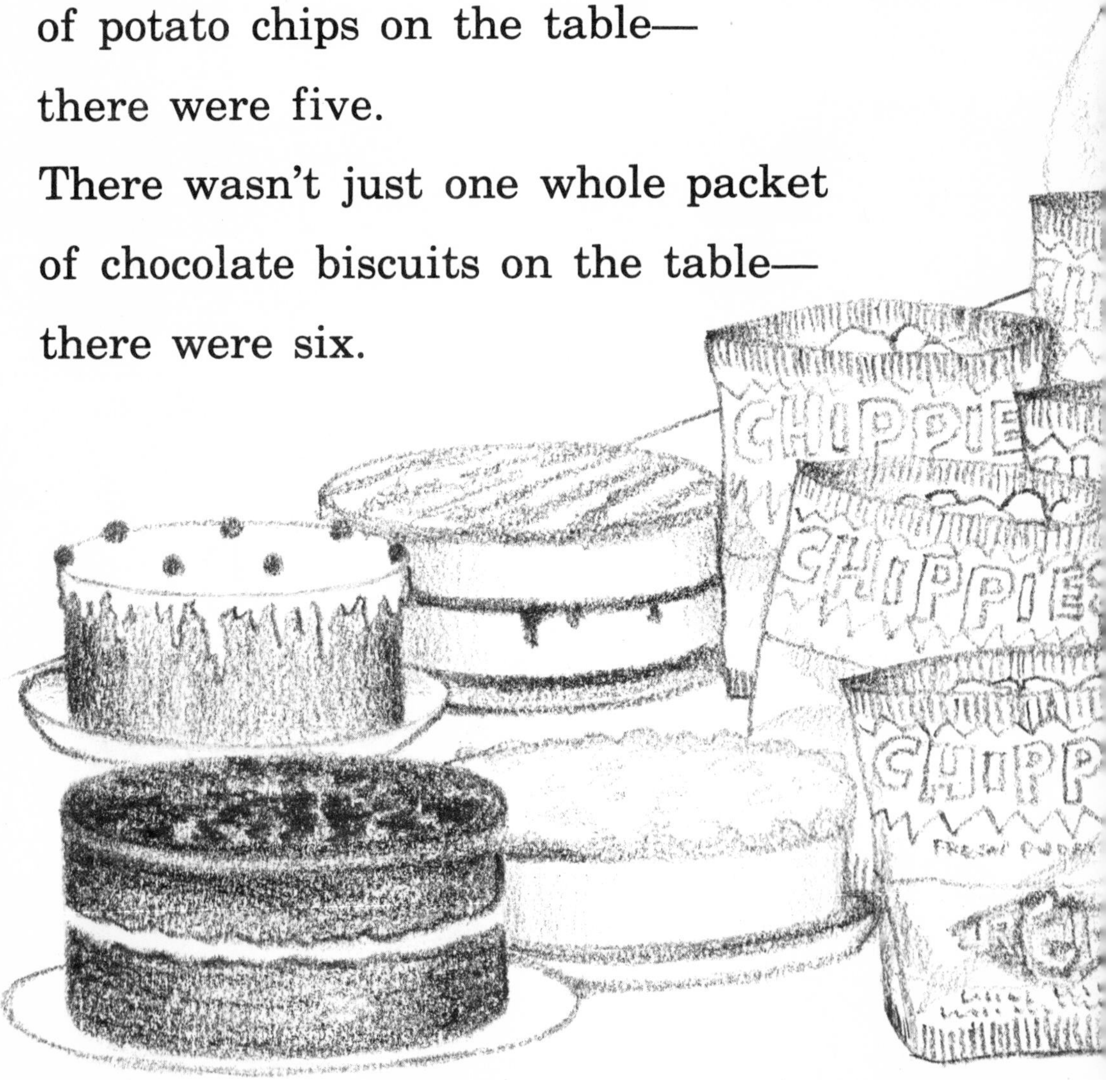
CHIPPIE
CHIPPIE
CHIPP

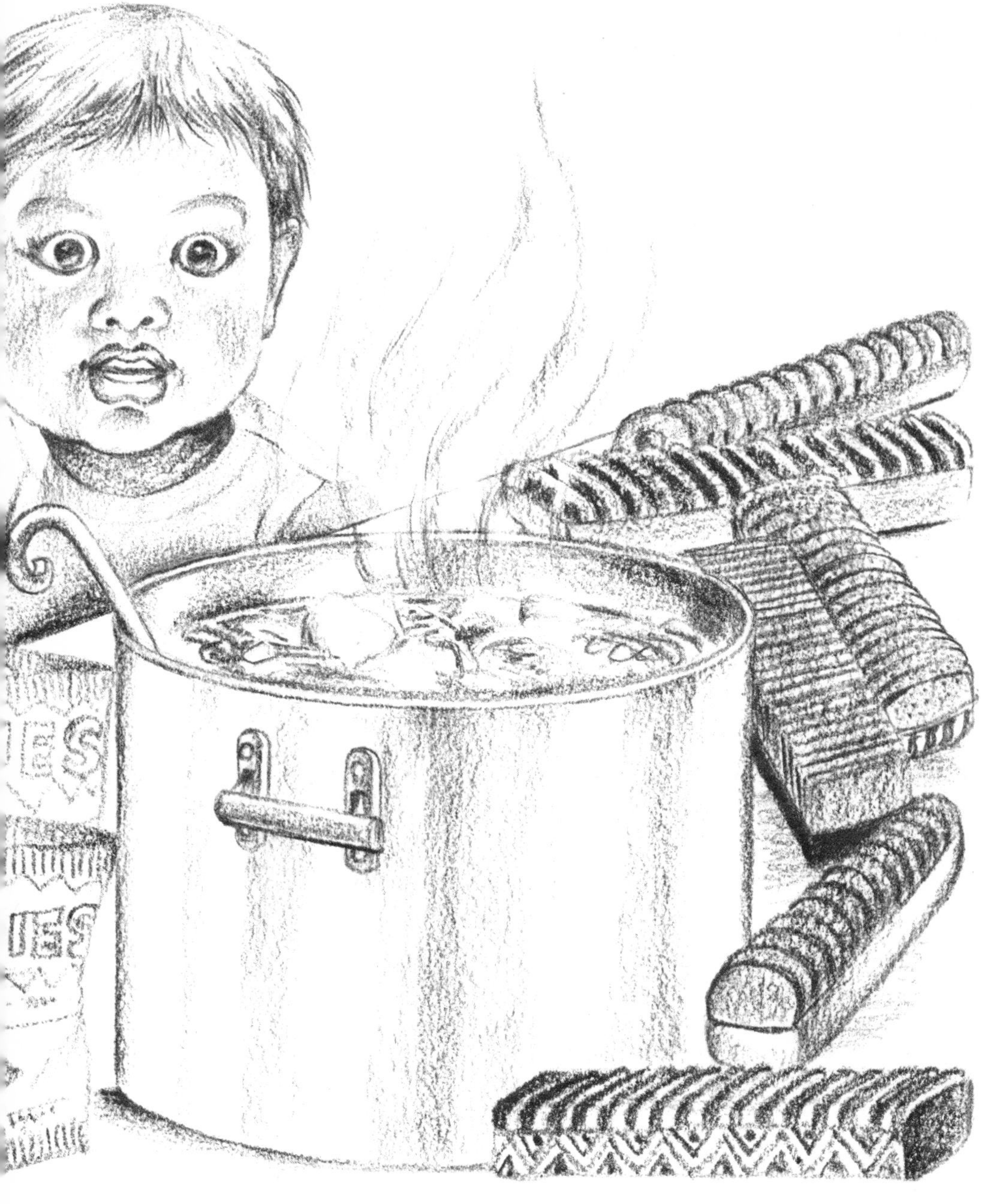

And there was a big, steaming hot pot of pork bones and puha!

Skipping Rhyme

by Marie Darby

Diddily, diddily, dandy,
I'm a stick of candy.
Lick me slow
And lick me fast.
How many licks do you think I'll last?
One, two, three, four, five,
Six, seven, eight, nine....

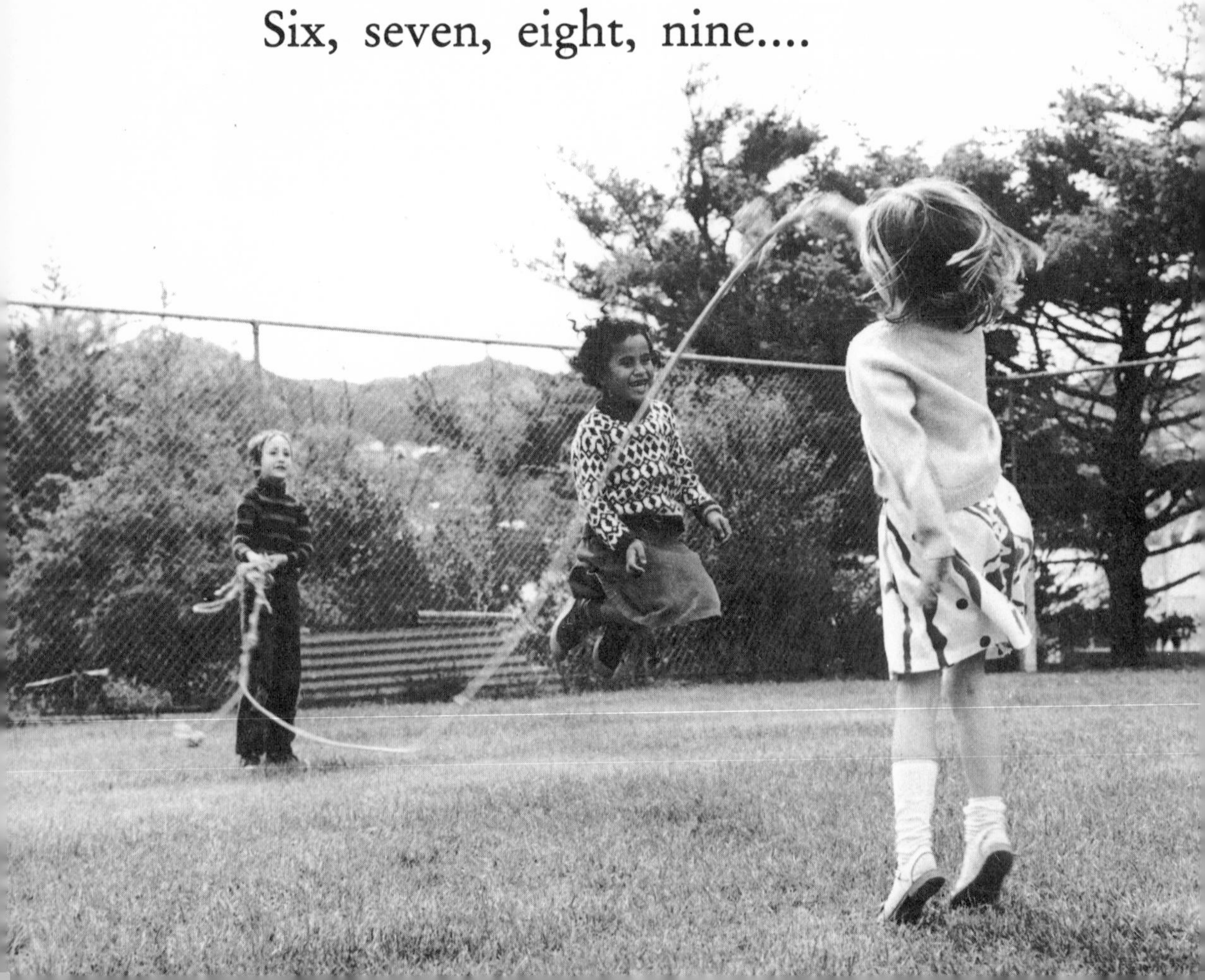